WESTERN SEA

LARTROXIA NORTH

DEMORNTE

Sebbei

LOMARN DESERT

Lomarn

Citadel of the Red Three

W9-ASA-971

LARTROXIA WEST

Ammuria

Lynurus

Wesvetin

Kamathae

LARTROXIA SOUTH

Lartroxia   Raven's Eyrie

Matnabla

Nostoblet   Burwhet

BAY of   MYCEUM
ARTROXIA   MOUNTAINS   Andalor

SORN-ELLYN

PELLIN

OLAN   JOSTEN   Yslsl's Tower

Prisarte

HOVNOSIA   FISTIA   MIDDLE SEA

THOVNOS   MONTES

Thovnosten   RACONOS

PARWI   WALDANN

QUARNORA   TRESLI

Castakes

OCALIDAD MOUNTAINS

Jhaniikest's Tower

WESTERN SEA   Breimen

Jadenball   WOLLENDAN

Selonari

KRANORILL   SALT DESERT

Arellarti

SOUTHERN LANDS

ICE SEA

Gods in Darkness

Other books by Karl Edward Wagner
Novels
Legion From the Shadows
The Road of Kings
Killer (with David Drake)

Short Story Collections
Death Angel's Shadow
Night Winds
In a Lonely Place
The Book of Kane
Why Not You and I
Exorcisms and Ecstasies

Anthologies (as editor)
The Year's Best Horror (Volumes VIII - XXII)
Echoes of Valor (Volumes I - III)
Intensive Scare

Gods in Darkness

THE COMPLETE NOVELS OF KANE

Darkness

BY

KARL EDWARD WAGNER

NIGHT SHADE BOOKS
San Francisco & Portland

Gods in Darkness © 2002 by the estate of Karl Edward Wagner
Cover art © 2002 by Ken Kelly
. Endpaper map @ 2002 by Night Shade Books,
drawn by Snow, based on an original map by Dale E. Rippke

This edition of *Gods in Darkness* is © 2002 by Night Shade Books

Cover and interior layout and design by Jeremy Lassen
All rights reserved. Printed in the United States of America.

Bloodstone © 1975 by the estate of Karl Edward Wagner
Dark Crusade © 1976 by the estate of Karl Edward Wagner
Darkness Weaves (corrected tex) © 1978 by the estate of Karl Edward Wagner

First Edition

ISBN
1-892389-24-X   (Hardcover)
1-892389-25-8   (Limited)

Night Shade Books
books@nightshadebooks.com

Please visit us on the web at
http://www.nightshadebooks.com

Contents

Bloodstone

For John F. Mayer —
Colleague and friend,
Brother in infamy…

Contents

Prologue

For miles uncounted the forest stood supreme. Giant trees reached their branches heavenward, fighting for sunlight and fresh air. Beneath their dense foliage existed another world than that of the open sky above — the twilight of the forest floor. There the cool gloom was broken only by scattered rays of sunlight that crept through the ceiling above, to melt upon the thick bed of leaf mold and pine needles which covered the floor. No undergrowth flourished, except in spots where an arboreal giant had fallen and torn a gap in the forest roof, through which yellow sunlight streamed. Then for a short time a cerement of underbrush might thrive on the rich humus beside the decaying trunk, until the branches above refilled the gulf and strangled the life-giving rays.

But the floor was far from a lifeless desert. A myriad of animal life, great and small, scrambled through the forest. Insects rustled through the carpet and up the trunks of the great trees. Serpents glided along the ground searching for rodents, whose dens were among the tangled roots. Several species of small furry animals picked their way through caves and grooves in the moss-hung debris of fallen branches and cast-off leaves of many seasons. High above, birds chattered gregariously, and somewhere a squirrel cursed in rage over some unseen affront. In the distance a crow croaked nervously and was still.

The doe heard its half-hearted call of warning and froze in the shadows, her fawn pressed against her flanks, shivering on extraordinary legs. Her wide eyes swiveled in alarm, and her taut ears tensed for sounds of danger. Cautiously she drew breath through sensitive nostrils, seeking a scent of wolf or bear or other predator. For minutes she paused, searching for some evidence of danger. None appeared, and visions of meadow clover beckoned. She stepped from the shadow of the trees once again, her fawn close behind.

Packed loam of the path recorded her pointed hooves but a few steps when a hissing arrow tore through her ribs. Gasping in agony, the doe staggered, then plunged along the path in blind flight. The fawn paused only a second before instinctive terror supplanted bewilderment, and on his stilt-like legs he pounded after his mother. A chorus of crows caught the scent of blood, of fear, and raised a raucous protest.

The hunter jumped from his concealment alongside the trail, another arrow nocked and ready. Bounding onto the gametrail, his patient eyes recognized the stream of blood, and he grinned jubilantly. "Lung at least — maybe heart, too, by the blood! Run while you can, bitch — you won't go far!" He drew a long knife and followed confidently the glistening trail.

Her hoofprints quickly left the path, but marks of the doe's passage were obvious by the crimson blotches splashed upon the forest floor. As the hunter surmised, she had not run more than a few hundred yards before death pulled her down. She lay in a sudden depression in the ground — a cavity ripped from the floor a few years earlier when an enormous tree had been uprooted. Her breath rattled now through red foamed nostrils, and her eyes seemed already glazed.

He clambered into the depression gingerly and cut her throat. Wiping the knife across her flank, the hunter cast about for the fawn. No sign of him. Something would get him by morning, probably, so at least he would not starve. He felt some slight remorse over killing a doe with fawn, but the day had been long, and his family in Breimen came first. Besides, he was paid to bring in deer for the market, not to observe forest idylls.

He sat against the bank with a tired but satisfied grunt, wiped his face on a dirty sleeve, and looked about him. A minute's rest — then gut her, rig up a drag, and pull the carcass into Breimen. And that would about finish it for this afternoon.

The bowl in which the huntsmen rested was several yards across, for the tree that had wrenched loose was an ancient one of immense size. Bare soil still scarred the depression, although material had begun to slide down from the edges. Something glittered upon the bottom of the hole. A lance of sunlight shone down from above to spear something bright, embedded in the humus — some object that cast back a silver reflection to the hunter's eyes. Mildly intrigued, he rose to get a closer look. The object that lay there in the dirt made him grunt in puzzlement and squat down to make astonished examination.

A ring lay embedded in the dirt. Around it the loam was streaked with white, crumbling material that seemed to be rotted bone, and reddish splotches which might represent rusted iron intermingled. Brushing away the loose surface, he discerned a few greenish lumps, recognizable only as corroded brass or copper. The body of some ancient warrior, possibly — although how long it had moldered here beneath the forest defied his imagination. Long enough for bones and accouterments to crumble away — and the tree that had overgrown the grave was centuries old.

With unsteady hand the hunter pulled the ring free of its bed of tainted clay and brushed loose the tenacious fragments that encased it. He spat and polished it against his leather trouser leg, then raised it to his eyes for appraisal. The metal was silvery in appearance, but seemed far harder — and silver should have tarnished black with antiquity. It seemed to be set with a tremendous cabochon-cut bloodstone — rich, deep-green stone with red veins traced throughout its depths. But it was a superb example of that gem, he judged, holding it to a ray of light. For the colors were somewhat more intense, and there appeared to be a quality of translucency to the stone that made it distinct from the normally opaque gem. The stone was huge -- abnormally large for a ring — and it seemed to fuse cunningly into its setting. Carefully he scraped free a last few stubborn flakes of bone-streaked clay from the inside of the ring and held it before his finger. Whoever had worn this ring lost centuries past must have been a giant, for its girth was several sizes too great for any normal finger to hold.

Uneasily the hunter recalled legends told by the Selonari of giants and demons who had stalked the forests even before they had settled here. And there were tales among his own people regarding the savage Rillyti, who supposedly never strayed far beyond the slimy shelter of their swamp.

But the hunter had a solid, practical mind. Saying a prayer to Ommem for protection, and to the spirit of the rotted skeleton for pardon, he dropped the ring into his pouch. Mechanically he began to gut his kill, all the while speculating pleasantly as to the price his find might bring him at the jewelers' market in Breimen.

I
Death by Firelight

An ominous black shadow in the leaping firelight, the big man crouched enswathed in his cloak and moodily sipped wine from a crockery mug lost in his huge fist. His close-fitting shirt and trousers of dark leather were freshly stained with sweat and blood, and the right sleeve was rolled back from a scarlet-streaked bandage encircling an arm thick with corded muscle. A belt bright with silver studs crossed his massive chest, holding fast an empty sword scabbard behind his powerful right shoulder. The sword itself stood before him, its point embedded in a gnarled tree root. Absently running a knuckle over the short red beard that framed his rather brutal face, he brooded over the many nicks and red brown smears that defaced the blade and cast shadows of violent combat by the flickering light. Seemingly he was oblivious to the others as they greedily spread out the loot to divide among themselves.

The Ocalidad Mountain Range that guarded the northern coasts of the forestland now called Wollendan had been infamous for its bandits long before the blond seafarers of the coast migrated through its passes to carve out cities from the great forests of the south. The dark-haired forest-dwellers who grudgingly yielded ground to their iron-guarded advance had made free use of the countless caves and unassailable fortresses the mountains provided, before the intruders had ever landed on their shores. Never in the memory of those who held the land had it been safe for a caravan to cross the Ocalidad Mountains. Yet commerce must flow from seacoast inland and back again, and the rich trade with the fabled cities across the seas made the gamble worth the effort. So men with wealth crossed the mountains, where men with swords waited to strip them of it, and the history of their measures and countermeasures was as long and colorful as it was bloody.

Earlier today this band had attacked a somewhat modest pack train crossing from the south under a small guard of armed men. The ensuing battle had ended in little better than a draw for the bandits, who lost a good number of men before the survivors of the caravan broke through the ambush to safety. In fleeing, however, several loads of goods had been left behind by the merchants, and the brigands were content to fall upon this booty and abandon further efforts against the remainder of the caravan. Retreating to their camp as nightfall overtook them, the bandits were now engaged in the difficult and dangerous business of dividing the spoils.

"A fine lot of jewelry here in this one pack," observed their leader, a scar-faced giant named Hechon. "Someone's out a bundle of money here. Wonder what it was all going for. Hey... maybe all the rumors are true about Malchion hiring some more troops to attack Selonari."

"That old tale's been blowing around these hills in one form or another long as I can think back," scoffed someone.

The contents of the jewel merchant's bag were carefully poured out on a blanket, where they tossed sparkles of firelight back into the circle of greedy eyes. A dozen pairs of hands twitched in eagerness to seize the treasure, but the bandits held back while Hechon fingered through the loot calculatingly. His would be the final word as to how everything would be divided among his band.

"Damn! Here's something interesting now!" muttered Hechon. A three-fingered hand reached down and lifted a ring into the firelight. Experienced eyes weighed the object. "Huh! Thought this looked strange! Ring's way too big for most people, and I can't quite call this metal. Not right for silver — too hard. Wonder if this is maybe platinum — that's a costly metal and hard as iron. I've heard tell they work it up north or somewhere. Thought this gem was bloodstone at first, too, but it don't look like any I ever seen. See how the light seems to shine into it a ways... you can almost follow the veins of red down into the gem."

"Let me see that ring." The big man seated apart from them spoke at last; Hechon's discovery of the ring had aroused him from his brooding aloofness.

Eyes turned at his low voice. Hechon looked toward him in shrewd calculation, and after a pause he tossed the bloodstone ring to him. "Sure, Kane. Take a look, then. If you're too tired to come stand around with the rest of us."

Kane caught the object in his left hand and held it before his eyes. In silence he studied the ring, carefully turning it about in the light, as if he saw a legend inscribed on its surface. He seemed lost in thought for a long while, then announced abruptly, "I want this ring as part of my share of the booty."

Hechon rankled at his tone. He had had second thoughts about accepting Kane into his band since the red-haired stranger had come to him two months before. He brought along a handful of others —

all that survived when their old gang of outlaws had been surprised by a troop of mercenaries sent out by the coastal cities to make the mountain passes safe for commerce. Where Kane had come from before that, Hechon neither knew nor cared. However, of Kane's deadly skill in battle the bandit leader did know, for the awesome might of the stranger's sword arm quickly made his name feared throughout the Ocalidad Mountains. And although Hechon immediately recognized the threat Kane posed to his leadership, he had judged his position among his own men too secure for the other to challenge outright... and in a raid Kane was worth a dozen lesser rogues.

Now Kane's confident appropriation of the bizarre ring struck resentment in Hechon's shrewd mind. Best to assert command now, he decided, before the others began to accept Kane's wishes as law in other matters. "I decide how the take gets split up," he growled. "Anyway, that's a valuable ring, and I've taken a liking to it myself."

Kane frowned slightly and continued to examine the bloodstone ring speculatively. "Bloodstone is scarcely a precious gem, and this ring's value is only that of a curiosity," he offered reasonably. "Still, I find it somewhat intriguing, and it looks like it might not be much too large for my hand. So maybe it's just a whim, but I want it. As to its dubious monetary worth, I'll take a big chance and accept this ring in lieu of the rest of my share of the spoils. That's leaving you others with an extra slice of obvious value to split up."

"You're not fool enough to gamble like that unless you maybe got some other ideas on that ring's worth," Hechon pointed out, now genuinely suspicious. "And like I say, I'm boss here, and I decide who gets what. So pass that damn ring back, Kane, and we'll get on with business. You'll take what I decide on, and right now I'm telling you that ring's going to be mine." The menace in his tone was a grating note.

Hechon glowered at Kane obstinately. Around them the other outlaws watched in nervous silence, almost imperceptibly shuffling away from the two. Abelin, Hechon's lanky lieutenant, carefully wiped his hands on his thighs and moved them out of Kane's sight, trying to read some signal in his leader's face. They would back him, Hechon decided.

In the strained silence even the voices of the night creatures seemed hushed and distant. Kane's eyes glowed with blue fire in the flickering light, cold death laughing derisively in their depths. Hechon had always felt a chill when he looked into those eyes, the eyes of a born killer. Uneasily he remembered the insane light that stirred in those eyes when Kane stood red with slaughter over those who fell before his blade in battle. Held next to his cheek in his left hand, the evil gleam of the bloodstone seemed to match Kane's uncanny stare. Even its scarlet veins seemed phosphorescent in the shadow of the firelight.

And Hechon knew Kane was not going to return the ring. Cold realization came that there was no course left him now. If he relented,

Kane would have outfaced him before his men, and his command over them would soon change fists. Kane's challenge must be answered, now and forever.

Kane seemed immobile, but Hechon knew the deadly speed with which he could strike. His sword stood before him in easy reach, impaled in a root. Narrowly Hechon watched Kane's left hand — his sword arm — but Kane still stroked his cheek with the ring. The bandit leader shrugged. "Well, if you want the damned ring that much, I guess you can keep it as your share." He seemed to relax, and he grinned about him at the others.

As he did, Hechon caught Abelin's eye for a significant moment, and his fingers spread in an evident gesture of helplessness. "After all, Kane," he continued, "it's worth more to me to keep you... "

Abelin's hand suddenly flicked to his neck and flew back balancing a long bladed knife from the sheath that hung between his shoulders. The bandit lieutenant's long arm straightened in unbroken motion to hurl the blade at Kane's chest.

But Kane had not fallen prey to Hechon's apparent acquiescence. Knowing the bandit chieftain's cunning, Kane had followed the other's eyes and caught the silent death sentence he had signed Abelin to carry out. And although Kane was left-handed, years of training had made his right arm almost as proficient as the other.

In the fraction of a second that Abelin required to send his blade flashing for Kane's heart, Kane hurled his powerful body to one side. As he leaped from his crouched position, the right hand that had strayed toward his right boot lashed out with the knife it found hidden there. Striking like a coiled serpent, Kane hurled his dagger across the fire like an arrow of light. Abelin's blade hissed past him as he twisted and thudded against the base of a tree. Still bending forward with his cast, the outlaw coughed in startled pain as Kane's knife drove its point through his heart.

Kane's lunge brought him to his feet even as he had thrown the knife. As the bandit lieutenant crumpled to his knees to realize that death had claimed him, Kane caught up his sword in his left hand, dropping the ring to the ground, and swung his boot into the fire. A blinding, searing wave of coals and burning embers exploded over the stunned bandits, driving them back in pain and confusion.

Hechon was reaching for his sword hilt the instant Abelin had drawn his knife. Throwing up his free arm to ward off the burning cloud of fire and ashes, the bandit leader whipped out the blade with frantic haste. Only barely did he raise his guard in time to turn back Kane's thrust.

Kane leaped across the fire, sword slashing like a fiery brand. Avoiding Hechon's return thrust, he struck again, swinging powerful blows that all but tore his opponent's hilt from numbed fingers. Forced to the defensive, Hechon backed away from Kane and strove desperately to stave off the attack until his men could shake off their surprise and come to his aid — if they would. Kane gave them no time to decide. As Hechon retreated around the scattered coals, something turned under his boot, causing him to sway off balance for only an instant. In that fraction of a heartbeat, Kane's sword eluded Hechon's failing guard and pierced his shoulder. Driven back by the blow, Hechon was helpless to block Kane's follow-through. A second later his smashed corpse flopped against the earth, spewing a torrent of crimson over the green-jeweled ring that glowed evilly in his dying vision.

Swiftly Kane scooped up the bloodstone ring from the darkened earth and straightened to face the other outlaws. Weapons drawn, they were milling about in confusion, uncertain what course was theirs to follow now that their leaders were slain.

"All right!" Kane roared, his reddened sword raised menacingly. "This ring is mine, and I'll kill any other damn fool who disputes my claim! Split the rest of the loot up among yourselves now! I've got what I want, and I'm leaving! Anyone who wants a quick trip to hell can try to stop me!"

No hand was raised against him. Retrieving his dagger and a handful of gold coins, Kane mounted his horse and thundered away into the darkness. Behind him the jackals quarreled over his leavings.

II
The Tower at Time's Abyss

The stones beneath his horse's hooves assumed an almost reassuring familiarity now, and Kane all at once was uncertain whether fifty years or as many days had passed since last he had ridden along this ridge. Trees grew sparse and stunted from the cracked and wind-sculpted rock, throwing odd shadows against the orange-red sun in the west. The wind that whipped through his hair and flapped the wolfskin cloak about his shoulders bore with it the cold scent of the sea, which verged as a blue ribbon into the hazy eastern horizon. Faint murmur of distant waves underscored the rush of the wind, and sharp cries of soaring birds rose in broken descant. These far-off dark shapes that hung and wheeled on the wind — were they ravens, hawks, or gulls? Or were they even birds? Kane was too concerned with keeping to the unfrequented and all but obliterated trail to give them further attention.

The ruins of a low wall crept into view, more sharply demarcating the ancient roadway he followed. Tumbled heaps of gray stone suggested fallen dwellings, and an occasional roofless structure now huddled against the crest of the ridge. As Kane rode closer to the ridge's summit, he could recognize the familiar details of her tower — a sweeping basalt spire that jutted perilously above a sheer plummet thousands of feet over the coastal plains far below. It seemed incredible that this tower had not plunged off into the abyss centuries ago, but Kane knew its fragility to be only illusion. For the city about this tower had lain in ruins long before the great ocean that once surged mightily against the mountain wall had receded, and still the tower had stood without change.

Lights began to glow within the tower's high windows, Kane observed, as he guided his mount along the final few hundred yards of cracked roadway that led to the summit. More strongly now the familiarity of these surroundings impressed him, imbuing him with a curious sense almost of homecoming. The eerie changelessness of her world was all the more strange to Kane because of the restless state of flux in which he perceived existence. It seemed to him that in Jhaniikest's tower there existed a focus of timelessness within the ever shifting patterns of the remainder of the universe, a refuge from time itself.

The tower gates swung open as he approached, throwing a mist of yellow light into the twilight that drifted over the ridges. Phantom guardsmen of a long-dead race clashed curious spears in stiff salute, and Kane's horse lolled frightened eyes and nickered nervously. Tired from days of hard riding, Kane eased himself from the saddle and led his snorting mount to the shelter of a roofless building near the tower's base. Tethering him, Kane saw that there was fodder enough growing through the cracked floor to occupy the animal until he could tend to him more fully.

Through slit-pupiled eyes the guardsmen watched impassively as Kane entered the tower portals. Behind him the doors closed with only a faint rasp, and he wondered when they had last swung open to admit a guest. Torches set along the wall afforded illumination as he crossed the entrance hall and ascended the stone stairwell that led to the levels above.

Jhaniikest stood by the head of the stairs, her half-folded wings framing the wide doorway. A smile of welcome drew thin red lips over needle-sharp white teeth as she held out her hand to him. "Kane! I saw you coming from above! All afternoon you've plodded along. I thought you had lost your way... maybe forgotten Jhaniikest over the years! I think it's been a century since last I saw you!"

"Not nearly that long, I'm certain," Kane protested, as he knelt to kiss the long-fingered, deceptively fragile hand. "Actually, I was thinking on the ride up that it had only been a few months since my last visit."

She laughed, an uncanny, high-pitched trill. "Kane... you're a total loss as a lover. Do you always tell your ladies that the years you've spent away from their presence have passed like days?" Her wide silver eyes appraised him in frank curiosity, the black vertical pupils almost circular in the darkened room. "You seem unchanged to me, Kane," she judged. "But then you always look the same — just like my shadow servants here. Come... sit beside me and tell me what things you've seen. I've already had the wine and hors d'oeuvres set out."

Kane accepted a flagon of wine from a slender serving girl whose bones were long drifting with the dust. Lips set in concentration as she balanced the heavy tray and its fragile contents, she seemed to him fully alive; he even thought he could discern the quick pulse of breath stirring the fine tawny fur of her breasts. Jhaniikest's sorcery was potent, he mused as he sipped the wine — demon wine conjured out of some unguessable cellar.

"Brought you something I thought you might enjoy," he announced, tugging out the pouch he wore beneath vest and shirt. Fumbling through its contents a moment, Kane withdrew a tiny packet wrapped in soft leather and offered it to her.

Jhaniikest caught it up with eager curiosity and ran her finger over the packet in brief speculation before she sliced through its tie with a sharp talon and spread the wrapping apart. "A ring!" She laughed in delight. "Kane... what a lovely sapphire!" Murmuring vague sounds of pleasure, she turned the splendid blue star sapphire about in the light, trying it on one finger, then another, admiring the effect.

She was an uncanny creature, Jhaniikest. Ageless offspring of a priestess of a vanished prehuman race and the winged god they had worshipped. Sorceress, priestess, demigoddess — for centuries she had lived in this tower that once had been temple for the race who had dwelt here. She had preserved this tower through her magic while the remainder of the ancient city crumbled into ruins, and she had summoned from death the shades of her people to serve her here. A goddess without a heaven. Or perhaps this was her heaven, for she had lived in this desolate tower for centuries, occupying herself with such unimaginable designs and philosophies as only the elder gods could comprehend. Kane had discovered her partly by chance a great many years before.

She knelt on her couch with her long legs drawn under her, membranous wings folded but stirring restlessly, as if buffeted by unperceived winds. Aside from her wings, Jhaniikest was not too dissimilar in form from a human. Her figure was almost that of a slender girl in mid-teens, although her limbs were disproportionately long, which raised her height to somewhat over six feet. Her chest seemed unnaturally deep from the thick bands of muscle that spread from the base of her wings down across shoulder and back and around to a keel-like breastbone. Small, firm breasts softened the sharp lines of her chest. Silver-white fur covered her entire body — fur short and fine as on a cat's face. Across her scalp and down her neck her hair grew long and billowy, a proud mane that any court beauty would envy. Her face was narrow, with piquant features, and there was an elfish point to her ears and chin. Jeweled ornaments glittered upon the silvery fur of her person — her only attire other than a golden belt of gems and bright silk scarves.

Her wings were Jhaniikest's most marvelous feature. Silver-furred bat's wings that reached from shoulder to hip and spanned to twenty feet when spread. Furled, they stood from her back like an ermine cape. Extended in flight, they shimmered opalescent in the sun. The inhuman strength of her compact and hollow-boned frame easily lifted her into the air, where Jhaniikest could soar for hours through the desolate skies. A winged goddess of a vanished realm.

The sapphire pleased Jhaniikest, as Kane, aware of her love of bright jewelry, had known it would. The gem, one of the finest he had gleaned in several years of banditry, was something her sorcery could easily surpass. But the goddess rarely received offerings in these years, and Kane had understood the delight his gift would bring Jhaniikest.

"What brings you to my realm once more, Kane?" Jhaniikest asked presently. "Don't tell me again that you rode this far just to give me jewelry and bring diversity to my days. It's flattering, but I know you too well. Kane's motives are never those he proclaims through a smile."

Kane winced. "Small thanks for my gallantry. Actually, though, it *was* a ring that brought me to your tower. A ring that seemed familiar when I first examined it. Not that I had ever seen it before, but a ring that I seemed to have heard of, or read about at some time in the past. Perhaps I acted rashly in acquiring the bauble, but if my memory hasn't begun to wander, this ring is the gateway to a world far beyond the dawn of mankind!

"I've left some things with you in the past, Jhaniikest. Priceless objects that I thought you might find interesting — that I knew I would lose myself before long. You will remember there were several old books — ancient volumes of sorcerous knowledge of the like seldom seen by others of my race. Once in studying these unhallowed manuscripts, I seem to recall I found reference to a bloodstone ring ... rather, a gem that resembled bloodstone. I've ridden several days to trace down that memory — although I've been planning for a long time to work my way around to visit you once again."

Jhaniikest tossed her head and laughed ruefully. "I see your ambitions are as boundless as ever, Kane. Well, I've kept all your things stuffed away somewhere. Those books are on the top level where you last saw them, probably, and you can page through them later. But before you turn scholar, you first shall entertain me. It's been a long while since I've had a visitor from the world outside my own, and my companions here have little to say that's of sparkling novelty."

Later that night, Kane followed Jhaniikest to the upper levels of the tower and into one of the chambers where she had gathered together many of the items she used in her own unfathomable pursuits. Finding the collection of scrolls and strangely bound volumes he sought, Kane seated himself at a lamp-lit table and began to examine the material, mumbling under his breath as he read.

Jhaniikest swung open the wide tower window. A gust of cold mountain wind stole through the gap and fanned the torchlight to a crackling slant of yellow. Twisting onto the ledge, she leaned outward over the abyss, fearless in her precarious perch. Moonlight glistened silver over her mane, glowed through the half-spread gossamer wings that curtained the aperture. Softly she sang a chant of high, tinkling syllables, watching with head atilt to see if Kane would wander in attention. But his brow remained set in an anxious frown as he concentrated over the crumbling pages of arcane glyphs penned by ancient and curious hands — although twice he gazed unseeingly toward her face as he distractedly reached for another volume. Suddenly his concentration deepened over the yellowed tome he was examining. Carefully he set aside Alorri-Zrokros's *Book of the Elders* and removed the bloodstone ring the pouch about his neck.

Laughter rose from his throat. Laughter reckless, triumphant in its rising tone. Laughter that unsettled the dust of silent years in the tower.

Startled at his outburst, Jhaniikest slipped to Kane's side, peering over his broad shoulder to discover the source of the jest.

"It's here — all here — as I remembered!" Kane pointed toward the time-stained page. "My memory has not dulled through the years... although Alorri-Zrokros's prose clings to any mind! Can you read this hand? It's an inferior transcription. See — there lies the history of this ring — a tale of an Earth centuries forgotten and of those who dwelt under stars unknown to man! There... the history of Bloodstone! Shall I read to you? Would you hear of the unimaginable power that waits to be unlocked by this ring?"

Harsh voice broken in eagerness, Kane translated the scrawled writing. Once Jhaniikest interrupted with a sharp exclamation of understanding. "Kane! Don't attempt this. I see only death for you in this madness! Let this ancient power lie buried!"

But Kane rushed on.

The bloodstone gleamed... glowed under the intensity of inhuman gaze. Deep within the green depths glinted subdued evil with the sullen promise of dawn.

III
Statecraft in Selonari

The knocking broke cadence with the throb of his skull, then seemed to drift apart, a persistent drumming now accompanied by strident chant. Then the lingering webs of sleep dissolved, and Dribeck recognized the summons at his chamber door.

"Milord! Milord Dribeck! It's well past the hour you told me to awaken you!" It was his chamberlain who tormented him. "Milord! It's close to noon! You said you must be aroused before noon! Milord, are you awake? Say something so I can be sure — "

"Go to hell, Asbraln!" Dribeck croaked. "I've been up... " He tossed back the fur robes as the knocking subsided. Unsteadily he sat up and swung his legs onto the floor. Dozens of needle-pronged flashes crackled through his skull, and he pressed his forehead against his palms, leaning forward with elbows balanced on knees. Tenderly he massaged, breathing a sigh compounded of curses and groans, until the ache retreated. He became conscious that something unclean had died in his mouth during the night.

Shenan's tits! That had been a night! All of Selonari must have lain awake at the noise! The major part of his gentry and mercenary captains had sat down to banquet. In the terminal stages of hangover, Dribeck regretted the improvident beakers of wine he had emptied. It was ruinous to match his brawny vassals cup for cup, but then his hold on their respect dictated that he stand in their eyes as full a man as any, for all his unassuming stature. In truth, though, Dribeck admitted that prudence had not tainted the wine's compelling savor at the time.

His face felt greasy, Dribeck noted, as he pushed back his shoulder length black hair and stroked smooth a tangled mustache. His jaw was convincingly stubbled, although to his chagrin its growth was too sparse even at 28 years to furnish a respectable beard. A great shame, that — a beard would add a note of strength, of dashing to his somewhat gaunt features. Not a weak profile by any measure — women found it virile enough, and men described his face as "watchful" or "quick" or "cunning." Strong enough an image for the ruler of a city-state, although Dribeck might hope for one more formidable in these times.

Shivering, he rose to his feet and pushed groggily through the curtains enclosing his bed. Pentri snorted in her sleep and half rolled to his vacated place. She was still asleep, or feigning it well — her exhaustion was gratifying, as Dribeck recalled her teasing laughter at his drunken loveplay. The rumpled furs revealed a long stretch of soft hip, but he checked his move to adjust the covering and stepped away with curtain askew. Pentri could catch cold, and Asbraln could eat his heart out. Cursing as his foot tangled in a discarded garment, Dribeck wrestled a robe over his spare frame and shuffled to the door.

Asbraln, a legacy of Dribeck's father and his tutor at arms and statecraft in younger days, swept into his lord's chamber. Glass crunched under his boot, and he regarded with raised eyebrow the strewn fragments of wine bottle. "You stated last night…" he began. His eyes widened for a second as they peered past the disarrayed curtains, and he turned his gaze quickly from the distraction. "Ah… you announced your intention to rise early to speak with Gerwein before returning to your guests."

Dribeck grunted sourly and massaged the back of his neck. Attendants were prowling about the chamber now, sorting through the debris to find fresh clothing for their master. Pentri cursed sleepily and burrowed beneath the furs. Giving her an envious look, Dribeck yielded himself to his servants' ministrations. There were better cures for a hangover than to plunge into the tangled subtleties of Selonari statecraft, he reflected.

"Any word as to Gerwein's present mood or thoughts?" he inquired of his chamberlain.

Asbraln spread his fingers. "She's angry — angry and suspicious. But that's not a new story. Our high priestess is unhappy with the increasing rumors that you intend to remove the tax exemptions the Temple of Shenan has enjoyed these many years. And this latest gathering of military power she interprets as a display of strength — an indication that you mean to enforce your taxation of Shenan's virgin coffers. I think she envisions a wholesale looting of the Temple wealth… and it's certain that she has unobtrusively increased the Temple guard."

"A lot of good that will be to her, if she thinks to stand against my will in this! But she must give some credence to any insistence that we strengthen our armed might against Breimen. The peace has been a tottering sham for years now, and it's common knowledge Malchion has doubled his mercenary ranks since last year."

"Gerwein is aware of this, milord. But she sees this as a threat to the Temple as well. She reasons that the expenses of another war with Breimen would only sharpen your eagerness to plunder the Temple's riches."

"Strikes me there's some contradictions in her suspicions," Dribeck mused. "Well, I'll talk with her, try to placate her. I'm meeting her in the Temple, which she'll take as some concession to her prestige. And while

I'm reassuring her, I can begin to plant a few thoughts in her mind on the consequences of Malchion's aggression. Her Temple would suffer more than sectarian indignities if the priests of Ommem held sway in Selonari. I think her balking at taxation will be less strident once she begins to think upon this as a holy war.

"So I'll calm icy Gerwein's objections somehow — at least until the next fancied insult provokes her. Then back to my guests... I'm leaving the day's entertainment to your overseeing. I intend to take leave of Gerwein in time to join in the games this afternoon. I've been accused of scholarship too often to risk any suggestion that the martial arts aren't the center of my life and interests. Anything else of pressing significance that I need to know about today?"

Asbraln paused a moment before suggesting, "Milord, there's a man who requests audience with you — a stranger named Kane. He claims to have a matter of considerable urgency and importance which he wishes to discuss with you."

Dribeck carefully readjusted the ties of his shirt. "Discuss with me? I assume you judged his case not to be altogether a waste of my time. Obviously, he must have enough confidence in his ability to claim my attention to warrant his passing bribes all the way up channels to my chamberlain. Well, what kind of man do you make him, and what's on his mind?"

With an air of wounded dignity Asbraln explained, "He's a strange man... savage-looking giant of a warrior, but a man of obvious breeding and refinement. Couldn't guess at his origins; he says he's from beyond the Southern Lands. I doubt he's from Wollendan, although his red hair and blue eyes remind you of that people. Age I'd guess around forty. Gives the impression of being extremely capable — and dangerous. I'd call him a mercenary officer — one several cuts above the average — who's seeking employment. At least, all he would tell me regarding his business with you was that he wishes to show you the means to increase your armed might beyond your wildest ambitions."

"Intriguing," Dribeck pronounced. "He comes at a fortuitous moment if his boast is true. More likely he's either crackpot or swindler — or perhaps an assassin sent by Malchion... or Gerwein? Disregarding these possibilities, I can take a few minutes to listen to him. From what you say, his sword might be worth my purchase, unless he sets too high a value on his service. Have this Kane brought to me at the games; I'll not need to grant formal audience to such a man as this. And see that he's closely watched while in my presence. If he's an assassin, he'll know his task is suicidal."

With uncertain stomach Dribeck steeled himself to attempt the breakfast his attendants were expectantly setting.

IV
A Stranger Brings Gifts

Arrows thudded a staccato rhythm into the wooden targets. Like a dull reverberation followed the shouts of spectator and archer together, a riotous clamor of cheers, curses, catcalls, advice. The mood was jovial, and the sour scent of beer made heady the cool air of Selonari's martial field. Already the games had progressed to the point where betting was fiercely earnest when Lord Dribeck returned from the Temple of Shenan.

His session with the high priestess had gone a little easier than expected, although Dribeck knew better than to hope Gerwein had abandoned either suspicion or ambition. Still, every day their confrontation could be delayed was a step toward victory for Dribeck and his party. Feeling more at ease, he greeted his guests with casual roughness suited to the situation and tossed off a foamy mug of beer, shouting for more to soothe a throat made arid from his tedious meeting with Gerwein. His stomach squirmed in protest before subsiding, for Dribeck loathed the taste of beer. But the alcohol seemed to blot over his lingering hangover, and he began to take in the celebrative spirit of the afternoon. Followed by a few of his closest supporters, Dribeck mingled with his guests, exchanging loud greetings and reckless wagers. He was becoming interested himself in the archery match when Asbraln approached to remind him of his half-forgotten appointment.

At Asbraln's introduction Dribeck turned a politely quizzical face toward the stranger while his mind considered the man speculatively. He was a formidable figure, this Kane, with a hulking, powerful stature that belied the feral grace of his movements. His rather brutal countenance managed to project a high degree of intellect to an eye discerning enough to penetrate its harsh savagery. The eyes … there was something chilling in their glint, a certain reflection of cold-blooded ruthlessness that underscored the impressions Dribeck had sensed. Kane was a hard-bitten warrior who had cut his way through many a battle and hardship, and his bearing indicated that he had led more often than followed. Whatever land he had last fought in, he had departed not without wealth: his garments of red wool and black leather adorned with silver studs, though not new, were not the garb of a common mercenary; nor was the sword whose hilt — unmistakably Carsultyal workmanship — protruded above his right shoulder a blade of usual quality.

On impulse, Dribeck extended his hand. The wrist his fingers closed upon was thick with sinew and muscle, while his own wrist was enshrouded in a long-fingered grip of measured strength. He wondered unpleasantly with what force might that grip tighten in anger as he retrieved his hand and gestured toward a servant to bring beer to the newcomer.

"Kane arrives bearing gifts," broke in Asbraln obliquely. He weighed the cracked leather volume apprehensively, wondering if its discolored binding might disguise some inconceivable assassination scheme. "This book," he explained lamely, as he offered it to his lord. Absently he brushed his hands across his stocky thighs, leaving faint grayish smudges trailing along the yellow wool.

Conscious of Kane's scrutiny, Dribeck opened the volume and concentrated over the unfamiliar characters. His thin face broke into a smile of enthusiastic appreciation. "Look, Asbraln! It's Laharbyn's *Principles of Sovereignty* — and in the original Carsultyal! An early transcription, by the writing!"

"I had thought you might find Laharbyn's work of interest," commented Kane smoothly. "Your interest in the finer arts is well known, so I presumed that a book might please you by way of introduction. Particularly since these works from Carsultyal's days of glory seldom reach this far west. Laharbyn has some intriguing observations on the consolidation of state power... You read Carsultyal, I see."

"Haltingly," Lord Dribeck acknowledged. "I've taken instruction in the six great languages. I'm grateful, Kane — this is an unanticipated treasure! Laharbyn I know -- chiefly through Ak-Commen's plagiarized *On Rule*. This will make a useful addition to my library."

Aware that he was in the midst of the games, Dribeck collected himself and instructed Asbraln to see that the book was placed in his chambers. His guests would not look favorably upon any show of dilettantism in this setting. Signing for Kane to accompany him, he resumed his jostled circuit along the field, his thoughts on the stranger. This was an odd gift to come from a man of Kane's profession. Possibly Kane was merely an individual of rare discernment and taste — not all wandering mercenaries were unlettered barbarians. But in view of his own political position in Selonari, Dribeck considered Kane's gift of the classic treatise on *Realpolitik* to imply broader meaning. The afternoon was proving more interesting than he had imagined.

"You intrigue me, Kane," Dribeck admitted. In step beside him the stranger nodded with a bland smile. "You're obviously taken some pains to achieve this meeting, and I wonder why. Any of my officers would have paid well for your sword, though I doubt your ambitions are that straightforward. Asbraln tells me you hinted of some means to strengthen my army... "

"Your astuteness has not been exaggerated," Kane remarked. He spoke the aboriginal language of the Southern Lands without a trace of accent, although the precise, almost pedantic, phrasing suggested it was not his native speech. "May I reflect your interest by stating that Selonari and its ruler intrigue me. As you've observed, I live by my sword — and by my wits. At present, I'm on my own and close to having exhausted the gains of my last venture, although in the past I've fought under the banners of the greatest lords — and under my own a time or two, as well.

"I set a high price on my services, a value judged from many years and many campaigns — experience that wins battles in the field and in the palace. It's a game that I love, and I choose carefully to whom I offer my sword. In brief, I seek out those battles where the adventure races to overshadow the rewards. Adventure to ease my boredom, reward to soothe my ambition... to the lord who can satisfy these motivations, I pledge my sword and the wisdom of countless battles that tempers its edge. And I feel certain that I converse with such a lord.

"It's well known in the circles I travel that Lord Dribeck of Selonari desires to add fighting men to his army, ostensibly to guard against invasion across the northern frontier by Breimen. A reasonable enough motive, since Lord Malchion of Breimen also is paying well for mercenary swords, and it's no secret that the men of Wollendan desire to extend their power all across the Southern Lands and into the Cold Forests. Then again, men say that Selonari must first conquer Selonari, before you can look toward Breimen. Selonari's ruler is young — he ascended his brother's throne before he reached maturity. And under the regency that followed his brother's untimely death, the shaky foundations of central power in the city-state crumbled yet further. Selonari's nobility are strong, and the Temple of Shenan longs to reassert itself as the center of authority. Or so men speculate in taverns and barracks all across the Southern Lands.

"All in all, men say Lord Dribeck's position is desperate, if not untenable — particularly since rumor hints he means to establish himself as absolute power in Selonari, despite the contrary wishes of certain powerful houses and of the Temple of Shenan."

"If you consider my position untenable, why have you come here?" queried Dribeck, with a note of anger.

"But I don't," Kane rushed to reply. "I only repeat rumors as they must have been reported to you. I admire a man who would rule by his wits more than by his soldiers. And I like the odds. There's no adventure in fighting for a lord whose victory is all but assured beforehand — and no profit. The lord whose hold on power is precarious... he pays well for the strength he needs to swing the balance to his favor. And will you dispute this logic which led me to Selonari?"

"I won't deny the truth of much you've observed," said Dribeck, after he had walked awhile in thought "But it seems you set a very high value on your services, Kane. Your name is unknown to me; you come without credentials other than a bold front and a polished tongue. And I'm still in the dark both as to what you propose to accomplish and what its cost will be."

Kane's reply was interrupted as Dribeck halted to watch the archers. The match was nearing conclusion. The targets — life-sized human outlines painted on planks — were moved back to well over a hundred yards' distance, and only a few of the many challengers remained in the contest. Scoring was based on a traditional set of values assigned various anatomical areas, higher points designated to the more vital regions, highest being the heart and eyes. There being no entrance restrictions, a great number of archers had begun the match — most participating only for sport and small bets with one another. But after eliminations progressed, only the most skilled marksmen remained to compete for the generous purse, and betting paced the mounting excitement.

"Are you an archer, Kane?" Dribeck asked suddenly.

"I can hold my own," he answered, offhand.

"That's my cousin Crempra there — third from the left, in brown with the high boots." Dribeck pointed toward a slender youth with no apparent familial resemblance. Crempra, who could not be as young as he looked, was stepping away from the mark in disgust. "Cousin just cost me some money with that last arrow. I was playing a long shot that he'd finish in the top five — should have tried for top ten, but Crempra told me he felt lucky. Out of his league, anyway, but the odds were nice. Look, can you handle his bow any better, Kane?"

Kane spoke cautiously, wondering where this was leading. "With a bow that I'm accustomed to, I could stand up against this field. With an unfamiliar one..."

"Crempra's is an excellent weapon," Dribeck pronounced, and waved for his cousin to join them. "You can have some free arrows to get the feel of it. You're unknown here, and there's a fine chance to set up side bets ... unless you aren't sure you can — "

"Hell, what's the bet?" Kane inquired, recognizing that backing down was not among the choices.

"That you can match the score of the five finalists — that's on a set of ten arrows at full range. Can't run through the whole series, but against the last set we can find a lot of takers who'll give us odds. Are you game?"

"Why not?" assented Kane as Crempra joined them. While Dribeck explained things to his cousin, Kane examined his bow. It was a fine instrument, he judged, a heavy weapon of moderate length after the style favored across the Southern Lands. Here in the forests, its power suited it to hunting or battle, although the bow would be too cumbersome for cavalry use.

Crempra was openly dubious but nonchalant. At Dribeck's urging he and Asbraln mingled with the throng taking bets, while the former gave orders concerning the arrangements. Dribeck seemed enthusiastic — he risked relatively little gold in the wager. If Kane won, the prestige would be Dribeck's as his backer. Should he lose, Kane would be at a disadvantage in striking a bargain with Dribeck.

Satisfied with preparations, Dribeck settled back to watch events unfold, angular jaw raised confidently, beer mug loosely held at waist level. The archery match was at last reaching an end, the final two marksmen loosing their last shafts. A wave of cheers signaled the winner — a Wollendan captain in Ovstal's service -- but already word of Dribeck's wager was drawing attention to the new diversion. Various of his acquaintances sauntered away from the crowd that milled about the winners to question Dribeck regarding the stranger. Judges quickly computed the minimum score needed to fulfill the wager; the match had been well contested, and the top five scores were high. Interest concentrated on Dribeck's proposal as the crowd waited for the other matches to begin.

It was going well. More reckless than he customarily allowed himself to be, Lord Dribeck became caught up in the general spirit. With mysterious allusions, he evaded questions concerning Kane and somehow created the simultaneous impression that the wager was both a sudden whim and a calculated ploy. It. was not a day for sober deliberation. Dribeck was a consummate gambler, this had long been known. Betting grew spirited.

A disregarded thought told him that more money was riding on Kane's untested ability than he had intended, that he had somehow implied far more knowledge of the stranger than he had any claim to. This awareness was now beside the point. Still, a shadow of unease whispered to Dribeck as he watched Kane's trial shots. The stranger had removed his sword to give full freedom to his movements. His stance was firm; Crempra's bow bent easily enough under the pull of his brawny shoulders. But his arrows were widely spaced, striking the target haphazardly, half flying wide or falling short.

Dribeck optimistically told himself that Kane was settling on a point of aim, familiarizing himself with the bow. Then the judges announced that the series would begin, and Kane chose ten arrows. Bets hastily concluded as the men concentrated on the archer and his distant target.

Kane's first arrow struck the center of the silhouette's chest. The next two feathered the heart. A fourth protruded from the throat. Two more shafts bit into each eye. Another squarely between. Then again to the heart. Before the tenth arrow was released, the only dispute that remained was whether the arrow to the crotch had been intentional or not. Kane's tally was almost twice that of the high score for the set.

A raucous outburst followed his last arrow. Outrageous handfuls of coins glittered and jingled from reluctant purse to eager hand. Awestricken applause mingled with clamors of protest, while older spectators argued over legendary contests that reputedly had attracted archers of greater skill.

"This really is a fine bow," Kane remarked, returning it to Crempra. "Should you decide to sell it, I'd be interested in talking with you." Crempra accepted the weapon with a bitter smile; he had bet against Kane.

"Brilliant marksmanship!" Dribeck congratulated, watching from the corner of his eye as Asbraln swept together a mounting heap of coins. "I was wondering how this might end after seeing your warm-up."

"No point in scaring off bets," Kane explained, which was not entirely true.

The uproar gradually dissipated as the games progressed to new events. Targets were rearranged for spear and knife competitions; elsewhere preparations began for bare-handed combat. Other fights took place which had not been planned, but none of them reached the stage of serious injury. It was a splendid afternoon, and Dribeck felt unaccustomed exhilaration as he downed another mug of beer. He was going to be drunk on his ass by nightfall, but he would not be alone, and it *was* a glorious afternoon.

"Well, Kane, if you have other talents that sparkle like your aim, I'll pay well to enlist them," Dribeck exclaimed between toasts. "Just what do you have in mind? Obviously a position of leadership. Granted. Shall I give you command over a company? Readily done — new mercenary troops are coming into Selonari every day, and I need experienced officers. There'll be a good chance to move to higher rank if you prove to be up to your own recommendation. I look for ability in my staff, and you'll find me as quick to recognize it as to reward it."

"Your offer is generous enough," Kane said smoothly, his manner implying his acceptance would be a personal favor. "But as I have hinted, I hope to discuss something more than military commissions — matters of far greater portent to your rule."

"Oh?" Dribeck had recognized that Kane's interest was more complex than simple pursuit of office. "Back to the mystery plan to make my army irresistible in battle? I had assumed you were grandstanding with Asbraln."

"This doesn't need to reach the public ear." Kate gestured toward the entourage.

Dribeck had already discarded the idea that Kane might be an assassin. He signed to his guard, who drew back. Withdrawing somewhat from the elbowing crowd, he propped himself against an overturned beer keg and looked inquiringly at the stranger.

"I'm a man of considerable learning," Kane began.

"So you've taken great pains to impress upon me."

"It was my intention to establish the validity of what I'll propose to you," Kane explained with a slight frown. "You're intelligent… a scholar of note. I'd only be wasting my time unless I've convinced you that my ideas are founded on careful study — on learning, rather than on ignorant superstitions."

Now completely baffled as to Kane's intent, Dribeck shrugged. "All right, I'll grant that you're well informed. But come to the point."

"I've spent a great deal of time in Carsultyal," Kane went on. "Her days of glory are long past, it's true, but that land was the center of man's exploration of elder knowledge. Most of the 'discoveries' that mankind built a civilization upon after the fall of the Golden Age were actually rediscoveries of alien science, pickings gleaned from the scrapheaps of vanished prehuman civilizations."

"Truth that has already all but passed from the popular mind," Dribeck nodded. "Man knows that he sprang forth on the Earth full grown, but in his conceit he has forgotten the reasons for his short infancy. Yes, I know the great works of Carsultyal. I've read of the fantastic discoveries of those early men -- the giants who fathomed the secrets of elder Earth to build a civilization overnight upon the prehuman ruins. I even have two volumes of Kethrid in my library, including the launching of *Yhosal-Monyr* and his voyages to explore the ancient Earth. It's a tragedy that the entire tale of that first great exploration is unknown to history."

"Tragedy? But then Kethrid lived for the poetry of the mysterious," mused Kane.

Withdrawing his thoughts from another path, he continued. "Good! Then you're familiar with much that I'm going to disclose to you. Do you know Alorri-Zrokros's *Book of the Elders?*"

"I know of it," Dribeck acknowledged, "though I've never seen a copy — nor spoken with one who has. Alorri-Zrokros's grand design of compiling a history of prehuman Earth was a brilliant conception. The zeal with which he pursued his researches bore unhallowed results, as his contemporaries record. Following that, little effort was made to preserve his work for those who might follow him."

"I've read Alorri-Zrokros," Kane stated. "I know his book well, and I respect the ancient wisdom he unveils in those pages. Knowledge is a tool — black knowledge a dangerous tool, but nonetheless a source of power to him who uses it with care."

Kane paused, seemingly in thought. Dribeck stared at him, awe-stricken interest in his gaze. A dozen wild speculations tumbled through his brain. He did not doubt Kane's assertion. Somehow no wonder seemed beyond the stranger's power to unfold.

"I read in the *Book of the Elders* of an elder race called the Krelran," Kane continued, "and of their ruined city which is known to man as Arellarti."

And suddenly Dribeck felt that the afternoon had been drained of its warmth and familiar laughter. There was no physical change. Just that a subtle and smothering veil seemed to separate them from the sunlight, from the human carousal, from the buoyant well-being he had known a moment ago. Annoyed at his sudden chill, he tried without success to dismiss it with a mental shrug. Unaccountably, Dribeck noticed for the first time the bizarre ring Kane wore loosely on his left hand — a bloodstone massive even against that outsize fist.

"What did the wizard have to say of Arellarti?" asked Dribeck uneasily.

"Much that would interest you — considering Selonari's proximity to the ruins. The Krelran were an enigma even among the mysterious elder races of prehuman Earth. Alorri-Zrokros has very little to disclose of their origins, their civilization, their position in the dawn world. They were not native to Earth — like others of that time, they came from beyond the stars — where, how, why is not known. The Krelran were few in number; so far as man has discovered, they built only one city, Arellarti. The ancient seas cut deep into the Southern Lands then, and Arellarti stood upon an island of a great inland bay. Alorri-Zrokros describes it as a wondrous and imposing citadel, standing only for a short time before its fall.

"For the Krelran found the ancient Earth a hostile world. Even in their solitude they became embroiled in the wars of the elder races. They defended their city well with their strange weapons; the alien science that had carried them from beyond the stars harnessed for them energies beyond human imagination. Great as their strength must have been, their enemies were more powerful. Arellarti was destroyed within its first century — by the Scylredi, Alorri-Zrokros postulates. The Krelran never recovered; their few survivors lived as savages in the shelter of the forested shore. The ancient sea receded until Arellarti was a lost island in a vast salt marsh, called today Kranor-Rill. Still skulking within the swamp and its vine-hidden ruins are the degenerate remnants of the Krelran race... the bestial anthropoid slime-dwellers you call Rillyti."

Dribeck rocked back on the beer keg, rubbing his palms across his knees. "Not all of what you tell me is new to us in Selonari," he pointed out. "The borders of Kranor-Rill are only a long day's ride from our walls, on the southern edge of our holdings. Though my people are not versed in the legends of the elder races, we know the Rillyti. Savage monsters — stand taller than a man, but their bodies are amphibian — heads like toads. They're semi-intelligent — fight with forged weapons, have a language of sorts. Dangerous beasts — but fortunately it's rare for one to stray from the confines of their swamp. And Kranor-Rill they're welcome to! As treacherous a tangle of slime and mud, vines and cypress, insects and vermin as ever defiled good land. The swamp is virtually impenetrable, and not far from its southern limits the Cold Forests begin. So there's not even a good reason for traveling around Kranor-Rill.

"As to Arellarti, our legends tell various stories of a lost city that lies in ruins within Kranor-Rill. And it's told that the city was built long ago by the Rillyti, that they still use its fallen structures as a temple for obscene rituals. They *do* creep forth on occasion and steal a girl from one of the outlying farms. Few men have braved the swamp and its ugly guardians to seek out Kranor-Rill's lost city; fewer still have returned to describe their adventure. Some men claim to have glimpsed Arellarti; their tales range from its being a shining city of gold to nothing more than a vine-choked jumble of broken stone.

"So Kranor-Rill is a stinking quicksand pesthole wise men avoid. The Rillyti are dangerous but rarely seen, since they shun the dry forestlands. Not even worth exterminating — if that were feasible. Wolves, panthers... these are the real dangers to those who live beyond the walls.

"Well, your account of Arellarti's forgotten past is intriguing, Kane. Perhaps, then, there's substance to the sinister and unsettling legends of Kranor-Rill. At any rate, you give a certain aura of ancient grandeur to that ill-famed region and its repulsive inhabitants. But just what significance do you attach to this? What bearing does prehuman history have on my present state of affairs?"

Kane inspected his empty mug and answered in a lowered voice, "Perhaps a great deal. We know that Arellarti was the fortress of an advanced civilization. The weapons of the Krelran were deadly beyond human conception. Now, suppose you had access to such power... imagine that Krelran weaponry were available to your army!"

"Absurd!" Dribeck commented, though his face showed interest. "Whatever weapons the Krelran commanded are age-old heaps of corrosion and dust by now."

"I'm not so certain," Kane went on. "Alorri-Zrokros hints that much of Krelran science lies preserved in Arellarti's ruins — that their most potent weapon was spared in the city's fall! The elder races controlled secrets of unfathomable mysteries, of incalculable powers! Is it so impossible, therefore, that some of their creations might have resisted the breath of time — might there not still exist some few artifacts of Krelran science that only await the touch of intelligence to be reactivated? I tell you, Lord Dribeck, I have spent years studying the great works of Carsultyal, and of other learned minds! I'm not only convinced that certain Krelran weapons survive in Arellarti, but I'm certain I can discover the secrets of their operation!"

"The odds are formidable on either assertion," reflected Dribeck, now plainly intrigued by Kane's argument.

"But the stakes are more than high enough to justify the attempt. If I can uncover just a few of their weapons… if I can reactivate only some minor portion of their ancient power… think of the value this would be to your army. The prestige, the fear of an unknown power! It would assure your leadership of Selonari — and Malchion would think long before risking his troops against such a force!"

"Arellarti is well guarded against intrusion these days," Dribeck pointed out, his thoughts racing in excitement. A calm voice of logic was speaking unheeded within his mind.

"It would be difficult — a dangerous mission, I'll concede. What I propose to do is lead a small force of picked men — well-armed to combat both swamp and Rillyti — lead them into Kranor-Rill. Alorri-Zrokros mentions that a path of sorts does exist. I've led a force through 'impenetrable' swamp before, and there I battled slinking natives with poisoned darts and treacherous snares. Logistically, this problem is similar and can be met with appropriate military solution. We'll enter Arellarti, and we'll unearth the secrets its ruins hold. What I find, I'll carry back to Selonari. And you'll have the weapons of elder Earth at your command."

"And what will you have, Kane?"

The stranger laughed. "Adventure… that for certain! And I trust your gratitude and confidence in me will lead you to reward me with a position of high rank. I'm not going to stay young forever… I hope that my years of fighting another's wars might leave me with more than a notched sword."

There was a note of mockery to his laughter, but Dribeck was well aware that he dealt with an ambitious man. "I'll give it a lot of thought," he promised. "Obviously, there'll be countless problems in organizing and carrying out your expedition — which I'm still doubtful that I'll back." But he and Kane both knew the proposal had captured his imagination. It was a long shot — hopelessly so, perhaps — but long shots paid a very high return for a paltry risk. Arms and equipment were mostly the property of the mercenaries… and it cost nothing for a mercenary to die.

With a thoughtful grunt Dribeck slid from the keg to rejoin the riotous throng. But the spirit of carefree buoyancy did not return to him.

V

The Rotting Land

Far south of Selonari, the forest confidently swept on. A blue-green sea of giant trees, flecked with ever broadening patches of white as it halted against the rocky coast the Cold Forests, where paths that led to the Ice Sea had seldom felt the tread of man. The forest's advance was not unbroken. Just to the south of Selonari grew a cancer. A festering abscess blighted the Southern Lands for tens of miles, swallowed the clear mountain rivers that fed its sickness, drained as a fistula through a wound in the Lesser Ocalidad Mountains and into the Western Sea. A rotting land, Kranor-Rill.

At Kranor-Rill the forest faltered. The proud, straight trunks gave way to stunted weaklings as the land began to sink. With an almost perceptible break, the forest ceased, the swamp began. Cypress was now the largest tree, its tortured roots gasping through the tepid slime, where even willow and sycamore drowned. Perhaps the soil still bore its taint of ancient salt sea, for even the fertile mulch of decay seemed unable to support verdure normally encountered in swampland. There was a poisoned maze of twisted trunks, of thorn-guarded scrub, of writhing vines. The vines — these were best suited to Kranor-Rill, thin creepers like drawn copper wire that tore with barbed kiss at those who brushed against them. Gargantuan lianas entwined about the trees — eventually amassing so thick as to choke their hosts — forming grotesque tangles of free-standing coils as their victims rotted in their grasp. Cowering, choking, poisonous, parasitic creatures — the vines were the spirit of Kranor-Rill.

It was a cold swamp, but not with the clean chill of the Cold Forests on which it bordered. The unwholesome warmth of an ocean of decay rotted the crisp cold to a corpse-like chill, like the buried incalescence of some deep and teaming crypt. From this rose a thick and ever present mist, a cloak of smothering vapor that clung to the morass, swallowed its chaotic vegetation, masked its unfathomed quicksand bogs. Kranor-Rill was a poisoned labyrinth whose oozing breath obscured the deadly hazards of its maze.

A golden-eyed serpent with scales like yellow mud broke through the green-scum crust of a dark pool and seized a man who passed too near its edge. Its wedge-like head gaped awesome jaws in a flash of hungry white as it struck, sinking double-tiered fangs into the soldier's thigh. Thrown to the mud by the impact, he had only time for a frightened howl of pain before the serpent embraced him in coils thicker than his heaving chest. Too late the mercenary sought his sword — his arm was pinioned tight against his side. Somehow his hand found a dirk. That hand stabbed convulsively, hopelessly, at the crushing coils that drew him irresistibly into the pool. Dark water stifled shriek of dread, muffled crack of splintering bone, cloaked glint of yellow coils. The crust of green scum drew a final, ruffled curtain to the scene.

It had lasted but a few seconds. The victim's startled companions broke from their frozen horror and rushed too late to the pool's edge. Across its fetid surface, scum boiled frantically, testimony to the death struggle writhing below. The enraged mercenaries jabbed swords and spears into the pool in useless retaliation, sinking to their knees in slime. A few thrusts seemed to strike resistance and brought eager curses, but the black water held its secret well. As the churning subsided, threads of dark crimson were seen tracing a pattern against the green scum. Whose blood diluted the swamp muck was never known — serpent and prey had vanished.

Angered at this newest setback, Kane drove his men back from the treacherous pool. Already they had paused to drag two men from unseen patches of quicksand, while a third had been engulfed by the morass before any hand could reach him. Two soldiers lost this quickly from his band! Worse yet, half a day had slipped past while they trudged through the reeking muck, and Kane was uncertain as to the distance that must yet be covered before darkness. Night in ruined Arellarti would be ordeal enough. But if night overtook them still shuffling through the swamp...

Kane cursed and slapped his arm. The bloodstone ring wriggled on his mud-slick finger and came perilously close to slipping off. It would have been wiser to keep the jewel in a secure pouch, but for reasons of his own, Kane stubbornly displayed the outsize ornament on his hand. A smear of blood on his arm marked the death meal of a swollen mosquito. Similar stigmata adorned like plague spots the exposed flesh of them all. Sourly Kane rubbed swamp slime over his already befouled face and arms, wondering if this provision in any degree slackened the incessant attack of the swarming insects.

"Two down — twenty-three to go," commented Banlid, Kane's paunchy second-in-command. "Kane, this stinking trail *is* going to lead us somewhere before dark, isn't it? I'm hoping it'll be the far side of this damn swamp!"

"It'll take us to Arellarti, and well before night," Kane growled, exhibiting confidence far in excess of his private feelings. Banlid had accompanied him at Dribeck's suggestion, and it was obvious that the Selonari acted as his lord's representative. It was an expected precaution, one which Kane accepted without resentment. "Regroup the men," he ordered. "This time maybe they'll keep to the trail and show a little more vigilance. The Rillyti can blend into this undergrowth as well concealed as that swamp python, and their strike will be as deadly!"

It was too much to expect that their intrusion could escape the attention of the Rillyti, Kane realized. But the risk was unavoidable, and he could only hope that the swamp creatures would be reluctant to attack so large a group of armed men — although their dim minds might consider this trespass sufficient provocation. Selonari had a few grim tales of skirmishes between man and Rillyti. Even allowing for the license of legend, the accounts were not cause for confidence. And it was only logical that the Rillyti would maintain some watch over the only direct path into their domain.

Doubtless the Rillyti knew numerous other pathways through Kranor-Rill. But Kane had learned of only one trail open to creatures not of amphibian stature and habits — and in places it seemed that even this one was beyond human capacity to follow. Alorri-Zrokros had written of a causeway built by the Krelran to span the inland sea, a bridge between their island citadel and the surrounding mainland. It was an earthen causeway, capped with reddish stone of curious texture. A hint of its construction lay in Alorri-Zrokros's suggestion that the inland sea was not a natural bay, rather an excavation blasted into the Southern Lands by the might of Krelran science. Kane had noted that the region's geology tended to support such a hypothesis.

But the causeway yet stood, outlasting the ages that had seen the ancient sea give way to tangled swampland. Following the vague description given in the *Book of the Elders*, Kane had discovered the vine-hidden entrance to the roadway at nightfall of the day previous. With dawn he had warily led his detachment of mercenaries into Kranor-Rill. Two men remained with the horses.

The swamp had almost overwhelmed the causeway, eating into its bank, burrowing beneath its bed, lapping across its surface, so that each slime-coated pool had to be probed to determine its depth. Often a seeming puddle proved to be a deep hole or bottomless quicksand. Such had to be carefully skirted, and twice logs were laid to bridge a gap where the swamp had rotted a full swath of roadway. Only in a few places could the original paving stones be trod upon. Long stretches of pavement lay buried under the thick mold of decay, and elsewhere thrusting trees and tenacious vines had erupted through the stones to form impenetrable masses of masonry and vegetation. Wherever their roots could cling grew knife-edged swamp grass and rubbery reeds high as a man's waist, and the space above was interlaced with tough lianas that dulled the intruders' swords and clawed back with grasping thorns. The boundary between swampland and causeway became a point that often defied conjecture, and only the adherence to straight-line design by the centuries-dead Krelran engineers made the decision one of reasonable certainty.

Progress was hideously slow, and the pitiless harassment of swarming insects and leeches made the march a torture. But Kane had chosen his men well, and though vitriolic, their curses did not become mutinous, even when another of their number met with mishap. He thrust his hand through the web of a gorgeous brown-and-yellow spider, whose bite left his sword arm swollen in scarlet agony.

At length the victim of the spider's fangs cried out incoherently and dropped to his knees. Delirious from the venom, he struck out at his solicitous companions, cradling his swollen arm and moaning in pain. With an eye toward the declining sun, Kane hurried to the man's side. An effort had already been made to draw out the venom — evidently without striking success — and Kane professionally estimated the soldier's chances as barely worth the effort of carrying him. The spider was of a species unknown to him, but evidently it shared the deadly antipathy that was Kranor-Rill's soul. Deeming it improvident to appear callous to his men, Kane ordered a short rest, privately wishing the victim might expire before it became necessary to transport him.

The pause was well timed.

One of the men who had moved somewhat ahead gave a sudden yell. "Damn! Here's one of them ugly things now! Hiding inside that mess of vines!" With a howl he retreated as a spear streaked past his chest.

Rising from the swamp itself, a band of Rillyti menaced them from the trail ahead — more than a dozen of the batrachian creatures. Over a head taller than a man they stood, with squat body far broader than any human trunk. Long spindly arms and thick bandy legs ended alike in splayed, webbed appendages — black claws arming the lengthy phalanges. A mottled hide of wart and scale, hued unwholesome yellow, brown and green after the swamp slime, covered their hairless bodies. Gnarled plates like armor spread across bowed back and barrel chest, stretched a sickly yellow over gross belly. A toad's head rose from wide shoulders, wattles and throat pouch, obscuring whatever neck supported it. They had lidless slit-pupiled eyes, gaping nostril pits, outsize lipless jaws rimmed with yellow vomerine fangs. These were grotesque, hideous creatures whose powerful, twisted forms echoed the malignant mess of Kranor-Rill. As they rose from hiding, black swamp water and gobbets of scum dripped from their hide and rubbery neck crests and glistened evilly on the long blades of bronze alloy that gleamed from webbed hands.

The Rillyti held their position, amphibian faces twisted in a fierce mask, yellow eyes clouded by a flashing nictitating membrane. A low grating rumble issued through bared fangs as their throat pouches puffed and slackened fitfully. Some carried short stabbing spears, to whose serrated tips a vomit-brown tarry substance clung. All were armed with the strange Rillyti sword — a finely curved blade as long as a two-handed broadsword, forged of tough bronze alloy that held a keener edge than steel — a lost alloy scavenged from Krelran ruins, Kane recalled, and a deadly weapon in their huge hands. The gummy matter adhering to their spears was a rapidly lethal poison of their preparation — corrosive, or it would be smeared on swordblades as well.

Kane considered it most fortunate that the batrachians had no more effective projectiles to dab with this venom -- their webbed hands were too large and clumsy to be skillful with a bow, nor were their bony jaws suited to use of the blowgun. However, the dense, almost impenetrable snarl of undergrowth made hand-to-hand combat the only feasible means of attack. Even now the soldiers could not use their bows effectively — too much cover for the enemy, too many tangled vines and branches for undeflected aim.

"They're not moving — looks like they're maybe interested in just guarding the trail," Banlid urged at Kane's side. "Let's get out of here before they rush us!"

"They're blocking the road because it leads to Arellarti. We must be close to!" growled Kane in excitement. "They're guarding just what I've come to find, and I'll gut any bastard who turns back on me now! We can take these slime-blooded toads easy enough! They're putting on a bluff, or they'd have attacked despite their aborted ambush! Turn tail now, and they'll run us down with ten times their number as night catches us on the trail!

"Come on, you swamp rats!" he roared, swinging his sword in a short flourish. "I'll show you how to gig toads!"

Kane rushed forward and almost was split in half by the first Rillyti to meet him. The instantaneous lunge of its thick legs launched the creature straight against Kane's charge, golden blade swinging downward as it bounded over the mud in a twelve-foot arc. Twisting desperately on the slippery footing, Kane evaded the impetus of its attack by a hairbreadth, and his blade of Carsultyal steel shivered against the bronze. The sword shrieked with a shock that numbed his shoulder, echoed through clenched teeth, but the power of his arm turned aside the onrushing blade. The Rillyti staggered as its lunge was checked, and before it could recover, Kane's weapon caught it across fist-sized eyes, topping the crested skull. With hoarse shouts his men leaped past the convulsing corpse.

"Their blood's red enough! Come on!" yelled Kane, a wild peal of laughter rising in his throat. And the swamp-strangled causeway writhed in chaotic, inhuman battle.

Evading the flailing death agony of the Rillyti, Kane turned to meet a second attack. A leaf-tipped spear jabbed for his belly, as the bufanoid feinted with its sword. Kane twisted away with feral grace, guarding the creature's blade with his own, and snatched at the spearshaft with his right hand. He meant to tear the weapon from his opponent's grip, but to Kane's dismay this stratagem had been foreseen. The shaft was coated with grease, and as the Rillyti jerked back, Kane's hand slid toward the poison-smeared head, missing contact with the serrated edge by the barest margin, when Kane hastily flicked his fingers free.

Determinedly the batrachian thrust again with its spear, this time following through with its blade. Kane parried grimly and without breaking the flow of his attack dropped in a crouch to elude the spear. Straightening with a snap, his right arm uncoiled with the precision of a cracking whip, and the dagger that he had drawn from his boot sank beyond the hilt in a slit-pupiled eye. Croaking in pain, the Rillyti dropped its spear to tear the needle from its eyesocket in a spray of ichor, its convulsive gesture ripping a jagged wound through the orbit. His adversary mortally wounded, Kane relaxed a fraction and nearly joined the swamp creature in hell. Toppling onto the mud, the Rillyti lashed out its sword with the last controlled effort of its dimming brain, and the swordtip sheared through the tip of Kane's boot as he hurriedly danced aside.

The batrachians were as slow to die as their primeval ancestors, and Kane saw at least one soldier spitted on the blade of a Rillyti as it tripped over its own dangling entrails. It was an ugly, vicious battle, as violent and deadly as the rotting land that surrounded the combatants. There was no open ground to speak of — only patches of clearing in a tangle of vines and undergrowth, ground made treacherous with leaning paving blocks, pools of muck and scum-hooded water. More than one mercenary ended his life forced into a slimy pool or quicksand mire. The Rillyti were stronger than their human opponents and fought on terrain familiar to them. But the swamp-dwellers were clumsy in their shambling movements, their webbed splay feet and bow-legs not equal to the deft footwork required for careful swordplay. Nonetheless, the slippery mud and chaotic swamp growth made footing unpredictable, which in large part offset the human beings' advantage in agility, while the Rillyti's hurtling rushes were a razor-edged terror, once the creatures had room to move. Only the raiders' superior numbers were keeping them in the battle.

Feeling a sticky warmth in his boot that he knew was not brackish water, Kane met the attack of another Rillyti. Again and again gray steel clashed against alien bronze, blades screeching like a woman's scream of ecstasy. The long-dead Carsultyal swordsmith had forged the temper well, for Kane's sword traded notches with the Krelran alloy, while several other steel blades snapped under the amphibians' powerful strokes. Kane had drawn a long-bladed knife from his belt, which he wielded with his right fist, although his new adversary fought with no weapon other than his sword.

But the Rillyti had other unexpected tactics, as he quickly discovered. As Kane lunged close to use the knife, the swamp creature gaped its jaws and lashed out with a sticky tongue of startling length. The maneuver sprayed Kane's face with a clinging stream of foul saliva. Kane choked and in reflex sought to wipe the acrid spittle from his eyes with his right arm. A second's inattention, and the hissing bronze blade all but struck home — Kane's last-instant parry deflected the other's weapon to block it against the swordhilt. The hilt stood up to the shock, but the force of impact all but wrenched Kane's weapon from his nerveless grasp. The blow benumbed the Rillyti's arm, as well, and Kane thought to finish the creature by quickly stabbing with his knife. The batrachian slithered away from the blade, taking a shallow gash through its tough hide, and its webbed hand struck Kane a solid blow.

Raking talons caught in Kane's mail shirt. On treacherous footing and already off balance, he was spun to the mud. A hanging vine tangled about his sword as he strove in vain to keep his feet, and Kane's numbed fingers relinquished their grip on its hilt. Gasping as his back crashed against an askew paving stone, Kane, swordless, saw the Rillyti raise its blade for a slash his knife could never parry. No chance to scramble for his fallen weapon. But beside him lay... a fallen spear! As he rolled desperately, Kane's left hand closed over the Rillyti spear. The swamp dweller was upon him, its fanged mouth agape in a bar of triumph. The sword was beginning its descent. Twisting on the ground, Kane hurled the spear straight into the yellowed maw.

From his semi-prone position it was a desperate, wobbly cast, with little force behind it -- but the distance was point-blank, the target lunging toward him...

Three items impinged on his hypersensitive consciousness, moving with dreamlike slowness before his adrenalin-charged mind... The spear streaking into the Rillyti's mouth, burying its poisoned fang deep into the back of its throat like a second tongue... The gleaming sword descending like a golden rainbow as he made a final effort to writhe from under its path... The bloodstone ring, loose on his finger, sailing away from his hand as he cast the spear, arcing over the embattled swampland...

With infinitesimal slowness these resolved into... A choking Rillyti, its attack forgotten, tearing at the shaft, trying to swallow, writhing a bizarre death dance, crumpling to the mud in agony, becoming still with uncanny suddenness... A bronze sword, deflected in its downward arc, grazing his shoulder as he twisted, exploding into glittering shards as it struck stone... A ring glinting in the late sun, falling through eternity, striking a pool of slime with a thick splash -- each droplet seen as it takes form and falls back — sinking into darkness.

With an insane bellow, Kane scrambled to his feet, fixed upon the spot where the bloodstone ring had disappeared. Automatically he scooped up his sword in passing, but no further notice did he take the battle. At the poolside where the ring had vanished he flung himself down and thrust his arms into the slime. Drawn white, his lips worked in soundless curses; his blue eyes were set in wild concentration. Blood dripped from a deep cut on his cheek — kissed by a fragment of the shattered sword — but he ignored it, even though the taste of blood was drawing a crawling horde of hungry leeches. Determinedly Kane raked his fingers through the fetid swamp muck, pulling up reeking fists full of wriggling mud and scum whenever it seemed he felt something hard. The pool was only a few feet deep here... if only the ring had sunk in a straight path as it hit.

"Kane! Holy shit! Have you gone stark staring mad!" Banlid shouted in his ear, shook his shoulder, interrupted his concentration. "Kane! Damn your ass, Kane! Snap out of it! We're up to our ears in battle!"

Angrily Kane cuffed the soldier away and returned to his searching. Once the rotting land had swallowed the ring, he could never reclaim it.

Alarmed, confused, Banlid jerked away from his leader. His racing thoughts reached a muddled decision that Kane had been struck on the head perhaps... clearly completely mad!

A wounded Rillyti, blood oozing from a deep stab in its chest, broke upon them. If its wound was mortal — as from its position it must be — the creature seemed not greatly disadvantaged. Croaking dismally, it spied the prone human, and its sword swung up. Banlid waited no further breath on his heedless leader and met the amphibian's attack. Few of the men other than Kane had won out in single combat with a Rillyti — ganging up on the swamp giants being the only effective strategy — and Banlid was close to exhaustion. Still, his antagonist was badly wounded, and as the mercenary feverishly defended himself, he sensed an insidious attenuation of the creature's assault.

For all this it was a tight duel -- the Rillyti lost all regard for pain or injury as it felt its strength drain from its wounds. In one final furious effort, it beat aside Banlid's tentative counterattack and leaped to grapple with him. Shakily the mercenary sidestepped its lunge, delivered a deep slash to its side, and finally hacked the Rillyti to pieces as it fell on its face, still trying to crawl forward.

Gasping for breath, he looked about for another of the monsters. None rose to attack him. Groggily he contemplated his leader, dull disbelief set in his flushed face. The madman would have let the Rillyti split him in two, had not Banlid interceded.

Kane had crawled out at full length on the pool's edge, his hips balanced there — trunk, shoulders, face buried in the tepid muck. He raised his face for air, expression still distracted, then ducked his head and churned the bottom slime with his hands. Banlid waited for matters to reach a head.

A sudden splash, and Banlid thought Kane had dived in completely. Rather it was his excited thrashing as he wriggled back onto the bank. He raised a mad countenance to the other. Slime and mud coated his face and hair, mingled with still flowing blood; a few swollen leeches dangled from the edges of his beard. Insanity burned in his cold blue eyes. His lips were twisted in a smile of triumph.

"All right... I found it," he announced in a low voice that held a harsh undernote. Carefully he wiped the ring on his filthy leathers, then slipped it once more over the middle finger of his left hand. Calmly he brushed his face clean with one hand and retrieved his sword.

Face impassive, he stared at Banlid, as if challenging other to comment upon his bizarre behavior. "Well, let's see how many are left," he remarked.

Banlid nodded, deciding it was wise to ignore the scene he had just witnessed. Kane seemed his usual self — Shenan knew how sane that might be — and the stress of battle did evoke strange reactions. The bloodstone ring drew his attention, and he wondered at the gem's eerie, sullen gleam. Was it some trick of the light, or did the stone appear to shed a more vivid luster than before?

VI
When Elder Gods Wake

The ancient causeway was torn apart by the violent struggle that had raged upon the swamp-rotted spine of red stone. Mutilated corpses of men and Rillyti lay strewn in grotesque heaps or floated in the brackish pools. Some of the Rillyti still twitched upon the sodden loam, like gigged frogs left to wither in the late afternoon sun. The bufanoid guardians were slain — reportedly one had fled into the swamp — but the toll of Kane's mercenaries was a grim one. Eight others had survived the attack, all relatively unscathed, for it had been the kind of battle in which a disabling wound meant swift death. The earlier victim of the spider's fangs lay forgotten where he had fallen, a Rillyti spear standing from his ribs; Kane wondered whether the arachnid's venom had proved fatal before the *coup de grâce.*

"If we turn back now, maybe we can make the — "

"No one turns back!" Kane interrupted Banlid. "We're almost in sight of Arellarti now, and we'll carry out my original plan! I knew we'd probably have to fight our way through Kranor-Rill — you men were told of our chances when I selected you. Our losses were worse maybe than I'd figured, but we've driven through their guards. I'll see that each of you receives a bonus when we return."

"Kane, we've only killed a few! Shenan knows how many hundreds of these monsters are lurking in this damned swamp!" Banlid protested. "We don't stand a prayer to see another dawn, if we press on deeper!"

"Want to try blundering back through the swamp after nightfall? Then pray the Rillyti overtake you swiftly — they'll grant you a cleaner death than Kranor-Rill has waiting! Sure, we've only seen a few of the Rillyti... they're scattered all through the swampland. But we've likely beaten the only organized force they'll have in our vicinity — those who stood guard over the causeway. It'll take a while for these toads to band together in sufficient strength to overwhelm us, and before then we'll be headed back to Selonari. And at Arellarti there should be room to use our bows. The ruins will give us walls at our backs — a redoubt we can defend with archery should the Rillyti get brave again. And unless the legends lie, we may uncover weapons that will give us the strength to destroy an army!"

Banlid recognized that further remonstrance was futile, probably dangerous. Grimly he acknowledged that Kane's logic was apparently sound, although the red-haired captain offered only the most sketchy plans for escaping from Arellarti, once they reached the place. The expedition held ominous promise of being a one-way trip, and with this unpleasant foreboding Banlid again regretted the role Lord Dribeck had forced him into.

The day grew a mile older, and the ground displayed no inclination to rise. Kranor-Rill yet surrounded them — the swamp seemingly endless, an omnipresence of poisoned life and malignant decay that became relentless rather than monotonous. But the sounds of the swamp had altered. The cacophony of animal sounds persisted, albeit at somewhat muted level, but new sounds now underlay. A bass croaking — distant, but seeming to gather from ever more hidden throats as they progressed. Unseen splashes, startling in their rush, that could only mark passage of creatures of considerable bulk, though no large animals had been sighted for some time. Sounds of dubious portent, where a greater imaginative effort was demanded to supply optimistic interpretation than one bleaker. Despite Kane's confident manner — reckless, a better descriptive — an atmosphere of clinging fear settled over his men.

A far-reaching shadow made twilight of the swampland and alerted them before the close horizon grudgingly yielded view. Already the causeway was rising above the morass, its glassy stones less obliterated now, and the terrain began to drop away as they approached the dull red walls that loomed above the rotting land. An island jutted from the sea of decay, and only their instinctive awe of its alien architecture held them back from storming its yawning portal — as exhausted swimmers strive toward an unknown beach, no thought for what dangers might lie beyond the surf.

Arellarti!

Dwarfed by the paired obelisks from which the massive gates had swung — now the broken pillars were festooned with vine, the gate blasted into blackened and curiously fused fragments of pitted bronze alloy — they paused to marvel at this swamp-guarded city of lost legend. Eagerly Kane clambered up the tangled lianas and gained the wall, nearly breaking his neck as a creeper tore free of the parapet. Heedless of his exposed position, he stood braced against the skyline, hands cupped to shield the setting sun that peered back at him from the opposite wall.

Arellarti was a city of stark and wondrous geometry. Its formulation lay severely circular, with diameter stretching somewhat over three miles to the far wall, so Kane estimated. Walls of the mottled red igneous stone formed a rim a hundred feet high to enclose the city. Cracked and aslant in places, the walls had miraculously escaped the centuries, although one quarter-mile section made a gap, where evidently the swamp had gnawed beneath the island. Beyond the gate, sunken stonework could be dimly glimpsed extending into the morass, possibly wharves for the long-vanished sea. Within the walls Kane could discern the outline of streets congested with debris and entwining vegetation, a perfect network of radial spokes and concentric circles whose precise engineering called to mind the deadly symmetry of a spider's web. So far as he could distinguish, the flawless geometry was extended even to the buildings that studded the concavo-convex city blocks, although distance and the general condition of extreme disrepair made this uncertain. Nonetheless, there seemed to exist an obsessive insistence that the bizarrely stylized architecture of one edifice be mirrored to the last alien angle by another counterbalancing structure. Briefly Kane noted that certain areas of smashed and toppled buildings appeared to lie in a punched-out pattern of destruction.

But his awareness of further details of the ruins was overawed by his attention to the monolithic structure that totally dominated Arellarti. A grin of triumph bared his teeth, and his bark of laughter caused wonder among his men below. Though an unknown few had ever crossed Kranor-Rill to spy upon these ruins, Alorri-Zrokros's description had been true. There at the center of Arellarti it towered like a vast hub — or like a bloated spider at the intersection of its wide-flung web, thought Kane, recalling his earlier image — colossal domed edifice over a quarter-mile across, whose smooth walls rose above the city to an apex of nearly a thousand feet. The city's seven radial streets converged on an open courtyard that surrounded the dome like a halo, and of an entrance there was no sign, the structure displaying the mathematically pure geometry that characterized all of Arellarti. Unless obscured by vines or effaced by time, any adornment seemed altogether absent from the dome itself, although the other examples of Krelran architecture showed bizarre patterns of geometric design etched into their stonework. Fissures and dark gaps that flawed the dome's soaring walls could be clearly seen at this distance, and the genius of alien engineering must have been marvelous indeed for the cyclopean structure to have resisted the crushing weight of centuries. In common with all else in Arellarti, the dome was constructed of red-mottled stone of evident igneous origin. As the late sunlight caught the city, Arellarti's precise symmetry — its glassy stones of burnt sienna, its measured streets choked with green lianas -- suddenly reminded Kane of a brilliant jeweled mosaic.

Grunting chop of sword against vine sounded close at hand. Less reckless than Kane, Banlid and the rest had pushed their way along the wall to the debris-choked stairway that ascended the parapet. Cursing as they methodically hacked through the obstructive maze of creepers, they wearily shuffled over steps which were spaced to a height uncomfortable for human gait. Near the top, their efforts dislodged a nest of hornets, and the stairway disrupted into a mad dance of frenzied swatting and swearing as the gold-and-green insects swarmed over them.

"Shenan's tits, Kane! We should have taken the ape's way up like you did!" complained Banlid, several angry welts puffing through the dirt on his bushy-bearded face. With a breathless cheer of self-congratulation, the men finally gained the rampart. Throwing themselves against the uncrenellated parapet, they gazed upon the ancient city through sweat-blurred eyes.

Abruptly one of the mercenaries wavered uncertainly. "I can't seem to breathe!" he murmured hoarsely, fear spreading across his pale features. His comrades looked at him in amazement, then in alarm, as he slumped to the stones in a stupor, sweaty hands weakly pawing at convulsive throat, his breath a strident wheeze. The sound grew higher pitched, became ragged, then ceased, his head rolled back and his limbs twitched aimlessly.

"Ommem have mercy — the hornets stung us all! We're all dead men!" moaned a Wollendan mercenary, as panic claimed the watchers.

"No, you're not! Stop your damned yelling before you shake the wall down!" ordered Kane. "Those hornets haven't poisoned the lot of you, or you'd all be flopping off the wall with him! I've seen this before — some freak of their blood makes a few people react like this to any harmless sting! Now get back and let me see to him — there's an off chance I can save him still!"

Pushing them away, Kane knelt beside the stricken soldier and whipped the dirk from his boot. Swiftly he felt along the spasm-knotted throat below the Adam's apple, sliced through surface tissue, and made a careful incision into the exposed cartilage of the windpipe.

"That's putting him out of his misery," commented someone. "Only you missed the big veins."

Kane gestured impatiently. "I cut open his windpipe so he can suck air. See... his chest is trying to pump air, but his throat's clamped shut with poisoned humors. If I was able to bypass the constriction, he can keep breathing until his breath blows off the poisoned humors, and the airways will reopen. I've seen this work a few times when a man was strangling from something within."

His men looked on dubiously, still uncertain that the hornets had not doomed them all. Although comatose, the victim's chest heaved more regularly now, and breath could be heard rushing through the wound in an eerie, bubbling rasp.

Kane watched the object of his handiwork with the inspired interest of experimentation. "Couple of you bring up some of that cane we've been chopping through all day," he ordered. "I think I can get a hollow tube down his windpipe an inch or two maybe. Ought to hold back the constriction and keep the hole open."

Two of the men disappeared down the stairway. The rest remained grouped around the victim, watching with interest. A few bets began to be offered as to his chances.

Howls of death and booming croaks rose like gobbling thunder from below and shattered their absorption with their unconscious fellow. Crawling from the cover of the swamp, a horde of Rillyti erupted onto the causeway. Their number may have been a hundred or a thousand — the computation was pointless in view of the handful who stood against them. Rising from the morass wherein they had stealthily gathered force, they swept onto the high ground like an obscene tidal wave of misshapen flesh and gleaming bronze. Their rush was irresistible. Even as those on the wall turned in horror, the second soldier was shredded under a dozen blades; his companion had utterly disappeared. In an instant the bufanoid army had bounded across the intervening space to storm the walls atop which the interlopers made a hopeless stand.

"We'll try to drive them back!" shouted Kane without conviction. "We've got the obelisk to our backs — that leaves only the one direction they can rush us from! They'll charge the stairway we've cleared for them, or one farther down — either way, that bottlenecks their attack! Bows ready! We'll pick them off as they come up the stairs! Shoot well if you'll live! There's a chance to slaughter enough to discourage their charge!"

And every man there knew that chance to be infinitesimal, and their prospects should they miraculously break the Rillyti onslaught even bleaker. To stain these stones with batrachian gore might make death sweeter, but no less final.

The Rillyti threw themselves at the wall, springing up the partly cleared stairway at as frantic a pace as the congested passage would permit. At close range, the archers fired into the foremost ranks. Roars of pain and rage boomed from the swamp creatures' throats as the powerful shafts skewered vital targets with withering accuracy. With each mortal wound, an amphibian pitched writhing into space and tumbled flailing against those behind. Their agonized contortions dislodged the others and checked their rush until the slain could be thrown over the edge. But the rush could be held only for a moment. Relentlessly the Rillyti stormed up the stairway, though the slaughter was great, and the steps grew slippery with their blood, the rubble below laden with flopping bodies.

Those who milled at the fool of the stairway shortly grew frustrated at the slow progress and thought to reach their enemy by a shorter route — although it was clear that the attack along the stairs moved inexorably nearer. A few with great hops caught the thick creepers that clung to the wall and began to climb. Others followed their lead, and quickly the wall was wriggling with a growing horde of clambering Rillyti. Although awkward and heavy, the amphibians used their clawed strength to great advantage — having some occasion to climb in their normal circumstances — and their ascent threatened to overwhelm the defenders in a short time.

Kane immediately noted their new line of assault, and he ordered his two worst archers to ward off this latest threat. With the slackened fire, the charge up the stairway accelerated alarmingly, but Kane knew an attack from more than one point would mean inescapable disaster. And the quivers rapidly grew depleted — only the arrows salvaged from the earlier skirmish had saved their supply from exhaustion before this. With their tough, warty hide and reptilian vitality, the Rillyti were difficult to bring down, often shambling forward in defiance of several well-placed shafts.

Desperately the soldiers hacked at the taut vines, seeking to check the assault on the wall. Often their efforts succeeded, for as the heavy batrachians recklessly flung themselves onto the lianas, the dragging weight became too great a burden. Weakened by the sword blows, one creeper after another tore loose from the wall and plummeted to the earth with its load of luckless climbers. But the lianas were on all sides, and many were too firmly rooted to be dislodged. It soon became necessary to fire down them point-blank, as the climbers struggled to the top. And then their swords had to meet flesh and bronze as the Rillyti reached the rampart.

The Rillyti gained the head of the stairway at about the same moment they broke over the parapet. With the detached calm that comes to fighting men who know death inescapable, Kane and his tiny force sent the last of their arrows drilling into those first to leap onto the rampart. In one corner of his mind, Kane saw the victim of the hornet's sting flung out from the wall, to plunge among the horde yet gathering on the ground below. He felt regret that he would never know whether his surgical efforts had been successful.

The killing that ensued was too one-sided to be termed a struggle. The two who sought to repel the climbers went down immediately, their reddened blades unable to dam the flood that swept over them. Another wave of Rillyti swarmed up the stairway, their rush unimpeded by silent bows.

"Make for the gate pillar!" roared Kane, knowing that they would be instantly overwhelmed by an attack on both sides. Not that the outcome would be altered. "Put the stone to our backs! We'll leave a few less toads to croak tonight!"

Determinedly they rushed toward the Rillyti who were just scrambling over the parapet. Gold blades swept up to bar their path; at their backs the rampart echoed the slapping tread of those who pursued them from the stairs. Kane led his men with a fury no strength could match. One batrachian was blasted from the parapet by the force of Kane's sword; another dropped under the gutting slash of his knife. A scream, and the man beside him reeled with a spear through his side. Kane whirled to lop off the climber's other arm as it reached over the parapet. Trailing scarlet droplets, the creature tumbled away from its hold, its webbed hand left locked about the vine.

Not yet in full possession of the rampart, the Rillyti fell away under their concerted rush. Face twisting in hate, Kane drove through their unformed ranks, dashing past the blades and taloned hands that clutched from the parapet. His desperate strength clove a path through, as none could stand before his blade. Behind him another of the soldiers died. Blood streamed from two shallow gashes that he never felt strike. And then they reached the gate pillar — Kane, Banlid, and a last mercenary, who slumped against the stone and slid slowly to the walkway as the Rillyti poison stole his last strength.

The timeworn obelisk at their backs, before them the amphibian horde was grouping for the final rush. The wall now crawled with Rillyti, bronze weapons poised to reave, bufanoid faces hideous in yellow-fanged grimaces of rage. Their cold, noisome breath seemed to brush against Kane and Banlid like the icy touch of death.

"We were fools not to turn back!" Banlid groaned. "While we violated their sanctuary, the swamp devils called together their hordes to ensnare us! Kane, we die now as no brave man should ever die!"

"I still have a last throw of the dice!" snarled Kane defiantly.

Taking a deliberate stride toward the advancing Rillyti, Kane dramatically extended his left arm — his hand a clenched fist. The batrachian ranks shuffled a step or two closer… then faltered! Croaking among themselves in subdued tones of confusion, the Rillyti suddenly halted.

Numb in disbelief, Banlid stared with jaw buried in double chin, not daring to guess how long this miracle might last. Initially, the shock was too stunning — some sort of garbled thought suggested that Kane's weaponless defiance had caused their confused hesitation. But a moment passed, and Banlid followed the gaze of those many bufanoid eyes.

He saw the massive bloodstone ring that blazed like a great inhuman eye upon Kane's fist and observed how the darting rays of the sun shone upon the gem, made the bloodstone glow like a living flame. He felt the sudden hush of awe that fell over the vengeful army of swamp creatures and sensed for himself the aura of unthinkable power that pulsed within the ring.

Like a scythe, this incredible reversal of mood passed through those Rillyti gathered about them and stilled their blood-mad roars, the murderous rush upon the wall. As knowledge spread among them, the batrachians fell into uncertain milling, their excited croaking softened under some indefinable emotion… *was it dread?* The sudden silence that crept over the beleaguered wall was eerie with the dying echoes of battle.

A specter in the macabre tableau, Kane took a slow step forward. A lifetime reached across the completion of that stride! And to Banlid's already overtaxed mind came another miracle beyond belief, transcending all hope. The foremost Rillyti moved back a step!

Another step. Now more of the creatures recoiled. *By Shenan… they were retreating!*

Deliberately Kane stalked toward them, fist extended so that all could behold the bloodstone ring. Reluctantly, inexorably as the ebbing tide, the Rillyti retreated before him, slunk back along the wall, stole down the stairway. Some broke for the swamp and disappeared into Kranor-Rill carrying news of unimaginable portent to their tribes. The major part of their number drifted back along the streets and into empty doorways, to watch intently from the shadows.

It was not truly a retreat, Banlid realized, but something different — an aura of ominous expectancy. Their harsh croaking — surely a rude language — imparted a further sense of waiting… of reverence… of fear… *Why?*

"I understand now why you scrambled like a madman to regain that ring," whispered Banlid, following uncertainly in Kane's shadow. "Is it some sorcerer's ring of power? What enchantment drives them back?"

Kane's face was transfigured in a storm of emotion. "The ring has no power yet — at least, I don't think so!" His voice was cracked, still shaken with unbearable tension. The nightmarish sequence of events had overstrained even his iron nerve, so that he dropped his normal veiled manner. "The Rillyti know this ring — they recognize Bloodstone! After centuries their race yet remembers the unearthly power this ring can command!"

The *Book of the Elders* had suggested such racial memory, hinting that worship of Bloodstone yet survived in certain demented rites among the Rillyti. Kane had studied the passage with obsession, brooded countless hours over the secrets hidden within other scraps of legend and black lore, seeking to wrest every particle of ancient knowledge from beyond the veils of time. A vast amount had escaped him, some areas beyond wildest conjecture. Sufficient facts were certain, however — enough to tempt him to fantastic risks. Alorri-Zrokros had maintained that the Rillyti would recognize the ring and honor its bearer; Kane was himself confident that this was indeed the ancient ring. But he had not intended to make the proof of the madman's visions rest on so terrible a test. Kane had fought free of death's grasping claws uncounted times. Still, this headlong plunge into unthinkable disaster, which his forced gamble had checked at the final instant, left him stunned in its aftermath.

Banlid watched the other man calculatingly. His thoughts pieced together numerous items of information regarding Kane — various bits of fact, threads of doubt that had never taken full form, the questions Dribeck had raised concerning the stranger. The Selonari lord has been astute in sending Banlid to keep watch over Kane — Banlid whose rotund frame belied the hardened fighter, as did his sleepy appearance mask a quick mind.

"The bloodstone ring you must have found and recognized as some sort of key to the ancient Krelran mysteries?" he questioned, as they descended the stairway. At Kane's distracted nod, he persisted, "Now that you've reached Arellarti, do you believe you can fathom its lost secrets? Can you command the power this ring may unlock?"

Kane's cold eyes were searching his now. The red-haired stranger was off his guard no longer. His answer came with sardonic tone.

"Yes."

But by this point Banlid had already begun to suspect the essential elements of Kane's designs.

"The Rillyti are overawed for the moment," he suggested. "Let's make a break for it before they lose their enthrallment!"

Kane shook his head. "They're not likely to. The power I've fought to possess lies nearby. Before another dawn, I'll explore Arellarti's secrets, or else there'll be no dawn!"

"You'll never succeed in carrying anything of value out of here on your own," Banlid pointed out. "We need to return to Selonari for more men."

Nervously he glanced toward the open gate, the ruined causeway leading across the darkening swampland. "Look, Kane... stay the night here if you're set on daring these devils to tear you to ribbons. But I'm heading back to Selonari right now — and on my own, if you mean to stay. Lord Dribeck will be grateful for whatever discoveries you've made for him. He's sure to send back enough men to help transport any useful artifacts to Selonari. You'll be made a lord, Kane — if the Rillyti don't finish you before dawn!"

"Go if you want to. I'm going to risk it," Kane replied.

Sweat chilled the small of his back as Banlid considered the stranger's ice-fire eyes. "Then I guess I'll try to get through." Could he dare hope Kane had not understood the full reasons for his fear? "If that ring gives you any kind of control over these Rillyti, see if you can persuade them to let me through the swamp." He reminded hopefully, "After all, I saved your life back on the trail when you were grubbing through the muck. I know you won't forget that."

"Hell, Banlid!" Kane muttered impatiently. "Go on and lose yourself in Kranor-Rill — I won't stop you! I don't know how much hold I've got over these toads… or how long it may last. But your chances here with me are better than if you try to follow that causeway after dark!"

"Well, I'll take the chance," returned Banlid. Resolutely he turned and trudged for the gate, trying to forget the numberless terrors that lay between Arellarti and the distant forests. The Rillyti alone presented enough threat, even if —

An envenomed blade drove through his back, ending his fears forever.

Pensive, Kane looked down at the spear-impaled form, half wondering that he felt no regret. Had the centuries stripped from him every vestige of humanity, then? "There was an outside chance you might have gotten through," he explained to the corpse.

If this sudden flash of violence perturbed the Rillyti, there was no indication. The swamp-dwellers had scattered, although many a hulking form could be seen standing apart or huddled in small groups. Though none came near him, their slitted eyes turned upon him a gaze of unfathomable interest. A low croaking passed among them — harsh rumbling syllables that conveyed a note of urgent excitement.

How long their awe of the bloodstone ring might maintain this nervous truce, Kane cared not to guess. He was gambling on the blighted wisdom of one whose visions brought madness coincident with lost knowledge. To win meant power whose limits Alorri-Zrokros had but hinted; failure would be disaster that similarly confounded human imagination. Since that night in Jhaniikest's tower, Kane had given no thought to the odds.

Warily Kane turned his back on the death-laden portal and stepped determinedly into the street. A few of the Rillyti stood in his path, but as he strode toward them, they shuffled away hastily. As he passed, Kane sensed that the watchers were following at a cautious distance. Continued beyond the gate as the swamp-buried causeway, the main avenue radiated through the Krelran city from its central nave. Garlanded with creepers and sparse undergrowth, its geometric perfection was only slightly hidden by leaning walls and heaps of debris. The colossal dome, now blotting out the setting sun, squatted at the city's heart, its curved walls arched above the peripheral structures in sullen mockery of a rainbow.

Reckless in the presence of that which for weeks had dominated his thoughts, Kane hurried toward his goal. His shallow wounds bled afresh as he clambered over mounds of rubble and impatiently hacked restraining vines. Even in his haste, he noted that the street was in far better repair than its antiquity warranted — though whether this was due to the permanence of Krelran architecture or because the city was not altogether untenanted he could not judge. Behind him sounded the leathery slap of webbed foot, the scratch of claw on stone. The Rillyti shambled in macabre procession and hunched in the shadows as he passed, peering with basilisk intensity from apertures in the time-blasted edifices. Kane absently noted rhythmic syllabism in their subdued croaking — dirge-like in its ominous tone of mingled dread and expectancy.

Framed by the eon-haunted structures that pressed upon the debris-piled avenue, festooned with lianas and spider-rooted trees that insinuated through cracked walls, the colossal dome awaited Kane at the dead city's heart. Fired by the dying sun — or by Kane's fevered imagination — the igneous stone blazed with volcanic hue, conjuring flame images of irresistible summons. It seemed to waver in Kane's vision, and though it beckoned with the compelling lure of flame to moth — promising doom, but with it an infinite moment of unimaginable ecstasy — Kane's purpose was unswerving. His obsession to cleave through the barrier of centuries, to command the secrets of elder-world science, totally consumed him, drove from his thoughts all caution, all doubt. Before him lay the key to incalculable power; every atom of his energy must be directed toward unlocking it. He limped, though unaware of the pain of his wounds, of the sapping agony of exhaustion. The ordeal of wrenching a path through the swamp and the hysteria of headlong battle at death's crumbling precipice had left his spirit numb to further shock. Now he was surrounded by scores of savage batrachians, alone in a lost city whose prehuman antiquity his very presence blasphemed. Kane's mind was twisted to a state of dreamlike clarity and obscurity, his thoughts a dichotomy of inspired certainty, enshrouded disregard. But a demonic haunting that transcended sanity had overshadowed Kane's mind ever since his eyes had first gazed into the bloodstone ring.

Nimbus about the flame, the open plaza encircled the monolithic dome. As Kane emerged from the avenue, it seemed as if the encroaching trees were stunted, twisted by the aura that emanated from the dome, their roots forced into octopoid contortions as they sought to penetrate the court pavement. At closer observation the giant dome was not unmarred by the centuries. Fissures traced patterns across its curvature; in some places, jagged apertures gaped to reveal a double wall, cross-braced with struts of bronze alloy. But not even the awesome weight of millennia had conquered this masterwork of alien engineering. Battle-scarred but erect, the dome rose in defiance of time, and only in a few sections did rifts breach both inner and outer wall. No doorway broke the hemispherical trimness of design. However, as Kane crossed the courtyard, he saw that the avenue led toward an opening in the perimeter, wherein a flight of steps inclined gently downward into darkness. Similar depressions could be seen on either side, and presumably Arellarti symmetry of design dictated subterranean ramps at each of the seven radial avenues. With the same reckless confidence, Kane descended the oddly spaced steps to the sunken entrance that waited in the dim light below. Sliding doors of bronze alloy stood apart across the semicircular opening, their massive slabs drawn back within the double wall. Entangled vines gave evidence of how long the doorway had lain open, awaiting entrance through its thirty-foot portal — *entrance of whom?* Kane stepped through.

The dome glowed, not from the sun — the fire was within. Sudden fleeting impressions, noted briefly as attention is swept past, drawn meteorlike to the heart of Arellarti: Vast open space, twilight. The sunlight filtering through fissures in the giant hemisphere in blobs of wan yellow, streaks of starlight dripping across the midnight dome of heaven. Trailing streamers of liana, like clouds against the sky, sick-toned and leprous-fleshed in the weak light. Strewn mounds of fallen rubble, soaring columns of bronze alloy, curved to brace the walls so high above. Pillars of cyclopean machinery, huddled in shrouds of fleshy creeper like brooding sentinels. Fantastic banks of ceramic and stone, metal and crystal — curiously patterned, multi-hued — all intertwined with mammoth lengths of copper that crawled throughout, like unthinkably huge serpents writhing from a nest of eggs.

An overawing all wonders… Bloodstone!

A gigantic crystal hemisphere nearly a hundred yards across filled the chamber's center, a smooth half-globe of dark green veined with red. Peripheral to its base was a circle of silver-white metal, linked by copper arteries to the looming columns of machinery. The heart of Arellarti did not beat; within the crystal its fires slumbered. But in the dim light Kane recognized immediately the kinship of this monolithic crystal to the bloodstone ring upon his finger. Passages of the *Book of the Elders* flashed through his consciousness and bombarded his senses with intolerable excitement as he understood the validity of its eldritch history.

No mine on Earth could have quarried so gigantic a crystal; Bloodstone, like the ring on Kane's hand, had come from beyond the stars. Here under this vast dome lay the culmination of Krelran science, the core of their ancient power. But that power lay dormant, buried by the centuries, and, as with the gemstone of the ring, only an aura of evil hinted of the immeasurable potential quiescent within the crystal's murky depths. No vestige of decay marred Bloodstone, nor did any vine cling to its gleaming curve. A crescent bank of the mottled red igneous stone stood close by Bloodstone, raised somewhat, as an altar before an idol. A bewildering pattern of copper and silver-toned metal, rods, cones and knobs of ceramic, and oddly hued crystal were set into its face, while within the apex of the semicircle lay a yard-wide disk of silver-white metal, from whose center a small black depression stared like a cyclops's eye. From the outer rim of this crescent dais gathered a maze of silver and copper cables, which joined into a central column of silver-white metal five feet across and fused a horizontal link between the instrument bank and the band of similar metal encircling Bloodstone.

It *was* an altar, observed Kane, noting the thick litter of human and batrachian bones strewn before Bloodstone at this point, the gruesome stains encrusted upon the crescent — grim evidence of the hideous rites men whispered the Rillyti held here. A humerus crunched to powder beneath his boot, testimony to the antiquity of the sacrifice. The anxious croaking of the Rillyti followed him across the dome's interior, a rumbling echo ominous as distant thunder. A monstrous congregation, they shambled behind him into their hoary temple. In the shadow they waited, squatting in puddles of tepid water, leaning on mounds of rubble, peering from behind tangles of leprous vegetation — their savage minds stricken with both anticipation and fear, as they waited to learn if the priest of legend had returned. Bronze swords in webbed hands promised the easiest fate that would await an impostor's unthinkable blasphemy.

Ignoring the Rillyti, Kane concentrated on what Alorri-Zrokros had written concerning Bloodstone — the macabre ritual his sorcery-trained mind had rehearsed, pondered over a thousand times since the reading. Only now his limbs seemed to move automatically, his thoughts incisive with inhuman clarity. The fading rays of daylight gave only splotchy illumination through the cracked dome, but he found this light more than adequate. No fear, no indecision encumbered his movements, and dimly Kane was aware that flashes of knowledge — patterns of thought not his own — were guiding him, drawing him into the ritual.

He mounted the few broad steps of the platform upon which rested the mottled stone crescent, blindly knocking away the skeletal debris. Unbearable tension charged the air like unborn lightning. The bank of instruments consumed his total attention. Jaw set in concentration, eyes hard with intensity, he studied the controls only briefly, so it seemed. Then his long fingers closed upon a silver rod and drew it down. A copper rod next, moved to the right; these ceramic knobs — too large for human grip — to be rotated thus. Kane's darting hands deftly performed intricate movements regarding which Alorri-Zrokros's instructions had been only vague. There was no uncertainty, nor did Kane pause to consult the careful notations he had distilled from the *Book of the Elders.*

A few levers resisted his strength momentarily, but time had done little damage to the alien machinery. Now the air was charged with more than psychic energy. Howls of fear bleated from the watchers as they were driven back against the shadow of the cracked and curving walls. Blinding bursts of light exploded from long-dead pillars of machinery; sheets of multicolored fire enveloped the serpentine coils of alien metal. A harsh stench like ozone assailed Kane's nostrils, and the air grew thick with reeking smoke as shrouds of fleshy liana peeled away in sizzling, sickly flame. Sparks crackled through the air, blazing within the colossal dome like an insane aurora borealis. A blast of luminous flame lashed out at a group of Rillyti who had cowered too near and left a huddle of blackened death.

Kane laughed in demonic exultation — a macabre figure bespattered in filth and gore, eyes ablaze like blue coals, red hair disordered with static, face transfigured in the chaotic blaze of light. Voice lifted against the crackling explosions, he screamed the chant Alorri-Zrokros had recorded, contorting his throat to shape the inhuman syllables. Rising from the shadow of the dome answered the booming chant of the Rillyti, their fear overcome by need to sound their centuries-unheeded invocation.

Bloodstone lay dormant no longer!

Energy pulsating through its arteries, the heart of Arellarti beat again after millennia of slumber.

Eerie fire dawned within its green depths, eternity deep — a glow rising like dawn viewed through dark emerald, shining shifting light upon the walls of the dome. A somewhat darker, more intense gleam, the veins of red pulsed into crimson life, and through its murky translucency these scarlet tendrils twisted fantastically to disappear within the depths of Bloodstone. Incalculable cosmic energies at last unleashed, Bloodstone blazed with a coruscating fire of life.

The frenzied chant of the Rillyti echoed in an inhuman chorus of wonder, of fulfillment, of terror. The final lines of his invocation writhing from drawn lips, Kane stood before the metal circle in the center of the stone crescent. Brushing his fingers over a slash on his shoulder, he smeared the fresh blood across the silver-white disk and anointed the circular depression at its heart. The ring already numbed his hand with an electric tingle as he moved to complete the elder-world ritual.

He knotted his left hand into a fist. The bloodstone ring projected from his clenched fingers, and now he noticed that this gem, too, glowed with life — a miniature counterpart of the titanic crystal ablaze before him. Then, as if stamping his signet to some inconceivable document — a wry thought that thus had been sealed many a sorcerous pact — Kane lowered his fist toward the center of the metal disk.

For the final inches some force seemed to draw his hand like an irresistible magnet. The bloodstone of the ring meshed into the central depression, meeting the blood-dampened metal with an electric crack.

In that instant Kane felt his every cell explode with what was at once unbearable agony and intolerable ecstasy — and transcending both. His entire body snapped into convulsive rigidity as the lightning of the cosmos blasted through his being. A scream was stillborn, never reached his paralyzed throat.

Bloodstone burst into a coruscant nova of raw energy and incandesced into blinding light that for one dreadful instant fully illumined its infinite depths. And from the sentient soul of Bloodstone a bolt of green light veined with red shot out — leaped out to enfold Kane, to bathe Kane in its uncanny fire.

For a long time there was a mind-wrenching chaos of indescribable sensations, tumbling thought patterns not his own, infinite blackness broken by flashes of formless image. Adrift for an eternity in a kaleidoscopic vortex of alien dream, his mind totally intermingled into a cosmic consciousness so impossibly alien that its every whirling mote of thought was incomprehensible — riotous images inconceivable because they were projections of sensory impulses for which there existed no equivalent human receptor.

Dimly Kane retained some shredded gossamer pattern of identity, vestigial awareness of being apart... insight such as comes to a dreamer who is at once conscious that he moves within a dream but is powerless to break from its spell or even to direct its course. He sensed the fabric of his mind, his soul being spread out, probed, examined, inspected with a condescending curiosity, impersonal yet intense.

This psychic vivisection of his consciousness angered Kane — or that ghost of his mind that now struggled toward coherent identity. He sought to group together his splintered consciousness, to repel the invading mind which relentlessly pored over the memories inscribed upon his soul. Resistance was encountered, fought against grimly as his enormous psychic vitality waxed strong. Decades devoted to occult studies had given Kane control of hidden resources, pathways of mentality unexplored by all but a few human minds. Startled by this unexpected sortie, the alien mind recoiled, and with a rush Kane reoccupied the strongholds of his consciousness. There followed a sense of baffled surprise at this unanticipated curtailment of its inspection, confidence that such defense could be overcome eventually.

Although the inquisitive dissection of his consciousness subsided, Kane still spun in a mental storm of alien thought. Fragments of image, splinters of sensation grew recognizable to him now, whether from the increasing familiarity of the new perspective, or because the enveloping sentience was shifting its sensory impulses to adapt to human perception, Kane could not tell. Inchoate phenomena were merging into a sequence, falling together like bright tiny bits of continuous mosaic. A picture began to unfold to which Kane's mind could conjecture interpretation from the recognizable fragments, although vast portions of the frieze remained formless patches of inhuman thought, tiles whose colors transcended the known spectrum.

Images coalesced...

Darkness. Indefinite period of waiting, longing. Movement. Progression through time? space? Danger. Energy. Danger narrowly averted. Interminable movement. Flight from danger? Danger in transit? Craving; anticipation. Ebb and flow of vast energies. Patience/despair/anticipation/hope. Termination of movement. Danger. Energy. Danger countered. Fulfillment. Hope.

Light. Transition.

(From a great height) Clouds, sea, land. White blue green red flashes of black. Danger. Closer. Across endless azure ocean to verdant land cloaked in towering dark forest. Danger hidden in forest and sea. Awesome violence of incalculable energy. Steaming rush of sea into glowing wound carved from continent. Destination/haven achieved. Fulfillment. Settling to earth. Hope/ambition.

(Images clearer now, moving with a curiously collapsed flow of time, stylistic representation often merging into pure symbolism.)

An island of raw stone arising from inland sea. Across choppy black water the misty shoreline encompasses horizon. Walls rising, jutting forth from the island like rubrous crystals of hoarfrost. Walls, buildings of *outré* architecture, network of streets. Beyond, docks and stabbing piers, a great causeway lancing the sea like a ray of light. A city bursting like some fantastic growth from the earth that was not its mother.

(There is a strange duality. A vantage point both fixed and transitory. Perception from shifting angles, the same instant viewed, projected from varying points. Simultaneous expression through lenses subtly differing.)

Moving forms through the rising city. The Krelran builders — dull-scaled creatures whose ancestry of their degenerate progeny, the Rillyti, was evident. Reptilian assurance, intelligence in their actions. Webbed hands mold-ing the city, leaders directing its architecture to exacting detail. Immense machines crawling throughout, gleaming, tireless as ants busy in their hill. Metal arms lifting colossal blocks of stone. From curious instruments brilliant lances of flame fuse the joints to seamless strength, carve out the precise angles, etch intricate patterns in the faces. Giant vessels like water beetles scuttle across the sea; bronze centipedes humpbacked with loads tread ponderously along the causeway, disgorge mountains of crushed ore and rubble. Mounds of unguessable material unloaded from elsewhere/above/within. All fed into towering hulks of machine/furnace, transmuted through unimaginable energies, reborn as blocks of red mottled stone, sheets and cables of various metals, materials unidentifiable. Raw substance metabolized into living cells of Arellarti. Workers transport, lay down the skeleton, the structure — create the exact geometries of life/organism. Overhead the vast shadow, rising and falling, wavering. Guard/nourish.

(There is something more here, something veiled. Many doors are closed in blackness, locked, and often their presence obscured. There are two minds that are one, and yet not the same. Each has doors, barriers, has keys that may unlock/open to reveal beyond/secret. Their doors are not the same, nor are their keys — but there are doors sealed with no apparent lock, and keys for which no door is evident.)

Need. The city grows to completion/fulfillment. Urgency. The dome lifts to the sky, enclosing/protecting, nerves/arteries develop apace. Danger grows greater with each day, each day because the city draws closer to completion and defiance of all danger. Hunger for energy burns/craves. Power drained perilously low to give birth to Arellarti. Urgency. Preparations must be complete/matured before attack while energy low. I/We/Being must gamble/risk more energy to accelerate completion before attack/before can defend. Presence known, earlier thrusts just to test strength. They may understand, plan to attack when vulnerability greatest.

Arellarti nears completion. Walls, structures, every cell/nerve close to organic unity. Dome is ready, cupping/enclosing like a protective/sustaining shell, translucent to perception from within/without. Final moment is near. Ship has already transformed/incorporated all but fraction of energy/unity. Embryonic surges of power begin to flow through nascent gridwork. Transmission/transformation/transmutation of life/awareness is beginning within new organism. The patterns are almost complete. I/We/Being come to life within new energy/structure.

Life flows. Energy. Birth/emergence/renewal. Sense the triumph of fresh life/energy rush through infant organism.

(There are two — union of duality. Separate the consciousness, know two parts of the whole. One lies within the dome, the crystal monolith. One lies within the ring. Both are one, together Bloodstone, linked together, parallel structure, obey the laws of crystal sentience/symmetry life, to leech the flow of cosmic energy. Within the dome is Bloodstone's consciousness, harnesses the energy of the greater cosmos, coordinates/governs the power/life. Within the ring lies its parallel self, independent/dependent parasite/symbiote, draws upon the energy of organic/[this plane] life of its bearer. The lord/priest/ servant of Bloodstone — external power to manipulate that which cannot be controlled internally — extension of the power/life. Both incarnations are one and essential to the unity. Dichotomy of size/energy cosmic too miniscule illusion/limitation of perception — both equal/essential to laws of symmetry of life/energy being...)

(Block)

Time is very almost [now]. Krelran flash across Arellarti in insane dream speed? slowness? The Master of Bloodstone directs the final preparations. Leader of the Krelran, there gleaming on his thumb where the webbing does not stretch, the bloodstone ring, symbol and instrument of his absolute power. The Master commands, his servants obey. His is the mind that oversees the raising of Arellarti, coordinates the directives that culminate in triumphant life/power.

Danger! Long-dreaded attack at most vulnerable phase! Dark ovoids of metal hover in the sky, hurl incandescent bolts of destroying energy upon Arellarti. A second assault from the sea — rushing teardrop vessels that overpower the ocean channel defenses, lash out at the walls with blasts of unnatural lightning. Too soon! Not enough power yet! Energy screens repel the enemy attack. Counterattack not yet effective. All power concentrated to defense screens. Not enough to hold — penetration! Sections of the city explode under the crackling energy blasts. The gates erupt with a splatter of cinder and fused metal. Hundreds of Krelran die with each failure of the defenses. They rush through the streets in terror-stricken madness. Arellarti writhes in pain.

Betrayal!

(All is chaotic; much is totally obscured. Treachery? Rebellion? Only the most broken images transmit the scene of panic and destruction.)

The Master has broken away! Now at the lowest ebb, greatest drain of energy... he has fled. Controls are locked, all power resources cut off. Trapped — only enough energy to defend the dome. Beyond the dome screens, the city lies in blazing death. Sacrifice unavoidable — last energy must power the dome defense screen.

The traitor escapes. The ship rises into the air. He tries to break through their attack. But he has doomed himself — there are not enough to control the ship, nor sufficient power to defend it long.

(Images separate into bewildering divergence. Only a few intense impressions stand out from the blurred chaos.)

Flight/pursuit/battle. Concussions shake the universe, metal hull fuses and sags. Cannot escape. Defense screens fail. Engines destroyed. Falling, falling. Attack moves away, they pursue the ship, they are burning it from the sky. Strikes the ground, final power absorbs blow, ripping through forest, bursts apart. They have won. Crawl from the wreckage... pain, strength failing. Across the forest, need to get clear. The ship glowing cinders under their fire. Cold. Cold/pain/weakness/dark...

The attack withdraws, watchful. Satisfied with destruction of ship, Arellarti in ruins. Power broken. Defeat. Only last defense holds. Cannot penetrate. Energy source cut off/locked shut, power grid destroyed. Helpless until [returns]. Need to maintain defense until final reserves exhaust...

The images grew dim, monotonous. Through deep twilight the fallen city was viewed. Survivors crawled about the ruins, broken and leaderless, slipped into degenerate barbarism. Centuries seemed to pass over the slumbering ruins. At times glimpses of strange shapes flashed by, but no new attack came. The sea grew stagnant and receded, left a marshy corpse across which a blighted extension of the surrounding forest crept. The swamp swallowed up Arellarti, stealthily crawled into its empty streets. Time began to rot away even the impervious mottled stone; the central dome itself was not spared.

All power exhausted, Bloodstone lay waiting within the crumbling dome — only the faintest glimmer of crystalline life yet burning. At times the Rillyti, savage misshapen descendants of the city's builders, fearfully entered the chamber to perform certain demented rituals before Bloodstone. In their murky minds still lived memory of their ancient power, of Bloodstone, but their rites were only superstitious remnants of the old knowledge, useless abominations, seemingly. The secrets of Bloodstone were lost to them — surviving only was twisted legend.

And finally Kane saw himself entering the dome, the indescribable hope/craving that observed/directed his actions. The sudden release of fantastic energy. Freedom from the centuries of powerless waiting. The resurgence of life.

Rebirth!

The alien union of dual existence suddenly returned. But with a significant difference.

Kane was no longer a drifting observer within Bloodstone's consciousness.

The coruscating stream of light that had engulfed him for only seconds receded into Bloodstone, and Kane slumped across the stone crescent in a sleep far deeper than death.

VII
A Priest Comes to Breimen

A flash in the firelight, the dagger spun across the room and stabbed its quivering fang into the overturned table braced against the far wall. The blade's tip was embedded into the edge of one of three tiny circles clustered about the smaller one in the center.

"Twelve more to my total, Teres!" exclaimed Lord Malchion jubilantly. "Make your last throw carefully — you'll need a ten at least, or Lian's gift warms my bed tonight!"

Teres left off from stroking the nervous slave girl's tousled hair, and squinted through the flickering light. "Lying lecher! I can see from here your blade's stuck an inch off the side of your twelve points!"

Lord Malchion drank a derisive toast, wine trickling over mustache as he upended the flagon. "Your eyes that bad, Teres, you'd better concede now, before you gouge up the wall. My blade cuts well into the circle — get your fat ass over here and see for yourself!"

Laughter rumbled from the several other men who lounged about the paneled chamber. "It's half into the circle, all right. You'll need a good throw, Teres," called Lian, as unofficial referee. Lian, a freelord from Wollendan's northern coast, had only this day pledged his sword and more than two hundred of his men to Malchion's service. The lean captain had presented his new lord with a honey-skinned slave girl, bartered — cheaply for her inexperience — from the tribesmen who roamed the fringes of the Salt Desert upon the Southern Lands' eastern shore. Malchion had responded to the gesture with a sumptuous banquet and, many gallons of wine into the night, Lian was amused to observe the Breimen lord and his heir quarreling over first night with the girl. A succession of drunken insults had led to a raucous contest, with chestnut-haired Cosmallen to serve the winner's pleasure.

"Come on, Teres!" Malchion taunted. "Look for yourself, if you won't trust a doting father's word! Come check it before I yank my knife free!" He chuckled with the ebullience of one who expects victory and waved for another cup of the sweet native wine. In younger days men called him "the Wolf," an epithet earned by his feral zest in battle and hunt. Four decades past the day he first drew blood in combat, his ferocity was undimmed, though physically Lord Malchion was beginning to mirror the years of hard living. The Wolf's stocky frame had grown fleshy of late, giving a false impression of corpulence that was denied by the unleached strength of his shoulders, his swaggering step with just the suspicion of a limp. Flushed with the exuberance of wine, his face seemed eased of the lines of age, the stains of riot; no gray streaked his yellow hair, although the disordered tangle of greasy locks began to grow thinner. Malchion stood firm like a great oak against the winds of time, but his teeth showed rot, and one suspected that unseen decay lurked elsewhere, as well.

Teres stood up with a tight-lipped frown and echoed his toast. Wine shone a rivulet along the straight scar that traced an oblique path across beardless cheek. "Shifty tub of guts! Leave your dirk where it stands, or I'll skewer your greedy hand to the board! Let it alone, and in a second you can contrast yours to a well-thrown score!"

The Wolf's cub proffered blue-gray tempered steel to Cosmallen's red lips. "Kiss my blade for luck, pretty-pretty, for you'll find my kisses sweeter than that sway-backed goat's!" Cosmallen uneasily complied.

Calculating the throw with assumed nonchalance, Teres shrugged tension from well-trained muscle and raised the knife. Despite the wine, there was smooth coordination in Teres's arm as it drew back and uncoiled with lithe strength.

The dagger flew toward target with apparent accuracy. But Teres had fumbled the release, and the knife struck the circle hilt first, its impact dislodging Malchion's weapon. Both blades dropped to the floor with a derisive clatter.

"Thoem! That was a lovely bit of work! Damn near stuck that in my foot, you did!" Malchion howled with amusement.

Teres's face was livid. "The knife slipped in my fingers! It was the lip rouge this bitch smeared on the blade! Damn you, you bloated bag of wine puke! Stop your idiot's giggling! No — keep it up — till you're apoplectic! I was fouled, and I'll damn well take another throw!"

"Oh, you were fouled — your head befouled with wine!" Malchion crowed. "You asked for her kiss, and you got it — the only one you'll have tonight! As final judge and chief arbiter, I declare myself the winner and this contest ended... before my wolfling's wild casts injure our gentle spectators! Watch the temper, Teres, and next time don't forget whose hands taught you to throw a knife, nor try again to match keenness of eye and head for drink with the old master! Sorry, dear daughter, but Cosmallen is the Wolf's prize tonight! Aahrr-rooo-oo!"

"Take her, then, scheming farthead!" snarled Teres through a gracious smile.. "What with wine and old age, I trust she'll sleep soundly... unless snores and foul breath disturb her rest!"

"Thoem, what a mouth to berate another's for foulness!" Malchion exclaimed in unruffled humor. "Were you my son, I'd feed you your ears for insolence! But as my daughter, your mindless insults only uphold the well-earned reputation of scold, of shrew!"

"Oh, enough of this 'were you my son' bullshit!" Teres yelled, hands clawed. "Try me if you dare test my mettle, and I'll tear off your greasy ears with my teeth!"

"Lovely thing when she's angry, isn't she?" Malchion grinned.

Teres muttered an incoherent string of curses and lapsed into silence, determined not to provide her father further amusement. She clamped her short fingernails between straight teeth in vexation, striving to present an air of aloof dignity.

She was a strange creature, Teres, who had devoted most of her 25 years to denying her femininity, and with startling success. Her features were heavily drawn, though not masculine, and might have been called pretty, but for the thin scar crossing one cheek and a nose twice broken and never perfectly set. Her blond hair she wore in a heavy braid, coiled back over one tanned shoulder, and her ears were pierced to display thick golden rings — neither so much a concession to femininity as an impression of the warrior styles among certain of the barbaric forest clans of Wollendan. Small, high breasts and slim hips were all but concealed under the rough warrior's garb she habitually wore. Years of riding alongside her father to war and to hunt, of drawing bow and raising sword for the most reckless venture, had trained her strength to the equal of many men's — while any weakness was doubly compensated for by the grace and ruthless courage of her sex. Withal, her compactly muscled figure called to mind the lean strength of a man five or more years her junior, but without boyish awkwardness. Teres's was not an unpleasant appearance, although certainly exotic — barbaric perhaps the happiest adjective.

A half-hearted knock announced the entrance of Lord Malchion's chief steward, Embrom. Heedless of the others present, he interrupted the seriocomic tableau to cross the chamber and whisper a few sentences for only his lord's hearing.

"Damn!" Malchion muttered. "The devil calls at the least fortunate hour, so they say. Still…"

He grunted and tossed off his drink with a decisive gesture. "The old master shows compassion for the young punk," he proclaimed somberly: "Teres, I grant you first blush of Cosmallen's yet to be revealed accomplishments. Count this as yet another favor from doting father to unappreciative whelp."

Rising, he nodded to his guests. "Gentlemen, if you will excuse me, exigencies of my disordered household require that I take leave of our learned discourse upon spiritual matters. My servants will see to your needs, should some of you care to further indulge in metaphysical speculations. My cellar library has many an unopened volume of vintage wisdom crying for perusal."

With unsteady dignity he completed his departure. From the halls beyond echoed an enormous belch, followed by an outburst of laughter.

Teres swore and chewed a knuckle, gazing at the long-limbed slave girl as if she would strike her. "That obese goat grants favors as gladly as starved hound bestows a fat chop to stray cat!" she growled. "Go to my chambers, Cosmallen. I'll teach you pleasant games after I've learned what disagreeable schemes dear Father is playing." She stalked from the room with a perfunctory good night.

Nervously Cosmallen glanced toward her late master for some sign of reassurance, but Lian only shrugged and looked into his wine. Reflecting sourly upon the life of uncomplicated luxury that was promised to await beautiful girls in rich courts like Breimen, she wandered off to ask directions to her mistress's chambers.

"That was something of a... ah, bizarre interlude," remarked Lian after a pause. "Whatever happened to that vaunted stern morality of Wollendan's barbarian heritage?"

"A lie, as with most cherished traditions," commented Ossvalt cynically. Malchion's most trusted counselor — or so men said — stirred a gnarled finger through his wine and smoothed his mustache with the reddened tip. "High moral principles," he continued, "are not the sacred heritage of barbarism, anyway — just the revered illusion of peasants in any society. Sour-grapes rationalizing by petty minds relating to all matters which they lack the power and the imagination to master themselves."

"And wine breeds philosophers," thought Lian, who was not yet sufficiently drunk to ponder cosmic vagaries of human reason. "When I purchased the girl," he persisted, "I hadn't thought I'd be provoking a drunken quarrel between father and daughter who'd drink first from the cup! Was Teres serious about bedding the wench, or was she only sincere in baiting her father?"

"Bright Ommem only knows!" shrugged Ossvalt, licking clean his mustache. "The tales of Teres are as wild as they are many, and since she revels in her infamy, half the stories are probably authored by Teres herself. Wild Teres, the old Wolf's cub grown up deadly as any she-wolf! Teres who dresses like a man, drinks like a man, yearns for battle like a man, rides like a man, fights like a man, curses like a man, loves like a man — excels a man in just about any pretension of virility, so she boasts. Her maids limp around all scratched and bruised, swearing she shaves her face each morning to remove the stubble. That's a lie, though she'd grow a beard if she could. First broke her nose when she was fifteen -- fell off her horse dead drunk trying to ride it through the great hall one night — but she claims it was a battle wound. Scar on her face did come from a battle a few years back — because she scorns to wear a proper helmet. Never lain with a man, but killed or maimed a dozen or more who've tried it, so she claims. Hell, you decide how much or how little to believe... I'd grow sober before I'd recount half her ringing saga!"

"Well, so much for the pristine warrior maid of legend," Lian pronounced. Although Teres's fame had traveled across the Southern Lands, he had found her presence more disconcerting than anticipated. "Still, the whimsy that leads Malchion to indulge his daughter's posturing strikes me as ill-advised. Can't say I'm looking forward to leading my men into combat with a girl ranked above me in order of command."

Ossvalt grew serious. "Understandable sentiments, perhaps, but I'd avoid expressing them in open conversation. Teres's position is unassailable, so far as Malchion is concerned — and the Wolf may grow old, but never question his control of Breimen! We're no squabbling rats' nest of grasping factions like our esteemed friends in Selonari!

"And if you will accept the well-meant advice of one who persuaded Malchion to send for you and your men, cease to think of Teres as anyone other than Malchion's son. To look upon her otherwise is indiscreet, and indiscretions have a way of proving unfortunate for the ambitious."

The remaining revelers were drifting away, leaving the two closeted. Ossvalt leaned on the other's steadier shoulder, sloshing wine on his bare arm, and continued his confidences. "Certainly Malchion considers Teres his son. She's his closest heir, and the Wolf means to pass on to her all this wealth and power he's fought to consolidate in Breimen. Teres is his only prospect — at least, if he's to have the egotistic pleasure of founding a blood dynasty. So Teres is his son — and since a woman has never really made it as a ruler among the clans of Wollendan, Malchion has spared no pains to mold his daughter into warrior lord. A work of art, that, in a twisted sort of way. Oh, the Wolf's cub has fangs as sharp and ready as the sire. Grizzled old Wolf and snarling she-wolf, to lead the whole damn pack. They're a splendid pair, those two — deserve each other, that's for sure!"

"But a libertine of Malchion's glorious stature must have fathered more than a few sons!" Lian interjected, relaxing his belt a notch.

"Don't know how closely you may have followed events on the southern frontier, Lian," Ossvalt explained, with a thoughtful slap to his expansive middle. "Being close to it all, you forget that the attention of the world may not be focused on Breimen. Anyway, you may recall that Malchion had two sons and a daughter by his first wife... all of whom died before passing infancy. Then Teres, whose birth Melwohnna never really recovered from. So he took a second wife when the first died, and Ahranli bore him a son and daughter. Then came the conspiracy of that unhanged traitor Ristkon and his friends, and the three of them were massacred in the botched assassination attempt on Malchion. Third wife was barren, or likely it's true that the Wolf picked up some dread disease whoring with his troops on one of his campaigns. Had a bastard son named Besntuin, for whom he had great hopes at one time. But Besntuin was a halfwit, and it was probably fortunate when he was stomped into the mud by outraged stallion, before he grew old enough to shave.

"So Teres is heir apparent by default. Got passed over rather callously in her early years. Hell, it was plain enough to a child, even, that Malchion was only interested in a son or three. Suppose that made some impression on her — be a son if you want attention. Never got a lot of that, with her own mother dead, and no other woman she ever got close to, really. Just the Wolf, and he was rough enough to crush any spirit but one that might be swept along with the flood. So Teres was a tomboy far back as anyone ever noticed, and it amused Malchion to encourage her mimicry of himself and his companions. Then after it came about that Teres was his only heir, he devoted his all-out efforts to reshaping her into a son. Taught her to hunt, to ride, to fight — personally oversaw her training in arms. She made him a good enough son, too — I've seen her in battle, and I wouldn't have wanted to face her even in my prime. She could probably fit in among your mercenaries without a hitch, if her sex wasn't known. Probably raise too much hell for discipline, though. Her father and his kind are the only company she's ever kept — treats other women just as a man would. I'm sure she even thinks of herself as a man. Life in Breimen is sure going to be interesting if she succeeds her father."

"Weird!" muttered Lian. "Another round?"

"Why not!" Ossvalt blearily agreed. "I tell you, Lian, we have fallen upon strange days."

Malchion, meanwhile, having made his departure, followed Embrom in thoughtful silence to his private chambers. The chief steward opened the chamber door for his lord, glanced about the room suspiciously, and stood waiting until Malchion dismissed him with instructions to be certain his privacy was not interrupted. Closing the door behind him, Malchion was alone in the room with the man who had come calling at this late hour of night.

The man who awaited him was featureless within the hooded pelisse that enswathed his massive frame. In the poor light, his face was hidden by the cloak, only the vaguest indication of profile being discernible behind the shadow. Even details of clothing lay submerged, for the cloak's dark blue folds fell to boot top. A series of stylized designs across the shoulder of the garment identified the wearer as an acolyte of some minor outland sect whose followers were known to make lengthy and seemingly pointless pilgrimages. Which did not account for the sinister aura that overlay the chamber like the enveloping folds of the stranger's cloak.

The late night visitor, unexpected but not uninvited, filled a second silver chalice with wine as Malchion entered. Part of the sleeve fell back from corded left arm as he replaced the ruby-glass decanter, so that lamplight shone upon the ring encircling the middle finger of that hand. The Wolf, whose undimmed eyes grew more alert with age, noted something altered about the ring, whose striking gem had impressed his attention on an earlier occasion. Absently he realized the nature of the changed appearance: previously the bloodstone ring had fitted very loosely over the finger, while now its circle was closed to the point that the silver-white metal seemed almost set into the flesh. The stranger, then, had found time to have a jeweler adjust the ring's fit.

"Fine hour to make a call," grumbled Malchion, accepting without thanks the proffered cup of his choice wine. "I assume your coming here was not witnessed."

"My information requires your urgent attention; I came when I could," Kane replied, wondering somewhat at the other's petulance. "Needless to say, all my movements have been governed by faultless discretion."

"The words of one of my most gifted spies — before he was assassinated two steps from what I had supposed was a secret entrance to this keep!" Malchion returned. "Well, how did it go, and what can you tell me?"

Kane shrugged back the hood. His face seemed haggard — strange, considering it had only been a few weeks since he had left Breimen bound for Selonari. "It all went smoothly enough," he began. "As I outlined the last time we talked, I slipped out of Breimen without notice, cut north to the coast, caught a ship and doubled west down the coast to Jadenbal. There I made port, got involved in a respectable tavern brawl, and left a discreetly traceable trail from the coast to Selonari. No problem making contact with Dribeck — he's as clever as they say, but what suspicions he may have had were allayed. Wasn't overly difficult to convince him that I was an unemployed mercenary captain a few cuts above the usual grade, and he became interested with little prodding in my yarn about fantastic weapons of elder-world science that lay waiting for someone to claim in a lost city within Kranor-Rill.

"He gave me a small command, which in turn gave me access to a great deal of information that will interest you. So when I decided I'd learned enough of importance, I led an expedition into Kranor-Rill to steal secrets from toads. As I'd expected, the Rillyti were not pleased. I led my men into their ambush, made sure there were no survivors, then escaped through the swamp by another route, stole a horse and rushed back to you. All at considerable risk, I may remind you, for which I expect your promised generous recompense."

"The price was agreed upon," Malchion reminded him.

Kane pursed his lips. "Aspects of our deal were somewhat vague," he persisted. "In view of the importance of — "

From the hallway sounded angry curses, punctuated by a howl of pain. The door was thrown open, hinges rasping in their sockets. Boot still outstretched, Teres half fell through the doorway. "Where are you, you pot-bellied pervert!" she yelled. "What secret debauchery are you — "

She caught sight of Kane. "Shenan's tits! He's with a priest! The weight of his sins grows too burdensome for the old fart!"

"Shut up, damn it!" growled Malchion. "Close that door before your drunken slobbering upsets everything!"

Embrom's tight face appeared behind her shoulder. "Kicked me in the crotch, she did!" he gasped. "You tell me how I'm going to keep her from busting in! If she was — "

"All right, forget it!" Malchion broke in over the uproar. "Close that damn door and keep it shut! Teres, since you're here, sit down and shut up!"

"Meanest-looking priest I ever saw, that's no lie," observed Teres, dropping to a chair and boldly staring at Kane. "What is it?"

"Kane, this is my notorious daughter, Teres, appearing in all her glory. She throws a dagger side-armed."

"Screw you," she commented dispassionately. "Pour a fellow a drink, how about it, priest? But you're no holy man, are you?"

"She has her father's judgment for character. Kane is — or was, until some drunken ass made public gossip of a secret conference — a most resourceful agent, one I've hired to penetrate Selonari's schemes. He's gained the confidence of that gutless wonder, Dribeck, after considerable effort, so he says, and he was about to enlighten me when you so adroitly joined us."

"Hey, this is a lot better stuff than you were pouring for Lian," Teres commended with a smack of her lips. "Pass the decanter, Kane, and I'll split the rest with you. Good vintage shouldn't be wasted on a bursting wineskin like my father — who's far drunker than me, though with his bulk he sits straighter, that much I'll concede. Kane, you just don't make it as a pilgrim, you know. Those eyes, those hands — you look ready to strangle the first fool who comes to ask your blessing. What dark alley did Malchion find you lurking in?"

"Men of my talents are drawn by the smell of battle," Kane replied vaguely, considering Teres with amused interest. "And this cloak serves to mask my features from Dribeck's spies — which it does well enough with the hood — not to entice gold offerings from the devout."

"Oh, a man of talents sits amongst us," Teres told her cup.

"We were discussing what you had learned of Dribeck's plans," Malchion reminded.

"No, we were discussing how much my information was worth in coin of the realm," Kane pointed out.

Malchion grunted in vexation. The other's insolence grew annoying at times, although Kane's bland self-confidence commanded the Wolf's respect. Breimen's lord had a good eye for ability and was quick to recruit the services of anyone he judged useful, which in part accounted for his success as ruler of the fastest rising city-state in the Southern Lands. He judged Kane's services a worthwhile investment, if the stranger were half as capable as he gave the impression of being, and his loyalty secure so far as gold could buy it — as good a guarantee as any mercenary could be held to.

"Look, Kane," he capitulated with drunken magnanimity, "you know my reputation. Ask around, and you'll hear that. I deal fair and square... pay off my debts and collect the ones that are owed me. I pay well for any information that's worth my hearing. We've made a bargain already, but if what you've learned is worth more than we agreed on, I'll be judge of that and pay a fair bonus."

"Fair enough," Kane nodded. "Across the Southern Lands you're known as a man who rewards most generously those who serve well — a reputation, I might add, that drew me to your cause in what seemed an imminent war."

"Seemed?" Teres snorted.

Kane frowned. "Yes. Uncertainty is no longer to be implied. I can tell you point-blank that there *shall* be war with Selonari. Lord Dribeck intends to maintain his northern frontier by reducing your own outposts along the border. Further, he sees a full-scale war of conquest against Breimen as the only means to consolidate his own authority over the snarling factions in Selonari's long smouldering power struggle."

"This much I've deduced… and had pointed out to me by Ossvalt and other counselors," Malchion sarcastically observed. "Worthless."

"It's not just conjecture, nor is it nothing more that another border skirmish. I've taken part in the training of his troops, and he's recruited well, from mercenaries and from the private armies of Selonari gentry. His army is well armed and disciplined, and will not long confine itself to drill and parades."

"Tavern gossip still. Selonari has blustered without effect for years."

"Dribeck plans to bluff no longer. He means to cross the Macewen River into Breim lands. I learned a good bit of his designs while I was in Selonari — as well as specific information of troops, armament, tactics…"

"Which interests me — at least, whatever information my other spies haven't already given me. But this is all part of our original bargain, Kane, hardly reason to open my treasury to you."

"I think you'll find my information more accurate and less public," Kane went on smoothly, building with confidence to his masterstroke. "Would I be boring you if I told you that Dribeck has ordered the assassination of Ossvalt and Lutwion as the initial move in his attack?"

Malchion's ruddy features blanched, then flamed anew. Teres jerked erect her sagging frame. "Lutwion! Ossvalt!" He blurted. "My most capable general and the wisest of my advisers! He plots their deaths!"

Kane nodded emphatically. "They're also two of the strongest voices to call for war with Selonari. He intends that their deaths will appear without connection to their political sentiments. Thus he may at once deprive you of their valuable services, while at the same time he removes two who urge you to take steps to counter his secret designs. He both disarms you and lulls you into inattention — and without your suspecting the cause, so that he can continue preparations for invasion."

"I see Dribeck's craftiness hasn't been exaggerated," growled Malchion. "But how does he plan to murder two of my closest associates without directing blame to Selonari?"

"Unfortunately, I could learn few details," Kane explained. "Dribeck admits no one to his full confidence; to press inquiry would have been unfortunate, as well. I only know that he plans their deaths by devious means. There will be no red-daggered assassin for you to capture and put to torture. Further, I know he plans their deaths for successive nights to make coincidence less alarming. And the murders were to take place soon after I left Selonari — he made a reference to the first night of the full moon. That's tonight."

Malchion swore and leaped to his feet, striving to clear his wine-clouded thoughts. "Tonight! Damn you, couldn't you have gotten word to me before this?"

"I haven't been in Breimen an hour yet," retorted Kane defensively. "If I'd fled directly from Selonari, I might not have made it to the river — besides which, Dribeck would have been alerted. He would have made new plans, and my subsequent usefulness would be lost to you. I gambled that I would reach you before his assassins could strike. Evidently my timing has held"

"Ommem knows how close you've cut it, though!" Malchion exclaimed, pacing about the room with anxious strides.

"Well, Ossvalt was deep in his cups with Lian, when I left them," Teres pointed out. "So he's reasonably safe in our own keep. But Lutwion left a few hours ago for his manor — you had some off-color comments on his early departure, I recall."

"Then he's in the greater danger!" Malchion concluded. "I'll send a runner to warn him, and a detachment of guards close behind — if it isn't too late! Ossvalt I'll see to personally!

"Raise your hood, Kane! I'll try to keep your identity hidden, but you're closer to this plot than any of us, and I'll require your presence until I can be confident where I stand!" He rushed from the chamber, howling for Embrom to summon guards.

"Come along, reverend pilgrim," called Teres, steadying herself against Kane's shoulder. "Let's see if Ossvalt needs a priest. Maybe we'll snare us a brace of assassins." The light of excitement shone in her blue eyes, and Kane wondered if she were less drunk than her gait evidenced.

The last revelers had grown tired, and the dark, paneled room was deserted when Teres and Kane returned to the scene of her debauched contest for the slave girl. Doubling back, they reached Ossvalt's chambers before the guard was fully alerted. Lian met them as they entered the corridor.

"Ossvalt! Have you seen Ossvalt?" Teres demanded.

"Of course," Lian answered, wondering what new madness his lord's daughter planned with Ossvalt and this foreboding priest. "He holds his cups well, but enough wine will sink any ship. Ossvalt required a little help with the stairs, so I convoyed him to his berth. Out cold when I left him just a moment ago, snoring like a rutting bull."

"Anyone with him?" Teres inquired.

"Alone with his dreams. What's wrong?"

"We've just learned of a plot to assassinate him — Lutwion, too — and probably tonight! Another of Dribeck's bloody schemes! Malchion's off sending word to the general, and he should have ordered guards to Ossvalt's side by now, as well."

"No worry yet," said Lian with drunken assurance. "No one's entered that door since I walked out, and it's a good fifty-foot drop from his windows."

"An assassin could have hidden himself inside," Kane suggested, speaking for the first time.

"True. I didn't bother to poke through his closets," Lian conceded. "Who are you?"

"An ally of dubious integrity, beyond which you don't need to question," Teres said. "You two want to wait for reinforcements while I hunt for an assassin?"

Pushing past the two men, Teres swung open Ossvalt's door and entered. Kane and Lian followed close, the latter with bared sword. Scuffle and clank of harness announced the approach of Malchion's soldiers.

Fully clothed, Ossvalt's corpulent form lay stretched face down across his bed. He made no response to their entry.

"Out cold till morning," judged Lian. Teres was prowling about the room, inspecting each shadow and nook with suspicion. The mercenary captain regarded her movements blearily, then with drunken gravity thrust his sword beneath the bed and knelt down to look for a body. Kane examined the windows for a moment; stone walls plunged sheer into distant darkness.

"As I said, his chambers are empty," Lian pronounced.

Teres grunted. "Leave the shutters open. This room has a sour reek of returned wine." To the entering guardsmen: "Captain, keep three men here beside Ossvalt; the rest in the hall. Do I need to remind any of you about sleeping at your post?"

Kane studied Ossvalt curiously. "I thought you left him snoring."

Lian shrugged. "So? He's rolled over since then. It's a rare man who snores when he sleeps on his belly."

Straightening from his inspection of the counselor, Kane remarked, "And a rarer man who can snore when dead — as this man is!"

VIII
Death in the Fog

"**A** misty night. The sky's clouded over thick as mud — even the moon lies buried. Only light is a greasy flicker of lightning now and then smothered by the clouds, too far away for honest thunder," Lutwion observed, gazing from the window of his manor house. "So it's an assassin's night, after all, even if the moon is wrong. Odd that Dribeck didn't set a moonless night for his assassins to strike. But the man is as unpredictable as he is cunning — a most dangerous combination, to my mind."

"Damn it, Lutwion, can't you stay away from that window?" complained Malchion, harassed and ill-tempered after a sleepless night and frustrating day. "Whatever killed Ossvalt, it must have struck through a window."

"Unless Lian knows more than he tells," Kane commented icily.

"Lian's trustworthy, damn it!" growled Malchion. "I know him, and he has no reason whatsoever to plot with that Selonari schemer. And your inferences had Lian frothing mad — stay away from him, or there'll be blood spilled!"

"Not mine, I think," Kane sneered. "I only put facts together, and if Lian felt insult, perhaps he knows his reasons. As I've said, Dribeck didn't take me into his confidence on this assassination plot, and I don't have to tell you his ways are devious."

"Well, Lian's not with us tonight," broke in Lutwion crisply. "I know the man well enough — he's a tough fighter, a capable leader, and I trust him. Though, under the circumstances, I admit I'd have reservations if another man were in his place last night."

The Breim general slid a bolt through shutters and turned from the window. His sharp features were seamed leather from years and campaigns, his blond hair thin and cut short. No other marks of age did he carry. His blue eyes were bright and alert; there was a spring yet in measured step, sinewy grace of movement, confident strength. His height was well under six feet, but surprisingly long arms and rugged compactness of frame indicated a man who could lead his soldiers into battle. The last two fingers of his left hand were missing half their length.

"And don't chase me from the window like a scolding nurse," Lutwion continued. "Ignorance of your field is the most dangerous error in any situation. After all, this is my own manor. I know my ground here; my retainers are all men I can trust. In addition to the guards you pressed on me, milord, I've positioned my own men throughout the building and grounds — as well as along the nearby streets. Even on this mist-blinded night, an assassin will have little chance to reach this room — and then he will find armed men waiting, rather than the wine-soaked old man whose sleep he made an endless one last night. I only hope he does try to reach me — perhaps he can tell us much before we finish our sport. As for the windows, let them tempt him. He'll have a good climb from the grounds below."

"He had a better climb to Ossvalt's window, and that didn't stop him," Malchion muttered. "If indeed he used the window."

"Yes, *if* indeed," mused Lutwion. "We know so little. Still, my guess is that the assassin hid in Ossvalt's chambers. He came out after Lian left, probably smothered Ossvalt while he slept, and escaped through the window down a rope, which he then jerked loose. Clear-cut work for any accomplished assassin. I suppose we can't rule out the possibility of sorcery in the murder, but I don't think even Dribeck wants to risk the consequences of unleashed powers of magic in this war. He knows our priests of Ommem can retaliate in kind, and from reports I doubt if he can count on like support from the Temple of Shenan — Gerwein's no friend of his, that's certain."

"I can vouch for that," Kane asserted, "though there seems an element of sorcery to Ossvalt's death. No one seen to enter or leave the room, no mark on the body, no sign of struggle — you would expect that even if he were smothered. The assassin might have had time to rearrange the bedding, but Ossvalt's face wasn't bluish — his features were even composed. You'd have sworn he died of natural causes, if I hadn't warned you of Dribeck's plot. And he wasn't poisoned, so far as we know, since he ate and drank along with everyone else that night."

"I've thought of that," Lutwion remarked, as the door opened to admit a servant with a tray. Nerves had tightened despite his careful knock. Guards stood watchful in the hallway beyond. "And while I'm not exactly fasting, what little I've eaten today has been tasted first by my cooks. Here's cold meat, bread and wine, if you're inclined. My own appetite isn't too keen tonight."

The servant was infected by the atmosphere of tension. His hand trembled nervously as he poured wine, and he clumsily brushed the decanter against a brimming goblet, as he bent to serve Kane. The cowled figure had noted the other's unsteadiness, however, and his left hand flashed from his pelisse to catch up the overbalanced goblet even as it toppled. Lutwion's eyebrows rose as he witnessed the stranger's startling reflexes. Mumbling apologies, the servant set down his tray and departed. Kane stared after him.

"Why don't you shed that cloak, pilgrim?" Lutwion asked. "My men are trustworthy, if you're concerned about secrecy."

"There is still the matter of an unknown assassin," Malchion explained. "I mean to use the priest here to spy further on Dribeck's plots, and if he's recognized now, his return to Selonari will be unpleasant. I'd rather no one knew his identity. Keeping him here tonight is a calculated risk, but he's closer to this plot than any of us, and I can't spare him. Meanwhile, I'm trying to preserve whatever secrecy I can about him."

Lutwion looked thoughtfully at the face hidden in the shadow of the hood. "Well, any fool should know he isn't a priest, but so long as you avoid any more exposure than necessary, I doubt if anyone can tell for certain just who is hidden in that pelisse. A spy in Dribeck's midst will be invaluable in the war — and it looks like we'll need to crush Selonari soon, now that Dribeck has shown his intent. A suggestion, though: I'd get rid of that ring. It's quite distinctive, even if prying eyes can't see your face clearly."

"Thanks. I admit your point is valid," Kane replied. "But the ring has proved to bring me luck in the past, and I'm inclined to take the slight chance of its drawing notice."

"Well, it's your neck. Ah! Something's stirred up the hounds! I want to check this!"

Ferocious baying met their ears as they raced to the ground level of the manor house. Men cursed and yelled, shouted challenges. Loud but brief, the alarm had diminished by the time Lutwion shouldered his way through the main door and demanded an account from the milling guardsmen.

A familiar laugh greeted them. "Lutwion, your security stinks!" grinned Teres, her teeth bright against a soot-smeared face. "I got all the way to your servants' quarters and just about had a window forced, before your pack caught my trail. You'll never make it to morning if you trust these men with your safety. The kennels look to be best guarded — pass the night there."

"I thought you wanted to keep an eye on Lian," Malchion reminded. There was pride in the smile he flashed toward his daughter.

"Lian is interesting only if you share his enthusiasm for Lian. I don't. Besides, he's no tool of Dribeck. I thought I'd come watch you men snare an assassin."

"Milord! She knocked two of our men out cold, and damn well split Osbun's scalp open!" protested one of Lutwion's captains sourly.

"An assassin would have split their skulls. Next time they'll man their posts more vigilantly," Teres purred.

"Yeah? Well, Osbun says he challenged you in the alley, and you identified yourself to him — then as soon as he let you approach, you slugged him with a bludgeon.

"So next time he won't be lulled by a voice of authority. It's a dark night, and I might have been disguised," Teres continued imperturbably.

Lutwion ordered his men back to their posts, his mood stormy. "I appreciate your interest," he said unconvincingly. His frown was genuine. "Thanks to your concern, my men are riled up, my defenses are revealed, and we've made enough uproar to frighten any assassin back to Selonari. That is, if he hasn't used this confusion to slip by my guards!"

"Hell, in the same breath you bitch at me for scaring off your killer, then for letting him sneak past!" Teres scoffed. She nodded at Kane. "Well, here it is again — Father's personal spiritual guide. Sometime I'm going to see what you look like without that tent, Kane.

"Oh, I'm sorry," she apologized without conviction. "And we're trying so hard to keep your identity a secret. Well, there's no one in earshot except Lutwion, and our good general won't abuse his knowledge."

Kane caught Teres's mocking blue eyes and wondered again at the destructive malice of her whims. "Which side are you on?" he murmured to her in low voice.

"An intriguing question coming from you, my pilgrim," she remarked with a bright smile.

"While we're about, might as well patrol the manor," Lutwion decided. "If we find our killer skulking about, Teres can show us how to deal with him properly."

Teres's appearance had somewhat lessened the tautness of nerve among those who waited through the night. Malchion argued that their precautions had thwarted Dribeck's assassin, since the original plot assumed that Ossvalt's death would appear natural, and Lutwion therefore would have suspected nothing. Which meant, as Teres pointed out, that now Lutwion dare not relax his vigilance. The general said little, being not surprisingly in a grim mood.

A night passed under threat of death seems interminable, and paradoxically, boredom wallows across the mind alongside fear's shrill and ceaseless chatter. But for the alert bearing, the darting glance into every shadow, distracted conversation often left unfinished, Lutwion might well be leading his guests on a leisurely tour of his manor. No furtive movements, no sinister figures met their inspection; guards had only negative responses to their queries.

Momentarily the general paused at the doorway of his bedchamber. "An obvious place for the assassin to wait, if our reconstruction of last night holds true," he told them. "Empty when we examined the room earlier this evening… but now? Well, I've stationed a guard within. The murderer will have to take second choice for a place to hide himself, if he tries to repeat his game."

But as they stepped into the chamber, no challenge greeted them. Teres laughed and pointed. A soldier in Lutwion's livery reclined upon the general's bed.

"Bright Ommem roast your liver, soldier!" Lutwion roared. "You never could have chosen a worse post to sleep on! I'll lash your back to raven meat with these hands!"

The guardsman slept soundly — nor would he ever waken.

"Dead! Dead like Ossvalt!" gasped Malchion, roughly shaking the prone form.

"Not long dead, either," Kane pronounced. "His flesh is warm and limber, but the heart is still."

Guards poured in from the hallway at Lutwion's bellow. Bleakly he directed them to search the chambers thoroughly, then joined the examination of the slain guardsman. Their efforts yielded nothing.

Kane inspected the windows thoughtfully. "Shutters are bolted securely. The killer didn't leave through here this time. The hall door then, obviously, but why kill the guard? Probably surprised the assassin, but why was there no outcry? Why wasn't he seen leaving?" His fingers drew back the shutter bolts.

"Leave them open, will you?" Teres requested over the hubbub of conjecture. "The room has a sour stench of death — " Her features froze as recognition dawned. "By Thoem! Just like the odor I sensed in Ossvalt's room last night."

The others turned toward her, bewilderment on their faces. "Maybe so," Kane began. "Though how this hypothetical stench of death might fit in seems a tenuous link at best. I'm not sure myself that there's anything more here than what you can expect from a corpse in a closed chamber... "

Knuckles jammed against teeth, Teres studied the slain guard intently. Falling to her knees, she stared closely at the dead face. "No, there's something here. Why were both bodies found as if asleep? Ossvalt maybe was killed in his sleep... but the guard, too? There has to be a link — and bugger my ass if I don't think I see it now!"

Flashing out her dagger, Teres tore loose a strip of cloth from the black shirt she wore. She breathed heavily upon it several times, then with cautious movements began to rub the dampened patch across the pillows. Rising, she thrust it under a lamp and cried out, "I know how they died!"

Malchion looked over her shoulder quizzically. "So you've found some dandruff!"

"Not dandruff, dumbass!" Teres snorted. "See those pale tiny particles! They're grains of poison." The others crowded about to share examination.

"See... they're tiny crystals! The Carsultyal wizards refine the powder from the roots or blossoms of some malign jungle flowers — they're masters of subtle poisons!"

"What do you know about it!" scoffed Lutwion, though his sweaty face was not drawn in ridicule.

"Vyrel, our moss-bearded physician, told me a good many bits of arcane lore to pass the time when I was bedridden in his care with my busted leg. He studied for a while in Carsultyal — long enough to acquire a few of their secrets and their vices. He used some milder preparations of this sort to dull my pain at first. Ommem! The dreams I had! And he used to inhale the fumes of his powders himself in an intricate sort of pipe — probably what killed him eventually -- and that's how I remembered the odor. This must be one of the deadlier of the preparations that the wizards play with.

"The assassin slipped into the bedchamber, sprinkled the powder from a sealed flask over the pillows, then walked away. A sleeper wouldn't notice them, they're so few and so tiny ... but some would be absorbed through his face on contact, killing silently."

"They're vanishing!" Lutwion exclaimed, pointing to the deadly particles.

"It seems they're volatile," Teres speculated. "They melt away in air — leave no trace after a few hours, other than the faint odor." As they watched, the crystals diminished to rapidly fading motes of moisture. "Guess the heat from the lamp speeds up the sublimation… like Vyrel's strange pipe."

The others nodded hypnotically, eyes glazed as they stared at the patch of dark cloth. Teres started to slump.

"The windows! Damn it, throw open those windows!" yelled Kane, who had drifted apart from their cluster. "Drop that cloth, and come suck some clean air into your chests! The fumes are more potent than you realize!"

Like sleepwalkers they obeyed, shuffling with groggy movements to the windows as the guards swung open the shutters. Duly they leaned their heads into the misty night, mechanically breathing in deep lungfuls of the fresh air.

"Like being drunk, almost — very drunk," Teres murmured, her head slowly clearing.

"If you'd kept at it, you'd never wake for the hangover," Kane warned. "The mystery of the guard's death is cleared up, though. The assassin, who obviously visited this room before the guard took his post, sprinkled too much poison over the pillows — probably so there would still remain crystals when Lutwion at last decided to sleep. In the closed bedchamber the vapors accumulated, so that the hidden guardsman grew sleepy under the poisoned breath. The bed tempted his faltering senses, and he fell into the deathtrap set for Lutwion."

"So it wasn't sorcery," mused Lutwion, recovering alertness. "Unless the killer is a wraith. Either he totally eluded my guards, or I'm left with the unpleasant conclusion that one of my men is a traitor."

Through the gaping windows coursed a call of alarm from the hidden depths of night. A hoarse shout of challenge muffled in the distance, with a rising tone of insistence. Angry summons for help, answered by converging clamor of excited cries, pounding boots.

"Milords!" came an anonymous yell from below.

"Milords! We've spotted him! Some bastard just tried to sneak past our lines! Headed away from the manor! He broke and ran when we sighted him but we're hot after him! He'll not slip through our outlying perimeter!"

"Good work!" roared Lutwion, leaning perilously from the window. "It's our killer! Take him alive if you can, but fog or no fog, I want that devil run to earth! I'm coming out!"

He whirled to the others, eyes alight. "Well, I'll soon know who the traitor is, if he's one of my men! Thoem, what a dismal night to track a killer! Every man after him, now! That slinking murderer must be taken, before he breaks past my net!"

Into the night they plunged. Lutwion vanished with several of his guards; his sharp voice cut through the darkness, directing his men in their search. Despite his orders, the military precision of his deployment, confusion was master.

Teres quickly separated from the others. Invisible in her black, close-fitting garments, her face smudged with soot, she merged with the night like a she-wolf on the hunt. A torch would only give away her position; the assassin needed no light, nor did she. Her sword rested easily in her grip; her heart raced dizzily in fierce thrill. Perhaps the drug still twisted her mind. A loom-

ing guardsman missed death by a hairbreadth, and she answered his curses
with laughter.

With every ruthless trick, the night fought their efforts to penetrate its
veil. No worse night could be designed for their deadly manhunt. Fog rolled
in oily streamers and touched cheeks with palpable breath, cool as a corpse's
caress. Lost cries, voices came muffled to dreamlike distance through the enveloping swirl. Dozens of armed men rushed madly about her, but none could
be seen. Phantoms of fog they were, frantic spirits that darted into view or a
heartbeat, then vanished. Misty jewels, their torches seemed glowing patches
of spider-silk, casting illumination scarcely far enough to touch earth.

The moon was swallowed entirely in the morass of clouds, roiling heavily
across the skies. Sporadic flashes of lightning made wan flickers behind the
cloudbank, silhouetting for an instant dim patterns grotesquely writhing
against the heavens. Belated thunder rumbled ominously, distant but growing near, fitful as a sleeping hound's growl. Through this night the search
dragged on, spreading outward now.

Teres felt the streets beneath her boots and sensed the darker shadow of
an unseen building. Her steps had taken her beyond the grounds of Lutwion's
manor, into the adjacent portion of the city. Voices yet called through the
viscous darkness. Lutwion had posted men along nearby streets and alleys;
his net was flung wide, and now it drew back. But had the assassin slipped
through its mesh? After all, Teres reminded herself, they knew not the face of
the man they hunted. If he were one of the general's retainers, might not he
have joined with his pursuers until a better chance for escape presented?

She froze in abrupt fear. From beyond her the fog was sundered by a shriek
of terror! A mindless scream of stark horror, of unendurable agony, burst
from the night; she could not say whether it came from one voice or several.
Almost as its ragged note rose forth, the unearthly anguish broke off, silenced
with grim finality. And Teres, who counted her nerve better than any man's,
caught her breath with a shudder.

Teeth fixed in lip, pain calling her to reality, Teres fought to quell the panic
in her heart. Slowly she drove the ice-tingle from her body, held her swordpoint
steady before her. Had she imagined it, or had she glimpsed a sickly flicker of
greenish light through the fog, just as the scream had reached her? Lightning
reflected? *Nerves?*

There was sudden stillness all around… for what seemed an interminable
space. Then she heard pounding footsteps close by. Lips drawn in a snarl, she
poised her blade for the killing thrust.

"Steady, Teres! It's Kane," breathed a voice from a shadow she could dimly
make out. She was too shaken to wonder until later how the stranger could
see her this clearly in the darkness.

"That cry!" she mumbled.

"Came from close by — there's an alley leading off here, I think," Kane
finished. "I was trailing someone who seemed in a greater hurry to leave than
to join in the search. Lost him near here only a few minutes ago. Didn't give
the alarm, because I figured he'd take off and escape cleanly before others

could get here. I was trying to cut across his trail when I heard that scream. We'd better stay together till we know what's behind this."

For once, Teres felt glad for companionship. Shoulder to shoulder they moved toward the point from which the cry had seemed to originate. Men with torches ran to join them, casting light over the grisly scene they discovered.

Four men lay dead at the mouth of an alley. Three were soldiers; the fourth was Lutwion.

Their bodies lay twisted in grotesque angles, contorted as if they had been hurled back by some unthinkable force. Flesh seemed shrunken, features frozen masks of agonized dread. There was no need to feel for life. On each body glowered a brand of blackened flesh, smouldering clothing — a matted crater etched into human tissue, bridged by splinters of charred bone. It was as if the dead men had been struck by a stream of molten iron.

"What kills like that?" someone moaned.

"Lightning?" wondered Teres. "Could they have been hit by lightning? I thought I saw a flash of lightning from this spot. Look — that man's sword is fused to his arm!"

"Lightning, could be!" growled Malchion savagely. "A fine coincidence, though, for Dribeck! More likely the scheming coward has meddled with sorcery for this deed! Well, by Ommem, I swear to you — Selonari will think lightning's blasted her towers when I march south! I'll roast Dribeck over a fire of his precious books and wash the streets with the blood of his people!"

He drew Kane aside, so that only Teres overheard their words. "Get back to Selonari as fast as you're able! I know your risk is triple now, but the plunder of that city will glut even your lust for wealth if you serve me well in this! Get me any information you can smuggle out — you know my agents there! My army will march for the Macewen as quick as I can muster, and I need to know every foul trick Dribeck's cunning mind is plotting!"

"You'll hear from me soon!" promised Kane. He melted into the fog.

IX
War Eagles Gather

"**I** tell you true!" swore Havern, red wine squirting through rotted teeth as he gulped too great a mouthful. "There's riot and plunder gonna be, like there never was before, no lie!"

"Gimme that bladder, fartmouth! You're slobbering more than swallowing!" complained Wessa, pawing at the wineskin with his good hand. "Damn… another leak! We'll have to finish this up!" He raised the skin to his lips and sucked noisily as a stream from the puncture sprayed over his filthy beard.

"No need to spare it, Wessa sweet. What I'm telling you is we can soon be fat and greasy as lords at an orgy!" He paused to blow his nose with his finger, narrowly missing the other. "Snurk! Let me have that back now, Wessa, come on."

"Here … fire your slosh-brains with more booze dreams!" sneered Wessa, surrendering the wineskin. "Back off, Havern, you gonna fall over and knock me in the river maybe in a minute. Thoem's left ball! See that mother of a rat there! He's a banquet for the both of us!"

Snatching a stone from the riverbank, he threw it after the rat, missing by several feet. "Damn! If I had the strength in my other arm! Been six years since that bastard's mace messed me up!" Whining, he began to suck the wine from his scraggly beard.

"That rat's gonna get his pack together and come back here looking to pick our bones, sure enough," warned Havern. "I'm telling you, though, we'll soon be gorging ourselves on roasts and sweetmeats, Wessa. All the food and wine our guts can hold, all the women our hands can fondle, all the riches our backs can carry away! Ours for the grabbing, that's no lie! Word's everywhere. Old Malchion's sending an army with his bitch daughter to march on Selonari. He's gonna burn that craphole to the ground, and there'll be looting like you never believed!"

Wessa reclaimed the wineskin. "Maybe so, but a man could get his head pushed out his ass with all the fighting," he said morosely. "No pity for a one-armed man in war."

"Your bad arm can hold a shield," Havern judged. "Who's gonna do any fighting, anyway, I want to know? Not us. We'll follow along old Wolf's soldiers, and let them do all the work of killing and dying. Once Selonari falls, we just step in and help ourselves. Safer than staying in Breimen, 'cause no guards gonna come running when you cut a throat! Hell, Wessa, every free rogue in Breimen's gonna follow along for a slice of the spoils!"

"Well, I figure we can't do much worse than what we are," Wessa conceded. His rheumy eyes grew crafty in greedy vision.

"You know it's gonna be the sweetest tit we ever chewed!" promised Havern, waving the flaccid wineskin grandly. They stumbled along Breimen's waterfront for a space in thoughtful silence, broken only by Havern's wheezing cough, and gurgling smacks as they squeezed at the bladder.

"Well, we found us one, Havern dear," observed Wessa with a cackle. "River left us a prize here, sure enough, and with luck we're first to find him!" He pointed to a dark shape bobbing face down against the rocks.

Eagerly they clambered to the water's edge and hauled the corpse onto the bank. "Someone's been up to deviltry," smirked Havern, as they pawed through the dead man's clothing. "Didn't bother to weight the stiff, so the current washed him back along the eddy. Knew this was a lucky night for us to scavenge!"

"Wearing livery of some lord, but this knife's too good for a servant, and here's gold growing stale in his almoner. Too bad the way his chest is all burned up, but maybe the vest can be patched over. Wonder what they done to him to kill a man like this! Shit, Havern, look at the bastard's face!"

"Pretty," remarked his comrade. "You know, I bet those boots will about fit me."

X
A Stranger Returns

Wind rippling his mane, the stallion wanted to canter, and Lord Dribeck decided to give his steed a good run, once he completed inspection rounds. Brisk exercise might relax them both, loosen the tightness in his belly. A short gallop across the martial field and down a forest trail — to Dribeck, who was a better horseman than most of his officers, the prospect would be an exhilarating interval from the tension that hung over Selonari like the thunderclouds of war.

"I had about given you up for dead," he remarked, "even with my high regard for your capabilities. The men you left with the horses at length reported your disappearance, and when the small search party I sent to investigate also failed to return, it seemed that Kranor-Rill would hold yet another secret in its depths. Reports from the vicinity give out that the Rillyti are prowling about even into the forest fringe, and there's more than the usual flow of tales concerning strange activity in the heart of the swamp — curious sounds, sinister lights glimpsed through the mists, and the like.

"Probably accounts for the enthusiastic response my call for new troops drew from the southern frontier. Well, I shouldn't be cynical. All of Selonari's people are rallying to the city. If Malchion takes Selonari, our settlements fall spoils, and our free farmers will be Wollendan serfs."

"Kranor-Rill and its deadly children very nearly did claim me," Kane reflected, riding beside Dribeck. Bath, sleep, fresh garments transformed him from the grim, swamp-stained wanderer who had wearily ridden into Selonari the day before, but there remained a haggardness about him that had not been present earlier.

To Dribeck's anxious questions, Kane had unfolded a terrifying narrative of his ill-fated expedition to the hidden ruins of Arellarti. Several days spent searching, the swamp-buried city had unearthed nothing of practical value. Meanwhile, the Rillyti had encircled their camp with ever growing numbers, until Kane was forced to break for the forestlands before the batrachian hordes decided to attack. Once beyond the city walls, Kane's party was ambushed and annihilated by the enraged creatures. Kane and a few others had fled into the swamp, where Kane wandered lost for several days, somehow eluding the Rillyti and the countless other perils of Kranor-Rill, until he at last crawled onto firm ground to return to Selonari. Evidently none of the others had survived the ordeal. At Kane's suggestion that further exploration might yet lead to some valuable discoveries, Dribeck balked, arguing that he had no more men to waste.

"I'll admit I'm relieved to have you with me once again," Lord Dribeck confided, as they rode past the confused mustering of new troops. "There's been hell to pay while you were gone, and frankly I value your assistance. Shenan knows, I'll need every resource I can draw upon, if my rule here is going to last out the month. There's madness loose in Breimen — old Malchion's henchmen murdered under fantastic circumstances — and the Wolf is using this as a final excuse for war. Had a spy planted in Lutwion's household, who might have known the truth behind all this wild talk of sorcery, but he vanished without a word to me. Malchion's marshaled his army for the conquest of Selonari, and I've only a few days to make a defense.

"Well, I've known for years Wollendan's blond raiders would someday decide to swallow up Selonari like they treated the other old states of the northern coast. I've never succeeded in impressing the danger upon the popular mind. The city could well be an ash heap in a few days, but my gentry still line up in their petty jealous factions, and the Temple refuses to submit to taxation. All I could get Gerwein to agree to, without forcing the issue at an untimely moment, was a 'gracious donation' of the Temple guard and a few tid-bits of their hoarded wealth. At least she sends me well-trained soldiery — not to disparage the stalwart freeman, but a professional soldier is worth any five amateurs, just intentions be damned."

He pointed to a thin and scar-faced officer, who directed the cavalry drill — mercenaries, by the mixture of nationalities his men represented. The tall man's blond hair was noteworthy among the ranks of dark haired Selonari. "That's Ristkon, Malchion's old enemy, who came so near to wresting Breimen from the Wolf," explained Dribeck with some pride. "I learned where he had fled after his rebellion collapsed, and approached him. Ristkon was aglow for the chance to avenge his old defeat — brought his own company of cavalry along."

"So hate is stronger than clan loyalties," remarked Kane. "You've found a doubly valued ally there. "

"I've a company for you to command, as well, Kane," Dribeck reminded him. "Coordination will be a major problem in meeting the Breim army, and the man who can surmount all this disorder might find himself quickly installed as my chief lieutenant."

"I appreciate your hint," Kane acknowledged through a grin. "The value of such promotion would seem, then, to balance on our victory. After all, few conquerors trouble to hang a defeated foot-soldier."

XI
Thunderclouds of War

The first arrows swept across the morning sky in a sudden gust, prelude to the impending storm. An engineer clutched his throat and toppled from the thrusting bridge into the river; others cursed as iron fangs struck at exposed limbs and challenged mail tunics. Stolidly, guards stepped forward to raise outsize shields over the workmen, trusting that their light armor would turn back most of the arrows, while the shoulder-high framework at the bridge's advancing edge would form a barrier against direct fire. From the Breim shore of the Macewen River hissed an answering barrage of arrows, striking the heavily forested bank opposite without observable effect.

"Well, we got midway across the Macewen before Selonari arrived to dispute our crossing," remarked Teres, squinting into the dense forest beyond the flood plain. "Dribeck must be marshaling his full strength to block us here, but I can't see for shit how many he's brought up just now. Be good to finish that bridge before his entire force gathers to welcome us to our new lands."

Malchion grunted noncommittally, intent on the progress of the bridge. Unofficial boundary between the holdings of the two city-states, the Macewen River sprang from mountain streams of the Great Ocalidad range, then cut southwest across the Southern Lands to reach the Western Sea at Serpent's Tail, flowing through the same precipitous gap through which drained Kranor-Rill. Breimen and Selonari stood along tributary rivers, the Clasten and Neltoben, which joined the Macewen farther downstream from this spot — some eighty to ninety miles from either city. Short of marching northeast to the foothills of the Great Ocalidads, there were only two stretches where the Macewen might safely be forded at this season. Word had reached Malchion from Kane that Dribeck had divided his army to guard either fording. The Wolf had then prepared to bridge the Macewen at a point where the river flowed languidly through wide channels.

Thus to the Macewen Breim wagons had carried preconstructed segments of floating bridge — pontoons like enclosed rowboats, wide sections of thick planks for decking, poles to drive into the river bed for anchoring the structure. By moonlight engineers had rowed across the river to fasten stout rope cables to trees on the far shore. While carpenters busily lashed and hammered together new sections, completed ones were floated into the stream, joined end to end along the taut cables, then lashed to slanting piles driven into the mud. Construction moved swiftly, so that as the sun warmed dawn to morning, the bridge spanned a good three-quarters of the river.

Then the death song of arrows announced the arrival of Dribeck's forces. Unable to judge the effectiveness of his return barrage, Malchion ordered his archers to maintain cover fire, as well as they might, with the far bank virtually out of bowshot. After the initial pause, progress on the bridge continued, although at slower pace, as the workers labored behind shieldwork, passing back to shore those whom a well-aimed shaft sought out.

Teres felt her pulse quicken as the scent of battle reached her flared nostrils. Her warhorse, Gwellines, stamped his hooves and snorted. Beneath her tunic of light mail she wore a jerkin of tough black leather, sewn with sections of scoured iron and cups of gray metal to enclose her breasts. Leather trousers of like pattern belled to cover booted calves. An iron casque covered her head, but left her face bare. Adornment of accouterments Teres shunned; in combat she relied on speed and lithe agility to offset her opponents' advantage in bulk, and extra weight she deemed a useless encumbrance. Her martial display, she boasted, lay in the deadly beauty of striking steel.

"Lian may have trouble holding the far shore, if Dribeck mounts too powerful a defense before the bridge is done," she commented, needling Malchion. Teres had argued for ferrying half the men across first, thereby securing both banks before turning to bridge construction. Such would have been Lutwion's counsel, she advised. Gruffly Malchion proclaimed that he had won battles without Lutwion's counsel, and he didn't need a spokesman for the general's ghost. They marched with siege machinery and supplies for reducing Selonari, and they'd save time and effort to bridge the Macewen now. Extra boats were needless freight. They'd invade Dribeck's lands before he could regroup his army from its encampment by the fordings.

The Wolf bared his teeth. "We'll have the bridge completed in another hour. Lian's got near two hundred men to defend the bridgehead, and that'll keep off this skulking band of archers. We'll cross in good time before Dribeck can do anything about it. Hell, there can't be fifty or a hundred men hiding in that forest cover, or they'd have rushed Lian before now." Sucking air through teeth with a half musical hiss, he considered the forest thoughtfully.

But on the Selonari shore there were more than a handful of soldiers that awaited the Wolf's army. Had any of Lian's scouts lived past the discovery, they might have reported that Lord Dribeck and over three thousand of his soldiers stood ready within the forest. Dribeck's own scouts had kept him informed of Malchion's march, sending word of his movements back by carrier pigeon. By forced march, Dribeck had led his army through the night to take position confronting Breimen's invasion of Selonari lands.

Shedding his blue cloak as the sun stole through the forest wall, Lord

Dribeck raised in his stirrups to get a better view of the advancing enemy. "Bridge is coming on steadily, though my archers have made things tense for them," he observed. "Malchion will try to cross by the time the mists start to dry away." From beside the Selonari lord, Kane made an affirmative sound. His long fingers stroked the blade of Carsultyal steel, as if to caress its lethal strength a last time before its edge was stained and blunted by combat. "Giving out that you planned to meet the Wolf beside the fording was a well-conceived ploy," he commended.

"When outnumbered, look to strength in strategy," Dribeck quoted. "Though there's no harm in having superiority in strength *and* in strategy. Still, there weren't too many choices for Malchion to cross the Macewen. With all his plans to lay siege, he had to cross within access to a serviceable wagon road, and that makes it easier to pinpoint his course south."

He paused to wipe his forehead. It would seem that a certain measure of calmness could be maintained so long as he contrived to view this intellectually, as a tactical exercise rather than deadly combat. But as the battle drew nearer, Dribeck conceded that emotion laughed at the frail bonds of intellect. Kane, on the other hand, seemed to feel no tension — if anything, gave the appearance of impatience. Dribeck shrugged mentally.

"When conflict is inevitable, then choose the battleground," he again quoted. Kane laughed softly. Dribeck had made use of this axiom in planning his campaign. Thus they awaited the Breim army within the forest depths, seeking only to slow their crossing, when they might have thrown back Malchion's tentative thrust. But sooner or later, the Wolf would force crossing, and Dribeck intended this to take place on his terms.

"Strategy is a fine game," murmured Kane, "but its brilliance is usually a matter of retrospect. War isn't a rational science, and steel and blood have decided many a battle that logic had won for the vanquished."

"Kane, your thoughts are as comforting as a raven's croak." Dribeck fumbled with a small flask. "Join me in a mouthful of brandy?"

Kane accepted the proffered flask. "To victory!" he toasted with a smile.

As Malchion had predicted, by the end of an hour the river was bridged. On the Selonari shore, Lian's men hurried beneath the desultory sniping to lash firm the final pontoon sections. Sheltered somewhat by felled trees, he and his detachment had concentrated on holding the bridgehead. After a few tentative sorties were driven back, Lian had judged the hidden archers too minor a danger to justify a concerted advance before the main body of troops could cross. A cheer rose from the beleaguered vanguard as the shores were linked.

Teres spurred her stallion to the riverbank. At her insistence, she was to lead the first thrust — nor had Malchion begrudged her this perilous honor. "Follow me, you puke-blooded sons of whores," she howled, brandishing sword in fist. "I'll lead you straight to Hell and glory, and strangle with my boot the first bastard who looks back before we set Selonari ablaze!"

The pontoons thrummed like war drums beneath the stallions' hooves, swelled to percussive symphony with the pounding boots, clanking, jingling of harness and steel, hoarse battle cries of soldiers, wild trumpeting of mounts. The bridge trembled and slapped spreading waves across the dark current, but bore stolidly the tread of an army upon its back.

Across the Macewen Malchion's army marched, thrusting a glittering tentacle of war into Selonari lands. Separating from the massed strength on the Breim shore came closed ranks of infantry, with companies of light cavalry few in number since the great forests precluded most cavalry tactics and left only a supportive role for the mounted soldier. Boldly accoutered officers rode or marched beside their men, yelling orders and encouragement against the uproar. Farther back on the shore reposed wagons of ponderous siege machinery, of supplies to sustain the invading army. Behind these waited the jackals, the vultures — bands of human scavengers voracious for the spoils of battle, allies not even of one another.

Perhaps a quarter of Malchion's army had crossed when Lord Dribeck launched his counterattack. The shower of arrows suddenly became a punishing hail of death, sweeping like a demon wind through the tight ranks. Horses screamed and fell, entangled flailing hooves with thrashing bodies of soldiers. Progress across the bridge faltered as jumbled bodies of the fallen and blood-slick planks made a chaos to dam the flow of men. Behind them the Breim archers could not return fire — for thus far the only targets were their fellows. At the bridgehead men cursed and died, fighting for whatever shelter was offered from the relentless rain of iron-toothed shafts.

"Push forward!" screamed Teres, defying the death that fell about her. "Break into the forest! You're nothing but targets here! Forward and close with these slinking bandits! Cram your steel through the archers' bellies, and they'll cease to strafe us! Forward, damn you! Make way for your comrades to cross over!"

Shields braced against streaking arrows, the Breim soldiers surged over the riverbank, across the flood plain, and plunged into the heavy forest beyond. War cries roared with harsh anger as they raced to slake their fury with the blood of the hidden enemy.

"Kane! Ovstal! Ivocel! Bring up your companies!" Dribeck ordered, as the Breim army rushed toward them.

The ranks of archers parted to give passage to the Selonari heavy infantry. Forward they marched, shields raised, weapons poised to strike — swords, axes, spears, maces — the backbone of Dribeck's army crunching forward to break the Breim charge. For as the battle reached into the forest, archery would be no longer effective, nor would the field permit sophisticated tactics or formation. This would be pitched combat, hand to hand, steel against steel, and muscle and nerve would decide victory now.

The two lines swept together and struck like two raging storm fronts. Lightning crashed and flickered as blade met blade, thunder rolled and echoed the mindless roar of battle, the clangor of striking steel, the howl of violent death. And the ground grew darkly sodden with the splash of crimson rain.

Sword flashing, Teres entered battle with a wild yell. Gwellines reared, eyes rolling, nostrils flared, as the tide of war washed over them. His hooves lashed

out, caught an enemy in the face. Teres's sword clove down, leaped back slinging scarlet spray. An axe swung upward and struck the shield almost from her
grip. Her spurred boot raked the foeman's eyes, her blade thrust, and he entered Hell a blindman.

Had any man felt qualms at slaying a woman, they vanished before the
fury of this hellion. Through their ranks she ravaged, guiding the warhorse
with her knees, though the stallion seemed to think like a man. Weaving between the great trees, Gwellines galloped, leaving many a Selonari crushed
beneath his hooves. Blows aimed at her were met by shield and blade, slipped
past and answered with deadly speed. Her soldiers rallied to her, fought recklessly at her side, and when a man stopped a thrusting blade from her back,
his slayer drew his last breath knowing the blaze of her wrath.

Into the forest they surged, where trees were giant pillars of this temple of
war. And the sacrificial altars were glutted. It was a chaos, a desperate melee
of man against man, a myriad of individual duels on which the outcome of
the battle hung, although in the turmoil, the maze of forest, there was no way
to guess which army had the firmer grasp on victory.

Resting a moment as the battle swirled about her, Teres tried to gauge her
army's status. It was a hopeless task at present. The steady pressure from the
forest beyond was proof that Dribeck had brought up his main army in the
night, though how many soldiers he held in reserve could not be known.
Noticeably absent from the struggle thus far was any sign of the Selonari
cavalry. Glancing back at the bridgehead, Teres saw that the Wolf's soldiers
had cleared the planks and were trickling across the Macewen. As their advance drove the archers out of bowshot of the bridge — and their fire was
nearly stilled already — Malchion's army would surge across. Then Dribeck
could send in all his reserves, but with little hope of throwing back the invaders. Since this moment was his only real chance to crush their advance, Teres
assumed he must already have brought up the greatest part of his army. Well,
Selonari had not enough strength; they could only meet her vanguard on, at
best, even terms. It remained for her to hold firm until Malchion's main force
could cross to support them, then they'd chase Dribeck all the way to Selonari,
where he'd be lucky if enough of his army survived to bar the gates.

She saw a horseman draw near — one of the few Dribeck had shown so
far — and recognized Kane as the rider. The stranger loomed more massive
in battle gear than in his priest's cloak. He fought like some elder god of war,
it seemed, face twisted in malevolent laughter, eyes glowing blue fire, slaying
her soldiers like infirm slaves. With surprise Teres noted that he carried no
shield; instead he swung a heavy mace in his right band, parrying, striking
with it as if he had full use of both arms. Their eyes met for an instant, and
even at this distance Teres felt stunned by their chill flame of death.

Kane wheeled his mount and turned to another portion of the field. Teres
wondered about his reasons for continuing his masquerade — to preserve
Dribeck's confidence, presumably, but after this battle the Selonari lord most
likely would share his secrets with the ravens. Perhaps Kane had found no
opportunity to desert, though he fought under Dribeck's standard as if he

were that schemer's champion. It occurred to Teres that her own men might well slay Kane without ever learning he was the Wolf's agent. But that, she decided, was Kane's risk, and she wondered if such might not be a fortunate twist of fate.

But there was enemy blood to spill. She pushed Kane from her thoughts and spurred Gwellines forward to where her soldiers were falling back, scattering men of both armies before her charge.

From his own steed, Lord Dribeck viewed the weaving battle with concern. Crempra's archers had been broken by the Breim advance. He had pulled them back, but now wondered if he would be forced to commit them once again — although he had hoped to hold them for a better moment. Still, he had advanced almost his entire reserve, keeping back only his personal guard. If many more of Malchion's soldiers came across, he would have to use Crempra's archers for infantry, throw in his own guard as well, and try to force the invaders back to the river. It would mean the final cast of the dice for him, but unless his first strategy came through, and soon, this desperate move would be his only recourse.

Then the anxious eyes that searched the far shore widened in hope. Confusion caught up Malchion's right flank as it waited to cross the Macewen. Down the graveled flood plain wildly galloped a company of horsemen, steel blazing in the morning sunlight. A cavalry charge on Malchion's unprotected flank!

Above the roar of his men Dribeck waved his sword and shouted in exultation. "Ristkon's cavalry! We've done it! Now the Wolf will know he's thrust his leg into the jaws of a trap! He'll gnaw it off if he's to escape us! For Selonari, men! Our steel can spare his worn teeth the task! At these yellow-bearded reavers, now, and we'll show them how Selonari welcomes thieves!"

He threw the remainder of his force full into battle, boldly committing them to his strategy. For when the point of Malchion's crossing had been fixed, Dribeck had sent his entire cavalry under Ristkon's command to ford the Macewen at the closest shallow. It had been a gamble — a mad ride downstream, across the fording, then back upstream — with only a few stretches of roadway to speed their progress. His archers had delayed the Breim crossing for as long as could be done without alerting Malchion to their true strength. It had been close, but the first of the gamble was won. To capitalize on this strategy remained for him still, and his carefully set trap might well prove unequal to the monstrous beast its jaws held.

Intent only on crossing the river, Malchion was caught altogether off guard by the cavalry assault. Milling in confusion along the bank, his soldiers were staggered by Ristkon's charge. Men yelled and fell over one another, tumbled into the current, seeking only to escape the murderous hooves, the reddened blades. Chaos shambled along the shore. A wedge through rotted log, the Selonari cavalry split the Breim army as they drove to the bridge.

Malchion howled commands, but the panic-stricken confusion upon the shore made a barrier of the packed ranks, and the Wolf was helpless in his numbers. For all the disorder, his soldiers heavily outnumbered the enemy horsemen, and he knew he could bring down his heel to crush the Selonari into the river. But first his men must recover from the shock of the charge, and Ristkon had not meant his to be suicidal.

Even as the army of Breimen recoiled from their thrust, the Selonari cavalry slashed through to the bridge. There the Breim soldiers fell back in dismay, uncertain whether to face the enemy on one shore or the other. Ristkon's men rode determinedly forward, and the pontoon bridge became the unlikely field for a cavalry charge. Meanwhile Dribeck had moved up his archers once again under the advance of his reserve infantry. Arrows raked the near side of the bridge, driving back the Breim soldiers who attempted to retreat to their fellows' aid. Cut down by arrows, crushed by hooves more frightful than the blades of the riders, Malchion's soldiers were swept from the bridge. The Macewen seemed choked with limp or struggling bodies of men and horses.

The Wolf led his army in pursuit, enraged with sudden understanding of Dribeck's strategy. But his way was blocked. For as they retreated, the rearguard of cavalry held back their pursuers long enough to break open skins of oil which they had brought. In minutes the bridge was ablaze, while in other sections the Selonari smashed open the pontoons, slashed and pried at the lashings. The bridge seemed to disintegrate all at once. Freed of the pilings, large sections drifted away into the current, some sinking, others trailing smoke — one with several soldiers yet standing on its decking.

Malchion's army was divided, and the Wolf could only howl in anger. The Macewen was too deep to ford here. Men and riders who shed armor to swim across were picked off by the archers when they came within bowshot — those who were not swept away by the current. The fastest of Malchion's remaining cavalry could not reach the fording and ride back to the battleground until hours after the issue was decided. Even had there been more material readily on hand, it would take hours to rebuild the bridge. In despair Malchion sent men across in whatever rowboats he had available, but these were subject to murderous archery fire, and eventually the Selonari captured and destroyed them all.

There was nothing to do but stand powerless with a good third of his army, a helpless witness to the battle as it resolved on the far shore. It was a torment that drove more than a few to plunge into the river and vent their rage in futile exertion.

The forest floor became a raging, tumultuous battlefield, its carpet torn apart, spattered with dark wetness, strewn with death. The final dice had been thrown in the game of strategy. Now the mindless demons of war ravaged amok throughout the field. The battle was joined in inchoate ferocity that only death could untangle. No retreat, no reserves — either in men or in fury.

And through the twisting dance of war, the earthshaking din of combat, Teres coldly appraised her position. With the influx of Ristkon's cavalry and Dribeck's reserves, the Breim invaders were well outnumbered. Strafed by arrows as they milled across the flood plain, their advance to the forest was crushed back by Dribeck's fresh troops, and through their rear slashed the

Selonari mounted horse. They were seized in a vice between forest and river, with Ristkon driving a wedge through their spine. Her army must brace its full strength to force open the vice, or be broken like a thief on the rack.

Down from the forest marched Dribeck with his personal guard. At his flank Crempra dashed about, exhorting his archers to waste not a shaft — nor leave a full quiver, when the conflict became too entangled to know friend from enemy, as soon it must. The Temple guard had fallen back to form a wall of steel about the archers, fending off the desperate rushes of the Breim army. In the midst of the invaders already, Kane and Ovstal still fought at the head of their companies. Ristkon could be seen, silvered mail gleaming as he rode, leading his cavalry across the Breim flank, where such of the Wolf's cavalry as survived made an attempt to group for countercharge. Two others of his captains were down, by Dribeck's counting, as had fallen Diab, commander of the Temple guard.

Swords and spears slashed at his flesh. The Breim soldiers fought grimly to break through Dribeck's picked personal guard as it ringed the Selonari lord. His death could swing the battle, and their attack became maniacal as the tide turned against Breimen. Dribeck met the attack of those who reached him with cool swordplay. He was not a born swordsman, nor had he the physical might to dominate in combat. But his lean frame was possessed of wiry strength and evasive swiftness, which hours of careful training had honed to make his sword arm respected. And though he was conscious of the double risk he took in joining this desperate battle, Dribeck knew his men expected his personal leadership. They would not follow a lord whose bravery or martial prowess was suspect, and Dribeck meant to die a leader — if death must take him — rather than dance his dismal days as the puppet ruler his predecessors had become.

A spear tore at his mail and fell back. Dribeck drove his blade through the wielder's face. Screaming, the soldier dropped to his knees, still clutching the spear, and blindly jabbed it at his horse's belly. Swinging from the saddle, Dribeck lopped off the man's arm and left him writhing on the ground, as another enemy leaped to stab him. Dribeck's sword caught the other's blade, then with a sudden lunge laid open his belly. He straightened in time to block another's sword with his shield, traded blows in rapid succession, then rode the assailant down.

So it went. The battle knotted tighter still, now hand to hand exclusively, as the invaders were driven from the forest and onto the flood plain. Ristkon had split the Breim army into unequal halves, and in a fierce drive had overwhelmed the last of the enemy horsemen. The smaller half of Breim warriors was being forced into the Macewen, where the invaders were cut apart in the churned mud of the riverbank. Many tried to cast off armor and weapons, to swim back across the treacherous current. Some escaped thus. The annihilation of this segment of Breim warriors took the heart from their fellows; those who could now sought to slip through the perimeter and escape into the forest, where the Selonari pursued them a short way.

Kane's horse fell, Dribeck saw, hamstrung by a dying footsoldier. The red-haired stranger somehow leaped clear of crumpling mount to land on his feet. Blood-mad Breim soldiers swarmed upon him, and Dribeck knew no ordinary warrior could live under that rush. But Kane had penetrated to the thick of the enemy's main body, and there was no hope of reaching him soon enough. Kane was a bear surrounded by hounds, and his sword and mace rose and slashed, striking with blurring speed and deadly certainty. His attackers were hurled back by brute strength, ringing him with smashed and contorted corpses like a bulwark over which new assailants slipped and scrambled.

Then reddened blades and stark faces swirled about him, and Lord Dribeck could spare no further thought for Kane. Doggedly he fought. His guard were fewer now; the enemy were fewer still, but seemingly heedless of their lives in an effort to bring down the leader of their foe. His shield hacked and dented, the arm behind it numb from countless blows, Dribeck's sword arm ached with relentless exertion — the pain less endurable than the gashes and bruises inflicted upon him. He set his teeth, breathed with a shuddering hiss and drew upon the last stores of endurance to keep blade and shield weaving. Slash, parry! Block, thrust! *Where were his men?*

The foemen fell back abruptly as a mounted warrior drove through them. A mace shattered helm and skull of one whose axe had all but torn away Dribeck's shield, then the other was at his side. Too exhausted for surprise, Dribeck recognized Kane, astride a horse he had somehow captured, his massive frame splattered with gore, but apparently little of it his own. Dribeck could not guess with what awesome carnage the man had fought through the Breim ranks.

With Kane came a number of Selonari soldiers — the battle too disordered now to distinguish one captain's company from another's. They threw back the Breim onslaught, giving Dribeck time to draw agonized breaths, wipe stinging sweat and filth from his eyes.

The drive to slay the Selonari lord had been the last hope of Breimen's army: it had failed. Now Dribeck's soldiers were massed about him. The defenders' losses had been slighter, mainly because of the punishing toll of Crempra's archers, and the untenable position Dribeck's strategy had forced upon the intruders. The Selonari army was now in full control of the field; the battle's outcome was established.

Hopelessly outnumbered, a knot of nearly a hundred Breim warriors fought on. Teres had tried to maintain their advance into the forest. She and her men had been driven back last of all, forced onto the flood plain to discover further retreat was cut off. Dribeck held riverbank and forest edge; his soldiers surrounded them beyond escape. Nor was there any reasonable line of retreat, should they break through the trap — only the river, awash with hacked and drowned corpses, or the trees, where Dribeck's cavalry harried those few who sought to flee through the hostile forestland.

They formed a shield wall and waited for death to come, weary, bleeding limbs set for a last hopeless struggle. Already the Selonari army smashed and tore at their perimeter, merciless as starving wolves.

Amazingly, Lord Dribeck ordered his men to draw back. Still surrounded, the Breim soldiers accepted the respite to take fresh grips on their weapons and glare back at their slayers. But Dribeck was not minded to lose more of his warriors. The turn of battle had opened another avenue for him, and he sought quickly to follow on it.

"Lady Teres!" he called out to the disheveled girl astride a foam-streaked warhorse. "Your position is hopeless — any fool can see that! Order your men to drop their weapons and surrender to me!"

Teres tossed her head, ears still ringing from a blow that had dented her helmet. "Why surrender? Are your gutless jackals afraid to face Breim steel any longer? Then stand clear and give us passage to the river — and I'll order my warriors to spare your stumbling alley scum as we go!"

An angry murmur went through his men, and some edged forward. Sharply Dribeck ordered them back. "Save your bravado, Teres! You know your position! I'm giving you a chance for life! Be a fool, and you'll all die before the afternoon sun sinks an hour lower!"

"We'll die with swords in our hands, rather than stretched on Shenan's altars! Or slaughtered for the amusement of your craven nobility!" she shot back.

"You can't pretend to believe your own propaganda!" Dribeck growled. Human sacrifice had been officially banned for generations, though what the Temple might do in secrecy was beyond conjecture. "I offer you your lives on my word! Before all my men, I swear that all who surrender now will be treated as prisoners honorably taken! You will be bartered to Malchion according to my terms; until then you will not be harmed. These are terms no army of aggression deserves, but I here declare this to be my command! Now decide quickly between life and death, for my archers grow tired of waiting!"

Gloomily Teres considered her predicament. Across the Macewen, cruelly in full view, stood the rest of the Breim army. They might stand across the Western Sea for all the help they could offer. At her side were the last of her men, a pitiful few. Most of her officers were slain; Lian perhaps had fled, since none saw where he fell. She called herself a warrior, and in the sagas Teres's heroes would have spat in Dribeck's face and died with sword swinging. It was the way a warrior died.

But sagas were for the night, when minstrels could weave heroic images from the shadows of the dead past. The day was beautiful, clear and bright with cool forest wind soothing her anguished brow. And Teres did not want to die.

There will be other battles to fight, perhaps, she told herself wearily. Then there was Kane — an enigma, but there was no question of his service to Malchion in the past.

"All right, damn you," she said huskily. "I surrender myself and my men to you — on the strength of your word, for what value it will prove. Gwellines is too good a warhorse to be feathered by Selonari arrows."

XII
Spoils of Victory

For two days after the battle the skies wept — the hammering rains that marked the close of the Southern Lands' short summer. In Selonari there was rejoicing — unbridled riot that made the festival of the Spring Moon seem a pauper's wake in reflection.

Victory!

At least, for the moment. Shaken by the decimation of his army, Lord Malchion had withdrawn to Breimen. He yet had better than a quarter of his army and the greater. part of its supplies. But even allowing for Dribeck's losses, Malchion was outnumbered, and to cross the Macewen in the teeth of Selonari's warriors was to invite massacre. Injured, and feeling the loss of his daughter more keenly than he evidenced, the lame Wolf began the dismal return to Breimen. There he meant to rebuild his army before beginning a second offensive. Meanwhile, Breimen must be protected, in the event Dribeck should attempt to march north against the city, an ill-advised strategy Malchion rather hoped his enemy might be rash enough to try.

But now no one would cross the Macewen, for the river rose high on its banks, mercifully sweeping the flotsam of war to its delta on the Western Sea.

Through the rain Dribeck's triumphant army slogged back to Selonari. Wagons were heaped to overturning with the plunder of battle — stacks of war gear, litters of the wounded. They had worked through the night despoiling the field, tossing the dead of Breimen into the river, burying their comrades in great cairns. The wounded were cared for — even, by Dribeck's order, those of the enemy — although in a battle such as this a man's injuries were generally either mortal or not crippling. Patrols grew weary chasing down the few remaining Breim fugitives. When Malchion's retreat became certainty, the bulk of Dribeck's army returned to celebrate the victory.

Laden with glory and plunder, the Selonari soldiers all but fulfilled

Malchion's threat to raze the city to the ground. To fight alongside
Death is heady wine for those who evade his sword, so that life becomes a new bride, to be sported with in full before dawn dispels the
magic of the first night. Toasts were drunk to the fallen, sweethearts
consoled by the survivors. Grief might underlie the gaiety, might come
tomorrow when the wine of victory became a sour taste. But on the
night of their return, Selonari belonged to the victors, and they overflowed streets and taverns in total abandon.

Teres kept her face an aloof mask and drank a little wine. The banquet table before her overflowed with choice fare, but the ache in her
belly could not be warmed by food. She and her men had been marched
trough Selonari's streets, displayed before a hooting populace alongside the rest of the victor's booty. Still, they had not been abused —
other than the insults and offal the people had flung. Her men were
imprisoned somewhere in Dribeck's dungeons; thus far he appeared
scrupulous in keeping to his word.

Teres was given the dubious honor of attending Dribeck's victory
feast. Stripped of her weapons and mail, she sat with back straight at
the high table, conspicuous in her battle-stained hacton and pants
among the richly dressed gentry. Darkly Teres pondered the wisdom
of her surrender. If someone would be fool enough to place a knife
just close enough, she'd snatch it up and bury it in Dribeck's pride-
flushed throat. But the attendants on either side were vigilant — coldly
solicitous, but guards nonetheless. Teres sipped her wine and consoled herself with the thought that Dribeck at least respected her
nerve, did not dismiss her as some shrinking girl hostage, who was
crushed into meek subjection by her captor's magnificence.

Damn it, this wasn't going to help her escape, though. Maybe she
should choke down her pride and whimper a little... throw them off
guard. No, she would not further degrade herself. Let the greasy fools
guzzle and boast to their sallow whores of their bravery! Dribeck
would soon grow overconfident; then let him learn what fury he
thought to hold captive!

Teres wondered again how she might speak with Kane without
arousing suspicion. The hulking stranger was deep in his wine, seemingly — a brooding figure amidst the laughter and loud voices. Dribeck
had spoken low to a court wench, who slipped to Kane's side, but found
her wanton advances distractedly answered. Teres wished he might
give her some sort of sign, some indication that he meant to help her.
Terribly alone as she was in the citadel of her enemy, this enigmatic
figure was the only friend she had.

For the most part, Teres was ignored by the others at the high
table — Dribeck's captains, the more important gentry, their women,
and a lady of haughty beauty she learned was Gerwein, high priestess
of Shenan. Conversation was in the clipped language of the Southern
Lands, of its dark-haired people who had settled here before the

Wollendan migrations. Teres understood it well enough to follow their speech, if she were so inclined, but their main topic was painful for her. Dribeck's several efforts to engage her — he spoke fluent Wollendan — she coolly rebuffed. So despite their curious glances, her captors were content to grant her the dignity of silence. Probably they regarded her as only another of the battle trophies on display for their celebration.

One pair of eyes stared at her in open hostility. Ristkon, Malchion's old enemy, murderer of her kinsmen, traitor to Breimen in the past — and doubly so today. No more than a small girl during Ristkon's conspiracy to seize Breimen, she remembered his smiling face well. A gash through the left cheek had scarred badly, drawing that side of his mouth into a mirthless grin. He had been a vain youth, with a face as pretty as a girl's and a tall body of pantherish grace; the disfigurement had twisted more than his smile. After his defeat, he was thought to have fled the Southern Lands and sailed north beyond Malchion's wrath. Dribeck had evidently unearthed him in some ill-famed port along the northern coasts. Contemptuous, Teres considered it a measure of Selonari cunning that its lord would step to recruit such filth.

As the evening progressed Ristkon's glare grew bolder, returning to her more often. He had addressed her in taunting words a few times, insults she pretended not to hear. To his companions he spoke now and again in low tones — words that brought snickers and guffaws, turned speculative eyes toward her. Teres deliberately looked elsewhere, though her ears strained to catch his whispers.

"Teres," he called loudly after one outburst of private laughter, "all these years I've heard tales of wild Teres, the Wolf's sharp-fanged whelp. Last time I saw you, you were just a skinny little brat, who liked to thrash the page boys and crawl around the tables on feast days like a hound looking for scraps. So I couldn't know then, and now that I see you again, I still can't be sure. I mean, your face is homely as a sergeant's, and you're husky enough to command a press gang, and by all reports you've never been seen in anything approaching decent dress for a woman. So I'm puzzled, and I hope you'll tell me — are you really a girl who doesn't know her sex, or just some beardless freak of a boy?"

Teres looked him in the face and curled her lip in unvoiced contempt. Her sneer mimicked the twisted set of Ristkon's features. The table began to grow quiet.

Ristkon flushed, making a pale streak of his scar. "Well, I have to know for certain, Teres," he said in strained civility. "You know there's a blood feud between our lines. Now, if you're a man, honor demands we settle the feud at swordpoint. But if it's true you're a girl, why, I can't kill a girl. So I'll be content to take you to my chambers and treat you as I would any woman who's taken as spoils of victory."

Teres's knuckles tightened around the wine cup. "I didn't realize you made such a distinction, Ristkon," she replied, in a tone that carried. "It's common knowledge that you're an accomplished murderer of women and children. I assume your ambiguous honor is equally confused about whom you take to bed."

Conversation was silent. Laughter at the other tables seemed miles distant. Ristkon's crooked smile was ghastly against his taut features. Slowly he rose to his feet, hands grasping the table edge as if anchored there.

"Take that mule-faced bitch to my chambers!" he choked. "I'll know if there's a woman under all that dirt and leather!"

"Ristkon, I am lord here," Dribeck interceded. "I gave my word no harm would be done to the prisoners."

The other seemed to bite off his first answer. He resumed his seat stiffly and quickly read the faces of his tablemates. "I don't plan to do anything to this bitch a woman wasn't made to take," he said with a malicious laugh. "Don't know why you're showing such courtesy to an enemy, though — you know how gentle the Wolf and his whelp meant to be with all of us! And I shouldn't need to remind you it was my cavalry that turned the battle to your advantage — else you'd know the Wolf's mercy firsthand. Teres is spoils of war same as any captured wench, and I'd think my part in the victory should give me booty of my own choosing. At least, I don't know of any reasonable lord who'd begrudge his captain a little sport after his invaluable service... unless he was more generous with a captured enemy whore than his own comrades."

Dribeck frowned. Many of the others showed agreement with Ristkon's point of view — nor was his argument unreasonable. He had plans of his own, however, that he dared not jeopardize. Neither did he care to lose face before his men, which seemed unavoidable whether he granted or refused his captain's demand. The sword was sharp and had no hilt; either Ristkon's will was stronger than his word, or he was niggardly in rewarding his followers.

There seemed an escape from the dilemma. Quickly, then. "I'm not forgetting your role in our victory," he answered smoothly. "But a captain shouldn't forget that his lord takes first share of the plunder. As it happens, I'm minded to bed my enemy's daughter myself. There are sweeter wenches and more willing, but it amuses me to humble this snarling she-wolf. Choose another for your sport, Ristkon, and be assured I'll reward your loyalty with more pleasing booty than this.

"Put her in my chambers for now." He gave orders to her guards, who led Teres away. She gave him a scornful glance in passing, ignoring the rest of the grinning throng.

Ristkon's derisive laughter followed her. "But you'll let us know what you find out, won't you! Maybe you'll want to muzzle the she-wolf — her bite is probably as venomous as her growl!"

The Wollendan renegade seemed appeased, Dribeck decided. Evidently he judged the humiliation sufficient revenge for the moment. More to Dribeck's concern, his handling of the matter had found favor among his men. It was a great joke, and suited the drunken merriment of the night. Tomorrow or the next day, the incident would have dimmed to nothing more than an amusing anecdote, and he could proceed with his new plans untroubled by consequences of the evening.

In another wing of the citadel, Teres restlessly paced about the chamber. Two capable-looking maidservants kept nervous watch over her, more to keep her from locking the door than anything else, since Dribeck's chambers were situated within the castle's topmost level, and far, far below his windows Selonari's brick streets blazed with festive light. A pair of guards waited beyond the door. Teres was not inclined to leap from the window like a fool; she meant to show Dribeck her claws first, should he come to carry out his boast.

Grimly she cast about her prison. A strong rope or the equivalent might let her escape through the window, but it seemed doubtful Dribeck would keep such on hand. The guards had already removed several weapons. It was possible others had been missed, and if she could lay hands on something without being seen... But the two women watched her closely.

The chambers were interesting, had her mind been less troubled. Appointments were rich, though short of opulent. There was a virile tone to the furnishings that created a casual, comfortable presence. One alcove was a small study, shelves stuffed with charts and books. She glanced at the maps, particularly the one depicting the Southern Lands, but found nothing of military significance marked there. The books were meaningless, except for one whose title she spelled out haltingly to be a history of the Wollendan clans. Her reading was confined largely to military reports, and she deemed that anything else of value could be read aloud by clerks. So Dribeck was the scholar that men said. Grudgingly she admitted that the man was not unskilled in more important matters, as well — she had seen some of his fighting ability. The bed — her eyes kept returning to it despite her resolve — was a great curtained affair, its mattress draped with fine fur robes.

Short of ransacking the various chests and closets, there seemed no chance of turning up a weapon. She doubted her wardens would permit such rifling. One cabinet was strewn with delicate items of feminine toiletry, apparel, jewelry. "Pentri's — milord's mistress," explained one of the maids, at her quizzical expression. She shrugged. Such finery she had chosen to shun. A mirror lay upturned, and absently Teres noted that her face *was* dirty. To give her hands something to do, she found a lavabo and washed herself. It was not so bad a face.

A murmur at the door, and Dribeck entered, waving the maids to stand outside. He approached her with a trace of hesitation in his stride.

"So... has the lord of Selonari found courage to 'humble this snarling she-wolf'?" Teres taunted, forcing her voice to calmness as she measured the distance between them. "Drunken oafs have pawed at me on occasion. Some of them were lucky enough to find comfortable positions later — fat custodians in some foreign emperor's harem. Or shall I swoon for the fierce-hearted warrior... the strutting victor whose word is not worth the breath that utters it!"

To her surprise, Dribeck sank onto a chair and frowned at her in annoyance. "Damn it, if I wanted to wrestle with an acid-tongued virago, I'd chase after Gerwein. She doesn't wear spurs to bed... so far as I know. I told you you wouldn't be harmed, and my pledge stands! I could easily have given you to Ristkon — saved myself a difficult moment. Well, I didn't, and as far as I care, you can sleep here the night without my presence. Tomorrow, when things are smoothed over, you can go to the quarters I'd planned for you — not a dungeon cell, either. Hell, did you think I felt some overpowering sexual attraction for you? Ristkon just wanted you out of some black malice, and I interfered with no thought but to spare you from his twisted revenge."

"Well, *you* pick your servants!" Teres retorted, wondering if this was a ruse to put her off guard. Somewhere she found spirit to resent his curt rebuff — an emotion which seemed illogical even to her. "Let me say that the thought of sharing a bed with you was only slightly less distasteful to me than the prospect of that traitor's embrace. And the surest way to demonstrate the sanctity of your word is to get your ass out of here right now. Your Pentri must be moaning for you this very moment."

Dribeck started, a ghost of a smile on his lips. "Pentri? Hmmm. The gossip in Breimen is stale... I've grown tired of the minx. She's down the hall with Kane, probably. My moody friend seemed unhappy without the immediate prospect of battle, so I sent Pentri to him to ease his melancholy."

"He needn't mope for long. There'll be another battle, and soon! Did you really think Malchion would give up this war, just because your trickery dealt us a temporary reversal? Before the snows come, your victory celebration will seem a sour mockery!"

Dribeck drew his fingers together before his face, cradled chin on thumbs, elbows on knees. "Perhaps not," he commented, dropping his hands. "That's what I hope to discuss with you. There is no point in continuing this war, really. Your defeat must have convinced you of what a mistake your invasion was. (Let me finish!) Breimen lost the best part of its army. You can bankrupt your treasury, arm every farmboy and alley rat, try to cross the Macewen again, and there'll be another bloody defeat for you. All right... say by chance you *were* victorious after your best effort has already failed. Selonari wouldn't fall easily. You'd be left with a decimated population, a bankrupt government, mercenaries running riot through your land, and your great prize would be a burned-over city-state. That's the best you'd come out; all odds are you'd never make it across the Macewen!

"Why do it? Breimen doesn't need Selonari's wealth, or our lands. Maybe the Wollendan tradition is to seize land as you desire, but you should damn well realize by now that Selonari isn't some backwater settlement you can march right over, like your countrymen overran the northern towns some years back. If you feel the need to expand your holdings — a dubious necessity — then move east. There's nothing but miles of timber between Breimen's borders and the slopes of the Great Ocalidads. Selonari has no interest in seizing Breimen's lands. If that were true, my army would be at your gates this night. What logic, then, in continuing the war?"

"War is seldom logical, I'm told," Teres returned. "My people's honor is at stake, for one thing... though I doubt you would understand the idea of honor. And Selonari's hostility toward Breimen is well proven. We know you mean to consolidate your control of this degenerate court by invading Breimen. Why else did you so carefully assassinate two of our leaders before we even thought to invade Selonari in our defense!"

"Your army had been marshaled for months! And I swear to you these so-called assassinations were done utterly without the knowledge or complicity of Selonari!"

But our spies tell a different story, she thought, smiling that she had a certain defense for his too persuasive arguments. "Well, now I know how good your word is," she replied ambiguously.

Dribeck frowned at her. "Well, you think about it for a while. You'll have the time. I've tried to act in good faith with you, whether your suspicious mind will let you recognize that or not. And if you're wondering about your fate, let me say I intend to return you and the other prisoners to Breimen, and I hope to do this as a gesture of faith that will include a treaty of peace."

"So you can hatch further schemes, no doubt."

He slid to his feet. "I won't waste the night arguing with a deaf mind. You think about it, though — might not corrupt your spirit to do that. Sleep on it. The two girls will see to your needs."

Dribeck looked back at the door. "It's really an interesting face, when it's clean enough to see your skin," he concluded.

Teres swore at his back. The maidservants stole back inside. Basic male tactic. Sweep a woman off her feet with flattery, then she'll believe every word you say. Some women might. And the next man to call her face "interesting" would die horribly.

XIII
She-Wolf's Fangs

After Dribeck's departure, Teres tired of prowling about the room. Throwing back the curtains, she stretched out across his bed, boots dug into the furs, her back arched against piled cushions. Little had she slept, despite the racking fatigue of these last days of nightmare. For all the exhaustion that gnawed at her, her nerves were too tightly strung, her position too uncertain to permit her to relax. Besides, this night of mad celebration might offer as good a chance to escape as she would ever be given.

She drew her knees together, clasping her hands about them to raise her back from the pillows. One of the two maidservants slumped down upon a couch; the other sat upright in a chair — taking first watch, Teres noted. Baiting her maids was one of her favorite amusements.

With unblinking stare, Teres gazed into the other girl's eyes. The other returned her gaze curiously a moment, then dropped her eyes in alarm. Teres continued to watch her face. The maid fidgeted with her garments and cast about the room for something to occupy her thoughts. Every few minutes she raised her eyes again, found Teres still watching her, and nervously looked away. At length she set her lips and boldly stared back, seeking to end the game. Teres held her eyes for a space, then pursed her mouth to form a kiss. Flushing, the servant girl glanced away, looked helplessly toward her companion, whose soft breathing indicated she slept.

"Come lie beside me, where you'll be comfortable," Teres whispered. "There's no need to pass the night stiff as a guardsman at his post." The girl colored and muttered something in vexation, too soft for Teres to hear. Anxiously she rose to search the room for something to take her thoughts from the prisoner. Teres smiled mischievously and began to hum disjointedly a scurrilous ballad popular among the troops, freely translating bits of verse to suit her spirit.

Challenge sounded in the hall. Men's voices drifted through the door. Someone protested about orders. Another voice explained that they were to finish their watch, give them a chance to share in the victory celebration. Teres, listening with interest, decided from the muffled sounds that her guard had just changed. To her memory, there were only two soldiers posted in the hallway, but with a fresh pair her chances of slipping past probably edged a hair closer to nil.

Stealthy footsteps approached; voices mumbled at the doorway. Feeling a thrill of alarm, Teres ceased her teasing and rose to her feet. The door rattled and swung suddenly open. Her breath caught.

Three men hastily entered. A pair of tough-looking mercenaries — and Ristkon, twisted smile as malevolent as the coiled whip on his shoulder.

His henchmen showed knives. "Not a sound!" he hissed warning to the startled maidservants. "Cry out, and my men will carve a smile across your throats!" He turned hot eyes on Teres.

Quickly his men bound and gagged the terrified maids. Dumping the girls in a closet, they reluctantly quitted the room.

Deliberately Ristkon placed his sword and dagger beside the doorway, well out of reach of the captive. Serpentine as the uncoiling whip, he sulked across the chamber toward her. "I said I meant to learn what manner of freak the Wolf's pup might be," he grinned. "And I've known a whip to turn many a bitch's snarl to a whimper."

"Hadn't you better get your stooges to bind me for you first?" Teres spat. "It's out of your reputation to take such personal risks!"

The whip licked lazily toward her boots. "You'll see that my lash cuts as sharp as your tongue," he warned unruffled. "Before long you'll whine and grovel like a well-mannered bitch should for her master."

"Dribeck will deal harshly with a minion who transgresses his lord's pledge!" she promised hopefully. Biting down a wave of panic, she backed toward the bed.

Ristkon laughed in derision. "What can Dribeck do? My men have replaced his guards. My noble lord and his brainless cousin have stepped into the night to clank mugs with his soldiers — to win their love, so he thinks. The others here are all besotted with drink and carousal. There's none to give a thought to you, and when you'll soon moan for me, your cries will be swallowed up in the night's riot. If tomorrow Dribeck finds his pampered prize somewhat less haughty, what can he say to his most valued captain? The fool has enough cunning to know he needs my horsemen in this war! Do you think he'll scruple at a captive's well-being to quarrel with his most powerful ally? He'll laugh and shrug it off, as if it had been his plan from the start!"

He strode closer, face livid with hate. "Do you know this weakling means to make peace with your father? After he promised me governorship of Breimen for my support of his cause! Well, I was driven like a dog from that city, and I'll return like a conqueror! And the

Wolf and his vainglorious line are going to whimper on their bellies before my feet!"

The whip snaked out, to curl about her waist. Its lash did not cut through the iron-bossed leather jerkin, though her breath stuttered at its force. Laughing, Ristkon yanked back on the whip, spinning her as its coils unwound. "Will you climb out of your man's leathers, she-wolf? Or shall I peel it from your flanks!"

Again the whip struck for her. She threw up her arms to guard her face, felt the bed press against her calves. Fury fought terror; wildly she tried to think. Ristkon stepped closer, drew back on the lash. Staggering, Teres let herself be pulled forward to his grasp. His smile somehow leered wider. He crushed her to his chest, still grasping the whip's haft. She felt his heart pounding, his breath in her hair. "Lost your fight this easily, have you?"

She clasped her hands around his back. No trace of flab had the years implanted to flaw his dancer's body. "A lord usually needs no such weapon to shed a lady's clothes," she murmured unsteadily, not daring to meet his face.

"A wanton so soon?" he rasped, and pressed his lips against hers, his vanity. flattered by her swift capitulation. She closed her eyes, hesitantly returning his harsh kiss. "My bitch has sheathed her claws... or more likely dreams of trickery! Do you fear my whip now? You've had but a taste."

"No man has ever mastered me," Teres whispered.

"The fastenings are on the back." She snuggled against him. The coils dropped from her waist.

The wine of Ristkon's breath made her dizzy. There was smug mastery in his sneering face. "Perhaps there is a woman inside these jabbing tits of iron," he muttered, hoarsely, fumbling with the fastenings of her jerkin. "We'll soon both know. Serve me well, wench. If you please me, perhaps you'll face the morning without your ribs shining through your back."

The hacton came loose down the nape of her neck. Docilely she raised her arms and let him tug the garment over her head. Underneath, she wore only a thin shirt, clinging to her flesh with chill sweat. "Not a boy, after all," observed Ristkon thickly. He ran his thin fingers across her firm breasts, trying to cup them, but she threw her arms around his neck, embracing him tightly. The whip dropped to the floor, atop her castoff jerkin. Roughly Ristkon tugged out her shirt and slipped his hands beneath the garment. She sighed huskily in his ear, feeling his throbbing neck pulse.

The cloth he drew off, and as he stared at her boldly, she loosened the ties of his shirt. "Stand back a pace," he warned. She complied meekly, as he quickly yanked his shirt over his head, suspiciously alert that she make no move while the cloth briefly blinded his vision.

Leaning against the bed pillar seductively, Teres worked her boots free. "Am I so displeasing to your eyes?" she whispered. Ristkon made an impatient gesture. Her fingers dug at the clasp of her pants. Watching his face with half-lidded eyes, she slid the leather trousers off her slim hips, wriggled them down her thighs, stepped out of them as they crumpled onto the floor.

Wearing only a brief undergarment, Teres swayed across the room. Ristkon's eyes branded her, but she held her smile. He tried to embrace her, but she laughed and touched his belt. Her fingers tickled his tight belly, then broke open the clasp. With a sudden wrench, she jerked his pants down to his knees. "Your boots," she breathed heavily.

Impatiently Ristkon fumbled with his clothing. "Stand away!" he mumbled, struggling with boots and trousers in haste.

Instead Teres drew back half a step. She hooked her fingers into the waist of her undergarment, and began to roll the thin cloth down her hips. Ristkon watched greedily as the furrow of her belly was bared. He bent forward clumsily, in an awkward half squat, as he blindly tore at the restraining trousers, bunched stubbornly over his boots.

Not daring to think of consequences, Teres shot her knee up. It slammed full into his outthrust face, smashing broken teeth into flesh.

With a choked cry — too startled to express his pain and rage! — Ristkon snapped backward, legs entrapped in his clothing. He fell heavily on his back, head striking the floor. Before he could recover from the stunning impact, Teres leapt upon him.

She snatched up the whip — there was no time to reach Ristkon's sword. A crimson spray whooshed from his ruined lips, as she drove her knees into his chest. The lash she twisted about his throat to choke off his angry bellow.

He twisted desperately, striving to throw her clear. But Teres had resilient strength in her willowy frame, and she was trained in the subtleties of hand-to-hand combat. She grimly fought for her hold, every spark of shame and rage strengthening her strangling grip.

The whip bit deep into his splotched throat — as she mercilessly twisted the garroting coil. Her knees pinned Ristkon's shoulders, but his legs lashed wildly, still ensnared in his clothing. This muffled the drumming of his heels, and presently their staccato pounding ceased.

Her hands shook as she at length relaxed their grip on the whip. She contemplated the purpled face a moment and felt loathing shudder through her. As she rose to her feet, the room wavered somewhat, though her thoughts worked in cool clarity.

Their struggle had been silent. If any sounds lead reached past the door, Ristkon's guards must have assumed their leader was at play. Perhaps she could bar the door...

Then what? Dribeck's reaction to the death of his captain might be anything. At best, she would merely remain his prisoner. Slumping upon the bed, she gnawed a favorite knuckle as she thought over her situation. Ristkon's interference had completely altered her status.

Fake guards waited beyond the door, Ristkon's weapons lay before her, her wardens were bound and helpless. The entire city had gone mad this night, and by Ristkon's words the citadel was abandoned to drunken revelers. Her chances would never be better — if she could get past Ristkon's henchmen alive.

A plan began to take form. Risky, but she grew weary of being Dribeck's victory prize. Some disguise might serve her in this.

Quickly she stepped to the cabinet where Pentri's effects lay scattered and rifled through them intently. If the Selonari knew her only as a rough-featured youth in stained battle gear, perhaps she should change her costume. Unfortunately, Pentri had left little here in the way of substantial clothing, and Teres dared not loose one of the maids and borrow her garments. Any second, any hint of suspicion, and someone might open the door to investigate.

With rapid movements she sponged the sweat and grit from her body, noting the red welts the lash had raised, the half-healed scratches and bruises of combat. Well, on this night no one would notice. She found a halter and loin belt that fitted loosely on her slim figure — extravagant affairs of silver wire and flame-tinted silk that made her feel like a tavern dancer. A green silk negligee, trimmed with fur, was as close to street clothing as Pentri had left. She slipped it over her shoulders, then frowned at her reflection. Not warrior's garb, at any rate.

Her hair was the most dangerous point, but there seemed little she could do about that. At least she had noticed a few blonde women among the dark haired Selonari. The heavy braid she rapidly unbound, to brush the long tresses smooth and arrange them under a jeweled headband. One half of her face, where the scar crossed her cheek, she let her hair spill over. Not too many would recognize her face, unless they caught the broken nose and looked more closely. A touch of color to her lips... It might work.

She would soon know. Wiping her palms, Teres drew Ristkon's sword and held it back in the folds of her gown. Coolly she swung the door ajar.

"It's an orgy. Come join in," she invited the soldier who confronted her.

She stood in shadow, the blade hidden behind her. The negligee hung open all down the front. It was an alluring invitation.

In a second the soldier would stop to think. But at the unexpected appearance of a seductive girl, he reacted automatically, without suspicion of danger. A smile starting to crease his features, he stepped through the doorway toward the girl. His hands reached for her.

Not giving him a second to reflect, Teres lunged with the sword. Its tip thrust through his heart, and the guard crumpled with a hoarse groan.

There were two guards. The other had stood on the side away from the half-opened door. He appeared in the doorway, even as Teres yanked back her blade to let his companion topple dying to the floor.

"What the hell!" he blurted. "What the hell!" His eyes took in the two corpses, the vengeful siren. For a stunned second he hesitated, his sword slowly rising, his throat contracting to shout alarm. Teres's blade struck savagely. His head half flew from his shoulders as he fell across the doorway.

Treading over the prostrate forms, she stepped into the hallway warily, and thus evaded the rush of the third guard. The mercenary had waited down the hall, to waylay Dribeck with some feigned dilemma should he return prematurely. Their swords met with a clang that should have alarmed the entire citadel.

Desperately Teres parried his blade, then slashed at his face. The soldier deflected her sword and retreated in confusion. Teres anticipated his cry for help and snarled as his mouth opened, "Sound the alarm, and how will Dribeck reward your part in Ristkon's insubordination? You knew your lord's orders — Dribeck will hang you, once he learns of Ristkon's treachery!"

"Reckon he won't learn!" grunted the mercenary. "You just sealed your death, bitch! Don't need no help to gut a woman!" He lunged forward.

Hampered by the billowing negligee, Teres barely eluded his thrust. The unfamiliar garments tangled about her, restricted her movements. And how long could this continue before someone heard the clash of steel? Recklessly she advanced, driving the guard back a few steps. His blade tugged at a fold of silk, as it sought her bare flash.

The guard staggered, arched his back in pain. By reflex as his swordpoint wavered, Teres ran him through, although the mercenary was already dying from the dirk protruding from his back. As he fell on his face, Teres gazed in wonder at the embedded knife-hilt.

"Pretty," remarked Kane, striding forward on bare feet. "Oh, very pretty indeed. What more have you done?"

Roughly he grasped the guard's body and dragged it into Dribeck's chambers. With raised brow he glanced over the carnage. "Damn! It *has* been a full night for you! Let's keep this unnoticed while we can. I'll mop up the blood in the hallway; you pour some wine over the smear, and maybe no one will look closer. You can get some wine, can't you?"

"Where did you come from?" Teres queried, bringing the wine.

"My room is in this wing, too — thank your fiery god that no one else is about right now! I meant to check on you, if chance presented... Ristkon left the banquet in too composed a mood. So I was wondering how to see you, when I smelled blood, stepped into the hallway and discovered you running amok. There seemed no point in prolonging the duel, so my knife found his back. Save us a swallow of that, will you? Quick now, to my room! Discovery here would be unfortunate."

"Where's Pentri?" Teres asked uneasily, noting the livid scratches across Kane's bare back. She carried her clothes and Ristkon's weapons balled in her arms.

"Get inside. You keep well informed, Teres. Pentri's asleep on my bed, with a smile on her hungry lips. I drugged her wine, and she'll frolic through her dreams for hours yet. She'll think the wine overcame her, and tomorrow she'll swear with all the fervor of her vanity that we two sported the night away. By the way, that's an impressive outfit. Now what the hell happened back there?"

Briefly Teres sketched an account of the evening. "Kane, you've got to help me escape!" she finished. "Dribeck said he'd be gone for the night, but new guards — someone is certain to wonder why the door is unguarded. They'll look inside, and Dribeck will turn the castle upside down searching for me!"

"I think I can get you out of here," Kane mused. "Short notice, but we seem to be committed now — and as you point out, discipline is at a nadir tonight. And it's certain your life is in danger until you cross into Breim lands."

"What about Dribeck's talk of peace?"

"More of his cunning. His losses at the river were greater than he admits. He knows Malchion can rebuild his army faster than Selonari can... and that the Wolf's next march south won't be so rashly conceived. So he hopes to stall for time — build up his army under pretense of truce. While Breimen is lulled, he means to attack your city without warning, solidifying his position here with this retaliatory invasion, using Breimen's spoils to reward his followers."

"I suspected his treachery myself," Teres swore bitterly. "I'll need a good horse to flee the city. But you're in danger, too! Will you come with me?"

Kane shook his head. "Unless I ruin it tonight, my position here is secure. I saved Dribeck's life in the battle, fought gallantly to win the day — so he believes. Tell Malchion that I'll stay at Dribeck's side, pass on what information I can, and trust that the Wolf's generosity is more boundless than his enemy's.

"But on horseback you're sure to encounter Selonari patrols — Dribeck hasn't left his frontier unguarded in the dizziness of his victory, don't forget. Once he learns you've escaped, he's sure to put a watch all along the border. There's a less dangerous way, I think. Look, how well do you know the geography of the Southern Lands?"

"As well as any commander of troops should!" the question rankled Teres.

"All right, then. As you know, the Neltoben River flows through Selonari, continues west and joins with the Macewen — maybe twenty miles upstream of where the Clasten River flows down from Breimen to empty into the Macewen. The river's high from the rains, but not too dangerous to navigate. Say we steal a small boat, put you aboard… with the fast current you'll be far past Selonari's walls by dawn, and with the rain nobody's going to notice who's on the river. You just drift with the current — the only fork is where the Neltoben's South Branch flows into Kranor-Rill, but that's only a mud-choked creek, so you won't confuse it. Follow into the Macewen, down to where the Clasten runs in. Then you'll know you're out of Selonari lands. Beach the boat, and there's a settlement there where you can commandeer a horse, then ride north along the Clasten to Breimen."

"Sounds good. How do I get out of here, though?"

Kane regarded her thoughtfully. "Rely on the camouflage you've already chosen. You don't look like the infamous Teres in that silk affair. I'll carry you, keep your face and that blond hair hidden behind my cloak. If anyone meets us, I'll explain that you're Pentri, and I'm going to revive you with some fresh air. No one's thinking too clearly tonight, and semi-clad girls aren't worth remarking on in this revelry. Outside, it's raining too hard to notice anything.

"And we've wasted time enough to be out of here already." Shoving feet into boots, Kane threw a cape over his bare shoulders, belted his sword to his waist. Taking some coins and a joint of meat from Kane, Teres wrapped them in a bundle with her own clothes and weapons. Kane added a flask of wine and examined the package critically. "Your boots, too?" he grimaced. "Try to keep that under my cloak. If anyone notices, I'd rather not try to explain this one."

He swept her up, letting his cape fold over to cover her head and shoulders, while her legs were bared by the other side, making it obvious that his burden was a private matter. Burying her face low against Kane's shoulder beneath the cloak, Teres supported her by hooking the scabbard tip into his belt and pillowed her head against the leather. So positioned, she felt Kane open the door and stride boldly down the hallway.

Teres's temperament was suited to direct action; this subterfuge tormented her overwrought nerves. It took all her endurance to lie limp in Kane's arms, her eyes blind to what was taking place about her, her imagination tantalized by the distant sounds that drifted through the darkness. *I will be calm*, she ordered herself, taking comfort from the sword beneath her head. If they were challenged, she and Kane could kill a hundred of the drunken fools before they fell.

There was a measure of security in the massive strength of the man; it seemed strangely comforting to feel the broad bands of muscle ripple beneath her cheek. Reddish hair bristled across his torso and limbs, his frame and features almost bestial in their rugged savagery. Yet the stranger was no apish barbarian; there was a sense of ruthless intelligence; his speech, his manner bore the stamp of civilization, of a man who sought both knowledge and power. She wondered to what limits.

Kane bore her effortlessly, although it was no delicate-limbed girl he cradled in his arms. There was unhurried confidence in his stride, and Teres vowed that her nerve would not prove of inferior temper.

Dribeck's citadel was somewhat grander than her father's keep, and to her unseeing mind its corridors were interminable. A few voices babbled in the darkness, and Kane grunted an occasional response. No one seemed to challenge them, or even to pay much attention. Well, why should anyone accost a man of Kane's position — ask his business — when it plainly was private? Logic explained; heedless, her emotions painted disaster in vivid colors. What if some meddling party of drunkards happened to…

Wind stirred the russet folds, dampness clinging to its breath. An indistinct question from close at hand. Kane's voice rumbled against her cheek, his tongue thick with drink. "To faint for a real orgy, these genteel wenches. Little cold rain in her face will wake her up — or I'll find something livelier in the taverns." A mixed response of knowing chuckles, sympathetic exclamations, advice to try the Prancing Mare for sights to quiver a well-bred lady's thighs. "Take the place apart!" muttered Kane, moving past.

Rain splashed against her bare legs, rattled upon Kane's cloak and blotted out sound as well as sight. Teres released her clenched teeth, relief washing over her like the rain. They had escaped the citadel.

Kane walked on a ways, then set her down. Peering about, she discovered they stood in an alley. The night was foggy; a cold drizzle fell patiently. Indistinct figures stumbled through the murk, intent on reaching warm shelter or oblivious of their state altogether.

"Walk from here," Kane muttered. "For a well-turned armful, you're solid as a wrestler. I understand how Ristkon lost the match."

Teres declined to comment, uncertain whether to consider this a compliment or not. "Now what?" she asked instead.

"Walk beside me to the river. See about finding a boat. Here, get under this." He drew her to his side, covering her with his cape. "No one's going to give a second glance to a couple of revelers trying to stay dry."

It was a snug fit — Teres was nearly as tall as Kane. He enclosed her with his right arm, drew her close to his broad chest, and pulled a fold of the cloak over both their heads. Clutching her pack in front of her, she contrived to jab him with the sword scabbard as they walked.

Water spread in wide puddles along the brick streets, cool beneath her bare feet, splashed over her legs as they waded through the night. Kane kept to the shadows, though the sizzling streetlights, the yellow-streaked windows and smoky doorways spilled ineffectual light into the street. As Kane had predicted, no attention was wasted on them by the few others abroad in the gloom. Rapidly they stole through the rejoicing city, pausing only once to strip a cloak from a senseless drunk.

Beyond the raucous uproar of the taverns, the riverfront was deserted. The river gate stood open, its guards drunk and gaming in the shelter of their barracks. Stragglers sloshed past unnoticed, bound to sample the pleasures found within Selonari's walls or in the rougher dens that spotted the waterfront and outlying fringe of the city. Stealthily they drifted along the quay, avoiding these few centers of clamoring merriment.

"Looks good," concluded Kane, pointing to an overturned rowboat beached along the shore. "Won't need bailing, either." The boat was about eighteen feet in length, with lifting bow and wide stern, an undistinguished riverboat showing signs of disrepair. Fresh gouges in the mud indicated it had been in regular use — presumably seaworthy, then. Battered oars were shipped underneath, and its bowchain was anchored to a tree. There was a dwelling nearby, but the owners were off in a tavern somewhere tonight, and no lights shone.

Kane busied himself with the lock, picking skillfully with a sliver of metal drawn from his boot. In a moment the chain was loose. Overturning the boat, he grasped the stern and raised it easily. "You want to catch the bow so she doesn't grate on the stones?" he suggested. Teres strained her back to the task and lifted the bow clear of the mud while Kane carried the vessel to the water's edge. "The launching had been done in silence.

"All right, you know your course. Don't hit a snag in the dark, is all," he warned her. "Keep to the current, and you'll reach the fork of the Clasten and the Macewen by noon or so. Use the oars if your shoulders can stand it — steer with the tiller be better, probably. Going to be light in a few hours, so you can see the drift."

Teres murmured acknowledgment as she tossed in her bundle and stepped over the bow. Kane handed her the stolen cloak. "This will keep you warm. Let me have that negligee. People saw me walk out with a girl in my arms; they'll see me return the same way. I'll find some tavern wench and carry her back with me — she'll never figure it out, when she wakes up in Dribeck's castle."

Handing him the garment, Teres covered herself with the cloak and dropped down beside the tiller. "You're taking the biggest risk now, Kane," she advised. "Ristkon's body may have been discovered already... Pentri found drugged in your room instead of abroad with you. You could walk right back into a trap."

"I've thought of that," Kane admitted. "Well, for these stakes I'll chance it. Good luck."

"Good luck to you," she replied. Her smile was concerned. "Kane, thanks for what you've done."

He shrugged, muttered something indistinct. With a shove, he sent the boat out into the current. For a moment she saw him gazing after her, then darkness engulfed them both.

XIV
Flight into Nightmare

The rain was cold, the mist from the river colder. Teres huddled under the clammy folds of the cape, limbs pressed together for warmth. The cloak was soaked through, but kept the rain off; underneath she wore only the brief halter and loin belt, and through the thin silk, the filigree chains and beads were chill against her flesh. She considered her packet of clothing, but left it under the bowpiece where it could stay dry. She could not get any wetter, at least, and should the boat capsize, she could swim better like this.

Through the night the river bore her along. In the darkness it was impossible to judge her speed, but the boat seemed to hurtle through the rain. Logs and bits of drift bobbed past, pulled from the shore as the Neltoben climbed along its banks. At first, Teres's heart caught each time a chunk of flotsam nudged against the boat. But their course and speed were about the same, and presently she ignored the other passengers upon the flood current. Occasionally she drifted near enough to discern the blacker shadow of the riverbank, and quickly she would steer the boat back into the middle of the stream. A few snags reached out, but these were rare, for the river had risen several feet, and the racing current swirled her craft past such obstructions.

A monotonous drizzle, the rain continued to fall. Dawn was drawing near, though, for the skies were tinged with gray. The shoreline became a dark wall, dreamily floating past her boat, and the mist grew thicker, whiter with the approach of light. At present. there seemed little to do to man the rowboat; the river appeared willing to carry her back to her land without effort on her part. It was not even raining heavily enough now to bail.

Wearily Teres slumped across the stern. Her hair was wringing wet and made a clammy pillow as she stretched out, trying to make herself comfortable. The patter of rain and the mumble of the river were soothing, hypnotic. *When had she last slept?* An eternity ago, it seemed. The ordeal of the last few days left her exhausted, drained of strength physically and emotionally. How pleasant it was to lie here, alone with the river and the rain and the coming dawn

Teres slept.

Dreams came to her, flowing like the river. Troubled scenes of battle, shiny blades flashing for her. She fought frantically, her movements slow, clumsy. She hacked at onrushing assailants whose bodies showed no wound, who kept coming toward her even as she slashed and chopped their unyielding flesh. Swords stabbed into her, tore her skin. She seemed to feel the pain, moaned and twisted as she lay, unable to waken fully.

Faces drifted past her consciousness, flotsam on the current. Familiar ones whose names she knew, anonymous faces who had swirled before her eyes in the fury of combat. Malchion — always taunting, laughing at her as he encouraged her. Ristkon — his face ghastly purple, twisted smile leering. His whip struck her face, scarred her cheek. His hands clutched, scratched, turned to spiders that crawled over her flesh. Dribeck, proud and disdainful -- never drawing a breath until his cunning told him how to act to best advantage. His words so convincing, his heart black with lies. Kane — his face hidden by a mask. Mysterious. Always present when fate seemed poised to turn, other times a phantom. His actions always readily explained. Behind the mask... what motives, what secret laughter?

The strange ring he wore. Its sinister jewel glowed before her mind's eye, impossibly large, intolerably brilliant, unthinkably evil. It shone through his mask, its malevolent gleam supplanting the blue murderlust that smouldered under his brow. Terror intense now, the nightmare touching her with insane fear. The bloodstone was enormous, immense as the sun. Kane disappeared within its depths. Its evil luster engulfed her, tore at her mind as she fought insensately, sucked at her soul with vampiric lust. There were other things dimly visible in its hellish luminance... writhing figures human, humanoid, utterly alien. They were slaves of the bloodstone, their souls feeding its fire through eternal agony. The gem was alive, sentient! Its aura was creeping across the land, sweeping the entire Earth into its pulsating flames. It saw her now, wanted her, reached out its glowing tendrils for her. Its touch probed her brain!

She screamed then and shot upright, almost capsizing the boat. Her mouth tasted of fear. Sick and shuddering, she sat hunched against the stern, groggily recollecting her thoughts as fire racked her cramped muscles. Light. The sun was high. The rain had ceased; the mist still hung. She was on the river.

She was not on the river.

In lost confusion, Teres looked about her. The rowboat no longer shot along the current; the riverbank did not rise against the sky. Instead her craft drifted listlessly through a tepid mire, and all about her rose a chaotic wilderness of slime-laden mud and vine-strangled trees.

Kane's warning! The darkness, her slumber! When the Neltoben River had risen in flood, its mud-choked South Branch had once more flowed with rushing water. While she slept, the boat had been caught in this deviant current.

She had drifted into Kranor-Rill!

Bleakly she recalled the dark tales of this unwholesome morass... the deadly creatures who crawled through its labyrinth, the treacherous stretches of unseen quicksand, its ruined city, said to have been built in the Earth's lost dawn, and the fearsome Rillyti, who conducted certain abominable rites with captured humans in the fastness of the swamp. She shivered; the late morning sun seemed cheerless through the swamp mist.

No time to panic now, she told herself, still shaken by the horror of her dream. Teres shrugged oft the cloak, tied back her straggly hair, found blood on her face where a low-trailing limb had slapped her. Bright Ommem, how far into Kranor-Rill had the boat drifted?

Far indeed, it appeared. Little current stirred her craft. Looking around, she saw only a maze of bayous leading away… *leading who knew where?* The rising water had covered most of the mud flats; cypress knees were flush with the surface; sycamore thickets were wreathed with floating slime at their bases. She might have drifted in from a myriad possible avenues.

Stoically Teres shipped oars and pulled back against the scum-flecked water. So long as she rowed against the current, her course must be directed out of the swamp. Unfortunately, the current here had grown so tenuous that she could not be certain of its direction, or even of its existence.

Her fatigue scarcely diminished by her troubled sleep, Teres's back and shoulders quickly grew tight with ache. It was a heavy boat for one not accustomed to rowing. Still, there was great danger here, and she forced her protesting frame to row, to row, to row.

One bayou proved to be a cul-de-sac, and she cursed bitterly as she retraced her course. Softened from the rain, her hands began to chafe and blister at the oars. With strips of silk torn from her loin belt she bound the oar handles, which helped somewhat.

Then the bow rammed against some submerged obstruction, jarring the boat. Startled, her wide eyes gazed intently at the planks, relieved that no snag had burst through. But the rowboat appeared hung against something — how? She had not rammed another mud bar surely.

Despite her nerve, Teres screamed when the webbed hands slapped over the side of the boat. Like sorcery-conjured demons, the Rillyti rose from the murky depths of the swamp. *How many?* Ten, fifteen … what matter? They surrounded her boat, paddled in scum-trailing circles about her, climbed from behind tangles of cypress roots, slid from dank thickets along mud flats.

The rowboat rocked violently. Teres dropped the oars and leaped for her sword, lying just beneath the bowseat. A sudden tilt all but capsized the boat, threw her dizzily against the bottom. She scrambled to her knees, nearly falling overboard as the boat lurched

A webbed hand shot over the side and clamped about her arm, Teres snarled in animal loathing, pounded at the imprisoning grip, sank her teeth into its foul scaly hide. The hand only tightened, scraping into her flesh with its rough claws. The rowboat tilted heavily, would have overturned had not webbed hands held it steady. With a wet flop, a Rillyti clambered over the stern, its bulging eyes hideous as they glared at her.

Teres went mad, tore at the clawed fingers that pinioned her, nearly disjointed her shoulder, as she sought desperately to stretch out for the sword. It waited just inches from her straining fingers. The other batrachian reached for her now. Her bare foot kicked out savagely. Clawing, biting like an animal she fought back. Against its armored hide her fists were useless. Another crawled into the boat and pinned her arms. Only the steadying hold of the Rillyti clustered about them kept the rowboat from capsizing a hundred times.

Tired of her struggling, the Rillyti cuffed her, almost breaking her jaw. Teres went limp, stunned almost senseless by the blow that clouded her mind with starbursts of pain, filled her mouth with the taste of blood. With thongs of leather the monsters bound her wrists and ankles, the knots clumsy but sound. Leaving her slumped across the bottom of the boat, they leaped over the side again.

As the fog in her thoughts cleared, Teres felt the vessel moving. The Rillyti were towing the boat into the depths of Kranor-Rill.

For a while Teres lay there, too sick with horror to move. Her thoughts — spinning dizzily, drugged from fatigue and terror — painted gibbering images of stark fear. They had not killed her outright; the creatures had bound her like a trussed lamb. Vividly the whispered legends of Kranor-Rill screamed through her mind. The loathsome rites the Rillyti performed on captured humans, the nameless god of elder-world evil to whom they sacrificed on moonless nights. She recalled the dark tales of their raids upon isolated frontier settlements, of the depraved bestiality that tainted their treatment of those whose misfortune was not to be slaughtered outright, of the unspeakable atrocities the mutilated corpses bore witness to, the hideous ravings of those mindless wretches who lived to mew and giggle at their belated rescuers. In dread, Teres remembered that the moon was waning these last few nights, and her sanity all but fled as she thought about the manner of her death.

This was not the way the she-wolf died, cowering on her belly in abject fear. The unyielding steel of Teres's will shivered at the blows of demon panic, but would not snap under its awesome pressure. Though it almost strangled her, she choked down the bleating scream that once released would never stop. She called herself warrior, not trembling court lady; if this was to be her dismal fate, Teres meant to die true to the identity she had chosen.

She lifted her head, forced her eyes to see what lay about her, drove the frightened images from her mind. *Her sword.* The monsters had paid no attention to her pack. It still lay under the bow, the bundle of clothing, provisions... and her sword.

Teres twisted about. She sat hunched in the stern; the sword was several feet away. Perhaps she could reach it, stealthily ease it from its scabbard, cut her bonds. There was no hope of escaping the Rillyti, she understood that. But with sword in hand she would shower the swamp with their blood. She would fight until they were forced to kill her... die a clean death with her blade reeking with her enemies' gore.

But first she must reach the sword. Carefully she shifted her position. Her captors swam alongside the rowboat, clutching its sides; this kept her movements within the boat hidden from them. Slowly Teres drew her knees under her and pushed forward across the bottom. Heart thundering in her breast, she waited motionlessly, praying her activity had not aroused suspicion.

She wriggled forward another foot to reach the mid-ship seat. Surely the Rillyti could sense her shifting weight — how long before they investigated? Pressing against the bottom, she writhed underneath the seat overhead. Her wrists were tied behind her back, so that she must slide her weight along the battered boards. Grit and splinters of wood abraded her bare flesh, the needling pain unnoticed in the tearing agony of suspense. She crawled from under the seat. Halfway there... what would happen when her weight tilted the bow into the water?

Inch by painful inch, Teres edged toward the bow, crawling a little, then resting to lull the monsters' curiosity. She could almost touch the sword now... and here was the most dangerous point. The pack had been jammed well up under the bowseat to stay dry, and with her hands bound behind her back, Teres would have to sit against the bow and reach up under the seat. This would raise her head in view of the Rillyti; it was daring too much to hope it would not draw attention.

Perhaps she could pull the sword to her. Cautiously Teres twisted around on her hips and stretched her feet toward the bow. She hunched closer. Her toes drew under the bowseat and touched the bundle. Another inch farther, She could feel the leather pack against her feet now. Her ankles were tightly bound, but she could hook a toe under the belt that circled the bundle.

She pulled her feet back, trying to lift the pack from the deck. The sword scraped against the hull. Teres sank her teeth into her lip, waited for a bufanoid face to peer over the side. Nothing. Could the creatures not have seen her sword when they captured her? She raised her ankles and drew back again, trying to keep the sword from clanking. Its scabbard hung crosswise against the bowstruts, jammed. Sweat stung her eyes. Carefully she shoved the pack back under the bow, rotated her ankles to free the scabbard, pulled it toward her once more. The scabbard came free of the strut; the bundle moved out into the open. Teres flexed her knees and drew her ankles to her hips.

A sudden splashing. Amphibian shoulders and trunks emerged from the water. They were passing over a shallow bar. Hostile faces glanced down at her, saw the sword only inches from her grasp.

She lunged for the hilt, but never had a chance. Cruel hands lifted her from the bow and dragged her roughly to the stern. The sword lay where she had dropped it. Ignoring the pain as protruding boards bruised her bare flesh, Teres stared at the fallen weapon in hopeless yearning. One of them threw a leather noose over her head, snugged it against her throat, and tied the loose end around the tiller. The booming croaks assailed her — angry, derisive — but she was too shaken to notice.

The day and the boat dragged on. Teres slumped against the stern, numb in spirit and body. The sword had been her last hope; now she could only expect death on some unhallowed altar, or an even more grisly fate. At least, no man would stand by to watch her passing — perhaps this unknown death would be a fitting climax for the legend she had worked to create. Poets and warriors of coming ages could speculate whatever became of Teres, the she-wolf of Breimen? This was trifling consolation to her, but every other thought her mind turned to led only to cringing madness.

The sun was sinking now, but she was dimly aware of its course. Under its wan warmth, her leather bonds dried and tightened, bit into her flesh. There was water slopping along the bottom, and she splashed it over the thongs when the pain aroused her from her stupor. Once she thought about soaking the hide strips, so that they might stretch and grow slack. But the leather had been wet before it was tied and would stretch no farther; after a while she abandoned the attempt.

Once there sounded a bellow of pain, followed by tremendous thrashing. Teres looked up to see one of her captors struggling in the writhing coils of an enormous serpent whose jaws were embedded in the amphibian's shoulder. Other Rillyti closed in, their golden swords hacking at the reptile, so that it was half severed in a number of places. Spewing dark blood, the serpent at last released its victim and slithered beneath the surface, where its contortions boiled the scum to foam. The stricken Rillyti floated listlessly, legs kicking in rough spasms. A pair of the creatures dragged its body behind them as they resumed their progress. Teres hoped the snake's wounds had not been mortal.

Hours passed in monotonous misery. Somehow the Rillyti found a path through the rotting maze. A few times they had to drag the rowboat across mud bars, but generally they simply carried it in tow. There was a wide circuit made at another point, where Teres observed a limitless morass of quicksand, too treacherous for even the swamp creatures to dare.

Through the tangle of vegetation, she caught glimpses of higher ground now and again. Its shadowy outline persisted, until at length she could discern an island rising from the swamp. In places now she thought she sighted a great wall of rubrous stone looming over the trees. Her mind worked in detached speculation. Perhaps she would walk the legendary streets of lost Arellarti before she died.

The hull scraped against stone, nudged into a moss carpeted quay. Clambering from the water, the Rillyti moored the rowboat against the overgrown quay and ascended the steep bank of the island. One of them unceremoniously slung Teres across its shoulder and followed the others.

Twisting her head, she secured an inverted view as she jolted up the bank and onto a stone causeway. Hundreds of the Rillyti were milling about, hurrying to examine the captive. Their bass cries echoed from the walls — dull bellows, hoarse croaks, rasping hisses — plainly intelligible communication to their pit-like ears. From their numbers, they must have made this ruined city their encampment.

Ruined city? Teres stared about in amazement, her mind slipping off its shroud of despair. The legends of the existence of this lost prehuman city were true. But it was more than the wonder of these cyclopean walls of unknown stone, the precise and alien geometry of its radial streets and windowless buildings, the monstrous creatures who shambled through this masterwork of eons-dead genius — it was not this alone that made her breath catch in astonishment. For Arellarti was not the dead ruin legend had pictured.

Arellarti was in a state of reconstruction.

Everywhere she passed, there was evidence of full-scale restoration. The streets were cleared of debris. No strangling encroachment of swamp growth remained — although traces of Kranor-Rill's invasion could be seen in bits of vine that clung like lost streamers in the cracks of the walls, or the phantom trails of suckers etched to the stones where once they climbed. Drying fragments of brush yet littered the streets in places, fugitive scraps from the enormous mounds which had been dragged away.

And the city was being rebuilt. Rillyti labored busily to erase the scars of time. Huge blocks of the strange stone were being hoisted atop the wall; broken obelisks rose again; jagged rifts were smoothed, filled in. Scaffolding was thrown up around many of the buildings, where cracked and slanting edifices were being dismantled, new stones laid to heal the decay. Where the scouring elements had effaced the bizarre engravings of the walls, crumbled away certain peculiar carvings and ornamentation, hulking workers were restoring the original patterns with meticulous attention. An entire army of swamp creatures worked with single-minded zeal to undo the corrosive marks of millennia. Arellarti was emerging from its long death, shedding grave-mold and cobweb as it rose from its swamp-buried tomb.

But the marvel of this reawakening titan of elder Earth could not dispel the horror of her plight. Teres sensed the colossal presence before she was able to see it, stretched helpless across her captor's shoulder as she was. Its shadow fell over them — shadows were filling all of Arellarti now, as the sun slunk away. Across the central courtyard they bore her, down an incline, and into the enclosure of a vast dome.

Teres caught shaken glimpses of the gigantic walls which soared away to darkness far above, of a limitless space encircled within — columns of bizarre design, gleaming banks of stone, crystal and metal, sinister coils of unfamiliar alloys. A fantastic structure of unimaginable complexity. It had the aura of a temple to some dark and nameless god.

The Rillyti laid her on the altar then — an altar it must be, for now she saw the god. A hemisphere of bloodstone, huge as the heavens, brooded in the center of this prehuman dome. She stared into it in dread fascination, struggling only weakly when they cut her bonds, tied her spread-eagled to the oddly positioned bars which protruded from the crescent altar, whose stone carried stains of frightful significance.

The bloodstone was alive.

In terror Teres remembered her nightmare, knew that her subconscious mind had felt the evil influence of this sentient crystal, as she drifted into its poisoned realm. Perhaps the bloodstone, sensing her intrusion, had dispatched its servants to bring her to its temple. She writhed against her bonds, mechanically, without hope of freeing herself. The altar's curious knobs and protrusions jammed into her back, making her wonder at its *outré* design.

The crystal was alive with energy. A green luminance made its depths translucent for an impossible distance; scarlet flame pulsed through its veined markings. The entire dome was lit by the crystal's evil glow, and vibrant energy seemed to radiate unseen through its lustrous tentacles of multihued metals, hummed and throbbed through the looming columns of machinery. Like the monstrous eye of some cyclopean god, the bloodstone glared from its setting, considering its shambling worshippers and the horrified sacrifice tied to its altar. From what alien dimension, in what benighted age, she wondered, had come this crystal of malevolent energy to this world?

Crowds of Rillyti were gathering in the shadows. Turning her gaze from the bloodstone, Teres saw the figure approach her — a robed batrachian of imposing stature. His fingers were closed upon a knife of white metal, and it threw back the wavering glow of the bloodstone as he stood over her.

The priest, for such he must be, began a roaring chant. Like an obscene chorus, the assembled Rillyti responded to his invocation, croaked a rhythmic litany that echoed ceaselessly across the dome. Teres heard their gibbering chant only dimly; all her attention was held by the glinting knife as it rose and fell, wavered about her pinioned form. The blade seemed to hover now over her belly, as the invocation rose in crescendo. Breathing a final prayer to Ommem — though in truth her god seemed to have forgotten her — Teres set her teeth, steeled her muscles, watched the flickering knife carve ritual passes through the air above her flesh. This was going to be worse than her imagination had pictured.

The chant trailed off abruptly. Teres closed her eyes, expecting the knife to descend. It did not, during the time of the breath she unconsciously held, and she opened her eyes to see what new depravity she must face. The priest had stepped back, so she stole another breath, one she had never thought to draw. The knife was lowered — at his side, not in her belly. The Rillyti appeared to cringe in fear.

Crackling light brushed her face, and Teres risked a glance away from the knife to follow the eyes of the worshippers. In the air above the bloodstone a creature of fire was taking shape.

God or demon? Teres wondered, unable to guess what meant the awed response of the Rillyti. It was a humanoid shape, she observed, dancing like witch's fire over the apex of the living crystal. A man of light, of energy, of the coruscant life-force that glowed within the bloodstone. Smoothly its outlines coalesced, a man of emerald and ruby-veined energy, a silhouette in three dimensions.

As its flickering outlines grew less blurred, the vibrant energy cooled and solidified. The figure floated from above the bloodstone, glided down its smooth sides, came to rest before the altar. The Rillyti were slinking away into the night, even as the shimmering film of energy drew away from the figure like a mask, revealing the man who had formed from the crystal's alien force.

But Teres had already found the silhouette familiar to her eyes; recognized the substance of this crystal that was not bloodstone, though it resembled that gem; remembered well where she had seen such a crystal before. And so it came as no sudden shock to Teres that the man who stood before her was the stranger called Kane.

XV
Lord of Bloodstone

Kane's eyes swept over the awestricken Rillyti, his manner domineering, commanding. Some voiceless communication seemed to pass between man and batrachian, and Teres sensed the silent anger that drove the creatures back into the night, resentful but subdued.

"What are you, Kane... man or demon?" Teres exclaimed.

Kane considered her thoughtfully for a moment, vexation mingled with indecision in his frown. "I've been called both," he answered distractedly, "though both races have damned me often enough. And I claim neither — although once men called me brother. With time you can decide in your own mind; for now it's enough that the Rillyti obey me."

His knife cut her bonds. Teres groaned and slid from the altar, massaged her wrists and ankles. There were angry bruises where she had lain against the protruding bars.

"This isn't an altar, of course," muttered Kane abstractly, watching her ministrations. "It's a control dais for Bloodstone. The Rillyti have declined into pitiful degeneracy since the days of Arellarti's building, and their superstitious rites have replaced whatever knowledge they may once have had of Bloodstone. I had forbidden these pointless sacrifices — it's a testament to Krelran engineering that the controls weren't completely jammed after centuries of such abuse. Still, old ways die hard, as they say. You were too tempting a victim for them to waste, which is some measure of the toads' degeneracy, I suppose, when you consider the evolutionary gulf between Rillyti and mankind.

"Teres, you present a complication to me just now. Still, there are ways I can turn this twist of fate to my advantage. I assume you must have blundered into the Neltoben's South Branch — I should have allowed for the river's rise. But then, you told me you were certain of your geography."

Her legs shook, but she turned on him angrily. "It seems, Kane, that your schemes are far more subtle than those of the ambitious adventurer

I first judged you! There's a sorcery here, and it appears I'm only a pawn in some diabolical mystery … and that I had the bad grace to upset some phase of your conspiracy. But what devil's game do you play, Kane? By what wizardry did you materialize from the bloodstone's rays? And since I doubt it was accident that you came when you did, why did you cheat your minions of their sport? A little water would have cleaned things afterwards, and you wouldn't have caused their resentment!"

"Toads obey me, or they die. I couldn't care less for their affection. As to my presence, I see what Bloodstone sees, and Bloodstone sees all within Arellarti." He paused, then added: "I intervened because… because your death was useless to me… perhaps because you interest me. My game — as well you name it — is an adventure whose goals you will soon understand. You err in accusing me of sorcery, but then the true nature of my power so defies human comprehension that men will call it magic.

"To ease your mind, though, I plan you no malice. Naturally, you will remain in Arellarti until my plans achieve a certain stage; after that…? Well, you'll no longer be in a position to upset my strategy, so you can decide for yourself. Meanwhile, I've commanded the Rillyti not to harm you — so long as you don't try to go beyond Arellarti's walls. I think you know what will happen then. And you would be wise to shun the presence of Bloodstone, for reasons that you probably are aware of."

Teres looked at him bitterly, hating Kane for his treachery, but unable to forget the debt she owed him. His words grew fuzzy; his figure blurred. She swayed dizzily, then caught herself against the control dais. Her strength was virtually burned out from this endless ordeal.

"Can you walk?" Kane asked with a shadow of concern. "I'll take you to where you can rest."

"I can walk… damn better than crawling serpents who steal the shape of men!" she snarled, but did not deny her fatigue.

Kane grinned. "Sure you can. Come with me, then — and if you fall, I'll let you sleep where you lie."

The days that followed had an unreal quality about them, like some fantastic dream from which she could not awaken. Dreamlike, certain moments were impressed upon her mind with indelible clarity, while other times Teres scarcely could recall what had transpired an hour earlier. Kane told her she had fallen prey to some fever, and he gave her strange, bitter powders to take, though these seemed only to cloud her thoughts further. To her own mind, it was more the alien evil of this elder-world city that twisted her thoughts, filled her head with bizarre images.

It was late afternoon when Teres awoke from a lengthy and mercifully dreamless sleep. She lay quiet for a moment, her eyes still shut, and felt the stones beneath her bed of furs. When she opened her eyes, she knew where she was, although the evening before she had fallen onto the rough bed without a glance at her surroundings. Extreme exhaustion had triumphed over her tormented nerves, and she had lapsed into a deep slumber almost instantly.

The room must be Kane's, she decided, since he was evidently the only human in Arellarti. Its furnishings were primitive, aside from a few curious relics he must have gathered from the ruins for study. It was reassuring to find her pack from the boat resting near her, and after cursory ablution Teres discarded her begrimed harem costume and drew on her familiar garments. The sword, of course, was not included, but she partook of the wine and meat she had packed several worlds ago.

Feeling her devil-may-care mood return — after all, what more could happen to her? — she tentatively pushed at the door of the chamber. It swung open readily enough, and she peered into the hallway, where a pair of Rillyti returned her gaze. Their manner was not hostile. Time to test Kane's word, she decided, stepping into the hall.

At her emergence, the guards gestured for Teres to follow. She complied nonchalantly, finishing the braid of her hair with an air of disregard for her surroundings. They descended a steep flight of spiral stairs — the ones, she recalled, whose odd-spaced steps had occasioned some difficulty last evening. Kane had chosen a tower for his lair in Arellarti, and she later recognized that a proclivity for heights was characteristic of him.

Kane knelt inside the dome, intent on a series of engraved bronze alloy plates he had laid out adjacent to one of the glowing columns. He looked up to greet her, his manner casual in the midst of this ancient city of alien sorcery. "Teres… awake finally!" He smiled, noting her change of garments. "Should I say you look like a new man?"

Her smile was venomous. "Some thief made off with my sword."

"I haven't enough toads for you to wreak havoc among them. Besides, you'll be protected from any predators that might creep past the walls." Ignoring her retort, he dismissed the guards. "I think you'll be interested in touring Arellarti. After all, aside from myself, you're one of the few humans ever to set foot within this city of toads. I believe the others never had time for reflection on Krelran architecture."

He reached for her arm, but Teres turned away. Shrugging, Kane stepped on ahead, the girl matching his stride. As they walked through the city, Kane told her something of Arellarti's history, his own connections with its mystery, his reasons for his undertaking — speaking at times guardedly, others exuberantly — like a lord extolling some newly conquered domain. Teres listened in silence for the most part, not able to draw him out on points he chose to leave a sinister veil upon. Despite her unease, her anger, she found herself fascinated by his narrative, and by the uncanny grandeur of Arellarti.

He paused alongside the towering obelisks, where Arellarti's ponderous bronze portals — recast in the shrieking furnaces of the city — were being levered onto ancient hinges. This vantage provided an overview of the lost city, so that Teres could gaze in wonder upon the spider-web geometry of Arellarti. Clearly evident was the frenzied reconstruction throughout the circular metropolis, work which she learned continued

through the night, lighted by brilliant torches whose flames were fed by
the energy of Bloodstone. Teres adopted Kane's habit of addressing the
alien crystal by proper name, "Bloodstone," for he assured her the gemstone was a sentient creature, an entity of godlike power.

Below them she could see the tireless Rillyti laboring over tasks which
ranged from the hoisting of mammoth blocks of stone to the painstaking
reengraving of a delicately carved helix or volute. In the gathering twilight the serpentine flickering brilliance of Arellarti's furnaces stone an
eerie light along the streets. Nourished by the crystal's awesome energies,
the furnace gave birth in travails of incandescent fury to the unknown
alloys and the obsidian-like stone that raised Arellarti from millennia of
decay. Raw materials came from salvaged debris and heaps of varicoloured
mud the batrachians dug from the swamp.

"Strange that these uncouth slime-dwellers can perform such organized and intricate labor," mused Kane. "Hard to realize that a race of the
magnificence the Krelran must have attained in that lost age could have
degenerated into these misshapen toads. I wonder how mankind would
fare, should some cosmic disaster blast our civilization into forgotten
rubble. Perhaps we would return to the trees and caves of our bestial ancestors — skulking apemen that a mad creator's folly transformed into
men — and not even legend would remember the dead majesty of our
race."

"How can the Rillyti carry out this project, and why do they bother?"
Teres wanted to know. "From what you say, they must have lived content
in their primitive villages — until you unleashed this slumbering evil!"

"Arellarti was their home of old," Kane replied. "Now they rebuild it.
Bloodstone is their god; they obey its commands. They are nothing more
than slaves to the crystal — an army of working bodies whose brain is
Bloodstone. They worship it, and like a true god Bloodstone controls its
servants to accomplish its private goals. Bloodstone commands; toads
carry out its will. I doubt they have any freedom to disregard its telepathic directives. Well, once they controlled Bloodstone; now they serve.
Another measure of how far their race has declined. Now I am Master of
Bloodstone, and through my servant, the Rillyti are my slaves as well."

Teres laughed scornfully. "Are you truly lord of Bloodstone, Kane? By
what power do you claim fealty? How can any human believe himself
master of this demon whose powers you call godlike — to any sane mind
it is a force of cosmic evil!"

He glowered, angered at her insinuations more than he meant to show.
Teres laughed inwardly, amused that she had broken his annoying attitude of detached calm. "By this ring I am Master of Bloodstone!" Kane
emphatically proclaimed. He clenched his fist to brandish the sinister jewel.

She glanced at the ring with unconcern. "I have seen ragged fools who
swore they wielded vast powers of sorcery within the sigils they wore on
dirty fingers," she scoffed. "And I know of a few such talismans which did
have some degree of magical potency. But your boast defies physical law,

since you state Bloodstone is not the work of sorcery. How can a tiny chip of gemstone make you lord of a crystal monolith whose powers come from beyond the stars?"

"Size is not a factor even in physical law," snorted Kane. "A spark can burn a city, a wheel can move a boulder, a sliver of iron can kill a dragon. Don't presume to suggest laws for alien science.

"There is much that even I don't understand about Bloodstone. There are gaps in my knowledge — considerable gaps, I'll grant you — which are lost within mystery beyond my understanding. Sometimes Bloodstone's wisdom has no equivalent in human comprehension; other times I know the crystal guards its thoughts and memories from my perception.

"My link to Bloodstone is of a symbiotic nature. I can draw upon Bloodstone's power, but without me — or more accurately, without the master of this ring — Bloodstone is only a lifeless crystal. For reasons that I cannot altogether comprehend, Bloodstone's life force is a combination of two sources. Somehow it feeds upon the cosmic flow of energy that holds our universe in balance — in space as well as dimension. But it also requires the power of organic life, which it obtains by..."

He faltered, coughed as if to clear his throat, and began on another thought. "So the bond between Bloodstone and the wearer of this ring is all-important. The ring itself is only a convenient method to maintain physical contact; the crystal in the ring is the vital factor. Both Bloodstone and the gemstone of the ring are hemispherical. Though it seems to defy your 'physical law,' the two crystals are equal halves of the single organism. The crystal in the dome draws upon forces of cosmic energy; the crystal in this ring transmits organic life force. The two forces — the two halves — make up the sentient entity that is Bloodstone. My mind and that of Bloodstone are linked through this chain, and we draw power through one another."

"Then you are slave to this twofold vampire!" sneered Teres,

"No!" Kane exploded, and she thought he would strike her. "No! Our minds are separate, independent! I cannot penetrate Bloodstone's thoughts beyond its secret veils, nor can Bloodstone rule my will like a sorcerer's hypnotic spell! My mind is my own, and I am master of our pact! And this is not only because I am indispensable to its existence. The Krelran, who created — or at least harnessed — Bloodstone, built external controls into the crystal entity. That 'altar,' where my toad friends were about to make sacrifice last night, is a master control for the entire crystal. He who knows the nature of Bloodstone can manipulate projections on that dais, and so control the energy within the crystal. To the Krelran, Bloodstone was only a machine, a complex and powerful machine, and no machine can be self-controlled. If I desired, I could shut off Bloodstone's energy... leave it the dormant crystal it was when I found it!"

He caught the look in her eyes and added pointedly, "Needless to say, the control dais is not without certain devices to shield it from ignorant tampering or wanton destruction. Should Bloodstone be impelled, it could annihilate the author of such hostile intent, were he not protected by this ring."

"The crystal would have lain dormant then, until Kranor-Rill at last swallowed these forgotten ruins!" Teres exclaimed in wonder. "What madness drove you to awaken this relic of elder-world evil!"

Kane answered with a sarcastic laugh. "You call it evil? Bloodstone exists beyond human concepts of good and evil. The alien crystal is a focus of cosmic energy; as such, Bloodstone is the key to power beyond human comprehension. I mean to unlock that power, to use it for my own purposes. In that ambition I am no more a 'master of evil' than any other conqueror — who is always a devil to his enemies, a god to his followers."

"Who will follow you, Kane?" There was loathing in her tone.

His voice remained confident. "A strong man will follow a strong leader. When the power of Bloodstone reaches across the Southern Lands, there will be many who will make a victorious cause their own. It is far better to join a conqueror's army than be trampled under his march! And my power will not halt along the coasts of the Southern Lands!"

"Impressive schemes for a lone adventurer who hides among his toads in a rotting domain!" she retorted with deadly scorn. "A man who is twice traitor dreams to rule a continent!"

Her taunts stung him. Kane's manner grew less reserved. "I only bide my time here! Bloodstone now has only the smallest fraction of its potential power. My slaves are at work repairing the damage of centuries, but that will only restore its power to its ancient level! Arellarti was never completed by the Krelran — their enemies destroyed them before the city could be finished. Had their work been perfected, and had not the ancient Master of Bloodstone in some manner inactivated the crystal (or so I find hints in Bloodstone's guarded thoughts), Arellarti could never have fallen, even under the devastating weapons of elder Earth!

"I mean to complete this venture of lost eons — to bring Bloodstone to the peak of its power! Today I am vulnerable, I freely admit it. Were my purpose discovered, a concerted attack could defeat me. But such a united effort will never occur. My neighboring states are at war. They will continue to waste their strength, until my initial foray will overwhelm them easily… unsuspecting and exhausted by their petty battles! I intend to establish the foundation for my empire here in the Southern Lands, and I'll find loyal subjects among the survivors. And soon no man will dare to proclaim himself my enemy. For once Arellarti has been completed to its projected design, the power of Bloodstone will be the power of the cosmos! There isn't an army, a city, a force known to man that can stop me then!"

"Others have made that boast!" Teres snapped.

His eyes were a chilling glow. "Yes, and some of them founded empires that yet stand!"

The night her sleep was poisoned by strange and unwholesome dreams, and when Teres broke from her fitful slumber she found the nightmarish spell yet held her. Phantom shapes leered at her in the darkness, slowly to fade as she gazed at the night with fevered eyes, her fist choking off the cry that hovered on her lips. Sweat covered her skin; her forehead was burning to her cool fingers, though the fur robes were inadequate to comfort her icy trembling. She slipped in and out of consciousness until daylight, too weak to seek the water her throat craved.

When Teres had not appeared by late morning, Kane decided to awaken her. He entered after her hoarse voice answered his tentative knock. A trace of alarm touched his features when he found her prostrate with fever.

"Go back to your toads and sorceries, and let me die in peace!" Teres growled plaintively. Her damp hands pushed him away, but there was no strength in her arms.

"Head's like a boiled egg," commented Kane, withdrawing his hand from her brow. He questioned her solicitously but received only vague reply.

"Damn it, Kane! Leave me alone!" she snarled, and struck at him weakly when he pulled away her furs and pressed his cheek to her bare back.

"Damn it, keep still!" he returned. "I'm trying to get some idea of what's wrong with you!" He began to thump her back carefully with the fingers of both hands.

"You're no physician... though only Thoem the Accursed knows what else you may be!"

"How do you know what I am and what I'm not! My years are greater than you imagine, and a man learns what he needs, if he thinks to defy both death and ennui."

Teres felt too dismal at the moment to berate him further. His touch was gentle, his manner concerned, and though she suspected Kane was only playing for her trust, his attention was not unpleasant. At this point she doubted whether anything could make her more miserable than this febrile torpitude.

"Your lungs sound clear enough," Kane declared. "I don't think there's a pneumonia — at least, not yet. More likely, you've caught the grandfather of colds, from exposure to the damp in your fatigued state. Or maybe you've inhaled some noisome swamp vapors — Kranor-Rill's very breath is poisoned in many places." He sorted through the chamber's scant possessions, muttering to himself. "I've only transported the barest of provisions to Arellarti, as you can see," he explained. "But I do have some useful drugs on hand." He measured out a grayish-yellow powder and stirred it into a cup of wine.

"If I may choose, I prefer a sword to poison."

"I understand why Malchion looks ten years older than his years," grumbled Kane in vexation. "Your judgment is as hasty as your logic is erratic. I know poisons that would send you to Hell in the throes of insurmountable ecstasy; only the slain know how sharp is the bite of cold steel. However, this drug will break your fever. It's a subtle compound of barks, molds, roots and other medicaments, with which I doubt your backward Wollendan physicians are familiar. Smile and drink it, or wither away with fever. The hours I can spare away from Selonari are rather limited at present, and I dislike leaving a delirious girl alone in Toad Hall."

The potion was bitter and probably contained a soporific, for Teres fell asleep shortly thereafter, musing upon Kane's knowledge of esoteric drugs.

He looked in on her a number of times in the course of the afternoon, the night and the day that followed. The drug was efficacious, for her fever soon broke, and the throbbing in her head left her. She slept for long periods, still haunted by bizarre dreams that merged into her waking thoughts. Kane's touch, cool on her febrile skin, she was aware of hazily — as if she were apart from herself, watching a fever-racked girl, cradled in his great arms while he held a cup to the stranger's pale lips. He talked to her, though she made little response — a rambling monologue her delirium fogged mind did not follow. There remained only an impression of names, lands and cities of distant continents, of lost ages. How many of the fragments of memory that came to her later were from his words or her imagination, Teres never was certain.

The fever left her one morning — at least, for a time. Strength returned to her limbs, driving away the dull lassitude that had held her so long in its vampirish embrace. Her depression chased after her distemperature, although some weakness persisted. The tower room stifled her, and Teres decided to taste the morning air. Kane, despite her confused feelings toward him, afforded intriguing companionship, so she set out to find him.

Her hulking guards evidently guessed her intention, or acted at Kane's command, for when she quitted the chamber, the watchful Rillyti pointed the way. Keeping well away from the grotesque creatures, she followed them to a low structure that fronted on the central courtyard.

Kane was inside, crouched near a deep crack that had rent both wall and floor of the rubble-strewn building. The light was uncertain, so that Teres could not at once discern Kane's action. When she drew closer, she wondered whether fever might not still be twisting her mind.

Rising from the fault in the floor, a vast and misshapen spider web slanted over a mound of curious debris. An enormous spider hung upon the web — larger than any tarantula of Kranor-Rill it was, and its thick black legs outspanned even Kane's outsize hands. The arachnid's bloated body seemed oddly proportioned, bulky as a man's fists held end to end, and the sparsely bristled chitin gleamed like a droplet of black blood.

Kane was intent upon the creature, so that he failed to look up at Teres's entrance. Kneeling beside the web, he appeared to be thrusting something toward the spider. Teres gained the weird sensation that he whispered to the thing, though the echoes of the place clearly played tricks with her mind, since she seemed to hear two faint and chittering noises.

She was almost touching Kane's shoulder before he noticed her presence. The spider uttered an annoyed rasping sound and scurried on its stubby legs into the deep crack in the stone floor, but not before its iridescent eyes had met Teres's with a gaze of iniquitous intelligence. She cried out, clutched at Kane's arm.

"He didn't like you," Kane mumbled, and held open his hand. "He left before he finished eating." Bits of melon lay on his palm.

"Spiders don't eat melon," Teres said shakily, unable to decide if this were not another phantom of delirium.

"This one does," laughed Kane at some secret jest. His eyes were dilated, for a moment unfocused. "Especially when it's seasoned to his taste." Blood seeped from a cut along his thumb.

Repelled by the shadow of madness that twisted about her, Teres fled the ruined structure. Outside she wandered, aimlessly — she could not say how long — before she felt Kane's presence at her side.

Though his face was strangely flushed, Kane had his wonted bland manner. In view of his casual attitude, Teres wondered how much of what she had witnessed had been fever dream, or whether transient insanity lurked behind the cold murderlust of Kane's uncanny eyes. She realized he was asking about her health, a mundane inquiry that seemed in utter contrast to the sinister aura of Arellarti. She made an unthinking reply.

"Then let's hope your recovery is a lasting one," Kane continued. "I'll have to leave you for a time now. My absences from Dribeck's presence are sometimes awkward to account for, and I've stayed overlong already. Still, I didn't care to leave you until you were yourself again. So I'll return to Selonari soon, though I'd far rather lounge around Toad Hall and partake of yellow sunshine."

"Damned considerate of you to endanger your dark schemes, just to wipe my brow," Teres muttered. "How does your plot progress?"

"Well enough," Kane smiled. "Malchion believes his daughter was secretly murdered, Dribeck thinks you're lurking somewhere within Selonari's borders yet, and efforts to renew the conflict rumble along frenziedly. By the time Bloodstone has attained the peak of its power, the land will be in such chaos I could take it with a hundred good men."

"I'm overawed."

Kane watched her sharply. "How long will this petulance sour you, Teres? Am I so much more to be despised than any other conqueror?"

"You are blackened by the evil you seek to wield, by the treachery of your tactics," she quickly answered.

He stared at her with impatient lines to his jaw. "A man wields the weapons he can master. The power of an army, the power of Bloodstone... tools of destruction, tools of empire. A man dies from a blade as surely as from... Bloodstone.

"You're an unusual girl, Teres, and I've known many women.. You'd think me mad if I told you more, but you're unlike anyone I've encountered in all my years of wandering. To say I find you fascinating is superfluous. You're a strong woman... one who admires strength when she sees it in others. We are similar, perhaps.

"Through Bloodstone I command power to carve an empire across the Earth, limited only by my own interest in the game! My triumph need not be flawed again by loneliness. I would share my power with one strong enough!"

"You're mad if you think I would sell my soul to you,"

"Am I?" Kane sought her eyes. "There's something in your eyes I can see when you look at me... something you try to force back. Think about it, Teres. To these clods you're a freak — at best you'll maybe rule a few years over your backwater city-state, an outsider to your subjects, a stranger to yourself. What's noble in that? Mine will be power such as no man has ever held — not just the tepid pleasure of ruling over the conquered nations of mankind! I offer to place you at my side, and you say I'm mad to tempt you. What paltry romantic stupidity!"

"Your high opinion of another's ethics bespeaks the obvious absence of your own conscience," Teres coldly commented.

"Ethics! Your moral scruples are a senseless wasteland of contradictions and stupidity!" he exploded. "I serve Kane, and no other gods or obscure values!"

"Obviously."

"Where were your high principles when you so joyously led an invading army to destroy Selonari?" he countered.

Her answer was ready. "Dribeck plotted against us. We fought back as men should — with honest steel and muscle — not alien sorcery!"

"The soldiers who fell doubtless smiled at the rightness of their dying." Kane's sarcasm was scathing. "Death is death. Victory is victory. The difference is strength... of men, of weapons, of strategy, whatever. Bloodstone is my strength, strength greater than any army. And victory always decides the morality of war — after the fact."

Teres made a disgusted sound. But after her indignation left her, in the hours she sat alone in the alien city, Kane's words haunted her, bedeviled her thoughts.

"Bloodstone grows more powerful with each day," remarked Kane one afternoon. He had just returned after an absence of days, and Teres found his company a welcome relief. The Rillyti ignored her, so long as she did not approach the city walls. But the gnawing concern whether they might disregard Kane's commands plagued her, and familiarity had not lessened her revulsion for the batrachians.

"I don't see how this obsessive restoration of Arellarti has any bearing on your crystal demon," Teres prodded. "Granted you want the walls secure against siege, and the causeway must be cleared for you to lead your army from the swamp, but why waste effort, as you do, on reconstruction of trivial ornamentation? For that matter, why do you repair these useless buildings? There are far more here than you and these creatures can occupy, and a number of these structures appear of totally nonfunctional design — not even windows or doors on some!"

"The Krelran were not an extravagant race," Kane said evasively. "Nor is Bloodstone of poetic temperament. Arellarti was engineered as a functional unit; Bloodstone directs its completion according to the original plan. That which is superfluous to man may be significant to Bloodstone."

Teres shivered. "At night when I look from the tower I can see its malignant nimbus hovering over the dome."

"The glow effulges as its energy waxes," Kane commented. "The life pulse of Arellarti beats stronger. Shun that region of the city, Teres, especially on moonless nights."

A caustic retort on his solicitude died in her throat. Instead, she remained silent at his side, looking out over the fire-hued city. "Why do you pursue this insane scheme, Kane?" she asked finally. "Either Malchion or Dribeck would give you wealth and honor, if you would serve them loyally. What more can you gain by unshackling this monstrous power upon mankind? I won't argue that power and riches are worth the struggle to possess. But how many of those men who have plotted and fought to build the empires of history ever found their prize worth the winning? Any Wollendan lord knows greater happiness — he has fortune and power beyond his needs, and the cares of a thankless and rebellious nation are not his concern.

"I'll not deny my attraction to you, Kane. You spoke the truth when you said we are much alike. We are both outsiders among the people we think to rule. I, too, admire strength, and ruthless demon though I know you to be, you are stronger than any man I've known!

"Kane, give up this accursed venture! Destroy Bloodstone, if you really can do that! Return with me to Breimen! If you do this, I swear to you I will never speak of your treachery, your sorcerous schemes, I'll tell Malchion only that you helped me escape from Dribeck, that when your position in Selonari became suspect, you brought me from hiding and fled with me to Breimen. No one will doubt this. If you serve us faithfully, Malchion will give you all that you desire. Nor will my father rule forever, and with a strong man beside me, my control of Breimen will be assured. Come away from this accursed city, Kane! Come away with me! We'll rule together — over Breimen, Selonari, or any other city-state we set our blades against!"

Their hands met on the ledge. Kane's voice was low. "Almost I hear myself assenting to your thoughts, Teres. And if my motivations were as simple and direct as you project them, then I might well destroy this power I've unchained here and go away from Arellarti to carve out a kingdom at your side."

Her face showed anger, but there was bitter pain in her voice. "But you won't, of course! Your greed for power is far closer to your black heart than any love you claim to feel for me!"

"Now you begin to speak like a woman. Try to realize that there is more to my seeking than a blind lust for power."

"And you speak like a man — defending your ego by pleading for my lesser intellect to understand!"

"I'm not sure any human can understand my mind! You first considered me an ambitious adventurer; later you saw me as a treacherous demon — Thoem knows what you think of me at this moment! Teres, you grasp but the barest shade of my thoughts, my motives!"

"I'm in a reckless mood tonight! Pray, shine light through the darkness of my poor ignorance."

He was silent for a long time. Evening gathered over Arellarti, where a dark star shone in the city's heart. Teres scraped her finger along the tower window, struggling with the tormenting dichotomy of anger and love she felt toward Kane.

"How old am I, Teres?" Kane asked suddenly.

The question seemed pointless. "Outwardly you look perhaps ten years my senior. But your manner hints of greater experience, and since you ask so ominously, let me hang another ten years of infamy on your shoulders."

"And if I told you that outwardly my body has remained unchanged for more than ten times the years you ascribe to me?"

Teres stared at him in disbelief, wondering what game he played with her. The Southern Lands stood along the frontier of mankind's emerging civilization; here sorcery was not the familiar force it might be on the greater continents. Teres had heard countless dark tales, but she had little firsthand knowledge of magic, aside from the trivial displays of hedge wizards… and the awesome secrets the priests of Ommem were said to guard.

"You don't look like those gnarled and ancient sorcerers I've heard about, who crouch in their towers for generations, mumbling foul incantations, glutting their depraved minds with secret and damnable knowledge. Though there's madness in your eyes, I find you human enough. Your blood ran red as any man's that day by the Macewen."

Kane's gesture was impatient. He had started to bare something of his soul to her and found her reception indifferent. "Your acquaintance with occult powers is limited, I think you'll agree. A man can be immortal, in that Time's destroying breath cannot wither his physical being. So long as such a man eluded death by violence, he might live to wander through centuries… watch present become history, history pass into legend, legend fade beyond the memory of man. Wounded, his body would heal without a scar, endlessly rejuvenated to the state it held at the instant of an insane god's curse."

"Immortality is not deemed a curse."

"What do mortals know? Flesh can heal, but the soul can be scarred! To be doomed to wander through eternity… branded an outcast, no land to call home, no man to name friend! Whatever he seeks to love — to grasp — slips through his embrace inevitably. Age consumes the bones of his hope. The loneliness! Only memories, cold phantoms to torture his dreams. And the hideous, smothering boredom that creeps more stifling with each decade, as the taste of life's frantic delights and transient interests grows stale and dry upon his spirit! It is a curse that waxes less endurable with each passing year. Imagine, if you can, how infinitely precious any chance to discover new adventure would become to this man!"

"Suicide is not an infrequent surcease to despair," she replied cynically.

"And suicide would be the ultimate surrender to the malevolent will of the god who damned him!" he fiercely proclaimed.

"Why was this man doomed to such an existence?" Teres asked uncertainly, wondering how much credence to give Kane's rambling discourse.

But Kane lapsed into reticence, evidently regretting his outburst of emotion. "Perhaps I share something of this man's spirit," he stated vaguely. "I seek more from Bloodstone than the serpent-fanged majesty of rulership, though I'll not deny the game of empire intrigues me.

"Bloodstone's power is as limitless as the energy that drives the cosmos, holds the dimensions of alien universes within their separate planes. There are countless channels into which I can direct this power. You've seen its energy transmute crude materials into wondrous substances; its furnaces could pour forth gold or diamonds, as readily as they transform swamp muck into steel-hard bronze. Bloodstone's power could annihilate a nation, or raise new lands from the depths of the sea. You're witness as it rebuilds a dead city. Soon you'll behold the destruction of armies!

"But another facet of Bloodstone's power holds greater promise and fascination. There are certain flaws and folds in the fabric of the interdimensional planes... points where lines in the cosmic lattice impinge upon one another. The cosmos is a realm that Bloodstone courses through, like a ship on some fantastic sea. Its creators harnessed its energies to give the crystal control over these gateways through the universe. Thus, by the power of this ring, I can direct Bloodstone to project my body through its energy field — through these interdimensional passageways — and into the point of focus where the passages open onto our world. By the same power, I can return to Arellarti when I desire. You've already seen me accomplish this — the night I returned from Selonari to spare your life, the other times I've left here and returned again. There are only eight points within the Southern Lands where this focus occurs, and three are yet too far from here for Bloodstone to transport me. Fortunately one such point is in the cellar of an abandoned palace in Selonari; another is a cave, just a few hours' ride from Breimen. It's curious that these points of focus all are in places about which macabre legends have grown up.

"When Bloodstone attains its full power, I can travel through any of these gateways... wherever they emerge upon the Earth. In the first days of its rebirth, Bloodstone could not have projected my body beyond these walls. But the time is not distant when I can journey beyond the Western Sea to any of the fabled continents of our world, lands where man has only begun to cast his shadow! And unless I misread the hints which flicker through Bloodstone's secret thoughts, its power can transport me to the stars and beyond! Bloodstone is a key to the limitless cosmos from which it draws energy; when the key is forged completely, it shall unlock the doors of the infinite... and I will be master of its secrets! What hold will the specter of boredom have upon me when the mysteries of the cosmos open to my touch!

"The full range of Bloodstone's power is incalculable. Even an imagination as jaded as mine falters incredulously at the images which flash like dying stars across the blackness of its mind! And I can only grasp the implications of its thought that have meaning to the human mind! What further mysteries pulse within its crystal depths defies all comprehension!

"Think well on this, Teres! Am I madman or traitor, because I hold the key to such unimaginable power... and dare to use it? Could any man ever offer to share with you a vision such as mine?"

Her sinister forebodings seemed less substantial to her as the force of Kane's zeal washed over her thoughts. His arguments were insidious; instinctively she knew them to be the logic of soulless evil, but reason could not always deny the rationality with which they were structured.

"I don't know, Kane," she replied uncertainly. "Somehow I know that your thoughts are subtle poison, hateful to all I believe in."

"And by what sanctity do your cherished values stand pristine from the tide of challenging ideas?" he asked sardonically.

"Let me think, Kane. Let me think for myself."

When it came, it was there. Perhaps it had been there already, held back by denial. Maybe it had come upon her gradually. Teres only knew that it was there, irrepressible the instant of realization.

Kane had returned at night. He evidently stole away whenever he could do so, although his absence could be disastrous if noticed. And Teres knew that the cursory attention he gave to affairs of Arellarti could not justify the risks he took in returning so often.

He had brought some wine, some few provisions to spice the unpalatable fare the Rillyti served them. They were sitting close, feeling the rush of the heady wine. Kane made some chance remark that brought laughter to Teres.

How long since last I laughed? mused Teres dizzily, wondering that so human a sound could ring in this alien city. Their eyes met, held in the silence after her laugh.

Kane leaned forward, cupped her head in his hand. Automatically Teres thought to pull away, but feeling a stirring in her breast, she held her ground. Their lips met softly, and her eyes closed as they kissed. As she sensed his presence enfolding her, her thoughts swirled in a vortex of conflicting emotions.

One half of her won out, and Teres returned the kiss insistently. In that instant she knew she would not draw away from his touch, nor hold back the feelings that coursed through her being. Her arms reached to take his shoulders, anchor against their strength as the long-denied storm of emotion engulfed them both.

They made love with a wild awkwardness that first night — exploring as if amazed at the newness they found in one another and in themselves. The surging power that overwhelmed them was almost brutal in its intensity, and their bodies tossed upon the fur robes as if in combat. Afterwards, the passion they had shared left both of them shaken — purged, and at once fulfilled.

An odd languor of contentment warmed Teres as she lay across Kane's chest, head under his chin. Her unbound hair spilled over their flesh like stolen sunlight, rippling through Kane's fingers as he stroked smooth their tangled tresses. Forgotten in their frenzy, Kane's dagger lay atop a pile of crumpled clothing. It would be so easy to snatch it up, to drive its point through this sated brute's unsuspecting heart.

But Teres knew she would not. Whatever villainy Kane might be plotting for tomorrow, tonight they were together as two people in love. *Love?* she mused. A sickly word, synonym for weakness — so she had thought. This could not be love they shared, for this was strength, not flutter-hearted mooning.

Kane's eyes met hers. She knew his look had followed hers to the nearby dirk, his thoughts drifting with hers. These was a smile on his lips as he sensed her rejection of the weapon's temptation.

Noting his smile, Teres twisted upon him, threw her knees astride his hips, and leaned forward as if to pin his shoulders. "Are you purring, you great grinning tomcat?" she hissed in his face. "Because I choose to lie with you, don't imagine in your smug contentment that you're my master. I propose to take you at your promise, Kane — to share as equals what fate gives to us each. But the day you expect submission from Teres… for that gloating conceit, I'll kill you with my bare hands!"

"Your warning is one I'll honor!" Kane laughed and sealed her lips with his. Then, as Teres felt their passion blaze afresh, she enfolded him in her velvet-soft embrace and jarred breath from him with the steel that lay within.

The autumn was fading, and night came sooner now than when Teres had ridden with an army from the gates of Breimen. So few weeks, she reflected, lying sleepless against Kane's shoulder. How disordered her existence had become. It should have taken longer to tear loose the pattern that a lifetime had woven.

Tendrils of evil light shone green through the tower window. It watches us here, mused Teres. Kane had laughed when she curtained the opening, but to her the baleful glow profaned their lovemaking. The light from Bloodstone reached into the sky now, like some demented moon that had fallen to earth, still shedding sickly luminance. Along the borders, men spoke uneasily of the uncanny glow that seeped through the nighttime mists of Kranor-Rill, so Kane told her. Their notice worried him little, however, since he confidently foretold the triumph of his plans before winter's advent. The second stage of the ruinous war between Breimen and Selonari was not far distant, nor would many more weeks pass before Arellarti would be completed according to the masterplan of its eons-vanished Krelran founders.

But with each passing day, Teres's spirit troubled her more. Kane's venture could only loose evil upon the Earth, of this she was convinced. And although his vivid dreams of immeasurable power tempted her desperately, it went against her soul to aid him in this effort. There was no escaping the recognition that Kane meant to overturn the world she knew... to make men slaves to this horror from Earth's savage dawn.

She loved Kane — or if this was not love they shared, she cared not to learn what love might be. For a time she had told herself that it was in her power to deter Kane from the evil he meant to do — persuade him to abandon this madness and go somewhere else with her. Even when she tried every wile, every subtlety she could command, Kane's obsession remained unswerving. Bitterly Teres accepted defeat in this battle, and the knowledge of her failure left her tormented with indecision.

Stealthily she slipped from Kane's side to draw closer the vagrant curtains. She glimpsed the gleaming dome through the shifting folds. Its coruscant glow loomed over Arellarti, washed like the tide about their tower.

Kane stirred fitfully in his sleep as she rearranged the furs to nestle against him. With a frown she noticed the sinister ring on his hand. It, too, shed soft luminescence, ominous in the night. Ordinarily her eyes shunned the malevolent ring, whose gem, Kane said, was brother to the giant crystal within the dome. Tonight she looked closely at the ring, noting in growing alarm that the pulsations of light in the scarlet veins of the gem matched the heartbeat she felt in Kane's chest.

He was deep in dreams tonight, so that a thought came to her. Cautiously she touched the ring, wondering if she might wrest it loose without waking him. The fit looked to be a tight one, but perhaps she could slip it free and smash it with a blow, before Kane realized her intention. The gem repelled her touch with unearthly chill. Tentatively she sought to twist the ring loose.

Teres bit her lip to stifle her scream. For the silver-white metal of the ring was fused to the flesh of Kane's finger.

XVI
When Death Is Unmasked

Her face was hot and pale, her eyes reddened, when Kane awoke to kiss her in the morning light. "What is it?" he inquired anxiously, when her lips brushed his with unwonted apathy. "Didn't you sleep?"

"I lay awake though much of the night," she answered. "I think the fever returns."

"Then I wish you had awakened me. My sleep was without rest, for I sank into dreams I like not to recall." His fingers caressed her face tenderly, swept away the trailing blond tendrils that streaked her haggard face. Her flesh recoiled from the cold touch of the ring.

"Your face feels hot and drawn, your heart beats quickly. Damn! I had hoped this recurrent fever had broken for good, though I've noted a decline in your usual vigorous spirits of late. Wait, I'll get something." He padded across the stones to the chest where his possessions were kept.

"I don't want any more of your weird drugs," Teres complained. "I'm sick of being imprisoned in this foul city, where the very air is poisoned by the fetid vapors of Kranor-Rill. Kane, can you take me along with you through Bloodstone?"

There was faint suspicion in his face as he looked up from the cabinet. "I've carried other objects close to my person through Bloodstone. Its power has now increased to the level where I could draw another person through the crystal with me, assuming we clung together like parting lovers." His eyes questioned her.

"Take me with you, then!" Teres pleaded. "Or do you consider me only your chattel? The atmosphere of this unwholesome place smothers my every breath, sucks like a feasting leech upon my vitality. Take me into the forest with you, Kane. Let me breathe fresh air, feel warm sunlight... spend an afternoon where the tainted aura of this elder-world horror does not lie. Please, Kane, I've lain too long in the shadow!"

Kane seemed to regret he suspicion he had nurtured. "Of course, Teres," he acceded. "The atmosphere of Arellarti is oppressive. I've been thoughtless not to give you relief from this noisome morass earlier. Small wonder your health is uncertain, when I've held you captive here these many days. There is a focus of cosmic stress that opens into the forest just north of here. Bloodstone's power should be sufficient to transport the two of us there."

There was a moment of terror when they entered the shadowy dome, where emerald light played about them, tinting their skin like ghastly corpse flesh. Teres swallowed her loathing fear and clutched Kane's arm as he strode confidently forward to the malignant crystal.

His hands adjusted the crystal knobs of the control dais in a manner she could not follow. Smiling encouragement — an iniquitous grin in the serpentine light — he led her to the glowing crystal. "Still game for this?" he asked.

Teres took umbrage at his bantering tone. "I can take anything you can!" she gritted.

"Stand close to me, then," he advised. "We have to share the force field of the ring."

Willingly Teres pressed her body against his massive frame, threw her arms about him as if in last embrace. From Bloodstone thrummed a high drone of power — felt in her head, though not audible to her ears. An electric tingling coursed through her then, and in dread she glimpsed a dancing web of green fire engulfing both their forms. Teres tightened her embrace in a final spasm, clinging to Kane as the vortex of energy burst over them, sucked them down... down...

Hideous vertigo. Blackness. Falling for eternity. Falling through eternity.

Blaze of white light. Teres staggered as firmness pressed her boots. Then she did fall, overbalancing Kane; they struggled in a wriggling heap onto leaf-strewn stone. Bloodstone, Arellarti, Kranor-Rill... all had vanished. About them now rose the yellow and gold forest of autumn, where sunlight warm and familiar sifted through the richly hued trees.

A tortuous outcropping of gray stone — whose leaning and queerly eroded columns hinted that more than nature had been at work here — marked this focus of interdimensional flux. As Teres grappled for support against him, Kane's boot tripped on a broken pedestal, and the frightened girl fell atop him to the stone. In her panic, she pinned his arms that sought to catch their fall and with driving shoulder threw him back against a splintered column. Rock smashed into his skull, obliterating his consciousness in a haze of black pain.

Teres examined him anxiously. A deeper red matted his thick hair where the stone had struck, but his chest heaved regularly. It had almost been accidental, Teres reflected, though her actions had not been the work of a panic-stricken girl.

She had persuaded Kane to take her from Arellarti with no formulated plan or intention — except flight, escape from the evil luminance of Bloodstone, and from Kane as well, since he refused to break away from this unhallowed bond. Teres thought only to reach the world beyond the fog-shrouded tarn, the world of men, of honest sunlight and firm ground. Where a lifetime ago a wild girl had striven to master the arts of war, as sung in minstrel's ballads, and never dreamed that she would be plunged into the black realm of elder Earth, whose legends were remembered in darker verse. Let Kane take her to the world she had left, then there would be hope to flee this cancerous terror. There was no other chance of escaping from Arellarti with its bestial guardians, and Kranor-Rill surrounding it like a poisonous moat. But how might she elude Kane? A hundred wild possibilities gibbered in her mind, but beyond the all-consuming need to escape, Teres had resolved nothing.

In the vertigo that claimed them as they passed between the planes of time and space — spewed forth upon this jagged knoll, to stagger and blink from the wrenching shock — Teres had seized her chance. Her need to escape made her movements almost instinctive. She tripped Kane as they swayed together and drove his head against the skewed rock. *And now?*

Her hand shook as she drew forth Kane's dirk. The haft was cold in her hands, its blade a white-hot sliver of light. She could kill him now, while he lay senseless. A cowardly way to slay so powerful a warrior, but she could never hope to match him in equal combat. And certainly he should be slain. Whatever her feelings toward this man — for he was a man, although his thoughts and motives might seem inhuman — there could be no denial of the treachery of his acts, nor of the alien evil he schemed to call back from the stars of Earth's dawn. He must die, if this horror were to be averted. True, he had saved her life on several counts; true, she believed she loved him, believed he returned her love. Balanced against the measureless suffering his mad dreams would hurl upon mankind... He must die, and her hand could strike the blow. The heroes whose legends she sought to emulate would not hesitate. Bright Ommem knew what crimes this man had perpetrated, should there be truth to his allusions to immortality. Kinder that a loving hand should wield the knife, strike here at the heart, a quick clean death before he awoke.

A stormwind of conflicting thoughts and emotions. Though its intolerable weight pained her arm as if she had held it forever, only seconds passed before she lowered the dagger. Almost despising her own weakness, Teres knew she could not kill Kane like this.

The bloodstone ring blazed on his hand, its luster sullen and unnatural in the sunlight. It seemed to watch her. Perhaps it did. With a bark of mirthless laughter, Teres saw the answer to her dilemma. Kane could do nothing without the ring. If she destroyed it, his power would vanish, his dark schemes crumble like sand. Probably he would never forgive her, but it was better to live with the curse of his hatred than with the stain of his blood.

She touched the ring with shrinking fingers, yet gripping firmly, as if she held a viper by its neck. Her discovery of last night had not been nightmarish illusion; in the daylight she could see that the metal of the ring merged with the flesh of his middle finger. She tugged experimentally, but without dislodging it any fraction.

No matter. If the ring would not come away from finger, finger could come away from hand. Gruesome work, but a finger was a petty sacrifice under these dread circumstances. Quick, before he was aroused.

Steeling herself, Teres pinned Kane's left hand with her knee and stretched forth his middle finger. The gem shone like some unthinkable fire, imprisoned beneath depths of green sea. She set the razor-honed blade against the base of the digit and started to press down.

Teres screamed. The knife flung smoking from her nerveless hand, its edge blackened and fused where it had cut into Kane's skin. At the instant of incision a bolt of insurmountable agony had contacted the blade, coursed like unseen lightning along her arm. She fell back, stunned and sickened from the lancing pain.

"What the hell!" rumbled Kane, jolted abruptly from his stupor. He glared about in confusion, saw the shallow cut on his hand, the seared blade, the stricken girl. With grim suddenness his thoughts reconstructed what had transpired.

There was deadly fury ablaze in his killer's eyes as he struggled to his feet.

Teres recovered faster. The war of anger and pain across Kane's face was not good to look upon. Flight was all that remained for her.

She scrambled clear of the contorted cluster of rock, broke into the open forest, and thus gained a fair lead before Kane could clear his throbbing head and give pursuit. His heavy tread made a dull pounding upon the forest floor as he plunged after her. Once he called to her, but neither wasted breath on further sound.

Teres had the fleetness of a vixen. There was stamina in her long limbs, and with her lead she believed she could rapidly outdistance Kane. The other's brawny frame seemed far too bulky for a foot race, even though she had observed the sudden quickness of his movements. Still Teres knew she was faster of foot than most men, and she hoped to lose her pursuer in the thick timber before they had run far.

A short distance proved her hope to be misdirected. Like a charging bull, Kane leapt from the rocks and rushed after her. His initial burst of speed closed her lead; then, seeing that he could not overtake her at once, he paced himself to follow her at short interval. There was driving strength in his thick legs and enduring wind in his barrel chest. He hung onto her trail like a great, silent bearhound.

Teres set as fast a pace as she dared, then concentrated on maintaining it. Huge trunks flashed by her, in blurs of gray, sometimes looming before her as if sprung up through sorcery. Roots and dead branches clawed at her ankles, but somehow she avoided them as well. The forest gloom kept the ground barren of undergrowth, the tall trunks shorn of low branches, or their race would be of different character. Teres could not have plowed through underbrush as easily as her relentless pursuer. Like children playing tag through some fantastic temple of infinite pillars, they dashed through the deep forest, their footfalls muffled by leaf mold, so that louder sounded their panting breath, drumming hearts.

Bleakly Teres realized she could not shake Kane like this. With unfailing strength he pounded along behind her, at times gaining a little, at others dropping somewhat back. But never did he lose sight of his quarry, and as the chase stretched on, it became apparent that he was slowly closing the distance between them. Fever and weeks of inaction had leeched Teres's stamina. She gasped for breath now; her second wind was gone. Aching fatigue cramped her muscles, made ragged the grace of her deer-like strides.

One of them must soon drop to the forest loam, she knew, and odds told her that person would be Teres, unless some miracle intervened, and quickly. She wasted brief effort trying to dodge through the maze of trunks, seeking to escape his sight, perhaps lose him in the forest. But Kane was too near to her now for this stratagem, nor had she the breath or agility to run an evasive course.

The forest abruptly opened upon a road. Her heart pounding too painfully for thought, Teres turned onto the road and used its firmer surface to gain a few strides on Kane. Fear alone gave strength to her agonized limbs now, and her chest ached too horribly to draw breath. On faltering legs she followed the roadway. With pitiless patience, Kane bore along in her steps like a wrathful nemesis, and it almost seemed she could feel his hoarse breath on her back. Though there was no hope of losing him here, the open road made running a fraction less difficult — maybe would give her another hundred yards of flight, before she collapsed to the earth to await Kane's anger. And if the gods of fortune could but grant it, perhaps there might lie a village hidden beneath the trees.

Trees whose canopied branches overarched the road made dazzling, dizzy mosaic of light and shadow to blanket the road, soft ground. Swaying ground.

A horse whinnied and reared. Men yelled startled curses. Blindly she had rounded a curve and burst upon a detachment of armed men. *Soldiers!* Her vision wavered too vertiginously to discern whose men they were, nor did she greatly care in her deathly exhaustion.

She dropped to her knees before the prancing mount, drew great sobbing mouthfuls of air into her flailing chest.

"What the hell's happening here!" demanded a familiar voice. Lord Dribeck calmed his pawing stallion and glared down at the gasping figure who had blocked his march. "Shenan's tits! It's Teres! Hers is a face that I won't forget! Scared out of her skin from the looks of things! And Kane! Another face that hangs in the mind! What are you doing here, Kane? What's going on!"

Kane gave no indication of being disconcerted. "I've caught a fugitive for you, milord," he explained, speaking slowly to draw breath. He wished now he had ended the chase in the forest, but he had been savoring Teres's hopeless fear, even though for the past mile or more he could have overtaken her. He might have ended her flight in another manner, but he had not meant to kill her, despite his anger.

"I thought you were scouting along the border," Dribeck was saying.

"So I was — until I intercepted some information which revealed Teres to be hiding along the fringes of Kranor-Rill. Didn't want to give her a chance to grow suspicious and slip away again, so I immediately rode south. By killing my horse I got to the abandoned homestead where she laired before she had time to be wary. She sought to elude me through the forest, and the rest is obvious. I see you also learned of her hideout, since you were leading a company of soldiers to capture her." Kane uneasily wondered how much inquiry his glib story would bear up under.

"No, I'm leading my men toward Kranor-Rill to investigate — and I hope to quell — this growing alarm along the southern frontier. We're getting persistent rumors of weird glowing lights that emanate through the swamp mists at night, that the Rillyti are building some sort of road across the quicksands... Well, you've heard them all yourself." Dribeck looked searchingly at Kane, his face thoughtful. To be sure, appearances substantiated Kane's bewildering tale.

"Dribeck, if you believe this villain's lies any longer, you deserve the doom he plans for us all!" snarled Teres, who had found breath to speak at last.

A flicker of pain crossed Kane's features before he could recover his mask. Dribeck noted this. Kane's face now registered careful amusement.

"What's this raving?" Dribeck inquired.

"Her tongue is as venomous as ever," Kane remarked. "And after weeks of solitary skulking, she'll astound our ears with pent-up poisons."

Teres continued doggedly. "You believe Kane to be your trusted captain, don't you, Dribeck? Well, you're not the only fool in the Southern Lands; Malchion thinks Kane is his most resourceful spy. And we've both been bitten by this serpent in our midst. While Kane has played us off one against another, he's been master of his own game! In Arellarti he's discovered some monstrous power that he hopes to control — an evil power that will enslave all mankind, if he succeeds in setting it free! And we're to be first spoils of his conquest!"

"Now here's an amusing device," commented Kane sardonically. "Turn your enemies against one another, is that your thought, Teres? Your lies show great imagination, but you've spun them too fast — and too extravagant for credence. You would do better if you'd keep the fantasy simple, less grandiose." Doubt was whispering to him now. *If this went much further...*

"I'm surprised that the girl would offer such an implausible tale," Dribeck observed pointedly. "Unless, of course, there were some hint of truth to her distracted accusations."

"Only desperation and a quick imagination," Kane interceded hurriedly. "Your tale of phantom green radiances and the like furnished the skeleton for this hasty fabrication."

"I'll unmask a desperate liar!" Teres swore, rising on unsteady legs. "That remarkable ring he wears. He uses that ring to control Bloodstone — so he believes! But the ring is fused to his flesh, as his soul is welded to Bloodstone! Order Kane to remove the bloodstone ring — and give it to you! Then we'll see how glib his tongue can be!"

"The matter is easily concluded then. Kane, pass me that odd ring you wear."

Nodding assent, Kane pulled at the ring. "Damn! It's a tight fit ever since I got the jeweler to cut it to size. That's why I so seldom take the thing off. Well, as you see, it's no more than a strangely styled ring that caught my fancy." He held forth his hand, brandishing the gem. "Now if we've indulged our prisoner's fancy long enough — "

"He can't remove the ring!" Teres persisted. "The ring is bonded to his flesh!

Make him show you!"

"Let me see the ring, Kane. Give me your hand, if the ring won't slide over your knuckle." There was firmness in Dribeck's command.

"Milord," began Kane, feeling himself losing this duel, " it seems pointless to humor your prisoner's ill-conceived slander any further. You will naturally recall how loosely this ring fitted before I had a jeweler attend to it — overzealously as it turns out."

Dribeck's gaze did not falter. Behind him not a few of his soldiers had rested hands on swordhilts. He now recalled the significant fact that the ring's alteration had occurred while Kane was supposedly lost in Kranor-Rill.

Kane made a thin smile, acknowledging defeat, perhaps. Then his face grew savage with another emotion. "As you demand, I'll give you my ring!" he growled. He thrust out his left hand, clenched into a fist, the bloodstone facing them like a vengeful eye.

Some scrap of memory, some instinct warned her. Teres yelled, threw herself to the side, striking Dribeck's mount. The horse shied, sidestepping suddenly.

From the bloodstone ring shot forth a coruscant beam of energy, emerald light veined with scarlet, that crackled past the space where the two had stood!

Behind them, someone screamed in agony, men howled in fear. A soldier pitched downward in a contorted jumble, his flesh blackened as if lightning had blasted him. The stench of ozone and charred tissue tainted the air. Kane cursed in fury.

What followed happened quickly. Kane twisted toward Teres and Dribeck. Two of the mounted guard charged forward with drawn swords. Kane's attention was diverted to this new threat. Again a bolt of energy flared from his ring, and the guardsmen crumpled. into a writhing, smouldering tangle. The foremost of Dribeck's swordsmen leaped to meet him and died hideously beneath the coruscating lance of energy.

Dribeck was not fool enough to face that which he could not fight. In the seconds that Kane's diversion gave him, he hauled Teres onto his saddle and spurred the stallion into the forest. As they left the roadway, a lethal ray shot past their heads and blasted a tree to glowing splinters. The horse lunged beneath the toppling branches, terror driving his hooves.

"Keep low!" Dribeck yelled needlessly. The stallion narrowly avoided collision with the trunks that flashed before them. Another ray of energy speared after them, laying waste to several trees. Its aim was wild. Kane had lost them in the timber.

On the roadway, alien death ravened mercilessly. The Selonari broke and ran, after a foolhardy rush to overwhelm this lone demon of destruction left half their number blackened corpses. Kane raked the forest with his murderous weapon, throwing full disorder to their retreat. Men died in terrible swathes.

But as they vanished, his killing rage was slaked. Feeling weak of a sudden, he abandoned the slaughter and withdrew to the slanting circle of stones, where Bloodstone could transport him back to Arellarti. Alone.

The mask was shattered. A land was raised against Kane. One man and the dark legacy of elder Earth.

XVII
What Manner of Man...

"I suppose we were lucky that Kane didn't have a bow," Lord Dribeck remarked with assumed casualness. "He never would have missed us then."

"And if your men had held their ground like disciplined troops, the archers could have skewered his treacherous heart," Crempra pointed out.

"Easy to say when you weren't there yourself," scoffed Teres. "When you see the bodies... It was demon lightning he hurled from the ring! It doesn't matter how well-trained or how brave your men are — caught in the open, an unknown weapon that burns and destroys whatever it strikes! Hell, anyone would run for his ass!"

A wild ride had brought Dribeck and Teres to Selonari that night. As they rode, Teres told a breathless narrative of all that had happened to her since she disappeared from Dribeck's chambers. Ristkon's part in that bloody escape Dribeck had already surmised, and he bore her no malice for the turmoil his death had caused. In view of the altered circumstances arising from Kane's conspiracy, Teres now found herself in the role of tentative ally.

Once in Selonari, she collapsed from exhaustion and slept soundly throughout the night, while Dribeck pieced together the fragmented information this reversal had presented.

With morning came a courteous summons to a council of war convened by the Selonari lord to consider the new menace of Kane's treachery. Somewhat refreshed, Teres donned the loose-sleeved shirt of deep blue silk, vest and pants of burgundy deerskin, which she found laid out for her. The fresh garments pleased her, and she spent more than usual care with her braid, wondering how such mundane concerns were possible after the horror she had known. An escort showed her to the council chamber. Waiting there was an edgy assemblage composed of Lord Dribeck, Crempra, Asbraln, Ovstal, and several other officers and counselors whose names she had not recalled. Adding to Teres's narrative, Dribeck laid out such information as he had gathered.

"Hindsight is of little use to us," he remarked, separating Teres and Crempra from the prelude to a quarrel. "Unhappily, hindsight is about all we have, right now. Putting facts together, it's obvious that Kane was indeed playing Breimen against Selonari for his own purposes. He provoked Malchion's invasion — which might or might not have taken place eventually — by plying him with all the fears, lies and rumors the Wolf's ear was ready to hear. To bring matters to a head, Kane pretended to warn Malchion of an assassination plot, then brazenly poisoned Ossvalt and tried to do the same for Lutwion. Teres has told us of his knowledge of strange drugs. When she fouled the net he had cast for Lutwion, Kane stalked him in the night, then killed him and his men with the power of his ring."

"There was another body found slain in that fashion," Teres interposed. "But we never identified him after the scavengers and the river had done their work."

Dribeck nodded. "I think I can hazard a guess. You mentioned that one of Lutwion's servants slipped away that night — you assumed he was the assassin. Actually I *did* have a spy insinuated into Lutwion's household, and the man vanished completely sometime about then. If I may theorize, perhaps my agent recognized Kane somehow, but with Kane's awareness of his knowledge. He tried to flee to pass on this information before Kane could deal with him, but Kane followed him from Lutwion's manor, and the bloodstone ring claimed another life that night."

"Why did Kane fight for us, though?" Ovstal wanted to know. "In the battle by the river, it was his sword and his leadership as much as any man's that carried the victory for Selonari."

"To the point that he saved my life," Dribeck added. "Perhaps a move to ensure my confidence in him." There was a strange tone to his voice for a moment. "And of course his position permitted him to pass scraps of information — mostly useless — to Malchion.

"But remember that Kane's is a mind of ingenious cunning. It shows in his entire strategy — the ease with which he manipulated all of us, from the moment he persuaded me to furnish him the expedition he needed to reach Arellarti. He might have written that book of statecraft he gave me at our first meeting. No, Kane's motives were more devious, and to make some bold statements, I think I follow his logic. Kane probably concluded that, left to the fortunes of battle, Breimen would conquer Selonari... and his judgment likely was sound. However, Kane saw little profit for him in such a victory; he desired a costly and drawn-out war, which would leave both powers too exhausted to pose a threat to him. Bluntly, Kane fought for Selonari to shift the odds — a great risk, but justified, as fate proved. Thus he gave

Malchion the misinformation that our army was encamped along the Macewen's fordings and lured the Wolf into a disastrous bridge crossing instead. And though both Ristkon and I took credit for the cavalry tactics that turned the battle for us, the idea was Kane's; I thought his modesty most selfless.

"Ristkon's insubordination played into Kane's hands after the battle. I had privately announced my hope to conclude the war with a treaty of peace, following the collapse of Malchion's invasion. Kane's reaction to this turn of events was one you can imagine; it was his intent to prolong the war. Probably he would have attempted to free Teres, anyway, since she was the key to my proposed truce. As it happened, Ristkon set it all up for Kane to take charge of. He helped Teres escape, sent her off for Breimen with assurances that my offer of peace was only a mask for my own invasion of Breimen, then boldly advised me that her flight was obvious rejection of any treaty. The maidservants gave a picture of Ristkon's attempted rape, but they were buried in a closet when Kane arrived. So his part in the escape was never known, and I just assumed Teres had somehow slipped past us in the confusion of the night, which is about what did occur.

"But Kane hadn't calculated on the vagaries of the river. Teres blundered into his lair, and for reasons that aren't entirely apparent, Kane kept her alive in Arellarti. Meanwhile, he must have informed Malchion that I had secretly executed his daughter, thus continuing his game of stoking the fires of war between us. Teres has told us of the threat Kane mounts in Arellarti. If she hadn't had the nerve to attempt an escape, very likely we'd all still dance like puppets for this master — until he chose the moment to set loose this elder wizardry upon our unresisting and battle-weary lands."

"The man is incredible!" Asbraln exclaimed. "Taken of itself, his conspiracy is a masterpiece of ruthless cunning, a work of genius! But aside from his political machinations, there's this insane plot to revive some centuries-buried alien sorcery! What manner of man do we fight?"

"That mystery may lie deeper than we guess," declared Dribeck. "Some of Kane's enigmatic references — seemingly mad statements — that Teres has recounted awakened several haunting phantoms of memory. I spent part of the night going through my library, and I found something which is perhaps more sinister than mere coincidence. I wonder if any of you have read the works of Kethrid?"

Crempra grimaced. "Cousin, this is not the time to parade your —"

"But it is!" Dribeck interrupted impatiently. "Perhaps a bit more attention to history would have served us well before now. Quickly, then, before I bore you, Kethrid was probably the greatest mind of his age. More than any other man, he influenced the rise of Carsultyal, mankind's first great city. It was the men of Carsultyal — and particularly Kethrid — who salvaged from the ruins of elder Earth civili-

zations the fantastic stores of knowledge that overnight lifted our infant race from the semi-barbarism which followed the fall of the
Golden Age to the advanced state of civilization we presently enjoy.
Without thought or thanks to those who gave us this learning, I might
add.

"Kethrid sailed the strange seas of man's birth, explored unknown
coasts, new lands... found there the fallen cities of Earth's elder races.
His adventures made an epic. The knowledge he brought back to
Carsultyal formed the core of that civilization, and from there this
rediscovered learning spread to all of mankind. Of Kethrid's final
voyage we know nothing, for neither he and his crew nor his great
ship, the *Yhosal-Monyr*, were ever seen again."

Dribeck referred to a richly bound volume. "Kethrid had a close
friend — an adviser, colleague, comrade at arms — a stranger who
journeyed with him and evidently had a major role in Kethrid's discoveries. His friend was named Kane, described as 'a gigantic warrior
with knowledge of strange secrets,' who was 'left handed, of fair but
cruel face, with red hair, and cold blue eyes whose gaze calls to mind
the murderous fury he shows in battle.' Of his past Kethrid knew —
or at least wrote — nothing, except an intriguing passage that reads:
'There came to my mind that Kane of infamous name, whose soul
was of the darkness of elder Earth, whose soul quested for the knowledge of the elder creatures who yet walked boldly and not in shadow,
gods and demons whose glory was faded; he who defied our creator
in that forgotten age of paradise; he who was doomed to wander eternally through the savage world of his making, driven by his curse,
branded an outcast by the mark of death that lighted his eyes.'

"This Kane was with Kethrid on that final voyage from which no
man returned. And the passage I've translated was penned by Kethrid
over four centuries ago. As you say, Asbraln... what manner of man
do we fight!"

Ovstal broke the silence. "Interesting, milord. Ominous, even. But
of dubious practical worth to us. I'm more concerned with this Krelran
weapon Kane means to use against us. Do your books tell us anything
here?"

Dribeck shook his head. "Such information is more the province
of sorcerous lore, where my tastes do not run. I'm hoping the Temple
may know something of Arellarti — the priestesses of Shenan boast
of occult knowledge, though their talents lie more in political intrigue
and the amassment of wealth. I tried to get Gerwein here this morning but got a curt reply to the effect that the high priestess grants
audiences, she is not summoned to them. You tell me what to do.

"Succinctly, our knowledge of Kane's plans, his power, his defenses
all lies in what Teres has told us. You've all listened to her story. So
what do we know? Kane has rebuilt a fortress within Kranor-Rill. He
commands an army of around a thousand or more Rillyti. In addi-

tion, he controls a weapon of unknown but obviously formidable power, which at present has reached only a fraction of its potential force. Kane plans to embark on a conquest of the Southern Lands ... and Shenan knows to what greater extent his dark ambitions will lead him.

"What may we infer? Kane's power is limited — at least, for the present — so that he fears the combined might of Breimen and Selonari. Hence his efforts to reduce our strength to proportions he can overwhelm with his initial strike.

"Our course, gentlemen, is evident to us all. We must gather what strength we can, and invade Kranor-Rill. We must destroy Kane and the evil he has released there before Bloodstone attains power such that neither magic nor steel can stand against Kane!"

"A difficult siege," Ovstal speculated. "The Rillyti are awesome opponents to face in battle. We must cross an impenetrable morass to reach them. Once we're there, Arellarti will be a most imposing fortress to breach, and a lengthy siege is out of the question. Shenan knows what diabolical weapons Kane can use for defense."

"Well, we know it's going to be a costly battle. Still, Kane must be vulnerable, or he wouldn't have plotted so craftily to prevent this sort of attack. We can advance along the roadway his creatures rebuilt to invade us, so we'll be able to bring up siege machinery. We've no choice. Give Kane the time he needs to complete his work there, and then there'll be no army that can stop him. Every hour we delay brings victory closer to Kane!"

"And Breimen?" Asbraln reminded.

"We fight a common cause. Likely we fight for the freedom of mankind! Our quarrel is pointless now — in fact, Kane was the instigator of our war. I'm relying on Teres to convince Malchion of this. Knowing the truth of Kane's deception, the menace he poses to both our lands, Malchion can only accept truce, unite with us in destroying Arellarti. Our combined strength is the very force Kane has feared all along. Let us sincerely hope his fears were well founded!"

Later that afternoon, Teres critically readjusted the harness of her stallion, for Dribeck had ordered him saddled, although she preferred to see to this task herself. The warhorse nickered a pleasant greeting, and Teres's eyes grew bright as she threw an arm about his gray neck. Her sword and other captured gear hung at his saddle. It was more than reunion for her; it was a return to the familiar face of existence she once had known, before Kane had drawn her into his own shadow world.

As she swung onto the, saddle, she noted that Dribeck had started to offer a hand, then thought better of it. "Dribeck," she stated gravely, "If I never have a better reason, I'll always remember you with kindness for taking care of Gwellines for me. I trained him myself, and he's the best damn charger this land has ever bred."

"He *is* a magnificent animal," Dribeck agreed, reflecting that these were about the first civil words Teres had ever volunteered to him. "I'd have ridden him myself, but he damn near killed the first of my men who tried to mount him."

"Got my sword back, too," Teres murmured. Its balance and smaller hilt had been painstakingly crafted to her specifications. "Hell, you even got my boots fixed last night! You know how long it takes to get a pair of boots to fit just right? No better friend when you've broken them in just so. Dribeck... thanks."

He almost betrayed his astonishment. It had been his hope to win her confidence; why, then, did he find her unexpected warmth so unsettling? He muttered some depreciatory formula. "I had hoped you might have better memories of Selonari hospitality this time, though these are grim days that have found us. I dislike your immediate departure when you've barely rested, but in view of this crisis I can't but admire your endurance.

"Did these garments suit you? You cut a rather nice figure astride that stallion." That wasn't necessary to add.

Teres frowned slightly. "I'm told my face is a memorable one," she retorted with more bitterness than she intended. She thought again of Kane, but roughly pushed the image from her mind. She had made her decision.

Dribeck shrugged, unaccountably crestfallen at her rebuff. "Well, my men will escort you to the border; beyond there, the other prisoners I've released should be enough guard to get you to Breimen. I've got archers posted by the few of Kane's gateways we know of, but there's a chance he might break through elsewhere and try to waylay you. Doubt if he'll try anything, but I'm ready to expect the unexpected from that man.

"Good luck with Malchion. I'm counting on your testimony to carry the truce through. Let me know what aid he'll send to us here. An attack on Arellarti is going to call for everything we can marshal against Kane. You know better than any of us what defeat will mean."

"I know," said Teres in a low voice. She touched her heels to Gwellines.

XVIII
The Wolf Lays Plans

Teres gaped dumbly, wondering if her ears had lied to her — or whether her father had lost his senses.

Her hearing was not at fault. Malchion drained his mug, clashed it against the table, and repeated, "We do nothing." Cosmallen refilled the mug and smiled uncertainly at Teres, who put her hand over her own cup.

"I don't understand," Teres declared in confusion.

It had been a taxing day. At her unexpected return to Breimen, Malchion, looking more dissolute than she remembered, had nearly cracked her ribs in a welcoming hug. On Kane's word he had assumed his daughter to be dead, and to find her alive and safe in his keep … truly this demanded a celebration. Teres had with great difficulty impressed upon him the gravity of her information and finally succeeded in conferring with Breimen's master in private.

Once she had her father's attention, to finish her narrative had been a major ordeal. With every new disclosure, Malchion would explode into a furious denunciation and shout hasty orders to Embrom, whom Teres would have to forestall until she had a chance to explain subsequent events. Malchion interrupted continually — missed points, made her repeat constantly, jumped ahead of her narrative, fired pointless questions. Her own temper blazed when the Wolf flatly refused to believe certain parts of her story.

Somehow Teres had finished the tale, untangled matters so that even Malchion could understand all that had transpired. She thought that her father even believed her narrative — at least, far enough to recognize the genuine threat to his rule. But then his seemingly irrational response: "We do nothing."

"You don't believe what I've told you?" she queried.

Malchion grunted and wiped his mustache on the back of his hand. "No, I believe you — at least, so far as Kane plotting some foul sorcery in that ruined city, and Dribeck ready to piss in his boots, for fear of what those toads will do to his army. Never did trust Kane, anyway — just used him as I could. No, I trust your word, Teres — it's just that you let that Selonari weakling twist your judgment to suit his schemes."

He hunched forward and stuck out his finger, toward her. "Look, Teres. You say Kane provoked this war between us and Selonari. Well, maybe he did goad me into attacking sooner than I might have, maybe he did set the both of us up. Point is, I'd planned to invade Selonari sooner or later, anyway; you know that, and as I recall, you were restless to get on with it. Selonari has lands and wealth our people need, and those black haired runts will always pose a threat to our frontier. If Wollendan is going to be the power in the Southern Lands, we can't have independent city-states like Selonari in our midst, that's all. What we've got here is a cultural conflict, and sooner or later, theirs is going to have to be swallowed up by our own."

"But Kane means to conquer the entire continent — Thoem knows what else he plans!" argued Teres, not wishing to dispute her father's statements.

"Well, now, maybe Kane does, or maybe he doesn't. Not wanting to disparage your judgment, Teres, but all this talk of Kane's invincible sorceries … we just have your word on how powerful this really is. Now, don't scream at your sire! Tell me, how much do you know, realistically, about elder-world races and cities and weapons and magic? Hmmm? All right, then, you just have Kane's word how great and powerful his forces will be, and Kane's word isn't worth the spit it takes to speak it. And what man wouldn't boast and bluster, trying to impress a gullible girl anyway — under the circumstances?"

"Damn your thick skull! I *saw* what he could do with just that ring! He butchered damn near fifty men!"

"Because none of those Selonari had balls or brains enough to step behind cover, take out an arrow, draw back on the bow, and kill that bastard dead as they get. Now, I'm not saying Kane isn't dangerous. The Rillyti alone should make a rough bunch to meet in open combat, from what I hear. What I'm saying is we don't really know that Kane stands as any real threat to Breimen or the rest of Wollendan.

"But we do know Kane threatens Selonari, and so Dribeck comes begging for us to help him. Well, bullshit! Of course he tells you mankind's in mortal danger; he wants our soldiers to fight his battles. Afterwards we'd find out how genuine Selonari's talk of peace really is. Well, the Wolf didn't rule this long to play the fool for that weak-armed schemer! Kane and Dribeck can fight it out as best they can — even Dribeck ought to be able to defeat one man and a lot of slime-eating toads. If they kill each other off, so much the better; I'll erect a monument to Kane's memory. Figure if Kane does make a decent fight of it, Selonari is going to come away too crippled to do much more than lick its wounds. Under those happy conditions, I doubt if there'll be much resistance to our army when we march south to avenge our earlier setback. Now do you see the Wolf's logic, cub?"

"Plainly. What happens if Kane defeats Dribeck and conquers Selonari for himself?" asked Teres darkly.

Malchion waved for another cup, his mood exuberant once more. "Dribeck's worry, not mine. Then we'll just take Selonari from Kane, is all. I mean, even if Kane's weapon makes him as dangerous a force as you make him out, he's still going to take a beating from Selonari before he can crawl out of his swamp. Fact of geography: it's a long march from Kranor-Rill to Breimen, and Selonari is between. He'll have to take Selonari before he moves north, or risk their cutting off his retreat and then have to fight on two fronts. If Kane gets past Selonari, it's a long dry march for a battle-weary army of toads to get to Breimen. By then, we can be ready. And if Kane turns out to be a genuine threat to Wollendan... well, there'll be a lot of swords and husky lads to swing them, waiting to show Kane how real men can fight!"

"Then you'll not even agree to a truce?" Teres's tone was dismal.

The Wolf made a flourishing gesture. "Sure, I'll accept Dribeck's truce, since that pleases you. Why not? I'm not prepared to renew the war just yet. Let Kane do our fighting for us. Afterwards... well, of course we'll know how to play that one, after the others have cast their dice. Never been a truce made that wasn't made to be broken sometime."

"Then I'll take your word to Dribeck: you agree to a truce, but you can spare no troops to invade Arellarti, since you're concerned first with Breimen's own defenses." She added hopefully, "Shall I say we'll be prepared to fight Kane, should he threaten our borders?"

"Say it however you like. Damned if a stay with those guileful bastards hasn't polished your tongue. But there's no reason for you to say anything to Dribeck; I can easily send some brittle-boned ambassador." He landed a whack on Cosmallen's bare thigh, causing the girl to slosh wine across the table.

"I'd rather go myself," Teres said dully.

"Well, I'm never one to deny my cub her whims, even when they're clearly pointless. And since that settles this 'grave crisis,' how about some serious drinking? After your adventures, the Wolf thinks Breimen should celebrate his cub's return in the proper manner."

"I'd rather not," Teres begged off. "These past days have been a grueling ordeal, and all I want to do now is stretch out on my own bed and sleep a few days through."

He gazed at her in surprise. "As you wish — not like you to drag away from a good night of raising hell, though. Well, I'll celebrate for the both of us."

"I'm sure," Teres acknowledged, and took her leave. Cosmallen met her at the door. "That's a beautiful shirt, milady. May I feel the silk?" Her slim fingers caressed her shoulder.

Teres decided her mind was tormented by too many thoughts, too many memories to reflect upon throughout the night. "Bring us some wine, and come along, Cosmallen. Perhaps I'll let you try it on."

XIX
Dreams in Arellarti

Night lay deep upon Arellarti, the moon and stars dim and distant. Hidden from their wan light the city crouched beneath the mist, its rubrous walls rising in perfect geometry, alien beauty in a rotting land. To the moon's affrighted eye, Arellarti appeared as some monstrous and deadly spider, its misshapen form tinted and obscured by the iridescent bubble of blood in which it hung. The causeway stretched off to the forests like a filament of web, holding Arellarti suspended over the poisonous tarn. Slowly the spider was ascending its web, reaching out to the sleeping land beyond.

The coruscant effulgence of Bloodstone illumined the entire city and spilled over onto the murky slime of the swamp. Its emerald rays gave a sick hue to the mottled red stone, which now might be seen to be flecked with green throughout its density. For in the darkness, the very stones of Arellarti seemed translucent, as if the light of Bloodstone shone not only *on* the city, but *through* the city. The walls of the colossal dome were alive with the radiance that penetrated them — translucent almost to the extent that the sentient crystal within could be distinguished as a darker shadow through the walls. Its brilliance was that of a blood-red star, dying in a nova of venomous luminance.

Bathed in its eerie light, Kane slumped wearily against the crescent dais, a still-warm pipe lying behind in a scatter of gray ashes. Heavy were Kane's thoughts, his spirit dark as the clouded night beyond the sullen glow of Bloodstone.

This began as an adventure, or so I believed. I thought no more of it than a means to raise an army of conquest — my major weapon arising from alien science rather than elder sorcery, my soldiers these bestial swamp creatures in place of human warriors. Men have fought for wizards and conquerors in the past; I reasoned that once my power was known, men would fight beneath my banner as willingly. Now the horror in which I have steeped myself creeps through the gloom of my spirit, so that even I sense the dread power that emanates from you. Could it be this time I've gone too far — that the revulsion men feel toward my power will prove greater than their lust to share in the spoils of conquest? Shall I stand more alone than before, with my entire race in arms against me, reviling the name of Kane?

Would that be so different from your present fate? Your only escape from your curse has been to wander ceaselessly, through lands where your name has faded from man's short memory, move on again when they have new reasons to remember. You will always be reviled, but my power will make you feared; never again will you be driven like a hunted wolf across the land. And from what I understand of your miserable race, there will be many whose souls can be gained for the yellow metal you prize so extravagantly, or the chance to seize another man's holdings without fear of retribution.

I thought I understood her. She loved me for a moment, then she grew to hate me. She would have given her heart to a conqueror, but it was not strength alone that she sought. When she recognized the alien evil I had bonded to my soul, she drew away from me in loathing... deceived me, joined with her enemy to destroy me. And at one time I could have abandoned this blighted venture, gone with her into her world, found happiness by her side.

For how long, immortal? Until she grew old and wrinkled, while you remained as you are now? Until you grew bored once more with playing warlord over these dull creatures — a petty ruler of a frontier land? I see in your mind that you have fallen to such stupidity in times past — and regretted it with bitter memories ever since. Have you then chosen to forget the lessons of your doomed existence? Have you decided to unman yourself with the dissembling cowardice, the whimpering self-doubts that your race proudly rationalizes as conscience? Such thoughts are not your own, Kane. It was the woman who poisoned you, deluded you... betrayed you. Can you deny now that love is the most cancerous of human weaknesses? A race whose emotions overrule rational thought should compensate for this failing and harness the stronger emotions. Hate and fear are far more dynamic principles than love; the former builds empires, the latter throws them away.

I might yet destroy you.

And would you?

No. I have gambled everything for the power you shall give me. And although the prize seems less glorious to me than before, my goal remains to create an undying empire, with all of mankind acknowledging as master the outcast Kane. If I succeed, perhaps I'll grow bored with this game, too, as I have with all others. Perhaps even the new worlds you promise to open to me will in time lose their novelty. And at that distant age, may I enjoy as much the destruction of all I've created as I hope to delight in the striving to win it!

Then if such amusement will lift you from this despondent brooding, take heart. Our enemies gather to destroy us, but already my power has so increased that we need not fear them. Soon the lattice will be complete, and I will no longer be a crippled, imperfect entity. I can draw upon the limitless energy of the cosmos, usurp this world from the rule of its sickly sun, search out through this new universe for the others.

What others?

The others of my race who dwell beyond the stars. I too know loneliness — trapped in this rotting wasteland for millennia, as was my fate. When I am at last complete, I can communicate with my brothers, wherever they may wait within the framework of the cosmos. We were so few, so long ago — it will be good to speak with my own kind once more.

Then are there human emotions secreted away in all those locked recesses of your consciousness? The shadow thoughts you seek to hide from my awareness? To return your sneer, do not allow your weak emotions to interfere with the battle we now begin.

The emerald light pulsed and waned like dancing flame, but Kane had broken contact with the living crystal and listened no more to its insinuating thoughts. The vapor from the pipe lulled his tormented mind into a form of sleep where in his glowing dreams he seemed to sense monolithic laughter swirling about him.

XX
Night of Bloodstone

On the assumption that any attack from Arellarti, should Kane move first, must cross Kranor-Rill along the reconstructed causeway, Lord Dribeck had positioned a small company of soldiers near this point of egress. Until he could muster sufficient strength to lay siege to the hidden city, Dribeck intended to rely on this advance guard for intelligence of Kane's movements. Whether these men could hold the forest end of the causeway against whatever force might issue from Arellarti was a dubious matter.

So it was, that when the earth trembled beneath their feet, and the air was charged with the drawn-out roar of thunder — though the noon sky was almost cloudless — the soldiers looked to their weapons uneasily and muttered a few prayers that the gods be with them on what might become a suicidal mission. But when the tearing rumble died away, and the ground stayed firm and secure, there appeared no sequelae more sinister than a muffled whisper, like the rush of distant waters. Their waiting lost its painful intensity, so that men relaxed to speculate upon the strange phenomenon and laugh nervously over the fear that had breathed upon them.

At length their captain ordered a scouting party to circle the swampland toward the direction from which the disturbance had seemed to issue. Night overtook them before they could return, and so it was not until the following day when they made their report. A broad channel had miraculously appeared, gouging a straight course through Kranor-Rill, to the South Branch of the Neltoben River, and on into its mainstream. River water flowed into the swamp's seepage, forming a deep canal into the center of Kranor-Rill.

The captain considered this information at length, uncertain what interpretation to put upon it. Dutifully he sent a courier to Selonari, to inform Lord Dribeck of this cryptic work of sorcery. By the time the messenger delivered his report, the reason for the canal's sudden construction was no longer mystery.

In the gray hour before dawn, Breimen awoke to horror.

Through the veiling mists of twilight, an uncanny fleet slipped from Arellarti's reconstructed quays, whose stone piers knew the caress of deep waters for the first time in centuries. Past the glistening banks of heaped slime and muck, shattered vegetation and steaming mud, along the still oozing wound in Kranor-Rill's belly, the flotilla advanced through the freshly torn channel that opened the stagnant waters of the Neltoben's South Branch, and into its deeper North Branch, still turbulent from the cataclysmic redirection of its flow. Emerging into clear stream at last, the strange craft hurtled over the outraged current at fantastic speed, their velocity scarcely diminishing as they left the flow of the Neltoben and the Macewen and turned upstream upon the Clasten River.

The region along the river was desolate, a wilderness broken only by a few tiny settlements, which hung along the banks like sloughing scabs. Heavy mists obscured the riverbed; the waning moon was hidden. Except for those creatures whose hours were of the night, mankind slept.

So it happened that there were few who witnessed the passage of the demon ships through the enveloping fog. Only vague outlines could be glimpsed, dim flashes where the vapors were pierced by eddies of night wind. And what could be seen was sufficient to drive the watchers from the riverbank in fear-haunted flight.

A spectral fleet coursed along the river, and devils manned its decks. Long, gleaming hulls of silvery metal shaped the craft into titanic spearpoints whose cleaving prows balanced above the surface upon elongated struts. Foam streamed past the streaking bowfins to be swallowed in the churning turbulence that surged behind the stern, where silent turbines drove two unseen screws. The phantom decks were open, and their plates bore the weight of thirty or more monstrous passengers — hulking Rillyti warriors in full battle array. There were close to twenty of these bizarre vessels racing through the night at speeds which surpassed the fastest horse's gallop. In single line they followed the lead boat, whose course threaded the channel unimpeded by the darkness and mist. A huge silhouette of a man in billowing cloak could be fleetingly glimpsed at the leader's prow.

And so doom descended upon Breimen.

Fear quickly replaced astonishment in the wondering of the guards who sleepily stood watch upon Breimen's walls of stone and timber. Out of the swirling mists appeared the demon fleet; silver fins retracted to the bow, as the strange craft slowed and thrust alien prows onto the riverbank. Their decks disgorged the Rillyti horde, and the predawn quiet was torn with fierce roars, thunderous splashing as the creatures leaped over the sides. Their bronze alloy swords glinted dully as the batrachian army advanced upon the darkened city, where the first shrill of alarm was summoning its people from dream to waking nightmare.

An awesome sight awaited the grim soldiers who hastily manned the city walls. Wreathed in mist like phantoms of drugged nightmare, the bufanoid invaders shambled toward the river gate. A mighty bar slid into place across the threatened portals, whose thick timbers were proof against any force short of heavy siege equipment — of which the invaders had none. Archers squinted for marks in the darkness, aimed desultory fire into the advancing ranks. The swamp creatures bore heavy armor upon their warty backs, and the arrows struck with little effect. A few venom-tipped spears arched back from them to the walls, sending its defenders behind cover, but these weapons were more suited to thrusting than to casting accurately.

Although the attack was not expected, word of Kane's treacherous plot had supplied most of the conversation in Breimen these past few days, and vivid accounts were advanced concerning his slaughter of Dribeck's men, the terrifying extent of his sorcerous powers. So it was that despite their initial horror, Breimen's soldiers prepared to withstand this inhuman invasion. Archers, shafts at ready, peered alertly through the gloom for sight of Kane, whose death would break the back of the Rillyti onslaught.

Frightened rumors notwithstanding, no man was prepared for what they beheld when Kane at last appeared. At the head of the amphibian's charge stood a glowing figure — a man-shaped specter formed of living energy — or perhaps encased in a wavering armor of baleful green fire. Like a vengeful demon, the shimmering figure strode toward the river gate, his army of blood-mad fiends at his back. Archers sent shaft after shaft into the glowing silhouette, a certain target in the darkness. His ominous progress did not falter, while crackling flashes along his energy web evidenced the accuracy of their arrows. The soldiers looked to their weapons, glanced for assurance at the heavy timbered gate — and waited for the creatures to storm the walls. Nor was their wait a lengthy one.

Scarcely had the alerted guard scrambled from barracks and dashed to the ramparts when horror reached for them. The demon figure halted before the barbican and extended his left arm. From the blazing circle upon his fist leaped a flame of coruscant energy — a lance of shimmering emerald and crimson-flecked light. As this eerie bolt of fire struck the barbican, the ripping concussion jarred the entire length of the wall. The gate buckled inward, its timbers blackened and shattered, iron bolts red-hot slag. Soldiers near the sundered portal were thrown back by the blast.

Through the smouldering gap charged the Rillyti, descending upon the dazed defenders in great hopping strides. Before the stunned and terror-stricken soldiers thought to block their rush, the batrachians were in their midst, golden blades slashing murderously, poisoned barbs stabbing into the disordered ranks. The suddenness of their attack had caught Breimen almost totally unprepared, and now the battle-mad Rillyti had blasted entrance into the startled city. Overwhelmed by the ferocity that leaped upon them, the defenders fell back in near rout.

Their plight would be all but hopeless once the swamp creatures controlled free entry into Breimen, and with this bleak knowledge the soldiers battled desperately to contain the enemy's advance. Determinedly they struggled with the Rillyti, whose size and strength made them deadly opponents even had they lacked their great swords and bronze armor. Reinforced by fresh troops and rallying townspeople, they massed to push back the bufanoid invaders.

The struggle grew more intense; men fell upon the Rillyti with seeming disregard for their lives and pulled the monsters down by sheer weight of numbers.

For a moment it seemed that the defenders might succeed in driving back the Rillyti thrust. Then Kane appeared in the smoking rubble of the gate. Death lanced from Kane's fist, tore through the packed ranks of defenders like lightning from Hell. Here was terror against which no courage could stand. Men were flung apart, smashed to the stones as charred and twisted clumps of flesh, weapons fused to lifeless grips. Again and again the deadly bolts sought life, blasted it with annihilating caress. The horror on the faces of the dead sickened the heart, nor were the screams of brave men dying in fear encouraging sounds to hear. The mass of soldiers crumpled and fell apart, dissolved into panic-stricken flight from the destroying rays.

One warrior, driven mad by the horror that stalked among them, crawled past the tortured corpses and sprang upon Kane from behind. His outthrust sword speared for Kane's back and drove into the coruscating web of energy that surrounded him — touched, but did not penetrate. In a crackling instant, the blade fused into molten slag and its wielder flashed into glowing cinder that crumbled as it fell. Faced with an invulnerable creature who stalked them with a weapon of hellish destruction, the regrouped defenders broke and fled. Behind them, cutting them down as they blindly ran, hopped the blood-crazed Rillyti, their invasion into the city's heart no longer challenged.

Once Breimen's walls had fallen to their attack, there followed not battle, but ruthless slaughter. Malchion had not yet recovered from his defeat at the Macewen crossing, and in his complacency over Dribeck's desperate truce, he had dropped the wartime vigilance which might have kept his city prepared — if preparations were possible against this onslaught of elder-world wizardry. Thus it was that the diminished Breim army had been taken unaware, thrown into disorder by the fearsome power of Bloodstone, the vicious savagery of the Rillyti, and their best had fallen in the battle before the river gate. Now only sporadic resistance met the intruders — disorganized reinforcements from other barracks, aroused townspeople with swords in sleep-dulled grip. Angry men who fought against the current of panic to face the inhuman reavers died under their irresistible weapons, or turned to join the flight.

The graying night was lit by the flames of massacre. In an effort to conserve Bloodstone's energy reserves — drawn upon heavily to blast out the channel through the swamp and to power the invasion fleet, in addition to his own utilization — Kane relinquished the energy screen which enveloped him. Surrounded by his massive warriors, he stood revealed in armor of bronze alloy, further protected by the darkness and tumult, although now and again a hastily aimed arrow struck close to him, or skittered off the unyielding metal plates. A fantastic statue of living bronze, he directed the pitiless attack through the writhing city, gleaming armor throwing multihued reflections of fire and blood, flashes of evil green.

Through the predawn streets his demon army surged, slaying every living creature who came before their blades, whether to do battle or in hopeless flight. The Rillyti were not unscathed. Despite the chaos, men rallied in desperate knots and sought to throw barricades across the streets. Their swords clashed bravely against the greater blades of the enemy; clubs and axes hacked and hammered, and at point-blank range their spears and arrows struck with lethal force. Again and again one of the towering batrachians was pulled down, torn to pieces by mob ferocity, hamstrung or gutted by a well-placed sword stroke, perhaps skewered by the envenomed fang of a captured spear. But there were hundreds of the bestial invaders, and the cost of their deaths was often a mound of human corpses. The circumstances of Kane's attack hindered the defenders' effective use of their superior numbers, and wherever resistance toughened, the deadly power of Kane's ring turned their stand into terrified rout.

Breimen was a young city, so that timber formed the bulk of its construction. Now flames shot to greet the dawn from uncounted sites, fired by Kane's energy bolts and by the torches of the Rillyti. Horrified townsmen sought sanctuary in their homes — sought, but did not find. In sheer lust to destroy, the swamp creatures smashed entrance into the frightened dwellings and slaughtered all within — freeman and slave, woman and child — leaving only flaming shambles, whose loot they bothered not to carry away. Fanned by the morning breeze, flames leaped from building to building, and there was no man to deny their hunger. Gibbering chaos marched the streets of Breimen, leaving a crushed and crimson trail to mark its passage.

Near Breimen's center waited Malchion's keep, a squat, unlovely structure of stone and timber, surrounded by palisade and dry moat of barbed spikes. Here men found shelter; resistance found a core to build upon. Roused from his wine-besotted sleep, the Wolf monitored the grim reports of those who had fled the enemy thrust. Malchion snapped orders in haste. All able-bodied men were to be taken into the keep and armed for its defense, until the proximity of Kane's advance forced them to raise the drawbridge. If walls and spiked trench thwarted their assault, there would be time for the rest of the stricken city to regroup, to draw strength from the outlying barracks. Runners were dispatched to spread Malchion's commands. Once a massed attack threatened Kane's rearguard, the Wolf would lead a sortie from the keep. Kane would be pincered between disciplined attacks on two sides, and the city whose belly he thought he had slashed through would close like a trap upon the inhuman army.

But Kane, who had planned a lightning raid, not a lengthy siege, recognized clearly that his position could be overextended. He had come not to conquer, but to destroy, and as the defense stiffened at Malchion's keep, he strode forward to deal with the enemy fortress with the power he commanded. Against the strafing archery fire, Kane was forced to reactivate his protecting cloak of wavering energy. Arrows spattered like spit on glowing steel as they struck the shimmering figure, this phantom of emerald flame who stalked through the smoke-clotted dawn.

Demon lightning, more potent than any he had yet unleashed, blazed from Kane's flame-sheathed fist. Its coruscant bolts met the palisaded wall in a shuddering blast. Timbers flared in consuming incandescence; stones fused, exploded into white-hot splinters. Those who could, fled the searing walls in blind fear;

those less fortunate danced spasmodically upon the crackling death pyre. In seconds Kane's raking energy had devastated the fortress walls and driven survivors to cover.

No Rillyti surged past the smouldering debris of the blasted palisade, though there was none to dispute their rush upon the keep. Kane's attention quickly shifted to the embattled fortress; again the energy of Bloodstone leapt from his ring. More brilliant than ever before, full into the foundation wall the lance of fire struck. A tremendous concussion shook the entire fortress; the defenders sprawled across the reeling floor, plummeted from their perches. Like a hell-spawned hammer, the annihilating beam carved into the foundations, slashing through the splintering rock like a white hot blade through a maiden's belly. Kane stood transfixed, a river of star-born energy coursing from his extended fist. Behind him, the Rillyti croaked in fright, cowered back from the exploding fragments that spun through the green-tinted fury of the walls.

The very stones seemed to scream in death agony, descant to the threnody of thundering explosion, crackling energy, terror-stricken howls. Half its length ablaze, its foundation wall torn away, the fortress of Breimen slowly settled against its wound. With a gathering rush, the entire keep crumpled onto its pyre, slammed against the blistered earth with a death roar like the last peals of thunder of a violent storm. Its hallways were jammed with hundreds of panic-maddened souls, fleeing hopelessly from the consuming rays. All but those who fought their way to the exits and leaped from leaning windows to seek flight through the horror-filled dawn — all but these few were crushed to screaming ruin, as the fortress toppled to blazing, broken rubble. Its promised security now closed upon them as a deathtrap. The smoke from the holocaust obscured the skies of dawn, tainted the creeping sun to a rubrous crescent against the flame-streaked horizon.

The shifting web of energy flashed off with the cessation of the spiking beam, for the fortress no longer existed. Kane slumped wearily, barely able to bear the weight of his armor. The destruction of Malchion's keep had drained Bloodstone's energy reserves to a dangerous level, so that their return to Arellarti would be imperiled, should Kane draw upon the crystal for any more power.

But his purpose had been accomplished. Breimen was a broken cripple now, and the power he had demonstrated would cause men to reexamine their decision to challenge him. Calling back his marauding army, Kane ordered a return to their fleet.

Along the path they had entered, Breimen was ablaze, with the fires spreading throughout the city. It was necessary to cut their way back to the river by a different, circuitous route, which they fought through with little difficulty — for the destruction of Malchion's fortress along with the bulk of his remaining army had broken the back of the resistance. Those whose suicidal charges sought to halt their progress were summarily butchered, and never were the invaders pressed to the extreme that Kane need call upon the final reserves of Bloodstone's energy — the power they needed to drive the engines of their waiting craft.

The fleet which departed the dying city was lighter by almost half its number. But the power of Breimen was vanishing in the pall of smoke that enshrouded the morning sky.

XXI
No Tears in Selonari

Someone was knocking at her door. "Teres?"

She sat up, bewildered by the unfamiliar surroundings, thinking for a moment that she had awakened in Kane's tower. No, she was alone. This was Dribeck's citadel, where she had spent the last few days since returning to Selonari with the Wolf's message and an escort of twenty-five of her own men. Dribeck had read between the lines of Malchion's decision — and noted Teres's following, as well — though he kept his thoughts to himself. Teres wished guiltily that her father had permitted her to bring more of the men she counted as loyal, but the Wolf half suspected her motives. At least there would be a handful of swords to offset this shadow upon Breimen's honor.

"Teres?" Still the rapping. "Teres? It's Dribeck. I need to speak with you."

She recognized the voice. "Just a minute," she called uncertainly. The stars were bright through her windows; she could only have been asleep for a few hours. Feeling alarm, Teres sat up on the bed, naked in the wan flicker of a single lamp. Drawing free one of the dark fur robes, still warm where she had lain beneath it, she wrapped it about her figure and padded to the door.

"What is it?" she murmured uneasily, slipping back the bolt.

Dribeck's long face was worried. "I'd better come in," he advised. "I've just been given some grim news."

Teres frowned as the other pushed past her, giving no notice to her lack of attire. His manner was haunted; he was numb from some overwhelming disaster. "Kane...?" she began in a strained voice.

"Yes." Dribeck stared at her with a stunned expression. Her heart is a warrior's, he told himself, so give it to her straight and have it done. "Word has just reached us, as survivors begin to arrive. Kane attacked Breimen two days ago with an army of Rillyti. There was a savage slaughter, and Malchion's keep was destroyed. When Kane withdrew, half the city was in flames. Breimen lies in defeated rains, and Kane retired to Arellarti with most of his army intact."

Teres slumped weak-kneed against the wall, her face ashen, the knuckles that gripped her robe blanched from stress. For a moment she was silent, unbelieving. Her lips worked, finally shaped words. "How?" she managed to utter.

Bleakly Dribeck related the terrified reports which the first to reach Selonari had given him. Teres listened without comment, white, immobile as a fur-draped statue. It seemed the wall must buckle from the immense weight that leaned upon it.

"My father?" she asked weakly.

Dribeck's voice was sympathetic. "He was within the fortress when its walls were blasted into rubble. It is doubtful that... " He did not finish the statement, nor was there need.

There was pain in her eyes, in her tone, though her face was calm. "The Wolf deserved a better death than that," she whispered. After a pause she added, "Or perhaps you feel his fate was a just one. After all, he refused to aid you — figured that Selonari and Kane could fight to the death, while Breimen played vulture."

Such had been Dribeck's thought, but he denied it, saying only, "A man fights by the rules he knows. A warrior's death should be in open battle, not as prey to black sorceries."

"Why Breimen?" Teres demanded of fate. Then, reflecting, "Was it revenge?"

"I think not," Dribeck assured her. "Kane's mind is too rational to risk everything for emotional gratification. It's doubtful that he knew of Malchion's neutrality. Probably he considered Breimen to have allied itself with Selonari, and he thought to counter this threat before Malchion marched south. From his tactics, it appears obvious as well that he meant to overawe his prospective enemies with a display of devastating power."

"Maybe," muttered Teres, thinking Dribeck knew only one facet of Kane's twisted psyche.

She seemed composed, so that Dribeck advanced a further point, albeit somewhat guiltily. "We're of course gathering information as fast as it comes in. My counselors are being roused while we speak — I've called an emergency meeting, naturally. Your presence would be of great value, but under the circumstances I understand your desire to — "

"To throw myself down and weep hysterically?" grated Teres, showing her teeth against her whiter face, two spots of scarlet emblazoned on the cheekbones like a demon mask. "So might a foolish girl honor the murder of her city and kin! A warrior sharpens his sword of vengeance! I'll be at your damned council!"

"As you wish," commended Dribeck, who had hoped for this response. "Come, then, when you are ready — you know the council chamber well enough by now." Asbraln was calling him from the hall, but he paused long enough to add, "Teres, I know my sincerity has at times seemed dubious, but... You have my genuine sympathy tonight — and my respect."

Teres barely acknowledged his departure. For a long while she remained braced against the wall, her arms clasping the furs to her body. At length she dropped onto the bed, realization of what had occurred finally creeping past the defense of disbelief. There was a sound in the lonely chamber then, a sobbing catch of breath, low and raking. But there were no tears in her eyes, so the choked sounds must have been curses.

Mechanically she drew on her clothing. This performance seemed commonplace as ever; might it be that nothing else in her life had changed?

She heard Dribeck's angry tone as she neared the council chamber. They had already begun, then — she had taken more time with her thoughts than she realized. The now familiar faces considered her gravely as she entered, but to outward appearances Teres was remarkably composed. Fear hung like a thick vapor over the circle of bleak faces.

Quickly Dribeck advised her of the most recent fragments of information, but when the conference resumed, Teres had the feeling its topic had changed. "The essential point — and subsequent information won't alter this — is that Kane was able to reduce Breimen to smoking rubble in a matter of hours, then withdraw to his fortress with relatively minor losses. Granted, Malchion was not expecting attack. Nonetheless Breimen was as well defended a city as Selonari, and although surprised and disorganized, the Wolf's army was probably as large as our own. Bluntly, the power that Kane wields makes lethal mockery of warfare as we know it. If Kane — when Kane decides to march against Selonari, we're fools to believe our city will fare any better against this alien sorcery.

"We can't let him choose his own time to strike. I say we must attack Arellarti at once!"

"Suicidal, at this point!" declared Ovstal.

"You know what will happen if we wait for Kane to come to our walls!" Dribeck retorted. "To carry the attack to him is our best chance. Damn it, we've been over this!"

"But then we counted on support from Breimen," Ovstal reminded.

"We can block off Kane's canal through the swamp," suggested Ainon, one of Dribeck's more powerful supporters among the gentry. "Barricade the channel with logs, so he can't bring his transport boats out. Those toads won't be worth so much after a long march through the forest."

"Hell, Ainon, use your head!" Dribeck remarked bitterly. "Kane carved that channel through the length of Kranor-Rill in less time than it takes to swim across! What kind of barrier would block him?"

"We should at least hold off for a few days," Ovstal persisted. "If it comes to a siege, we'll need every man we can muster. Malchion wouldn't help us before, but maybe now some of these Breim refugees will join with us."

"How many men do you think that will be?" commented Crempra, wincing under Teres's glare.

"Ill-bred, but accurate, cousin," Dribeck admitted. "We can't spare time to wait for dazed bands of refugees to trickle in. Kane needs that time more than we do. My guess is that he dangerously overextended his power on the Breimen raid. Otherwise he wouldn't have crippled his enemy and then withdrawn — rather he'd have totally annihilated the city, or occupied it, perhaps. We strike now, and maybe we can hit before he recovers his strength — at least we'll attack before Bloodstone's power increases to whatever potential the crystal can attain."

"My men and I will join your assault," growled Teres, speaking for the first time, "and with us will march any man of Breimen who still has spine to swing a blade."

"I'm sure we all appreciate the spirit of your offer," Ovstal replied ambiguously. "But there's another problem. Courage and steel can't do battle with the weapons Kane commands. Our army marches into unguessable danger, and the men know it. Now, maybe it goes against your vaunted logic, but it's human nature to trust in thick walls and familiar weapons."

"You're saying...?"

"I'm saying the men might mutiny if you try to lay siege to Arellarti right now. They're brave men, but you can push them too far. Here in Selonari they can fight on secure ground."

"It may be that we can work a bargain with Kane," Arclec put in hastily, seeing Dribeck flush with anger.

Dribeck turned his wrath upon his wealthiest counselor. "After what Kane did to Breimen, knowing with what forces he's allied himself, can you seriously consider trying to bargain with Kane?"

There was no answer from the tight-pressed lips of those present.

"Since we must fight, let us fight that battle where we have a slim chance of victory," Dribeck went on.

"There's no denying our casualties will be unprecedented. But a man who is impaled upon his enemy's sword in dying disarms his enemy — and so is avenged by his comrades. It sickens me to propose that, in order to kill the serpent, we must suffer his strikes until his fangs are drained of venom. But unless someone knows a better strategy, these pitiless tactics are all we can fall back upon.

"As to mutiny, I think once tales spread of the massacre in Breimen, then men will know how vain is their trust in Selonari's walls. Kane once observed that bravery and desperation are at times inseparable.

Comment?"

"Might as well die on the attack as on the defense," quoted Ovstal somberly. "With planning, with luck... maybe we can counter some of Kane's advantage. Spread our forces, make him waste his power in striking at small targets. Better yet, close with his minions, so he'd hesitate to fire. These bolts of energy are his deadliest weapon, so far as we know. Without that ring and in open combat, we'd have the numbers to chop apart his army. Be best if we could draw him out of his fortress. Lure him into the open, then attack with everything we can muster. Good trick if we could do it — but Kane's a damn clever strategist himself, that I'll give him."

"Can't we find some counterspell to protect the men from Kane's sorcery?" demanded Arclec, thinking of his position in the army's van.

"There may be hope," Dribeck announced. "I'm going to speak with Gerwein again. Last time she hinted that the Temple might have access to powers of magic as potent as Kane's frozen demon. She was vague, whether temporizing or truly uncertain what help she could give, I couldn't say. If the latter, she's had time now to search through the Temple's moldy vaults for forgotten secrets. If the former, let's hope the massacre at Breimen will warm her heart to our crass political endeavors."

Asbraln shook his head gloomily. "Ask help from the Temple, and the price won't be an easy one. It's been a hard battle to block Gerwein's ambitions as much as we've done."

Dribeck made a bitter face. "As we've said, these are desperate days before us. If Gerwein can be of help against Kane, we can't afford to ignore her aid. I only hope the cost won't make our victory a black one for us. But then, defeat looms blacker still."

XXII
The Vaults of the Temple

Gerwein was a model of imperious grace for so early in the morning, mysterious in a long-skirted gown of burgundy silk, patterned with patches of cream leather, and cunningly pierced to suggest the beauty it enswathed. Her raven hair was combed in long, softly curling tresses; her dark eyes were as inscrutably calculating as a cat's stare across a dimly lit room. Teres did not like the cold impersonality of her delicately chiseled face.

"The wild she-wolf," she stated, her gaze flicking over the rough-attired girl. Teres challenged her unwavering eyes. Gerwein could not have been more than five years her senior. "Do you bring her as bodyguard, Lord Dribeck... or do you think to sway my sympathies with the help of one of the goddess's sex?"

"I thought you might find it of benefit to speak with the only person who has firsthand knowledge of Kane's hidden power," replied Dribeck, keeping an even temper with difficulty, after a sleepless night of care.

"Perhaps. Yes, maybe we would have things to say to each other. But this morning I perceive a haunted urgency overshadowing your usual polished manner, milord, and cries from the street inform us of Kane's most recent work of infamy. Has the madman whom you welcomed among us returned to our gates so soon?"

Dribeck gave her a vivid account of all they had learned concerning Breimen's fate, watching her face for some show of unease. He was disappointed. The high priestess's air of mocking sophistication was unbroken, although she questioned them both on point after point.

Finally Gerwein fell silent, pondering the information they had given. Her beautiful face was unchanged, but she had come to a decision. "Come with me, if you please," she directed, rising from her chair of state. "It is rare that outsiders intrude beyond the Temple's halls of worship, but I see these are strange times."

Into the secret reaches of the Temple they followed her, through winding hallways that twisted past rooms with incense-laden air and groups of girls in pale tunics at study or at leisure, performing meaningless rituals or mundane household tasks, The hallway led down flights of stairs, became torchlit as the chevroned windows disappeared. Now the rooms were more often closed and locked, some with doors whose timbers seemed inordinately massive. From behind one such door escaped the muffled sound of weeping, and Teres thought she saw a quick, cruel smile dance across Gerwein's lips.

They were well underground when the priestess paused before an iron-bound portal. "Knock," she invited. Dribeck complied.

A sharp face appeared at the spyhole, ducked, and then with a scraping of bolts, the door was opened. The room within was surprisingly large. Dribeck's harried countenance lit in admiration at the sight of the vast wealth of books and manuscripts stored along the extensive shelves. A trio of priestesses of middle to declining years were examining a number of musty volumes laid out upon a heavy table. A silver-gray disk of polished metal, perhaps five feet in diameter, lay flat against the table's center. Dribeck assumed it was a mirror — until he bent over and saw that the burnished circle cast no reflection.

"The Temple archives," announced Gerwein. "Repository of centuries of tedious records and arcane wisdom. In these fallen days, we daughters of Shenan have all but lost our ability to discriminate between the trivia of routine and the priceless knowledge whose secrets our cult once mastered. My sisters have labored ceaselessly these last days in the effort to distill knowledge of the elder Krelran race and their demon Bloodstone from this moldering dune of ancient parchment. Selonari is fortunate — as is the world beyond, it would seem — that our search has not been altogether in vain."

"What do you know of Arellarti?" Dribeck could not help blurting.

"Much. We hope to know more, once we can find a certain ancient manuscript that dates from our city's earliest days. So far, that volume has eluded us." Her smile was coldly triumphant. "But we've learned enough already from references in the other writings to recognize the nature of this crystal devil called Bloodstone. And more important — having learned this, we have discovered means to combat its power. It is likely that we shall be able to nullify the deadly energy bolts Kane controls through his ring... and I see my suave Lord Dribeck betrays his interest!"

"If you can counteract that one weapon, we can destroy Kane!" swore Dribeck, too intent to fence with the high priestess.

"Unless Bloodstone has other powers, and more deadly. But I think we're learning enough to do battle with Kane on even terms. From your statements, Teres, I see Kane once revealed a significant aspect of Krelran power, though your unlettered mind failed to grasp what he meant. You spoke of Bloodstone's power as 'sorcery,' and Kane said that you were in error, and by design or condescension to your ignorance, he never troubled to explain the distinction.

"Kane's power is that of science, not sorcery — although with elder-world science the distinction becomes blurred. But then, to untutored minds the distinction is difficult to grasp, for this lies in understanding the forces at work, and in the laws they obey. For example, to produce a deadly sword to wield in battle, a master smith will use secrets of his craft to smelt choice iron into steel, forge steel into tempered blade, then balance, hone and haft the blade to the best of his art. Similarly, a wizard may utilize the secrets of his craft to forge a sword from starfire and incantations. Both swords seem magic to some club-swinging apeman, such as legend places on lands unknown to our civilization, but clearly one is born of science, the other spawned by sorcery. I leave it to you to judge which weapon would prove more potent."

"I'll trust to honest steel," snapped Teres, angered by Gerwein's gibes. "I've heard the legends of your magic swords, and they seem to serve their masters ill enough by the saga's end!"

"She took me literally," breathed Gerwein in polite wonder.

"I don't consider myself untutored," broke in Dribeck, himself annoyed. "Now that you've made your point, where does it lead us?"

"Your pardon, milord. It leads to a war of science against sorcery. And to our advantage, we understand something of the principles of Krelran science, while I doubt Kane is greatly acquainted with the sorcerous powers of Shenan."

"I'd not care to stake my life on that," Dribeck warned.

"But then you are. The important thing is that Krelran science borders on realms we humans consider sorcery — although perhaps my analogy of the savage persists. Science has laws; magic obeys laws. The source of the power each draws upon is different — or is it, if we question far enough? Matters too devious for our attention today. But what we understand of Bloodstone's power convinces us that it is closely akin to the laws of sorcery, and as such it is within our power to combat Kane through the magic of Shenan.

"This disk, which I see you recognize is not a mirror, was laid in the Temple vaults centuries ago, its use almost forgotten — as with so many other artifacts of our lost glory. It may be the defense you seek against Bloodstone's death beam."

Dribeck considered the metal disk skeptically.

"Lift it," she suggested.

It was chill to his touch — how cold he did not realize until his fingertips came away with stinging white stigmata. With painful effort he hooked his grip beneath an edge, and while its mass should not have been more than a few tens of pounds, the disk of unknown metal seemed to weigh as much as the stout oak table.

Her laughter was even colder. "A simulacrum, it would appear. We have rediscovered its secret, and it may be that Kane will soon find the power of Bloodstone is not invincible. And there is much else we have learned, which will dismay Kane when the battle begins. Of course, the rituals are complex, for the forces involved are of a major order. We will require time, many items that we know where to find.

"You will have to revoke the ban on human sacrifice, however, unless you wish to battle Kane with swords alone. Don't look so grim, milord. We also know where to find our virgins — frail blooms we've nurtured since birth. The details will not concern you; it is enough that no child known beyond these walls will die."

Grimly Dribeck speculated as to why the Temple maintained such an unspeakable reserve, when human sacrifice had long been forbidden... and how they had obtained the infants originally. Even less pleasant was consideration of the payment which the Temple would demand for their intervention. The line of thought sickened him, tainting the hope he had begun to experience. *But what choice was there?*

"I'm wondering what you mean to gain from this, Gerwein," he somberly conceded. "Altruism is not characteristic of the Temple, so I know you aren't helping me out of love for Selonari."

Gerwein might have been discussing the setting of a banquet table. "I'm not naive either, Dribeck. I'll expect an end to your obsessive attempts to tax the Temple, of course. Otherwise I won't demand any political concessions or promises that I know you'll renege on once the danger is past.

"Let the magic of Shenan's daughters save our land from the dread fate Kane intends for us. I think the people will remember well by whose hands they were spared. And I think they will be less enthusiastic for your calculating attacks upon our return to power after this. The game, as you well know, milord, is called prestige."

XXIII
Giants in the Dark Sky

"There's death in the air, and the men feel its breath," observed Dribeck dismally. "This is unlike the prelude to any battle I've ever fought."

The lord of Selonari stood at the sinking shores of Kranor-Rill as light faded. The familiar echoes of axes and shovels and the rumble of fighting men making camp were reassuring, although the usual raucous shouts seemed muffled and sober beneath the pall of unknown dread. Taking with him every man who would bear a weapon, Dribeck had begun his march south the dawn following his conference with Gerwein. Final preparations had taken little time, since he had already gathered his army to him, and the men were held at battle ready. By the close of the third day, their encampment was pitched and respectably fortified, a great wedge with apex positioned at the causeway's terminus.

"There's little joy in a battle where black sorcery and 'alien' science struggle like giants in the dark sky and brave men become no more than scurrying ants who die unnoticed beneath their tread," Teres responded somberly. She and Dribeck sought out one another's company these days, finding solace in their companionship. An unspoken admiration had grown between the two — so different in temperament, but alike in that both were outsiders in their social order.

Teres thought of herself now as ruler of Breimen, nor did the hundred or more refugees who joined her banner dispute her leadership — although it was questionable whether her legacy was anything greater than a pile of ruins. If she lived through this battle, if Bloodstone were destroyed... then she meant to see to Breimen. But first she must try to avenge its fall.

"Our chance of victory may hinge on Kane's attacking us," Dribeck again pointed out. "Here Gerwein's sorcery may offer protection from Kane's energy blasts — at least the men are willing to gamble on it. If we have to besiege Arellarti, I don't know how much help she can give us."

He threw a worn glance over the forest camp, with its earth and timber bulwarks, lines of tents, swarming knots of soldiers. Cook fires were just starting to twinkle beneath the darkening trees. "I doubt that Kane has any reliable means to reconnoiter — much beyond knowing we're here. His toads can't mingle with the men, and I'd like to think no human has sunk low enough to spy for him. Aside from its military merit, I'm hoping this wedge formation will give him an inaccurate profile of our true strength. If we can play upon his confidence in his own power, it may be he'll decide to attack first and avoid the possibility of our projected siege wreaking havoc upon the city he's gone to such pains to restore."

"Think Kane will attack tonight?" queried Crempra, who had wandered over with Asbraln, the latter a fierce and aged eagle in battle gear that had last seen combat a decade ago.

"Reasonable to expect — if he'll attack at all," Dribeck concluded. "The longer he waits, the stronger we can build our fortifications. Besides, he's a creature of the night, and the darkness will work in favor of the Rillyti. Although I doubt they can outflank us in our position, the swamp creatures prefer stealth to direct confrontation. He planned his attack on Breimen to occur before dawn, remember."

"At night, when Ommem's power ebbs to its lowest," commented Teres. "Kane is no stranger to the occult world; it may be he thought to counter any appeal my city might have made to the shining god of Wollendan. If so, this night is the dark of the moon — the time Kane hinted Bloodstone's power was greatest. How will your moon goddess Shenan serve you tonight?"

"Gerwein warned us that the time is not propitious, but that's beyond us. However, she still believes their magic will be potent." Dribeck looked toward the tents of the priestesses.

Teres followed his gaze. With surprising efficiency, the daughters of Shenan had reorganized the voluminous paraphernalia with which they had loaded several wagons to overturning. Their every requirement was immediately fulfilled by order of Lord Dribeck, and a small knoll had been cleared of trees for them. Soldiers labored to set up their tents and equipment, surrounded by busy feminine figures clad in varying styles from the simple tunics of acolytes to the more elegant gowns of the ranking priestesses. At the peak of the knoll, struggling workmen were hoisting the eerie metal disk to its mounting place atop a low stone altar. The altar of dark, unflawed stone had been transported from the Temple's depths — whose vaults had yielded other things, as well, that were strangers to the light of day.

Teres frowned at the pale-skinned maidens whom the priestesses quickly hustled into the tents, leading them by the manacles which linked wrists and neck. Their steps were resigned, but their blinking eyes mirrored fear. "And we declare our cause more just than Kane's!" she spat in disgust. "I wonder if our victory will be worth its cost!"

Dribeck's face was determined, although there was dismay in his eyes. "As you've said, there's little joy in this battle. Our weapons must be iniquitous if we are to avert a greater evil still."

The twilight deepened, merged into night. Cordons of sentries patrolled nervously. Nor did sleep come to the encampment, where uneasy soldiers made whispers as they honed steel. The demons of battle were stirring the night breeze with their leathery wings, and there was not a man who did not sense the building tension.

"He comes!" breathed Gerwein, her eyes glazed with concentration, and no man questioned her knowledge.

"Drawn by the scent of your sorcery," mused Teres half aloud, hackles tingling at the weird spectacle which unfolded before them.

The torches flashed and flared. Rippling like pennants in the chill breeze were the priestesses' silken robes. Tents flapped like angry wings beyond the torchlit circle. Teres shivered, not entirely from the wind, yet with battle imminent, she disdained the warm but hampering folds of her cloak. Dribeck spoke softly to Ainon, who left to attend to the lighting of bonfires erected along the fringes of Kranor-Rill.

Tied across the altar, the naked girl writhed without hope., She could not be much past her mid-teens — an innocent, frail flower nurtured in the Temple's secret halls, to be plucked at the moment her keepers judged the bloom to be ready. The fear had left her now, and she seemed to lie entranced by the priestess's rising chant. Teres tried to console herself with the thought that this girl had never really known life, but the revulsion she felt did not diminish. The girl had never uttered a cry.

Higher, more insistent, rang the incantation, now in a language Teres had never before heard. Gerwein's slim fingers dashed curious substances into the flaming brazier, which oozed bittersweet vapors that curled like mist over the priestesses' contorted dance. The girl lay still, seemingly asleep — but for the too rapid rise and fall of her breasts. Gerwein tossed a final spray of powder into the flame, then with a harsh cry drove her fist to just short of the girl's left breast, though Teres would have sworn her hand was empty. The sacrifice's eyes started wide, her mouth convulsed into a silent scream, her body strained against the fetters — and in that instant the brazier spat a shower of sparks and went out!

The metal disk had suddenly blazed luminous in that moment. A ghostly streamer of light, shining from its pale surface, fell upon the contorted sacrifice. For a second it enswathed her staring figure; a phantom shape seemed to swirl through the luminance. Softly the wraith of light withdrew from the girl, withdrew into the circle of polished metal, now glowing brightly. Gold, pale light of death. *How like the moon*, thought Teres in awe.

On the altar lay the lifeless husk of a girl.

Gerwein's lovely face bore a cold, cruel smile of triumph, though she was perhaps a trifle shaken by her spell.

Shouts of alarm sounded from the sentries.

"Now let your sorcery protect us, if it can!" gritted Dribeck as he rushed to lead his men. A cordon of Temple guards closed a shield about the priestesses' knoll.

The effulgence of Arellarti was even brighter, Teres observed — a baleful green luminescence through the ever present mists. Like a ribbon of clotting blood, even the stones of the causeway radiated with pulsant light. Through the fog she could see hulking shapes that shambled along the uncanny road-way, dark shadows against the crimson radiance.

Warning shouts from close at hand. The flaring bonfires exposed scores of the monstrous batrachians rising from the muck and slime of the swamp. Kane had deployed his minions in a stealthy advance. Now, as they swept onto the forest earth, he brought up his main column to follow the initial surprise with crushing force.

"There are your targets!" bellowed Crempra's strident voice. "Against the light! Give it to them now!" Questing arrows hissed through the night.

Roars of pain and of rage told of the archers' accuracy, even when the darkness cloaked the bite of their shafts. Murderous swords raised, the Rillyti emerged from the swamp in great leaping strides. Arrows rattled and streaked across their gleaming armor, penetrating only with a direct hit at close range, while others lodged with crippling effect in the tough hide of exposed limbs.

"Try to hit their eyes!" advised Crempra, noting the luminous reflection of their widened pupils in the firelight. His arrow flew true to its mark and brought a Rillyti crashing to the mud, clawing at the intolerable agony that lanced through its brain.

To the bulwarks the swamp creatures rushed, oblivious of the fallen in their lust to kill. With fierce bellows they struck the barrier and vaulted over in powerful bounds. Men died beneath their alien-forged blades or answered their threat with equally deadly steel.

Quickly Crempra pulled back his archers from the overrun trenchline to give way to the heavy infantry that surged forward to halt the onrushing Rillyti. A venom-coated spear tugged at his sleeve. His heart caught in fear until he made certain his arm bore no scratch. Gingerly he cut away the tainted area of torn cloth, then hurried to reposition his archers.

From the causeway, the main bulk of the Rillyti horde was issuing into the forest. There the point of the wedge confronted them, and intense fighting raged in seesaw fashion. The archers maintained withering fire onto the lus-trous roadway, taking heavy toll despite the bronze alloy armor of the am-phibians. But as increasing numbers of the Rillyti gained the high ground, supported by those who had spread out through the swamp, combat along the apex of the wedge waxed fierce and bloody. Each time the batrachians appeared on the verge of overrunning the line of fortification, a fresh surge of steel and sinew would drive them back again over the red litter of death. In the howling melee, the archers were helpless, and further advance by the Rillyti threatened to push them beyond bowshot of the causeway.

Something strange and deadly strode down the causeway. A demon of green flame shimmered through the mists and struck terror in three thou-sand hearts with the dread promise of searing death. Arrows touched the eerie figure without halting his inexorable advance. The Rillyti roared wel-come, drew away from the beleaguered encampment.

Kane had come. The Master of Bloodstone had come to destroy those who dared challenge his power. And behind him marched the main force of his inhuman army, held in reserve while his vanguard tested Dribeck's defenses.

Kane extended his left arm, and courage failed the warriors along the bulwarks. Desperately they fled the ground they had so bravely contested a moment before. A lance of destroying energy hurled itself from his flame-wreathed fist. With a thunderous concussion, the front line of Dribeck's fortifications leaped into air, showering the night sky with a hail of smouldering fragments and baked clods of earth. Those who had not fled shrieked in final brief agony as the emerald lash fell upon them. Again the terror of ancient Earth reached out its incandescent claws to claim the souls of men in its pitiless fury.

Confident in his power, Kane stalked forward. This night he meant to crush all ordered resistance within this region — to extend his rule of fear across the conquered city-states. Once it became certain that to resist Bloodstone was to die, Kane expected to gather an army of men to replace the Rillyti, warriors whose allegiance would follow the tide of victory.

Bloodstone whispered that it was only hours from the fulfillment of its design. Only a few days had been needed to mount its energy potential to an even higher level than before commencement of the attack on Breimen. Under these conditions, even while he sensed the presence of sorcery, recognized that Dribeck's position was far stronger here than were he to besiege Arellarti, Kane in his arrogance determined to annihilate the Selonari force on its own terms. This was to be an object lesson in the futility of resistance to Bloodstone's incalculable might.

The Selonari had thrown up hasty fortifications, which checked the Rillyti thrust for the initial moment. The Master of Bloodstone intended to obliterate the entire forest encampment with his searing blasts of energy and to loose his ravening batrachian army upon the disordered survivors. The dread lance of flame shot forth from the ring, and the jutting prow of bulwarks flared into withering destruction.

A weird and unexpected barrier abruptly stood before him. In a soaring arc, the sorcerous disk lofted itself across the embattled encampment, seeking the alien force in obedience to the priestesses' conjuration. No visible agency moved the shining disk; like a miniature image of the moon, it swung across the nighted sky, hovering at the height of a tall man to obstruct Kane's passage.

Kane paused, for a second uncertain. Dead-white as the full moon of winter, the cold circle of light hung in the air before him, a challenge to his advance. Here loomed sorcery, potent sorcery whose nature was unknown to Kane. That its presence threatened him was undeniable, but the character and the potential of the menace he could not guess.

Destroy it! came the sneering whisper to his mind. No longer hesitant, Kane struck. A bolt of shimmering violence streaked from the bloodstone ring and speared the center of the hovering disk.

The circle of light seemed to vibrate, its luminance more brilliant for an instant, like an inconceivable silver gong that when struck, emitted a frequency far beyond human perception. It should have flared into a spewing mass of fused metal. Instead, its burnished surface bore no blemish.

Kane recoiled, his arm weak with numbing chill. The energy screen wavered, almost extinguished. With vampirish greed, the pale disk had absorbed the destroying beam of energy, sucked in the stream of power, with a lusting hunger for more. Almost it seemed to reach for him with an awesome thirst.

Feeling the first shadow of alarm, Kane returned to the attack. Again the lance of green fire leaped forth — brighter, more powerful than before. A mighty wall of stone would have been pulverized to molten cinders by the blast, yet the saucer of light only increased its pale brilliance. Prepared for its reaching hunger, Kane's shimmering energy shield braced him against the leech-like force.

Kane retreated, aware of the peril he faced. The soldiers had paused in their flight, daring to hope that Selonari's magic promised succor. Shaken by the failure of their god to destroy this sorcerous shield, the Rillyti croaked nervously. The battle held its breath.

Angrily Kane signed to his servants, wondering if physical force might prove effective. Spears and clubs hurtled against the lustrous disk. Its cold effulgence grew more intense, and the missiles that streaked toward its surface silently vanished at the instant of impact.

His mind grappled with the dilemma. Thus far, this wizard's shield seemed to be only a defensive weapon — although this made it dangerous enough. Without the destructive power of the bloodstone ring, his inhuman allies would be heavily outnumbered by Dribeck's army. Victory could easily desert him.

The torchlit knoll drew his attention — the brightly patterned pavilions beneath the Temple's pennant, ridged by heavy guard. Fantastically gowned priestesses postured about the glowing altar, their distant chant inaudible, but their attitude of invocation expressive. Recognizing the source of the power which challenged him, Kane responded decisively. Turning from the metal disk, he directed a tremendous flame of energy toward the figures on the knoll.

Faster than thought, the luminous circle flashed before him. The destroying emerald bolt struck the interposing disk and was absorbed into the sorcerous shield. Reeling at the numbing, suctioning force, Kane redirected his attack. Again and again the lance of death leaped from his fist. Relentless as a shadow, the hovering disk followed his every movement, drawing the searing energy into its being with magnetic certainty.

Kane sensed Bloodstone's baffled rage. *Destroy it! Tonight my power grows almost limitless!*

Determined to end this impasse, Kane turned upon the hanging circle of light. No probing test of strength, no intercepted thrust, this! Now let their sorcery feel the awesome might of Bloodstone!

A blinding torrent of coruscating power poured from Kane's fist, energy far greater than that which had shattered Malchion's fortress, beyond that which had blasted a deep channel through the width of Kranor-Rill. Into the hovering disk tore the full destructive force of Bloodstone. Kane vanished in the consuming flow of energy — a humanoid point of incandescence that stood at the gate of this devastating release of unimaginable power.

Incredibly, the metal disk withstood the onslaught, defied a continuous beam of destructive force whose diameter was greater than that of the pale saucer. Now indeed it seemed a diminutive simulacrum of the moon. Its dead-pale light waxed brighter and brighter — reached out. *Was the disk not growing in size as well?*

Suddenly it came to Kane that the luminous disk was not merely absorbing the energy blasts — it fed upon them! Bloodstone's incalculable energies were not overwhelming it — rather, the simulacrum was drawing power from the rays. Like an inconceivable vampire, the disk sucked in the cosmic energies of Bloodstone, grew larger, brighter, more powerful. *Hungrier.*

Its silver-white luminescence crept toward Kane, reached out for him, as the blinding disk drew closer, *closer,* ravening down the torrent of energy that fed its lust. Kane felt the cold brush of its caress now; even through the energy web, he felt its deadly, devouring chill. The pale light of a demon moon swept over him, relentlessly seeking to engulf him in its consuming vortex.

Kane cried out. Bloodstone understood the trap into which it had fallen — knew this vampirish simulacrum was feeding on the very power that should have destroyed...

With shattering finality, the shrieking barrage of energy ceased. The explosive silence was a shock; eyes blinded by the incandescent torrent saw painful afterimages, stars of blackness.

The moon disk hung alone on the causeway. Of the Master of Bloodstone there was no trace.

"What happened?" demanded Dribeck. "Is Kane dead?"

"If not dead, then defeated... for the moment," Teres put forward grimly. "I think Bloodstone snatched him back to Arellarti at the last instant — Kane mentioned that the causeway is an extension of Bloodstone's power radius. If so, we'll likely see more of Kane before the night is spent."

Dribeck glanced toward the hovering moon disk. "If he returns, our shield awaits him. For now, his army still threatens us."

Leaderless, the Rillyti had shaken off their stunned hesitation, so that once more they pressed their assault. Fearful to pass close to the luminous disk which had defeated their master's seemingly invincible power, the batrachians clambered from the causeway short of the menacing light and churned through the fringe of the morass to reach the dry ground. Purposefully they advanced, the fearsome legions of Kranor-Rill, obedient to Bloodstone's silent command.

Now the combat surged in fury. Men poured back to the yet smoking ruins of the bulwarks, blades slashing with a fierce will. The power of Bloodstone was broken; the all-conquering bolts of destruction had been defeated by the magic of their goddess. After the banishment of such horror, near hysteria gripped the soldiers. Even the once terrifying Rillyti seemed no more than misshapen, bestial swordsmen after this cataclysmic confrontation of alien science and dread sorcery.

No milling rabble of sleep-fogged, unprepared soldiers, no fear-crazed mob, unmanned by Bloodstone's murderous power. These were battle-ready troops, fully armed and fighting with feral spirit, from seasoned veteran to fuzz-cheeked youth. The Rillyti now were committed to desperate combat, pitted against men who fought for more than life — who battled to preserve their land and people from Bloodstone's evil shadow.

To the smouldering bulwarks the batrachians rushed, their golden blades aflame with hatred for mankind. In their savage brains burned the unrelenting command: *Kill the human intruders! Kill the soft-fleshed weaklings! Kill them all!*

The struggle swept over the sundered fortifications and drove the men back as ever more Rillyti lurched from the swamp. Armored as they were, their weapons of deadlier reach than the blades of men, the bufanoid killers tore through the line of soldiers like blood-lusting devils. Their greater stature, their inhuman strength — coupled with a total disregard for their personal safety — made the creatures the equal of any four human warriors.

Steel against alien bronze! Steaming human gore clotted with cool bufanoid blood in spreading stigmata across the torn earth. The soldiers fought doggedly, attacking the amphibians in small bands, while the Rillyti battled each for himself. To the humans was the advantage of intelligence over the bestial savages, and they were further aided by their greater agility. The awkward amphibians were unstoppable in head-on combat, when their powerful slashes could batter down any guard, split a man half in two. But if their vicious lunges could be evaded, a quick blade might thrust deep and recover before the creature could parry. Once the strategy proved itself, soldiers harried the towering monsters like a snapping, snarling pack, engaged their weapons long enough to let another man swing a hamstringing blow. Crippled, not long did a batrachian flop upon the forest earth before vengeful blades hacked out its life.

In uncanny, desperate battle the degenerate remnants of an elder race — one that had mastered the stars — locked in mortal strife with the young race who boasted to be Earth's new masters. In darkness they fought, beneath the deeper shadow of the forest, where the wan light of the stars, the smoky flare of the fires dared not creep. Chaos ruled the battlefield as combatants slashed blindly, swinging wild blows, dying from unseen wounds. Here the Rillyti had an edge, for their bulging eyes pierced the darkness more surely than human sight. But their looming bulk could not be mistaken, even in the near absence of light. In blind ferocity man grappled batrachian, slew or was slain. The ground became strewn with the fallen, though no man knew for certain the number of the dead, nor witnessed the manner of their passing.

Crempra had scrambled up a tree early in the strife, and from this vantage he could view such of the swirling struggle as could be discerned. Dribeck's nimble cousin was an indifferent swordsman, and the roaring melee was not to his liking. Five quivers of arrows dangling in near reach, he braced himself on his perch and loosed his bow with deadly effect on any Rillyti unlucky enough to enter the light of the bonfires.

So it happened that the gigantic batrachian whose half-deflected stroke had driven Teres to her knees in a daze halted its killing blow at the top of its arc and howled in death agony as a feathered shaft spouted black ichor from its eye. Teres rolled away from the toppling monster, scarcely taking time to wonder at this last-instant succor.

The harried remnants of her soldiers closed about her once again, while she shook the fog from her head and recovered her sword. The blade was sticky with bufanoid gore, and the shield she bore was chopped and beaten. Only her sudden speed had spared her life in numerous duels with shambling assailants thrice her weight. Undaunted by yet another brush with death, she cursed her men for pausing to rest when the murderers of their nation waited to die. Her words spurred them on. Led by this vengeful she-wolf -- whose snarling face showed the scar of past combat, but no shadow of the fatigue that tortured them now — the haggard handful of Breimen's perished army stormed back into the struggle.

Dribeck fought shoulder to shoulder with Asbraln, who made it evident that he considered Selonari's lord an unblooded stripling consigned to his protection. There was yet firm strength in the aged shoulders — or Dribeck had always thought of him as aged — and the doughty chamberlain swung his archaic two-handed broadsword with greater skill than Dribeck could equal. The younger man forgot his chagrin when twice Asbraln's heavier weapon struck back the Rillyti blade that would have ripped Dribeck apart.

The Selonari lord had waded into the thick of the battle, his personal guard thinning as the fighting roared and clashed through the night. Strategy? Only to kill — to kill your foe before you died in his place. There could be no other strategy; the darkness cloaked this war to the death, and with both forces totally committed, it was a grappling contest of brutal ferocity. Dribeck loathed the primitive savagery of the battle — it offended his reasoning nature. But his mind now abandoned its concern with tactics, so that he fought with the instinctive logic of survival.

Who lived? Who lay dead? The living were anonymous writhing shapes in the darkness nearby, bestial curses and yells beyond the close perimeter of vision. The dead — they were the limp and slippery debris that rolled beneath your boot. Only where the priestesses' knoll shed a circle of light could a fair glimpse of the battle be caught. There, Dribeck noted in relief, the cordon of soldiers still formed an unbroken ring, bulwarked now by scores of the slain.

Long ago he had planned this battle with care, counted the numbers, directed the preparations. Then it had seemed that his army well outnumbered Kane's minions, that it was only a matter of tempting Kane to come to him, that without Bloodstone the battle would be fought on human terms. But this smothering darkness made victory an invisible prize, and to know whose hand now closed upon it required speculation for which he had no time. The puddles of light gave no more than tormenting hints. For all Dribeck could be certain, he and his men battled alone, an island lost in the Rillyti tide.

Asbraln staggered and fell back beneath an amphibian's charge. His broadsword rang as it blocked the descending blade of bronze, but the man was winded. Automatically Dribeck lashed out his sword and severed the webbed fist halfway up the forearm. The creature howled, blinded him with its spurting blood, and as Dribeck hesitated, the spear in its other hand skittered past his shield. Its point had force enough behind it to tear through the mail tunic and gash his twisting side.

With a gasp of dread, Asbraln laid open the Rillyti's belly with an upward thrust through its crotch. Ignoring the monster's death throes, the chamberlain clutched his lord's shoulders. The other heard Asbraln cry out the name of Dribeck's father, whose name the older man seldom spoke. "The spear! Milord, you're a dead man!" groaned Asbraln.

Dribeck wiped the stinging blood from his eyes, dully waited for the first searing lancination of the Rillyti venom to creep through his limbs. But fatigue was the only agony, and the shallow gash on his ribs seemed less a pain than this breathless weariness. His men were watching him in stunned pity. It seemed appropriate that his final words should be such to stir future generations, if he could utter something immortal before consciousness left him. "Well, damn it," he muttered, unable to compose his thoughts.

Asbraln had recovered the spear, raised it in grief-clumsy hands. He laughed in a choked rumble. "One of our own," he announced, pointing to the iron spearpoint.

With a shrug, Dribeck dismissed the incident. Constant confrontation with violent death this night left him too numb to sense any realistic emotion. Logically he understood that chance had again spared him a grisly death, but he was too drained to feel any particular relief.

The wounds of combat were fading. It came to him that his panting company had stood for several minutes, slumped from fatigue, binding their wounds. No Rillyti had challenged them. Voices of others sounded close at hand. Torches were flickering across the tangled battlefield.

"I think," Dribeck hazarded, "that once it gets light, we may discover that we've won this battle."

But there were other eyes that looked upon the conflict, alien sight to which the darkness posed no barrier — a malevolent force that pierced the night and perceived the torn and death-laden battlefield. It saw that its army had been overcome, its fierce legions strewn upon the bodies of their slayers, scattered in flight into the fastnesses of the swamp.

The Rillyti are broken. Your power is checked. How shall I defend these walls when the sun brings their army against us?

The sun will find none but the dead. In a few hours all shall be completed. Already my being courses with the driving energies of the cosmos, so that their puny sorceries have only for a moment thwarted me. Did you imagine that I have revealed to you all of the power that lies within me? Now you shall know, arrogant man, that there are yet secrets which defy even your conception!

Now through the forest swept the army of Selonari. Carrying torches, they searched among the trees, pausing amidst the piled dead to give aid to a comrade, to dispatch a floundering batrachian. Outnumbered beyond hope, the fragmented

Rillyti army slunk away into Kranor-Rill, driven like scum before a cresting wave. Desperate knots of men and bufanoids yet struggled in the darkness, but when their fellows came upon them, steel gleamed in a score of hands, and the duel became a slaughter. For all that, the human advance was not an unbroken flow. Countless vortices of swirling violence marked the suicidal stand of some blood-maddened batrachian, whose savage blade might rend and tear, long after it seemed possible for any creature so wounded to fight on.

Such islands of strife, however vicious, could not stem the crushing advance. Pressing upon the swampy land's perimeter, the worn but jubilant troops watched the last of the Rillyti turn and flee, their mindless ferocity finally mastered by human might.

Then struck gibbering horror — inconceivable term that drove sanity from the frightened souls of men.

Phantom shapes were emerging from the mist, streaming along the sullen stones of the causeway — an army of maggots vomited over the dead tongue of some impossible serpent. Spectral figures of green flame they were — shadowy creatures whose substance was the coruscant energy of Bloodstone. Like a rippling point of fire they flowed across the rubrous stone, an unending army of captive souls.

The shadow creatures of Bloodstone. A demon array of shimmering flame — monstrous shapes of things dead, but denied the freedom of dissolution. Their semi-translucent bodies took strange and horrid forms, some terrifying in that their alien figuration was of ages beyond human memory, others equally abominable for the dread familiarity of their aspect.

There were creatures who resembled the Rillyti, but of taller, more erect stature, with limbs of more subtle build, and peaked skulls of intelligent mien. *Reptilian.* These were the Krelran, the centuries-dead builders of Arellarti. Nor were theirs the only shades of the vanished races of elder Earth. Octopoid monsters writhed forward; clearly the six thick tentacles which slithered down from bloated trunks provided unnatural locomotion for creatures that hinted of the ocean's black depths; two whiplike tentacles extended menacingly from the humped shoulders of each trunk, above which sprouted a rounded head bearing six lidless eyes like a coronet, and a toothless maw that gaped like a death wound where the face should have been. Other bizarre shapes, fewer in number, joined the onrushing horde. Chitinous spider-like creatures, large as a horse, clicked across the stones on four spindly limbs. Four more such limbs thrust forward, metallic claws clashing, from the upward-curling cephalothorax. Fluttering through the air on moth wings of fire came humanoid beings whose angular bodies were clothed in shaggy scales, whose faces were set with great compound-eyes like glittering mosaic. Hairy beasts like misshapen apes slouched forward, long arms swinging to the ground.

Here were creatures of the distant past, shadow slaves of Bloodstone since the dawn of Arellarti. They seemed to be fiery wraiths in the life image of their millennia-lost bodies. Such was not so for the teeming bulk of their army. These were shapes which appeared withered and twisted with gnawing decay — distorted, skeletal things, molded of the same shimmering energy, which gave them the aspect of forms enshrouded by devouring flame. Most of these corpse-like shapes were batrachian, an eerie devolution ranging from the elder Krelran to the bestial Rillyti. But many were the spectral images of human lamia, whose energy-wreathed silhouettes included brutish dawn races, along with scores of men, women, even children, of the present peoples of the Southern Lands.

For Kane had not been altogether accurate when he dismissed the Rillyti sacrifices as useless superstition. These were creatures whose souls had been stolen by Bloodstone's searing tongue of energy, enslaved throughout the centuries, imperfect shades of those whose souls had been offered to the monolithic crystal as it lay dormant — crudely fed to their god through the Rillyti's unholy sacrificial rites. But there were many other shapes in this army of abominations, and these were somehow the most terrifying of all.

Marching shoulder to alien shoulder with these creatures of horror came the naked figures of many men — those whose souls Bloodstone had captured through the destroying power of Kane's ring. Horribly familiar were many of these shapes, some whose blackened bodies yet lay warm upon the blasted bulwarks. The dead of Breimen were there — men who had died from the searing energies of the bloodstone ring — as were the soldiers of Selonari who had fallen when Teres revealed Kane's treachery to Dribeck. Death at the burning touch of Bloodstone was far more hideous than ever it had seemed, for those who died under its caress of shimmering energy fed their souls to its unhallowed power. Bloodstone thirsted for organic life as well as cosmic force…

Teres shuddered with loathing. Among the dread horde of Bloodstone's shadow slaves she had recognized the glowing profile of Lutwion. And although full realization of this horror now menacing them did not come at once, fragments of understanding suggested themselves to the men, threatened to plunge frighted reason into the protective darkness of insanity.

Through the oily mists rushed the lamia of writhing energy — naked, silent, eyes staring pools of flame. Their numbers were myriad, but they bore no weapons save the outstretched limbs that blazed with glimmering fire. Shaking off its pall of fear, Dribeck's army awaited this new horror; a thousand grim faces prepared to learn whether steel could master these dread specters of elder evil.

In a sudden wave they burst upon the awestricken men, a grotesque spume of emerald and crimson-veined shadows. Swords slashed and thrust into their macabre vanguard. Bodies that appeared phantasmal now proved substantial. Resistance met the searching blades, though not the touch of flesh. Steel sheared through the wraithlike figures with the sickening feel of clinging jelly — gristle-boned, repulsive substance whose consistency suggested an unthinkable congealment of noxious mist. Bloodless phantoms with rubbery strength in their limbs, fangs and talons like sharpened horn.

The shadow creatures would not die.

They yielded to steel's ripping might, but they would not fall. With mindless fury they threw themselves upon the soldiers, submitted to their desperate blades with awful disregard for individual preservation. Swords sliced through them, their wielders overbalanced by the uncanny resistance the weapons struck. But grievous wounds saw neither blood nor nameless ichor, nor yet did the creatures falter in the face of any number of mortal wounds.

Bloodstone's enormously amplified power, now spiraling to impossible limits with each passing moment, had achieved the cosmic transmutation of energy into matter. The crystal entity had clothed its captive souls in a semblance of matter — an inconceivable substance of primal nature, whose characteristics were neither wholly of matter nor of energy — a blasphemous caricature of life, which, not living, could not die.

Teres had led her decimated company to the front line of this hideous attack. Yelling in revulsion as she thrust, she plunged her sword into the unfeeling breast of one who had been her countryman days before. The blade darted through, then back. Barely staggering from its impact, the specter reached for her. Teres recoiled in dismay and slashed at the grasping arms. The blade sprang through, severed one entire arm and the other at elbow. The butchered limbs dropped, but her assailant stepped closer, bloodless stumps waving. With a burst of loathing, she lopped off the creature's head. It bounded to the earth, but the decapitated figure yet groped for her. She froze for a stunned instant, and the apparition lunged for her. Teres sidestepped and slashed through its thigh. The leg fell away, precipitating the maimed shadow creature to the ground. Blindly it hunched forward on its belly.

In horror Teres saw that her comrades were likewise beset. A buffet knocked her sprawling, as one of the moth-winged creatures soared past. Behind her the lepidopteran struck, and bore a soldier to the earth. Its taloned hands gashed his face and throat as they grappled, while the man's blade stabbed ineffectually. Another shadow creature — a withered batrachian shape — reached down for her. Teres slashed for its legs and rolled agilely from under its toppling weight. There was nothing insubstantial about these monsters' strength, she realized, hacking the lamia apart as from the ground it clutched for her.

Another human shade — *did it seem familiar?* Wildly Teres swung her blade in a downward arc, clove through head and shoulders, through chest to belly level, before the rubbery flesh stopped the steel. She yanked free her sword, then doubted her eyes… as the two segments swung back together, sealing the ghastly wound. Setting her teeth, she chopped out again and dismembered the thing.

The shimmering form of a young girl stalked toward her. Teres remembered her near death upon Bloodstone's altar, and horror stayed her arm. Something at that instant clutched her boot, and Teres looked down to see a dismembered hand had caught her ankle in vise-like grip. The ground was crawling with severed segments of the shadow creatures, writhing blindly forward with maniacal intent. She hacked at the repellent thing, parted forearm from wrist; spider-like, the hand climbed onto her calf. Then the girlish apparition leaped upon her, clawed fingers raking for her eyes, grappling for her sword. Bitterly Teres repented her involuntary hesitance and fended off the shadow girl's attack. There was cold strength in the arm that sought to wrest free Teres's blade, and the claws that gouged her cheek were dangerously real. Twisting, Teres planted a boot in her assailant's belly and drove her back. The jolt dislodged the scrambling hand from its purchase on her thigh, and for a moment Teres tore free. Pitiless now, her sword slashed again and again to dash the decay-pocked specter piecemeal upon the earth.

Retreating to regain her breath and conquer the nausea that shook her, Teres looked upon a battlefield of nightmarish terror. In a seething stream, the shadow creatures of Bloodstone stormed across the burning roadway. Surely only a small fraction of their myriad had engaged the human army thus far, and there seemed no way the thousand or more warriors could long stand in the face of such overwhelming numbers. Already they were falling back beneath the irresistible pressure of the energy phantoms' relentless advance.

Arrows, spears were useless. Fear-driven swords were taking a terrific toll on the weaponless foe, but to what avail? Hacked and dismembered, the shadow creatures continued to wriggle forward, driving the soldiers before them. The forest floor was alight with loathsome scuttling things. A malignant intelligence directed their onslaught, so that even the disjoined fragments conspired against the embattled humans. A lepidopterous torso, limbless and decapitated, yet fluttered about the line of combat, striking the unwary onto the outstretched grasp of the enemy, until someone sent it plummeting on sheared wings. Near her, a fallen soldier died with throat ripped open by the vomerine fangs of a severed bufanoid head. A mangled torso rolled beneath another soldier's retreating step and pitched him onto the horror-covered ground. An ape-like shade, sundered across its belly, continued its horrid advance with torso swinging between hairy arms, while its hips shambled off at another angle.

Men were dying under the shadow creatures' assault. The glowing figures could not be killed — only disabled through arduous tactics, which drew a man's efforts while more of the creatures rushed upon him. The demented wraiths were swarming over the desperate warriors — clawing, biting, choking the life from their victims, oblivious to the wounds that tore their unnatural flesh. The plight of Selonari's army was enough imperiled, with just the human and batrachian phantoms to contend against, but the terrifying presence of these other creatures from Earth's lost antiquity had shattering impact.

The monstrous octopoids were deadliest. Their bulk was over half again that of a man, much of that in the powerful tentacles which lashed out to crush and strangle. Severed, the serpentine tentacles slithered forward like fiery pythons, no whit less dangerous until chopped into stubby fragments. Equally menacing, although few in number, were the arachnoid creatures with their darting speed and chitin-edged claws. The moth-winged specters, also but a few, presented danger in their unexpected attack from the air, while the taloned digits and stabbing mouth parts made them formidable opponents. And the shaggy ape creatures carried strength enough in their slouching frames to rip a man apart.

This then was the hideous battle that raged into the timber — the soldiers yielding ground grudgingly, driven back nonetheless. The relentless onslaught of the shadow creatures slithered over a new litter of bodies, corpses distinguishable from those slain earlier by their mangled aspect. And although dawn was yet hours distant, the night was broken by the eerie, evil luminescence of the shadow hordes.

Teres caught a glimpse of Dribeck in the emerald radiance; the Selonari lord was fighting gamely in the face of blackest defeat. Wanting suddenly to stand beside him, she cut her way through the tireless van of Bloodstone's spectral creatures.

A blade slashed toward her, a clumsy stroke so unexpected she barely did parry. Her astonishment vanished quickly at the new threat as she engaged her opponent's bronze alloy sword, a Rillyti weapon wielded now by a hand that weeks ago was human. Thinking ruefully of the shield she had earlier discarded for long dagger — the shield had been useless against bare-handed assailants — Teres lunged to attack. Her foe parried clumsily; evidently its guiding intelligence was too limited for the intricacies of swordplay. Instinctively she thrust her swordtip through its chest — and almost lost an ear, when the lamia's awkward slash followed what should have been a mortal wound. Teres cursed her momentary lapse — battle fatigue was dulling her thoughts — and lopped off the extended sword arm. As she methodically disabled the creature, she noted that elsewhere along the line of combat were the phantom shapes taking up fallen Rillyti weapons. Those of steel they left untouched. She grimaced. Even with their clumsy swordplay, the creatures would be deadly opponents, invulnerable as they were to all but wounds that severed completely.

Dribeck went down. A crawling arm, sundered at the shoulder, had clamped webbed fingers upon his ankle. He swore, slashing idly at the dragging weight, as a man-shaped phantom hurtled upon him. Hindered by the tenacious grasp, Dribeck lost his balance and fell, the shadow creature struggling atop him, hands locked about the man's throat. Dribeck's steel sliced through the glowing arms, and his sudden lunge knocked the unsupported creature away from him. He struggled to his feet, but the strangling hands still closed about his long neck. Fighting for breath, he hacked the forearms off at the wrists — to no effect. In panic Dribeck dropped his blade, clutched the spectral hands in his own, sought to tear them from their choking grip. The rubbery flesh-substance was slippery under his sweaty fingers.

Dribeck's tongue was starting to protrude when Teres reached him. Those who remained of his personal guard were too hard-pressed to note their lord's distress. Despairing of breaking the stranglehold, she set her dagger point between thumb and forefinger and sawed through the tough flesh. Unable to appose, the disjointed segments fell free, and she flung them off into the darkness.

Weak but still conscious, Dribeck staggered to his feet, while Teres beat down the assault of another shadow slave. He retrieved his sword and, supported by Teres, withdrew from the battle to recover his strength.

"My thanks, Teres!" he gasped, massaging his bruised throat. "But I think you may have saved a life that will never see the dawn! The men fight well, but fatigue now tortures us all. One by one, we fall to the ceaseless onslaught of this demon horde — nor do we rise again with the unnatural vitality that our deathless enemy draws upon."

"Will you call retreat?" she suggested. "We can still escape."

Lord Dribeck shook his head wearily. "A useless escape. Kane's power has already exceeded my most pessimistic calculations. Another hour, another day… who can say! Kane boasted that Bloodstone's power would become limitless! It's likely that this battle will be the last chance mankind will ever know to escape the shadow of Bloodstone. While a handful of us survives, I dare not throw away that slim chance of victory!

"We've pushed Kane hard, gained ground on him. We nullified his deadliest weapon, handed his Rillyti army a bloody defeat and we're taking toll of this phantom horde. I can't count how many men we've lost, but I'm still hoping we can outlast these murderous shadows somehow. Butcher them all to wriggling fragments, and maybe we can walk over the glowing scum to find Arellarti without further guards.

"And there's still Gerwein," he added. The priestesses' knoll thrust like a bastion along the faltering Selonari lines, but the advancing shadow creatures had not overrun it. About the camp of Shenan's daughters, Dribeck had concentrated the bulk of his troops, for he judged that their sorcery might well hold the only chance for victory. Beleaguered as never before, the cordon battled valiantly to withstand the merciless assault. Dribeck could discern Gerwein's tall figure, leading the frantic priestesses through some unguessable incantations. Still white forms, stretched upon the ground, attested to the altar's black hunger. Gerwein, then, had not accepted defeat.

"I have my breath again," declared Dribeck, squaring his lean shoulders. "It's pointless to seek to maintain our battle line any further, and I don't want the Temple's hill to be cut off. Come on, we'll retract our line to the knoll and make a stand against its base."

Teres did not listen. Her eyes were wide with insupportable horror.

Following her gaze, Dribeck mirrored her fear.

The dismembered segments of energy-substance no longer writhed in blind disunion. From the wriggling wake of the shadow slaves' onslaught, impossible monstrosities were taking shape. Disjointed limbs crawled against mangled trunks, pressed together — and were one. Haphazardly at first seemed this terrible union to occur, but now there was demented purpose to the gruesome reanastomoses.

A one-armed torso lurched erect on mismatched legs, clasped against its stub of forearm another arm, severed above elbow, and with this dubiously jointed limb snatched up a rolling head and joined it to its nuchal stump. So it went throughout the battlefield, strewn with this ghastly debris. Little attempt was made to match the component segments, so that inconceivable travesties of coherent life took shape. Human heads and limbs clung to batrachian trunks, and the reverse. Dread-winged conglomerations flopped across the ground, unable to take flight. An apish creature shambled with octopoid tentacles upon its shoulders; a human shape bore spider arms. Many of the depraved recombinations were incapable of erect ambulation, having blindly conjoined with limbs of too great disparity — or fused arms to knees, thighs to shoulders. These thrashed about, powerless to break this *outré* reconjunction, or oblivious to the unnatural mismating.

Other abominations shambled across the forest field that were an even greater outrage to natural order. A hemisected man shape, cloven from shoulder through crotch by a mighty blow, wriggled forward in centipede fashion, an impossible disarray of limbs jutting from its sectioned plane. Most terrible of all were the octopoid creatures, reconjoined in a blasphemous, crawling chaos of tentacles, claws, human and amphibian limbs, human heads protruding like cancerous growths from their rubbery flesh. Scarcely less monstrous were the horrid reshapings of the spider creatures. Nor were the snapping heads affixed to disjointed arms good to look upon as they scrambled crab-like over the corpses.

Taking new and frightful shape as they crept onward, these fiery monstrosities of unthinkable configuration inexorably advanced to reinforce the teeming shadow army, whose onslaught threatened to overwhelm the line of warriors with each passing moment.

Lord Dribeck tore his sickened gaze from the crawling horde of madness. "To the priestesses' encampment, then!" he ordered in a shaken voice. "Where I fear we must make our final stand."

Pulling back the men, together they slashed their way toward the knoll. The task seemed all but insurmountable. The hard-pressing ranks of the shadow creatures bore down upon them like engulfing quicksand, clung tenaciously, smothered them with crushing numbers. Even as the Selonari line contracted, they left a trail of mangled bodies embedded in the avalanche of emerald horror.

They had hacked through half the distance to the embattled prominence when final disaster caught them. A sudden surge of the more monstrous shadow slaves overran their withdrawal, smashed through the ranks of battle-worn soldiers. Their line had broken; now the knoll was cut off. Bloodstone's shimmering minions thrust past the breach and streamed through to encircle the fragmented human army.

"We must reach the Temple's knoll!" yelled Dribeck. "Try to cut through to the others!" Desperation added new strength to fatigued limbs, and the rallying warriors closed the rift somewhat. But their endurance was cracking under the unrelenting strain, nor was there a man among them not scratched and gouged by the phantoms' talons, or carrying the deeper wounds of bronze blades. The column contracted, buttressed against the monsters' rush, but now the spectral shapes, enclosed the human ranks, ravaged through the rearguard where the wounded had been taken.

They would not see the dawn, Teres realized, and though she had often thought to die in battle, there was no heroism in being torn apart by these mindless shadow creatures. Recklessly now she fought, too exhausted to curse, but with a feral snarl on her bleeding lips. Ah, for Gwellines — his hooves would wreak havoc amidst these glowing carrion! But the stallion was tethered with the other mounts, deemed useless in this night combat. Wistfully she hoped the horse would be spared; he was about the last vestige of her once settled existence.

Teres went down under clutching arms. Dribeck's sword sliced through her assailant's shoulders, then a misshapen human/bufanoid hybrid leaped upon his turned back. Doggedly he struggled under its weight — the creature's mismatched components made its attack clumsy, albeit vicious. Cutting away the choking fingers, Teres lurched toward him, but staggered as a legless torso trapped her foot in its webbed fist. She turned upon the dismembered trunk, hacking down as it sought to climb her legs. Dribeck had dropped to his knees, now beset by another misshaped foe as well, his sword arm pinned by its grasp. A tentacle lashed out at Teres as she struggled with the crawling hands that ensnared her legs. Her last-instant slash cut through the serpentine coil as it struck for her throat, but a sudden blow from a jointed spider-claw stripped the sword from her deadened grip.

She lunged for the fallen blade, stumbled from the dragging anchor that clutched her ankles, and threw herself headlong to seize the blade. Frantically she chopped at the loathsome claws that held her; they would not let her rise. The tentacled monster loomed over her, reached once more for her throat. Teres sliced upward, her last strength failing, and recognized in unbelieving horror that atop the grotesque, multi-limbed arachnoid carapace reposed the head of Lutwion.

Then there was moonlight.

She thought her reeling senses had shattered with madness in that fearful moment. Impossibly, the moon had suddenly turned full. Pale luminance streamed down from its cold, ashen sphere, cast shadows upon the sickened earth.

But it was not the moon that coursed through natural skies — she realized that with wonder. Its luminescence was far too intense. The white brilliance hurt her eyes, struck her upturned face with palpable force. She could sense the unearthly chill of the moonbeam's touch, cold that seemed to leech the warmth from her sweat-soaked skin.

And the globe that shone down upon them was not the dead surface of the moon that mankind knew. There were subtle shapes writhing upon its pale eye. In sudden fear, Teres looked away.

The attack, the relentless advance of the shadow creatures, halted. Their mindless faces seemed to contort with terror as they looked upon this unnatural effulgence.

Teres saw that their emerald flesh-substance was blackening, beginning to slough away in leprous scabs that dwindled while they fluttered to the ground.

The shadow army broke and fled — running, crawling, scurrying, as best they could — retreated from the incredulous humans, fled for the causeway. Although the distance was not great, they would not cross it.

Like vengeful lances the too-brilliant moonbeams stabbed down upon the routed horde. Their unnatural flesh withered and seared under the cold rays, as if they were worms writhing beneath an intolerable heat. First to go were the wriggling fragments, like blackened slugs as they contorted in agony, crumbled apart and melted into the earth. The larger segments lasted longer, but got no farther. Nor did the creatures who fled on staggering limbs fare much better. Under the pitiless luminescence their charred limbs faltered and collapsed as the burning decay eroded their substance. As they bucked and rolled across the forest, their death struggles carried them only a little way before dissolution overtook them. A few blindly sought the shadow of the trees, but to no avail; the moonlight seemed to search the fugitives out in defiance of natural law. Some of the monstrous conglomerates of alien and human shadow substance almost reached the foot of the causeway. There the last of them fell, formless blobs of searing, shriveling flesh that gave up their stolen life force in silent agony — collapsed into crumbling mounds of char, melted to a dark star upon the earth, which slowly faded away into the nothingness from which the shadow slaves were spawned.

Dawn was touching the horizon as the alien moon slowly dimmed. Stunned and bleeding, the remnants of Dribeck's army looked in disbelief for their vanished enemy. And if victory belongs to the survivors, then few were the victors of this nightmare battle.

XXIV
The Final Mask Falls

Gerwein's face had aged ten years during that night. At dawn the battle-worn survivors had tended their wounded as well as might be, then collapsed upon the forest earth in utter exhaustion. As strength returned, they had searched the field of combat, still too fatigued to bury the uncounted dead. Of the shadow creatures no trace remained, but the earth was heavy with the corpses of men and Rillyti. From this battle there would be raised a row of cairns great as the stony peaks of Serpent's Tail.

The shambles of the encampment was restored to a semblance of order, but far fewer were the tents now spread beneath the rattling victory banner. A watch was posted, strategy discussed tentatively — though with the morning sun above them, the men cared only to draw grateful breath and lick their wounds.

A gaunt Lord Dribeck, his injuries cared for, sat before his pavilion deep in thought. Teres dozed fitfully on a pallet inside. Thigh tightly bandaged, Asbraln rested in the sun — Dribeck had ordered the chamberlain taken from the battle after a deep leg wound incapacitated him. Crempra, who had sprained his ankle falling out of a tree, reposed beside him, basking in the warmth of victory with no apparent concern for the next day.

Gerwein came to him there. It was a measure of the gravity of her visit, in that she felt compelled to call upon Dribeck. He had hurried to congratulate the high priestess over the sorcerous vanquishment of Bloodstone's shadow horde, only to learn Gerwein was prostrate with exhaustion in the aftermath of her incantations. Leaving word of his gratitude, Dribeck had intended to return to the Temple's encampment after the noon hour, then to discuss his projected siege of Arellarti.

Her proud face was drawn with strain; something that might be fear shone in her magnificent eyes. Her cold disdain seemed broken by some overbearing concern, and she brushed aside his speech of thanks — when once the priestess would have given her soul for this moment. Perhaps she had.

"I must speak with you," she announced in a strange voice.

"Of course," Dribeck acceded. "In my tent, then. These are all who remain of my counselors, so we might as well make it a formal council. We need to consider our next move against Kane, now that his power lies crushed by your magic."

Gerwein pursed her lips in a taunt line, entered the pavilion, and dropped onto a chair. The others followed her within. Starting from her stupor, Teres had her sword half drawn before awareness returned; sheepishly she sat up. One of the priestess's attendants placed in Gerwein's hands a brittle-leafed tome and withdrew silently.

"This is the lost volume to which I made reference on your visit to the Temple archives," Gerwein began, before each had taken his place. "The pages of our crumbling volumes referred to a yet more ancient manuscript which told the full history of Arellarti, of Bloodstone — as far as any man has penetrated its secrets. Parts of this knowledge had been excerpted, appended to the older compendia of our Temple's lore. Thence came the knowledge we used to combat Bloodstone's powers: the secret of its annihilating energy, which is somehow akin to both the energies of the cosmos and of life — vampirish of the living entities whom it destroys. The shadow slaves of Bloodstone — stolen souls, whom it enslaved on the plane where elder science merges into sorcery. These were dead creatures invested with a depraved sham-life, and thus they were vulnerable to Shenan's shining wrath, for such mockeries of living death are hateful to the sight of true gods."

She rested the heavy tome upon Dribeck's battered camp table and opened its pages with a gesture. "My sisters discovered this as we were making ready to depart Selonari. It's a palimpsest, or we would have known it earlier. I can't guess its age, although it predates the more than five centuries our people have held these lands. It's written in the Old Tongue, the language of those whose day was before mankind became a race. I think the history must have come from the giants, who ranged far across the dawn Earth and knew many secrets of the elder ages, though someone must have transcribed this, for the giants cared little for writing. One of my parsimonious ancestors, who did not read Old Tongue or else deemed this lore of little value, erased the parchment to record her memoirs. Much of the ancient script is still legible; my sisters restored it somewhat, and I was able to read these lost pages as we journeyed.

"I was disconcerted by what I learned, but in my pride I did not give full credence to these faded lines. It seemed that my sorcery could triumph over this resurrected demon of alien science, despite the sinister insinuations of the manuscript. So I kept silent upon my new wisdom, thinking it would be advantageous to make the disclosure as a dramatic stroke when Kane was vanquished by my magic.

"But the battle went not as I had thought. More potent sorceries were demanded than I had ever planned — you cannot imagine the powers that clashed invisibly, the frightful sacrifices this narrow victory cost! And now I understand that this ancient writing is not wild exaggeration! That we are aligned against powers of which we have known but a frightened glimpse! That the price of our defeat is far more hideous than ever we had guessed!"

"You mean Kane could indeed conquer the earth?" demanded Dribeck. "Can he enslave all mankind?"

Gerwein laughed bitterly — a sharp, unpleasant sound.

"Kane! He knows not what power he has awakened! The doom I speak of is a far blacker evil than a world empire with Kane as tyrant — that would mean little more than a change of masters for much of mankind!

"But let me read. I'll translate as well as I can these archaic lines, since I doubt if even Lord Dribeck knows Old Tongue:

"And in that distant age to our world and to this land came Bloodstone, from beyond the stars that shone in the elder night. In flight came Bloodstone, driven before the vast war between its brothers and the races of the stars, who had risen against the dread hunger of the crystal entities, and did battle to sunder the strangling fetters of abominable tyranny which that unnatural race had spread across the stars. Seeking refuge from their anger, Bloodstone determined to dwell upon our world, and with its final stores of energy from the land it blasted a great burning wound, and into this wound flowed the waters of the sea, and there was formed an inland sea, wherein Bloodstone had carved an island, and upon this haven did it come to rest. There in the fastness of its island, Bloodstone directed its Krelran slaves to build for it a fortress city, raised from strange elements that Bloodstone's power had transmuted from certain substances, these it took from the earth and the sea and the air and the fire. Nor was this city, as any other the Earth has known, before or since, for its design was not so much structured to give shelter to the crystal and its slaves, but to call down from the stars the limitless energies that were the life force of Bloodstone. Thus did his minions labor long and arduously, giving fullest attention to every minute detail of their master's great design, whether to the precise angles of some gigantic and doorless edifice, or to a tiny etching upon some bizarrely faceted carving. For once this extension of its power lattice could be completed, then could Bloodstone freely drink of those immeasurable energies that hold together the universe, known and unknown, that hold apart this plane of existence from dimensions and from worlds beyond this that we know, that are the life principle of all nature, whether rock or flame or living creature.

"Further, it was the intent of Bloodstone to call out to its brothers beyond the stars, where their danger now was great as the wrath of their enemies, and to summon its crystal race, as many as survived, to come to our world, where their enemies had not followed, and here to descend, and to carry out the dread design from which they had been driven by the power of their enemies. Thus would Bloodstone and its kind have brought down from the stars a monstrous doom upon our world, feeding upon and enslaving the elder races that here dwelled, in the same manner that it treated its Krelran slaves, and no power upon the Earth could deny their might. But the elder races of Earth had knowledge of Bloodstone's evil intent, nor were these other beings without wizardry of their own, some having themselves ridden from the stars on great engines of their devising, some having origins of which we may not speak. The greatest of these, the Scylredi, from their castles beneath the sea, and the Tuhchiso, who dwell in far deserts, and the Brveen, whose home is the cliffs where the Great Serpent's Head drops down upon the salt marshes, then made truce from their smouldering wars, and they made an alliance one with another to destroy the work of Bloodstone. Thereby did follow a mighty and terrible war between these elder races and Bloodstone, and great was the destruction of that fearful combat, despite that Bloodstone was much weakened from its flight and its building of Arellarti, and that its power lattice was not completed, so that it could not draw upon the energies for which it thirsted sorely. Even then it may have been that Bloodstone would have withstood their attack, but when its powers were concentrated to its defense, then did the master of the Krelran, Bloodstone's chief servant, who wielded in a strangely wrought ring upon his fist the dual self of Bloodstone's being, rebel against the slavery in which Bloodstone held his people, notwithstanding the high station he bore among them. This chief of the Krelran slaves with secret thoughts approached Bloodstone, and manipulated the master controls of the crystal's power structure to cut off that thin stream of energy by which the crystal was nourished, doing this before Bloodstone could once more hold his mind in thrall. And here was Bloodstone vulnerable, for according to its dual nature of crystal and organic life, it could not control its power through itself directly, but only through the agency of its slave, who under Bloodstone's power was both extension and organic identity of the crystal consciousness. No hand but that of its chief slave might command the mechanisms of the control dais and live, nor could Bloodstone destroy its rebellious slave, for he was part of the crystal's life structure. Thereby was Bloodstone crippled before its enemies, and its rebellious servant then sought to flee, with others of his kind, in the great ship that had carried them to our world. But the fury of these elder races spared no work of Bloodstone and followed the fleeing ship, and destroyed it, and with it died the servant of Bloodstone. Thus was the bond of life broken for Bloodstone, and the ring that bore its dual self was lost; and the giant crystal fell dormant within its ravaged city, which the elder races were not able to destroy utterly, as they did the alien ship. For centuries now has Bloodstone lain silent in the ruins of Arellarti, while the great elder races that conquered it have fallen from their ancient state of might, and it is said that Bloodstone lies not dead, but in repose, dreaming of that day when, by an evil miracle, its power may again throw a light of horror upon our Earth."

Gerwein closed the book, pushed it away from her. "It goes on to describe Arellarti, talks about the powers of Bloodstone and the like — the sections which were excerpted and abridged for the volumes we uncovered earlier. The part I translated for you tells us where we stand, though.

"In short, you suggest that Kane's power has been broken. This is doubly false. In truth we speak of Bloodstone's power, for Kane is no more than its pawn. He erred, as did we all, in believing the Krelran had harnessed the power of Bloodstone to serve their race. Our conceit kept us from recognizing on whose neck the shackles truly weighed. And now we realize how little our hollow victory means — if after such losses we can name it victory! While we were barely able to check Bloodstone's attack last night, our strength has been sacrificed for but little gain. We defended our lives — the lives of a few of us — and now what force have we to attack Bloodstone! Yet Bloodstone is no more than a short span of time from the fulfillment of its design and the attainment of power that well may be without limit! Do you think this inconsequential setback we dealt Bloodstone last night could have crippled such might?

"But the final despair is to understand the doom Bloodstone means to wreak upon all mankind — if its horror will not reach even farther! The others of its race shall be summoned, and man shall be a mindless slave to these devouring gods... and what hope is there to break such chains? I believed my pitiful sorceries could defeat Bloodstone, but last night it took the most potent of spells just to withstand its languid thrust! Once it achieves the peak of its power, no magic forces known to man can resist Bloodstone! It took the incalculable strength of three elder-world titans to destroy Bloodstone when its power was at ebb — and even they could not altogether annihilate it!

"Our cause is doomed," she declared quietly. "We are pitted against an enemy whose power truly is beyond our conception. Against such measureless force mankind cannot hope to prevail."

It seemed the dark silence which followed her pronouncement would never be broken. Not even a bird or warrior's shout was heard within the tent. It was as if the pavilion had been hermetically sealed by their despair.

"Let us die in the attempt," said Dribeck at last.

The others remained silent. Nor was there any answer they could give.

"I have no more than several hundred men who are fit to march," he continued, his voice unnatural. "Still, I'll lead them to the walls of Arellarti though we're but children throwing stones at an ogre's castle. Likely we'll all perish before some new and terrible weapon... before we ever reach the city portals. Yet there's a chance we might fight through — reach Bloodstone's fane — destroy it somehow, I don't know — maybe force Kane to show us how. The odds are not ones I care to ponder, but they seem a far more tempting gamble than to wait for Bloodstone to deal with us as it wills.

"At least the evils of which we know have been vanquished. The shadow army is destroyed, there can't be more than a few score Rillyti skulking about, and we can counter Kane's death ring. I'm assuming we can take your moon disk with us — is there any other way your sorceries can aid us?

"We'll try to arrange for the simulacrum to accompany you, though I doubt its magic could withstand the fury of Bloodstone's limitless energy for very long." Gerwein's chin lifted resolutely; her eyes flashed determination, if not hope.

"There *is* one desperate spell which remains to us that may be effective — a spell that will force Bloodstone to the defensive. But this is magic of terrible potence. I had hoped not to resort to such evocation, since the forces that will be unshackled will be almost beyond the limits of sorcery to control. There is no longer a choice to make, it seems.

"As you know, Shenan, goddess of the moon, is mistress of the ocean tides. Kranor-Rill was sea before it rotted into morass, and thus its boundaries once were part of the tidal realm. There is a spell, a most dangerous spell, that will loose the ancient tides upon the lands where once they held dominion. I intend to send the waters of the Western Sea into Kranor-Rill… to hurl the power of the tides against Arellarti!"

"Can the sea destroy Bloodstone?" demanded Dribeck with desperate interest.

"Who can say?" returned Gerwein. "The tides are as powerful a force as our race knows. Perhaps the sea can conquer Bloodstone — or at least so devastate its walls of living stone that the power lattice will be shattered and we can win a delay from our doom. If nothing more, Bloodstone must concentrate its power to counter our threat, and in that interval you may have some chance to strike a blow for its glowing heart."

"Better than I dared hope for," Dribeck observed bleakly. "Cast your spells with the greatest art you command, Gerwein! I'll hold my attack until we learn what fate wills."

"What the goddess wills," Gerwein corrected, with a flash of her old assurance. Rising to leave, she reached for the book.

"May I examine this?" Dribeck asked. "I'm not altogether unlearned in the Old Tongue."

The priestess shrugged. "As you wish, milord. But I warn you, those pages hold only despair, and there's enough of that in the air we breathe."

XXV
When Mad Dreams Die

Teres continued to sit in brooding silence for a long while after Gerwein's departure. Dribeck spared little time to wonder at her unwonted mood. His limping cousin he sent to oversee preparations for the final battle. His army was hideously mauled, such of it as remained, and it would be a worn and battered band who fought for mankind's last hope. Thinking to glean some undiscovered thread of knowledge — a buried secret that would command the tide of victory — the Selonari lord bent his attention to the moldering manuscript. With difficulty he translated the antique script.

So engrossed was he that he paid scant mind to Teres's sudden and pointless question: "Do you think Kane can read Old Tongue?"

Dribeck looked up in bewilderment. "If any man within a thousand miles of here could, Kane is probably that one," he replied abstractly. "I begin to believe Old Tongue may be his native language!"

Teres did not enlarge, and Dribeck was immediately back to his task. He failed to notice when she rose with set jaw and strode from the tent.

But he was aware of her when she returned, for he had shoved the tome aside in irreverent frustration to stare gloomily at the blue skies and green forestland without. She had saddled Gwellines and led the restless gray stallion into his field of vision. His eyes grew strange as he recognized her undaunted figure, now proud beneath a shirt of light mail.

The doorway framed her as she entered, the fire of her braid softening to gold when it passed from sunlight to shadow. Her blue eyes looked straight into his, their reckless light steady with decision. "I'm taking that book to Kane," she stated.

Dribeck's face showed no comprehension.

"I've thought it all through," she explained simply. "Kane is the keystone to the power of Bloodstone. If Kane dies, the crystal is dormant once more. And Kane has the power to destroy Bloodstone, if he wills. At least he told me he could.

"Kane doesn't realize the doom that lies in the crystal's evil soul, though he knows Bloodstone withholds secrets from him. Bloodstone has betrayed him. Kane would never have revived this alien horror had he known its true nature; he believes the crystal is no more than an invincible weapon that he can wield as he pleases. So did we all think until today.

"I intend to reveal to Kane the nightmarish truth which underlies his mad dream. This ancient book will bear proof, if he doubts my word. Bloodstone's servant turned on his crystal master once before, and brought ruin to its dark scheme. I figure Kane will not be pleased to learn he's been this creature's fool.

"If he won't — or can't — destroy the crystal... perhaps I can get a knife between his ribs," she finished grimly.

Dribeck frowned, logic and emotion both howling at once in his tumbling thoughts. "In the first place, you'd be killed before you reached Arellarti. In the second place, Kane himself will kill you on sight. You may recall that your interference foundered a meticulously crafted plot, that Kane had only murder in his heart for you at your sudden parting."

"I'll chance both," Teres replied levelly. "What few Rillyti he has left are probably pulled back to defend the walls; the other dangers of the swamp I'll have to risk. Kane will know I'm coming as soon as I tread the causeway, and if I'm alone, I think he'll grant me safe passage — out of curiosity, if for no other reason. And perhaps he'll see me for other reasons, as well. I think his actions when I escaped arose from his sudden murderous rage. We... meant much to one another... for a breath of time. He remembers."

"And does Kane still mean something to you?" grated Dribeck, surprised to know jealousy.

"I don't know," Teres mumbled. "For all the evil he's done, I still don't know. You yourself seem to admire him still... I don't know."

He realized distantly that this was true. "Gerwein has evoked the ancient tides. The Western Sea will rush upon Kranor-Rill and engulf Arellarti. You'd die with the rest."

"Gerwein's sorcery won't prevail over Bloodstone," she snorted. "I know its power because I've seen Arellarti. The witch's spells are false hope and wasted time. Even were they not in vain, I'd still chance it. Kane is the fulcrum of victory, and I'm the only one who can reach him."

I can't let emotion twist my thoughts at this point, reflected Dribeck, but he said, "I can't let you take the risk."

"Look, damn it!" Teres snarled in flashing anger. "I'm not asking you to *let* me do anything! I'm telling you what my intentions are, and then I'm acting on it! Kindly remember that I'm not one of your captains or gentry! My city may be in ruins, my army may be but a handful, but I now rule Breimen, and my status concerning you is that of an ally on equal terms! Well, as such I've notified you of my battle plans, as courtesy dictates, and I don't need your leave to follow my own strategy!"

"All right, I'll concede your right to direct your actions as you judge best," grumbled Dribeck. "It's rather that — "

"That I'm a woman and you're a man — and a man protects and gives orders, and a woman obeys and gives thanks for her champion's protection! Well, you know where you can shove that idea! I'm taking that book to Kane, and if I die, then I'll die my own master! I'll trust to my own good sword arm for protection — and be better served!"

Which stung perhaps worst of all. "Climb off my back, Teres, damn it! I'm not going to stop you! I won't even deny that your plan is as sound a strategy as any that's left to us. I just wanted to be certain you know the odds you're taking on. Start when you're ready, and good luck to you!"

Still angry, Teres snatched up the palimpsest and stalked from the pavilion. She secured it within her saddlebag, then swung onto the stallion, still not meeting Dribeck's eye.

"Good luck, Teres!" he called, this time meaning it. But he could not tell whether she heard him.

Gwellines snorted and shied as his hooves crossed the torn, muddy earth which surrounded the causeway's terminus. Uneasy, Teres noticed that the crimson aura of the igneous stones was a visible haze even by daylight. She spoke soothingly to the stallion, stroked his pulsing neck, and when she touched spur to his flank, Gwellines struck hooves upon the unnatural pavement. As he cantered forward into the rotting land, tiny sparks danced eerily where iron scored the glassy surface.

Like a streak of molten light, the roadway bore into the depths of Kranor-Rill. For miles it stretched, an unwavering line that lifted above the fetid mire and labyrinthine hillocks of vegetation. Even now Teres found spirit to marvel at this masterwork of supernormal engineering. Her sword lay ready for whatever danger might challenge her intrusion, but no springing threat was visible. There was a strange quietness overhanging the swamp. Within the tangles of leprous undergrowth nothing stirred. Not even a serpent basked upon the causeway, and the expected swarms of malicious insects had vanished. It was as if the venomous denizens of Kranor-Rill had withdrawn into the deeper reaches of the swamp, had retreated from the alien evil that radiated from the lustrous stones.

As she rode, her anger cooled and her thoughts returned to Lord Dribeck. Teres regretted that their final words had been scathing; the Selonari lord had become as close a friend as there remained to her, and it pained her that this bitter memory would be their last one.

No! She would not resign herself to death.

The swamp lay all about her, writhing, mist-cloaked desolation. The stark severity of the roadway soon grew to monotony, and with the stagnant fog swallowing the horizons, she quickly lost all conception of time and distance. She seemed to ride endlessly through a glowing tunnel in the blood-tinged mist, while half-seen and sinister shapes loomed and crouched beyond the uncanny silence that encircled her. Haunting her was the knowledge of insurmountable danger that tightened like a hangman's noose with every crash of Gwellines's hooves, lurked half-formed in her imagination, gnawing with acid-venomed fangs on the strained fibers of her nerves. An unbearable sensation of menace hung like a deepening chill upon the charged atmosphere.

And even before its familiar walls jutted through the dank vapor, Teres could see the nimbus light of serpentine evil that reached out from Arellarti.

The monolithic bronze portal stood open, dwarfing the giant figure who slouched, arms folded, against an obelisk. His arrogant smile greeted her, but it seemed to her the insolent strength of his massive frame had weathered gaunt, haggard, eroded by some nameless and vampirish force.

"So you've come back, she-wolf," spoke Kane in a tired voice.

For a space she had no words, forgot the hazily rehearsed phrases she had considered during her ride.

Kane had been aware of her coming since she first spurred her mount onto the causeway. With mixed emotions he had allowed her to approach. The rage he had known at Teres's betrayal had been fleeting, a wound he suppressed by the memory of her companionship. For in Kane's world, hate was as constant a force as the numberless sands that drifted across a desert. After so long an existence within its shifting dunes, he little felt the stinging, arid winds which remolded the changeless waste. Love was rare, elusive. Seldom did Kane chance upon love in his blighted wandering; fewer still were the times his hand had closed upon its subtle mystery.

He wanted Teres; that was enough. But while he might dismiss his own anger toward her, Kane understood that the same might not be so for the girl. Teres had repudiated him once before, and since that moment Kane had only given her further cause to hate him. That her return to him now was of uncertain portent Kane bitterly realized. Yet he welcomed Teres, while in his mind Bloodstone's insinuating voice urged him to destroy her.

"I had wondered if you might return," Kane went on. "Have you then reconsidered my offer to you? Two armies that would have opposed me have been destroyed, and the desperate sorceries of Shenan's daughters will not shield Lord Dribeck after tonight. Or do you come on his behalf? Dribeck always impressed me as a man of intelligence. If he recognizes the hopelessness of his position, I'll be willing to come to terms with Selonari. As you can see, few of my toads returned from last night's skirmish. But then, it's been my plan all along to replace my ugly servitors with a human army. It would be advantageous for us all if Dribeck decides to throw his lot in with me. I've no wish to devastate my future properties any further."

Teres slid from her saddle while Kane talked. There was a glint of irony to his eyes that made her wonder. Only a few of his Rillyti warriors were in sight, so that she pondered a sudden thrust with her blade. Kane seemed to know her thoughts, by the sardonic mockery of his aspect; he remembered that she had balked at killing him once before when he lay helpless, and he dared her now to strike. Teres was not certain she could... despite the doom that impended. She must try first to reason with Kane; if that failed... then, if steel could slay him, her hand must make the attempt.

"Dribeck still means to fight you, Kane," she announced confidently. "If you believe last night's battle destroyed either our military strength or our resolve to crush this alien horror you serve, then you'll soon learn your error. Nor do I return to be consort to your iniquity. I've come to warn you, Kane — warn you of the evil your ill-conceived ambition has set free."

"A dialogue we've had often enough," he pointed out sarcastically.

"In the past you argued with a half-knowledge that was a trap deadlier than pure lies! Your egotistic confidence blinded you to the truth of your situation. What do you really know of Bloodstone, other than the fragmented guesses of a madman's writings and the veiled lies Bloodstone whispers to you?"

Her hands shook as she withdrew the palimpsest, for her fingers held the most potent weapon left for mankind's defense. "You won't believe me, I know. But maybe you'll recognize the truth from this book!" She offered it to him. His expression was one of dubious curiosity.

"Kane, the Krelran weren't *masters* of the crystal! They were Bloodstone's *slaves!*"

Kill her! Destroy her and her book of lies!

Kane winced as the command thundered through his skull. The ring on his fist tingled, burned, throbbed with the lethal intensity of a coiled serpent. And perhaps because of the desperate rage that screamed at him, he hesitated no longer. From her hand he tore the ancient volume. He glanced at it cursorily, then concentrated over the nearly effaced script.

Night was stealing over the forest. Dribeck returned from the Temple's encampment, his faced lined and ashen from what he had seen there. The weirdly illumined knoll was a phantasmagoria of writhing figures and wailing incantation. Fear crouched ominously upon its slopes, and the rising power of Gerwein's spell swirled through the dying twilight like black lightning. The cries of those who lay stretched upon Shenan's altar were like the mournful call of a lost night bird, chilling in despair, more a dirge than a moan of fear.

Dribeck shuddered, not liking to think of that spreading mound of pale, cold forms. "However this turns out," he remarked to Crempra, "Gerwein will not profit from her magic. Did you see the faces of the men? Only their fear of Bloodstone keeps them from putting the entire pack of those witches to the sword! If we live to return, Selonari will shun the Temple for many a year. All this foul sorcery, whether Bloodstone's or Shenan's, has sickened the land. Gerwein will find no grateful hearts after this night — only bellies cold with loathing!"

"Darkness doesn't come tonight," Crempra observed. "The light of Shenan's hell-moon shines over our camp, and Kranor-Rill is ablaze with misty flames of emerald and scarlet. See how the light pulses ever brighter!"

"Bloodstone's power must be close to its peak even now," said Dribeck without hope. "Gerwein fears for the success of her magic. Already her spells should have lured the Western Sea into our land, but Bloodstone combats her witch-tide. Now her evocation becomes more intense, more potent than she might dare. The power of Bloodstone interferes without faltering, holds the tides in their natural ebb and flow. Unless her magic can exhaust Bloodstone, overcome its unyielding resistance, we will have to attack Arellarti with no power more miraculous than the might of our sword arms. Shenan knows how we can succeed after the fearsome power of her magic has failed to conquer Bloodstone!"

He gazed at the roadway with troubled eyes. "Still nothing from Teres?"

Asbraln shook his head.

Dribeck sighed bitterly. "She was our best hope, though I sicken to think of her danger." For the hundredth time in the last hour he silently berated himself for his angry words at their parting. The girl had gotten to him, he could no longer deny that even to himself. Her defiant independence drew him to her as a man admires the fierce self-reliance of a wild and untamable creature. She knew the odds against her, but on her own initiative she undertook this perilous quest. And he was witless enough to insult her courage, try to shelter her like some shivering court wench who would whimper and cling to her protector at the first hint of danger.

"It must be a good twenty-mile ride to Arellarti," he mused aloud. "She should have returned by now." A hundred unpleasant fantasies whispered in his mind. Even if she were still alive, unless she could escape Arellarti, she would die in the destruction of the city — should Gerwein's spell be victorious in this unseen conflict of science and sorcery. Still, she had known the risks of her mission.

"I'm going after Teres," someone announced in Dribeck's voice.

Crempra was gaping at him.

"I have to know what's happened to her," he explained lamely. "Need to reconnoiter the city's defenses, anyway. Gerwein's magic isn't going to work."

"Hell, cousin!" Crempra blurted., "Send out a scout, then! No point in you throwing your life away. Someone has to lead us."

"Doesn't look like my life is destined to be long and peaceful, anyway you cut it," Dribeck retorted, his mind set. "I'll chance it like this."

"One man couldn't get through. Maybe a small force of cavalry," suggested Crempra.

Dribeck threw him a sharp, glance. "Maybe so. I'll put about fifty men on our best mounts. Try to get in and back before… well, before whatever horror this night will bring, breaks loose."

Crempra shrugged fatalistically. "Guess even with this ankle I can still ride as well as anyone. Just might get a chance to use my bow once or twice, before we're wiped out to a man."

Dribeck looked with surprise upon his cousin. "You're the one who boasts of discretion in battle. You should stay to command, if I don't return."

"What is there worth leading? And who'd follow me? No, cousin, I don't suffer from your compelling desire to rule. Someone else can endure that responsibility — I'll enjoy the pleasures he's too harassed to sample. If you're determined to lead a suicide raid on Arellarti, I'll ride along. Before we all die, I'd at least like a glimpse of our enemy's fortress. Do you realize Teres is the only one of us who's actually seen Bloodstone?"

From his cot, Asbraln was making anxious sounds about joining them. But his thigh wound would burst open if he tried to mount, and Dribeck firmly argued him down, reflecting all the while on the resolution that underlay his cousin's customary flippancy.

"I'll get the men mounted, and we'll ride immediately," said Dribeck, wondering if he could get volunteers. Since their position was untenable, anyway, perhaps he could find enough men willing to join a commando raid. "We'll ride hard," he continued. "Get in, find out what's there, and get back. If Gerwein fails, we'll bring up the infantry and siege machinery. No time for that now, and I don't want to risk it against the chance of sudden flood. Maybe we'll make it back. If not... Asbraln, use your judgment. Ivocel is a capable captain and comes of a good house — he's as close to a ranking officer as you'll have left." Absently he realized that very likely the future leadership of Selonari would no longer be of concern to himself, or to anyone for that matter.

"For long there have been some who have questioned it," proudly remarked Asbraln, as his lord dashed off into the evening shadow; "but there's man's blood in his heart, beyond doubt!"

Crempra struggled to force bandaged foot into boot. "Damned stupid way of judging that!" he grimaced. "Just because he jumps out of character and throws his life away on a thoughtless gamble. If that's your idea of heroism, you've never really thought about it."

Asbraln snorted. "No heroism in forever following the calculations of one's cunning mind. A man ought to attempt the illogical, if there's fire in his heart. So why are you going with him?"

Crempra laughed mirthlessly and did not answer.

Kane's face was strangely lined when at last he closed the book; his hands were calm, but it was a feat of will to hold them from tearing out in blind anger. Only his blue eyes flamed with ice-fires of inexpressible rage.

There was no doubt. The hints and forebodings which Bloodstone's ceaseless whisper had suppressed now burst to the surface of his tumultuous thoughts. Even while he forced himself to read, to understand, Bloodstone's desperate commands had shrieked through his brain, urging him to read no further, to destroy the book, confusing his thoughts as he groped to awareness. Countless rational arguments told him to ignore what he read — poisoned thoughts masquerading as his own.

Were Kane not convinced of the manuscript's authenticity, its accuracy, the frantic efforts of the alien crystal to block his recognition of his true status were damning.

"Alorri-Zrokros was not omniscient," muttered Kane in an unreal voice. "Or my transcription had certain fatal inaccuracies."

"Now you know the truth," breathed Teres, wondering what this victory might avail. "You aren't Master of Bloodstone — you're its slave! It's lied to you from the moment you so rashly brought it back to life -- maybe before, even — duped you into serving its will, while it lay yet powerless. While it secretly conspired to enslave all mankind to sustain the hideous appetites of its evil race! You thought you would be ruler of a world empire, Kane, but your role will only be chief foreman of the numberless slaves. You resurrected a monstrous evil that the entire might of the elders gods sought in vain to destroy! You've made yourself the most wretched traitor mankind will ever know!"

Kane made a grinding sound deep in his throat, and Teres cringed at the unreasoning fury that blazed from his brow. He rushed past her, his visage the mask of a madman who knows the curse of his madness. Awed by the forces she had unchained, Teres dashed after him, oblivious to the few batrachians who watched in fear.

"Bloodstone!" Kane roared, bursting into the central dome. "Bloodstone!" His wrath was not to be contained by cold telepathic converse.

I warned you to destroy her. Do you find pleasure in your awakening?

"Someone's going to be destroyed before the day grows darker!" snarled Kane, stalking toward the control dais.

Stop this senseless rebellion, Kane! What if your insignificant vanity has been crushed? You are useful to me as you are. Continue to serve me of your free will, and my power will yet bring to you all the wealth and luxury you lust for.

"I'll be slave to neither god nor devil — nor to a freak of alien science! You played me for a fool, Bloodstone! For that I'll kill you, even though your lies promised me power greater than the gods!"

Stop this, Kane! You can't harm me now! Control your petty anger before you force me to take action!

"Your slave turned against you once before! I can destroy you with these hands that returned you to life!"

Then I was too weak to halt his treacherous attack! Now no hand can turn against me!

"I know the restrictions of your power! I form an all-essential link in your perverted life-force! You can't destroy me without destroying yourself, but I don't need you to live!" He reached the crescent.

Fool! Do you think I can't command obedience from a pitiful slave like you!

"Too late for your lies now!" Kane's hand touched a crystal knob.

Pain! Unendurable pain burst through every shrieking nerve in his contorted frame. Kane heard himself screaming — a wordless cry of agony that came unbidden to his tortured throat. For a endless stretch of time the pain racked his helpless body, stabbing white-hot fangs into every atom of his being.

It ended sometime, somehow, he realized dimly, feeling the warm stones pressing against his crumpled form. An echo caromed through the burning dome, and he supposed it was the sound of his scream. The agony had vanished, left his shaken body sick with the memory. Teres was running toward him. Drunkenly he called for her to stay back. She ignored him.

While I may not do you physical harm, as you now know, I can give you much pain — unbearable pain that will not relent, even when your cringing mind is no more than a soulless lump of pulsing jelly! You wear a slave's shackle on your hand, Kane, and you are my creature. Continue this futile rebellion, and I'll blast your soul with such agony that your mind will shrivel and crumble. You'll serve me better if you yield to my power, but even a mindless tool can be used by a master's hand — until a better tool is provided. When my brothers come, you'll find that you're not irreplaceable. Think on this while you ponder fruitless rebellion.

Now kill that girl before she causes me further inconvenience!

"Get out of here, Teres!" Kane gritted, his spirit one of unquenchable hate. "Bloodstone will kill you!"

She knelt beside him, tried to drag him to his feet, but his knees would not yet brace. Although she knew nothing of Bloodstone's thoughts, she had sensed the conflict from Kane's words, understood that some unendurable shock had felled him as he seized the control rods. "I won't leave you here!" she swore, not questioning the resolution she felt.

"Run, damn it! You're the one who's endangered!" He got his feet under him and slid upward against the dais.

Shall I force you to obey? Never mind — my other slaves will follow my bidding. The sorcerous attack of my enemies grows more persistent now. A vain attempt, but it angers me to waste power in staving off their frantic efforts. Once I have reached my brothers, and can spare attention to their annoyance, I mean to annihilate this source of resistance.

Think well on what you have learned, slave. If you forget this stupid tantrum, and serve me well... you'll find that I am a benevolent master. Resist, and you'll still serve me — but without pleasure for either of us. Once you might have broken your bonds, my fool, but now there is no power in your world that can conquer me!

The jeering thoughts withdrew.

"Kane!" gasped Teres. "The Rillyti!" Entering the shimmering dome were ten or more batrachians. The bared blades in their webbed fists left no doubt as to their intent. Inwardly Teres despaired, for against these monstrous assailants her sword arm would win her only moments more of life.

A cutting rasp, and Kane stood with blade in his hand. "Run between those two columns of instruments!" he growled, pointing. "That'll guard our flanks and rear, and the toads will have to meet us head-on!"

They raced to the glowing instrument banks, just as the Rillyti lumbered down upon them. Kane thrust Teres behind him, caught the blade of the first attacker and tore it from its grasp with the unbridled rage that drove his arm. The creature's head split like cordwood, and Teres's sword stabbed out to disembowel another.

"Stay back!" Kane yelled. "They don't dare kill me! It's you they want!"

Teres cursed him. "I'll kill my own snakes! They're wild enough to cut you in half with a misaimed blow!"

That might solve some problems, she reflected suddenly. *Right now — a quick thrust through Kane's back?* She knew she could not do it. Not while he fought against her murderers — no matter how much depended on his death. Uneasily she recalled the unforeseen consequences of her attempt to cut off the bloodstone ring, and she wondered if Kane could be slain by common steel.

The Rillyti, pressing their attack, tried to bear Kane down under their weight. They must not kill the man, but the girl must die, and since she was protected by the other, their onslaught was poorly executed. Several of their number now flopped across the slippery floor, testament to the deadliness of the human blades; others drew back to minister to flowing wounds. About the combatants, Bloodstone's flame pulsed ever brighter as the demon of alien science battled the forces of sorcery marshaled to defeat it.

The attack abruptly creased. Teres almost fell past Kane as she lunged for a retreating assailant. Leaving their dead, the swamp creatures shambled from the dome.

Your pet may live, until I have time to deal with her as she deserves. A few of her comrades ride toward my gate, but they shall not ride back. You may return to my favor by destroying these rash intruders... No? Remain and sulk, then. My other slaves will deal with them.

Their sorcery is nearing the limits of their powers to command it, but the seas obey my will instead. I have no time for these petty distractions now. The moment draws close when the stars will assume the optimum configuration -- then shall my brothers join with me and I with them! These vexing sorceries shall vanish like blown dust when the moment comes!

"Kane! What's happening!" demanded Teres, as the batrachians withdrew from their attack.

Kane explained. "Dribeck sends a mounted force against Arellarti. It must be a small band, since Bloodstone only sends the remains of its Rillyti army to ambush them. The crystal is too concerned with other matters to waste attention on such a trifling threat."

"Can you use that ring? Destroy the Rillyti — or turn it against Bloodstone?"

Kane shook his head. "Impossible. Since Bloodstone powers the ring, I can't direct it against any target the crystal refuses."

"Can't you do anything to stop it?"

"I'll try something — wait for a chance!" he promised. The fury in his eyes bore witness to his intention.

The coruscating brilliance waxed more intense than ever, seared the eyes. Even the sullen stones of the walls were pulsing with molten light.

"The stars are right," groaned Kane. "It's reaching out for its brothers, seeking through the wilderness beyond the stars for its race! Can you sense the flow of incalculable energies through the gem? Bloodstone is reaching out through both time and space as it searches! Now its power warps the laws of the physical universe!

"No longer does it trouble to cloak the secret recesses of its mind. I can see them now, know the hidden thoughts of this creature's iniquitous soul. There! The cyclopean laboratory where Bloodstone and its brothers take form — are born! The weapons of a blighted alien science turn against their creators! The unthinkable destruction of their wars! There are thoughts here I cannot grasp... I dare not...!"

The intolerable radiance made ghastly the twisted mask of his face. "Quickly, Teres!" he warned. "There's too much danger in this place!" Without waiting for acquiescence, Kane clutched her shoulder and propelled her from the dome as if she were a frail child.

Something more than anger haunted his face, once they were outside. What horror has he looked upon? wondered Teres fearfully. Around them the entire city was pulsing with unnatural luminance.

"Can you die by your own hand?" she asked unsteadily.

Kane laughed, a cruel bark reminiscent of his accustomed spirit. "Probably Bloodstone would try to stay my hand. I wonder how many of my actions of late were of my own volition. I don't really know... How closely it guards its slave! But I'll not die before the crystal dies — dies with the knowledge of its defeat!"

"With you dead, then Bloodstone would be powerless," Teres said pointedly.

"For the moment, perhaps. But I don't plan to sacrifice my life, if I can help it!" He held her with his eyes. "Or do you think to slay me?"

She shivered. "I don't know that I can — even to save mankind! But if I knew that you would reconsider, willingly serve Bloodstone in return for the scraps it tosses to you..."

"I'll serve no master but myself!" spat Kane. "Mankind has given me little cause to feel loyalty toward the race, but no creature will use Kane as its pawn and live to reap the spoils of its game"

They had neared the gate. Now the rising nimbus of light made the night as midday. Kane abruptly froze, his mind distant, listening

...to a silent scream of terror.

Bloodstone had reached out beyond the stars. Pulsing with the flow of cosmic energy, it called to its brothers. Called to those who had shared its unnatural birth in distant millennia. To those who formed the complete network of its being. Those who had battled alongside it in the desperate wars of long ago. Who would be waiting through the centuries to share a unified existence once more. Waiting for the fulfillment of the perfect lattice...

Bloodstone searched... and found nothing! Bloodstone called out... and received no answer. Frantically, while the giant crystal grid of Arellarti pulsed and flamed, Bloodstone sought through the corridors of interdimensional space. There was nothing.

Bloodstone was alone.

Knowledge came that its brothers lay with the dust of an eons-forgotten war. And that knowledge brought... madness!

Its alien mind was structured on the logic of symmetry, the fulfillment of geometric perfection. In the shattering realization that it stood alone, incomplete, imperfect, the inconceivable rationale of the crystal entity fell into chaos. Power suddenly surged without control through its lattice depths as Bloodstone's insane mind flung raving energies across the universe.

Even Teres sensed its demented shriek, and Kane reeled as if he had been bludgeoned. Bleats of terror echoed from the swamp beyond, and she glimpsed crashing bufanoid shapes as they burst through the morass in panic. The effulgence of the walls pulsed into a blinding torrent of mottled crimson, and all the earth seemed ablaze with scintillant flame.

"It's gone mad!" yelled Kane, clutching his head in pain. "The others of its race are dead, and Bloodstone's soul has gone amok! It lashes out in the mindless rage of a beheaded serpent — deadly still, but blind to the attack of its enemy!"

Gwellines reared against his tether, trumpeted in fear at the screaming brilliance. With savage strength Kane halted his plunging, so that the stallion knew Teres's hand, and calmed somewhat. In an instant Kane swept the startled girl through the air, and slapped her onto saddle. The gate was yet open.

"Ride fast, Teres!" he commanded. "There is only death now in Arellarti! Ride to the forest and beyond! You and the others can escape! Bloodstone and I have not finished this game!"

"I'll not go and leave you to die! Gwellines can carry us both!"

"There'll be no time! Bloodstone is berserk, and sorcery ravens down over Arellarti! This chaos will be my only chance to destroy the demon I've set free! I'll try to escape through the interdimensional projection — there'll be no time for anything else!"

He caught her arm. "If there is a tomorrow for us, will you come with me, Teres?"

She looked into his baleful eyes, and the words she wanted to say hung in her throat. "Kane, once we could have shared a life together. Even now I can't deny the attraction I feel toward you. But there is too much between us now — too great an abyss — for love to bridge!"

Kane's lips drew back. His eyes searched her face and knew the pain there. "Words I've heard too often! Ride on, she-wolf! Tie your fate to Dribeck, if you will — or whatever whim your spirit thinks it desires. You'll not forget Kane, I think. Now ride, before doom overtakes you! For either Bloodstone or Kane must die this night!"

His hand struck Gwellines, and the stallion plunged for the open gate. Along the molten causeway he tore, bearing off his desperately clinging rider at a reckless gallop. Alien horror shambled forth from Arellarti now, and the warhorse sensed the urgency of flight.

Teres could barely rein in her mount as she burst upon Dribeck and his band, still bewildered that the Rillyti ambush which had closed upon them had broken into terrified rout, midway in the creatures' attack.

Dribeck brightened with unexpected relief to see Teres racing toward them through the blood-fed stream of light. "We put the toads to flight!" he shouted, as the horse reared in a shower of sparks.

"Go back!" warned Teres, before he could speak further. "We can do nothing in Arellarti. Kane has turned upon Bloodstone, and devils wage war in the night!"

Now all his dreams had been plunged into nightmare, and the lure of adventure had become a spider web of horror. The power that had promised him mastery of the stars was a lie to chain him into soulless slavery. Madness reigned at the death of a mad dream, and the cold strength of his fury was all that reaved the shackles of insanity.

Kane entered the dome and strode heavily toward the dais. The berserk crystal knew him, sensed his intent. A crackling ball of emerald flame flared about him — the suicidal rage of a scorpion, which stings itself when entrapped by an enemy it cannot face. Kane stalked forward, heedless of the stabbing coils.

Bloodstone still fought against the forces of Shenan's magic — holding sorcery at bay despite the cosmic madness that howled through its alien mind. Dimly it was aware of Kane and marshaled its tortured energies to defend itself. But its broken power was no longer irresistible.

Kane felt its phantom voice gibber in his mind. A thousand reasons sought to turn his steps aside. A thousand promises tempted his soul. Hideous threats struck out at him, in berserk chaos coupled with the gilded pleas.

He ignored them all.

Then came the invisible pain, but no more was it of unendurable intensity. Kane staggered, bit his lips to bloody froth, unfelt against the greater agony. He did not scream. The dark force of his hatred, his rage threw a shield about his mind, burned back the gobbling tentacles of pain which sought to crush his spirit.

His lips moved, spitting curses in a score of languages, roaring defiance at the stricken monster whose demented throes strangled him, ripped at him with searing agony. Through waves of torment, like a desperate swimmer who would not drown, Kane forced his buckling legs to hold him upright, to take inching steps forward.

Streamers of energy wreathed him as he fell across the stone crescent and clutched at the projections for support. Now the pain was not psychic alone, for Bloodstone's flailing claws tore blackened welts across his skin. In its berserk dementia, the crystal struck at its own flesh. Its frantic howls threw Kane's mind into confusion, disrupted his thought as he strove to recall the task he must perform.

Kane braced himself against the relentless onslaught! His was a mind centuries wise in the psychic mysteries, his spirit indomitable from centuries of constant struggle to survive. No man could resist the might of Bloodstone, even crippled as was the crystals entity now. The wrath of Kane was more than human. He found the strength through hate.

His fist smashed down against a protruding rod. Bloodstone screamed in pain — and in sudden fear.

Not pausing, Kane struck out with bleeding knuckles, thrust an entire row of metal rods deep into the stone crescent. His other hand pawed against the crystal projections and slashed fingers on the slowly turning ceramic knobs.

Intolerable lancination shuddered through him, and he clung to the projections of the dais to keep from slumping to the floor. The bloodstone ring burned into his flesh, as if his entire hand had been plunged into molten iron. Grimly he fought back unconsciousness, knowing its relief would only mean death. With pain-fogged movements he reset the rods and projections of the blazing crescent. He forced himself to lock in the controls, to overload the monolithic circuitry.

Now the brilliance of Bloodstone was a hungry glare that seared his blurring vision. Agony throbbed through him in cadence with the burning waves of pulsing incandescence. The heat was not an illusion. Beneath his touch the stones were blistering his flesh. The entire power web of Arellarti was blazing with uncontrolled energy, rising like the molten cone of a volcano from the steaming swampland.

Kane had jammed the external controls, which governed the colossal energies that Bloodstone sucked from the cosmos. The nightmarish creation of elder science was trapped in the full torrent of the power it fed upon. Like an unbraked millwheel caught in an inconceivable flood, Bloodstone was snared in a vortex of energy that raced out of control, pent up with no outlet, raging power that would tear it to atoms.

The stones trembled beneath his smoking boots. Kane could hear a distant roar, a rumble beneath the whining howl of Arellarti, as if some unimaginable storm were bursting through the darkness beyond the blazing city.

Fool! Your betrayal will destroy us together!

That was the last coherent thought Kane was to sense from Bloodstone. Desperately he worked over the dials and protrusions which controlled the powers of interdimensional projection. Regardless of its amok insanity, Bloodstone would have to respond to the settings of its instruments — for all its malevolent soul, it had been designed as a machine by its creators. Or would it respond? Could it, even, with the damage Kane had inflicted?

The crushing roar of doom rushed closer, and Kane knew this slim chance was all that remained. Would there even be time for a vengeful Bloodstone to transport him to a nearby locus? Though he might die in the crystal's disintegrating embrace — or wander disembodied through the interdimensional gulfs — Kane made the gamble.

Once more the coils of coruscant energy wrapped about him. Kane was borne through the crystal gateway to the abyss beyond natural space and time…

Abruptly released from the immoveable barrier that had so thoroughly repelled its sorcerous tides, the waters of the Western Sea plunged inland — as if through a sundered dam of vast height.

On their knoll the daughters of Shenan wailed in sudden fear, for the force of their most dangerous spells had broken loose at the collapse of Bloodstone's resisting power. Bursting past the vanished obstruction, their sorcerous might recoiled with pent-up potency far beyond their calculations.

Not a phantom tide, to steal upon the stronghold of their enemy, obeyed their compelling summons. A tidal wave more than a hundred yards high smashed through the great fault at Serpent's Tail and drove across the rotting land like the fist of the avenging gods!

Those in the forest fled in terror for the higher ground, fled to escape the witch-tide that ravaged through its ancient shores.

With irresistible might, the mountain of water ripped across the trembling marshlands. Envenomed creatures, stunted trees, choking lianas, bottomless quicksand — all the blighted dwellers of Kranor-Rill were devoured by the ravening wave.

When it struck the superheated stones of Arellarti, there was a mountainous concussion which seemed to tear the earth apart. In the forest beyond, trees shook, leaned, turned broken roots to the stars. Those who ran were thrown to the earth by the enormous shock and threw back frighted gaze to witness the shrieking nova.

Within its almost molten dome, Bloodstone shattered into a billion splinters of glowing energy.

The crested wave broke past this knob of pulverized stone, and the night was once more robed in star-flecked darkness. Like a stinging wash of antiseptic, the sea reached in, then drew back again, leaving behind a scoured land, purged of the evil that had rotted there.

Epilogue

It was spring of another year, and Teres awoke before dawn, knowing a strange restlessness. Old dreams return; ghosts will not lie. Sleep does not come when memories will not fade.

Silently, so not to wake those who slept, she stole from her chamber. Gwellines was restless, too, and nickered a friendly greeting as she saddled him. Past dawnlit gates of Selonari, his hooves trotted south.

Morning came, warmed into noon. The forest was bright with the fresh verdancy of spring. Teres's spirit soared bright and airy as she rode beneath the trees. There was a warm, clean taste to the breeze, so that she reveled in the freshness of the season, like some reawakened woodsprite.

The sun had started its decline when her quest was achieved. With an eerie sense of pilgrimage, she dismounted and approached the contorted stone circle where once she had parted from Kane. Memories came back ever stronger and softened her eyes in recollection. Strange, how moments of happiness were as haunting as the remembrance of terror. An insistent curiosity led her back to the spot where these two emotions had merged.

She walked about with wide and searching eyes. Beneath her foot sounded the soft crunch of last year's leaves, dissolving into the rocky soil. *Here he would have come...*

Suddenly she stooped, caught up the dully glinting object half buried in the leaf-strewn stone pocket, where a reviling hand had slung it.

"Bright Ommem! I knew it!" Teres cried with a glad laugh.

She rolled the bloodstone ring about on her palm. Its gem was lifeless now, its weight that of an empty shell. The white metal seemed pitted and distorted, the bloodstone opaque and shot through with a thousand cracks, as if it had been exposed to some unendurable heat, to some intolerable stress.

When she closed her fist upon it, the bloodstone ring crumbled like ancient bone.

Dark Crusade

To Bob Herford —
So, we'll go no more aroving
So late into the night…

Contents

And the hapless Soldier's sigh
Runs in blood down Palace walls.

— William Blake, *London*

Prologue

"There's no refuge there."

"What?"

The hunted man spun about, warily studied the shadows. There, in the dark corner of the buttress, a black-robed figure he had not noticed a moment before — when on failing legs he staggered toward the shadowed walls of the ancient tower. From the darkened streets down which he fled came shouts and clamour of armed pursuit. In the black silence beneath the tower, there was only the hoarse rush of his breath and the soft splat of blood as it dripped from his arm. His sword raised clumsily in the direction of the voice.

"There's no refuge for you there," repeated the black-robed figure. "Not in the Lair of Yslsl."

A bony hand snaked from the shadowy robe and gestured toward the black stone tower that rose into the starless night. The wounded swordsman followed the gesture, gazed upward at the dark mass of the abandoned tower. It was older than the city of Ingoldi, men said. Older even than the fortress, Ceddi, whose weathered fortifications had once incorporated the black tower. Abandoned now, the ancient tower was the subject of countless foreboding legends. But tonight guardsmen with torches and ready blades made the yawning doorway and its cobwebbed spiral stairs a welcome shelter.

"What do you know, old man!" growled the hunted man.

"Only that the guardsmen who followed your blood-trail will not hesitate to search the tower. There's no escape for you in the Lair of Yslsl, and brave Orted will make this final stand with only bats and spiders to shield his back."

The swordsman squared his bull-like shoulders. "So you know me, old man."

"All across Shapeli men know the fame of Orted. And all Ingoldi is talking of the trap that closed upon you and your wolves today, as you dared enter the city to plunder the Guild Fair."

The bandit laughed bitterly. "Not a one of the common folk of Shapeli would raise a hand against us — and one of my own men betrayed me."

He stepped closer to the black-robed figure. "And I know you, old man — a priest of Sataki by your black cassock and gold medallion. I thought the Satakis stayed in the dusty halls of Ceddi, shut away from the common world."

"We haven't forgotten the world beyond Ceddi," returned the priest. "Nor are we friends of those who oppress the poor to build up worldly treasures."

There was surprising strength in the gnarled fingers that tugged at his bloody sleeve. "Come. We'll give you shelter in Ceddi."

"Is this another trap? I warn you you'll not live to spend the bounty you seek!"

"Don't be a fool. I could have given the alarm already if I desired your death. Come. They are almost upon us. There's a way past the wall close by here."

With nothing to lose, Orted yielded to the pull on his sleeve. The priest withdrew through the shadows of the tower, leading across the rubble-strewn court toward a ruined wall. A paving stone pivoted downward at the angle of the wall, and steps led downward still. The priest descended confidently. Ill at ease, the bandit leader followed. Very little was known of the Satakis, but such rumors as there were of the ancient cult were not pleasant ones. Still, the torches were very close, and the arrows in his shoulder and side were leeching away his strength.

As he entered the gloomy passageway within, the entrance silently swung shut. Orted turned to see whose hand had closed it. He sensed the priest's quick movement behind him.

Then nothing at all.

Sensation returned after a space. The back of his skull ached. Cold stone pressed against his bare flesh. His limbs were outstretched, immobile. He opened his eyes.

Above him floated a naked man, spread-eagled in the blackness.

Orted shook his head, fighting pain and vertigo. His vision cleared. He looked into a black mirror, high on the ceiling above him. The naked man was himself.

He was spread-eagled across a circle of black stone, piniored by thongs about his wrists and ankles. His limbs lay along grooves cut into the stone, and in the mirror, he recognized the ring of glyphs carved into the perimeter. It was the same as on the gold medallion the priest had worn — the avellan cross with its circle of elder glyphs.

But he was on the cross, and this was the altar of Sataki.

Orted growled a curse and strained at his bonds. Even had he not been wounded it would have been useless.

The black-robed figures circled about the altar looked down at him, faces expressionless blurs in the shadow of their cowls.

Orted raged at them. "Where are you, you pox-eaten whoreson liar! Is this the refuge you promised! Why didn't you leave me to face the guardsmen — that would have been a clean death!"

"It would have been a useless death," sneered the familiar voice. "Sacrifices are rare to find in these dismal times, and my brothers too few, too old. It has been months since we last were able to lure into Ceddi some fool whose disappearance would not be noticed. For all your life of villainy and plunder, bold Orted, your final act will be one of service. Not in many years have we offered to Sataki a soul as strong as yours!"

They ignored his curses. as they began their evocation. The bandit howled in rage, writhed against his bonds — but his cries could break their-low-voiced chant no more than his sweat-soaked limbs could snap their fetters. Orted, a man who had no gods, called out to Thoem, to Vaul, to such other gods whose names he knew. When they ignored him, the outlaw beseeched the aid of Thro'-ellet the Seven-Eyed, of Lord Tloluvin, or Sathonys, and others of the demonlords whose names are not good to speak. If they listened, they were not moved.

"Our god is far older than those to whom you plead in vain!" came a mocking whisper from the priest who painted the sigil of Sataki across the bandit's chest with a brush wetted from his flowing wounds.

Bittersweet incense clouded the air, its narcotic fumes dulling his senses, soothing his frantic struggle to break free. Their droning chant, unintelligible to his ears, grew vague and distant. In the black mirror overhead, his reflection became clouded...

No. From the mirror above him a black fog was taking form, blotting out his reflection in a shroud of nebulous substance.

Orted screamed then — arching his body away from the altar, heedless of the trivial pain of his wounds.

Something was being torn from him...

The circle of priests ceased their chant, drew back in anticipation...

But that which they anticipated did not occur — and not even the hoariest annals of their ancient cult gave warning of that which did.

A thousand misty tendrils streamed down from the circle of black glass high above. Like spiderwebs of jet, they spun down to enfold the contorted figure on the altar. And on the tendrils of shadow, the half-glimpsed shadow of *something* crept down to engulf the stricken man. Altar and sacrifice were totally obliterated in a writhing mass of darkness.

Those of the onlookers who had not fled or died from fear could not guess how long the shadow clung there. Huddled in supplication they buried their faces in their robes. As there are names it is not wise to utter, there are visions it is not well to see.

And after a period of dread a voice commanded them: "Rise and stand before me!"

Lifting terror-stricken faces, the priests of Sataki beheld a wonder beyond comprehension.

I

The Man Who Cast No Shadow

The Guild Fair at Ingoldi was in its third day. Located centrally to the trade routes that crossed this region of tropical forest, the city was an ideal setting for the annual event. From across Shapeli craftsmen journeyed to display their work to the speculative eyes of merchants and traders of the forestland and beyond — wind-burned sailors whose merchant ships plied the Inland Sea to the west, dark-tanned horsemen whose caravans crossed the grassy plains of the southern kingdoms where the forestland turned to savannah on Shapeli's southern border. Even for those who were neither craftsman nor merchant, the Guild Fair was a grand event — a holiday from an existence of bucolic drudgery. From innumerable towns and settlements, those who were able to make the journey travelled to Ingoldi for a week of carnival.

In stalls and pavilions, from wagons and hastily thrown up awnings, all across Guild Square and overflowing along the streets that entered the square, buyer and seller hawked and haggled for the products of the forest. Rich fur pelts and leatherwork, finely woven cloth of cotton and linen. Sturdy chests of tropical hardwood to hold your purchases safe against your travel, or a delicate comb of ebony and adder skin to grace your lady's hair. Tablewares of tin and copper, pottery and blown glass, wooden trenchers and silver plates. Exquisite jewellery of silver and gold, emerald and opal — and to guard it, hardwood bows and iron-barbed arrows, knives and swords whose blades are of true Carsultyal steel — by Thoem, I swear it!

Taverns and impromptu wineshops served the thirsty crowd with ale and wine, brandy and more curious spirits. Street vendors hawked fresh fruits and produce, or spicy stews and kabobs, cooked before your eyes on charcoal braziers. Beneath the tolerant eyes of the city guard, cutpurses and con men roved through the throng in search of prey. Enterprising whores with harsh laughter and automatic smiles sought to lure tradesmen from the business of the day. Acrobats, mimes, and street singers added their frantic distractions to the milling crowds.

The Guild Fair was an imbroglio of gaudy colors, exotic smells, strident sounds and jostled bodies. All Ingoldi was engulfed in the festival atmosphere, and the abortive attempt of Orted and his outlaw pack to raid the Guild Fair the day before was already a topic of outworn interest.

To Captain Fordheir, who commanded the city guard, the matter was still of pressing interest. Fordheir it was whose archers had yesterday made a bloody shambles of Orted's carefully planned raid. Tempted by the bounty on the famous outlaw's head, one of his band had earlier revealed Orted's well-laid plans to the captain of the guard.

Ingoldi was an indolent, sprawling city — after centuries of peace, its walls outgrown and dismantled for building stone. With the Guild Fair at height, an incalculable fortune in coin and costly, readily transportable wares was concentrated here — with only an undermanned city guard to protect it. It was a daring scheme, but the common folk applauded the bold outlaw and would not rally behind the mercenary guard or the rich merchants. Why face outlaw steel to protect gold that could never be yours?

Orted thought to have a hundred of his men intermingled with the throng as he rode into Guild Square. The informer's eye had been keen as an adder's fang, and less than half remained untaken when Orted and the rest of his band charged down narrow Trade Street. Suddenly guildsmen's wagons were barricades, and overhanging shops housed archers. It was quick slaughter for all but a few.

To Fordheir's chagrin, Orted himself had thus far eluded him. When the trap closed, Fordheir saw the bandit leader, already hit twice, crash his horse through the lattice window of a shop. Somehow the wounded outlaw cut his way past the archers within, then bolted down the twisting maze of alleys and hidden courtyards beyond — losing himself in the confusion of mob panic. They hunted him throughout the afternoon and evening, but withal Orted somehow won free.

Fordheir scowled as he remembered how the blood-trail inexplicably vanished near the ancient walls of Ceddi. The outlaw had almost been in his grasp there, and someone had helped him. His men perhaps, in which case Orted doubtless was far from Ingoldi — or possibly someone in the city now sheltered him.

Fordheir had long pondered the inconsistency of the outlaw's popularity. Orted was a hero to the common folks — a daring rogue who only stole from their masters. Fordheir snorted at the conceit — what profit was there in robbing from the poor? Besides, he knew enough of the outlaw to be aware of the ruthless, less picaresque side of his depredations.

Captain Fordheir, on the other hand, and the city guard were only despised mercenaries — hired by the merchants and the aristocracy to maintain such order as there was in Ingoldi. For pittance pay that necessitated bribe-taking to maintain one's person and equipage, the city guard kept the citizens of Ingoldi reasonably safe from each other. The populace held them in scorn, and the gentry loudly demanded to know how Orted had managed to escape. It was, reflected Fordheir, his blond hair thinning and his joints stiff with age, enough to make him yearn for the days of his youth and the interminable border wars of the southern kingdoms. But an aging mercenary has to eke out his years as best he can.

Wearily he stretched in his saddle, wriggling his toes in the cramped boots. He and twenty mounted guardsmen slowly made their way into the city after some hours of fruitless search along the outskirts of Ingoldi. Emerging from the forest, the city's nondescript skyline of pointed roofs, crooked chimneys, and domed mansions of the wealthy was a welcome sight. The dark walls of Ceddi made the gloomy fortress a thing apart from carnival Ingoldi.

It had been a sleepless night, a long afternoon. Fordheir's tired joints ached, his belly was sour, his temper frayed. Grudgingly he admitted to himself that he had let the outlaw leader slip through his hands. Well, a good meal, a pitcher of ale, and his cot at the barracks would improve matters somewhat.

A horseman approached them at gallop. By his dark green shirt and trousers, a stripe of red along the leg, Fordheir recognized the rider as one of his men. He wondered what the guardsman's haste might bode.

The rider was out of breath as he drew rein. "Lieutenant Anchara ordered me to find you, sir. A group of Satakis are haranguing the crowd. He's afraid there might be trouble."

Fordheir swore. "If those damn pinch faced priests don't have sense enough to stay hidden in their stone-pile during Guild Fair, it's none of our lookout if the crowd tears them to pieces!"

"It's not that," the guardsman said with a trace of worry. "Lieutenant Anchara thinks they've got the crowd behind them."

"Thoem's balls! One day it's bandits, the next a bunch of crap-headed fanatics! Does Anchara really think we need to bust them up? He's got men there — why doesn't he use them!"

"I couldn't say, sir. But something's definitely in the air. Lieutenant Anchara thinks he saw some of Orted's men in the ranks about the priests."

"Lieutenant Anchara thinks! Why doesn't he ask Tapper if they're Orted's men! That's what we're paying the little snake for!"

"The informer has disappeared, sir." The guardsman's tone was unhappy.

Fordheir spat in disgust. "On the double, then. Let's see what kind of fool's errand this is!"

As he led his men through the streets to Guild Square, Fordheir tried to make sense of this latest disturbance. So far as he knew, the Satakis generally kept to their crumbling citadel and left the outside world alone. From time to time the disappearance of a street child or drunken beggar was whispered to be the work of the Satakis, but no one had ever been concerned enough to inquire within the fortress.

Tradition had it that their cult worshipped some elder world demon, and that Ceddi (which was said to mean "the Altar") had been raised on the stones of a still older fortress, of which the Tower of Yslsl was a survival. The cult was as ancient one, certainly; at present all but passed into extinction. Religious fanaticism had burned out some centuries previous when the Dualist heresy had fanned the flames that brought down the vast Serranthonian Empire. Today those of the Great Northern Continent who felt obliged to follow a god commonly worshipped Thoem or Vaul, or some combination thereof, and Sataki and Yslsl were names alien to any known pantheon. The seldom seen black-robed priests were held in some distrust by the populace, and few cared to venture close to Ceddi after twilight. While almost nothing was known about the cult, there were certain rumors and conjectures of an unpleasant sort.

Guild Square was as crowded as Fordheir could remember having seen it. Over a hundred yards across, the vast paved square was jammed to the point where walking was a labor. There was an atmosphere of suppressed energy, of building excitement about the crowd. Forcing passage to where Lieutenant Anchara waited with another contingent of the guard, Fordheir decided he didn't like the feel of it. Too many heads were turned from the business of the Fair, intent on the small group of black-robed priests who had appropriated a stage platform near the center. This far away, Fordheir could not hear their words — but the murmurs of the crowd were not reassuring.

His lieutenant gave him a nervous grin as he drew rein. "Hope I didn't cause you to break off anything important…"

Fordheir shook his blond head. "You didn't." Anchara had served under him in the old days in the southern kingdoms. Fordheir respected the man's judgment, and now to his mind as well there came a sense of danger.

"How long has this been going on?"

"About an hour ago I noticed that a bunch of them had climbed up on one of the stages, started their damn preaching. Few people tried to shout them down, but if you look close you'll see they've got some damn ugly-looking bastards cordoned around the stage. There were a few scuffles, nothing much, and I was wondering how to handle it or if I need bother, when I came to notice a few faces in the cordon. Damn Tapper demanded his money and lit out like all hell was after him, so I couldn't be sure — but I'd swear that tall bastard with the earrings there is one Tapper fingered and gave us the slip."

Fordheir studied the cordon of thuggish guards. Their dirty and ill-sorted garments had one thing in common — each wore a broad armband of red cloth, on which was emblazoned in black ink an "X" within a circle. Fordheir vaguely recalled that this was the sigil of Sataki.

"You're right," he said. "It is a tough-looking gang to be playing watchdog for a bunch of crazy-assed priests. Wonder where they got the money to hire them?"

"I'd swear they're some of Orted's men."

"We could check it. How long have people been listening to them?"

"Well, like I said, at first there was some catcalls and that was silenced pretty quick. Then people close by started looking to see what the row was all about. And some drifted away, but more stayed, and the crowd just kept building up as more and more folks come over to see what everybody else was listening to. They've about got the square jammed solid, and nobody can get to the stalls or anything."

"Then we'd better bust this up," Fordheir decided, remembering who paid his wages.

The harangue of the black-robed priests had been working to a crescendo. At this distance Fordheir could catch only a little of what they said. Oft-repeated was the word "prophet" and certain phrases: "a new age," "a world reborn in darkness," "a prophet sent from Sataki," "he who will lead us." Fordheir's eye was drawn to the tall priest who stood in their midst — silent, motionless — enswathed in a great hooded cape of black silk, on which the sigil of Sataki was emblazoned so that its band of glyphs fell like a scarlet circle about his torso, and the avellan cross rose over his chest and back so that his head was the center of its "X." The words and gestures of the other priests more and more were directed toward their silent brother. Highly charged with excitement, the attention of the crowd focused on this enigmatic figure.

Suddenly the impassioned harangue of the priests broke off. Fordheir heard their cry: "Behold! The Prophet from the Altar!"

With a dramatic flourish, the silent priest flung off his cape.

Anchara gasped and pointed. "Thoem! Do you see that!"

Fordheir saw. Everyone saw.

With the majesty of a demigod, Orted stood before them. The leonine head with its mass of brown hair and clean-shaven features was unmistakable — albeit more carefully groomed than was his wont. Arms akimbo, clad in close-fitting trousers and blouse-sleeved shirt of black silk, he loomed larger than life. The gold sigil of Sataki hung over his broad chest, flashing in the late afternoon sun. His glowing black eyes passed over the many hundreds of faces before him, seeming to meet each man's gaze.

He cast no shadow.

"Block off every street out of the square," Fordheir ordered. "And send a rider to the barracks for every available man. I don't understand this, but Orted's no fool."

Grimly he contemplated forcing a wedge through the packed square. "Bring up archers," he went on. "We can't risk his escaping into the mob."

"Sir." Anchara's voice was uneasy. "He doesn't seem to cast a shadow."

"I know."

Guild Square grew quiet after the initial hubbub of surprise as the crowd recognized the outlaw leader. The carnival air was overshadowed with an atmosphere of wonder and expectation. In the hush Orted began to speak in measured tone, his resonant voice ringing clearly.

"I am the man who once was Orted, called bandit and outlaw by other men. I am that man no longer. A god has entered into me, and his will is my will, my words are his words. Listen to me, for I am Orted Ak-Ceddi, the Prophet of Sataki!

"The World of Light is doomed, and the Gods of Light shall perish with it, and the Children of Light shall be utterly consumed in their fall. Before Light there was Darkness, before Order there was Chaos. Light and Order are fragile abnormalities in the natural state of the Cosmos. They cannot long endure. The Gods of Darkness and Chaos are far older and vastly more powerful. Against their wisdom and strength the usurper gods must fail.

"The wars they wage are beyond human comprehension, but the time is close at hand when the victor shall conquer, and the defeated shall be destroyed. The day is close upon us when our world shall be utterly swallowed in darkness, when man's futile gods shall be destroyed, and with them their temples and the fools who seek shelter therein."

Evening shadows were closing over the square, giving dramatic emphasis to the sombre words of the man who cast no shadow. Fordheir could taste the aura of fear that claimed the awestricken listeners. The man's voice was hypnotic, compelling. Fordheir felt a sense of hopelessness creep through his thoughts.

"There is but one hope of salvation."

The tightly packed crowd waited in utter silence.

"The Children of Light shall perish with their gods — but the Gods of Darkness shall preserve all those who honor them. Our world shall be reborn in Darkness, and there shall be a rebirth for all who have pledged their souls to Darkness. For the Children of Darkness there shall be a new age, and they shall share in the spoils of victory. They shall know the pure freedom of Chaos, and they shall themselves live as gods. No pleasure shall be denied them, no longing shall pass unfulfilled. Vanquished gods shall be their slaves, fallen goddesses their concubines, and the Children of Light shall be as dirt beneath the feet of the Children of Darkness!"

Exultant shouts began to echo across the square.

Orted Ak-Ceddi waited for the excited cries to swell, then raised his arms for silence.

"Sataki, greatest of the Gods of Darkness, has entered into me, and he bids me tell you this: That he, Sataki, who has all but been forgotten by mankind, has not forgotten mankind. That, he, Sataki, has forgiven mankind his negligence, for he understands that mankind has too long been misled by false gods. That he, Sataki, has determined that mankind shall be led forth from his ignorance, so that many thousands shall share in the triumph of Darkness. That he, Sataki, has chosen me, Orted Ak-Ceddi, to be his Prophet, and to lead mankind into the new age!"

"The men are in position, sir," Anchara whispered, reining nervously alongside. "The streets are cordoned, but if the mob turns on us…"

Fordheir felt his belly tighten. "I don't pretend to understand this," he stated grimly. "But I understand our duty. Have the archers prepared to fire on command. If we can conclude this cleanly, we will. But we will conclude this."

Orted Ak-Ceddi again raised his arms for silence.

"Sataki bids me tell you further: That it is his command that all mankind shall honor his name and his altar. The day of final victory is near, and Sataki commands that the Children of Light shall be destroyed by the Children of Darkness, even as the Gods of Light and Order are vanquished by the Gods of Darkness and Chaos.

"Therefore, this is Sataki's will: That each man must choose — Sataki or death! To all men who honor his name, Sataki gives the riches and pleasures of this world, and the promise of eternal majesty in the new age to come! To all men who refuse to honor his name, Sataki gives naught but death in this world, and eternal degradation in the new age to come! Their goods and their wealth shall be forfeit to Sataki, and all his followers shall share equally in that bounty! And the only law shall be: Serve Sataki and do as you desire! And the only command shall be: Serve Sataki or die!"

The crowd was in a rage — fights erupting throughout the square as reactions differed to the Prophet's impassioned oratory. Matters were getting out of hand, Fordheir decided, abandoning hope for a quiet arrest of the outlaw-turned-zealot. He gave a command to the archers, who had moved in as close as the press allowed.

A rush of arrows streaked past the stage, to the peril of those standing close by. Half a dozen shafts struck Orted Ak-Ceddi. His powerful body staggered under their impact, as their iron barbs glanced off his torso. Screams and angry shouts rose from the crowd. The Prophet held his feet.

"He wears good mail beneath his clothing," marvelled Anchara.

"Would you slay me, fools!" bellowed the Prophet. Abruptly he ripped the arrow-torn shirt from his chest. "Steel cannot pierce the flesh Sataki has touched!"

Orted Ak-Ceddi wore no mail. His bare flesh was unmarked by any wound, old or recent.

"More sorcery!" Anchara breathed. "Steel cannot fight sorcery!"

"We'll damn well know for sure!" Fordheir growled. "Prepare to move forward."

The archers had hesitated, stunned by what they witnessed.

Orted's shout carried over the tumult of the crowd. He raised his arms triumphantly. "See how Sataki protects his prophet! So shall Sataki protect and reward all who serve him! Choose now — Sataki or death! Will you serve Sataki!"

"Sataki!" roared the crowd. "Sataki!" the Prophet shouted back.

"*Sataki!*" the roar was louder — and louder into a chant.

"Then to the unbelievers, death!" Orted commanded against the roar. He pointed to the archers. "*Death!*"

"*Death!*" chanted the crowd.

Seeing their danger, the archers tried to withdraw to the main body of the guard. Too late. The press was too close, as the mob turned on them, hurling stones and clubs. The archers fired pointblank into the enraged mass of bodies.

There were so many targets, but an archer can draw and loose only so fast, and thus...

Fordheir drew his long sabre, turning sick at the sudden wave of slaughter. Violence claimed the massed square in countless individual struggles. The first stalls and pavillions were surged over by the looting mob. From his platform, Orted Ak-Ceddi exulted them on.

"Can we break them?" Lieutenant Anchara wondered.

Less than a hundred horsemen against a blood-mad mob? Captain Fordheir knew that ordinarily the odds would favor him. This time?

"Draw sabres," he ordered. "Forward to clear the square."

The guard pushed forward, horses at a walk, against the rioting thousands. The failing sunlight touched their grim faces and razor-honed sabres. Angry faces snarled up at their approach.

"Disperse! Clear the square!"

The mob wavered, pushing back into its already packed ranks to avoid the menace of hooves and steel. A few looters began to break for the alleys.

Then a clarion command. "*For Sataki! Strike and kill!*"

"*Sataki!*" the mob echoed. "*Death!*"

Stones and clubs began to fly, and a sprinkle of arrows. Knives and weapons sprang to defiant fists.

"Forward!"

Sabres slashed downward into enraged faces. Hooves struck out at writhing bodies. Before the horsemen, the forefront of the mob crumpled, stretched bleeding and broken across the stones. But pressure from the rear forced the mob relentlessly forward. They were too tightly packed to flee, and the press was too thick for the guardsmen to maneuver.

The city guard struggled forward and into the clawing masses — crimson-drenched sabres rising and falling with deadly skill. Still the mob surged forward, breaking the mounted ranks in suicidal rushes, trapping small groups of horsemen within its seething mass. Horses screamed and went down, carrying their riders to brutal death. Stones and hurled weapons cleared saddle after saddle. Like scorpions against an army of ants, the guardsmen slew and slew, and in slaying were pulled down.

In an eddy of the slaughter, where the mob cared more to pillage the jewellers' pavilions than to face slashing steel, the last of the city guard regrouped. Less than a score remained, exhausted and wounded. They were surrounded by the howling mob — murderous beasts united by the Prophet's unleashing of man's inborn lust for violence.

Lieutenant Anchara was half-blinded from a gash over his eye. Mechanically he tied a bandage about his head. "Can we break free from them?" he asked dully.

Fordheir glanced toward the distant streets, where murder and looting already spread, and the maelstrom of feral bodies that struggled about them. He ached in every joint, and he wished for a pitcher of ale.

"I don't think we can," he said. "For every man there comes a time for death. I think that time has come for us."

II
The Man Who Feared Shadows

The thin-faced man ducked through the open doorway of the Red Gables in Sandotneri of the southern kingdoms. Instantly he turned and craned his long neck to examine the street he had just quitted, where men went about their business in the heat and dust of late afternoon. Furtively he turned again to stare at those who sought refuge from the sun in the inn's public room. A bony hand wiped sweat from a sunken face where hunted eyes glared from dark hollows. He gazed questioningly at the innkeeper, who shook his head. Then, with a final scrutiny of the room, the frightened man darted for the stairs and disappeared into the rooms overhead.

"That one looks like he's scared of his own shadow," commented one of the drinkers at the bar.

The innkeeper looked at him significantly. "He is."

"How's that?"

The innkeeper shrugged his squat shoulders. The Red Gables was not a hostelry where the affairs of its guests greatly concerned the management. Still…

"Scared of his shadow. Bolts his door soon as the sun gets low, stays there until it's broad daylight. Keeps the room lit bright as day — must burn up fifty or more candles in a night, I don't know."

"Burns candles all night?"

"Yeah. Got ten, fifteen maybe burning all at once, got them all around his bed. And three oil lamps. Damn good luck he doesn't burn the whole place down. I'd throw him out, but his money's good."

"So what's he afraid of?"

"Shadows."

"Shadows?"

"That's what he muttered one morning when he stumbles down here, crazy drunk and looking for more. 'Shadows,' he said."

"But it's the light that makes the shadows."

"No, it's the light that lets you see what the shadows are up to." The hosteler tapped his balding head. "He says."

"Seen them like that before," another allowed. "Things coming after them. Generally it's things that come out of a pipe or too many mugs of old 'here's how.'" He tossed off his mug.

"Sometimes they come from elsewhere," said the black-robed figure no one had seen enter.

The frightened man hurried down the hallway, a heavy bronze key ready in his hand. The Red Gables was one of the few inns in this quarter of the city to offer rooms whose doors were equipped with such locks. It cost more, but there were some who would not begrudge the expense. Thus it was with some sense of security that the frightened man fumbled with the lock and slipped into his room.

He closed the door and gave a small scared bleat at the sight of the man who waited inside.

His visitor was not a reassuring figure. At rather more than twice the thin man's bulk, he sprawled half out of the room's single chair. His massive frame exuded an aura of almost bestial strength. The figure might have been that of some great ape, clad in black leather trousers and sleeveless vest. Ruthless intelligence showed in the face, framed by nape-length red hair and a beard like rust. A red silk scarf encircled his thick neck, and belted across the barrel chest, the hilt of a Carsultyal sword protruded over his right shoulder. The savage blue eyes held a note in their stare that promised sudden carnage should that huge left hand reach for the hilt.

But it was with relief that the frightened man breathed, "Kane!"

The big man raised a craggy eyebrow. "What's wrong with you, Tapper? You're as jumpy as a cat in a butcher shop. You haven't made some slip…?"

Tapper shook his head. "No, nothing wrong, Kane."

"I hired you because the word was you were a man with nerve," Kane's voice held a note of warning. "You act like a man who's about to break."

"It's not this business, Kane. It's something else."

"What, then? I'm running too close to the edge here to risk everything on a man who can't carry his end."

Tapper nodded nervously, licking dry lips. Maybe it was time again to start running. If he could make the coast…

"I'm all right," he maintained sullenly. "Thoem, Kane! You don't know what it was like getting out of Shapeli. The Satakis are everywhere — nothing can stand up to them! I showed my heels to Ingoldi hours before they slaughtered the guard and looted the city. Got away from Brandis the same night they surrounded the town and burned it. I barely escaped the slaughter at Emleoas by putting a Sataki armband on and joining the looters — and I passed over what they'd left of General Cumdeller's mercenaries in riding for the border. The Prophet's got tens of thousands under his banner, Kane. When it's a choice between join the pillagers or die in the ashes, they don't even need to listen to that devil's spiel to swear their souls to Sataki!"

"There's a hundred miles of savannah between Sandotneri and the forests of Shapeli," Kane reminded him drily. "I hardly think Orted Ak-Ceddi will look for you here."

Tapper started, glancing at the other sidelong to judge whether Kane's remark implied more than scornful jest. Although Tapper's betrayal of the former bandit leader was not common knowledge in the southern kingdoms, Kane was incredibly well informed.

The frightened man shuddered, tried to repress memories of weeks of terror-haunted flight. Sataki's shadowy tentacles reached far. Time and again the Prophet's hordes had rolled over towns where Tapper sought refuge. And the nights… The nights were worst. The bounty gold had not lasted long, nor had the money that came to hand afterward.

Then out of Shapeli and into the southern kingdoms, where the shadow of the Dark Crusade had not reached. For the spy and the assassin, there was always ready gold in the southern kingdoms. Gold enough to reach the coast, to buy passage to the Southern Continent or lands beyond.

The southern kingdoms was a geographic designation more grandiose than actual. South of Shapeli's forestland, the Great Northern Continent curved westward as a broad region of savannah around the Inland Sea to the north and the Southern Sound on the south — then northward past the western shore of the Inland Sea, where the grasslands rose into the Altanstand Mountains. Beyond their rocky bourne the greater portion of the continental mass sprawled out over some four thousand miles, eventually to join the Northern Ice Sea. Centuries before Halbros-Serrantho had attempted to unite this northern portion of the continent, but the Serranthonian Empire now lay broken in decay, and the only other formidable attempt to lay claim to the whole of the Great Northern Continent was the fading memory of Ashertiri's ill-fated war with Carsultyal in mankind's youth.

The southern kingdoms might number fifty or a hundred, depending on the most recent marriages and inheritances, annexations and secessions, alliances and civil wars. Scattered across a 2500 mile stretch of sun-scorched veldt, the stubbornly independent hereditary holdings were constantly at odds over territorial and water rights. Fierce border wars and deadly court intrigues were hallowed tradition in the southern kingdoms. A man like Tapper might grow wealthy in a single night. Or he might die in an instant.

Tapper uneasily considered his visitor. But the gold he needed demanded certain risks, and the frightened man knew darker fears than the dangers of political conspiracy. He noted with dread the greying skies outside the bulls-eye panes.

"How'd you get in here?" he asked in alarm. The window, unshuttered but securely bolted, overlooked a fifteen foot drop to the street below.

"I got in," Kane told him unhelpfully. He scowled impatiently while the other man fretted about the room, lighting candles from the oil lamps that burned throughout the day. The tiny room stank of tallow and soot and fear.

"You don't like the dark," Kane observed sarcastically.

"No. No, I don't. Nor shadows."

"A spy who fears the dark!" Kane sneered. "I'm rather afraid I made a mistake when I entrusted you to…"

"I'm all right, I tell you!" Tapper insisted. "I took care of my part!"

Kane smiled. "Ah! Did you now? Let me see."

"You've got the gold?"

"Of course. I told you I pay well for useful information." Kane drew a heavy almoner from his belt. It chinked when he tossed it in his broad palm.

"All right. You know the kind of risks I'm running," Tapper muttered, sitting on the edge of the bed.

"We're both running. What do you have for me?"

"Well, it's true that Esketra is receiving Jarvo secretly in her chambers," Tapper began.

"Which I knew when I hired you."

"No — only surmised. You wanted me to find out how Jarvo passed from his house to the palace without being seen by any of your men."

"Well?"

"I've found out how."

"For that information I *will* pay."

"You were right when you guessed it would have to be through some hidden passage," Tapper told him. "And you'd figured right on the rest of it, too."

"Esketra *does* have the chart?"

"Esketra *did* have it," Tapper grinned. He drew a square of folded parchment from inside his doublet. "But not since this afternoon."

Kane tossed him the almoner. "There's more for you if this is what I hope it is."

"It's what you were after," Tapper proudly assured him, extending the yellowed sheet. "Got the whole story *and* the map from one of her maids — who'll be wanting more of your gold, too. When she couldn't see Jarvo as she wanted without compromising herself, Esketra got into Owrinos' secret papers and stole the old chart of the palace's hidden ways. She traced a passage from her chambers to under the wall and out through the royal crypts at the temple of Thoem. Jarvo had a tunnel driven to connect his house with the cellars of the apartment block across the way. When he wants, he slips past your watchers and ducks off for the temple — makes his way to Esketra's chambers through the old network of passages. Esketra kept the chart as guard against getting lost in the maze — then never bothered to risk replacing it. The maid stole it from her."

Eagerly Kane unfolded the ancient parchment. The document was all he had dared hope for — an architectural diagram of the Palace of Sandotneri, outlining completely the network of secret rooms and hidden passageways within the huge stone structure. Every palace has its hidden ways, and frequently their builders died because of their knowledge. It was a secret closely guarded, entrusted by father to heir. Sometimes its complexity necessitated a map, such as this that now lay outspread before Kane's scrutiny.

"Excellent!" he complimented the thief. "But you'll need to see it's returned before it's missed. I'll make a copy."

"Returning it will be an added risk."

"For which you'll be paid. Send down for pen and paper. I'll copy this immediately."

Kane waited impatiently for writing materials to be brought up. This had been a rare piece of fortune.

Owrinos was presently king of Sandotneri and the lands to which that city lay claim. But his health was failing, and without male heir his throne must soon fall to a cousin. The matter of succession was hotly contested by two powerful branches of the royal family, whose factions were popularly designated the Reds and the Blues. Kane, a foreign mercenary who had risen to generalship of the Sandotneri cavalry, was a powerful supporter of the Reds. Jarvo, who claimed distant kinship to Owrinos, was a firm adherent of the Blues, whose faction was gaining in prestige. He was also a bitter enemy to Kane ever since Owrinos had appointed Kane to generalship over Jarvo in recognition of the outlander's brilliance in recent campaigns.

At best Kane had hoped with this piece of intrigue to discredit Jarvo and the Blues by exposing the younger officer's liaison with Esketra — denouncing such as an effort of the Blues to win influence through seduction of Owrinos' daughter. But Kane's greatest hope, based on certain information and careful deduction, had been to get his hands on just such a document as now lay on the table before him.

Kane concentrated on copying the yellowed parchment, while Tapper anxiously paced the room and stared at the candles. His huge hands plied pen and ink with far greater dexterity than might have been expected from a mercenary. In his mind's eye Kane envisioned the hidden passageways filled with his men, secret doors springing open to emit his assassins…

A sudden pounding at the door brought an end to Kane's dreams of *coup d'etat*. He sprang to his feet with a curse. In his concentration he had not noticed the stealthy approach of men in the hallway outside, nor the ominous subdual of the crowd noises downstairs.

The door shuddered under another blow. The men outside were not bothering to ask admittance.

Kane cracked the window. In the darkened street below, men with blue scarves at their throats looked up and pointed. Kane closed the window.

The door shuddered again. It was a sturdy door, but the men outside were using a ram.

"Kane, what are we going to do?"

"Keep calm!" Kane snarled. "We'll bluff it out!"

Giving the chart and nearly finished copy a last close look, he stuffed them into the fireplace and applied a candle. The aged parchment burned readily, and Kane had already stirred the ashes into dust when the lock surrendered and the door crashed inward.

Armed Blues tumbled into the room to face Kane and the long blade that menaced them in his left hand.

"Yes?" suggested Kane evenly.

Pushing past his men, Colonel Jarvo strode into the room. The officer's girlishly handsome face smiled with triumph. A fine blue cloak swirled impressively about his silvered mail. A head shorter than Kane's six feet, Jarvo's broad shoulders and thick limbs gave him a stocky appearance that contrasted to the grace of his movements.

"General Kane, I hereby arrest you for the high crimes of treason and conspiracy. And this man with you," he added, indicating Tapper. "Surrender your sword."

Tapper's half-drawn weapon dropped to the floor,

Kane's blade did not waver. "What game is this, Jarvo?" he growled, his back to the wall. "If you want my sword, you know how to get it."

Jarvo gave him a venomous look, remembering tardily that he should have brought archers. "Useless, Kane. Your game is lost. Thirty of my men surround the inn."

"Did you think I'd come here alone?" Kane sneered. "Fifty of mine await my call."

"You bluff, Kane," Jarvo said with more confidence than he felt. After all, Kane's presence here was of Kane's planning, and his own coming a rash act born of the moment.

He pressed on confidently. "Your man was seen in close conversation with one of Esketra's servants. His manner was furtive; it was suspected that the maid was stealing her mistress' property and passing it to him — but when we put her to question she confessed theft of an unexpected sort. Your rat's hole had earlier been marked, and when it was reported to me that you were seen entering the Red Gables, I lost no time surrounding the place."

Kane stared at Tapper in feigned surprise. "You mean this man has been receiving stolen jewellery? Well, I'll admit I was suspicious of his offer to sell me a fine emerald pendant for so little. But the price demanded I at least examine the gems…"

"Kane, the game is over," Jarvo insisted tiredly.

"Of course, if I'd recognized the jewellery as belonging to Esketra…"

"Kane, Kane. The wench told all as the rack unjointed her limbs." But Jarvo knew that, while the connection was damning, the maid had only known of Tapper's part in the matter. Kane was powerful enough to make a stab at blustering this through, might well succeed. Further, his own indiscretions with Esketra would discredit him when brought out.

Jarvo indicated the fireplace and the ashes smeared on Kane's boot. "I see the object of the theft has flown into the night — but we still hold the thief to give evidence."

"Certainly," Kane agreed. "And my men and I will see that he's safely imprisoned for questioning."

"I'll see to that," Jarvo promised.

Kane shook his head. "In all candor, Colonel Jarvo, in view of your openly expressed antipathy and the severity of the charges you bring against me, I must insist that my men and I share in the prisoner's custody."

"Oh, Kane. We waste time." Jarvo wished he could emulate the other's icy calm. In spite of his hatred of the outlander, there was much about Kane that Jarvo wished were part of his own make-up. In a quiet moment he had once reflected he might like Kane, if he did not envy him so.

"Stand close by me, Tapper," warned Kane. "I fear these men don't mean to see you have fair trial."

The frightened man obeyed — knowing Kane might well intend to kill him with a sudden thrust, but certain that the Blues would show him no mercy.

Jarvo vacillated, not wishing to stake everything on one throw of the dice by rushing Kane.

In the strained tableau, a candle sputtered out. Tapper uneasily watched its final string of white smoke.

Jarvo remembered something curious his spies had told him. "It's awfully bright in here," he observed. "Surely we can do without all these candles."

He signed to one of his men, who cautiously moved to snuff the room's candles — wary of Kane's blade, for all of them here had seen its bloody artistry.

"Kane..." muttered Tapper in a shaky voice.

"It's all right," Kane purred. "I'm here."

"Kane, you don't..." Tapper trailed off miserably. A quick look from Kane promised instant death at the first foolish move.

Jarvo grinned. "And all these lamps. Surely three are too many for this small room."

Another. of the Blues extinguished two of the oil lamps. Only one lamp remained now, burning on the window ledge beside Kane. Tapper crouched beside it, moaning softly.

"Come talk to me, Tapper," Jarvo pleaded soothingly. "There's plenty of light out in the hall."

"Stay here!" Kane warned. He would have to kill Tapper soon now, he realized. He had hesitated this long — not willing to touch off a violent climax to his carefully laid plans, if he could possibly preserve the situation.

The lamp flickered. It was low on oil. Tapper could see the level of fuel in the blown glass bowl.

"I'm going to wait out in the hallway," Jarvo said. The man could break, or Kane could damn himself by killing him — either way. "Soon the lamp will go out, and then it will get very dark in this room. Very, very dark. But I'll be out here waiting in the light."

"Wait!" Tapper darted away from Kane. "Look, I..."

"Take this lamp too, Jarvo," Kane said.

His blade snagged the lamp's fingerhold, slung it across the tiny room. Jarvo whirled in the doorway, just as the glass vessel smashed against the jamb. The lamp exploded, spraying flaming oil over the side of his face.

Yelling in agony, Jarvo stumbled backward from the room. He clawed at his face, smothering the gnawing flames in the folds of his cloak, as his men fell back in confusion.

The room was plunged into total darkness. Tapper began to scream.

The window crashed open. There was a brief glimpse of a huge figure hurtling into the moonless night. The door banged shut.

Catching the sill to break his fall, Kane dropped the remaining distance to the street. Like a great cat, he hit the pavement — blade slashing. Two of Jarvo's men died before surprise had left their faces.

"Reds! To me!" Kane roared. "Come on, Tapper! Jump for it!"

He cursed the man, striking down another of the Blues. "Reds! To me!"

A clash of hooves, and a half-dozen riders bore down the narrow street. The remaining Blues broke for the shelter of the inn.

Kane caught an empty saddle and swung up. "Tapper! Damn you, jump for it!"

The Blues were starting back into the street, realizing the Reds were but a few.

Kane swore. "Well, they've got him — and that's the game! Let's ride! There's hell to pay now!"

And inside the Red Gables, Jarvo's men helped him to his feet. He was sick with the agony of his face. One eye saw nothing but a red haze of pain.

"Kane's escaped!" someone told him. "He had men with horses waiting."

Jarvo cursed from more than pain. "And the other man?"

"No one else came out the window."

"Then he's still here — and we've got him!" Jarvo laughed mirthlessly. "No one's come out past us. Bring a light here!"

Someone brought a lantern. They kicked open the door, shone the light into the silent room.

Tapper's body, slack and broken-necked, was already slumping to the floor. And although it melted an instant after the lamplight silhouetted the macabre struggle, the sooty shape that gripped the thin throat in murderous hands was clearly Tapper's own shadow.

III
Goldfish

The garden smelled of roses, yellow and hot in the westering sun, and the chalky undercurrent of baked flagstones washed by the whispering spray of the cool fountain. On the terrace below, where the cascading spring spilled down from ledge to mossy ledge to collect in a deep pool, Esketra laughed softly. Silver-grey willows stirred long lacy fronds in the warm lazy breeze of evening, echoing the laughter of the girl who stood beneath their shade. A shimmer of bright color on the silver and black surface of the pool. Popeyed and ungainly and pompously finned, the goldfish danced and darted for the crumbs that trickled from her long graceful fingers.

Grotesque little creatures, mused Jarvo sullenly, and for all their extravagant fins and scintillant color, beautiful only at a distance. He scuffed his boots impatiently and cleared his throat.

Esketra pretended to notice him for the first time. Her grey eyes widened and her wide lips made a bright smile of greeting. "Why, Colonel... No, it's *General* Jarvo now! How good of you to call upon me — after so long an absence."

"I thought discretion appropriate," Jarvo answered levelly. The late sun pierced the tracery of the willows, so that splashes of light and shadow alternately masked and limned the white face and waist-length coils of luminous black hair, the slender figure that swayed within the grey gauzy kaftan. Jarvo forgot that for a week he had begged in vain to see her.

"Yes," Esketra drawled agreement. "Discretion. And...?"

Jarvo stepped into the shadow of the willows. "Can we talk here?"

"There are only my goldfish to eavesdrop here," laughed Esketra, looking across the sun-dappled garden.

Standing beside her, Jarvo spoke in a low voice. "I've covered our little intrigue quite well, I think. It is known only that the maid had stolen the map to pass to Kane's henchman. Those two are dead, and Kane has fled no man knows where. The tunnel has been cunningly sealed over, and there's no one who can link either of our names to this bit of treachery."

"Masterfully handled, my general," approved Esketra, intently studying the bandages that enswathed the left half of his face. She dropped her eyes. "Perhaps we should forgo such rendezvous for a time — until new scandals command the tongues of court gossips."

"That wait will be difficult to endure," murmured Jarvo, seeking to draw her close.

"You'll endure it if you love me!" Esketra insisted, evading his embrace. "What? Would you have my name bandied about like some barracks doxy's?"

Jarvo fumbled clumsily. "No — of course, I'll do as you say. We must be careful."

"You'll be busy," Esketra told him. "With your new command. And Kane is still at large."

The right half of Jarvo's face smiled grimly. "Took to his heels with those of his men who were loyal to him. Fled beyond our borders. For all I know, Kane's slunk back to whatever strange land he came from. His treason and disgrace have broken the Reds. Those who haven't declared their sudden affection for the Blues have seen fit to make a discreet withdrawal from court. The Reds are discredited. Even should Kane dare to return, the damage to their reputation is beyond repair."

"What a strange man he was!" Esketra shuddered. "Did anyone ever really find out anything about his past?"

"No," said Jarvo, which was not entirely true.

"But Kane might return," Esketra persisted. "His ambitious were obvious. A man of his intelligence and capability might…"

Jarvo squared his shoulders and drew himself up to full height; the extra heel of his cavalry boots brought him even with Esketra's brow. "Kane is finished," he snapped. "If he's fool enough to return to Sandotneri, I'll make an end to the hulking bastard and all his cunning schemes!"

Esketra laughed softly and held a crumb low over the pool. A golden head struggled above the surface, caught the morsel from her long fingers, fell back with a splash upon its slower fellows.

Jarvo flushed. Within his heart he knew that Kane's precipitous flight had been an error on his rival's part, that had Kane known of Tapper's death, he might well have brazened it out. At best the uneasy stalemate would have continued; more likely there would have been open war between the two factions. Jarvo feared Kane, and so hated him. His present victory was a hollow bitterness, for it had been a windfall — Kane's blunder, not his own merit. He wondered if Esketra sensed this, saw beneath his bluster and mocked him.

"So my general will protect me from Kane," smiled Esketra, with a bland inflection that was neither sarcastic nor adulatory. She scattered the last handful of crumbs petulantly.

"And what of these ominous rumblings we hear from Shapeli? Is it true that some madman has raised an army from one half of the peasantry and massacred the other half?"

"So it is rumored." Jarvo shrugged. "And the refugees who clamour at our borders swear such rumors are fact."

His face hurt and his palms were sweaty. He rubbed his hands on his trousers and edged closer to Esketra. Except for the purl of the fountain and the rustle of the willows, the garden was silent. At a distance, along the high garden wall, workmen grubbed at a blighted tree. The sound of their mattocks against roots did not reach the pool.

"You will, no doubt, be away on our northern borders for a time," Esketra went on. "To personally assess the danger from Shapeli. Kane would have done that."

Jarvo tasted gall. "Orted's peasant army presents no threat to Sandotneri," he growled. "A mob of poorly armed louts can't face a charge of heavy cavalry."

"Did I not hear something of a mercenary army the Satakis slaughtered?"

"Cumdeller was a fool! He thought to challenge Orted on his own ground — in a forest where a snake can't pass between two trees without sucking in its breath. It's four days march across open savannah to reach Sandotneri — four days for trained infantry. For the Satakis there would be no march back."

"But a new general would be expected to make a personal appraisal of the situation," Esketra persisted.

Jarvo stood silent. The breeze rustled his fine blue cloak and cooled his silvered mail. It carried a scent of her perfume upon the breath of roses, and his palms still sweated against his tight trouser. Esketra remained an arm's length from him and showed him her exquisite profile.

"You were badly burned by Kane's fire?" she wondered, gazing sidelong at his bandaged face.

Jarvo's mouth felt dry. "The surgeons applied unguents and compresses to soften the scarring. They say my left eye will never know day from night."

"Blinded," mused Esketra with a shiver. "Maimed because you sought to preserve my name from blemish. I owe you a great debt of gratitude."

She held her slim fingers over the surface. An iridescent-scaled body lurched from the pool, nuzzled for her fingers. She held nothing in her hand, and, still groping, the bright fish tumbled back into the pool. The other goldfish, assuming it had accepted a morsel, set upon it.

Esketra laughed with the willows and the fountain. She extended her fingers for Jarvo's kiss.

"Be certain to come see me," she smiled. "When you return from your tour of the northern frontier."

IV
Shadows That Slay

From deep within the forests, terror crawled forth. Its tentacled advance was as crushing and relentless as the numberless and strangling roots of the shadowy forestland — massive roots that twined endlessly through the soil, pried apart the crumbling rock beneath. Terror was power. Irresistible power of uncounted arms raised to destroy; power directed by one sinister mind that commanded its numberless creatures to pillage and to slay. Power was terror.

From out of the night and the forest, the Satakis ringed the city wall. For hours now Erill had listened to their chanting. From her vantage atop a flat roof she could see their torches flickering beneath the massive trees. Torches more numerous than the stars in the cloudless sky, enclosing Gillera as surely as the star-flecked night enclosed the forest.

Erill smelled the soot of their torches, reflected that soon the cloudless skies would be obscured with the smoke of Gillera. Bitterly the girl cursed the lord mayor and his aldermen for their stupidity in believing the city walls could withstand such a siege. Further she cursed the spiteful turn of fortune that had left her carnival troupe caught up in the advance of the Satakis, trapped here in Gillera. As an afterthought she cursed the invidious fate that had destined her to become a mime in a threadbare travelling carnival.

She had seen a lot, lived a lot, for a girl not past her teens; that she would live to see more seemed to her problematical. If hers had been a hard life, its experience had in turn hardened Erill, tempered her with a resourcefulness and resilience that told her when to cringe and when to twist the knife. It was a toughness that served her well in the decade since her dimly remembered parents sold her to a brothel in Ingoldi.

Old Wurdis, who bossed the motley troupe of acrobats, conjurers, grifters and mimes, found her hidden in one of the wagons as they rolled away from Ingoldi and its inhospitable officials. Having no cause to love that city or its authorities, Wurdis let her remain with the carnival. He never forgot to re-mind the girl that every member of the troupe must do his part, earn his keep, pull his share of the load. His nagging homilies forever in her ears, Erill learned to do one thing and another for him and about the carnival. When someone left an asp in Wurdis' boot one night, another assumed management of the loose-knit caravan, and Erill made her own way.

She was thin, with the flat muscles and agile limbs of an acrobat, and her figure seemed to have attained such fullness as it ever would. She had a firm jaw, a square chin, fall lips and straight nose, and the sort of mobile features that remained expressive under a painted mask. Her hair was a close-curled shock of blonde, and her eyes were a shade of green that matched the fillet of jade beads she always wore.

Jade also was the tiny pipe from which she sucked the last tingling lungful of opiated hashish. Erill blew a wreath of smoke toward the wavering torches beyond the wall, coughed softly, and despondently examined the oily lump of ash in the stained bowl. It was only ash, and crumbled beneath the stub of reed taper. Erill cursed again. It was her last.

"You'd be advised to keep your wits about you tonight," admonished Boree, joining her along the parapet. "If the Satakis carry the wall, there's a chance to make a break during the street fighting."

"What the hell difference does it make, Boree?" Erill scowled at the pock-faced fortune teller whose wagon she shared. "There's no refuge in Gillera. We're trapped here. The Satakis will roll over these ancient walls in a single rush — and they'll massacre us all because these damn fools dared to resist them."

Boree shrugged her mannish shoulders. "Where there's life, there's a chance."

"Chance, hell."

Boree drew a flat ebony box from the purse at her belt. She released its lid, slipped the deck of lacquered black squares into her palm. "See what your chances are," she invited, extending the deck to Erill.

Erill made a motion to take the cards, then waved them aside. "Hell, I'll take my chances as I find them."

"Or as they find you," Boree intoned sombrely.

"Go haunt someone else tonight, will you?" Erill snapped. "Whatever's coming, I just want to get enough of a load on so I won't feel it when it hits me."

"Just take the cards," Boree persisted.

If only to get rid of her, Erill accepted the deck of twenty-seven black cards, shuffled them expertly, cut three from the deck and lay them face down on the parapet.

Boree's long-nailed fingers flipped them over. Erill tried to peer past her shoulder, but the older woman's black tangle of hair obscured her view. Silently Boree returned the cards to their ebony casket.

"Well?"

"You're too hashish-sotted to do it right," the dark-haired woman told her gruffly. Not meeting Erill's gaze, she quickly turned and left the rooftop.

Erill swore and hugged her shoulders. She wore only a thin bandeau and slitted cotton skirt of calf length. It seemed suddenly cold, alone here in the night. The last night of her life, most probably.

Damn Boree! Erill had wandered up here for solitude and hashish-tinted oblivion. Boree's gloomy presence had restored a grim sense of reality to the night.

"I don't want to die," Erill whispered to the night.

"Of course not," the night answered.

Erill caught her breath, spun about. The hashish... of course.

"Nor is there need for you to die," the night assured her.

Erill pressed a knuckle to her teeth, felt for the triangular-bladed poniard she wore at her belt.

A portion of the darkness detached itself. It was a figure in a black robe, face hidden in shadowy cowl. Erill had seen the priests of Sataki in her girl-hood in Ingoldi. She knew that she looked upon one now.

"Only those who oppose Sataki shall die," the cowled figure whispered. "It is the rulers of Gillera who thus deny Sataki's power, and not Gillera's people. What a pity that the masses must suffer for the sins of their rulers."

Erill stared at the shadowy figure, still uncertain whether this was reality or some hellish apparition born of the opium-tainted hashish.

"The choice is yours," whispered the priest, advancing as she pressed her back to the parapet. "Sataki or death. Choose now, girl!"

Erill's hand closed upon the hilt of the poniard, then froze there. For now the moonlight shone brightly enough to see that there was nothing but shadows without the black cowl.

"Choose!"

"Sataki!" breathed Erill in a gasp, as the creature of shadow loomed before her.

"Wisely chosen, girl. But be certain that there is no turning back."

Erill nodded dumbly.

"Take this." A shadow-filled sleeve extended above her outstretched hand. A cold smooth weight fell against her palm. It was a jet-black disc of stone. Vaguely Erill knew it for a replica of the gold medallions worn by the priests of Sataki. Her skin shrank from its alien touch.

"No one will pay you heed," the whisper continued. "You shall serve Sataki in this."

The shadow whispered further commands, made snickering promises and insinuations that burned through Erill's consciousness like acid on bare flesh.

Erill cried out, as one from nightmare. With a dry laugh, the black robe collapsed upon itself, rustled hollowly onto the rooftop, dissolving as it fell. When she gaped in terror at her feet, the roof tiles were barren of cloth or flesh.

A hashish nightmare?

A cold, sinister disc of jet lay clutched in her palm.

Dimly Erill heard a voice within her soul, shrieking for her to hurl the evil medallion into the night. But the shadow had given her certain commands, and she could only obey. With dream-like steps, Erill turned from the parapet and descended into the fear-laden streets.

There had been an attempt to enforce military curfew, but the mobs of refugees seeking vain asylum within Gillera had so overflowed the city that the effort was abandoned. Inns, hostelries and caravanserai were all filled beyond floorspace. When disused buildings and empty hovels were filled to the point of collapse, refugees spilled into streets and squares in makeshift huts, tents, wagons, or whatever fell to hand. Others filled alleys and doorways with nothing but their tattered garments for covering. The city fathers had at first thought to swell the ranks of Gillera's defenders by admitting all who sought shelter within its walls. When they at last closed the gates to all without, the flood of refugees had overburdened Gillera's facilities for food, water and sanitation. While the city's high walls might withstand the Satakis, Gillera could never endure a lengthy siege.

Terror strangled Gillera in a thousand chill tentacles. The city was doomed. All within recognized its inexorability. All that remained was the hour of its coming. The Satakis were merciless. No army, no city could stand before them. The choice was capitulation or annihilation. Gillera had chosen to defy the Dark Crusade.

The chants of the Satakis carried from the nighted forest and over the beleaguered walls and into the terror-haunted streets. A hundred thousand within listened to the voice of doom, knowing in an hour or a day or another day that doom would engulf them.

Dull faces watched Erill without interest as she passed by them. Taverns overflowed into the streets, until their stores of wine and ale were exhausted. Men and women reeled and sprawled along the streets, heedless in the final haze of dissipations. Houses stood barred and barricaded, frightened eyes squinting past shuttered windows. Temples were mobbed with wailing throngs, beseeching Thoem or Vaul to protect them from the terror of the hordes of a far older god. In the hidden recesses of secret fanes, certain horrible mystic rites were performed with anxious speed.

Now and again a voice called out to Erill, inviting the girl to share a cup or an embrace, begging her for food or coin, challenging her to join in prayer or sacrifice in this final hour. Erill passed by, seeming neither to hear their voices, nor to see their fear-twisted faces. A shadow had spoken to her, and all else seemed no more than a dream and the echo of a dream.

The night was cloudless, the stars cold and bright. Yet it seemed to Erill that a legion of shadows marched across the heavens, writher across the lurid moon. Coiling down from the abyss of night, the shadows danced and slithered from beyond the stars, crept behind her in a hellish pack as she followed the winding streets and alleys of Gillera.

The soft scuff of her sandals came distant and dimly to her ears. The rest of the city seemed enveloped in black cobweb, muffling even the throb of her heart. Her skin was pale with the night's chill, but the only thing Erill felt was the cold, evil disc that burned her clenched fist.

The city gate was a glaring brilliance of light that stung her eyes. Erill hesitated a moment, then strode forward.

The relic of wars of past centuries, the gates of Gillera, were ponderous valves of cast bronze, heavily fortified from twin barbicans. Grim-faced guardsmen manned the fortifications, knowing that an attack must come from this quarter, unless the Satakis were prepared to sustain ruinous casualties along the wall. While a human wave with scaling ladders might carry a portion of the wall, they would have to cross the outer defenses of dry moat and stake-set earthworks under murderous fire from archers behind the parapet.

Tense figures stared out into the night, watching the growing sea of wavering torchlight. Within the gateway, soldiers and armed citizens milled about, talking in low voices, seeing to various tasks, catching snatches of sleep. A few gave note to the ashen-faced girl who wove a course between the jostling bodies — from her set features, presumably seeking a lover or kinsman amongst the massed defenders. There were many such, seeking a tearful farewell on this night.

Erill's mission was otherwise.

Before the brazen gates Erill halted. Cold seeped through her breast, her heart no longer seemed to beat. The hateful blaze of fires and cressets scathed her flesh. A number of heads turned curiously toward the blonde girl who paused before the beleaguered portal.

Moving as in dream, Erill hurled the onyx disc against the massive bronze doors, and cried out the phrases the shadow had whispered to her.

A last-instant presentiment of doom. Shouts as those nearest to the girl whirled to seize her, silence her.

Then darkness smothered the fires and the torches, and from the stars the shadow pack crawled down to slay and to slay.

Erill screamed, fell back — shielding her face in her arms. To see a man writhe beneath the strangling embrace of his own shadow is a monstrous thing, nor does the vision seem less hideous when it is mirrored over a hundred times.

The blackness, riven by choked screams, was absolute, and clotted the area of the portal like some vast and misshapen spider. Erill heard her own voice screaming, felt the hypnotic spell of the shadow lift from her soul. It was like an awakening from nightmare, and into a reality that offered no refuge from the embrace of horror.

Through slitted eyes she saw the shadow horde — grotesque densities of deeper blackness than the night — fling aside their dead, stream toward the bronze gates. The sigil of Sataki, swollen to colossal proportions, overspread the brazen valves where Erill's hand had cast it.

Shadow hands drew at the iron bolts; shadow forms heaved against the massive valves. With the deceptively slow majesty of a falling tree, the brazen portals of Gillera swung ponderously open.

Drained, half-senseless, Erill slumped amidst the twisted bodies of the slain, as the shadow pack streamed past the yawning portal and into the darkness beyond. Dimly she was aware of a wild roaring, as of two monstrous winds. One was the panic-stricken cries of those within Gillera, suddenly aware that something from beyond the dark had opened their city to their slayers. The other was the blood-lusting howls of the Satakis as they poured past the unguarded gates.

V

Sharks

The leaden waters of the Inland Sea thundered fitfully against the iron-hard fangs of the promontory overlooking the small harbor of Bern's Cove. The tide was at ebb, and the sour-sweet smell of seaweed and brine and fish hung on the desultory breeze. It mingled feverishly with the stale-sour stench of the refugee camp strewn out along the beach like jetsam of some darker tide.

Several months earlier Bern's Cove had sheltered a few hundred fishermen and their families. Today uncounted refugees swamped the tiny village and the rocky beaches beyond. Tents and huts and brush lean-tos afforded shade to those who could claim such luxuries; others huddled in the sparse shade of the storm-sculpted headland. The equatorial sun made the beaches shimmering expanses of white-hot flame, summoning forth a miasma of sweat and refuse and filth and fear. Typhoid was already killing faster than heat or starvation, and there was a dread whisper of cholera.

As Sandotneri closed its borders to the ever-increasing flood of refugees from the Prophet's conquests, those who sought to flee the Dark Crusade crowded the scattered towns and fishing villages along the western shore of the Inland Sea. Those who could, bought passage on whatever vessel might take them aboard. Ships were few; the cost of passage quickly soared. Most waited on the beach — waited for more ships to come to port, schemed and begged for the cost of a berth, endured the heat and misery for the hope of flight. Most simply waited. And waited.

Within the village itself, floorspace for a reed pallet rented nightly at a sum that would have purchased any dwelling in Bern's Cove a few months before. Food and drink sold for whatever price a merchant cared to demand. Fishermen who owned any vessel larger than a rowboat were in a quandary whether to reap the certain wealth their catches brought from those who clamoured for food, or instead to dare the sudden storms of the Inland Sea for the gold of those who begged passage to distant shores.

Between the village and the refugee camp, a hastily thrown up patchwork of awnings and pavilions contained the overflow of merchants and opportunists of every sort who gathered wherever the misfortunes of war meant ready wealth. Northward, beyond the sea and savannah, the forests of Shapeli lay under the shadow of the Satakis. That this shadow of dread might soon engulf those beyond the forest's fringe in no way troubled the appetites of the vultures.

Beneath the shade of a sailcloth awning, Captain Steiern mopped the sweat from his round face with a silken scarf and sipped wine from a golden flagon. Returning the flagon to the heavy wooden table beside him, he leaned back in his chair and smiled at the anxious faces that crowded beyond the shade.

"Who's next?" he inquired lazily. The oaken chair creaked beneath his beefy frame. Golden coins made a bright chink as a mate counted the last of them into the strongbox upon the table.

Below the promontory, Captain Steiern's caravel, the *Cormorant*, rode her anchor and tempted the hopes of those on the shimmering beach. Her lateen sails were neatly furled, and at the distance no one could see their careless patches or the cracked mast. The *Cormorant* had made harbor that morning, and despite the exorbitant demands of her captain, already her decks would soon be crowded with passengers.

"Come quickly now!" Steiern called. "Only a few berths remain, then I dare take on no more. Who's next? Show me only ten marks of gold or whatever barter that's equivalent. Ten marks, my friends, for safe passage to far Krussin. Ten marks for your lives and your freedom."

"Ten marks should purchase that leaky barge of yours," scoffed a disgruntled onlooker.

Several of Steiern's burly hands scowled, but the captain only sipped his wine. "Well then, my would-be ship-owner," he said evenly. "Save your gold to buy the next leaky barge to make port. Could be another ship will put in before the Satakis hang you all up to dry. Come, my friends, ten marks for safe passage to Krussin, far from the Prophet's armies."

"Krussin, hell!" grunted the other. He turned to the radish-faced man beside him. "Let's get away from here. That tub is doing well to float at anchor, let alone cross the Inland Sea in summer."

"Well, what choice is there?" demanded his comrade, following the taller man through the crowd. "Either plague or starvation, or the Satakis — we rot here unless we find passage. Thoem curse Sandotneri for closing her borders to us! The southern kingdoms will regret the thousands they turned away, when the Prophet burns a swath through *their* lands!"

"That madman and his rabble won't venture beyond Shapeli," growled a third bystander, alike turning away in disgust. His ragged gear marked him as a former officer of the municipal guard from one of the many cities to fall to the Satakis.

The three — the other two evidently merchants who had fled with little more than their lives — paused to scowl as a luckier refugee pushed through the crowd to pour a heap of gold coins upon the captain's table. Steiern swept them up with rapacious fingers. In the lull between breakers they could almost hear the drone of flies.

"Orted won't venture beyond Shapeli?" inquired a new voice from behind them.

The trio turned to glare at the newcomer. He led a black stallion that must have stood seventeen hands. A man with such a mount might well have ten marks for passage, so that they looked at him with some calculation and little favor.

"No, Orted won't," snapped the former guardsman. "He's mad as a tomb beetle, but he's too shrewd a leader to risk his peasant mob against the cavalry of the southern kingdoms. He'll have to be content to consolidate his power in Shapeli."

"Then why do men pay ten marks for passage with Captain Steiern?" the newcomer asked sardonically.

"Because it's death to remain in Shapeli — unless you join the Satakis," growled the tall merchant, with the tired patience of one who explains the obvious.

"And the Satakis are certain to swoop down on Bern's Cove," whined the other, wiping stringy white hair from his red face. "Orted will crush the border towns, if only to punish those who have fled his Dark Crusade. The Prophet is mad — or possessed!"

"True," agreed his companion. "It goes beyond power-lust or greed. Orted is stark mad. He won't be content with Shapeli. He'll want to extend his power into the southern kingdoms. There will be no stopping the Dark Crusade."

"Mounted steel and a march under the hot sun will stop him!" sneered the guardsman. "If Orted leads his rabble onto the plain, Sandotneri's cavalry will cut the Satakis into crow bait."

"A fat lot of good that will do us," grumbled the shorter merchant. "By then we'll be dead — caught between Sandotneri and Shapeli. For it's certain the Prophet will invade the southern kingdoms."

"Then it's certain he'll get a welcome he'll never forget," the guardsman insisted. "You can't face a cavalry charge with a mob of peasants — and that's all Orted's invincible army amounts to."

"Friend, you appear to be a man not without means," inveigled the taller merchant, scratching his hatchet jaw. "Perhaps you can help us book passage with Captain Steiern. I have certain rich holdings near Krussin. My associate here has well-placed relations along the coast there. We have but a part of the fee; your loan for the remainder will be generously repaid once we make port."

The stranger turned his back and swung astride his mount. Holding rein for a moment, he stared down at them thoughtfully. "You've saved me a voyage — I return your favor," he told them abruptly. "There's no refuge for you aboard the *Cormorant*. I've ridden all along the coast, and I've seen Captain Steiern play his game in every port along the way. Once beyond the harbor, his passengers are shark bait, and the *Cormorant* sails on for the next cargo of fools."

"Ten marks, my friends!" came Steiern's voice. "Surely ten marks is not too dear a price!"

"Thoem!" muttered the tall merchant, his face ashen. "But wait — what favor have we done you?"

"Like you, I've been seeking passage to another shore," the rider replied. "But your words suggest that there's work for me right here."

Kane spurred his stallion northward.

VI
Red Harvest

"Thoem! Their army covers the earth!"

Jarvo scowled and snorted, "Army, hell! Look at them, Ridaze. They're nothing more than a mob."

The sun beat an amber flame across the limitless savannah. It was still burning its arc across the eastern sky, and by the time it reached its zenith the sea of tall grass would shimmer in yellow-green waves. The last rainfall had been weeks before. Climbing thunderheads of dust rose from the northern and southern horizons, signalling the advance of the two armies.

Crawling across the northern horizon marched a seemingly endless wave of human flesh. Two hundred thousand? Five hundred thousand? Jarvo could not tell Scouting reports indicated the latter estimate, possibly more. A fraction were mounted, the vast majority on foot; Jarvo disdained to consider such rabble in terms of cavalry and infantry. Wagons and impedimenta were scattered at random throughout the surging mass of bodies. The Prophet's army had all the order and discipline of a rioting mob in search of a fight. Jarvo was surprised it had held together for the two-day trek south of Shapeli's forested demesne.

"We should have spared ourselves a day's ride, and let them walk all the farther," grumbled Ridaze, doffing his armet to mop his face. "A few more days under this sun, and our work would be all the simpler. Any of the Satakis left standing would be too wilted to do much but wait for our blades to come reaping."

"There's too many of them to risk allowing a closer approach to our borders," Jarvo reminded his subordinate. "Let those who escape us run back to Shapeli, and not skulk around Sandotneri's marches."

Ridaze lifted an eyebrow. "You think some may escape us?" The other officers chuckled.

"Too many here to kill in a day," Jarvo grinned sourly. "See to your men now, and remember: no looting until the rout is complete, then as you will. Oh — and take no prisoners."

"Not even the cute ones?" another officer leered.

"That counts as loot," Ridaze laughed.

"Good hunting," Jarvo, dismissed them. His colonels saluted and rode off to where their commands waited.

Jarvo frowned, scratching at the thick scar that disfigured the left side of his face. The hot sun tightened and seared the leprous tissue. Beneath its black patch, sweat stung the eye that had no more vision than the boiled egg it resembled. Despite the heat, Jarvo replaced his vizored helmet.

Some months had passed since that night at the Red Gables. The burns had healed — healed with severe scarring for all the ointments and assurances of the physicians. Esketra had been very sympathetic. Jarvo had seen her only three times since their rendezvous in her garden. Each time she had been on the arm of a different court gallant; she had expressed very touching concern for him. A score of attempts to meet with her alone had been politely, firmly rebuffed. Jarvo told himself he had no reason for jealousy. They must maintain discretion for yet awhile longer.

Kane had dropped off the face of the earth; not even the ghost of a rumor as to where he had vanished. That pained Jarvo far worse than the agony of his face, for he found he hated Kane more and more, each time he passed a mirror.

With Esketra's unaccountable aloofness making life in Sandotneri intolerable for him, Jarvo welcomed the reports from the frontier that Orted Ak-Ceddi was massing his ragtag army for an invasion of the southern kingdoms. It still seemed incomprehensible to him that a leader of Orted's reputed cunning would embark on such a fool-hardy expedition. The whole of Shapeli now lay under the Satakis' control. With so many conquests to consolidate, Orted was mad to grasp for more.

Perhaps it was no more than the familiar pattern of a tyrant whose victories only inflamed his greed for yet more conquests. Perhaps the Prophet was truly insane. Jarvo shrugged. It mattered little to him why the Dark Crusade dared venture beyond the confines of Shapeli's dense forests.

There were disturbing rumors that the priests of Sataki had employed certain sorceries to facilitate the Prophet's conquests. Jarvo was inclined to discount such rumors, although the dearth of information concerning the cult of Sataki was a source of unease.

More to the point, countless horrified accounts from those who fled Shapeli afforded hard evidence that the Prophet relied on mob violence of an unparalleled scale for his victories. Overwhelming numbers and ruthless terror were the extent of Orted's tactics. Messy but effective — on the Prophet's own ground. Today the field was one of Jarvo's choosing.

The savannah was relieved by an almost imperceptible rise and fall of the terrain. While it was inaccurate to consider the Sandotneri position that of high ground, there was sufficient rise to command a prospect of the advancing Satakis. As their horde slowly crept forth from the haze of their dust, Jarvo felt the first twinge of uncertainty. Their army covered the horizon. Jarvo had never before seen half so many bodies assembled in one numberless mass. The Dark Crusade must have emptied the forests of Shapeli.

Weeks before, the Satakis had overwhelmed the last towns along the forest's edge and the coast. Scouting parties had watched closely thereafter. At word of the Prophet's impending invasion, Jarvo had ridden north from Sandotneri with ten regiments of light horse and five of heavy cavalry. Mustering the frontier outposts of their garrisons increased his ranks by an equivalent of another ten regiments of light mounted — about half of that archers. Thirty thousand men against easily ten times that number. Trained warriors against an undisciplined mob.

Jarvo felt a fierce rush of pride to command such an army. Momentary doubt vanished even as it formed, and his only misgiving was that there was small glory in the slaughter of peasants. Rising in his stirrups, Jarvo gave the signal to attack.

There was no formal battle line to the Sataki front — only a vast polymorphic mass of bodies advancing on foot. Now they milled in confusion before the impending charge of Sandotneri cavalry. Trained officers might have forced them into some sort of effective defensive posture, but the Satakis had scrupulously massacred whatever armies and garrisons that had vainly defended Shapeli's cities from their onslaught. Such officers as Orted had were chosen from the worst cutthroats and bullies of the rabble. While their commands were obeyed out of fear, none of the Prophet's generals had any effective knowledge of warfare, to say nothing of how to receive a cavalry charge.

Wary of some hidden ploy, Jarvo opened the battle with a tentative thrust of four regiments of light horse along the enemy van, and split his six regiments of mounted archers into a two-pronged sweep of either flank. His heavy cavalry he entirely withheld until initial contact could furnish certain measure of the Sataki army.

The Sataki front struggled to present a firm wall of defense to the Sandotneri attack. Scattered companies of horsemen detached themselves from the main body of the army, galloping forth to meet the charge of light horse. Behind them, the mass of foot compressed along the van to form a wall of shields and spears. Desultory archery fire spattered from behind the mass of bodies — more of a danger to the Sataki horsemen than to the Sandotneri charge, still well beyond range.

Silver and deadly in the morning sun, the Sandotneri light cavalry swept toward the approaching wave of riders. Each trooper wore a hauberk of fine chain mail, and carried a round buckler and the long cavalry sabre common to the southern kingdoms. Like all warriors of this limitless savannah, they were horsemen almost from birth.

The Sataki horsemen were mounted on such horse as had fallen to them in the conquest of Shapeli, armed and armored with whatever spoils came to hand. While outnumbering the four Sandotneri regiments, they galloped to meet them with somewhat less precision than a stampede.

Maneuvering swiftly, the Sandotneri archers closed from either flank. They were two darker masses in the distance, as in place of drawn sabres they wielded the short composite cavalry bows of the southern kingdoms — heavy weapons whose iron-barbed shafts could penetrate mail. Clad alike in hauberks, the archers also carried sabres in saddle scabbards, and could act as a reserve once the supply of arrows was exhausted.

Watching from his vantage, Jarvo waited with his five regiments of heavy cavalry as his center, the remaining regiments of light horse drawn up on either wing. He studied the imminent contact with heart-stopping intensity — unwilling to commit further men until he felt certain of the enemy.

Across the sea of grass, the Sandotneri horse slashed through the Sataki riders as a scythe reaps ripe wheat. Sabres flashed beneath the rising sun; riderless horses plunged away in flight. The amber grassland stirred beneath a rising mist of yellow dust; the tall stalks were crushed and trampled, drenched in sodden blotches of scarlet.

The Sataki horsemen were no match for the veteran troopers of Sandotneri. Unskilled both in horsemanship, and in the use of weapons from horseback, they might have fared better on foot. In a slashing tumult, the Sandotneri rode through them — sabres emptying saddles with sudden finality. The skirmish — it could hardly be termed a battle — held for only a few minutes of swirling carnage. Then the survivors broke away, attempted to turn back for the main body of the Prophet's army.

A number of the horses did return to the Sataki line.

Now, cutting across the Satakis' flanks, the mounted archers strafed the discomfited front ranks with devastating effect. The short composite bows — laminated horn and dense wood and sinew — drilled their iron-headed shafts through plundered mail and improvised shields. In the packed masses of humanity, every bolt found its fatal target.

Return fire — badly aimed arrows and hurled spears — took negligible casualties amongst the streaking archers. Officers yelled in vain for their men to hold their spears to await the impending charge; in a panic, the Satakis threw away the best defensive weapon they could claim.

Demoralized by the slaughter of their own mounted force, raked by the deadly fire of the Sandotneri archers — the Sataki line reeled back in disorder. The yet advancing masses behind them checked their retreat — bringing the advance to a milling halt as van and center entangled.

From his saddle, Jarvo grinned crookedly beneath his demon-mask vizor. There would be no cunning artifices from the Satakis today. The numberless horde stumbled in helpless fright from stings and scratches; it was time now to begin the killing.

"Lancers! Forward, *ho!*"

A thunderous shout answered Jarvo's command — followed by the deafening clangour as six thousand armored warriors couched their steel-headed lances. Battle horns quickly relayed the command. Jarvo was holding nothing in reserve now. Once in motion, their charge would follow the battle plan previously agreed upon.

A monstrous metallic avalanche, the charge of heavy cavalry rumbled across the, trampled veldt. The pounding hooves of their great warhorses gouged a dusty swath through the dry sod. Steel plate armor — burnished, silver-chased, etched and blued — threw back six thousand scintillant reflections of destruction to the climbing sun, and the smooth steel heads of their lances glinted like stars of a tropic night. Lance and heavy shield for each man, and slung from saddle or scabbard — broadsword, ax, or mace, to deal with those who withstood their dread charge.

Five regiments of armored, battle-hardened warriors — the most awesome fighting force of the age. Developed over centuries of internecine warfare upon the vast plains of the southern kingdoms, their heavy cavalry represented the elite military power in the land. Ordinarily a charge such as this would have been directed against a similar mounted force of some rival kingdom — with the temporary solution of one of the interminable border disputes or wars of succession in the balance. The Satakis had no comparable force, only a teeming mass of human flesh to await the Sandotneri charge.

The first regiments of light horse — virtually unscathed — swung aside before their thunderous charge. Archers fired a last few arrows into the crumbling Sataki vanguard, then rode to contain the flanks as the charge tore into the center. Behind the hooves of the heavy cavalry, the reserve regiments of light horse galloped to support the armored force, as the charge carried past the Sataki line.

Faces dull with panic gaped stupidly at the looming wave of steel. Mouths made black circles of dumb terror. Even before the wave broke over the poorly ordered line of battle, men hurled their weapons in blind fear, flung down their clumsy shields and sought to flee.

The Sandotneri charge clove through the Prophet's peasant army as a warhorse's hooves scatter a dunghill. Already drained from the ordeal of their long march, utterly demoralized before this unstoppable onslaught of steel-fanged death — the poorly armed rabble broke and fled. They were not soldiers, but a mob united by greed and by fear — a mob that would plunder and murder, yet a mob withal. They had neither the heart nor the ability to stand before disciplined, heavily armed troops. They could do little but die.

Even flight was denied them. As the routed front of the Sataki army sought to retreat, the howling fugitives collided with those in the rear — still advancing like some blind and brainless behemoth, unaware of the annihilation that awaited. Panic spread instantly as the terrified fugitives forced through the melee, outdistancing their mounted pursuers only because it took more time to slay than to flee in the thick press.

Even as the entire Sataki horde sought to turn and flee, any semblance of orderly retreat was impossible — and any hope of a rally or rearguard action rather less likely. Burdened with ponderous trains of baggage and impedimenta, wagons of women and children, the Dark Crusade was less an army on the march than a tribal migration. The fugitives were thrown back against their own masses, hemmed in by their baggage train and the press of panic-stricken humanity.

Early in the charge, Jarvo left his lance impaled in a peasant's back. Now the Sandotneri general mechanically hewed about him with his broadsword. Only the resistance of packed human flesh brought up the Sandotneri charge, impeding it as a morass of weed clutches at a bull. For all the armed resistance they encountered, the cavalry might have ridden through unchecked.

Ranging like wolves in the fold, the light horse moved around their armored comrades, cutting down the Satakis until their arms ached and their bloodlust grew as dulled as their sabres. Strategy and tactics were vain conceits now; the task was only to hack at the shapeless and bleeding mass that sought brokenly to writhe away from its dismembered fragments. Archers exhausted their shafts, little troubled to tear them out of the dead. This was a day of meat cutting.

Across the gore-drenched field of battle, Jarvo led his troops. Some resistance flared in tiny pockets — a few had the desperate courage to die with steel in their teeth instead of in their backs. But the outcome of the battle was not in doubt — if ever it had been. The balance of war is inexorable: When one army turns and runs, there can only be one gory, unequal conclusion.

Jarvo wondered where Orted Ak-Ceddi might be — whether their leader was dead or in hiding. Jarvo had promised ten marks of gold to the man who brought him his head — with or without the Prophet's shoulders attached. Throughout the battle there had been no report of the Prophet's whereabouts.

Ridaze eventually furnished the answer. Bored with the slaughter, he paused to interrogate a few captives. Presumably they used their last breaths of life to speak truly.

"Not here," he explained to Jarvo. "He didn't even come. The Prophet ordered his generals to lead his Dark Crusade into Sandotneri — and stayed home, snug in his palace in Ingoldi while his followers took the measure of our cavalry."

Jarvo spat out a mouthful of dust. "At least then, the stories of Orted's cunning weren't exaggerated."

The Sataki mass was broken — the survivors fleeing across the veldt in a thousand directions, pursued by mounted slayers. Jarvo decided it would be too much effort to hunt them after nightfall.

It was midafternoon.

VII
Nexus of the Crisis

Rising from the treeless horizon, the full moon burned over the trampled savannah like a white-hot coal above a troubled sea of blood. Against the horizon, beneath the white orb of the moon, a horse and rider rose from the distant veldt.

The tableau was one of eerie silence. Replete and torpid, carrion birds that had assembled before twilight croaked somnolently to one another, as they roosted beside their unfinished banquet. Silent save for quarrelsome snarls and yelps, dingoes and jackals prowled through the field of carnage. Now and again a ripple of ghoulish laughter or the explosive crack of a bone marked the presence of a feasting hyena.

The tens of thousands of dead made no sound at all.

With the approaching drum of hoofbeats, those who feasted turned their eyes toward the interloper. Vultures stretched their wings nervously. Lips drew back over gory fangs in jealous greeting. Curious wallabies and other small nocturnal creatures halted, then slipped shyly away from the oncoming rider.

The tens of thousands of dead made no move at all.

Slowly — for in the clear night air distances across the savannah seemed dreamlike and unreal — the rider approached the silent battlefield. Dark against the moon and the horizon, he might have been Death in black mail astride a black stallion. A faint breeze rustled through the high grass where the fury of battle had not torn apart the sod, carrying the scent of butchered flesh and spilled blood and violent death.

The rider slowed to study the sea of blood, then urged his snorting stallion to wade along its shores. The black stallion's heavy tread sounded like muffled drumbeats on the torn and spattered sod.

Here and there the carcass of a horse, stripped of saddle and harness. The victors had taken their own dead and wounded — there could not have been many by the signs of it — and left the field to the vanquished. A plain of the dead — men, women, children by the thousands and thousands. Peasants and gutter trash for the most part, scarcely a one of them with the aspect of a veteran fighting man. Just meat to dull cavalry blades. Crude homemade weapons and rags and tatters in place of decent blades and mail. The dead had not been despoiled, nor were there spoils here worth taking. It was a field of dead meat, and of interest only to the thousands of scavengers who would glut themselves until only bare bones remained. Then the grass would grow again, richer and greener for the nourishment, and the bones would vanish beneath the verdant sea.

Beyond the great mass of the slain, a less dense moraine of dead marked where the battle turned to retreat, and the retreat broken into rout. Away across the savannah the flood of war had washed, leaving its drift of broken bodies, cut down from behind as they fled in panic from mounted steel. The trail of death littered a swath that stretched across the far horizon, disappearing toward the shadowy forestland many miles distant. Until the pursuers tired of butchery, that trail of bodies would extend unbroken to the forest — unless there were no more to be slain.

Shadowed beneath the rising moon, the rider picked his course amidst the dead, picturing the battle that had been fought here, and the horrific slaughter that ensued. Before his practiced eye the battle was reenacted. The dead stirred and rose, fought their final battles, and died again. To his ears came the echoes of that battle, the dim ghosts of shouts and death cries.

Vultures croaked and sidled away with wings upraised. Predators snarled and. slunk back from their spoil. He paid them no more heed than he paid to the slain. His thoughts were elsewhere now, and the field of carnage no longer held interest.

He had looked upon a thousand such battlefields; it might be that he would look upon a thousand such more. The rising breeze moaned a ghost-song through the waving grassland, and its death-scented breath fanned his billowing red cloak. Following the trail of death, Kane dwindled against the far horizon.

VIII
Origin of Storms

The winds of the tropic storm lashed Ingoldi. Even within the massive fortifications of Ceddi, the monstrous blasts of thunder pounded through the stone walls and rolled along the gloomy hallways. Gusts of water slashed through the balistraria, washing across the stones. Sky-spanning chains of lightning flickered eerily past the narrow apertures, to add their sporadic glare to the flaring cressets along the passages.

No less than the fury of the storm was the rage of Orted Ak-Ceddi.

A year had wrought strange transformations upon the former bandit chieftain, even as a hundred thousand pairs of hands had raised Ceddi from a crumbling pile to a towering and unassailable fortress, had moulded Ingoldi from a sprawling city into a military citadel.

The man who cast no shadow yet showed the panther-like quickness and the steel-thewed strength of the hunted outlaw. Months of unbridled dissipation had nonetheless begun to leave its mark — clothing his raw-muscled frame with an insidious smoothness of fat, suffusing his ruddy features with shadows and lines of debauchery. His eyes, formerly alight with quick cunning, now blazed with the black flames of fanaticism, and the ponderous dynamism of absolute power.

For the moment the certainty of that absolute power was shaken, and with uncertainty arose consuming rage. With the assumption of godlike power comes the awareness of godlike passions. Not the impaled agonies of all Orted's captains could slake the Prophet's wrath.

Alone he brooded in his chambers, staring out across the storm-swept citadel beyond his tower windows. In his demonic rage, not even the priests of Sataki dared approach him. In the courtyard far below, the violent winds flung about the scarecrow limbs of the impaled officers who had failed him — giving false life to their cold flesh.

"Defeat!" Orted spat, glowering at the puppets that danced for him even in death. "Massacre!"

It mattered nothing that his generals had attempted to argue that an invasion of the southern kingdoms was suicidal folly: that his unbroken chain of victories within Shapeli were only monstrous extensions of mob violence, and that crude numbers, no matter how overpowering, could not hope to prevail in an actual drawn battle against superior discipline and weaponry. The Prophet had quickly silenced such doubts of victory by pointing out that failure to obey his commands was suicidal folly of a far more sinister degree. Sataki commanded that the southern kingdoms be subdued. Sataki must be obeyed.

That his protesting generals had had the temerity to escape his wrath by being among the first to die beneath the charge of the Sandotneri cavalry only blackened the Prophet's rage.

Orted flung open the lattice panes of a window, let the storm beat upon his livid face, the wind lash his perfumed coils of brown hair. Lightning shattered the storm-haunted night, bathing his rigid frame in its hellish glare, splashing a stark highlight to the tossing corpses far below. Stygian darkness, then flickering bursts of intense flame. Orted's movements seemed spasmodic, unreal in the stroboscopic luminance. His thick neck straining, mouth a ghastly rictus — Orted Ak-Ceddi screamed his wrath and his defiance against the howling storm, screamed into the lightning-blasted night, where no living soul dared venture.

"There shall be no defeat!" he roared against the storm. "I shall conquer! I must conquer!"

A titanic bolt of lightning shattered the night, blinding him in its elemental flame — even as its tumultuous thunderclap deafened his hearing.

For a moment Orted Ak-Ceddi saw utter blackness, heard naught but the throbbing of his heart. Then from behind him in his chamber:

"To conquer you must have heavy cavalry."

Orted whirled at the low voice. The door of his private chambers stood open. Limned at the threshold by the flickering lightning — a silhouetted figure, massive, all but filling the doorway. A pair of eyes blazed a hellish blue beneath the storm-tossed mane of red hair.

"I am Kane. You need me."

IX
The Forging

The shrill laughter of the children chittered through the roiling dust of the parade ground. Drawn by the expanse of open ground beyond Ingoldi's walls, they gathered in shouting packs to watch the bright glitter of the cavalry drill, and to play their endless games of kick-ball. Within the Prophet's capital, the faces of their elders might be haunted and strained, but here beneath the city wall, heedless of the danger from hooves and steel, the children romped about with all the unaffected gusto of their youthful innocence.

Kane had demanded a parade ground on which to train the Prophet's cavalry. Kane demanded; Orted Ak-Ceddi commanded. A hundred thousand pairs of hands obeyed. A square mile of tropical hardwood forest was torn out of the earth. Roots were painstakingly grubbed forth, rocks and boulders hauled away, the denuded plain meticulously levelled and filled in, the soil packed to stony firmness. Where there had been jungle, there was now a square mile of packed earth, flat and barren as a table top.

Kane was impressed. He remembered the deadly piranha that infested the rivers of the southwestern portion of the Great Northern Continent, and the voracious march of the army ants that swarmed through the jungles there.

The parade ground stood ready and waiting when the first regiments of cavalry began to sift through the forest barrier to converge on Ingoldi.

"The Dark Crusade is a colossus — a giant," Kane told Orted. "But it is a helpless giant for all its hugeness and its strength — for it is a giant without weapons or armor. I can forge the weapons and armor your giant must have if it is to conquer.

"Give to me the gold and the power that I require," said Kane. "And I shall forge the Sword of Sataki."

"Who are you?" the Prophet whispered, and in his secret thoughts he wondered: *What are you?*

Gold and power. Orted Ak-Ceddi had both in abundance. To win yet more, he gave Kane whatever the stranger demanded.

Kane cast the gold to the four winds, and from lands beyond Shapeli men answered his call.

"From what I've seen of your army," Kane said, "I'll have to rely heavily on mercenary troops for cavalry. There's only so much one can do in terms of time and training. I rather hope some of them might make effective pikemen."

"They are the Children of Sataki!" stormed Orted dangerously.

"They are rabble," Kane replied. "I cannot forge a sword from mud and dung."

"Your mercenaries will not be true believers!" the Prophet thundered.

"They will be soldiers; that is sufficient," Kane told him. "As to their religion, they'll believe whatever you pay them to believe. A sword has no soul."

It was a critical point. Kane misread its implication.

Gold. Orted Ak-Ceddi had the plunder of all Shapeli to fill his coffers. He had made a fool's gamble and lost an army. Kane took his gold and bought him a second army — brighter and deadlier than the first, for Kane spent the gold wisely.

It was a game Kane knew well.

To the south, Sandotneri held the frontier behind a wall of armor and steel. Content with the slaughter of the Prophet's army, Jarvo felt no inclination to risk further punitive expeditions into the trackless forests of Shapeli. In his palace in Sandotneri, King Owrinos languished interminably upon his death bed — cancer gnawing like a worm. Court intrigue intensified as to his successor, and the hero of the marches of Shapeli cut a most impressive figure on parade. With such to concern him, Jarvo left the frontier to those of his officers who seemed least favorable to his cause, and wondered how Esketra could appear so infatuated with a shallow sycophant like Ridaze.

With only a half-hearted watch to see that no new army marched forth from Shapeli, the frontier guard little cared who might choose to ride into Shapeli. At first only lone horsemen and small bands of riders; then — as clandestine gold filled the campaign chests of the garrison commanders — no one challenged if an army rode by night.

Elsewhere, along Shapeli's western coast, ships crossed and recrossed the Inland Sea to the western mass of the Great Northern Continent. There, from the decadent kingdoms that had sprung up amidst the ruins of the vast Serronthonian Empire, certain men heeded the call of gold, looked to swords and battle gear, took passage for the forests of Shapeli.

Upon the northern and eastern coasts of this peninsular subcontinent beat the rolling breakers of the Eastern Sea. A thousand leagues across its azure waves lay the continental mass of Lartroxia, where men named this same expanse of water the Western Sea. Ships could and did cross this great span of ocean, but such crossings had grown less and less common as both of the northern supercontinents lapsed into centuries of barbarism. Kane had no need to cross an ocean for the men he sought.

Even within Shapeli, Kane found those who could be forged into the metal he required. Some among the Satakis — through native talent or rudimentary training —could handle weapons, sit a horse, and not endanger comrade more than enemy. Kane chose them from the rabble, armed them, trained them.

A general amnesty — proclaimed by Kane over Orted's objections — lured a scattering of half-starved ex-guardsmen out of hiding.

"They defied Sataki!" the Prophet exploded.

"They have since repented; be magnanimous," Kane said. "I need trained men for my officers."

A core of trained officers — professional soldiers — and about them a framework of veteran warriors. This was the key to Kane's ambitious design. From this core he could build an army, swelling its ranks from the Sataki masses — to such degree as the best of them could be trained.

With gold and power, it was only a factor of time.

Meanwhile the forges of Shapeli blackened the sky, as craftsmen worked day and night turning out the weapons and armor Kane demanded. Kane ransacked the whole of Shapeli to fill the stables at Ingoldi, lavished shiploads of gold to bring in the mounts he still required.

It was a formidable task. It would have been impossible without the thousands of mercenaries who answered Kane's summons.

To think of such men as knights or samurai would be inaccurate. While some claimed aristocratic lineage, in an age of shattered empire, and no dynasty of note in centuries — of uncounted petty kingdoms and principalities — such pretensions were a conceit. Nor were these landed gentry who owed allegiance to some feudal lord, although there were some with considerable holdings and private armies. It was an age of near anarchy, when a man might take whatever he could hold, and force of might overruled all laws temporal, spiritual, or natural. Long a bucolic backwater of city-states and agrarian villages, Shapeli had only rejoined its era.

The arms, armor and horse of such a soldier represented a huge investment. The skill to use them effectively demanded years of training. Yet in an age of constant warfare, such professional soldiers could grow wealthy from selling their services, or from private endeavours of a less glorious nature.

Call them free companions or *condottieri* or mercenaries. They were a warrior class, without code or values other than each man's personal creed, owing allegiance to whatever cause paid well. Their ranks were open to any man who could claim the prerequisite weapons and accoutrements. Those who also had the necessary skills might, with luck, live long and eventful careers.

These were the men Kane summoned. Most came to him with their own arms and mounts; some only with their scars. They were an army that lacked only coherence to be ready to fight.

For the Satakis, it was a different story. Kane selected the most promising, turned them over to his veteran officers. He hoped that several months of training and drill might hammer them into acceptable light cavalry. As for the rest — perhaps a few worthwhile regiments of pikemen and foot soldiers. Incredibly, the Prophet's followers still numbered in the hundreds of thousands — Shapeli's forests had sheltered a population of some millions before Orted launched his Dark Crusade. The best of the Prophet's army had been thrown away against the Sandotneri charge. Kane supposed the dregs that remained might be dangerous enough to a cornered foe.

"They can hold a sword; they can fight," argued Orted Ak-Ceddi.

"They can stop a sword well enough, I trust," Kane sneered.

For months Kane drilled them on the parade ground at Ingoldi. With surgical precision he excised the useless, gave command to the best, organized and reorganized. The long hours of toil at last began to show results. Upon the steel core of his mercenary force, the mismatched components and raw material slowly welded together into a fighting unit. Under the guidance of veterans, the Sataki regiments took shape — a fusion of battle-hardened mercenaries and newly trained recruits from the Prophet's hordes.

Kane was, for the most part, not displeased with their progress. The Sword of Sataki made an impressive show, at drill or on parade. Kane knew the test of battle was yet to come, and that this was the only test that mattered. He was withal reasonably confident of his men.

Indeed, someone might have pointed out that the greater portion of Kane's officers were men who had served under Kane in Sandotneri. Doubtless, had Orted remarked upon this, Kane would have told him, and truthfully, that he needed officers whom he knew he could trust.

It was with some satisfaction that Kane turned from reviewing the day's cavalry drill, and leisurely rode back across the parade ground with several of his officers.

"The Sword of Sataki has been forged, I rather think," he remarked to his staff. "There remains only the task of honing it."

And blooding it, he told himself.

Despite the heavy rainfall in Shapeli, the tropic sun quickly dried out the packed earth. Through the thin dust lazily drifted the laughter of children at their play. Heedless of the riders' approach, the children played their game of kickball almost under their hooves. Shrieking gaily, they propelled the bounding objects across the hard clay.

"Watch it!" Kane pulled rein, swerved as a small girl recklessly chased the rolling kickball across his path. The huge black stallion reared, pawed its deadly hooves. With a frightened squeal, the child darted away.

"That's General Kane!" breathed excited voices. "Now you've done it! Run!" The gang of children scattered like leaves.

The girl stood her ground — wanting her kickball, but not daring to approach while Kane calmed his stamping mount.

Liking her mettle, Kane leaned from his saddle, caught up the kickball by its matted hair. Casually he glanced at the battered features of the young woman's head, almost unrecognizable from dirt and clotted gore. The bare feet of the children had all but pulped this kickball in the course of their game.

Kane handed down the grisly object to the anxious girl — her blue eyes big with wonder at receiving attention from so important a man. "This one has about had it," he told her, and pointed to the row of impaled heads along the city wall. "You'd better put this back and get yourself another kickball."

Each morning the heads of persons suspected of disloyalty to Orted and hence to Sataki were put on display. The children of Shapeli were quick to find new sport with such grim trophies.

"Oh, no, sir," replied the girl, gravely accepting the battered head. "I want to keep this one. She's my mother."

X
At the Tower of Yslsl

Ingoldi lay beneath the veil of night, pierced by the stars that seemed too close and too bright in the tropic skies. It was yet an hour before the false dawn, and the streets were deserted. Houses were silent behind bolts and shutters, and even the Defenders of Sataki, the Prophet's special police corps, seemed to be asleep at this hour.

Hooves made a hollow echo along the empty streets. If any awoke at the sound, they waited without breathing for the hoofbeats to pass by. It was the hoofbeats of a great black stallion, and no man cared to encounter horse or rider at this lonely hour of the night.

Kane, sleepless on these nights, rode alone through the deserted city, wrapped in his thoughts. Such nocturnal ramblings were of little solace, for Kane hated Ingoldi.

The capital of the Satakis bore little resemblance to the city of two years ago. A good third of Ingoldi had been burned in the aftermath of rioting at the Guild Fair; most of what remained was razed by order of the Prophet. Magnificent temples and mansions of the wealthy were despoiled and carted away piecemeal by the Satakis.

As the Prophet's hordes streamed into his capital in the wake of his victories, houses and public buildings that had stood for centuries were demolished. From the blocks of barren rubble, ungainly dormitories and communal dwellings sprang up like huge and featureless fungi. The city's picturesque courts and narrow, winding streets were swallowed up in the rebuilding, supplanted by broad, avenues of geometric pattern — military thoroughfares for the marching horde. Outlying gardens and villas were trampled into the ashes and muck, and in their place arose a high wall to enclose the unlovely new city and its elbowing masses.

Two years ago, a sprawling and indolent city, shaped by centuries of dreamy transformation. Today it was a teeming and ugly military barracks, born of directed violence. It reminded Kane of some colossal anthill, flung together for no purpose other than to house the faceless units of the Prophet's killing machine.

Even Ceddi, ancient citadel of the priests of Sataki, had not escaped the transmutation. Its crumbling stone walls and angular towers — old when the city of Ingoldi sprang up in its shadow, eventually to encircle the sombre fortress — were razed and cannibalized for building stone. Higher walls and grander fortifications arose from the ancient foundations. Blocky, featureless halls and towers replaced the broken spires and antique edifices of ancient Ceddi. Only beneath the earth, in Ceddi's hidden cellars, were the Prophet's renovations without consequence.

Kane knew the city and its sinister fortress of old. It pained him to see the architectures of past ages smashed beneath the utilitarian juggernaut of the Dark Crusade. The sacrifice of untold human lives meant nothing to Kane. A stone wall, being a somewhat more enduring entity, impressed him the more deeply with its loss.

Kane suddenly sneered at his own melancholia. He had looked upon the passing of too many lives, too many walls of stone, to allow himself to brood upon it tonight.

He drew rein. There was one edifice where the ghosts of lost ages lay undisturbed. He stood before it now: the Tower of Yslsl.

The black stone tower had waited here long centuries ago, when the priests of Sataki first penetrated Shapeli to raise the log palisade of Ceddi. They came to burrow down to the buried fane of their deity, to restore the worship of the prehuman god or devil whose secrets had been revealed to their leaders. Of the tower and of what hands had raised it, their legends retained only nebulous hints. Of Yslsl, even less was remembered.

The walls of the tower rose as solid and foreboding in that distant age as they stood today. The builders of Ceddi incorporated the tower within their log palisade, as a redoubt against the attacks of the savage tribes within the great forest. While there seldom were specific incidents, the tower was center of countless dark rumors and unwholesome superstitions. It was never occupied or put to use for any length of time, and when stone walls replaced Ceddi's palisade, the Tower of Yslsl was not included within the enceinte. Nor was it within the Prophet's renovated line of fortifications.

There had been no attempt to cannibalize the tower for its building stone. At least, if such an attempt had ever been made, it was not repeated.

In the shadow of the Prophet's citadel, engulfed by the featureless hives of his minions, the Tower of Yslsl nonetheless stood apart from these things, as it had stood apart from the older city, and before that from the untrod forest. Silent and sombre, the Tower of Yslsl brooded in this night as it had through nights before the dawn of man.

The tower regarded Kane, and Kane regarded the tower.

Restless yet, Kane dismounted. Angel snorted, shied fretfully away from the tower. Kane spoke soothingly, stroked the stallion's neck until he grew calmer. Surrounding the tower was a circle of desolation, a cleared area of rubble and broken walls. Kane left his mount untethered; Angel would wait for him there, and no one would dare approach Kane's stallion.

The tower was round and without apparent taper, rising somewhat over a hundred feet, and perhaps a quarter of that in diameter. It was built of massive blocks of black stone, resembling basalt, perfectly fitted in unmortared joints. Even after untold centuries, at no point had the joints eroded beyond the thickness of a sword blade. Except for its deepset doorway, the tower walls were unbroken by window or aperture of any sort.

There was a door, iron-bound, of timber blackened and iron-hard with age — fitted there in a previous century during one of the sporadic efforts to utilize the empty tower. The Satakis had replaced the iron bolts and cleared away the debris within, with the object of once again using the structure as a redoubt. Once the new fortifications were completed, the Tower of Yslsl was again abandoned to dust and shadows.

The door opened to Kane's hand, and he stepped inside. Within there was deeper night, but this did not greatly appear to inconvenience Kane.

Arising from the barren earth, a spiral stairway climbed the interior wall. Of curious design, each step was an unbroken intrusion of the wall at that point — jutting out into open space to a breadth where two men might pass with care. Efforts to erect floors at levels along the wall had been made at various times. Timbers had rotted and fallen in; the wall remained. The Satakis had removed most of the debris, so that, gazing upward, Kane had an unobstructed view of the tower interior.

The free-standing stairway rose in a precise spiral. If there was a taper to the interior wall, it was not discernible. The walls were some four feet at the doorway, a sheer face interrupted only by the stairway. A half-circle of starlight shimmered from high above.

Leisurely Kane climbed the stairway. He had climbed these same steps on a number of occasions, and he made his way with confidence.

At the summit, the stairway opened onto a semicircular ledge — a half-moon floor which appeared to be of one mammoth slab of stone. Above this, the tower walls continued another ten feet, then abruptly terminated. Over the centuries, various authorities had argued that the tower must have contained a roof and interior chambers at the time of its building — timber constructions that had rotted away with time, even as had latter day efforts at such embellishments. It must have been thus, for otherwise the tower could be of no comprehensible purpose. Explanations as to how its engineers raised that titanic half-circle of stone to the tower's hundred foot peak were less satisfactory.

There was yet another wondrous mystery to the tower. Set into the curving wall at the top of the stairway, there where a man might stand on the half-moon ledge and contemplate it, was a huge sunburst of jet.

The circular pattern extended from the ledge to the top of the tower wall, and resembled nothing more than a stylized representation of the sun. The sunburst was set flush with the stone of the wall, but was a lustrous rather than a dull black — obsidian, as opposed to basalt, although the resemblance here to either igneous mineral was superficial. Some suggested it was carved from a separate stone and cunningly set into the wall; others claimed it was instead the achievement of some lost process of annealing and polishing. Despite its age, the sunburst showed neither scratches nor chips.

It was popularly believed that Yslsl had been a sun god, that this was his temple, and that here was his symbolic portrayal. It was a convenient explanation, although sceptics argued that the symbolic sunrays were too suggestive of tentacles, and that such vague legends as did survive hinted that Yslsl was anything but a sun god.

Kane, had he cared to do so, might have given them more definite information. And he might have told them that this tower had an exact counterpart on the other side of the earth — in a land whose people made similarly foolish efforts to overlay the dark legends that still persisted. Of other such towers, Kane could only speculate.

Tonight when he reached the semicircular ledge, Kane saw that he was not alone.

Crouched beneath the jet sunburst, a slender girl stared wild-eyed at his approach. Kane looked at her curiously.

She held a poniard as if she knew how to use it, but Kane made no move toward his own swordhilt.

"Put your sting away," he told her, not caring to deal with a terror-stricken girl on this narrow ledge.

"General Kane, is it?" hissed the girl, making no move. "Why do you follow me here?"

Kane laughed. "Why do you lie in wait for me?"

She thought a moment. "If you didn't follow me, then what business could you have here in the Tower of Yslsl?"

"If you aren't an assassin, what business could you possibly have in the Lair of Yslsl?" Kane countered.

"That's easily answered. I came up here to leap off."

"Then what should you care whether I followed you or not? Leap away and have done."

She laughed bitterly and returned her poniard to its sheath. The eyes beneath her jade fillet were haunted. "I don't have the nerve. I never do. Some night I'll miss a step in the dark, and that will serve as well."

Kane shrugged and stepped onto the stone floor. The girl drew away, watching him closely. She was pretty in a thin-but-not-fragile way. Kane ignored her after a casual glance. He had been seeking solitude, and the girl had broken in upon his mood.

"Why did you call this the Lair of Yslsl?"

Kane studied her. "Do you really want to know?"

There was a note to his voice that brought her about. "Sure, tell me. I got over being terrified over a year ago in Gillera." She wished he'd turn his eyes from hers all the same.

Kane touched the black sunburst. It was unnaturally cold to his fingers. "This is a doorway, if you know how to open it. And beyond the doorway, Yslsl waits patiently as a spider in his lair."

"What is Yslsl?"

"A demon, of a sort," Kane replied vaguely. "There is no appropriate term in your language. Think of this world as but one chamber in a vast castle, and think of Yslsl as something old and evil who dwells in the next room — something cunning who has found a way to open a tiny doorway through the wall in between. Only he can't crawl through to you, so he has to wait in his lair for you to crawl through to him."

"But why would anyone ever try to do that?" she protested.

"Suppose you knew that leading out of the Lair of Yslsl were other doors, leading to other rooms — rooms filled with riches and wonders beyond your wildest dreams — and that you could enter these other rooms. If you got past Yslsl."

"But what if Yslsl caught you?"

"That," Kane said, "no one knows. No one has ever escaped the Lair of Yslsl."

She shivered, as much from the eerie wistfulness of Kane's voice as from his words. "Can you open the doorway?"

"I can."

She shivered again, staring thoughtfully at the black sun. "Then open it for me, Kane. I have nothing to live for."

"It would be infinitely better to step off this ledge, and die a quick, clean death below, than to step past this doorway. You'll find no refuge in the Lair of Yslsl."

The girl cursed him, deciding that Kane had only been playing with her with this fanciful tale. "Neither is there any refuge in death!"

"So I'm told," said Kane with harsh bitterness. "So I'm told."

Kane whirled, descended the stairs in a rush. She was still wondering over his sudden anger, after his hoofbeats had died away into the night.

XI
Mourning of the Following Day

"**G**et rid of him."

"Kane?"

"He'll destroy you."

"Nothing can destroy me."

"He'll destroy us all."

"Don't be fools."

"What do you know of Kane?"

"I know that Kane can lead my army to victory."

"Your army! It is Kane's army."

"Fools! It is my army. My gold buys their allegiance."

"But it is Kane who leads them."

"And Kane obeys my commands."

"But if Kane should disobey?"

"Kane is but one man. He can be replaced."

"Then do so now."

"And who shall lead my army into Sandotneri?"

"Lead them yourself."

"Fools! Does a god concern himself with battles!"

"Kane is dangerous. You dare not trust him."

"Kane is but a sword. He shall slay as I command."

"He will turn on you."

"When he does, I shall find another sword."

"You should get rid of Kane now."

"Do you command me? Fools! A god does as he wills."

"But Kane? You dare not trust him."

"Dare not? Waste my time no more with your bleatings.

"Kane is not what he seems."

"I only care that Kane will lead my army against Sandotneri tomorrow."

"And against you on another day."

"That is another day. Kane shall not live to see its dawn."

The room smelled of perfume and spilled wine, caught on a warm breeze from the roses below the open window. Within there was darkness and the soft billowing of gauzy curtains. The night was utterly silent, muffled by the high, thin clouds that cloaked the sky. Even the scrape of leather on stone was a sound no louder than a short breath.

He had ordered the guards to another quarter of the garden walls, clambered over the coping as they obeyed. He felt like a cheap sneak-thief and a fool, but he had to talk to her. The spies' reports had been fragmented and sent in a panic, but enough was clear. Kane was returning to Sandotneri, and he was not coming alone.

He climbed the ornate stonework to her balcony with breathless ease. It was a way he had gone on many breathless nights, well remembered for all the months that had intervened. She had told him to wait until she called for him again, but the months had dragged on and dragged on. True, there was great need for discretion — all the more so now that her father lay in his final coma. No hint of dishonor must tarnish her name, he realized that.

Silently he lifted himself to her balcony window. All was quiet within; she was sleeping at this late hour. He would softly call her name, as he had done on those other nights. She would awaken with a smile, dance over to the window and greet him with a lingering kiss that promised...

He knew it was daring to steal upon her like this. She would forgive him, smile at his boldness — just as before. He would be marching north at dawn, riding out to meet Kane. He might never see her again.

But no! He would conquer Kane and whatever army the Satakis sent with him. He would return to Sandotneri, victorious once again. Owrinos clung to life by a spider-silk now; it was a matter of hours. With her smiles to greet him on his triumphant return, he felt certain the choice of Sandotneri's next ruler was assured. But he *must* talk with her alone...

He craned his head past the dreamily billowing window curtains, formed his lips to call her name. The clouds parted then, threw a pallid splash of moonlight past the swaying curtains onto the scented silks of her bed. His breath caught, and the only sound he made was the shudder of his heart.

She was not yet asleep, but neither she nor her lover had a thought to spare for the frozen mask of pain that stared past the curtains, nor did they hear the dull fall of his body to the garden below, and the blundering footsteps that fled from there.

Kane rides alone through the night.
Where do you ride tonight, Kane?
Tomorrow you lead an army on the road of conquest.
There's no rest for you tonight, Kane.
At night you're haunted by age-old dreams;

There is no refuge for Kane in sleep.
By day you're driven by the curse of your past;
And so you play your games.
Again you'll lead your army on the road to death;
Again you'll smash at cities and reap the red harvest;
Again you'll curse the gods of destiny;
While you shift the fates of kingdoms,
To play at your game.
How many times, Kane?
How many of these nights before the dawn of war?
How many armies have you led?
How many battles have you fought?
How many times have you riven the web of destiny?
And what have you ever won?
Ride on through the night, Kane, alone,
Like a comet that comes and destroys,
And drives on.
Play the game to the end, Kane.
Maybe this time.

XII
The Blooding

Marching south from Ingoldi, Kane led his army along the newly completed system of military roads that crossed the Prophet's forested domain. Old roads and market trails had been broadened and straightened, new connecting strips hewn from the forest. While Shapeli's dense forest served as a natural barrier to an invading army, neither was it possible to lead an army out of the forest with any order or dispatch. Taking advantage of the dry season, Kane moved his men expeditiously across Shapeli on the new road and to the forest fringe. Beyond the forest there were no roads, only an endless expanse of sun-scorched veldt.

At Sembrano, on the edge of the forest, Kane paused to form his regiments and to allow his baggage train to catch up. There, on the second day, he was joined by twenty regiments of foot, mustered from the Sataki strongholds to the south of Ingoldi. Another ten regiments of foot soldiers had been dispersed along the line of march to secure the road against retreat and pursuit; Kane had no intention of leaving the door to the Prophet's capital standing open. Shapeli itself was held by forty regiments of infantry — the bulk of the Prophet's nonprofessional army — with the poorly armed and accoutred masses to shore them up in the event of siege.

The fate of the Dark Crusade hung on victory for Kane and his newly formed army. If the Sword of Sataki was broken by Sandotneri, Orted knew he would have to withstand punitive countermeasures from the southern kingdoms. Thus the Prophet of Sataki stood fast in his citadel and awaited the outcome of Kane's *chevauchée.*

Kane came down to Sembrano at the head of his entire mercenary army, including those of the Satakis who had responded to training sufficiently to flesh out his cavalry regiments. This gave Kane a strength of eight regiments of heavy cavalry and twenty-one of light horse, or nearly 35,000 men. Of these, the heavy cavalry were formed almost entirely of the *condottieri,* who brought with them the essential equippage and training. The ranks of light cavalry were filled with more of the Satakis — untried and unblooded —

than Kane felt confident of, and he trusted his core of veterans to hold these regiments together. Included were seven regiments of mounted archers — again mainly comprised of mercenaries, the Satakis being indifferent archers.

This then was the Sword of Sataki, a disparate army of hardened professionals and unblooded recruits. Kane had seen to its forging. Very shortly he would try its temper against the proven edge of Sandotneri steel.

Kane was fully aware that a surprise assault on Sandotneri itself was impossible. By now Jarvo's intelligence would have informed the Sandotneri general of Kane's presence in Shapeli, and that a considerable force of armored cavalry was moving against the frontier. Kane knew that Jarvo would have to bring up his own cavalry to counter the Sataki threat. Kane's intent was straightforward: to engage the Sandotneri army and destroy it — thereby leaving the city vulnerable to siege by the Prophet's masses of foot soldiers, who might march on Sandotneri unmolested.

At the Prophet's insistence, Kane was to be accompanied by the twenty regiments of foot that were drawn from Shapeli's outlying towns, thereby giving Kane an additional paper strength of 24,000 infantry. Kane considered these regiments a liability, inasmuch as they would be an anchor to his mounted advance. Orted argued that they would serve as an occupying force to lay siege to Sandotneri. Kane gave in on the matter. He intended to march upon the city anyway, in order to draw Jarvo into an open battle, and under the circumstances the loss of a few days in cutting across the frontier was of little consequence. Privately Kane intended to abandon the foot soldiers to their fate should their drag imperil his cavalry, and that Orted had withheld his personal forces from the advance suggested the Prophet was willing to sacrifice another contingent of his followers.

Warfare upon the broad savannah was akin to a battle upon the high sea. The open veldt stretched untold miles without significant natural barriers; there were no defensive positions that could be outflanked. Similarly, there was no point in capturing vast tracts of grassland; these could not be held, and only served to overextend the lines of supply and communication. Further, while there was abundant fodder for their mounts, forage for the troops was limited to the agrarian estates of the outflung demesnes. Water was confined to scattered wells and to the treacherous water-meadows that buried the region's rivers and streams.

The savannah was a limitless sea of tall grass, across which the mounted armies swiftly coursed like vast armored fleets. Speed and striking power were all-important. Here, as in a great sea battle, warfare was a lightning-quick, swirling combat between heavily armed and highly mobile troops. The object was to destroy an opponent's fighting force, thereby leaving the enemy kingdom open to the invading army.

Infantry lacked the mobility that such tactics demanded. Nor could the unsupported foot soldiers withstand a charge of heavy cavalry. In the absence of fortifications or natural barriers, an army that could not maneuver with its foe could be quickly outflanked and encircled. The savannah was a lonely expanse of emptiness; it swallowed entire armies as the sea devours whole fleets.

Kane left Sembrano before the summer's early dawn, advancing along a line of watering places that led to Sandotneri. He intended to engage Jarvo's army as quickly as possible, and a direct drive on the city was certain to force the encounter. Heavy plate armor was no protection from the broiling sun, and Kane meant to attack before his men were too exhausted to fight.

The Sword of Sataki advanced behind a tight cavalry screen — consisting of six regiments of light horse swinging over a front of some ten miles, with patrols as far as five miles in advance of the contact troops. Another two regiments of light horse were detached as flankers. Behind the screen, the main body advanced in a double column, each of three regiments of light horse, followed by four of heavy cavalry, then three more of light. Behind them rolled the ponderous baggage train, and, eating dust as tradition befitted, the twenty regiments of foot. A final regiment of light cavalry was spread out as a rearguard.

The order of march was a compact one, for Kane expected Jarvo's attack and intended to keep his forces concentrated for instant deployment once his outriders made contact with the Sandotneri army. He was prepared to sacrifice the baggage train if need be — it was primarily necessitated by the presence of the foot soldiers — and his main concern with the infantry column was to keep it out of the way of his own maneuvering.

The double columns advanced in a well ordered line of about a mile across behind the cavalry screen, with the last of the foot trailing along less than a mile to the rear. Despite loud complaints from the Prophet's newly recruited infantry, Kane brought them a good twenty-five miles the first day, to Charia's Wells. The Sandotneri garrison there was already in Kane's pay, and the small outpost capitulated without a fight. Kane bivouacked there for the night, carefully positioning his pickets and vedettes.

By dawn the next morning the columns were again in motion, disposed along the same order of march. There were a number of desertions among the foot soldiers as the day progressed and the sun grew hotter. Kane ordered the rearguard to sabre any and all stragglers, which discouraged further attempts. While Kane had no use for them, neither did he care to have them fall into Jarvo's hands and tell all they knew of Kane's plans.

Kane drove them another twenty miles that day — a leisurely pace for the cavalry, although the raw foot soldiers were hard pressed to keep up. That night they bivouacked at Tregua Spring, a small village whose few inhabitants fled before them. The night passed without incident, and in the morning the vedettes still reported no contact with Jarvo's force.

The third day's march dragged on uneventfully. Desertions and complaints were fewer. They were well into Sandotneri's lands, and excitement and tension increased as each mile took the army closer to battle. They made another twenty miles that day, and bivouacked at Adesso Wells. There was a fair-sized outpost here, but the advance scouts found it newly deserted when they approached.

Kane doubled his pickets that night, assuming that Jarvo now was informed of his position and had pulled in all frontier garrisons to reinforce his main body. Sandotneri was only some forty miles distant — a day's hard ride for cavalry. Jarvo would have to move very soon.

About midnight excited scouts reported to Kane that Jarvo was encamped about ten miles to the south of their line of march, at the village of Meritavano. The Sandotneri general had been mustering his army within a day's ride of the city; the swiftness of Kane's advance had been unexpected, and he had only this day taken to the field to halt the Sataki drive.

Reports came quickly thereafter. Jarvo was confident of victory, and had good reason to feel so. His army had sustained only trifling casualties in the slaughter of the Sataki horde a year previous. The Sandotneri force this time was of greater strength — reported to be comprised of twenty-four regiments of light horse and six regiments of heavy cavalry.

While Jarvo was aware that Kane led a considerable body of cavalry, it was after all a pieced-together army, untested in battle. Spies had given only vague information as to its strength, and Kane's cavalry screen had effectively concealed the nature of his troops. Jarvo's scouts had seen the straggling line of foot soldiers and the lumbering wagons of impedimenta, giving the impression that the Sataki army was a mass of infantry supported by several dispersed regiments of light cavalry. It was known that Kane had some heavy cavalry under his command, but, hidden as it was within the center of the column, its strength was grossly underestimated. A year ago the Prophet had had no armored force; it stood to reason that he could not have mustered more than a regiment since then at best.

Jarvo was confident.

Kane knew Jarvo well. And Kane knew that Jarvo would be overconfident.

Kane was on the move before dawn. By the time the climbing sun burned the light dew from the somnolent grassland, the two armies faced one another. The hour of the blooding was inescapably at hand.

Jarvo already had his ranks formed and on the advance. His plan had been to swoop down on Adesso Wells and encircle the Sataki army as it struggled to get under way. His strategy was sound, based on the information, as it was, that the invading army was primarily infantry with only token cavalry support. While he should have taken warning from the rapidity of Kane's advance, Jarvo felt there was little reason to suppose this army was much better trained than the last one the Prophet had sent to slaughter.

The Sandotneri general was somewhat disconcerted by the rapidly approaching dust cloud that bore down upon him from the northern horizon. His confidence still unshaken, Jarvo quickly deployed his regiments — six regiments of mounted archers along the first line, supported by his heavy cavalry as center, with six regiments of light horse on either wing, and the remaining light cavalry behind center as a reserve.

The field was a monotonous stretch of savannah, unbroken by natural barriers or fortifications. It might have been a yellow carpet spread upon the floor of some immense, blue-vaulted chamber. There was an imperceptible rise to the plain toward the northern horizon, falling away to the marshes below Meritavano a few miles to the south. Jarvo counted this of no consequence.

A thin plume of dust obscured the Sataki advance, making it impossible for Jarvo to see with accuracy much beyond the front ranks. It seemed to him that Kane had deployed his troops across too long a line, and he supposed this was because Kane's cavalry screen had not effectively fallen back upon the main body of infantry.

Not caring to give Kane time to correct this error, Jarvo ordered his front line of archers to attack.

Kane's brutal face twisted into a tigerish smile as he observed the Sandotneri line. Kane knew its strength as well as Jarvo, and he knew that his was the superior force — *if* his army could fight. While another man might have been unnerved at doing battle with troops he formerly had led, to Kane the situation was not a novel one.

At this point the front lines of the two armies were somewhat over a mile apart, both sides still advancing at a walk. Kane had deployed his columns into a wide crescent, positioning his archers on either flank with the remaining fourteen regiments of light horse in two lines across the front. Deployed in a third line were his eight regiments of heavy cavalry, held in reserve until Jarvo committed his own armor. Somewhat to the rear, his infantry formed up into five marching squares with pikes and pole-axes bristling about their perimeters.

As Jarvo's mounted archers swept away from the Sandotneri front, Kane signalled for his archers to attack from the flanks. It was a tentative contact on Jarvo's part, Kane decided, probably as much to feel out the Sataki force as anything. Conservative by nature, Jarvo was following the strategy that had routed the Satakis in their earlier battle.

The move reflected his contempt for the Sataki army. While archers might take heavy toll of inadequately protected foot soldiers, against other cavalry their value was more of harrassment. A direct hit of the light, iron-headed shafts might penetrate mail, but not the steel plate armor of heavy cavalry. On the other hand, the mounts of the light cavalry were without the bardings that protected the horses of the armored regiments. Sweeping archery fire could destroy a formation with crippled and unmanageable mounts, and Kane countered to guard against this.

Preceded by a black rain of death, the two forces swirled together across the yellow plain. Kane's archers were distinguishable in the distance by their black scarves and their broad armbands of red cloth, emblazoned with the black sigil of Sataki. Jarvo, Kane noted sardonically, seemed to have ordained his own blue scarves for the whole of the Sandotneri army.

The charging archers wheeled about like countless dust-devils through the high grass. It was a lightning-swift engagement — emptying saddles across both fronts, more often sending horse and rider careening to the earth. An archer typically carried twenty-four arrows in his quiver. On this terrain, any man of them could fire six arrows a minute with accuracy — more than that if circumstances required. Quivers were emptied in a matter of a few minutes; after that it was a matter of returning to the lines or scavenging on the field.

Both sides took moderate casualties, although far from crippling. Kane's was the superior force, and the Sandotneri charge failed to penetrate. The opposing horsemen exchanged fire until their quivers emptied — then withdrew to their respective, slowly advancing lines. It was a sudden, indecisive engagement — calling to mind the curtain of lightning that precedes an approaching storm across the horizon.

Jarvo, angered by the standoff and impatient to take command of the battle, ordered his heavy cavalry to charge the center of Kane's line, at the same time sending his regiments of light horse against either horn of the crescent to protect his flanks. The returning archers wheeled past his own flanks to advance with the reserve force. The reserve was to follow as a second wave, and join the attack wherever the Sandotneri line seemed to be breaking.

Jarvo's plan of action was to break through the cavalry ranks — thereby cutting Kane's line in two, and penetrating to the unsupported infantry in the rear. It was a good plan — assuming that Kane's cavalry would be hurled back against the panic-stricken masses of foot. The dust that obscured Kane's advance, however, hid the fact that the infantry was well to the rear — and that immediately behind the screen of light horse Kane waited with eight regiments of heavy cavalry.

The Sandotneri charge rumbled toward the Sword of Sataki, driving Kane's retreating archers before it like foam before a breaker.

Astride his stallion, Kane snarled commands to his trumpeters. An aide handed him a goblet of brandy. Kane tossed it off, with a wild laugh crushed it in his gauntleted fist. Locking down the vizor of his armet, he caught up his lance and urged Angel forward at a fast trot.

Trumpets blared all along the crescent, relaying Kane's commands through the thin dust that veiled battle pennants. Officers shouted orders above the deepening thunder of a hundred thousand hooves.

Riding several hundred yards ahead of Kane's heavy cavalry, the first and second lines of light horse abruptly divided at the center, wheeling toward the right and left horns of the crescent. As the gap at the center broke apart, the retreating regiments of archers galloped through, passing between the open ranks of the armored third line to reform at the rear. As the archers dashed to the rear and the opening in the center expanded, Kane's third line closed ranks and surged forward. Through the yellow curtain of dust, Kane led his armored cavalry onto the open savannah.

Near 10,000 steel lance heads glinted in the sun, like the sudden smile of a hungry shark. In an instant of fear, Jarvo knew he had fallen into Kane's trap. There was no turning back.

The earth shook beneath their charge. Pounding hooves — driving the ponderous mass of armored warrior and steel bardings — tore through the dense sod, ground the dry soil into numberless explosions of flying dust and pulverized rock. Like two monstrous avalanches of scintillant steel and driving muscle and bone, the opposing armies rushed together — now at full gallop, ripping apart the earth in a frenzy to smash and to slay.

Less than half a mile separated the two lines of heavy cavalry as their charge broke into full gallop. Great chunks of shuddering distance hurtled past beneath their thundering hooves. Time hung in an eerie stillness against the onrush of space. Seconds dwindled into meaningless splinters of eternity. Time was unreal.

Encased in steel universes: sight fixed on the lance-lines ahead, sound deadened by the tearing roar of hooves, smell obliterated by dusty heat, tongue choked with tension, sensation only of headlong hurtling through space. What does a meteor know of time in the instant of its final flaming plunge?

Steel and space... and time?... is *now*.

Sound is sundering steel and molten screams of rage and agony. The explosive death of a volcano, vomiting its fiery blood into the icy sea. Two waves of steel smash together. Time is still; space is motionless. Steel is totality.

Steel against steel. Muscle and bone direct us, steel protect us. Steel against steel.

Lance into shield, into breastplate and pallette, into peytral and cuello. Steel lance heads bite and glance, wooden shafts shudder and splinter. They clashed together like the fanged jaws of some unthinkable leviathan, closed with a maniacal fury that ground and shattered its endless rows of bright fangs.

Edged weapons were all but useless against plate armor. Driven by the hurtling mass of steel and thew, the leaf-bladed lance heads could pierce steel armor of man or horse with deadly effect. Even if the lance head turned, or the shaft splintered, frequently the impact in itself was murderous — flinging an armored opponent from his saddle at full gallop. Should the unhorsed warrior survive the fall, the crushing weight of his armor might leave him helplessly pinned. Nor was the danger entirely at the point of the lance. An inexpert lancer, because the grapper transmitted much of the shock to the felt-lined lance arrest secured to the right side of his breastplate, might be flung from saddle by the same impact that drove into his opponent.

Kane tore through at the head of his charge — an awesome figure in black plate armor, forged to fit his massive frame. His black stallion, gigantic in matching steel bardings, loomed like a frothing, iron-hooved demon. His men knew he led them, and they followed into hell without further thought.

The dull thunder roll of drumming hooves — then the instant of collision. A lance pointed toward Kane across the closing gap of timeless space. Kane shifted his own lance suddenly, struck the other lance, felt it glance harmlessly across his vamplate — then his lance head angled upward to slide past his assailant's shield, strike the angle of armet and gorget. The lance head caught for an instant, the shaft bent under their combined momentum — then sprang free, and the Sandotneri rider tumbled backward from his saddle, neck already snapped.

The clangour of his fall suddenly echoed across the entire front — a strident protest of steel drowning out the bass rumble of hooves, as the two lines collided.

Kane, his lance only momentarily engaged, galloped past the unstrung puppet of steel. Already a second lance was thrusting for him. Kane swung his lance to guard; the other lance head instantly lowered, struck Kane's stallion. The hemispherical boss of the peytral deflected the point. Kane's lance, glancing from the other's shield, struck the Sandotneri cavalryman in the center of his breastplate. The steel lance head drove through breastplate, chest, and backplate. Kane's lance lifted the impaled warrior from the saddle, held him for an instant in midair — before the wooden shaft snapped.

Kane cursed and hurled the broken half into the path of a third oncoming lancer. Lunging aside, Kane deflected the enemy lance with his shield, as his own broken lance entangled the charger's driving legs. The Sandotneri mount stumbled — at full gallop with a double burden of heavy armor and rider, it could not recover. Horse and trooper crashed head over heels as Kane drove past, unslinging the massive battle-ax from his saddle.

Another lancer thundered toward him, as Kane flung up the heavy ax. Kane twisted, caught the lance head on his shield. The shaft splintered at the impact, jarring Kane against his high cantle. His assailant held his saddle with no less difficulty. Kane swung the ax in a murderous arc as they came together. The heavy spike pean gouged through the barred vizor of the other's armet. Kane hauled on the haft, almost losing grip, as their horses pounded past each other. The spike tore free in a splatter of brain.

By now Kane's charge had carried him through the Sandotneri line. A scatter of light horse followed as a second line, but Kane ignored them for the moment. Hauling on the curb bit, he managed to wheel Angel to the right, checking his headlong charge. He had an instant's respite to draw breath and to survey the dust-veiled field. The Sandotneri charge had shattered against Kane's armored regiments. Already most of the struggling warriors had lost their lances, were smashing at one another with ax, mace and flail. Here and there Kane saw great two-handed broadswords in use — heavy blades whose crushing power served even when edge failed against steel plate.

The melee resounded like the forges of hell — a deafening cacaphony of smashing steel, pounding hooves, crashing bodies, war cries and howls of death-agony. Dust and torn sod swirled like a yellow blizzard.

Beyond the struggling mass of armor, the regiments of light cavalry engaged in a lightning storm of sabres and plunging hooves. They rode clear of the armored melee — their sabres were toys against armored horse and rider, and mail hauberks were no defense against the crushing weapons of the heavy cavalry.

The dust obscured details of the battle, but Kane could see that the horns of his crescent, reinforced as his front lines of light horse swung to either flank, had engulfed the entire Sandotneri charge. Jarvo's force was encircled. The battle was now one vast melee, and Kane had the advantage of numbers. Jarvo's only hope to escape annihilation was to break through the Sataki trap, reform his men for a fighting retreat.

And now Kane saw that the infantry squares were cautiously advancing to join the fray. The Sataki charge had overrun the Sandotneri charge, carrying the battle past the initial line of contact. The torn earth was littered with bodies in armor and mail, many still alive but crippled within the weight of their armor, pinned beneath fallen mounts. Remorseless as jackals, the foot soldiers swarmed over them — driving poniards and misericordes through mail and joints between plates, smashing in armets and breastplates with hammers and axes.

Kane hoped in their frenzy the louts could tell comrade from foe.

Now members of Kane's personal guard sifted through the chaos of steel and straining flesh, regrouped around their general for new orders. The battle was beyond the stage of strategy — a seething maelstrom of individual duels and hand-to-hand fighting. Kane dispatched several aides to order the foot soldiers to attend and help remount any of the Sandotneri troopers who might still fight — then plunged back into the melee.

Ax and shield. Hammer and mace. No lance now — the struggle was too close to wield them. Some of the armored warriors were driving into the beleaguered Sandotneri light horse — ripping through them in the dense fray like grotesque metallic sharks. Enclosed within the Sataki crescent, the Sandotneri cavalry could not maneuver. Horses screamed and reared, smashing into their comrades as riders could not manage their panicked mounts. In the press, there was no room to fight back against the garrotting Sataki encirclement.

While the Sandotneri army had not been seriously outnumbered at the start of the battle, Jarvo in his confidence had committed two deadly blunders. He had allowed his flanks to be engulfed, and he had failed to withhold an adequate reserve.

Kane ranged through the chaotic battle, trying to seek out Jarvo. The pall of dust thickened with each passing minute, enveloping the entire field in a smothering blanket. He could see no further than a score of yards in the yellow haze. The battle surged over a square mile of torn earth and broken flesh, and his enemy eluded him in the swirling vortex that left the field strewn with an ever growing litter of death.

There was no scarcity of work for him closer at hand. Looming through the yellow murk in his black armor — now dusty and splashed with gore — Kane looked like the god of war stalking through the revels of his worshippers. If his presence in the thick of the fighting inspired his men, it also drew the desperate attacks of the trapped enemy. With Kane down, there was yet a hope of victory.

Kane wielded his battle-ax like a wand of death, cleaving shield and brassart with its wide blade, smashing through breastplate and armet with the thick spike on its opposite side. The haft was steel-strapped, turning the edges of slashing swords and axes. His shield was bashed and notched from the blows of maces and flails, of questing blades. His armor was scored and dented from desperate blows that slammed past his guard. When they could not bring down the raging demon in gore-spattered armor, they struck at his black stallion — their blows glancing off chanfron and crinet.

Kane smashed them down as a lion scatters jackals — killing until they dared not close with him, fled before his lethal rush. He was in his element — tireless and implacable as he cut through the milling Sandotneri warriors, strewing the torn earth with broken bodies and smashed steel. Kane's attack was that of a berserker — headlong and unstoppable. Yet a careful observer would note that this was no suicidal frenzy — rather that each movement, each blow and parry was finely calculated by a keen and highly skilled intellect. And that awareness made Kane all the more terrifying to them.

The battle carried southward, toward Meritavano, where the Sandotneri army had camped the night before. Across the wake of dead and wounded, the Sataki foot soldiers followed with gore-clotted poniards and axes. The Sandotneri army, struggling to break out of the Sataki vise, was not merely being decimated; it was being eliminated.

Still in the thick of the fighting, Kane heard the sudden blare of trumpets from the dust beyond. Jarvo was trying to rally his men. Kane smashed down a last mailed foeman — his blunted ax could not penetrate the mail, but the force behind it, caved in the man's chest — paused to let his personal guard gather about him. Suddenly the field seemed barren of Sandotneri horsemen.

After a moment reports came back to Kane that Jarvo, leading the last desperate remnants of his heavy cavalry, had managed to disengage Kane's armored troops and cut a retreat through the ring of light horse to the south. Those of the Sandotneri who could follow, turned and fled through the break.

Kane snarled commands, called for his trumpeters to sound pursuit. Kane might have spared his breath. Sensing the kill, his cavalry were already slashing at the heels of the fleeing Sandotneri. It was a day's ride to the safety of the city walls, and it was manifest that Jarvo was without any reserve troops to reinforce his retreat.

Gathering his personal guard to him, Kane plunged after the fugitives — striving to throw out flankers to cut off the exhausted enemy. He galloped past the deserted Sandotneri camp at Meritavano, sourly noting that already his men were more interested in pillage than pursuit. Just to the south of the village, Kane drew rein amidst a milling body of his men.

Pushing through them, Kane rode as close as he dared. A low curse escaped his lips. Men near him heard it, shivered.

The land to the south of Meritavano was an expanse of reedy bog and water-meadow, fed by one of the savannah's buried rivers. Caught between the village and the flanking Sataki cavalry, Jarvo had tried to lead his men across the water-meadow — looking deceptively solid in this the dry season. Now horses and riders thrashed helplessly in the deep mud — the weight of their mail and armor dragging them beneath the surface of the marsh, leaving them floundering about in the muck, unable to rise and win free to the dry land beyond. On the far side, a dismal few mounts and riders dragged themselves free, staggered off through the tall grass.

"Send the foot soldiers in there," Kane ordered. "Have them strip to the skin, so they won't sink in over their butts. They can use their poniards well enough, I've seen. And bring rope — as much as there is. Salvage what they can of horses and armor, before it all sinks into the morass. And bring me Jarvo — dead or alive."

The Satakis leapt to their muddy slaughter with all the unrestrained zeal of children frolicking in the rain.

They slithered through the marsh until darkness claimed the day and the field. Toward twilight one muck-smeared searcher proudly handed Kane a battered helmet with vizor worked into a snarling demon's mask — pulled out of the scum of a deep pool.

Kane stared out across the darkening morass.

XIII
Siege

King Owrinos of Sandotneri gave a last spasmodic shudder, uttered a great liquid sigh, smiled and lay still. It might have been a delicious stretch and yawn before settling into contented sleep, but his smile was fixed for the ages, and the blood that bubbled from his lips clotted and dried. The king would never again awaken, not even at the shuddering impacts of the massive stones that were pounding his palace into rubble.

His daughter, summoned by the court physicians when the hemorrhage erupted, gazed at the emaciated corpse and shrugged. Owrinos had taken too long in his dying. After so many months of anticipation, his death was only an anticlimax to the impending doom of his besieged city.

"Sandotneri looks to you now, Ridaze," Esketra murmured. "General Ridaze."

From close at hand — a jarring concussion, the tearing rumble of a collapsing wall. Esketra could smell the musty tang of pulverized plaster and brick, hear the distant moans and shouts.

"What's left of it," she amended.

Ridaze's handsome face was grim with concern. "Kane's trebuchets are smashing the outer walls to powder. Esketra, we must take you to a place of safety."

"Lead on," Esketra said dully. "We both know there is no place of safety in Sandotneri."

The city had been stunned when the first panic-stricken riders brought word of their army's defeat at the hands of the Satakis. For the first hours there was disbelief, loud denials as the rumors gobbled about the city streets. Then came the pitiful knots of fugitives — the scattered survivors of the rout, battered and filthy and half-dead from their flight. And the next day brought the victorious Sataki army.

The Satakis sacked the outlying settlements and villas, as Kane took up a position before the city walls. Kane sent emissaries to speak eloquently of the advantages of peaceful surrender. Their arguments failed to persuade in part because the people of Sandotneri trusted to their walls and to some last minute deliverance from their neighboring kingdoms; in part because, with Owrinos in a coma and Jarvo presumed dead, there was no single personage with authority to surrender the city.

Kane set to work constructing siege engines from the tackle and timber carried in the baggage train. By the next morning his massive trebuchets were bombarding the city with boulders and chunks of masonry, while his sappers mined beneath the walls. Meanwhile, several of his cavalry regiments were detached to escort the unwieldy mass of the Prophet's assault force from Shapeli. Its heavy cavalry destroyed, the beleaguered remnants of Sandotneri's army dared not risk a sortie against Kane's armor.

Kane waited for the city to know it was doomed. He could afford to be patient for a while. He had ample provisions and water for his horses and men, and he was confident that no new army would come to raise the siege. Of those of the southern kingdoms whose holdings bordered on Sandotneri's demesne, certainly no help would be forthcoming. Ripestnari, whose lands bordered Sandotneri along the Inland Sea, was a traditional enemy; Desdrineli, to the south, was at war on its own western marches and could spare no troops; Vegliari, further to the south, had been laid waste by a long and bloody civil strife and was on the brink of schism; Bavostni, on the Eastern Sea and sharing part of the marches of Shapeli, had only years before lost a bitter territorial war with Sandotneri — and was at present Kane's major outside source of men and equipment.

They would stand by while the Satakis gobbled up Sandotneri. That they were next in the path of the Dark Crusade was a threat too distant to consider. After all, Shapeli was leagues away across the savannah, and certainly Orted Ak-Ceddi would be satisfied when the conquest of Sandotneri secured his borders, and restored his military prestige.

And so Kane waited for the mass of assault troops to join him from Shapeli — amusing himself in the interim by bombarding the city. Initially there was answering fire from the city's own defensive engines, but Kane's trebuchets quickly found their range and annihilated them.

His design was primarily psychological warfare for the moment, inasmuch as Kane saw no point in breaching the walls before he had the reinforcements to throw into the defenders' fire. His own men were too valuable. Instead Kane was content to demoralize the besieged city with the evidence that his trebuchets could pound their walls and their palace at will. These siege engines were of massive construction, capable of hurling immense weights with deadly accuracy — range being adjusted through the movable weight on the short arm of the pivoted beam, or by shortening the sling on the longer throwing arm.

Nor were all the missiles of stone. In this region surface rock was scarce, but other ammunition was in ready supply. Heavily laden wagons returned from the plundered battlefield. Dead horses were better eating than the Sataki rabble was accustomed to, thus had value. The stripped bodies of the Sandotneri officers could be loaded into a trebuchet sling. They made little impression on the city's walls, but their effect on the defenders' morale was devastating.

Kane grew bored with the sport. It served to remind him that Jarvo's body had never been found. Spies and deserters from the city reported that the Sandotneri general had not been among the fugitives who limped back to their capital after the disaster at Meritavano.

The defeated general would have found a cold welcome there. Kane's crushing victory had plunged Jarvo's name into disgrace. Jarvo had left the city garrison under the command of his rivals, so that they would not share in the glory of his victory. His artifice had spared their lives, and now they repaid his memory by loudly proclaiming the defeat was entirely due to Jarvo's incompetent leadership.

Owrinos' death left Sandotneri without even a titular monarch. General Ridaze, at the last minute ordered to remain with the city garrison, had been elevated to Jarvo's former position. With Esketra's favor, Ridaze was the uncrowned commander of Sandotneri. It may have been that Ridaze found the sudden realization of his ambitions not so magnificent as he had dreamed.

Kane remembered Ridaze as a capable officer, popular with his men and rather more so with the ladies. Dark, dashing, daring, the romantic ideal of a cavalry officer — but of no particular genius or ability. Ridaze would present no problem; he was out of his depth.

Kane rather wished he knew for certain that Jarvo was safely buried beneath the morass at Meritavano. Kane despised Jarvo as a man, considered him unimaginative as a general — but the man had a certain plodding tenacity that, given the smiles of fortune, made him a dangerous opponent. His swordplay was characteristic: good enough to hold his own against a better man, unaware that he was outclassed, and let his opponent falter but once... Kane had seen any number of masters of the blade cut down by stolid journeymen who got lucky when it counted.

The siege wore on tiresomely — Kane unwilling to storm the walls, Ridaze not daring to attempt a sortie. Kane kept to his pavilion — letting his officers keep his army in order, moodily sipping brandy and considering his next move. In the distance, gouts of dust and splintered masonry exploded intermittently from the ruined palace. Kane brooded upon the destruction. It seemed only a short while ago that he had schemed to discover the secret passageways of that same palace; now he was smashing it to rubble. He always seemed to be smashing at things he could not have.

Kane swore and looked for another bottle of brandy. The familiar depression was getting worse after each battle now. He wondered how much longer the game would continue to amuse him, to stave off the awful weight of centuries from his spirit. The inaction and resultant letdown always made the boredom more intense than before. Kane found himself musing once again upon the Tower of Yslsl. For too many centuries had festered that haunting, deadly temptation...

The twilight brought with it two events to rouse him from his sombre mood.

A delegation ventured forth from Sandotneri under flag of truce. General Ridaze wished to discuss terms of honorable surrender.

A dark mass of humanity rolled across the northern horizon. The Sataki horde had come to Sandotneri.

Neither occurrence was unexpected. There was, however, something else that Kane had not been prepared for.

Orted Ak-Ceddi rode at the head of his Dark Crusade.

XIV
Treaties and Evocations

This turn of events did not please Kane. Kane had assumed that the Prophet would remain comfortable and secure in Ceddi, dreaming of the rich plunder his minions would faithfully haul back to his fortress — and more to the point, leave the direction of the Sword of Sataki to Kane.

His presence was ominous. And yet, the evening began quite well for Kane, as such evenings have a way of beginning.

From the shade of his pavilion, Kane leaned back in his chair and dispassionately awaited the approach of the envoys. He had both feet propped upon his campaign table, so that he sighted their anxious faces between his booted toes. The envoys were scared and stiffly formal. Kane wore leather cavalry trousers and a sleeveless aketon he normally wore under his armor, and was drunk enough not to care. Compared to the gallant finery of the Sandotneri envoys, Kane looked like an apish thug. The sardonic intelligence in his eyes left no doubt as to who was master of the situation.

"The siege is at a stalemate," began their leader. "You haven't enough troops to storm our walls. We lack sufficient cavalry to break your siege. Nothing can be gained by us through enduring your bombardment, nor by you through continuing a pointless siege, and thus risking exhausted provisions and attack from our allies."

Kane cut into his speech. "Before you bore me further, I should tell you that my vedettes have already informed me of the approach of a new body of the Prophet's foot soldiers. Since they number past a hundred thousand, you doubtless have observed their advance from Sandotneri's towers. And since that doubtless has provoked this conference, let's have no more nonsense about a stalemate."

"These new 'foot soldiers' are Sataki rabble," sneered the envoy. "I shouldn't have to tell *you* that Sandotneri's walls are well defended."

"Thank you, I know Sandotneri's defenses quite well," Kane said evenly. "And I know my siege engines can breach those walls whenever I command it. You, of course, have never had the misfortune to witness what the Sataki rabble can do to an enemy city once they're within its walls, although I'm certain you've heard countless lurid and grisly tales. I assure you anything you will have heard can be only euphemistic hints as to what you may expect to see before tomorrow's sunset."

The language was overladen with gutturals and always made Kane thirsty. He emptied his goblet with a flourish.

"You bore me," he said expansively. "This siege bores me. I feel inclined to be generous in my terms. Who is empowered to accept them in Sandotneri's behalf?"

The leader of the delegation glanced toward his colleagues, who looked away helplessly. "Until a new king is crowned, Esketra acts as regent, and General Ridaze is her military governor."

Kane nodded, offering them a wolfish smile. "Well then, have Esketra and General Ridaze come to me this evening, and we'll sign a treaty of surrender."

"What terms?" demanded the envoy.

"My terms," Kane told him. "Don't distress yourselves — I'm inclined to offer the standard terms of honorable surrender. I'll discuss them with your superiors."

He added, cutting off their protests, "If I don't hear from you by nightfall, by tomorrow the Satakis will hold festival in Sandotneri's streets. You won't like their terms at all."

His mood much improved, Kane watched their agitated departure. In a surge of proprietary concern, Kane ordered the barrage to cease, then called for a clerk to draw up articles of surrender as he dictated them. The procedure was nothing out of the ordinary. With the almost continuous state of warfare in the southern kingdoms, the rituals attendant upon victory and defeat had been almost formulized by convention. With the ease of long experience, Kane dealt with cessation of hostilities, surrender of armaments, payment of reparations, secession of territories, recognition of suzerainty, and other such matters as fast as his clerk could copy.

It was a tidy document, not unfair under the circumstances, and Kane was rather pleased with it. They could either sign it or not, and with the Sataki horde converging upon the beleaguered city, he expected they would sign it readily enough. It pleased Kane to have the matter thus neatly concluded without recourse to the Prophet's rabble.

Kane read over the document once the ink was dry, decided the work should serve as a very model for such documents, told his clerk to draw it up in triplicate, and called for his steward to bring a new bottle. By this time the cavalry escort he had detached to fetch the Sataki assault troops was riding into camp — a dark mass of tired men, women and children straggling miles to the rear. As before, the Sataki army was a numberless mass of humanity — driven by zeal and by fear.

Kane ignored the Prophet's horde, until his returning officers reported to him that Orted Ak-Ceddi rode with them, Kane looked toward the slowly advancing sea of bodies that crawled out of the deepening gloom — sensing a vague premonition.

The approach of a large party under flag of truce from Sandotneri cut short his speculation. Even in the distance, Kane recognized Esketra's tall figure riding side-saddle on a fine cream gelding. He smiled and got up to put on his best brocaded houppelande. Awaiting the delegation, Kane dispatched a messenger to Orted to inform him of the city's imminent surrender. He would conclude this matter quickly, and then discover what had drawn the Prophet out of the safety of his lair.

It was not a cordial reunion, but then Kane had not been on friendly terms with any of them even when he was general of Sandotneri's army. Esketra was manifestly terrified and chose to hide her fear beneath a shaky mask of hauteur. Ridaze was pallid with restrained fury — the corrosive fury of a man who has achieved the pinnacle of his ambitions for no purpose save to be humiliated before a hated rival. The others of their escort seemed to be surreptitiously pondering whether Kane wore mail beneath his houppelande.

Kane dispensed with icy formalities. "I think this is straightforward enough," he told them, proffering the articles of surrender.

The envoy Kane had dealt with previously examined the document, reading it aloud to Esketra and her general. Stone faces, pressed lips, angry eyes — condemned prisoners listening as the judge proclaims their sentence.

"Impossible!" growled Ridaze.

Kane raised an eyebrow. "Nonsense. Basically the same terms we offered Bavostni four years ago. It only pinches when it's your neck that's in the noose."

The twilight was deepening. Kane gestured toward the darker sea of bodies that was even now encircling the city walls. They couldn't see their faces in the distance, but they could hear the dread Sataki war chants that roared from uncounted thousands of throats.

"If you think I demand too costly tribute, imagine for yourselves what all those grubby hands will find to grasp when they loot Sandotneri on the morrow. So long as you adhere to these terms, I guarantee you your lives and safety. Once the mob breaks through, I won't even guarantee you a clean death."

They hesitated, but Kane knew it was only a last minute denial of the inevitable. They knew they must accept his terms, else neither Esketra nor Ridaze would have ridden into Kane's camp.

"You will note," Kane pointed out, "that the treaty acknowledges Esketra as Owrinos' heir and Ridaze as her chief minister — subject, of course, to the sovereignty of Ingoldi."

"Puppet rule!" spat Esketra.

"That has an ugly sound," purred Kane. "Think of yourself as a titular monarch. There are worse ways to dangle from a string than as a puppet."

"For the welfare of Sandotneri, I suggest we sign," spoke Ridaze stoutly. Their present position was untenable, and Kane's terms did guarantee their nominal rule. Later the situation might change, and a treaty was only a scrap of parchment.

Kane watched their reluctant signatures, then signed his own name with a flourish and stamped the document with the sigil of Sataki. A fine piece of work, he reflected, and neatly concluded.

"It's grown dark," Kane observed. "I think some refreshment to honor the occasion. I've directed my steward to set out a cold dinner for us. We can wait within my pavilion while your envoys proclaim the signing of our treaty to the city."

"I do not care to accept any further hospitalities from you," Esketra told him coldly.

"I'm sorry — did you think that was an invitation?" The menace cut through Kane's urbanity. "It wasn't. You two are my guests until I've seen how well the citizens of Sandotneri honor our new treaty. I hope your envoys will be persuasive."

With icy grace they retired into Kane's pavilion, where a light supper was being laid. Kane gave certain orders to his men, dispatched a second messenger to the Prophet to inform him of the formal surrender, then joined his unwilling guests.

It bothered Kane that he did not share the exultant spirits of his chief officers, as they gathered about to celebrate the surrender. An outsider might have mistaken Kane for one of the defeated parties, for his distracted and brooding aspect as the evening wore on. Kane was not in doubt as to the source of his unease: Orted Ak-Ceddi. What was the Prophet doing here? And why had he not yet communicated with Kane?

To this point all of Kane's cunningly laid plans had worked to perfection — the signed treaty making Kane virtual master of Sandotneri was the successful fulfillment of but the first phase in his grand design. There was reason for jubilation, but Orted's unexpected presence here only reminded Kane that the Prophet was still an unknown factor.

Kane had gone to pains to discover all he could, of Orted Ak-Ceddi. He knew that for all his pose as a popular hero and champion of the downtrodden, Orted the bandit chieftain had been a ruthless outlaw who left a wake of murder and rapine wherever his band passed through. Precisely what hold Orted had on the obscure cult of Sataki — or vice versa — was an enigma to Kane. Basically Kane saw Orted as a cunning opportunist who had seized the role of Prophet of Sataki as a guise to cloak his mass-scale depredations under the pretense of religious crusade. Mass power through mass hysteria — the rank and file proud to die for the glory of the holy cause; the elite content to reap the power and the wealth paid for with the blood of the faithful.

It was a familiar story. Kane saw nothing in Orted that would indicate the bandit-turned-prophet was anything beyond the characteristic pattern. Orted was crafty and rapacious; no question. Orted had a good command of guerilla tactics and mob violence, but lacked any competency with regard to waging a full-scale war against a disciplined foe; that was where Kane came in. Orted thought enough of his own well-being to let his minions do the work and run the risks, while he stayed home in luxury and security, and contemplated the fruits of their labors; this last was *why* Kane had interceded. Why then was Orted here? Had Kane misjudged him? It would bring matters to a head too soon, if Orted chose to take an active command of the Sword of

Sataki.

Perhaps, Kane mused, the Prophet had deemed the situation well-in hand, determined he could safely come to witness the triumph of his new army. But that would indicate a grandstand play, full of pomp and bombast. Orted had come unannounced. An inner voice whispered to Kane that he had somewhere made an error. The eldritch chanting of the Sataki horde seemed to underscore his gnawing doubt. Despite his earlier resolve to taper off, Kane found himself drinking toast for toast with his officers.

Hoofbeats again approached the pavilion. Curb chains jangled, and Kane waited expectantly — sensing a new tension from the sentries without. Then deeper blobs of blackness crowded the shadow beneath the awning outside. Followed by several of his priests, Orted Ak-Ceddi strolled through the doorway of the pavilion.

The Prophet had taken time to wash off the dust of travel before joining them, and he made an impressive entrance. His brown mane hung in precise perfumed coils, and his leonine features were languid beneath a cushion of dissipation. He wore tight leather trousers and blouse-sleeved shirt of black silk, with the gold sigil of Sataki dangling beneath the open throat. Orted favored them with a smile of sardonic amusement, and for an instant his eyes locked with Kane's.

They made an eerie study in contrasts, these two men who led the Dark Crusade. Orted, lean-hipped and broad-shouldered, pantherish in movement and strength. For all the months of debauchery there remained steel beneath the soft veneer of fat and the perfumed foppery. Behind him stood his black-robed priests, faces half-hidden beneath their cowls. Kane, barrel-chested and massive of limb, ogreish in strength and cat-quick for all his size. There was demonic intelligence in his coarse-featured face, and despite his apparent relaxed posture, Kane exuded menace. Behind Kane ranged his major officers — hard faces wary, casually shifting goblets so that swordhands were free.

Between them, Esketra and Ridaze, sensing the sudden tension — their aloof faces drawn with uncertainty.

Orted's black eyes hold the gaze of Kane's blue eyes. Eyes dark with cosmic evil: eyes that blazed with azure murder-lust. The secret touch of an elder god: the Mark of Kane. Orted broke the gaze, and broke the tableau.

"Orted Ak-Ceddi, Prophet of Sataki," Kane made needless introduction. "Esketra of Sandotneri and General Ridaze. I trust my aides have informed you that we have just formalized the treaty of surrender."

Kane gestured toward the document displayed on the map table. Orted's eyes glanced upon it casually, then darted back to rest upon Esketra. Esketra gave him a haughty smile, but her eyes were coolly speculative.

"Yes, General Kane. They informed me." Orted held out his hand, and a priest brought him the document. Carelessly the Prophet read through it. "Yes, everything seems in order."

It was a good effect, although Kane knew the former bandit was illiterate. Orted returned the parchment to the priest.

"I hadn't realized you were empowered to make treaties, Kane," he remarked, signing for a steward to bring him a goblet.

"As general of your army, such is understood," Kane said suavely. "After all, decisions have to be made in the field, and you scarcely can spare time to have my couriers forever at your heels in Ceddi, trying to haggle over various trivial issues. Of course, every agreement I undertake is subject to your approval."

"Of course. Such is understood," Orted agreed. "You know how well I trust your good judgment."

The Prophet gulped down his brandy. "This is quite good. I'll have more." He glanced about the richly furnished pavilion, as the steward refilled his goblet. "Don't go too far," he admonished. Behind him, his priests stood aloof and motionless as shadows of the dead.

"Well, Kane," Orted said, wiping his chin on his sleeve. "You've done very well for yourself here. I'm extremely pleased with what you've accomplished so far. You and your men have performed great works for the glory of Sataki. You have destroyed the army of Sandotneri, captured the city, and taken only moderate casualties in your victory. I congratulate you."

"Thank you," acknowledged Kane, every nerve straining to catch the menace he knew lurked behind Orted's brandied smile.

"You have, however, made one error in this," the Prophet spoke with deceptive grace. "To be sure, I don't fault you for it. You were acting as best you understood."

How much has the fool guessed? Kane's expression was blandly inquisitive. From his hand to his knife hilt to Orted's heart would be but a blurred instant.

"An error?"

"Yes. Sandotneri has twice defied the Dark Crusade. Sandotneri has massacred untold thousands of the Children of Sataki."

The Prophet's voice suddenly oozed with venom. "There can be no peace with Sandotneri! For these sins they must die!"

From out of the night, the throbbing chant of the Satakis — rising ever higher for these last moments — abruptly was stilled. Vaguely then, the keening moan as of a distant cold wind through skeletal trees. It was as if a hundred thousand throats raised one shrill scream of horror beneath a smothering shroud of leaden mist.

A shiver of indescribable ecstasy veiled the Prophet's eyes.

The muffled death-cry of a city rose to a banshee howl. Terror ravened the night, and those who heard knew that death had unveiled its face.

"You devil!" Ridaze snarled.

Lunging for the doorway, Kane saw what he intended, but made no move to interfere. The others were entranced by the tocsin of dread that shattered the night.

Ridaze drew a poniard from the sleeve of his doublet. In one desperate leap, he flung himself upon the enthralled Prophet, stabbed the needle-like blade into his heart.

Kane exulted in that instant, knowing that even if Orted wore mail, that enraged blow would drive the poniard between the metal rings.

Orted staggered. The triangular blade snapped; its broken tip sprang away across the tent.

Ridaze recoiled, his face slack with disbelief. No trace of blood showed on the pierced silk.

Orted ignored him — even as the priests instantly swarmed over Ridaze. A rush of black robes, flashing grey blades, then gushing crimson. Ridaze sagged to the ground, disbelief still written in his dead face.

Kane spun past them — it was over in an instant — still following his initial impetus toward the doorway. Within the tent Esketra screamed brokenly, his officers blundered after him, the priests stood clustered about the laughing Prophet.

The night was starless black. Kane could see the circle of torches where the Satakis ringed the city. Where Sandotneri's towers and walls should rise, the others saw nothing at all. No light. No towers. Nothing but absolute darkness.

Kane, whose eyes pierced the darkness as keenly as ever his mother's, saw the dancing shadow horde that writhed, sated, away from silent Sandotneri and into the starless gulf of night.

XV
Omen

Daylight dissolved the pall of night and unveiled a city of the dead. No assault, no plague, nor poison could have wreaked such wholesale annihilation of human life. Kane, riding at dawn through the murdered city, thought of the ravages of poison gas — although he knew too well that no such mundane death had claimed these victims.

The dead lay everywhere — grey, contorted faces, eyes stark with horror, tongues swollen and protruding, limbs frozen in final convulsions. Soldiers sprawled upon the ramparts; children crumpled beside their toys, merchants slumped across their wares, mothers fallen over their dead infants. In street, or household, or tavern, or bastion, or alley, or stall…

For one dread instant, the portals of the dark world had yawned, and something alien and evil had crept forth — and feasted.

Now the Satakis swarmed like maggots throughout the corpse of Sandotneri — despoiling the dead, pillaging the silent shops and houses, stripping weapons and armor that had been no defense against elder horror. Commandeered wagons groaned beneath the weight of the plunder, broad peasant backs bent from sacks of loot. The wealth of Sandotneri was being stripped from the corpse, dragged off piecemeal for the forests of Shapeli.

Kane, inured to such scenes and to such horrors, nonetheless appeared depressed as he rode to meet Orted Ak-Ceddi. The Prophet gazed about him with the smug satisfaction of an artist who views his own masterwork. Kane had seen nothing of Orted in the chaotic hours since the Prophet and his retinue had swept out of Kane's pavilion, taking the terror-stricken Esketra with them. Kane had spent the remaining hours of the night deep in thought, while the Satakis rioted in triumph through the city of the dead, and Kane's officers attempted to maintain order amongst the men.

From time to time, throughout the night, Kane called to him certain of his men whom he knew he could trust, spoke with them in hushed council. Some departed that night on missions known only to themselves and to Kane.

By dawn, his spirits somewhat improved, Kane mounted Angel and rode into the city, where men told him he might find Orted Ak-Ceddi. Kane found him, smiling benediction upon the revels of his followers.

"Your face is grim this morning, General Kane," greeted the Prophet. "Surely the vision of massacre does not appall you."

"The massacre was needless," Kane replied. "The city had surrendered to us."

"Surrendered to you, Kane," the Prophet reminded him. "Not to me."

"I had signed a treaty."

"And the treaty was disregarded. There is no novelty in that. Surely nothing about the deed can blacken the name of Kane."

Kane glanced sharply at Orted wondering how deep the mockery might lie.

"No, Kane — don't scowl so. You have done as you promised, and I am well pleased with you. You have forged a true sword for Sataki, and you have wielded it gloriously against the enemies of the faithful. You understand war and its waging to perfection, Kane — but you cannot understand the sacred mission of the Dark Crusade. You are a sword, Kane — and as you once told me, a sword has no soul. Your duty is to conquer the enemies of Sataki, Kane. What I choose to do with the conquered enemy is according to the will of Sataki. Don't concern yourself with matters beyond your understanding — and beyond your authority."

Orted paused, gestured at the windrows of slain defenders along the wall. "Word of the doom that befell Sandotneri will speed like a blight throughout the southern kingdoms. Sandotneri defied the Dark Crusade; Sandotneri is no more. I think, Kane, Sandotneri's fate is a warning that will serve you well — when you lead the Sword of Sataki across the southern kingdoms."

"I have no doubt the warning will be understood," replied Kane, meeting the dark glow of the Prophet's eyes.

"Very well, then." Orted grinned without humor. "I believe Ripestnari is the next obstacle in our path."

"When it falls, the other border kingdoms will probably capitulate without resistance," Kane agreed.

"Then see that Ripestnari falls," Orted dismissed him. "You understand your duty."

"Perfectly," said Kane.

XVI
Broken Sword

The dead man in the grass made a hoarse, gobbling croak as the dingo sank its teeth into his leg.

It startled the dingo. The wild dog had been eating human carrion for the past week. Not once had its meal offered protest. Ears taut, it regarded the dead man suspiciously in the dying light.

The noise subsided, save for a low rattling moan. Emboldened, the dingo took a firmer grip on the bare leg.

This time the dead thing gave a bellow like a bull sinking beneath quicksand, thrashed its filthy limbs in aimless paroxysms.

The cry brought an answering shout from the billabong close by. A running body pushed through the grass, coming toward the kicking dead thing. There was easier prey than this, and the dingo took to its heels.

Cautiously the girl approached the moaning thing in the tall grass, her poniard glinting with the last rays of the sun.

"What is it, Erill?" came a shout from the wagon drawn up beside the billabong.

"It's a man, Boree!," she answered. "Alive, I think."

With a curse, the older woman caught up an ax and loped toward her. "Don't touch him!"

The man was naked, except for a torn jupon, coated with old blood and dried filth. His bare limbs were cracked and blistered from the sun, lacerated from the saw-bladed grass. Beneath a crust of muck and caked scum, a number of old wounds festered under foul scabs, and bright blood oozed from the bite on his leg.

He made a mewing sound, and wriggled brokenly toward the near by waterhole. If he was aware of their presence, he gave no sign. A faint trail of bent grass indicated the man had been crawling for some distance — evidently his last strength had failed just before he could reach the water he sought.

Boree made a thick sound in her throat. "It's a soldier, from the great battle."

"Ours or theirs?" Erill wondered.

"Who cares. Best to put the poor bastard out of his misery, and have done." Boree hefted the ax.

"No!" Erill protested sharply. "He doesn't appear badly wounded. Maybe he only needs water."

"Needs a lot more than that, honey. Could be all busted up inside. Hell, what are you going to do?"

The smaller girl bent to tug at the man's shoulders. "Give a hand here, Boree. We'll drag him down to the pool. I've seen too much of death."

"Then one more shouldn't bother you," grunted Boree. "Here, give me his shoulders, and I'll pull him. You grab hold his feet. If anything's busted, he's past caring."

She cursed as she raised the man's shoulders. "Hell, honey. He won't want to live even if he has the say. Half his face is all chewed up."

"Boree, will you just shut up and pull."

Straining, for the man was thickly built, and a limp body is a difficult weight to manage, the two women stumbled to drag him to their camp. Days before, their wagon had been part of the Sataki horde that converged upon Sandotneri — not so much from their zeal for the Dark Crusade, as because to remain behind might be construed as disloyalty to Sataki, and disloyalty did not escape the notice of the Defenders of Sataki. Now, turning from the plundered city, a lame horse had detached them from the straggling horde. By degrees they followed apart from the main body, returning to Ingoldi because there was no other place to go.

Erill had pondered the idea of fleeing to the south. But now that Sandotneri had fallen, the Sword of Sataki rode like a destroying wind across the southern kingdoms. The Dark Crusade was engulfing the land, and there was no place to flee. And so they slowly made their way back to the forests of Shapeli, camped here tonight with another day's wagon journey to go.

Gingerly they laid the man down at the water's edge. He had barely strength enough to gulp a few mouthfuls of water, then lapsed once more into unconsciousness. Erill stripped off the tattered jupon and began to lave the filth from his tortured flesh. The man lay senseless throughout her ministrations, even when she scrubbed against his encrusted wounds.

Boree, who had gone on with cooking their dinner, came over to see if he still lived. She shook her head, then scowled, squinting in the failing light.

"That's an old wound there on his face. It's all scar."

"Looks like an old burn scar," Erill commented. "I don't think he's badly wounded — mostly thirst and exhaustion."

"And fever," Boree remarked. "Burned up with fever. That'll kill him, even if he doesn't get blood poisoning from these wounds."

"They're not deep — only look bad because they've festered," Erill told her. "And there's awful bruises all around them."

"Crush injuries," Boree judged. "Likely then he wore armor. Unless you slip past a joint, takes a hell of a lot to bash through steel plate."

They looked down at the unconscious face, its scarred half unnaturally pallid against the fever-flushed skin of the right. It would have been a handsome face.

"Erill, do you know who this is!" Boree breathed suddenly.

"Yes."

"Erill, that's Jarvo! It has to be!"

"I know. I guessed it when we picked him up."

Boree licked her thick lips. "There's one huge bounty on him. Alive or dead."

"We'll keep him alive," Erill told her. "If we can."

"Bounty's the same."

"We aren't keeping him for any bounty."

"No bounty?" Boree tried to see the joke.

"We'll hide him, nurse him back to health."

"Erill, are you out of your mind!"

"No." Erill's face was as hard as her voice. "Once the Satakis used me as a tool to destroy a city. Now I'm going to salvage a sword to destroy the Dark Crusade."

"Oh, Erill," murmured Boree. "Oh, Erill."

XVII
Children's Hour

"**N**oochee! Noochee! Noochee!"

Jarvo spun around at the jeering shouts of the children, saw that they only played along the alley. He relaxed, then uneasily glanced about to see if anyone had taken note of his guilty start.

"Noochee! Noochee!" A whimper, then shrieks of laughter.

Noochee. He was an *inuchiri* — or *noochee*, as current slang had foreshortened it. There were only two kinds of people left in the world: the Satakis and the inuchiri — literally, "those who betray the one faith." As easy to say, the living and the dead — for where the Dark Crusade cast its shadow, there were no alternatives.

Jarvo froze, in the next instant tried to look nonchalant. Across the street, two guardsmen in red surcoats emblazoned with the black avellan cross of Sataki — uniform of the Defenders of Sataki, the Prophet's security police. Were they only lounging there, or were they watching him?

They might wonder why the cry of "noochee" had brought him about. Feigning mild curiosity, Jarvo continued his movement and strolled over to where the children laughed and played at the mouth of the alley. Glancing from the corner of his good eye, he saw the red-coated Defenders leisurely cross toward him. For a moment Jarvo considered bolting down the alley. Two things held him back. First, that would confirm their suspicions, bring out their shrill whistles to signal a noochee chase. Second, the alley was a dead end.

Jarvo gazed into the darkened alleyway, as if curious to see what sport the children found here. For a moment the darkness hid the far end, then his eye adjusted to the gloom.

At the far end, the children had nailed together an X-shaped framework of scrap timber, in imitation of the avellan cross of Sataki. A girl — she couldn't be much past six — hung upside down from the framework, her scrawny body straining against the inexpertly hammered nails. Her face was distorted from agony and bruises, and her mindless whimpers barely carried past the alley mouth.

"Noochee! Noochee!" shrilled the pack of children, squealing and darting from the mouth of the alley, pelting her with bits of offal and debris. A chance hit might provoke a new bleat of pain.

"Noochee! Noochee! Noochee!"

Jarvo started forward, felt a hand grip his shoulder. He whirled. In sick loathing he had forgotten the two Defenders.

"No problem, friend," one of them grinned. "It's a sure enough noochee brat. We arrested her family the other night, but the kids only flushed her out of hiding this morning."

"Thought they'd set up their own little Justice Square, just like the grown-ups," his comrade chuckled. "Crazy the way kids will pick things up."

"Been watching them all morning," the first guardsman added. "Gives a few of the grown-ups a start now and then. Just like it did you. But just a noochee brat."

Jarvo grinned crookedly. The Defenders were staring at him, and in a way that let him know what might be suspected of passers-by who sought to interfere with a noochee execution. He felt his belly tighten. There was a poniard hidden in his boot — in the interest of public safety, the Prophet had decreed that private citizens could not go armed except when on crusade. The Defenders wore steel helmets and hauberks, and went heavily armed. If their scrutiny penetrated Erill's paints and waxes, there was no question of fighting it out.

"What's your name, friend?" the first one asked.

"Insiemo," Jarvo answered, giving the identity Erill had coached him to assume.

"Face like yours I ought to remember. Where you from?"

"The Theatre Guild. I mostly work on sets and stuff, don't go out too much."

"Where you headed, Insiemo?"

"Got a break. Going for a drink."

"What happened to your face?"

"I was part of the first wave that went over the wall at Emleoas."

"Yeah? The west wall, huh." Casually spoken.

"No." Jarvo sensed the trap. "The west wall was the river wall — not even enough mud there to stand a ladder on. We went up over the east wall, after we'd laid down a sharp fire from the ridge there. I got to the parapet just in time to miss the flaming pitch that cleaned off the ladder beneath me. Well, I missed most of the pitch."

"One of the first bunch, huh." There was a trace of respectful sympathy. "Well, I guess I can't blame you for not walking around in public much."

"It'd look worse without the wax and greasepaint," Jarvo volunteered.

"I'd noticed you were sort of made up."

"Got it!" The other guardsman, silent during the questioning, smacked his fist into his palm. "Jarvo!"

Jarvo froze, his face doubly a mask.

"Huh?" the first one blurted.

"Yeah, sure! Jarvo!'" exclaimed his comrade, pleased with himself. "This is the guy who plays Jarvo in the new pageant the guild is putting on this month: *The Invincible March of the Sword of Sataki*. I caught it on three nights already."

"I haven't seen it yet."

"You'd better. It's the best one yet."

"I didn't think anyone would recognize me out of costume," Jarvo commented lamely, hoping his voice wouldn't stumble over commonplaces.

"Wouldn't have guessed — it if you hadn't mentioned you were from the Theatre Guild. Guess with that scar-face, you were tailored for the part. Not really tall enough though, but that don't matter much up on stage."

"Well, I'd better get that drink before I have to get back on the job," Jarvo suggested. "Give a cheer next time you're in the audience."

"Yeah, sure. It's a great pageant. The Theatre Guild may not turn out weapons or armor, but you guys still really do your part for the Crusade. I've gone back to the barracks every night after seeing this new one, thinking I ought to join up with the Sword of Sataki and share in the glory."

"Well, the Defenders of Sataki have an essential duty to perform, too," Jarvo said, edging away.

"You said it, Insiemo. Only thing is, we never get the cheers those cavalrymen do when they ride by."

Jarvo made a sympathetic grunt, escaped for the shelter of a corner tavern. It had been a bad idea, after all, to venture alone into the streets of Ingoldi. Erill would be furious with him. But after too many weeks of inaction, skulking around Erill's wagon in the Theatre Guild, Jarvo had to get out on his own, or lose his mind. Conscious that they were still watching him — the Defenders of Sataki watched everything — he ambled into the tavern.

He hadn't been thirsty before, but now his mouth felt gummy. Jarvo called for a stoup of ale, found it so expensive he wondered if he had enough money. He paid for it with bright, new-minted coins that had the sigil of Sataki stamped on one face and the profile of Orted Ak-Ceddi on the other. The coins purported to be silver, but clattered like they were mostly tin. The Prophet melted down into bullion the gold and silver his conquests brought him, ostensibly to mint his coinage — increasingly debased as the precious metals went into the vaults of Ceddi and to supply the Sword of Sataki. The taverner looked unhappy with the new coins, but the two Defenders lounged only a few yards away, and it was not wise to complain.

Carrying his ale, Jarvo crossed to a bench in the shadow of the wall, where he could look out through the open window. A taste of the ale proved it had been watered. Jarvo sipped it without protest. The commonroom was virtually deserted.

Fear. It haunted the faces of every person on the street. Serve Sataki or die, that was the law. It was written on walls and banners throughout the city, throughout Shapeli. Probably throughout what was left of the southern kingdoms, for each week brought news of yet another smashing victory for Kane and the Sword of Sataki. The Prophet said he would impose the law throughout the entire world. Maybe he would.

Jarvo sipped his tepid ale, stared at the painted mural on the tavern wall. It depicted Orted Ak-Ceddi leading his heroic followers in the first great battle of the Guild Fair. Sabres gory with the blood of the helpless townsfolk, the rat-faced thugs of the city guard cowered and tried to flee. Jarvo turned again to the window.

Fear. The Satakis either destroyed or assimilated everything in the path of the Dark Crusade. There was no middle ground. You pledged your soul to Sataki, and joined the triumphant horde. Or you defied Sataki, and joined the even greater horde of the dead. But vigilance was needed to make certain Sataki's newly pledged faithful were not secretly inuchiri. A man might lie to save his skin, thinking he could escape on another day. The Defenders of Sataki kept a constant guard against such treachery. Disloyalty to Sataki meant certain and hideous death — in Justice Square, or in the secret cellars beneath Ceddi.

Noochees hid everywhere. They plotted against the Dark Crusade. They spoke blasphemies against Sataki. They whispered treason against Orted Ak-Ceddi. When the Prophet commanded that his faithful must labor on some great project for the common good, the noochees grumbled. When the Prophet collected the booty of his conquests from the faithful to buy more soldiers and armaments for the common defense, the noochees complained. When the Prophet demanded that the faithful learn the chants and rituals of Sataki, the noochees showed no zeal. It was well that the Defenders of Sataki were so adept at ferreting out noochees.

Jarvo decided not to press his luck further. He'd proven to himself that he could walk through Ingoldi with impunity. It was time for other things now.

As he left the tavern, the hopeless moan from the alley suddenly rose to a piercing note of agony, cutting through the howls and laughter of the children. Jarvo saw smoke leaking from the alley mouth, and thought for but an instant that he only smelled burning refuse.

"Crazy damn kids!" The two Defenders pounded for the alleyway. "Burn the whole damn city down, if you aren't careful! "

"Noochee! Noochee!"

XVIII
Dream and Delirium

When Erill was angry, her eyes narrowed and flashed as bright and green as the band of jade beads across her brow. Right now she was angry.

"Damn you, Jarvo! I've warned you not to go out on your own yet! And what do you do but blunder into two Defenders first thing!"

She *was* mad. She made it her rule to call him Insiemo always — against making a slip sometime when other ears might hear and wonder.

"I've been cooped up here for months," Jarvo shot back. "Damn it, woman! I'm grateful for all you've done, but I'm not going to stay forever hidden under your bed, while Esketra suffers hell in that devil's harem!"

Erill set her jaw and squinted harder. "Damn it all, I don't care what in hell you do to risk your own bloody neck! Can't you get it through your thick skull that if you screw up, they'll trace you back to us here — and we'll all make a farewell performance on the scaffolds in Justice Square!"

That cut, because he'd realized it beforehand, and had taken the chance nonetheless.

"I'm sorry, Erill," Jarvo muttered, subsiding before her anger. "You've run a hell of a risk for my sake, and I've no right to put you and Boree and all your friends in danger. But, damn it, I can't keep hiding out here without doing anything. When I think of what Esketra has to endure…"

Erill cursed herself, scowling at him. She had been crazy as hell to let him find out his Great Love was alive, languishing in silks and furs in the Prophet's tower in Ceddi. His spirits were at such a low ebb after he'd learned that Sandotneri was no more than a city of ghosts. She'd told him of Esketra's captivity in desperate hope that he might shake off the black mood that gnawed at his soul more ravenously than any fever. It had brought Jarvo out of his melancholia well enough — and ever since he paced about restlessly, concocting mad schemes to rescue Esketra from the Prophet's fortress. While in delirium he had cried out Esketra's name again and again, and now that he was whole, he still spoke of her constantly. Erill found herself hating a woman she had never seen.

She broke her stony silence. "Look, there's some things I've got to take care of. Will you promise me to stay around the guild until I get back?"

"I won't even step out of the wagon to piss," Jarvo growled.

She left without farewells, and Jarvo didn't look up. In a foul mood, he told himself he shouldn't feel guilty. Erill was, after all, gutter-bred and gutter-raised. She had saved his life at the risk of hers, and he was grateful. But Erill was too lowborn to understand the needs and the duties that honor demanded of nobility, just as she was too coarse-natured to conceive of a love as deep and unselfish as the love he bore for Esketra. Erill and her friends had done much for him, and Jarvo felt the same lofty gratitude that any great lord extends to his loyal retainers.

It could be no more than that. It must be no more than that.

Jarvo retained only a foggy impression of those first fever-racked weeks. He had lain inside the wagon, somewhere between coma and delirium, while Erill forced him to swallow broths and eucalyptus teas and elixirs of cinchona bark and other powders that Boree procured. All the while they camped beside the waterhole, fearing to move him until his fever broke. Other stragglers from the Sataki horde passed by their camp. When any questioned, Erill explained that the stricken man was her lover, one Insiemo, sorely wounded in the great battle at Meritavano. No one questioned further. There were thousands so wounded, many with faces wrapped in bandages as was brave Insiemo's.

After several days, there were periods when Jarvo remained conscious long enough to gaze upon the wagon interior, the blonde girl who anxiously attended to him, the dark-haired older women whose pocked face always scowled. Gradually the mists of delirium lifted enough for him to understand his situation. It was then that his despair tortured him more cruelly than any fever.

Jarvo remembered the battle, the hopeless realization of defeat, the desperate attempt to rally his routed forces, the final horror when the headlong retreat was dragged down to hell in the treacherous mire below Meritavano. The memories tortured him still, waking or delirious.

Exhausted from the battle, racked with agonizing wounds beneath his dented armor, it had taken some moments before he realized the full horror of their doomed rout onto the marsh. The tall grass was suddenly high reeds; the firm sod was bottomless mud. His horse wallowed in the hidden mire, throwing Jarvo over its neck and into the clinging morass. Helpless in his heavy armor, Jarvo could not rise from the slippery muck. His struggles only dragged him deeper into the sucking depths of the bog. In a burst of panic, Jarvo knew he was going to be pulled beneath the fen by the weight of his armor — that scum and foetid slime would trickle through the vizor of his armet, drowning him in filth as he sank within his steel casket into the bottomless morass.

Then unseen hands pulled desperately at his sinking body. Frantic fingers unclasped his demon-mask helmet, flung it off his head. Troopers of his light horse, less encumbered in their mail hauberks, had crawled out to him. Loyal to death, they worked frenziedly to drag their leader out of his armored coffin. It was a tense struggle, as arrows fell upon them from the Sataki pursuers massed on the dry ground. Finally, exhausted and weak as a newborn infant, and nearly as naked, Jarvo sprawled on his belly in the churned mud, gasping for air.

Some of his men were struggling to the far bank of the water-meadow, dragging themselves wearily through the high grass in hope of flight. Jarvo knew Kane would send his cavalry to skirt the marsh, cut off their retreat. There was no escape from that quarter, nor could he remain where he was. Better to drown in the fen than fall into Kane's hands.

There was one desperate chance, and Jarvo took it. Slithering across the muck like some ungainly salamander, he began to work his way through the marsh — following the course of the reed-buried river, away from the sounds of massacre. All was confusion behind him, as Satakis crawled out to slaughter the mired calvarymen. Swimming through scum-covered pools, slithering between the high reeds, Jarvo was well beyond the circle of slaughter by the time darkness concealed hunters and hunted, slayers and slain.

The following days were a confused haze that Jarvo remembered with no more clarity than the first days he spent in Erill's wagon. Exhaustion and the agony of festering wounds were a constant torment — until fever blotted out all other sensation. He remembered drinking from foetid pools in a vain effort to quench his searing thirst, devouring raw the snakes and frogs and blind crawling things that were all he could catch to eat. He remembered the torturing bites and stings of myriads of insects, the blistering touch of the sun. Once a queen snake coiled before him; its bite would bring merciful oblivion, but instead he killed it with a rock and ate it.

Jarvo supposed he was quite mad for much of that time. Beyond his immediate need to escape, he was never certain what plans he may have had. At first there was the need to return to Sandotneri, but that was impossible with Kane's certain siege, and at some deeper level Jarvo knew Sandotneri must fall after his disastrous defeat. At times, when he could rally his thoughts at all, it seemed to Jarvo he must instead go to Ingoldi — that the only way to expiate his disgrace was to seek out Kane there and kill him. Only rarely did his dream of vengeance remember to take in Orted Ak-Ceddi as well. After several more days of aimless wandering in a northward direction, the only thing Jarvo could remember to concentrate on was the need to escape capture. And finally that awareness dissolved as well. There followed an indefinable interval of pain-haunted blackness that ended finally as his fevered vision began to focus on Erill's face.

By the time Jarvo could feed himself, or endure an hour without dripping with fever-sweat or shaking with chill, he had grown a heavy straw-colored beard. With the patches of scar-tissue, the beard gave him a decidedly mangy appearance, but it would be more days still before he would care. By then Erill had passed on to him such information as she dared give him as to the fate of Sandotneri. Jarvo lay in dull despair, wondering why he had been spared. More than ever he swore vengeance on Kane.

It was in this bleak mood he learned from Erill that Esketra yet lived — carried off by the Prophet to serve his will in Ceddi. Jarvo was silent for many hours thereafter. When he spoke again it was with a new calmness, for he had a use for life once more. He would return to Ingoldi with Erill and Boree, and there bide his time for the opportunity to rescue Esketra.

It could be done, of that Jarvo was certain. To believe otherwise was a torture beyond any enduring. All that remained was to study the problem, bide his time until he found a way. True, Esketra had been false to him. But he could forgive her that, knowing that her heart would be his once more, when he daringly stole her away from the Prophet's citadel. Their world was no more; their love would be a new world.

Thereafter he filled his days with a thousand mad schemes. He would storm the citadel with a secret army. He would organize a rebellion. He would burst upon Orted in his tower, cut him to pieces as Esketra watched with glowing eyes. He would steal into the citadel by night, spirit her away with the audacity of a master thief. He would set a trap for Kane, overpower him in an epic duel sparing Kane's life while he forced him to procure Esketra's release.

The plans and variations were beyond number, ranging from vaguely feasible to hopelessly fanciful. They each ended with the same vision of triumph and bliss. Erill listened patiently to most of them, occasionally offering sarcastic comment. Whether from bitter tonics or airy hopes, the fever at length gave way, and Jarvo's strength returned.

They had to return to Shapeli — or risk being hunted down as inuchiri by the Sataki patrols that passed about them increasingly, as Kane led the Sword of Sataki ever onward into the southern kingdoms. Erill had originally planned no further than to try to nurse Jarvo back to health, then help him escape to wherever he might muster a new army to lead against Kane. By the time he was strong enough to leave, she found herself rather wishing he would stay. Her protests to his insistence in going to Ingoldi lacked vehemence.

After all, there was no place of safety from the Dark Crusade. Moreover, General Jarvo was by now presumed to be worm-meat beneath the marshes — and even should he have somehow escaped that day, was there any place a less likely refuge than Ingoldi? Finally, Jarvo was going to Ingoldi. If Erill would take him in her wagon, that was fine. If not, he would get there on his own.

So Erill brought him to Ingoldi. On his own, she knew he would never survive. Jarvo laughed at her fears. Erill held her temper, warned him that he had no conception of what awaited them in the Prophet's capital. Jarvo laughed again. Like much of laughter, it was born of ignorance.

A carnival wagon with two women and a maimed veteran does not excite immediate suspicion, even in Shapeli. Erill took measures to insure such suspicions might never fall — for the Defenders of Sataki were eternally vigilant, and seldom did they scruple over distinctions between whispered suspicion and veritable guilt.

Jarvo became Insiemo, a loyal follower of Sataki whose face had been scarred at Emleoas. His old wounds kept him from serving in the Sword of Sataki, but he had joined the Sataki horde that had called down the doom that engulfed Sandotneri. Old wounds had flared anew on his return from Sandotneri. Erill had met him then, offered the shelter of her wagon to the stricken hero, and they had become lovers after a fashion. Boree had sneered at this; Jarvo agreed the charade would lull suspicion. Humanitarian gestures were suspect in Shapeli.

Allowing for regional dialects, the language throughout Shapeli and the southern kingdoms was the same. Jarvo's accent was suspect. Erill coached his pronunciation until he could pass for a native of one of the border towns, whose accent had taken on a mongrel aspect after the years of social upheaval in Shapeli.

Jarvo had been clean-shaven; Insiemo had a full but scabby beard. Jarvo was blond and carefully groomed; Insiemo had a dark beard and shaggy hair streaked with grey. Jarvo wore an eye patch; Insiemo's left eye glared blindly at the world. Let them stare at the ruined eye, Erill told him — and they will little note your other features. Greasepaints and stains darkened Jarvo's complexion from fair to swarthy. Strips of gum extended the scar across his nose and onto the unburned side of his face; waxy make-up made it appear he sought to hide the scarring as best he could. That camouflaged the wax extension that made a straight-bridged nose a hooked beak.

Erill considered such refinements as gum pads within the checks to distort the facial lines, or silver arches within the nostrils to flare out and tilt the nose upward, or clips and gum inserts to alter the shape of the ears. She decided against all these. They took too long to adjust and required constant attention, while close or prolonged scrutiny might discern them. Best to keep with a relatively simple appearance that Jarvo could maintain for weeks. It was a good disguise, made all the more effective because there were few left alive who knew Jarvo by sight. Jarvo was dead, and Shapeli was crowded with maimed veterans such as Insiemo.

He needed a cover. Erill and Boree had maintained their carnival contacts throughout all the upheaval. It kept them eating, and beat the Sataki labor teams. Now, as the war moved away from Ingoldi, the Theater Guild began to flourish. There were patriotic pageants to stir the morale of the masses, morality plays to remind them of their duties to Sataki, and of the new age that would come when the Dark Crusade was victorious. Erill was an accomplished mime, and had no difficulty picking up her former career. Jarvo was strong, could use his hands after a fashion; there was enough work to justify his presence at the guild while he waited for his chance.

The weeks were a torture for him, skulking in the background — thinking always of Esketra, but unable to do anything. He consoled himself by gathering detailed information on the Prophet's fortress and on the workings of the Dark Crusade. It occurred to him that his information would be invaluable to an invading army, but for Jarvo it was only a potential means toward entering Ceddi and rescuing Esketra.

His task was far more complicated than he had ever imagined. Ingoldi lived under a pall of suspicion and fear. The Defenders of Sataki watched everything, and what they missed a faithful citizen might whisper to them.

There were rewards for denouncing noochees. And Ceddi was absolutely closed to unauthorized persons. No one went in, no one came out, except under tightest security. No one outside of the priests of Sataki even knew for certain what went on inside the Prophet's citadel. Presumably the doomed prisoners who were dragged into Ceddi's secret recesses found out, but none ever came out again.

After months of frustration, Jarvo had not even seen Esketra, only knew from gossip that the Prophet's favorite concubine still lived. He clung to sanity by mentally enacting a thousand mad schemes — dreaming of hidden passages, scaled walls, secret notes, hidden spies, and other vain hopes. Lately he had thought of risking everything and trying to join the priesthood. No one knew for certain how the priests of Sataki recruited new brothers.

When the new pageant was being organized, and someone suggested that Insiemo was a natural to portray villainous Scarface Jarvo, Jarvo accepted with only weak protests. It was a piece of audacity that appealed to his growing recklessness. It was a secret jest, no more than thumbing his nose at an enemy's back. But Jarvo knew he must soon find some release from tension, or he would run amok.

So the months had dragged on for him. Defeated and disgraced, nursed back to strength from the brink of death, now living in the very shadow of his enemy's citadel, dependent upon a barely grown girl — a carnival mime of strange moods and uncertain temper. And while he skulked about helplessly, Kane was laying waste to the southern kingdoms, Orted Ak-Ceddi was piling his storerooms with blood-bartered loot, and Esketra was slave to the Prophet's foul lusts.

And Erill flew at him because he was so bold as to venture forth without his nursemaid.

So Jarvo scowled and sulked, aroused from his grim brooding only when Erill finally returned to the wagon.

Her face was worried.

"What is it?" he asked sharply.

"Trouble, I'm afraid. I just got word from the guild directors."

"Trouble from the censors?" That could be very bad.

"Wish that was all it was. No, the new pageant has met with the highest official praise. It's a stirring portrayal of the victorious advance of the Dark Crusade. All the faithful should see it twice."

"Then what's the sting?"

"We're too good. The Prophet has called for a command performance, to be given within the great hall of Ceddi."

Jarvo leapt to his feet with an exultant laugh. "That's too good to be true! Finally! It's the chance I've needed all along to get into Ceddi! I'll at least be able to see Esketra, maybe get word to her, maybe even…"

"It's to be a victory banquet — in honor of Kane's return."

XIX
Goddess

Bree's practiced fingers reshuffled the black lacquered squares, pushed the deck across the table to Erill.

"Try it again, honey."

Erill scowled, shook her blonde curls in vexation. "Twice is enough, damn it. I've got things to do. Why don't you leave me alone?"

Boree's face was expressionless, but her eyes were shadowed. "Once more."

"Go to hell. You won't even tell me what you read the last two times." Erill held the spill to her cold pipe, puffed it alight.

"Hard to read the cards tonight, honey."

"Then it's bad, and you don't want to scare me. Well, reading the cards again won't change my fate."

"I may have made a mistake somehow."

"Then it's not worth wasting my time."

"Please. Once more."

Erill swore and accepted the black deck. It angered her that her hands trembled.

Jarvo looked at his hands and cursed. The tremor didn't go away. *Nerves*, he told himself, and set his jaw determinedly.

That betrayed him. A spasm shook his muscles; his teeth chattered for an instant. Not nerves, fever.

Vaul! Not tonight...

Savagely Jarvo wiped at the sweat that oozed from his pallid face. He wondered again how it was possible to sweat when his guts were an icy ache. No matter. The familiar fever and chills gripped him, once again — treacherously, when he was certain his strength had fully returned, certain the nights of shivering beneath sweat-soaked blankets were past and gone. No matter; it was back.

Erill must not know. She had given up trying to dissuade him from appearing at the Prophet's command performance — but only because she knew no arguments could stop him. If she found out he was suffering another relapse, she'd rail at him to stay away — his illness would allow another to take his part without suspicion, and surely in his state…

Jarvo grimaced. He could hear her angry voice now. Erill could be very persuasive. No wonder that husky Boree always gave way to the girl's stinging temper.

He glanced toward the westering sun. It lacked some hours yet before the troupe would assemble for their admission into Ceddi. Perhaps by then his bout would have left him. The episodes were milder, and the intervals farther apart now.

No matter. He was going into Ceddi tonight. He would see Esketra tonight, if he never saw another sunrise.

Cautiously Jarvo slipped into the wagon, opened the chest beside his bed. The familiar phial waited conveniently on top. Forcing his hands to steadiness, Jarvo poured out a measure of powdered cinchona bark, washed the bitter drug down with a swallow of water.

Orted Ak-Ceddi inhaled a tiny portion of pulverized coca leaves from the back of his thumb. Snorted, sneezed, swallowed. He gulped a mouthful of brandy to remove the bitterness that penetrated before numbness settled over his nose and throat.

The tingling rush of cocaine glowed through his cramped limbs, obliterating the dullness of sleep as a flame touches spiderweb. He rubbed his face, refreshed as the last vestiges of hangover melted away. Beside him on the bed, Esketra made plaintive noises without awakening. Orted looked down at her naked body, dispassionately, as a sated reveller stirs and contemplates the remains of a feast, dully wonders how the banquet was passed.

Pulling on a silken robe, the Prophet padded across to a high window, drew aside the heavy curtains. Daylight flooded the chamber, but no shadow fell back from the man who stood framed in the aperture.

It was well past noon, not surprisingly — it had been dawn when Orted had called to Esketra and left the banquet hall. Kane had wished him a good night; it annoyed Orted that his hulking general seemed unaffected by the hours of carousal.

The memory of Kane drew Orted's eyes to the veil of smoke beyond Ingoldi's walls. The smoke of a thousand fires. The Sword of Sataki had returned to Ingoldi, driving before it a numberless army of neophytes from the conquered cities of the southern kingdoms. Orted thought upon the treasure-laden train of wagons that had rolled endlessly through the gates of Ceddi. Were it not for the expenses of waging war, his fortress would surely lie buried beneath an avalanche of gold by now — even as the walls of Ingoldi swelled to bursting from the ever-growing press of new worshippers.

Tonight another great banquet in honor of the endless victories of the Dark Crusade. In honor of Kane.

Orted frowned at the smoky pall of Kane's camp. What was the hidden motive of Kane's return? The Prophet's spies reported that certain elements within Shapeli already whispered that Kane might rule an empire as well as lead an army…

Orted dug another pinch of powdered coca leaves from his golden snuff-box. Kane had served him well — thus far. But each knew they played a deadly game, and neither intended to lose. Orted snuffed, rubbed his nose, and smiled thinly. A game, but the rules were his own, and Kane might have cause to regret his triumphal march into Ceddi.

Replacing the snuffbox, Orted reached for his goblet.

Kane drained the chalice and set it negligently aside. The die he had just cast showed two. Reaching across the table, he moved one of the featureless jade cubes one space across the hexagonally patterned gameboard.

Across the table from him, Colonel Alain, his second-in-command, grunted in his yellow beard and cast the die in turn. Five. He studied the board in silence, finally moved one of the jade cubes one space across, to confront the piece Kane had just moved.

He pursed his lips. "Challenge."

"Accepted." Kane turned the jade cube over, revealing a three. Alain did likewise with his piece: a four. Kane removed Alain's piece, reversed his own and edged it into the vacated space. Alain ruefully scratched his beard; of his twenty-one pieces, Kane now had captured nine, against losing two.

"Go on with your report," prompted Kane, reaching for the die.

Dolnes tore his attention away from the gameboard, shrugged his squat shoulders. "That's all of it."

Kane cast a three, hesitated an instant, then withdrew an advanced piece one space. He turned again to his spy.

"Is it? You're certain she's the one?"

"As certain as I can be," Dolnes assured him. "You got to remember it's damn near impossible getting any kind of information. Things have just been too torn apart and kicked around here. No records of anything, generally too few survivors left to talk. You got to find people who might know, who might remember, and who might even talk about it. And asking questions is about as safe work as doing stand-in for a sabre drill dummy."

"I know the difficulties," Kane said coldly. "If it were simple, I'd not be paying you so generously." He added: "Paying for results."

"Well, she's the one you want — near as I can tell without asking her."

"That isn't necessary," said Kane, moving another piece. "Challenge."

"Denied," Alain grudgingly decided. He withdrew his piece to the rear, and Kane occupied the contested space.

"What does the die determine?" Dolnes asked, unable to contain his curiosity.

"From which face of the hexagon a piece can be moved," Kane told him. "You can find the girl, I assume."

"Of course." Dolnes studied the strange board. "How are the pieces ranked?"

"One is of the highest order, descending to six. There are as many of each rank as each piece's numerical value."

"I'm not familiar with this game," Dolnes commented, intrigued.

"It's quite old," Kane told him drily. "I want this girl brought to me. To-night. Without fail. Colonel Alain will assign you men for the task."

Dolnes nodded. "The pieces all look alike. How can you tell the value of each piece as you move them about?"

"Through memory," Kane advised. "Coupled with a lot of deduction and guesswork. And you can always challenge."

"What if you guess wrong?"

"What do you think?" said Kane.

XX
Her Lips Are Painted Red...

The command performance of *The Invincible March of the Sword of Sataki* was a huge success. That the audience was drunkenly exuberant may have helped. Certainly the aloof, black-clad priests would never have given vent to such raucous applause.

Within the Prophet's citadel, one end of the great hall had been cleared, and a stage set up. As the evening wore on, wagonloads of sets and costumes rolled into Ceddi, accompanied by actors, chorus, and as many others of the guild who could find excuse to share in the Prophet's lavish entertainment. By the time the main courses were picked bones, the audience was in a boisterous spirit, and the performers were anxious to begin.

The pageant itself was a long, loud, tumultuous affair — basically a series of tableaus and processions, interspersed with dramatic speeches and noisy sham battles. A narrator supplied continuity, and interpreted the action while the chorus shouted chants and battle songs, musicians battered their instruments, and the stage crew dashed about with sets and sound effects. The overall effect was somewhere in between a morality play, a travesty, and a free-for-all. The audience responded with enthusiastic shouts and catcalls.

The performers were elaborately costumed and masked, clad in lightweight stage armor and brandishing wooden weapons. Cavalrymen galloped about with wickerwork horses suspended from their shoulders. With as many as forty or fifty performers onstage in a given battle — all shouting and laying about and rushing back and forth — the uproar was deafening. Most parts were indistinguishable, so that the slain rank and file rose again between scenes, to do battle and be slain again. Key figures in the drama often had speaking roles — usually soliloquies and dramatic speeches — delivered center-stage with extravagant gestures and posturing.

The character portraying Orted Ak-Ceddi had the lead role — a tall figure in black silks who made numerous stirring declamations, and who always charged fearlessly about in the fore of each battle. However, most of the audience preferred the Kane — a beefy actor in oversized armor, who forever rushed about shouting commands and imprecations, crushing all who stood before him. Minor roles went to important officers, brave and courageous men all, and to the leaders of the enemy forces, rotten and cowardly to a man.

The role of Jarvo, portrayed by one Insiemo, was typical of the latter — part buffoon, part dastard. While Jarvo's armor would turn up again on half a dozen other players as the pageant wore on, the Sandotneri arch-villain was easily recognizable by his scarred face, gruesomely exaggerated with stage make-up. In addition Insiemo wore an absurd blond wig, heel pads within his sollerets to increase his height, and spoke in a high, lisping voice. It was an excellent impersonation, a favorite of the audiences, and his efforts were applauded with loud boos and yells.

Jarvo made a short, cackling speech about how he would blaspheme Sataki and crush the Dark Crusade. Laughing fiendishly, he cavorted about the stage butchering unarmed peasants and mothers who crouched over shrieking children.

A pause to shift sets and for the dead to scramble back to the wings, during which the narrator droned on, and the chorus chanted dirges and calls to battle. Kane and Orted appeared at center stage, made long and improbable speeches, embraced in friendship. Kane raised his sword. Newly resurrected actors in mail and armor rushed to join him, stage horses swaying about their hips. Kane marched them all about the stage, their ranks swelling, everyone loudly singing "The Sword of Sataki Is Drawn." The audience cheered and joined in.

Again a shift of sets. From the opposite wing, Jarvo and his band of killers strutted onto stage. At the sight of the Sword of Sataki, boldly riding forth from the other wing, the Sandotneri cavalry halted in disorder. Jarvo squealed and rushed about in fright, shouting for his men to protect him. Useless. The Sword of Sataki swept across the stage, knocking over the panic-stricken Sandotneri troopers with joyful mayhem. Jarvo capered all about, seeking escape — only to blunder up against Kane's charge. Shrieking for mercy, for Sataki to forgive him, Jarvo died wretchedly beneath Kane's wooden ax and a tumult of shouts and jeers.

The pageant had an hour yet to drag on, but Jarvo's part was finished. Grimly he stripped off his costume and armor, while Kane and the victorious Sword of Sataki marched about the stage and sang "The Sword of Sataki Strikes True." Technically Jarvo should remain with the troupe to assist with sets and costumes, serve as an extra in forthcoming battles — but everyone connected with the guild who could con a pass was here for the performance, and he would not be missed.

As part of the gala, the celebrators wore fanciful masks — covering only the upper half of their faces, so as not to interfere with dining and drink. Jarvo peeled off his wig and stage make-up, appropriated an elegant, not-too-threadbare doublet from the costume store, and carefully adjusted the mask he had brought with him. It was a waxen caricature of his own face.

So accoutred, he slipped away from the backstage confusion, moving into the shadows of the great hall to mingle with the servants and guests. After the pageant, there would be acrobats and dancers, more drinking and general carousal. The performers could join in, so long as they held in the background. No one would remark upon him, and in the milling throng he could find a way to reach Esketra.

Beyond that, Jarvo had no firm plans. His first great gamble was won, however — neither Kane nor any of the others had seen anything amiss in the Jarvo who pranced about the stage. Why should they suspect, after all? Jarvo was dead. Yet, with Kane…

No matter. Luck was with him tonight. The fever had subsided to only a heady surge of his blood. He had penetrated undetected into the stronghold of his enemies. When he reached Esketra, they would find a way. In the drunkenness and revelry, and the confusion of packing up after the performance, anything was possible.

Accepting a goblet of wine from a servant, Jarvo confidently swaggered through the shadows surrounding the banquet tables. There were several hundreds of seated guests — officers of the Sword of Sataki, along with officers of the Defenders of Sataki and of the growing regiments of the Prophet's infantry. Others of the Prophet's flatterers and advisors joined in the banquet, along with other important personages. Also seated, but not joining in the hilarity, were numerous of the black-robed priests of Sataki. Whatever their thoughts of the raucous dissipation that reigned in their ancient sanctuary, their faces remained hidden within the shadow of their cowls. Beyond the tables were gathered a jostling fringe of servants and retainers, personages of lesser rank, stray entertainers, guards, and, doubtless, spies.

Jarvo took a position beside a column from which he could view the high table. Kane was there, his massive presence unmistakable despite the lion mask. He sat at the right of Orted Ak-Ceddi, the latter wearing a mask of featureless black. Apart from the increasing gaiety, they appeared to be arguing tersely. For all Jarvo's anxiety, they were completely ignoring the pageant.

To the Prophet's left — Jarvo's blood roared through his temples. The kite's mask could not conceal the proud features of Esketra.

Kane's temper was smouldering beneath the double mask of lion fur and of politesse. He wanted better than supercilious evasions to his questions, and the Prophet was not to oblige him.

"But it's foolhardy to continue our advance," Kane growled.

"Why not?" Orted demanded. "We're winning every battle. Keep after them until the last city has fallen."

"Yes, and we take casualties with every victory, too. I need more men, more horses, more…"

"I've sent you reinforcements by the thousands."

"I need still more. The farther our front moves from Shapeli, the more men I have to detach to guard our rear and to keep supply lines open. Damn it, I've cut a near thousand-mile swath through the southern kingdoms as things now stand."

"And you can go a thousand miles farther," Orted cut him off.

"Do you have any conception what that kind of distance means in terms of an army on horseback? This isn't a jog across the parade ground. It means long weeks, months in the saddle — foraging for food and water as supply lines grow uncertain, cutting across mile after mile of hostile country."

"This is the Dark Crusade, Kane — not a raiding party. If you can't solve simple military problems, I'll find someone who can."

"The solution is evident," Kane snarled. "I need more cavalry, and I need time to consolidate the territories we've won."

"I'll see that you get what you need," Orted promise curtly.

Kane swore and looked to his flagon. He had intended to talk this out in private, but the Prophet had avoided him during these few days.

"Certain of your strategy is incomprehensible," Kane pressed him. "Already Ingoldi is crowded beyond all reasoning. And yet you insist that I send ever more new converts from the fallen kingdoms. As it is, you've more people here than can live within the walls."

"Then I'll raise new walls," Orted said.

"So you'll have the largest city ever built," Kane said. "For what purpose? These people have to eat, they have to have places to live, they…"

"They are the Children of Sataki. It is enough that they dwell before the temple of their god."

Kane studied the Prophet carefully. There had to be some insidious logic underlying the man's fanaticism — some motivation for self-gain behind his rhetoric and platitudes.

"It would be better — after these neophytes have been thoroughly indoctrinated, of course — to send them back to their cities. Granted that it is impossible to hold vast expanses of conquered territory, it would be wise to have loyal Satakis occupying the cities at my army's back. I've conquered kingdom after kingdom, one after another — but if the unconquered kingdoms to the west ever unite their armies, cut between us and our line of supply…"

"Then you'll just have to see that that never happens," Orted warned him. "My commands are unchanged. I can't expect you to understand them; I insist that you obey them. Otherwise…"

And neither did he find it necessary to complete his sentence.

The pageant thundered to a close amidst loud ovation. The performers took their bows, then broke to partake of the leavings of the banquet, while a new troupe of musicians and dancing girls took over the entertainment. Kane and Orted Ak-Ceddi maintained a sullen truce while silks and bare limbs whirled frenziedly, and servants dashed from wine cup to empty wine cup.

Eventually the dancers had to rest. In the lull, Orted stood up to deliver an impassioned and interminable oration — expressing Sataki's gratitude for the brilliant leadership of Kane, the unyielding courage of the Sword of Sataki, the wholehearted loyalty of the Children of Sataki, the ceaseless devotion of the priests of Sataki — and that he, the Prophet of Sataki, was also grateful and proud of the common effort — and that while great things had been accomplished, further effort and further sacrifice were yet called for to push the Dark Crusade to final victory. Cheers and applause and a few impromptu demonstrations frequently interrupted his address. Afterward, Kane rose to offer similar comments — expressing his own humble pride and sense of personal fulfillment in being able to serve Sataki in his own small way, as well as the feeling of purpose and glory each soldier shared as they fought courageously to advance the Dark Crusade in the face of the forces of oppression and tyranny who would crush the one true faith and its freedom-loving faithful — if they but could. More applause. Kane at length sat down, very thirsty.

Musicians and dancers returned. The revellers settled down to earnest drinking and merriment.

Through it all, Jarvo watched impatiently from the shadow. The thought galled him that a suicidal attack might even now slay Kane and the Prophet. It would save countless innocent lives — if he succeeded. It would not win him Esketra.

Let it be Esketra.

The white-and-black-speckle feathers of the kite's mask covered her face like ermine — the sharp, hooked bill curving down over her patrician nose. Behind the tufts of feathers, her grey eyes stirred listlessly about the hall — drifting everywhere, seeing nothing. Her black hair was an ebon vignette about her pale perfect features. Cold, aloof, desirable as the kiss of a final dawn. She toyed with a platter of sweetmeats and small birds, cracking their bones in her sharp tiny teeth.

Minutes dragged by. Realizing he must not draw attention to himself, Jarvo drank sparingly and exchange pleasantries with others of the revellers. The banquet began to assume that frantic state of drunkenness that presages a long night of debauchery. Guests were leaving their places at the tables, wandering over to converse with friends. Small knots of men and women gathered in cliques, moved about the great hall. Servants hustled to clear away empty tables to make room.

Another chamber off from the great hall was opened as a ballroom, and the boisterous crowd quickly overflowed into the new space. Musicians plied stringed instruments, tambourines and flutes, and a number of couples began to form a dance. As guests streamed into the ballroom, others remained in the great hall to pick over the remnants of the feast and stay closer to the wine. A group of cavalry officers commandeered several of the musicians, began to sing loudly "Joyously They March to Their Deaths," beating time with their cups.

Kane remained in the great hall, drinking and singing with his officers. Orted vanished in the general confusion — Jarvo thought he was led away by a laughing blonde who wore a woodsprite's mask. Esketra let herself be taken into the ballroom on the arm of an officer in a devil's mask, and Jarvo followed as close as he dared.

Esketra and her escort joined the dancers, and Jarvo was forced to wait along the fringes of the ballroom, to maintain a guise of drunken conviviality with other garishly masked guests. It was sheer torture to be this close to

Esketra, stand helplessly while she was whirled about the floor on the arms of her captors. He wondered how many of the other women in the room were prisoners from the Prophet's seraglio, how many the willing consorts of this gang of cold-blooded plunderers and murderers.

She was wearing a long, full skirt of gauzy grey and silver stuff, her midriff bare, with a tight fitting jacket of similar material cut just below her breasts. Her bare limbs flashed as the dance swirled her skirts, and Jarvo's skull pounded with rage each time a new partner embraced her. After tonight — fortune willing — Esketra would be free. Later he, Jarvo, would have an accounting with her captors.

It seemed possible that he might join in the dance, work his way to her. Jarvo was reluctant to try it. Her astonishment on recognition might betray them. Best to approach her alone.

He waited, and his patience at length was rewarded.

The night had grown late. More and more of the guests were departing with the approach of dawn. In the great hall, the singers were hoarse and exhausted. Not a few revellers snored in corners or half across tables. In the ballroom the dancers grew weary, slipped away couple by couple for more private pursuits. The servants left their masters to their drunken stupor, and most of the performers had long since dispersed.

Esketra, declining the arm of her last partner, turned her scowling kite's mask about the ballroom. She seemed vexed over some matter, from the brusqueness with which she rebuffed the remaining revellers. On none too steady legs, she strolled from the dance floor and made her way through the dwindling crowd of merrymakers. As she passed from the ballroom into the hallway beyond, Jarvo started after her.

He followed her past the scattered couples and comatose drunks who spilled out into the adjacent hallways of the fortress. Esketra seemed to have a definite destination in mind, as her steps took her farther into the recesses of Ceddi.

Jarvo waited until there were no other guests in view, then called softly: "Esketra!"

She was starting for a stairway that led to the upper levels. At his call, she turned sharply. Her lips were deep red, her skin pale, but her expression was hidden behind the kite's mask. Her voice was cold with suppressed anger.

"What is it?"

"Esketra!" he repeated stupidly, rushing to her side.

Her eyes were cold behind the mask. "What do you wish with me?"

"Esketra! Don't you know me!"

"You are masked, my drunken buffoon. And may I add that I consider your mask in disgustingly poor taste."

"Masked?"

"Yes, fool. Remove it if you wish to speak to me — or else hurry back to your wine barrel."

Jarvo hesitated, wondering what words to speak.

With impatient fingers, Esketra yanked away the waxen mask that mimicked Jarvo's own face.

"Esketra!" he breathed, stepping toward her.

She recoiled. "Drunken swine! Do you wear two such fool's masks!"

"I wear no mask for you, Esketra."

"Oh." She pressed a trembling hand to her lips. "Oh, *no!*"

"I've come to take you away, Esketra."

"You're dead, Jarvo."

He laughed, understanding her shocked revulsion. "Kane made his worst error there, beloved. I survived the battle, hid myself in the fens. Two friends found me, nursed me to strength, brought me with them to Ingoldi. I've been living with them in the Theatre Guild for many weeks, laying plans to get you away from here."

She stared at him fixedly. Her flesh did not respond when he held her close. Jarvo felt a shudder pass through her, understood what a shock it was for her to see him here in the heart of her captors' stronghold.

"To get me away from here?" she said in a hushed voice.

"Yes!" Jarvo looked around, mastering his own rush of emotion. No one was yet in sight. "And tonight is perfect. With half the fortress dead drunk and the rest asleep, we can bundle you in a cloak, slip past whatever guard remains. Hundreds of guests have been staggering home all night. A quick change of garments and mask, and we'll look like all the others."

She stared for a moment more, then slowly nodded. "Yes, of course. You're here to rescue me."

"In another hour you'll be free again!" Jarvo exulted. Let the problems of getting out of Shapeli await, another day. He knew in a rush of confidence that his ploy would get them safely out of Ceddi.

"Of course," Esketra murmured, suddenly throwing off her frozen state. "I'll need other garments, as you say, and a different mask. Wait here, my chambers are close by. I'll get what I need."

"I'm coming with you."

She pushed him back. "Too dangerous! They'd suspect if they saw you with me. Stay here. I'll just get what I need and hurry back to you."

"But if…"

"Do as I say! Wait here for me! Do you want to throw away this one chance?"

"No. I'll wait, of course. But hurry!"

"I won't be but a moment," she promised, blowing him a kiss as she fled up the stairway. "Just wait here for me."

Jarvo waited until her footsteps receded — then the agony of suspense destroyed his momentary bliss, dragging each second into an hour. He paced the hall, alert for guards or other guests. They were far within Ceddi, presumably near the Prophet's living quarters. No one else would dare come this far — but that made his own presence here suspect. He cursed silently, looked about for concealment.

What can be keeping her? Impossible to know how long since she left. How long had it been? How long would it take?

A thought shook him — a vision of Esketra darting into her chambers, and finding the drunken Orted Ak-Ceddi. Jarvo envisioned the leering Prophet crushing the struggling girl to his sweaty chest, forcing his will upon her — while he paced about here like a fool!

The thought was beyond enduring. Stealthily Jarvo climbed the stairway up which Esketra had gone. He would follow her — be ready to rush in, if any man sought to hold her back.

The stairway opened onto a level above, and hallways stretched darkly in all directions. Doorways led off from the hallways at random intervals — evidently the living quarters for Ceddi's masters were in this area, as Jarvo suspected.

He paused uncertainly, cursed himself. He had no way of knowing which way Esketra had gone. If he sought to follow blindly, he might get lost, miss her as she returned for him. He started back. No, he had come this far for good reason; he would risk following along the hallway for a distance. He would not go farther from the stairway than he could retrace his steps.

He had gone only a short distance, when his straining ears caught the familiar clink of weapons and mail. Guardsmen were coming down the hallway.

Jarvo glared wildly. No time to run, and his presence here would not bear interrogation. A doorway close at hand. Unlocked. Jarvo pushed it open, stepped into the darkness within — just as a party of guardsmen, rounded a bend in the hall.

Leaving the doorway cracked, he waited to see if they would pass without alarm. Voices drifted through to him.

"Keep silent. We'll take him before he can run."

That was Orted Ak-Ceddi. But how...

"Oh, the poor fool won't go anywhere. I made him promise not to follow."

"It seems impossible that Jarvo could have been lurking here all this time!" Orted muttered.

"He said he had help from the Theatre Guild," Esketra said, laughing softly. "What's impossible is that the scar-face lout believes he's rescuing me. The mistress of the wealthiest and most powerful ruler in the world — and the silly fool thought he'd save me from my fate!"

"If we take him alive, you can explain to him the jest," Orted chuckled. "Softly now!"

XXI
...It Looks Like She's Been Fed

A dozen guardsmen crept past him — hastily summoned after Esketra burst in upon Orted and his blonde companion from the banquet. The Prophet, who was expecting a jealous outburst from his leman, did not let surprise slow his reactions to her breathless revelation.

The world crashed into fragments over Jarvo, pinning him in its ruins. For a timeless interval he stood paralyzed, heart silent, breath stilled, mind stunned. Had any man found him thus, they might have carved him like a roasted goose, and evoked no more response. As it was, his frozen shock saved his life — had his paralysis been less, Jarvo would have flung himself from concealment and lunged for Esketra's pale throat, though a dozen blades hacked him down.

They passed him without suspecting his presence. A soul cannot scream its agony, so that there was only a soft rustle as Jarvo slumped down against the wall, buried his face in his hands, the pain too intense to endure.

All his hopes and ambitions, all the fool's illusions that had lifted him from the ashes of his blasted existence, all were dead mockeries. The knowledge whose awareness he had so long ignored and rationalized to suit his idiot gropings could no longer be denied — ripped through his shattered defenses. For a black moment his mind reeled on the brink of catatonic madness.

Then came rage.

Let die the heart.

Let die the soul; let die the brain.

No life. No love. Hate is all.

Jarvo never remembered in what manner he fled Ceddi.

A blind man wanders unscathed through a burning city.

A drunken fool laughs in a ditch while thousands battle to the death.

Guards pay no heed to a ghost.

Jarvo wandered away from Ceddi, unheeding as the hue and cry echoed behind him.

He stumbled past drunken guards, besotted revellers, too sunken in debauchery to grasp the significance of the strident tocsin of alarm. A germ of animal cunning guided his reeling course away from those who might halt his flight.

A tragic buffoon. His face a mask too grotesque to be real. Too mindlessly drunk to evoke more than a sneer.

Grovel, little clown. Life spits in your tears.

He lurched through empty hallways, past the snoring revellers and the groping dancers, past the fumbling guards and the blindly rushing priests. The alarm was shouted throughout the spidery corridors, but in the milling chaos no one paid note to the pallid-fleshed dead man who staggered through their midst — glaring with an unseeing eye through his grotesque demon's mask.

There was a gate before him, open into the night. Jarvo blundered through, and into the cool darkness — never wondering that the guards who should have barred his way lay in puddles of scarlet, and stared back through glazed eyes. The dead do not challenge the dead.

Jarvo wandered through the darkness, paying no heed and paid no heed. About him in the night, the gods of war danced and howled. Horsemen tore past him. Armed men fled through the streets. Houses hid behind barred doors and shuttered windows. The cries and shouts that usurped the stillness before dawn did not reach his throbbing brain. He neither knew nor cared that death held its crimson revels in Ingoldi this night.

His soul was dead, but rage stirred from the ashes. No instinct of self-preservation guided his blind steps, for the will to live was dead. Rage animated his fever-seared flesh, and the flame of vengeance rose from the cinders of his soul.

He reeled through the fear-drenched streets of Ingoldi, unseen and unseeing in the bleak hour before dawn. Fever clawed at him, lost before the agony of his spirit. Slowly the dullness of his shock left him. The pain grew worse, but his fury left him oblivious to all other sensations. He was like a man who has received his death-wound, feels nothing in his berserk lust to slay his slayer, though his hands are slippery with his own lifeblood and his feet trip upon his dangling entrails.

He was walking along the shadow of the walls of Ceddi, and before him loomed a deeper mass of shadow. It was the Tower of Yslsl.

The door was ajar. He went inside. Within was darkness and silence.

Stairs spiralled upward into the night. Without volition, he climbed into the night. He came to the top of the stairs.

Fever and madness stabbed through his faltering consciousness. Jarvo stood upon the ledge at the tower's summit, staring blindly at the crawling sunburst of jet that glowered from the blank wall.

He had a fleeting instant of coherent thought. *What had drawn him here?* This was no place of refuge.

The writhing sunburst held his chaotic consciousness. In a flash of madness Jarvo saw that it was a doorway, that beyond it something waited, something called to him to open the doorway. Something beyond sensed the intolerable agony of his soul. Something hungered for that agony…

Jarvo stumbled away from the chill stone. The brink was at his heels. He flung himself forward, as his feet shot out from under him, his legs skidded on the edge of the stone.

For an instant his hands clawed at the smooth stone of the ledge, his legs kicked over emptiness. Then his outflung arms threw his balance forward. Clawing and kicking, he scrambled onto the ledge.

For a long while he lay there, too numb from fever and shock to crawl to his feet. His narrow brush with falling to his death cut through the trance that shackled his brain. Fear of falling — the instinctive fear that an infant knows before it draws its first wailing breath — jarred him back to awareness, hauled him forth from the abyss of madness.

The light of dawn was greying the circle above him, when Jarvo finally roused himself from his stupor. He came to his feet as one who awakes from an opium dream — thinking back over the scenes he has witnessed, wondering at the blank intervals in his memory, uncertain where dream and reality impinged. He rubbed his face wearily, tried to take stock.

He was in the Tower of Yslsl. Small wonder no one had come upon him while he lay here. He remembered briefly the strange illusion he had had of the black sunburst of stone. Nightmare born of fever and pain.

The rest of the evening was not nightmare. Grimly, as a man palpates a broken limb to assess whether he can force it to bear weight, Jarvo recalled the events of the night. The memory of Esketra's betrayal was like the pain of a bone as it is set. The pain was unavoidable. Once confronted, his thoughts could move on.

Jarvo swore. They would be combing the city for him now. His disastrous blunder had made Ingoldi a death-trap for him. Escape was imperative — or else certain capture and death.

With the realization of his danger, a new rush of dread made him cry out. He had told Esketra where he was hiding, who had helped him. Orted's vengeance would not be limited to one fool with a scarred face…

Recklessly Jarvo clambered down the spiral stairway. His life was worthless — but he must not allow Erill to share his doom.

Was there time? How long had he lain here? The Prophet would strike swiftly.

He flung back the heavy door and burst into the dawn-lit streets. He had run only a short distance before he encountered the first sprawled corpse.

Dumbly Jarvo gaped at the dead — recognizing guardsmen of the Prophet's army, Defenders of Sataki, and now and again a fallen cavalryman. Parts of the city were aflame, and the trail of death led toward the main gates.

Jarvo was in no state to fathom such mysteries — but it was evident after a glance that the tension between Kane and Orted Ak-Ceddi had passed the breaking point.

Jarvo paused only long enough to strip a dead Defender of his crimson surcoat and hauberk, wind a strip of bloody cloth about the scarred-half of his face, clap on steel helmet, and buckle on sword. Only a few cautious citizens were stirring from behind bolted doors, and no one challenged the red-bandaged Defender who ran through the corpse-strewn streets.

The Theatre Guild was not distant, and it was obvious to him that smoke was drifting from that quarter. He could see the overturned wagons and ruined stalls as he skidded around the last corner. A milling crowd of townsfolk was gathered about the smoking carnage. Jarvo felt his belly tense with chill.

A pack of children were scrambling about the wreckage. They paid him no attention, as the adults sidled quickly away.

"What happened here!" he demanded.

"Don't you know?" a small girl wondered. "They raided a noochee hideout here during the night. Then General Kane rode out of the city, and nobody could stop him. But you know that."

"Did any noochees escape?" Jarvo blurted — then stared at the girl. "Of course not," she said, trying to adjust the fillet of jade beads.

XXII
Let It Bleed

While it was days before Kane fitted all the pieces together of that night, it was Jarvo's unforeseen presence in Ceddi that threw all his plans into chaos.

The uneasy alliance between Kane and Orted Ak-Ceddi could end only in the death of one or the other. Both understood the situation; each had his own view as to whose death it must be.

The potentially explosive balance had existed this long for only two reasons.

Orted was loath to eliminate Kane so long as he depended on the continued victories of the Sword of Sataki. Kane's officers and the majority of his professional cavalry were loyal to Kane. Until the Prophet could supplant Kane's mercenaries with enough of the faithful followers of Sataki, to move against Kane was to risk disastrous mutiny.

Kane, on the other hand, was reluctant to move against Orted openly until he understood the nature of the Prophet's demonstrated sorcerous powers. Initially Kane had misjudged the former bandit, had assumed the man was either a greedy opportunist or a rash zealot. Either way, Kane's design had been to dupe the Prophet into financing an army under Kane's command, and, at the first convenient moment, to send the Prophet to the professed rewards of his afterworld. But there appeared an unknown factor. Orted Ak-Ceddi was not, entirely, a fraud. Kane needed to know more — but the Prophet's growing interference was forcing his hand.

Kane struck first to break the deadlock.

He had conquered half the southern kingdoms with the Sword of Sataki. Already an empire beyond the dreams of the most avaricious conqueror lay under Kane's heel. Eventually, Kane knew, the whole of the southern kingdoms would fall to him. Coupled with Shapeli, more than a third of the gigantic Great Northern Continent would be under Kane's rule. From there, in time, the old provinces and kingdoms of the Serranthonian Empire. Then the remainder of the supercontinent.

But for the present, Kane's army was overextended. Kane required more men and weapons, and he needed time enough to consolidate his victories. Instead, Orted demanded that he press on against the southern kingdoms, insisted that the conquered populaces be transferred to Shapeli. The latter was incomprehensible madness; the former was to invite military disaster.

Kane struck.

It was to be a straightforward *coup d'etat*. During the night of the great banquet, an artful courtesan in Kane's employ would entice Orted to leave at the height of the revels. Then, when the night was far gone and the fortress deep in debauchery, Kane's assassins would burst in upon the Prophet as he lay besotted with drink and drugs.

Orted's flesh might be proof against steel, but Kane's assassins were not so limited in imagination.

Esketra, stung with jealousy when Orted vanished from the festivities, was already on her way to his chambers when Jarvo accosted her. She burst in on the Prophet, even as Kane's assassins were dispatching the guards at a little-used entrance to the fortress. By the time they reached his chambers, Orted was stalking Jarvo with a party of his guardsmen.

Kane, waiting with a core of trusted followers in the great hall, misconstrued the sudden alarm and appearance of armed guards. Assuming that his plot had miscarried, and that the Prophet was moving to bottle him up within Ceddi, Kane and his men bolted. Blades were drawn, challenges and accusations shouted, and in an instant the uneasy balance erupted into open battle.

In a wild melee, Kane cut his way through the bewildered guards, out of Ceddi and through the city. Fierce fighting ensued, as Orted quickly reacted to the long expected crisis, sought to trap Kane within Ingoldi, away from the main force of his army. Kane was not to be entrapped that night. By dawn a wake of Sataki dead marked his passage through Ingoldi, and his camp beyond the city wall was deserted.

Kane examined the limp body that lay on the cot. He looked over at Dolnes and grunted. "She's alive, I'll grant you. What happened?"

His henchman picked at a fresh scab on his dirty forearm. Outside Kane's tent, the sounds of men and horses echoed across the bivouac. Ingoldi lay a hard day's ride behind them, and he had been pressed to catch up with Kane's retreat.

"I'm not at all sure. When we came for her, the mob was tearing the quarter apart. Evidently the Defenders had arrived before us — someone had denounced them as a nest of noochees. There wasn't a lot left."

"So I gather," Kane commented sourly.

"It wasn't anything we could have planned for," Dolnes protested. "We were lucky enough to find her still alive. They'd left her nailed to the side of a wagon when they finished with her. The mob didn't like us pulling her down, and we had to bust a few heads riding clear. By then, all hell was busting loose at the main gate. We came after you, and it was a close thing. I don't guess the ride trying to keep up with you did her much good either."

Kane looked closely at the bruised face. "I'll be damned," he muttered. "Girl, you should have jumped one of those nights."

"What is it?"

"Never mind. See Colonel Alain about your pay. But first call my surgeons to my tent. It may be that you'll earn your gold after all."

XXIII
Doorways

If being alive were a good thing, Erill decided she was lucky to be alive.

As from a nightmare, she recalled the assault on the guild by the Defenders of Sataki, remembered shouts and screams in the night, the rending and crashing of broken doors and overturned wagons, the helpless terror as brutal hands caught at her, the unending waves of pain...

Between black intervals of pain and terror, certain indelible visions burst through. Boree, swinging a gory ax, beaten down under a rush of mailed bodies. Her friends struck down without knowing the reason for their murder. An endless succession of leering, grunting, snarling faces. Pain lancing her flesh. The dull wonder as she saw the nails pressed to her pinioned flesh, watched the dreamlike, inexorable swing of the wooden mallet.

Their angry, gloating voices gobbled in her ears. Dimly Erill understood. Jarvo had found Esketra. Esketra had betrayed him. Jarvo was trapped in Ceddi, and Erill was hanging from iron nails. If she was conscious when Kane's men pulled her down, dragged her away from howling mob, she had no memory of it.

The morning wind from across the sea was cool on her face, and the waves of the Southern Sound washed over her bare feet. Erill glanced down at the fading scars that marred the insteps of her feet. A month ago she could not have walked for the torn flesh and broken bones. She looked at the puckered scars across both her palms, remembering how she had been unable to so much as feed herself for many days. So pain and the memory of pain must fade; given time enough, Erill supposed she could endure any ordeal.

She looked wistfully across the sea. Beyond the waves lay the Great Southern Continent, an easy voyage across the Southern Sound. The ruins of fabled Carsultyal slumbered there — mankind's first great city. Kane spoke of it often. His broadsword was forged in Carsultyal, centuries ago. Such antique blades were worth more than their weight in gold, for never since Carsultyal's fall has such steel been forged. It might be pleasant to journey to Carsultyal, perhaps lose herself in the cold wastes of the Herratlonai, the desert Kane said lay southeast of there. Nothing lived there anymore, nothing at all. The wind-etched wasteland had never heard of the Dark Crusade.

Perhaps Kane would let her go there. Why not? Erill had given up trying to guess Kane's motives.

She had awakened to find herself in his tent, her wounds salved and bandaged at Kane's direction. She had been unconscious for several days — lost in a sort of dream state born of delirium and the laudanum Kane got her to swallow.

They had ridden miles beyond Shapeli, Erill lying comatose in the baggage train. There had been hard fighting along the way, but Erill knew of that only afterward. The Sword of Sataki was broken by rebellion, as Kane gathered such of his regiments to him as remained loyal to Kane and not to a madman in Ceddi. For now, Kane held a broken sword by the hilt — as his mercenaries overpowered the factions recruited from the Prophet's faithful. By the time Erill had recovered sufficiently to be aware of her surroundings, Kane was temporarily camped at Intantemri, one of the southern kingdoms strongholds he had taken before his break with the Satakis.

She awakened to the awareness of Kane's eyes. He was seated beside her cot, so that when she opened her eyes, the two fixed flames of blue ice were no longer part of the drugged darkness, but stared at her from his coarse-hewn face. It was not a pleasant awakening. Erill closed her eyes, waited for this nightmare to pass as well.

"You are awake now," Kane said.

She was awake. There was a compelling force to Kane's will that lifted her from oblivion, as a powerful hand hauls a drowning child from an ebon pool.

She opened her eyes, took in her surroundings without comprehension, without connecting this world to the world of pain and mob terror. That awareness would come later, as her wounds healed, as she was borne along in the wake of Kane's rebellion.

"I want you to answer my questions," Kane said.

If he asked, she must answer. Her own will was still lost in the ebon pool.

"Once you were in a city called Gillera," Kane murmured.

Erill winced. There was another pain, another scar.

"It was night," Kane persisted. "The Satakis had surrounded the city."

Erill whimpered, tried to pull her eyes away from Kane's baleful stare, found she could not.

"I want you to tell me everything that happened to you that night."

"No," she moaned.

"Tell me what happened that night."

"*No!*"

"Erill, you *will* tell me."

Kane's eyes held her will, and though she had not screamed when the wooden mallet drove the iron nails into her flesh, Erill cried out then. But Kane's eyes commanded, and eventually she told him all he desired of her.

Even now that night of horror chilled her more than the memory of her crucifixion. Erill looked again at the sea. Untying her skirt and bandeau, she carefully laid the garments on the dry sand, then plunged into the warm surf.

The sea was clean. Its waves carried her effortlessly, its salty breath stung her kisses, its pulse was her heartbeat. Erill loved the sea.

Kane warned of sharks, of deadly riptides.

Erill loved the sea, and didn't care.

He was a strange man. Erill knew little about him.

Even in Ingoldi, little was spoken of Kane's past — unusual for so prominent a figure. To while away the boredom of her recovery, Erill had asked others about Kane. Some said one thing, some another; no one had much to answer. Kane was a good general; they followed him. It was all a soldier need know.

Kane was a mystery. The mystery intrigued Erill during the long months of battle and intrigue, attack and retreat. She suspected he might answer her if she questioned him about his past. For that reason Erill never asked.

"Why do you keep me with you?" she once asked Kane.

"I don't. Go where you wish."

"There's no place to go."

"Then stay."

It was not inertia that kept her with Kane. Erill sensed that she rode within the eye of the storm, that all about her the wars of the Dark Crusade, the horrors of the shadow world, laid waste to everything that stood.

"Where is there refuge, Kane?" she one night asked, inspired with the fumes of hashish.

"In this world there is no refuge," Kane told her.

"And in another world?"

"I cannot say. I know only this world. Yet I think in any world it must be the same."

She blew a wreath of smoke. "Then I'll seek refuge in dream."

"Seek no refuge in dream. A dream is unattainable."

"I know that a nightmare is attainable," she said bitterly. "Is there refuge in nightmare?"

"A nightmare can be conquered."

"If it doesn't conquer you."

Erill swam back to the beach, let the wind and the sun dry her thin body. The sea, she noted, left a taint of salt on her skin. She drew on her clothes, and went back to where Kane dug in the sand.

"Why did you seek me out, Kane?" she later had asked him.

"You are a fragment of the puzzle I sought to unravel."

"A fragment?"

"You had knowledge of the Satakis' shadow-spell."

"I know nothing of their magic."

"But you told me much."

"Are there other such fragments?"

"There were. It is a difficult puzzle. My first conception was wrong. That error was costly. I had to obtain full understanding in order to regain control."

"Then have you now solved your puzzle?"

"I have."

"And have you regained control?"

"I will."

"Can you explain it?" Erill asked on another night, as the dry wind moaned across the savannah, and shook the tent.

"Perhaps," Kane considered. "You remember when you asked me about the Lair of Yslsl?"

"I thought you jested with me."

Kane laughed mordantly.

"You said that the world was a room in a huge castle, and that Yslsl waited beyond a doorway that we could enter although Yslsl could not pass through."

"Well enough," Kane nodded. "The allegory is over simple, but it serves."

"But what has Yslsl to do with Orted Ak-Ceddi?"

"Remember that the castle is huge, limitless perhaps. There are many other rooms. Certain beings — call them demons or gods, for convenience — live in some of these other chambers. One such being is Yslsl. Another is Sataki."

Kane frowned, as if not wholly satisfied with his metaphor. He muttered something in a language Erill had never heard spoken — not surprisingly — then continued.

"There are many doorways such as the one in the Tower of Yslsl. The laws that govern the doorways vary, just as the beings who wait beyond differ in many ways. One of the keys to sorcery is the knowledge to open certain of these doorways, and to control and command the beings on the other side. That knowledge, carefully applied, can lead to great power; a false step means annihilation."

"Like demons and magic circles," Erill followed.

"Good," Kane approved. "Your concept of the wizard and his pentacle is valid here — although generally the wizard is evoking a being who has little interest in what takes place in this chamber we call the universe. Remember the castle is vast. Many of the dwellers beyond have no awareness of or interest in our small chamber. Others watch our universe hungrily, making the doorways to their realms as accessible as the laws of the cosmos make possible. The places of the earth where their doorways impinge soon become ill-omened and shunned by the wise."

"Like the Tower of Yslsl."

"And the Altar of Sataki beneath Ceddi — *Ceddi* is 'altar' in Old Tongue." Kane paused, shrugged. "In the cellars beneath Ceddi lies the Altar of Sataki. The Sigil of Sataki is a simulacrum of it. It's a doorway similar to the black sunburst atop the Tower of Yslsl. The priests of Sataki learned its secret many centuries ago, unearthed it, founded a degenerate cult about it."

"But who built the doorways?"

"The *ch'eyl'ryh* — the beings did themselves," Kane explained. "At least that's my belief. They're structures like a spider's web, or an ant lion's burrow — only of a more complex order. Elaborately constructed snares for predators whose existence is to lure and entrap unwary prey.

"Not much knowledge of them survived. I think Yslsl and Sataki are similar entities — and that conditions in that region of Shapeli were suited for their doorways to open close together, just as certain regions are prone to volcanic eruptions while others are not. The chief distinction is that Yslsl attracted no cult of worshippers to keep his rituals alive. Sataki did, although his cult was never of any importance."

"Until Orted espoused it," Erill murmured.

"Until Orted," Kane nodded. "And there the puzzle begins."

He was silent for a moment, listening to the voice of the wind.

"That was where I miscalculated. I knew Orted's reputation, saw that the Dark Crusade was a powerful force for conquest — and assumed Orted was using the facade of a religious war to build for himself an empire.

"I was wrong. Orted Ak-Ceddi is exactly what his priests proclaim him to be. He is a man into whose flesh their god has entered — or if you prefer, he is a man possessed by a devil."

Erill remembered her shudder at Kane's words. She shivered now at the thought, although the wind was warm, and the sea was dry on her flesh. She climbed the dune and gazed down to where Kane and his men dug about the ruins of what had once been Ashertiri, destroyed in the ancient wars with the sorcerers of Carsultyal.

"The fragments of the puzzle are scattered, hard to find," Kane had told her that night. "Much of it I can only reconstruct through conjecture, but I think I have it all now.

"The cult of Sataki was dying out. It had never been powerful, but now only a handful of fanatics kept its rituals. The priests made sacrifice to Sataki — luring victims into Ceddi, stealing children, waylaying drunks and beggars — offering them on the Altar of Sataki, intoning the spells that opened the doorway for the doomed sacrifice.

"Somehow they captured Orted. He was wounded in a raid on the Guild Fair, or they couldn't have taken him. They placed him on their altar, chanted the ritual of sacrifice. The doorway opened. Only this time, Sataki came through.

"I don't know how it happened. Under certain conditions such reversals can occur. A rare juxtaposition of the stars, perhaps; a transient flaw in the fabric of the cosmos. My guess would be that Sataki was near extinction from lack of worshippers, lack of sacrifices — ravenous, a starving lion. Orted was no ordinary man; he was physically powerful, a dynamic personality, intelligent, a leader, with enormous strength of will. Either Sataki took advantage of some freak of chance to reach through the doorway — or else Orted's soul was so powerful he drew the weakened god into himself.

"The reversal lasted only a short space in time. Then the doorway closed. Only a portion of Sataki's life-force was trapped on our side of the doorway — incarnated in Orted Ak-Ceddi."

Kane smiled at a bitter jest. "Sataki stole Orted's shadow, but he cloaked him with unearthly flesh no iron can penetrate. I wondered at the absence of the Prophet's shadow, but this is not an uncommon phenomenon of the supernatural. Vampires cast neither shadow nor reflection, a trait other super-natural creatures share — nor is the trick to eliminate a shadow any difficult spell. A tawdry trick to awe the masses, I dismissed it. Nor did the Prophet's heralded invulnerability impress me. If Orted could not be harmed by any weapons, why then did he not place his invulnerable body in the fore of his battles? Another shabby artifice, so I thought — an illusion he dared not test in battle."

"But can he be wounded, then?" Erill wondered.

"Not by iron or steel," Kane said. "But he feels the impact of a blow — I've seen that. I sent assassins to his chambers, and they were armed with silver blades, lances of fire-hardened wood, stone hammers. For Orted fears some manner of weapon, or he would surely now lead his army against me."

"He will send his army of slaying shadows instead," Erill warned him.

"Not unless I let him ensnare me," Kane said. "That was the whip he used to hold me in obedience — the threat of his shadow horde. And that was the essential fragment of the puzzle that you furnished me."

"Certain laws and procedures must be obeyed before any act of sorcery can have power. A wizard cannot conjure forth a demon with a simple wave of his hand — no more than a warrior can slay his enemy by asking him to die. You were a pawn at Gillera, but your experience that night revealed a portion of the spell. Other pawns, other witnesses furnished more information. I knew the Satakis' shadow magic had to have restrictive limitations — else the Prophet would have needed no army to carry out his conquests."

Kane toyed with his swordhilt. "It is a variation on the rites of sacrifice, evoking minions that dwell on the threshold of Sataki's realm. It requires darkness, it requires a simulacrum of the Altar of Sataki, and it requires the evocative power of the ritual chants. At first the Satakis used it only on individuals marked for death. They hunted down a man in my employ who once had betrayed Orted; a priest followed him to Sandotneri and struck when the poor fool let darkness catch him.

"Later the cult drew power from new worshippers; they could invoke the spell upon a limited area, even smother torchlight with their power — but they sometimes had to use a pawn to place the simulacrum. and to utter the final chant, when no priest or shadow-sending could get close enough to perform the task.

"Their power increased as their numbers increased. The culmination was when the Prophet himself led a horde of worshippers to destroy Sandotneri — as vengeance and as a warning. For all the horror of the unleashed shadow-army, the action was only a mass scale extension of the sacrificial rites that are chanted by a circle of priests about the Altar of Sataki."

Kane's voice was edged with triumph. "A deadly spell, but only if I were careless enough to allow the Satakis to invoke it. And I've taken careful measures to guard against that. Neither mundane assassin nor shadowy priest can approach me at night — and Orted knows my calvary would butcher any chanting horde he tried to send against me. Jarvo taught him that lesson in a manner the Satakis won't forget."

Erill's eyes clouded at Jarvo's name.

Kane marked this, but made no comment. He knew now that Erill had sheltered Jarvo in Ingoldi. Now rumors flew that Kane's old enemy had escaped during the chaos of revolt, had reached the as yet unconquered realms of the southern kingdoms, was seeking to raise a new army to lead against Kane and Orted Ak-Ceddi.

Kane bore Erill no animosity for her part in prolonging Jarvo's annoying existence. He felt that Erill had had opportunity to reflect upon her interference, as she hung from the nails before the mob.

"What will you do now?" she had asked.

"Wait for the revolt to spread throughout Shapeli," Kane replied. "Orted can't face my army on the savannah. I've destroyed whatever elements of the former Sword of Sataki remained loyal to Sataki. I control the conquered provinces of the southern kingdoms. I can't allow Orted to live — he's too dangerous an enemy. If the people of Shapeli won't rebel and do it for me, I'll have to fight my way into his stronghold and pull it down on his head."

Kane added thoughtfully, "And that won't be easy."

"And what will Orted do?"

"Have his hands full controlling a populace whose religious zeal will cool without the threat of the Sword of Sataki. Orted took a big chance insisting that all those conquered peoples be brought into Shapeli."

"If it was a risk, why did he take it? He could have delegated their rule to territorial governors, as in any empire."

Kane laughed. "That was the final error I made in judging Orted. I'd always assumed that — fraud or fanatic — Orted's goal was an empire. It wasn't. That's why I couldn't predict his actions."

"What is his goal, then?"

"Orted's methods to power were used to attain the goal, but it was Sataki's goal all along. He needs millions of faithful souls for a final evocation. I wonder just how many more worshippers the Prophet will require to furnish enough power to open the gateway one final time — to let Sataki come all the way through."

XXIV
Beneath the Sea of Sand

Kane clambered over the edge of the excavation, into the sandy pit below. "That's it!" he shouted. "Hold your shovels! Break that seal, and we're all dead men."

His men stood back sharply, as Kane knelt at the bottom of the excavation, began to paw through the damp sand with his fingers. They had been digging through the ruins of Ashertiri for a good week now, uncovering buried wall after sunken edifice, as Kane directed. Precisely what Kane sought here, no one was certain.

Yesterday they had unearthed what appeared to be a jumble of fused green stone. Kane exulted, directed them to dig farther down. Hours of labor revealed what evidently had been a tower of some emerald-hued ceramic substance, of which all but the very foundations had been blasted into slag by some inconceivable energy. After levering away slabs of rubble, they at length uncovered what appeared to be the buried floor of its lowest level.

Kane's excitement rose as their shovels laid bare a hexagonal slab of metal set in what had been the center of the cellar floor. Under Kane's clawing fingers was revealed a hexagon of silver metal, some eight feet across. Barely perceptible cracks divided the hexagon into six triangular segments, and at the center, where the apices converged, was an intricate seal stamped in what might have been crimson glass.

"'Leave me now," Kane told them, studying the crimson seal. His order was obeyed most willingly.

Erill gained the edge of the pit as they scrambled away. Her curiosity drove her past the retreating soldiers, and she peered into the excavation in time to see the triangular sections of the silver hexagon slide smoothly back into the stone of the floor.

Steps led downward into cold darkness. An invisible exhalation from far below swirled upward, like shimmering heat waves about glowing steel. Kane completed a complex gesture above the gaping pit — then stepped down into darkness where no living thing had entered in millennia.

Erill sensed rather than heard a menacing hiss from deep within the earth. Even Erill had a limit, and she scuttled back to where Kane's men awaited his return.

The minutes dragged past. The sun touched its zenith, began to curve downward. No one ventured closer to the excavation.

Kane returned rather suddenly, bearing with him a small casket of silver-grey metal, its hasp secured with a seal not unlike that of the door disclosed beneath the sand. Kane appeared as exhausted as any of them had ever seen the man.

"Bury it," Kane ordered. "Bury it completely."

Their shovels flung sand back into the excavation in a steady avalanche. Erill got a quick glimpse of the bottom of the pit. The silver hexagon was closed, its crimson seal unbroken. Then the sand of the dead city once more buried its secrets.

"What is it, Kane?" she asked, studying the silver-grey casket.

"Something that doesn't like shadows," Kane said.

XXV
Nemesis

They left the haunted ruins of Ashertiri the next dawn. During the night, exhausted messengers rode into camp carrying grim news to Kane. The rumors, for a change, were true.

Jarvo had gathered a new army.

A season had passed since Kane's abortive *coup d'etat* in Ceddi. While Kane and Orted maneuvered for command of the Dark Crusade, Jarvo had been at work amidst the unconquered states of the southern kingdoms. His efforts had been most effective.

Kane had conquered half the region because the separate kingdoms could not oppose him as a united force. Centuries of internecine wars, smouldering jealousies and hatreds had kept them apart. Certain of the kingdoms had thought to ally themselves with Kane in order to destroy traditional enemies; others had found resistance to the Sword of Sataki impossible, had capitulated without battle. One by one the Dark Crusade had engulfed them.

The disruption caused by Kane's rebellion afforded the remaining kingdoms pause to consider their plight.

The excesses of the Satakis were by now too well known to allow for any consideration of peaceful alliance with the Dark Crusade. Moreover, the relentless conquests of the Sword of Sataki made it obvious even to the most thick-witted ruler that the Prophet would not halt his advance until every city had fallen to him.

Into this atmosphere of growing panic, Jarvo had forced his presence. As the general who had dealt the Satakis their only defeat — and compared to subsequent Sataki victories, the disaster at Meritavano appeared a close battle — Jarvo suddenly enjoyed immense prestige. He was a compelling figure — his features scarred, his spirit one of implacable vengeance. He had penetrated into the Prophet's very citadel, and escaped to proclaim to the world the atrocities of the Dark Crusade.

Scarred emotionally now as well as physically, Jarvo seemed a destroying angel. Crowds and councils listened to him with rapt attention. The populace saw in him a savior, the army considered him an invincible leader, rulers sought his favor and counsel.

It was the power Jarvo had always dreamed of gaining. Now that he attained it, he no longer cared.

The solution he offered was straightforward: Counter Kane's cavalry with an even greater army.

Breaking all precedent, the free states of the southern kingdoms formed a temporary alliance, the Grand Combine. Individual kingdoms massed their armies under Jarvo's command.

When word of his coming reached Kane at Ashertiri, Jarvo was advancing with an army of 200,000 men, including almost fifty regiments of heavy cavalry. It was the largest professional army ever to take to the field on this continent.

Kane could not hope to face it. The army of the Grand Combine was almost twice the strength of the Sword of Sataki at its peak. There had been constant attrition with each new conquest; now revolt had cut its strength yet further. Kane's entire army barely numbered 25,000.

Kane had no course but to run.

And because Kane needed a place to run to, he sent emissaries to Orted Ak-Ceddi.

It was a desperate move, but then it was a desperate situation. Kane knew the Combine's army would annihilate his own force if it ever came to open battle. While he could avoid battle so long as he retreated across the broad savannah, Jarvo would pursue to the end. The conquered provinces had been laid waste, stripped by the Satakis; no new provisions and supplies were forthcoming from Shapeli. Kane could only flee across a barren land, pursued by a vastly greater, better supplied army. Kane's strength would dwindle with each league, and it would only be a matter of time before he was overtaken, crushed by a superior force.

If that much was evident, so was the subsequent fate of Shapeli. Jarvo was an implacable foe, and the Grand Combine was pledged to destroy the Dark Crusade, root and branch, and to liberate the conquered kingdoms of the eastern plains. This time the dense forests of Shapeli would be no protection — the Combine's army was too powerful to be halted, and Jarvo had sworn to reduce Ceddi to rubble. The Grand Combine would force its way into Shapeli, if they had to uproot every tree in the forest, and the Prophet's depleted army could not hope to throw them back.

Annihilation was inevitable — for Kane and for Orted Ak-Ceddi.

There was only one chance, and Kane proposed it: To make their truce and to fight the Grand Combine together.

To Kane the logic was beyond denial. If the present situation were maintained, it meant certain destruction for them both. If the warring factions of the Dark Crusade were reunited, there was a chance to wrest victory from an otherwise hopeless position.

Kane commanded 25,000 veteran troops — all that remained of the Sword of Sataki. Orted Ak-Ceddi, counting in the Defenders of Sataki, could prob-

ably muster three times that number of trained and fully equipped foot soldiers. Drawing upon the Sataki horde, the Prophet could raise a militia of
hundreds of thousands — the crucial point being one of supplying effective
arms to enough men who could be trusted not to turn against the Sataki
hierarchy.

In the open, such an unwieldy coalition would stand no chance against
the might of the Grand Combine. Within the forest, it was a different matter.
Jarvo could only advance as fast as the conditions would allow. Presumably
he would force a spearhead along the military road into Ingoldi, clearing trees
to expand his march, laying waste to towns and strongholds in his path.

The Sataki militia could not stand against the Combine's troops in battle —
poorly equipped rabble were sword-meat for trained soldiers. Kane's proposal was to use the militia as a constant harassing force to slow the Combine's
advance — driving them in suicidal waves against Jarvo's troops as they cut
through the forest. As such, they could do little damage, but men under attack cannot fell trees. While the slaughter would be appalling, Jarvo's advance would bog down, his troops would be exhausted by the time he finally
reached Ingoldi. There, from the protection of the city's fortifications, Kane
could coordinate an effective defense, using the Prophet's infantry to hold
the walls, counterattacking with his cavalry force.

If all went well, Kane knew he had a good chance of withstanding Jarvo's
siege, forcing the Combine's army to withdraw — and once in retreat, the
invading army could be decimated as it pulled back through the hostile forestland. If so, it would be more than simply staving off extinction — it would
be a matter of winner take all. For the kingdoms of the west had staked everything on the army of the Grand Combine; if Kane defeated Jarvo's invasion,
it would leave the whole of the southern kingdoms open to conquest by the
Dark Crusade.

Thus everything hung in balance for the Dark Crusade. The logic of war
was evident. Under these circumstances, Kane was certain Orted Ak-Ceddi
would agree to the proposed truce.

Orted agreed.

"Can we trust him, though?" Alain protested.

"We can trust Orted for the same reason that he must trust me," Kane
answered. "Because each of us depends on the other if he is to stay alive."

He paused, remembering. "There was a time that I went into a tavern to
kill a man. We were rivals, blood-enemies — sworn to kill the other on sight.
He was good; I couldn't take him at once. While we were fighting, the tavern
was surrounded, the city guard rushed in. They were sworn to kill us both on
sight.

"And so we fought back to back, he and I — while the guard tore at us
both. Neither of us feared a treacherous blow from the other, for the guard
would instantly cut down either of us alone. We killed maybe twenty of them,
before the handful that were left broke and fled."

"And after that?" Alain prompted.

"Afterward," said Kane, smiling at the memory, "I killed him."

XXVI
Desperado

A thunderhead of dust towered above the horizon, following Kane relentlessly as he retreated toward Shapeli as if he fled before a storm of inconceivable fury. Jarvo was pursuing hard on their trail, crushing all that did not flee. Kane managed to outdistance his nemesis, but only by holding to a pace that killed horses and left his men hanging to their saddles as drowning sailors cling to broken timbers. Kane wondered if the Combine's cavalry fared any better; probably they did — having set out with fresh mounts and full provisions.

The time lost in arranging the truce with Orted Ak-Ceddi was of itself almost Kane's undoing. The Combine advanced at a speed Kane had not imagined possible for so vast an army — even considering that Jarvo rode unchecked by the terrain and without fear of ambush. As for pursuing Kane, once the Combine's army converged on his trail, it was only a matter of following the swath of trampled earth and the litter of dead mounts and abandoned gear. A day's lead dwindled like wax in flame as the killing race stretched on. By the time they reached the forest, Kane doubted that Jarvo was more than a handful of hours behind.

No use now to think of tearing up the roadway, of throwing barricades and ambuscades in Jarvo's path. Too late to organize resistance — time only to ride headlong for Ingoldi. Sleep in your saddle, stuff handfuls of whatever is left to eat in your mouth as you ride. Horses have to stop for food and water and rest; men don't. No more fresh mounts, and every dead horse means a dead man when the Combine catches up. Ride on for Ingoldi, and pray its walls won't be your tomb.

After Sembrano, on the forest edge, Kane was able to stretch his lead over Jarvo. Ingoldi was a ride of several days from the border and through hostile territory for the army of the Grand Combine. Jarvo had to funnel his gigantic body of troops into the forest-spanning military roads, wary of ambushes and pockets of resistance that did not exist. His objective was secure and his enemy bottled up. Jarvo would slow his pace to save horses and men for the impending assault on Ingoldi.

Let the quarry run itself to exhaustion. Now that the end of the hunt was at hand, it made little difference to Jarvo whether he reached Ingoldi this day or the next. The battle could have but one outcome.

Kane grimly watched the gates of Ingoldi close behind the last of his haggard horsemen. It was afternoon, and his men had ridden through the night. With luck, Kane estimated they would have as long as the next day to prepare for the Combine's assault. Jarvo could not have carried siege engines with him at this pace. It would take days to construct such weapons, and if Orted's soldiers could hold the walls until then, Kane's men and horses should be rested enough to make a sortie.

Not that any sortie would break Jarvo's siege, Kane mused, but such tactics — lightning raids, then a dash back within the walls — could inflict costly casualties, destroy the Combine's new siege equipment. The best hope for them now would be to seek to hold out until the Prophet could summon his followers from the outlying cities of Shapeli. A peasant army could threaten Jarvo's rear, if their number were great enough. In time, the Combine's army might be crushed between two fronts.

Kane wondered whether the Prophet's followers would answer such a call — or whether those beyond Ingoldi would wish Jarvo luck in crushing a vicious tyrant.

An honor guard of Defenders of Sataki approached him. Their leader informed Kane that the Prophet awaited him in Ceddi.

"Don't go!" Erill whispered.

Kane grinned tiredly. "We have to coordinate our defensive strategy before Jarvo comes to add his voice. I'll get some rest afterward."

"Hell, you know what I mean. Don't trust him."

Kane looked at her, shrugged. "Orted knows we have to fight together if there's any chance at all. If he means treachery, he'll have to hurry before Jarvo puts an end to our quarrel.

"Alain, I'll need you with me. Dolnes, you know the city." He called off others of his staff, added: "And I'm sure Orted won't object if my personal guard rides in with me."

"Kane," Erill said. "Take me."

"Why?"

"Why not? I've ridden this far."

"As you wish." Kane had never asked the girl why she stayed with him during the gruelling race. She might have gone her own way, or remained in one of the towns along their retreat. He knew she felt neither love nor gratitude toward him, nor had she cause to. Erill was too hard to show any emotion, not even fear. She only wanted to be in at the kill.

Kane's officers led their exhausted men to their former barracks, to try to catch a few hours rest before the coming battle. Kane, accompanied by what remained of his personal regiment, followed Orted's honor guard into Ceddi.

The Prophet received him graciously. Their meeting was no more cordial than form required. They had discussed strategy and tactics on many a previous occasion — each knowing that their alliance must end in only one way. This occasion was no different.

It was growing dark by the time they ended their conference. Orted had agreed to all of Kane's proposals — evidently content to place the conduct of the defense in his hands, just as he had earlier entrusted the direction of the Sword of Sataki to Kane. That suited Kane, who had feared interference.

Food and drink had been served to the council, and to Kane's tired guard in the courtyard below. Sleep seemed most imperative now, and Kane decided it was time to find his quarters. He stood up to return to his men, wondering as he made his excuses what had become of Erill.

Esketra lay in her scented bath, watching the sheen of bubbles as they swirled and shattered. Her rich black hair was piled in thick coils, held in place with golden pins. She would wash it again in the morning, let her handmaidens brush the silken tresses, soothingly work in the perfumed oils. Now it was evening, and she did not wish to wait for it to dry before going to Orted.

The Prophet had been in a strange mood these last few days, she mused, trailing her fingers over her soft white skin. He was in a state of repressed excitement — more like a man who envisions the fulfillment of some long-cherished goal — rather than a ruler whose empire is teetering on the edge of utter ruin. Perhaps Kane's return to Ingoldi had rekindled Orted's confidence in his ultimate victory.

Victory. Against the invincible army that Jarvo was leading against them. Rumors said it was the greatest army ever amassed, that this newly formed Grand Combine would overwhelm Ingoldi's walls as a wave washes over a child's sandcastles, that their orders were to spare no living soul of the Prophet's Dark Crusade. Those noochees who repeated such lies in the hearing of the faithful were very shortly in better need of their breath. Still the atmosphere of impending doom did not clear.

Perhaps she had been wrong in joining her fortunes to those of Orted Ak-Ceddi. But who could ever have imagined that little toad Jarvo as a threat to the awesome power of the Prophet? What if Jarvo did destroy Ingoldi? What would he do to her?

Esketra smiled, remembering his stupid, fawning worship of her. She would cry, hint at horrid cruelties, and Scarface Jarvo would puff out his chest and play the savior. One tear from her eye, one glimpse of her beauty, one promise of a kiss from her red lips — and little Jarvo would kneel at her feet. Then let the gods guess who was conqueror and who the slave. The fortunes of war hung in balance, but for Esketra it would mean victory however the balance might swing.

It was time to dress. She rose from her golden tub, reaching for a towel. Her handmaidens should be here — where were the little bitches loitering? Angrily Esketra called for them, dabbing at her sleek skin with her towel.

Someone entered her bath. When she lowered the towel from her face, Esketra saw that it was not one of her servants.

It was a scrawny girl in dirty riding clothes, her face streaked with dust and sweat, lined with fatigue. Her eyes were green as a cat's.

"What are you doing in here!" Esketra demanded.

"I bring a message from Jarvo," the strange girl said, stepping forward cat-quick.

"Jarvo!" By the gods, had he already entered the city!

"Jarvo sends you his love," the girl said, extending her hand.

Esketra glanced to see what the girl had to give her.

It was a poniard.

As he left the council chambers, Kane wearily paused at a tower window. It was dark now, he noted. Tomorrow would probably bring the army of the Grand Combine to Ingoldi's walls. Before then, some rest. He would need all his strength if he were yet to stave off defeat. The chances were bleak, but he had survived far worse.

Absently Kane gazed out across the city. His eyes narrowed. Smoke and flame already flared into the night.

A quarter near the wall was ablaze. Surely not Jarvo already...

Kane cursed. Those were his barracks that were afire. His men... In the distance he could hear the dull animal roar of the attacking mob.

"Alain!" Kane shouted. "Get the others! We're riding out! Now!"

A sweep of Kane's arm, and his sword flamed in his left fist. Already they were alone in the hallway — the Prophet's counselors had discreetly withdrawn as they left the upper chambers. Kane had been in this situation too often not to realize what portended.

A rush carried them into the great hall — ominously deserted. The main door stood invitingly open — leading into the courtyard, where Kane's personal guard should await his return. Not daring to hope that Orted had been an instant too slow in closing his trap, Kane plunged into the darkened courtyard.

His men were lounging about the enclosure. They gave a startled greeting as Kane and his officers burst out of the great hall with drawn blades.

"Mount up!" Kane shouted. "We're getting out of here fast!"

As if to mock his command, the massive iron portcullis of the main gate crashed down with a thunderous knell. Behind Kane, the iron-bound doors of the great hall slammed shut with a clash of bolts.

Kane spun a glance about the courtyard. The few small doors that led back into the towering citadel were closed as well. Short of forcing the gate or scaling the fifty foot walls, they were trapped within the courtyard.

Laughter tumbled down from a tower window. Orted's laughter. Kane saw the Prophet silhouetted high above, gloating from his tower window.

"Are you in such a hurry to leave, Kane?" the Prophet jeered. "You must not miss the evening's crowning spectacle!"

"Orted, you bloody fool!" Kane yelled up at him. "Have you gone completely mad!"

"No, Kane!" the Prophet roared. "You're the fool this night! Have you forgotten the warning I gave you at Sandotneri?"

"You're insane, Orted! You need me to defend your city from Jarvo!"

"Jarvo will die on another night, Kane — when he tries his steel on my shadow horde! He rides to his doom, even as you have already ridden to yours! Fools, did you think you could intrude upon the Altar of Sataki with impunity! Were you mad to think I could ever forgive your treachery to Sataki, Kane? You and your traitor band are all inuchiri — and you know the penalty you must pay for that sin!"

"Orted, you're mad! You'll destroy us both!"

"Wrong, Kane! I'll feed the shadow horde instead — on your souls tonight, and on the souls of Jarvo's proud army on another night! Then let the world shudder before the might of Sataki!"

Kane's men milled desperately, about the enclosure, as the Prophet's taunts and laughter echoed across the court. The trap was a solid one. Given time, Kane knew they could batter down one of the interior doors, storm the barbican and raise the portcullis. They would not be given time.

Already the dread chanting of the priests reached the ears of the doomed soldiers. Orted had only held them here to await the fall of night, so that his priests could invoke the spell that summoned the slaying shadows. The evocation would not take long.

Kane ignored the Prophet's triumphant laughter. Kane had made a final error. He had assumed he was dealing with a rational mind, with Orted the bandit chieftain, who would have to agree to the logic of Kane's proposed alliance. Instead he dealt with a vengeful god.

Kane lunged for Angel, dug into the saddlebags, as the black stallion pranced nervously. The tension in the night was like the aura before a lightning storm.

His fingers touched a carefully wrapped packet. Moving with reckless haste, Kane tore away the rolls of padding — revealed the silver-grey casket he had taken such pains to obtain from the buried ruins of Ashertiri, knowing he must someday destroy Orted Ak-Ceddi, or be himself destroyed. He had hoped for other circumstances than these in which he was now ensnared, but there would be no other chance.

Chanting an invocation as he worked, Kane snapped the crimson seal that locked the casket's hasp. He felt power stir within the metal box. Deadly power, but Kane would take Orted with him.

Tendrils of blue light were already seeping through the airtight cover of the silvery casket. Kane had no need to warn his men to stand clear. Shouting out a spell in a tongue far older than lost Ashertiri, Kane stalked across the *enceinte* toward the citadel's central tower. He seemed to hold a blue-white star in his outstretched hands. Even though he cast the spell, Kane felt the skin of his hands sear from the power that stirred within the casket.

Averting his face, Kane shouted a final phrase, flung the metal casket away from him. Already a square of glowing silver, the ancient box exploded in an incandescent ball as it fell through the air. Kane leapt backward, praying that his spell would control the awesome force he had set free.

The courtyard crackled with a stark, searing light — brighter than the sun. A star seemed to explode against the base of the citadel wall. Horses reared in unmanageable fright. Men flung arms across singed faces.

Bathed in an aura of elemental flame, the salamander stretched its swelling limbs and stared lazily about.

Kane shouted a command in the tongue of the wizards who millennia ago had imprisoned the fire elemental. Slowly the salamander turned about, heeding the potent phrases. Its grotesque head swiveled toward the stone wall, and it waddled forward in obedience to Kane's command.

Elemental flame touched stone, and the wall erupted in a spraying fountain of lava. The salamander stalked forward into the gap. Molten globs of stone tumbled upon its obscenely bloated form — dissolved into incandescent fragments from the unearthly heat of its elemental substance. Dragging its tail like a loathsome comet, the fire elemental burrowed its way into the heart of the fortress, digging a molten path toward Ceddi's hidden cellars.

The chanting of the priests, Orted's gloating laughter — all ceased. Half-blinded by the incandescent flame, Kane's men now listened to the terror-stricken shrieks of those within Ceddi. The salamander had disappeared into the lower depths of the colossal fortress. From its glowing burrow, blue-white flame stabbed into the night.

"Keep close to the outer wall!" Kane warned. "I'm not sure what will happen when it..."

And in the hidden fane of the Satakis, the salamander crawled forth to find the Altar of Sataki — as Kane had commanded. And Kane commanded the salamander to destroy...

Elemental flame lashed out at the alien stone. For an instant the black mirror, reflected a white-hot circle of energy — behind which *something* seemed to stir, to reel back in agony...

The stones of the courtyard seemed to leap upward beneath their feet. The fury of an exploding star seemed to burst from deep within the earth. Men and horses tumbled head over heels, flung to the ground in a terrified mass of stunned and bleeding flesh. Behind them, a section of the courtyard wall buckled outward into the moat.

Like a child's castle of blocks, Ceddi's central tower crumpled inward upon the seething mass of flame and molten, rock that was until seconds ago the eons-old temple of a god who dwelt there no more.

For an eternity, stones seemed to crash down and down and down. Explosive echoes tore apart the night. Then a moment of utter stillness — before ears deafened by the holocaust began to hear the anguished shrieks and crackle of flames from within the sundered fortress. In the distance, frightened shouts called from streets where darkness now returned.

A third of Ceddi was rubble. Kane noted with chagrin that the Prophet's tower yet stood, tilted from the blast. But Orted would laugh no more. His god had forsaken him.

There was no hope now except in headlong flight. Kane pulled himself to his feet, relieved to see that Angel had escaped injury as well. Not all of his guard had been so lucky.

Kane swung astride the black stallion, unsheathed his blade from the scabbard at his shoulder. "All right, you bloody bastards!" he growled. "Off your butts, and let's ride! We're not wanted here any longer, and you won't want to wait around to complain to Jarvo for your back pay!"

When the explosion flung her off her feet, Erill had been calculating her chances in slipping past the guards at a rear gate of the fortress. She had decided her chances were about zero — but that it would not be much longer before someone looked to see what lay beneath the scarlet waters of the golden bath. While Erill was not worried about the consequences of her action, now that she had carried out her little vengeance, she had no particular desire to make atonement.

The blast flung her about as an angry child throws her doll. Luck and her training as an acrobat saved her a broken neck. The guards at the gate had neither advantage.

Not bothering to speculate, Erill was dashing through the wreckage even before the earth ceased its heaving. She kept running through the frightened confusion in the streets beyond the citadel. By the time her legs were aching from the strain, she had reached the city wall.

The ramparts were manned by the dead. Orted had ordered the bulk of his troops to attack Kane's cavalry regiments as they slept in their barracks. Only a skeleton force had been left to man the city walls. Jarvo had been closer on Kane's heels than Orted had gambled.

Erill clung to the shadows, studying the battle with an experienced eye. The dead men on the wall were struck down by arrows — probably in the first moments of the assault. Coming upon a city torn apart by treachery and unleashed sorceries, Jarvo had attacked instantly with only the vanguard of his troops. Now the battle appeared to be centered at the main gates further. From the signs, it appeared that the Combine's army had already forced entry. In that case, Ingoldi, Ceddi, the Satakis, and the Dark Crusade were doomed.

It amused Erill. The world was crashing into final and utter chaos. It seemed she had survived.

An abandoned watchtower was not likely to be disturbed again this night. Erill slipped within, opened the cannister of powdered coca leaves she had plundered from Esketra's chambers. It was the final act of the game, and she had a splendid view.

Kane had ridden only a short way, when the full realization of the disaster struck him.

The city was in arms against the noochee traitors of Kane's cavalry. Bloodied bands of his men met him as he rode — telling gruesome tales of massacre. Not suspecting suicidal treachery from the Satakis, Kane's exhausted men had flung themselves down and slept soundly. Orted's soldiers had set fire to the barracks, slaughtered the cavalrymen as they stumbled forth from the smoke and turmoil.

For all that, Kane's men were hardened fighters, and quick to grasp their danger. Frantic knots of men had broken through the trap, enough to swing certain massacre into a pitched battle. With the city raised against them, the desperate mercenaries had rushed the main gate, thinking to escape into the forest. In the darkness and chaos of battle, they had not realized they were only opening the city gate to Jarvo's army.

Reeling back from this new attack, Kane's once invincible army was cut apart and ground under. The Combine's troops were slaying all within the city — while the fanatical Satakis were determined to slay the noochee traitors to the last man.

Kane was trapped in a vice, and the jaws were closing too rapidly for escape. There was a shaky chance to survive if they could retreat across Ingoldi, force the rear gate, and reach the forest. The Combine's troops could never hunt down all the scattered fugitives. Some might escape, eventually flee to less hostile lands.

Then new word from the other bands of stragglers, Orted Ak-Ceddi, injured by falling stone but still deadly, had ordered the fanatical Satakis to destroy Kane and all that remained of his army — to sell their lives that not a single inuchiri traitor should escape the dying city.

Ahead of them, Jarvo and the army of the Grand Combine. Behind, the Sataki fanatics who had escaped the holocaust.

Death glowed in Kane's eyes as he turned to what remained of his command. The men knew their doom was upon them, but waited to learn if Kane could pull off one last miracle.

"Let's see if there's any wine left for us in Ceddi," Kane growled. "Then I'll see you all in hell — and let's make certain the place is crowded."

They wheeled their mounts about, and rode back through the death-laden streets of Ingoldi, toward the smouldering wreckage of Ceddi. A last few hundred soldiers — all that remained of the powerful Sword of Sataki. Exhausted, wounded, armed with whatever weapons they'd had time to seize, wearing mail and odd pieces of plate armor — riding horses equally battle-weary. They were professionals who had lived their lives by the sword.

And this was the last battle.

They drove off the milling townspeople as they rode — frightened fools who had been caught up in a nightmare beyond their understanding and beyond their control. They fled, and found death elsewhere.

Kane's men did not have to ride far to come upon the mass of Sataki fanatics who trailed them. No time for thought, no time for fine points. Kane spurred Angel, and they hit the Satakis at a gallop.

The night became a nightmare of smoke and stench, of flashing steel and snarling faces, of blood and sweat, of tiny wounds you barely felt over the ache of fatigued muscles. The wound that counted was the one you never felt at all.

Kane drove through them like a vengeful juggernaut, until Angel's frothy flanks were as drenched in blood as his crushing hooves. Men rushed at Kane, and Kane struck at them, smashing them to the earth with as little thought as a harvester wields his scythe. Their blades and bare fists tore at him, gouged flesh, chewed apart his mail hauberk. A flung stone carried off Kane's helmet, and a suicidal assailant tore away his buckler by dragging it down as his fellows chopped at Kane's arm. Carsultyal broadsword in his left hand, Kane caught up a cavalry sabre in his right. it was no longer a matter of slash, thrust, and parry; it was kill and kill and kill until death put an end to even berserker rage.

One by one, Kane's men went down. He no longer saw their faces either. Kane was beyond grief or anger. Emotion required energy, and Kane's entire being was concentrated on destruction.

They had reached the leaning walls of Ceddi now — Kane and the last of his personal guard. The Satakis would not fall back before them; they had to cut a path through them each step of the way. They were but a handful now, but the Sataki dead were like drift in the wash of a flood. Red-coated Defenders, black-robed priests, peasants and city dwellers — one united by fanaticism, united now by death.

Kane had but one great wish — to reach Orted and tear his black heart out with his bare hands. But Orted was not with the last of his faithful. Nor was he in Ceddi, when Kane forced his way into the ruined fortress. Kane knew where Orted would be. The Prophet had ordered his fanatics to throw away their lives in holding the battle away from Ceddi — while with characteristic cunning, Orted Ak-Ceddi had fled with whatever he might carry off.

That knowledge drove Kane to new fury. It was one thing to die in a hopeless battle; it was another to know that the enemy whose mad treachery had brought this doom upon him was making good his escape.

Kane reeled in his saddle, fatigue and a score of wounds leeching his strength. He was a lion, being pulled down by a horde of rats. He slew all in his reach, but there was a limit even to Kane's endurance, and his enemies were beyond numbering.

An instant's lull in the battle gave Kane pause to see that there were new foemen in Ceddi. The first wave of the Combine's army had swept through the city, the invaders were now streaming into the ruined citadel. Kane slew them with the same impartial efficiency he slaughtered the Satakis.

Spurring Angel out of the overrun courtyard, Kane saw that Ceddi was encircled. Jarvo's army, little concerned as to what awesome force had shattered the Prophet's fortress, was pouring over the last of the Sataki fanatics. And as Kane looked about, he saw the last of his personal guard had fallen.

No time to draw breath, let alone for contemplation. Kane charged into the Satakis who mindlessly clawed at him. A child rolled under Angel's hooves, thrusting with a spear. Angel screamed and crumpled — throwing Kane over his neck. Kane landed on his feet, cut the boy in half with a backward slash.

For an instant the mob closed over him. Kane's two blades flickered like crimson flame. They fell back from him, torn and reeling. Kane staggered away, bleeding from yet more wounds. He fought his way along the fortress wall, using it to guard his back. On foot the end was imminent.

There was a note of savage hatred in the shout — enough to draw Kane's attention to its source. Jarvo.

Kane snarled defiance. His enemy had recognized him from the light of the burning fortress.

In a frenzy, Jarvo was trying to cut through the melee that separated them. On horseback, armored, with his men about him, Jarvo would ride him down like a dog.

Kane lurched backward, wondering if he might seize a riderless horse. He was a dead man trapped here in the open.

Then darker shadow touched him like a chill breath as he turned. He had fought his way to the Tower of Yslsl.

Even in the rush of battle, the tower stood empty, its door standing open — a few bodies close by. Why venture within? There was no place to hide, not even a way to defend it.

Jarvo's shout, and the clash of hooves. In another instant it would all be over. Kane wondered if he could take Jarvo with him. No chance. Jarvo was too good a warrior, and Kane was too cut up even to get out of the way.

The doorway beckoned. There was a second, stranger doorway within, at the head of the stairs...

Kane had often wondered. How true were the legends? Could he remember how the doorway was to be opened?

It was hard to think any longer. Hard even to stand up.

Another second, and he could rest.

Kane stumbled through the doorway, heaved the ironbound door shut, worked the stiff bolts even as the ancient door shook to an impact.

Kane steadied himself against the cool darkness. Were there stars far overhead? If so, they were spinning.

The door thudded under new impacts. Dimly he could hear Jarvo's angry voice, shouting for a ram.

Kane began to climb the stairs.

XXVII
In the Lair of Yslsl

One instant the stench of the burning city, the cool fusty smell of the ancient tower... One instant the chaotic roar of the battle below, the inexorable smash of the ram against the splintering tower door... One instant the hard pressure of Kane's gore-streaked flesh against the cold black sunburst of stone...

Then the cold was all around him, and he was engulfed in infinite darkness. Kane was falling... Blind mote of consciousness falling timelessly...

And something thrust a thousand ice-tendrils into his soul...

Never... From nothingness the ice-whisper crawled through his consciousness... *Never shall I have feasted as now...*

HUNGER

And substance emerged from nihility...

Kane was in a passageway — greylit, its edges cobwebby vague, reminding him unpleasantly of a spider's tunnel-web. His steps drifted dreamily forward, silently, without volition. Ahead of him the corridor stretched grey and endless. Behind him — he slowly forced his head around...

Behind him the corridor dissolved into emptiness — a precipice upon infinity that followed upon each step. Unbidden his feet groped forward, and the precipice slid a step closer. There seemed to be stars glowing far below in that abyss...

Kane fought vertigo and shuffled forward...

The polar bear reared in the ice-cavern. Its angry cough rumbled into a challenging roar as its wrathful eyes recognized the intruder. With deceptive clumsiness the bear rolled toward him on its hind legs. Its taloned paws reached out to crush him to its furry chest.

Reacting automatically, Kane ducked the lethal swing of its forepaws. He darted back from the bear's rush, and his boots skidded into emptiness. With catlike agility he flung himself clawing forward onto the ice-ledge. For an instant he skidded toward the edge — then his desperate fingers clutched cracks in the glacier. He struggled back onto the ledge, and his thrashing boots, sheared away clods of rotted ice that fell silently into the abyss, into the mists that shrouded the glacier's base a thousand feet below.

The polar bear shuffled forth from its lair even as Kane scrambled to his feet on the narrow ledge. Kane felt for swordhilt, but the scabbard hung empty. His knife remained at his belt — but against half a ton of feral strength...

The ledge snaked along the misty palisades — too narrow, too slippery for escape.

The bear towered above him. Kane snarled, and the blade was a blue flicker as he lunged.

Almost three hundred pounds of human muscle and bone slammed into a thousand pounds of white-furred beast, and the impact staggered the bear's killing rush. Kane's dirk, a foot of honed steel, sliced hilt-deep into the beast's massive chest. Kane twisted the blade free — a rib had turned it from the heart. A gout of blood washed over blade and hilt, made it slippery as he stabbed again against the crimson-blotched chest.

Then tearing claws, finger-length, spike-tipped, made tatters of his thick fur cloak and leather vest, gored through the flesh of his shoulders and back. Kane hissed in agony, stabbed yet again with his blade. Breath shuddered from his lungs as the awesome forepaws began to enclose him in an irresistible death-hug. Teeth champed into his shoulder, numbing one arm.

Howling against the pain, Kane hacked his blade yet again, deeper still into the gore-matted shaggy chest. Blood shimmered mistily on the ice about them; mist pulsed a roaring throb in his skull.

Something else was in his skull... Something that fed...

The polar bear coughed and relaxed its fangs, spraying blood from its black-tongued muzzle — blood that was not Kane's. It sagged against him suddenly, dragging the man down beneath its gigantic bulk. The blood-slick daggerhilt tore away from Kane's grasp. Ripping forepaws still hugged him in a lethal embrace, but now their strength seemed less irresistible.

Kane desperately writhed from under the toppling bear, sliding toward its haunches as it sprawled forward against him. The mortally wounded polar bear pitched slackly toward the edge, hung for a long moment struggling feebly against overbalance, then slid like an avalanche over the ice-ledge and into the silent mists that waited far below.

Kane stumbled forward.

He was in a cavern, damp and smelling of carrion. Gelatinous fungi leaked wan, phosphorescent light onto the dripping stalactites. The floor was treacherous with slime and foetid pools of uncertain depth. Cold water drenched his bare flesh, as he sloshed along the passage. The broken chains on his bloody wrists clanked dismally.

He barely remembered that crimson instant of intolerable rage when the hopeless note of her disappearing screams had driven him mad, and the rusted chains that shackled him to the stone had snapped like rotted cord.

For worm-twisted miles he had followed the mocking echoes of her cries, bleak despair smothering the fires of his wrath. Those who had left him here — had they purposefully let her come to him to attempt hopeless rescue?

A pale figure sprawled in the pool just ahead. Kane plunged toward it recklessly, knowing at once the familiar lithe figure and ash-blonde hair. He called her name.

Vacant eyes stared up at him from a slime-crushed face. But the consummate horror was that she still lived...

Recognition seemed to light in her stark eyes as he knelt beside her mutilated form. His fingers pressed her lacerated neck, and there was only horror on her slack features.

Its attack was silent — dropping from the gloom above where it had climbed on its suckered limbs. Feral instinct cut through Kane's grief, and he sprang away at the last instant. The great hump of rubbery flesh grazed his naked skin as he twisted, but its murderous leap had missed him.

Stagnant water sprayed, and the devil-leech recoiled from its leap — its springy form unshaken by the drop. It reared upright like a man — like a child's mud statue of a man. Stubby legs and arms ended in sucker-tipped knots of appendages like outsize maggots, and its underbelly was slimily undulant as a slug's underside. Above its thick shoulders its neckless head hunched forward like a cobra's hood. Malevolent intelligence gleamed in its squid eyes, set far back of its outthrust suckered maw.

The devil-leech sprang for him, its ungainly bulk uncoiling suddenly from its fall as if driven by steel springs. Kane's footing failed on the fungus-smeared stone, as he tried to fend off its attack. In an overwhelming rush of cold, blubbery muscle, the devil-leech was upon him.

Kane grunted and struggled for a grip on the rubbery bulk. His fingers slithered uselessly on the slimy flesh, fighting the clutch of the demon's suckered paws. Its relentless mass squeezed against his squirming flesh, crushing him to a jelly-like carpet of fungi. Kane thrashed about with desperate strength, trying to tear away. He succeeded only in wriggling deeper into a stagnant pool; foul water sprayed over his gasping face, choking him.

Toothed and suckered like a giant lamprey's mouth, the devil-leech's maw sought his throat. Kane's fingers tore futilely as the cobra-hood head hunched downward. The foot-wide circular mouth with its rasp-toothed writhing tongues bore down, down...

His hands slipped, and the devil-leech's stubby arms suddenly pinned him down. The lamprey-maw darted for him. Kane writhed. The suctioning mouth fastened on his bare chest.

A thousand dull knives rasped into his flesh, as the circular mouth shredded the flesh of his chest. Scarlet welled for an instant, and then the hideous suction was tearing at his soul. Kane screamed.

Feeding feeding something else is feeding...

The mindless rage that had earlier snapped iron surged through him again.

Bellowing in fury, Kane recoiled with all his enormous strength. His arms tore free. His frantic fingers ripped the feeding mouth from his chest. Blood spread from the circle of macerated flesh. A circle like those that blotched her white, still flesh.

Kane flung up his knees and sent the devil-leech floundering back from him. He sprang to his feet — howling a one-noted roar of hate. Naked, bare-handed, he leapt upon the creature — this demon that had bloated on un-counted sacrifices in its foetid lair. His powerful hands gripped fast on either side of the devil's maw. The file-edged tongues gashed his fingers to the bone; the rubbery lips writhed to clamp shut. Kane set his grip and pulled, throwing his huge shoulders into the effort.

Boneless flesh stretched to the utmost. The devil-leech tried to wriggle away from the madman. Splits cracked into strained flesh, widened — then with a gathering wrench tore open. Black blood gushed forth as if from a putrid wound, covering his arms.

Kane laughed, somehow keeping his death-grip on the leathery rasp-toothed jaws. He pulled all the harder, tearing the boneless flesh apart as a man might part a coconut hull. He stood, in a pool of gore now, as the devil-leech's efforts to escape grew ever weaker. Arteries — if the demon had blood of its own — must have parted. An ocean of foulness welled up from its ruined throat as Kane's mad laughter echoed through the cavern…

But he was walking through the cavern again. No, it was a corridor — a dank passageway of coarse stone blocks. The passage was unlighted; the dark-ness close and foul with the stench of unwashed bodies. Kane's hands seemed dragged down; his gait was a clanking hobble. Massive chains shackled him.

Kane tried to halt, and the iron collar at his neck snapped his head for-ward. There were soldiers ahead of him, leading him by his chains. He had not seen them at once in the thick gloom. Trying to think. Kane let them jerk him forward along the passageway. Except for a scrap of rag, he was naked — his body scored with half-closed wounds. Pain and fatigue made his legs all but too weak to bear his weight.

Bolts clashed; hinges groaned. An iron-bound door was thrust open. Torch-light spilled into the passage. Kane blinked stupidly, blinded by the sudden light as his captors hauled him within.

The familiar, hated profile of Jarvo greeted him from within. The stocky general was seated in a low-backed chair beside a glowing brazier. A swordhilt protruded from the smouldering coals. His one good eye was alight with tri-umph, and his youthful face — the side not immobilized by scar — was twisted into a smile. Not wholly cloaked by shadow, the chamber's gleaming instru-ments of torture waited behind him.

Jarvo grunted in satisfaction. "So you're conscious again, Kane — or have you only feigned delirium these past hours?"

"Hours?" Kane heard his voice ask. His thoughts struggled for clarity. How was he here? Delirium…?

"So you'll pretend not to know?" Jarvo considered him thoughtfully. "Perhaps you don't. As a ploy, it's pointless. Yes, hours — more than a full day since the final battle. Since my men and I broke through into that old tower where you'd sought to hide. You were lying there senseless, half dead from your wounds. Had you thought to make a last stand there, Kane? Then you'll regret you didn't use your last strength to fall on your sword. My surgeons staunched your wounds, nursed life back into you with their elixirs."

Jarvo's scarred face sneered wrathfully. He clawed at his seared profile. "Have you forgotten so soon, Kane? Did you think to escape, with so easy a death? Orted Ak-Ceddi slipped from my grasp, but our people will at least see justice meted to you! You, Kane — you, his general who forged the sword by which the demon-cult of Sataki terrorized our lands!"

His voice, which had started to rise, now fell, its tone deceptively calm. "When I was chosen to lead the Combine's armies, I swore I'd pull the Prophet's fortress down on the bodies of his crazed priesthood, that I'd hang a follower of Sataki from every tree in Shapeli, and that Orted and his henchmen would die in agony before the eyes of my army. Well, Ceddi lies in ruin, the carrion crows are feasting the forest — and though Orted has eluded me, his general is my prisoner!"

Jarvo came to his feet, his good eye staring at Kane's face. "In a few hours it will be dawn. At dawn you will be dragged into the central square. There before my victorious army your limbs will be broken on the wheel, your skin will be flayed from your flesh, and, after a time, you will be burned at the stake. My torturers are artists; they assure me that with stimulant drugs and careful work you may live until nightfall."

Jarvo's hand blurred toward the smouldering brazier, came away with the sword — its blade white-hot from the coals. His voice cracked with hate. "And here's something to think on through the night!"

Kane tried to fling his head aside. Chains held him. Glowing steel slashed across Kane's face, cauterizing as it sheared through smoking flesh. Agony forced a hiss through his clenched teeth. The stench of his burning flesh choked him. Kane sagged backward, one half of his face a charred and bleeding horror.

"I return your favor," Jarvo growled, "and leave you one eye to see. Take him back to his cell."

Half-blinded, sick with pain, Kane scarcely was aware as his captors dragged him to his cell, flung him inside and locked the ponderous door. Weighed down with chains, he sprawled on the filthy stones of the pitch-dark cell. Agony lanced his skull. Jarvo's quick slash had torn away his ear, laid open his face to bare bone, split open one eye like a burst egg.

In a few hours they would come for him. He would die a hideous lingering death — humiliated before his enemies. They would gloat on his suffering, laugh at the screams of agony even Kane's iron will would not be able to lock in. And there was no hope of escape. Shackled, half-dead from his wounds, helpless in the grasp of his victorious enemies, not a man left alive who would lift a hand to help him.

This was the end. There would be no escape. A life that had outlasted centuries would end in agony and shame. Dismally. Hopelessly.

Feeding... something is feeding...

Kane clutched at his skull. Even through the pain of his mutilated face he could sense the icy tendrils pierce his brain, sucking energy from the agony of his tortured soul.

What was it... What had he done... He should not have fallen prisoner to Jarvo. There had been a hope of escape — desperate escape. It was so hard to think. Pain and despair dulled his mind. What had happened... A battle, Jarvo had said...

Kane remembered the battle. The chaos of blood, steel and flame as Jarvo's army stormed Ceddi and ended Orted's Dark Crusade in a wild night of violence and destruction. With fury Kane remembered the Prophet's treachery, his insane refusal to accept a truce after Kane's abortive *coup d'etat,* that had given the Combine its chance to rout the once invincible Sword of Sataki.

Kane remembered the last stand of his personal guard, trapped in the dying fortress between Orted's fanatical troops and Jarvo's advancing army. As the last of his men fell, Kane had hewn his way to a moment's respite. And then? Kane remembered the black despair of that moment, when, reeling from exhaustion and a dozen wounds, he had realized he was cut off. There had been the old tower... Even in the desperate melee of battle, men had been loath to approach the chill stones of this ancient redoubt; those who guarded it now fled their posts before Jarvo's advance. Kane had fought his way to the tower, bolted the ancient door in the face of his pursuers.

Why... He had done so knowing the door would hold them only short minutes — that he would be cornered. Why had he chosen the tower to make his final stand? Kane struggled to think, to remember. He had sought the ancient tower in some last desperate hope. *Why? Why... the tower...*

The Tower of Yslsl — No! The *Lair* of Yslsl!

Yslsl!

Wizard of a lost age — or demon? Only the vaguest of legends remained. His black stone tower had stood here even before the first priests of Sataki had crept into Shapeli, so it was said. Or was it true, as some held, that Sataki and Yslsl were both brother demons in the pantheon of some forgotten elder race? But the cult of Sataki still lived — although for centuries it had all but perished — and to Yslsl there remained only tenuous myths. And his tower. Or, as the legends said, his two towers...

When Ceddi had been built from this benighted forest-land, its first inhabitants had included the ancient tower within its log palisades. Though cold and menacing, its stones stood solid — and the city's founders had had more immediate dangers to face than foreboding legends. Generations later the tower yet stood — solid, cold and ill-famed as in the earliest days. Ceddi now had grander fortifications, and the old redoubt had been virtually abandoned.

There were *two* towers, so the legends held. One here, the other half a world away. And between the two towers dwelt Yslsl — the demon-wizard whose interdimensional web was linked to this world through these two foci of energy. Perhaps his web touched other worlds as well…

One might enter the Lair of Yslsl, enter and cross through to where another strand of the web was anchored. There was a ritual that would open the portal, a spell known to eons-dead priests and to students of such lore. One might journey through this interdimensional corridor if one knew the spell. But to do so one must confront Yslsl…

Kane, whose knowledge of the occult spanned centuries, knew the spell — and the danger. But with his enemies breaking through the tower door, there had been no other chance.

And Kane remembered. Remembered chanting out the spell with breath in frothing gasps. The smash of the battering ram splintering the iron-bound door. The chill of his slashed flesh pressed to the black sunburst of stone set into the wall at the head of the spiral steps. The falling into blackness…

What had happened…

Jarvo said they had found him stretched senseless on the stones. Had his last desperate hope been only a fool's gamble with an ancient legend? Or was he even now enmeshed in the Lair of Yslsl — tortured by the illusions plucked from his mind by the vampiric demon?

It was so hard to think… Concentrate through the burning agony of his mutilated face, the dull pain of his wounds, the sapping lethargy of despair…

Lie here, Kane. It is hopeless. Lie here and let them come for you…

Yslsl!

The pain — it was real, too real. How could one feel pain if this were only illusion? And the nightmarish sequences he had lived before awakening in chains — there had been pain. Dreams, too? Delirium? Jarvo had said he had lain delirious.

Illusion! It was illusion. It *is* illusion! The corridor…

"Yslsl!" Kane screamed. His voice echoed eerily. "Yslsl!" Outside the cell he heard his guards stirring anxiously.

No! There is no cell! There are no chains! Yslsl, I entered your lair!

Fool — you fell senseless on the tower floor. In a moment your captors will lead you to your death.

Then rage burned through the cobwebby fetters of despair. Kane reeled to his feet, forcing his mind to clarity.

"Yslsl! Where are you!"

He must will himself from this illusion — must *believe* this was illusion — or he would die within the illusion, and Yslsl would feed upon the shrieking disintegration of his soul.

"Yslsl!"

Kane lurched forward, headlong for the iron-bound door. *Now. Now he must break the illusion!* There was no cell, no chains, no door… He flung himself for the door — looming huge, substantial, immovable…

He was in a corridor, his footsteps carrying him onward as in a dream, and behind him the corridor vanished into an abyss. No chains, no wounds. Illusion. It had been illusion…

Kane sensed baffled rage — and for an instant, awe. Then gloating — and hunger. Ravenous, gluttonous hunger.

"Yslsl!"

Laughter, deep laughter.

A shape moved toward him. A girl. Dancing nakedly toward him, long hair like starlight swirling about her supple form. Her face — beautiful, cruel as a goddess.

"Poor Kane," she sang like a child. "Poor Kane, he's quite insane."

"Who are you!" Kane demanded.

"Who are you?" she mocked. "Don't you know? Don't you know?"

"Yslsl?"

"Poor Kane. Poor mad Kane. Yslsl? Do you want Yslsl?"

"Are you Yslsl!"

"Perhaps *I* am. Perhaps *you* are. Do you want Yslsl?"

"Yes, damn you! Where is Yslsl!'"

She laughed and pirouetted. Her starlight hair was a spinning nova. "Poor Kane, poor Kane. He's quite insane. Yslsl's in his brain. He feeds on your pain. And now you're insane. Poor Kane. *Why don't you die!'*

Kane grabbed for her. She darted away, but he caught her wrist. She spun against him, sinking her teeth into his hand.

Unendurable pain stabbed through him. Kane gasped and released her. The girl vanished in a snowfall of laughter-light.

Kane clutched his bitten hand, expecting to see blood. There was only a purple-green bruise, a swelling that grew as he watched. He shook with pain, as the swelling ballooned like an evil fungus — then burst.

And from the putrid abcess erupted not blood. Spiders. Tiny, black-green spiders crawled out of his flesh. Spiders bright and glittering as bits of glass. He felt their needle-point mandibles chewing free from his flesh. They crawled up his arm in a vein of bright-black chitin.

Kane screamed, tried to fling them off from his arm. The spiders hung on tenaciously, biting his clawing fingers. Lancinations of fire seethed through his envenomed flesh. The spiders were biting him as they crawled. Each bite burned into a purple-green swelling, a swelling that expanded and burst. And erupted with more spiders. To climb and bite... crawling for his face now...

Take a step back, Kane...

No! Behind him yawned the abyss. *This is illusion!*

The spiders were gone. His hand and arm were whole. Kane shuddered and plunged forward.

Laughter. Demonic laughter.

Goat-horned, toad-faced, the demon squatted in the mist ahead. A bloated dragon-toad, its scaled bulk utterly blocked the passageway. Its laughter roared deafeningly down the passage, and its mouth gaped ever wider — impossibly wider. An incredible length of sticky tongue snaked out toward Kane. In loathing Kane recoiled.

No! I can't step back!

Heels at the edge of the abyss, Kane forced, stand rigid, as the demon's tongue licked toward him. Now the creature's gaping toad-maw filled the entire passageway. Yellowed vomerine fangs stabbed from ceiling to floor like rotted stalactites and stalagmites. Foetid breath gushed forth from its gullet to sicken him. Kane swayed.

It wasn't a passageway at all. He was standing on the demon's foul tongue, gazing into its gigantic obscene maw. The passageway beyond was the creature's throat. He was walking into the leviathan's slobbering jaws... Horror and revulsion staggered him.

Run! Go back!

No! Yslsl, this is another illusion!

Go back! You'll be eaten!

Illusion!

Kane lurched forward from the advancing edge of the abyss. Down the slimy tongue, into the dripping jaws, into the yawning throat, where eyeless vermin crawled over his bare feet. The jaws began to close. Kane felt himself propelled downward into the demon's gullet.

Illusion!" Kane roared. He charged blindly ahead, past the filth that swarmed over him.

He was in a passageway, and at his heels the edge of nothingness remorselessly followed.

"Of course this is illusion, Kane. You're insane."

Orted Ak-Ceddi grinned at him. "You're insane, Kane — can't you understand? Completely mad mad mad. This is all illusion — and so are you."

Kane lunged for him. The Prophet waited with a supercilious smile. Kane's powerful hands locked about Orted's thick neck.

It wasn't Orted. It was a girl, face contorted in fear. He knew her — Lyuba, whom he had loved. Lyuba, dead and dust for centuries... by his hand...

"Kane! Stop it!" Lyuba gasped, writhing in his grip.

But his hands would not let go. They closed of their own will, relentlessly. Kane tried to tear his hands away, but still his strangling grip tightened. Lyuba's beautiful face purpled hideously. Her eyes burst from pressure. Her tongue protruded longer, longer...

It was a serpent's tongue. Kane held a serpent by its scaly throat. With a sudden twist, the scarlet serpent writhed free of his grasp, sank its fangs into his chest.

Kane yelled in pain, tore the fanged head from his chest. The serpent exploded into coruscant light, blinding him. Kane reeled backward...

No!

"Who is he?" The voices were suddenly all around. "What's the matter with him? Is he all right?"

The ballroom was filled with people, laughing and disporting themselves in swirls of jewels and costly robes over the obsidian floor. A number of faces were turned his way. Their expressions showed alarm.

"Are you all right?" asked a girl in a gown of strung pearls.

"Is something the matter?" her escort demanded. He wore an owl's mask.

"I... don't know," Kane heard himself say. Where was he? Did he know these people? What had he just done?

A pair of dancers blundered into him. "Watch it, old fellow," laughed one of them. "Had too much, have you?"

"What are you doing here, may I ask?" queried the consort of the pearl-dancer. "Are you one of the guests?"

Kane frowned. Was he? "I'm all right now."

"I think there's something wrong with him," someone suggested in a worried tone. "Who is he? Does anyone here know who he is?"

Who was he? Panic welled within him. Who was he? How had he gotten here? Kane couldn't remember anything beyond the last minute. He stared wildly about, seeking to escape. The dancers were calling for help.

Wait, some shred of memory. Yslsl…

"Stop it!" Kane screamed. The dancers halted and stared. "*Stop it!*" The ballroom shimmered.

It wasn't a ballroom. It was a dolmen. He lay on his back on a massive stone slab. Kane tried to move. He couldn't. His flesh was cold, rigid. His head was propped upon something; his eyes were open and he could see his recumbent body.

His flesh was shrivelled, gnawed with age. Rusted mail and rotted furs enswathed his mouldering body. He had no breath to scream.

Figures were filing into the dolmen, gazing down at him. Dead things, whose decayed features he could recognize enemies who had died at his hand in years past. Liches like himself. They filed around him, staring down, their rotted faces alight with secret mirth. They chanted a dirge.

"Poor Kane. He's quite insane."

"Poor Kane. He died in pain."

"Poor Kane. There's maggots in his brain."

Not maggots — something fouler… Yslsl.

Kane's frayed lips croaked a snarl: "Yslsl!"

Then there was nothingness. Kane, naked and alone, floated in the nothingness. Coldness, pain, nothingness.

His thoughts drifted, and his thoughts were pain. "Am I insane? Am I insane? Shouldn't I know something? Shouldn't I be somewhere? And where is here — and is it anywhere? And who am I — and am I anyone?"

And cosmic horror wrenched at his soul — horror surpassing all that had haunted him. He did not know.

He did not know. Where. How. Why. When. Who. If. Ever. Who.

"Insane insane (Yslsl's eaten his brain) insane insane"

And fury burned bright in his crumbling soul.

"I am Kane!" he roared at nothingness. "I am Kane!"

And he was walking down a passageway. And at every faltering step the passageway vanished behind him.

"No. *I* am Kane."

Before him crouched a hulking, red-bearded man. His brutal face was twisted in anger, and the flames of death danced in his cold blue eyes. Kane thought he saw his own reflection — then saw the other figure move of his own accord.

"*I* am Kane," said Kane to Kane.

Kane's lips drew back in a snarl. *"Yslsl!"* And it was almost a prayer.

Kane lunged for Kane's throat. Kane sidestepped his rush — but Kane's lunge was a feint. Twisting as he attacked, Kane slashed his open hand at Kane's neck. Kane partially evaded the killing blow, at the same instant knocking Kane from his feet with a sudden twist of his leg.

Kane fought for balance, grappling with Kane as each struggled for hold. An elbow caught Kane in the face, smashing his nose and blinding him with pain. He swung his hip at the last instant, as Kane sought to follow his advantage — making Kane miss a second blow with his open fist.

Breath gusted from their throats in jarring sobs. Skin ripped from their bodies as steel-strong fingers clawed for grip. Each sudden feint, each covert hold was known to them both. Strength, speed were identical — the same as was the killing rage that hurled Kane against Kane in desperate haired.

At the feet of the embattled twins awaited the abyss, inexorably following each struggling step of one combatant...

Slinging blood from his eyes, Kane broke Kane's strangling fingers from his throat with a crushing jab to the other's larynx. Coughing in agony, the other recoiled, his guard an instant too slow to deflect Kane's kick to his solar plexus. He slumped backward into the passage, scrambling to elude Kane's pressing attack. Kane bore into him, hammering a blow to his heart, to his face.

He staggered drunkenly on nerveless legs. Implacably Kane seized his throat, flung him around. The other butted his head into him with frantic strength, and Kane felt the edge of the abyss at his heels. Desperately Kane lunged sidewise and into the passage, suddenly flinging his opponent past him. Already plunging forward, the other could not check himself as the precipice glided closer. Arms flailing, he plummeted over the edge.

For an instant Kane saw something obscenely man-like, its face a mass of writhing translucent tendrils, clutching its taloned hands for the edge of the precipice. It clutched only nothingness, and into nothingness it fell — a spinning, slowly diminishing mote among other motes that Kane saw were not really stars...

The passageway screamed with soundless horror; its outlines wavered. Fighting to keep his feet, Kane saw just ahead — what seemed to be an opening in its infinite length. Not daring to imagine where it might lead, Kane plunged through...

And in battle-flamed Ceddi, an ancient tower door splintered under the last blow of the ram; and vengeful Jarvo leaped past its wreckage — to stare in uncomprehending fury at an empty chamber of dust and echoes...

And half a world away, a ragged girl suddenly gasped and clutched her father's arm. "Father! There! At the top of the stairs! There's a man lying there!"

"What!" Her father followed her pointing finger in alarm. When the storm had forced them to seek shelter for the night in this ancient pile of stone, he had looked around the tower uneasily — for there were legends — and seen nothing untoward. Still, the wavering light of their fire was uncertain, and that last burst of lightning had been near enough to seem to set the tower aflame.

He called out, received no answer. Taking a brand from the fire, he climbed the spiral stairs cautiously, hand on the worn sword that was all that remained of his old estate. His daughter followed, more curious than fearful.

"Is he alive?"

"Yes, though badly wounded. A knight, by his gear. He's been in a desperate fight — robbers, perhaps. We'll bind his wounds as best we can."

Kane opened his eyes, looked at them, fell back into a stupor.

"Will he live?"

"By the look in his eyes, he will — to the ruin of whoever brought him to this."

The girl hugged her scrawny ribs. "I saw madness in his eyes."

Her father grunted. "I'll try to drag him down to our fire. Can you lift a little? He's a giant."

"What's on his hands?" She shuddered.

"Let me see." He lifted a bloody hand and swore, wondering at the crumbling fragments that clung to fingers and nails.

"Whatever he fought, it must have been dead a long time."

Darkness Weaves

To the memory of Toad Hall,
and the Toad Hall crowd,
and Toad Hall days.

Contents

I say to you againe, doe not call upp Any that you can not put downe; by the Which I meane, Any that can in Turne call up somewhat against you, whereby your Powerfullest Devices may not be of use.

—Letter from Jedediah Orne: H.P. Lovecraft, *The Case of Charles Dexter Ward*

In their castle beyond night
Gather the Gods in Darkness,
With darkness to pattern man's fate.
*****

The colors of darkness are no monotonous hue —
For the blackness of Evil knows various shades,
Full many as Evil has names.
*****

Vengeance and Madness, inseparable twins,
Born together and worshipped as one;
Nor can the Gods tell one from his brother.
*****

In their castle beyond night
Gather the Gods in Darkness;
And darkness weaves with many shades.
(Fragment attributed to Opyros)

Part One

Prologue

"**H**e's evil incarnate! Stay away from him!" Arbas glared at the young outlander across from him and took a deep drink from the mug of ale the stranger had bought him. At present he felt only contempt for the free-spending youth who had sought him out here in the Tavern of Selram Honest.

Arbas — called by many Arbas the Assassin — was in a foul mood. A sudden and ill-timed (suspiciously ill-timed, it seemed to Arbas) run of bad luck with the dice earlier this evening had stripped from him a comfortable pile of winnings and all his ready coin as well. The adoring tavern maid, who had been slipping teasing fingers over the lean muscles beneath his leather vest, then turned coldly aloof and left him with a scornful air. Perhaps it was a disappointed air, Arbas mused sourly.

Then had come this stranger, whose upper-class manner was in dubious contrast to the rough dress he displayed. The stranger had simply introduced himself as Imel and volunteered no further information other than cautiously chosen gossip. Seemingly he was an altruist solely devoted to keeping Arbas's mug filled to the brim with strong ale. Unconvinced, Arbas decided to let the fool throw away his money. He was not a man who got drunk easily. Eventually Arbas knew that the other would in some very offhand, so very casual manner, begin to talk about some rival, some black-hearted son of a bitch — someone for whose demise Imel would pay.

Arbas had been professionally estimating exactly how much Imel might be able to pay when the stranger had abruptly demolished all the assassin's calculations. Somehow the conversation had shifted to the one man whose death the Combine authorities so fervently prayed for. With a start Arbas realized that the outlander was seeking information about Kane.

"Evil? But then, his character is not my concern. Anyway, I'm not searching the slums of Nostoblet to recruit a household treasurer. I simply wish to talk with him, is all — and I was told that you can tell me how to reach *him*." The stranger spoke the dialect of the Southern Lartroxian Combine with a burr that marked him a native of the island of Thovnos, capital of the

Thovnosian Empire about five hundred miles to the southwest.

"Then you're a fool!" retorted Arbas and emptied his mug. Beneath his hood the stranger's thin face flushed with anger. Silently damning the assassin's impertinence, he signalled a passing tavern maid to refill Arbas's mug. Carelessly he tossed her three bronze coins from his purse, making certain that Arbas noticed its weight. The tavern maid did, and she brushed against Imel's shoulder as she poured, smiling as she swung away.

"Fickle bitch!" mused Arbas illogically, studying the crimson imprint of her rouged breast on the Thovnosian's gray cloak. The assassin slowly sipped his ale, but gave no indication he had noticed the almoner. "Someone talks too much for me. Too damn much! Who told you I could find him?"

"He asked me not to give his name."

"Names, names, please mention no names. By Lato! You'll give me the name of that loose-tongued lying bastard who sent you to me — or you can go look for *him* in the Seventh Hell, where *he* damn well belongs! With that price on his head, there's not a handful of men in the Combine who'd not sell their souls for a chance to turn him in."

About them the tavern was bustling with activity. The cadaverous form of Selram Honest could be seen near the door to his wine cellar. A smile was etched through the grease of the gaunt proprietor's face as he looked over the noisy crowd. Most were in a festive mood, loudly going about their pleasures, gambling, whoring, carousing. Boisterous thugs from the ill-lit streets of Nostoblet, reckless mercenaries in the dark green shirts and leather trousers of the Combine's cavalry, strange-accented wanderers passing through the city for unguessable purposes, seductively clad street tarts whose hard laughter never echoed in their too-wise eyes. Two blond mercenaries from Waldann were about to cast aside the bonds of long companionship and draw knives over some lethal quarrel intelligible only to themselves. A pretty-faced whore with curious scars spiralling each bright-rouged breast was expertly rifling the purse of the incautious seaman who embraced her. A balding, filthy onetime sergeant of the Nostoblet city guard was amusing several jeering rednecks with his whining plea for a drink.

Here and there small groups of men sat hunched over their tables in low whispers, hatching plans of which the city guard would give much to learn. But the city guard seldom ventured into the riverport alleys of Nostoblet except to collect bribes, and Selram Honest cared nothing for his guests' affairs, so long as they had money for his hospitality. Each man's business was his own. No one paid the least attention, therefore, to the hushed exchange that was taking place between Arbas the assassin and the stranger from Thovnos.

At least, no one with the possible exception of a one-eared soldier in nondescript harness, who had entered the Tavern of Selram Honest not long after Imel. The burly warrior's decrepit battle gear and glowering visage insured his solitude from enterprising whores or talkative drunks. On the hand that raised his alecup occasionally to his lips, there shone a carven silver ring set with a massive amethyst. The crystal flashed violet in the smoky yellow light of the tavern. But the silent man sat far across the crowded room from

Arbas and Imel, well out of earshot. And if his gaze seemed too frequently turned in their direction, perhaps it was drawn by the dark-haired girl in multi-colored silks who danced upon the table somewhat beyond the two.

Imel remained in silent speculation for a moment, ignoring the smouldering anger in the assassin's dark face. This man was more difficult, more dangerous than he had at first judged him to be, and he was uncertain as to how deeply involved Arbas might be with his mission. At least for the present, he knew he must rely on the assassin. Diplomacy, then. Satisfy his suspicions, but tell him nothing important

"Then it was Bindoff who sent me to you," said the stranger, smiling at Arbas's startled reaction on hearing the Black Priest's name. "Now have we a deal?"

Arbas's estimation of the Thovnosian underwent a radical change. He had half-assumed the stranger was a bounty hunter and was considering a lonely spot for a knifing — but that he even knew of the Black Priest's connections with the man he sought was a telling point in his favor. Bindoff had guarded that secret with characteristic thoroughness. Perhaps, then, the man had in some inexplicable manner gained Bindoff's confidence. It might be worth the risk.

"Have you, say, twenty-five *mesitsi* gold ?" Arbas asked casually.

The stranger faked a hesitant pause — no merit in giving the assassin reason to think to ask for more. "I can raise it."

Arbas licked the foam from his mustache before replying. "All right, then. Bring it to me here two nights from tonight. I'll arrange for you to meet Kane."

"Why not tonight?" Imel urged.

"Not a chance, friend. Anyway, I guess I'll do me some checking on you before we go anywhere." Noting the stranger's annoyed impatience, Arbas quoted: "Happy in his folly, the fool embraced the devil."

The stranger laughed. "Spare me the scriptures. What is there about this Kane, though, that gives him so evil a reputation? Surely one of your position is unjustified in casting aspersions on anyone."

But Arbas only chuckled and said, "Ask me again after you've met Kane!"

I

Those Who Dwell Within Tombs

Fed by cold springs and tiny streams of the high Myceum Mountains far to the east, the River Cotras cut its twisted path through miles of rocky foot-hills, until at last it reached the wide belt of lowlands that circled the Lartroxian coast. There it began its rush to the western seas — a fifty-mile stretch of deep navigable channel through fertile farmlands and rich forests. The city Nostoblet stood along the banks of River Cotras, where its waters first rushed from the low hills onto the coastal plains. By virtue of the wide river channel, Nostoblet was an inland port, receiving both exotic trade goods from the merchant ships that plied the western seas, as well as the wealth of the eastern mountains, brought down the roaring waterway on rafts by the half-wild mountaineers.

The hills behind Nostoblet were thinly forested and scarred by great outcroppings and canyons, where long ago mountain streams had slashed through the soft rock. Stone cliffs stood out in endless profusion, some rising hundreds of feet above the valleys below them. An almost uncrossable bar-rier, they guarded the plains of South Lartroxia, marking the limits where, as some scholars maintained, the ancient seas had once rolled.

The cliffs in the hills behind Nostoblet had been honeycombed with tombs in many places. The comparatively recent southern spread of the worship of Horment had instituted the custom of cremation of the dead. Consequently these tombs had been out of use for over a century now, and the paths that led to them had been unwatched by human guards for almost as long.

The people of old Nostoblet had always been a practical folk, whose reli-gious habits had not required them to furnish lavish tombs for their dead. The custom of the wealthy in those days when the tombs were in use had been to lay their dead to rest in simple wooden boxes, which were set in niches within caverns that had been cut into the cliffs. None of the corpse's personal belongings were interred except the clothing he wore and occasional bits of jewelry of negligible value. Consequently there was nothing to tempt a would-be graverobber to slip past the few soldiers who had guarded the tombs in the past — or to brave the inhuman guardians. For the tombs of Nostoblet were infamous for ghouls and other worse dwellers, and the ghastly tales of their hauntings made all of Nostoblet scrupulously shun the area even to this time.

It was along the tortuous trails which ascended these cliffs that two men laboriously picked their way one stormy night. Lightning shattered the night's total blackness at frequent intervals, illuminating by its glare the rain-slick rock path that they followed along the face of the bluff. Its unpredictable flashes lighted the pathway far better than the feebly burning closed lantern Arbas carried.

"Careful here!" Arbas shouted back. "The rocks here are really slippery!" Ignoring his own advice, the assassin half slipped on a glistening boulder, and in struggling to keep his footing he very nearly threw the useless lantern over the edge.

The Thovnosian muttered savagely and concentrated on staying on the path. One slip on the streaming rocks would mean certain death among the rubble at the base of the bluffs. From somewhere in the darkness below, he could faintly hear the broken roar of rushing water pounding through the flooded stream bed.

Still there was no trace of fear in his voice as he growled, "Couldn't you have arranged for Kane to meet me somewhere dry?"

Arbas looked back with a wet grin of sardonic amusement written upon his dark face. "Changing your mind about meeting him, are you?" He laughed as his companion answered him with a torrent of curses. "It's a good night for our purposes, actually — the storm should give us cover from anyone who might try to follow us. Anyway, you know well enough that Kane couldn't show his face anywhere in the Combine with that price on his head. And even if it weren't for that, he's not too likely to come running for just anyone, unless it's damn well worth his while."

He added pointedly, "You still haven't said why you want to see Kane, you know."

"That's something for Kane to hear," retorted Imel.

Arbas nodded solemnly. "Uh-huh. Something for Kane to hear. Uh-huh. Well, don't let me be spoiling any dramatic secrets now. Wouldn't want that, of course."

But the Thovnosian chose to ignore him and lapsed into silence for the remainder of the climb.

Dark openings arose from the face of the stone wall to the right of them now. These were the doorways of the abandoned burial caverns, hand-hewn passages forced through the soft rock by slaves long dead with their masters. More than high enough to permit entrance of a tall man were these silent openings, and by the lightning flashes it appeared that the vaults within were considerably more spacious. Once-sturdy gates had barred access to the tombs in the past, but all seemed to have been forced at some time over the years. A few of the stronger doors stood ajar on frozen hinges, but most were missing entirely, or hanging at crazy angles — broken relics of rotted timber and corroded metal.

Imel speculated uneasily as to what hands might have torn asunder these stout portals to plunder the tombs they had protected — and why. It was a bad night for such thoughts. The darkness within the burial chambers was a far deeper gloom than that of the night, and time had not fully dispelled the stale odor of mouldering decay that tainted the damp air. His nerves crawled each time he nervously stepped past a gaping doorway, and his spine prickled with a sensation of hidden scrutiny. Now and again he caught the elusive sound of tiny scurrying and soft shuffling from within. Imel prayed it was only large rats startled in their lairs that he heard. But then the storm played eerie tricks upon the senses.

"This should be it. I think," Arbas announced shortly, and he led the way into the musty shelter of one of the burial caverns. Arbas turned up the lantern, which had miraculously remained burning, and Imel observed that the cavern took the shape of an L. There was a preliminary passage some twenty feet long, then at right angles a second and larger passage about fifty feet in length. The eight-foot walls of this first section had been cut out to form a triple row of niches. Only a few of the mouldering coffins that were laid in these niches remained intact. Most were broken apart and their contents scattered — although whether this was from age or vandalism the Thovnosian could not immediately tell.

A double curtain of hide was hung across the passage just after it made its bend. The curtain had been placed there to cut down the chill draft from outside — and to shut out the light from the lantern within. For as he stepped through the curtain, Imel saw that the chamber had been recently furnished for human occupancy.

Here in this ancient, shadow-haunted burial chamber Kane had made his lair.

"Well, where is he?" asked Imel brusquely. He was eager to get down to business and thereby shake off the dark, half-felt fears that had haunted him ever since he had entered the funerary district.

"Not used to waiting, are we now? Well, he'll get here in his own time. At least, he knows we're coming tonight," said Arbas, and appropriated the chamber's sole chair.

Cursing the assassin's insolence, Imel cast about the chamber for another seat. There was none. Still the chamber had been astonishingly well furnished — particularly so considering the difficulty and the danger of surveillance involved in bringing anything to these tombs. In the corner on the floor was a good bed of several large pelts and a mattress. Along with the chair there was a table with two lamps, several bottles, items of food and — most amazing of all — a number of books, scrolls, and writing implements. Scattered about the floor and empty niches were various other items — jars of oil, a crossbow and several quivers of bolts, utensils, more food, a battleaxe, and an assortment of rather ancient daggers, rings, and other bits of metalwork. There was a bed of ashes, still quite warm, where Kane had risked building small cooking fires. A stack of unburned wood indicated the use Kane had found for the coffins whose resting place he had preempted.

Heaped in a pile were the discarded bones of the coffins' tenants, and as Imel looked at this mound he felt the hackles of his neck rise. He had never been known as a squeamish man, and there had been no indication that the spirits of these dead were to be reckoned with. Rather, his disquiet stemmed from the state of these mouldering bones. It was enough that they had been gnawed — this could have been done by rats — but beyond that, they had been meticulously cracked apart and the marrow scraped from within. Something human — or vaguely human — would have devoured the rotting corpses like thus, reflected Imel. He shuddered even though the bones were old and crumbling.

Idly Imel stirred a curious finger through the litter of antique ornaments and metalwork. He was slightly disappointed to discover nothing of consequence. "Kane been pilfering tombs for this junk?" he asked, startled at the loudness of his voice.

The assassin shrugged. "I don't know. He's been holed up here long enough to go stir-crazy, but I'd guess he was just collecting the stuff to keep busy. Maybe he's thinking about making something with it. Maybe write up a catalogue for the pedants at the academy up in Matnabla. You know, I mean what would you do up here all the time? Kane's ... I don't know." He broke off in a mutter and became interested in his dagger.

Imel sighed in frustration, searching about the chamber for diversion. He noticed a cryptic pattern of intricate design and archaic pictographs arched over the threshold. Based on what he had seen thus far, he shrewdly guessed that this represented some manner of charm against the supernatural. Without comprehension he studied the talisman for a space, scratching slowly at the unaccustomed stubble he had let grow over his features.

The noise of the tempest outside, coupled with his unnatural surroundings, was making Imel more nervous by the minute. He crossed over to the table where Arbas nonchalantly honed his dagger upon a stone Kane had placed there. Leaning over, he looked at the books there in admiration — although more for their monetary than intellectual value. Curiously he leafed through several of them. Two were in the language of the Combine, and of the others, only one was in a language that looked even vaguely familiar. One very old one was extremely unusual, for the strange characters on its pages did not quite appear to have been handwritten. Imel wondered what type of book would seem so interesting to Kane that he would have transported several of them to the crypt. It was surprising enough to see that Kane could actually read, mused Imel. What little information he had compiled gave Kane the reputation of being a rugged and skillful warrior — a violent personality by all accounts. In Imel's experience, such a man usually was contemptuous of anything concerned with the arts.

Idly he looked through one of the two volumes written in the language of the Combine. Suddenly his eyes were held by a page filled entirely by a strange diagram. Startled, he slowly read the script on the page opposite and found his suspicions verified. With horror he shut the book and abruptly set it down. A grimoire. Was Kane then a sorcerer as well as a soldier? Imel remembered

Arbas's warning and began to feel fear.

He looked at Arbas and found the assassin grinning at him over his dagger. Sidelong he had been watching Imel and had seen the sudden terror in his eyes. Anger at revealing his emotions flooded Imel, washing away the fear — fear, he told himself, that any sane man feels when confronted with the paraphernalia of black sorcery.

"Stop your stupid smirking!" he snarled at Arbas, who merely chuckled in reply. Cursing fervently, the Thovnosian paced the chamber. By Tloluvin! He was a fool ever to have undertaken this mission — a fool ever to have became involved in *her* insane schemes! Realizing that he was fast losing control, he halted and struggled to regain his composure.

"Is Kane going to get here or not?" he demanded.

Arbas shrugged; he seemed to be getting impatient himself. "Perhaps he doesn't realize we're here yet," he offered. "Let's just take a lantern and show its light out on the ledge for a bit. I doubt if anyone other than Kane is around here to see it on a night like this." So saying, he picked up his battered lantern and moved toward the curtain wall.

They had just gone through the curtain and were starting toward the tunnel's mouth when an extended burst of chain lightning split the midnight skies and threw a flickering bluish light on the figure just entering the crypt. Startled, Imel was unable to suppress a gasp at the sight of the looming cloaked figure silhouetted darkly against the lightning-blasted torrent. Arbas's words at their first meeting flashed through Imel's mind: *Look for him in the Seventh Hell!* Truly this nightmarish scene could justifiably be that of a demon — or Lord Tloluvin himself — emerging from the Seventh Hell.

For the space of a heartbeat the lightning gave hellish illumination upon the figure. No features were discernible in the glare. He appeared only as a black shadow, the wind whipping his rain-drenched cloak and garments, his powerful body braced against the storm. His drawn sword glinted in the lightning, as did his eyes — sinister spots of fire in the darkness.

Then the lightning burst faded, and the figure stalked into the crypt. "Get that light under cover!" snapped Kane.

Arbas moved the curtain aside, and Kane stepped through, flinging off his sodden cloak and shaking a flood of water from his massive body. Cursing in some strange tongue, he poured himself a full cup of wine, drained it, and began pouring another. "A beautiful storm, but drying out from it in this dank hole is not to my liking," he growled between cups. "Arbas, see if that fire can be rekindled. The smoke won't be a danger tonight.

"Sit down and have some wine, Imel. It's excellent for cleansing the damp from your insides. These Lartroxians keep surprisingly good vineyards, I'll always grant them that." Pouring a third cup, he moved to where Arbas worked with the fire.

Gratefully Imel slumped into the chair and, seeing no other cup, gingerly drank the heavy wine from its bottle. He had been unnerved by the past hour's events, and the liquor warmed and steadied him. Missions of this sort ran against his nature, and he wished again, as he so often had before, that he could have talked *her* into sending someone else. That despicable Oxfors Alremas, perhaps. Not that he cared to rate Alremas superior in his missions of intrigue and cunning diplomacy. Still the Pellin lord's self-esteem at times grew insufferable, and Imel wondered how Alremas's aristocratic sensibilities would fare under the abuse he had himself thus far sustained.

Arbas soon had the fire ablaze with the dry wood from the caskets. Most of the smoke was sucked without by the storm winds, and it was not too uncomfortable. The flames lit the crypt as it had not been before, and Imel was able now to get his first good look at Kane.

He was a large man, a little over six feet in height, although he seemed shorter because of the extreme massiveness of his body. Thick neck, a barrel chest, strong, heavily muscled arms and legs — everything created in him an aura of great power. Even his hands were overlarge and the fingers long and powerful. Less brutal, they might have been called an artist's hands. Imel had once seen such hands before — on a notorious strangler, whose execution he had attended. As an embellishment on the Imperial law, the severed hands had been displayed alongside the impaled head in Thovnosten's Justice Square. Kane's age was hard to guess; he looked perhaps like a man of thirty in body, but he seemed to be older somehow. Imel had expected to find an older man, so he estimated Kane to be in his fifties and well preserved. Kane's complexion was fair and his hair light red, cut evenly to moderate length. His beard was short, and the features of his face were rugged and heavy — too primitively coarse to be considered handsome.

Kane sensed Imel's inspection and suddenly locked eyes with him. Abruptly there returned the chilling sensation that had earlier pulsed through Imel during the lightning burst. The eyes of Kane were like two blue-burning crystals of ice. Within them stirred a frozen fire of madness, death, torment, hellish hatred. They looked straight through Imel, searching out his innermost thoughts, searing his very soul. They were the eyes of a maddened killer.

With a cruel laugh, Kane turned away, releasing Imel from the spell of his eyes. His mind staggered back, and it was with effort that he suppressed blind panic. In a daze, his hand groped for the wine bottle. Gladly he made use of the wine's restorative virtue.

She who sent him on this mission to Kane had always instilled in Imel a feeling of revulsion. *She* was but a twisted, broken vessel of hatred, kept living by her depraved lust for vengeance. To be sure, no man could approach her without feeling the dark fire of her insane hatred. But this revulsion was nothing compared to the terror that had blasted Imel when he looked into the eyes of Kane. Insanity gleamed there, but in complement with a cold murder-lust. Insensate craving to kill and destroy — consuming hatred of life. With such eyes would Death receive the newly dead, or Lord Tloluvin welcome some hideously damned soul to his realm of eternal darkness.

"Now then, Imel, what business do you have that concerns me?"

Imel snapped out of his musings as Kane addressed him. Looking up, he found Kane had quit the fire and was half-sitting on the table across from him. He was watching Imel closely, a mocking smile over his brutal features —

the hellish blaze of his eyes subdued but smouldering still. His long fingers were toying with a silver ring. Imel assumed it was one from the pile of artifacts.

"I think you'd better have a very good reason for demanding to see me. Not that my time in this hole is in anything like short supply, but your coming here has put myself and Arbas in some danger." He held the ring to the light appraisingly. Seemingly he was intrigued with its intricate carvings. "You're sure, of course, that no one followed you…"

Casually Kane drew the lamp closer to him, the better to examine the ring. Imel frowned in vexation. "Interesting…" Kane muttered, extending the ring into the light. A soft violet glow emanated from the huge amethyst. Imel recognized the ring.

Cold fear seized him as realization dawned. Imel's hand streaked for the sword at his side. He had but touched its hilt when an arm whipped around from behind him, and a dagger point painfully tickled the flesh of his throat. Arbas! He had forgotten the assassin.

"Don't kill him just yet, Arbas," said Kane, who had not moved throughout. "You know, I think Imel knows that ring."

The assassin tickled his dagger point as the Thovnosian wanted to rise. Imel subsided. "Now how do you figure that?" Arbas asked with assumed bewilderment.

"Well, I think it's the way his face turned pale when he saw it. Or what do you make of that?"

"Could be he's just startled by that large a sapphire."

"No, I doubt that. Anyway, this is an amethyst."

"Same thing."

"No. I think you're on the wrong track, Arbas. I'll bet Imel was just thinking that the last time he saw this ring, it was on someone's hand he knew. Say, maybe that big skulking bastard who was following you two."

Arbas's voice was edged. "Following us! Now, Imel, that makes me look sort of gullible." He dug the dagger point deeper. Imel's breath came in ragged gasps as he attempted to contract his throat from the stinging blade.

"This is a Mycean blade," the assassin explained in Imel's ear. "Those mountain clansmen spend weeks forging their steel, shaping it just so. They say the steel will grow weak and brittle like a lowland blade — unless it takes a long drink of an enemy's warm blood every ten days or so."

"From here I'd say the workmanship was Pellinite," Kane observed.

"That's because it was a Pellinite craftsman who fitted the haft for me," rejoined Arbas in an offended manner. "Anyway, the nobleman who owned the knife before I killed him had always sworn it was a Mycean blade. The steel is unmistakable — watch how it glides through Imel's throat."

Kane shook his head and stood up. "Later, perhaps. Let him breathe now, though. As it happened, there was only one man who followed you, and I was waiting for him. I think Imel will talk freely now." His eyes held Imel in their deadly stare, now burning bright with anger. Imel knew he was very close to death. "Who was he? Why was he following you?" Kane did not waste adding a warning not to lie, and Imel probably couldn't have anyway — held in the cold grip of those eyes.

"An officer who accompanied me from Thovnos. He was my bodyguard. I've been through the slums of Nostoblet trying to find you, and I felt it necessary to have him accompany me at a discreet distance. Tonight I ordered him to follow me when I went with Arbas."

Kane considered him at length. "Yes, because you didn't trust him — and with good reason. Once he got you alone, Arbas would have killed you without compunction for whatever valuables you carried — had I not told him to bring you here. Curiosity on my part. All friend Bindoff could tell me was that you were a younger offshoot of somewhat impoverished Thovnosian gentry, a man of dubious integrity but reputedly adroit — and that you came to him with rather curious credentials and asked where to find me.

"So you are justified, but not pardoned. With every good soul in all South Lartroxia thirsting for my blood, I can take no chances. Your coming here was a risk; your coming with an escort was a worse risk. Maybe luck favors me this night, for I could discover no evidence that your friend was followed. At any rate, I was forced to wait in the rain even longer after I'd dealt with One-Ear, to be certain *he* wasn't followed. You see, I didn't trust you either, Imel. So I was waiting out there in the rocks beside the path. Watched you and Arbas go by, and then met your friend. I think I may have given him a bad fright. He did have an interesting ring, though."

With deceptive carelessness he tossed the ring onto the pile of odds and ends pilfered from the tombs. He signed the disappointed assassin to release the Thovnosian, then demanded, "Once again, What's your business?"

Imel slowly let out his breath as the dagger point withdrew. Trickles of sweat stung as they slid over the scarlet line across his throat. His neck felt dry where the assassin's hot breath had hit. Gathering his shaken wits for an effort on which he knew his life hung, Imel began, "I was sent here by one who desires your services — and who is willing to pay for them royally."

"Really? That's a bit vague, but it has a nice ring. Be more precise, though. In what form?"

"Wealth, power, position — a kingdom, perhaps."

"Now you begin to interest me. Let's hear the details. Particularly with regard to my 'services,' as you put it."

"Certainly. But first, what do you know of the affairs of the Thovnosian Empire?"

"Of its current affairs very little. It has been some years since I visited the islands."

"In that event, you will pardon me if I embark upon a somewhat lengthy tale to explain my mission."

"If I find it interesting," Kane murmured — then exclaimed softly, "Damn! Look here!" An evil-hued tomb beetle clattered to the table and lumbered determinedly toward the flickering lamp. Kane caught the large scarab up and fascinatedly watched it crawl from hand to hand. "Messenger from the dead. They love to burrow inside a rotting skull." He glanced up at Imel's strained face.

"Go ahead. I'm listening."

Imel's Tale

Netisten Maril today rules as Monarch of Thovnos, from which throne he is also Emperor of the Thovnosian Empire — an island federation south and east of the Lartroxian coast, beyond the Middle Sea that separates the continents of Lartroxia and the Southern Lands. As you may be aware, the Empire was formed two centuries ago from this broken subcontinent of eight major islands, some 2000 to 3000 square miles each — along with a dozen or so smaller islands and countless bits of land too small for mention. As the largest and most powerful island, Thovnos has been the seat of empire for most of the Empire's history, and Netisten Maril is a true descendant of a line that has long bred strong, capable rulers.

When his father, Netisten Sirrome, died, there was but one other claimant to the throne — Netisten Maril's older half-brother, Leyan, who was the bastard son of Netisten Sirrome and a seductive noblewoman from Tresli. Because he was illegitimate, Leyan did not bear the dynastic name and had no chance of succession — unless Maril should die without male heir. Thus he was dismayed when at an early age his younger brother married a distant cousin from Quarnora and soon had her with child.

His young wife bore him a daughter, M'Cori by name, and soon after became pregnant again. But as her time again drew near, she sickened and died without giving birth. Gossip suggests that Leyan had her poisoned to prevent a new heir, but she was always known to be a frail child, and perhaps the strain of bearing two children in quick succession proved more than she could endure.

Maril was unapproachable for months thereafter, his spirit tormented by several strong passions. First was a terrible fit of frustrated rage — for he himself had laid her womb open and wrenched out the son who lacked only a few weeks of natural birth. But he had loved her deeply, and as his rage subsided to despair, he was tortured with guilt — blaming himself for forcing his young wife too hard to bring him a son. Time slowly healed the passions that tore at him, but he was left a hard and loveless man — with a temper made worse that had never been mild. He seemed to push all thought of past or future marriage from his mind, and the child M'Cori suffered from neglect. It was Leyan who cared for her needs — not so much from pity, but because he himself had fathered two sturdy sons, Lages and Roget, and favored the idea of marrying a son to their cousin, M'Cori — thus securing the succession for his line if not for himself.

The passing years favored his enterprise, as Maril remained unwed, and M'Cori grew into girlhood — a child of startling beauty and a lack of guile that bordered on simple-mindedness. She felt a touching gratitude toward her uncle and a clinging devotion toward his sons. Lages and Roget grew into strong young men and were their father's pride — skilled in arms and leadership, well favored in appearances, adept in the graces of nobility. Leyan saw them as true princes of the blood. He was stricken when Roget, the older and less rash of his sons, died a hero's death at twenty-two while leading his uncle's army against rebels on the island Fisitia. He was avenged by his brother, Lages, who made up with quick temper what he lacked of Roget's quick wit. M'Cori shared in the mourning for Roget, for the three had grown up together as brothers and sister. But when mourning was done, she and Lages had become lovers.

Then four years ago Leyan saw happen that which threatened all his carefully laid plans. Netisten Maril was in love again.

From the ill-starred northern island of Pellin came a woman of unearthly beauty. Efrel was her name. She was of the best blood; her family had given their name to the island kingdom where they had ruled for long centuries. When the Empire was formed, it was thought that the Pellin lords would be its rulers, as their blood was the oldest and most noble. But Pellin had fallen on dark days, and the aged kingdom was no match for the younger, stronger kingdoms to the south. Indeed, all threats to Thovnos's domination have come from its young neighbors and not from remote Pellin — although it is no secret that the lords of Pellin have always dreamed of someday holding the reins of empire.

But the island Pellin has had an evil reputation since the earliest days when man first crossed the Western Sea to settle in this region. Our history is old, and very much of the centuries preceding the Empire's foundation has become obscured by myth and legend. Nonetheless, the strange stone ruins that are to be found mouldering in certain shunned locations among the islands defy all understanding. Of the race that built these monolithic citadels we know nothing. Legend insists that these ruins were here before the coming of man to the islands. Certainly the crumbling stones are of marvelous antiquity, and no man can guess what ages have passed since these cyclopean fortresses were raised, nor at whose hand they were destroyed. There are curious myths that hint of frightful carvings depicting colossal scenes of combat among monstrous sea beasts from a mad god's nightmare. The first seafarers who settled the islands left unsavory rumors of things carven upon certain of the eroded stones — hideous scenes they took pains to obliterate forever with frightened blows of hammer and chisel. No such carvings today remain to verify these myths. It is on the island of Pellin that these lichen-covered ruins are to be found in greatest concentration — nor are they in so advanced a state of decay as those on the southern islands.

Certainly it is not solely due to the immeasurably deep waters to the north of Pellin that no fisherman will cast nets there, that merchants sail many leagues off course to avoid the region. This area of the Western Sea is named the Sorn-Ellyn, which is said to mean "bottomless sea" in an archaic tongue. Its depths have never been plumbed. Legend says that the Earth has split asunder there, and that the waters of the Sorn-Ellyn flow down into the cosmic ocean upon which our world floats. A pretty concept, of course, and derived from folk myths of our universe's creation — though philosophers have since learned more bewildering theories to dispute.

Less easy to dismiss are the wild and unsettling stories told over the years by those few men who have ventured across the Sorn-Ellyn and returned — or so they claim. They spread fantastic tales of ghostly lights glimpsed at night from far down beneath the sea, of weird shapes only half seen that moved about on the black waves on nights of the full moon. Some claim they have heard an eerie whining sound that echoes from under the sea — a droning that makes men cry out in agony and drives ships' dogs insane with fear. Horrible sea monsters are said to haunt the Sorn-Ellyn as they lurk in the waters of no other sea — loathsome creatures that can drag beneath the waves an entire ship and her crew. The oldest legends speak of an elder race of demons who dwell in the black depths of the Sorn-Ellyn, eager to destroy all fools who dare trespass within their sunken realm.

And with these dark legends of the past there are mingled more recent tales that seamen speak of with fear yet in their eyes. Such reports are scoffed at by day, or told for a safe shudder over alecups — but not mentioned at night and at sea.

One such: A few years back a captain from Tresli was sailing home with a rich cargo of Lartroxian grain. Wishing to expose his cargo to the ocean damp no longer than necessary — and to make port ahead of his competitors — he chose to sail north across the Sorn-Ellyn, rather than take the circuitous route through the islands south of Pellin. His crew was uneasy, but the captain bribed them with extra pay — knowing the higher prices his grain could command if he returned before his rivals.

As they entered the Sorn Ellyn, the lookout sighted wreckage. Sailing closer, they discovered a splintered section of hull from an Ammurian vessel, and tied to the half-submerged timbers was a lone survivor. The sailor had been adrift for days after his ship was lost, but it was not only exposure and lack of food and water that had reduced him to a screaming, mindless madman. He went berserk when they lifted him aboard. Throwing off those who tried to minister to tortured flesh, he shrieked insanely of slimy black tentacles and faceless demons from the sea. As they tied him to a bed, the crewmen were sickened by the horrible scars that pitted his shrunken body — as if the man had been wrapped with links of red-hot chain.

Little could be made of his pitiful raving, but enough came through so that the captain was forced to turn his ship and speed away to avoid certain mutiny. And strangest to tell, during the first night after his rescue the castaway suddenly awoke from nightmare-tortured sleep, threw off the bonds that restrained him, and with maniacal strength burst past those who tried to hold him. Laughing and gibbering, he threw himself into the sea. A seaman who watched him swim out of sight swore he saw a strange light glowing beneath the dark waters, and several others claimed to have faintly heard an eerie humming sound coming from far below.

There are many other strange stories — enough to indicate that there is something unwholesome about Pellin and the sea around it. And this same shadow of evil hovers over the royal family, for it is acknowledged that the Pellin lords have long delved into mysteries best left unsounded. It is commonly known that Efrel's great-grandfather murdered his youngest granddaughter and bathed in her blood to restore his youth. Of his success we shall never know, as his angry son eviscerated him shortly thereafter.

Deep beneath the cellars and dungeons of Dan-Legeh, black citadel of the Pellin lords, there is said to lie a great subterranean chamber. Within this vast cavern the Pellin lords have for centuries tortured their enemies and pursued their infamous study of sorcerous lore. The few outsiders to enter this chamber and emerge again with whole mind have told of a great pool in the floor of the cavern — whose waters rise and ebb with the tides. Into this pool's black depths have disappeared many of those secrets Pellin has not deigned to share.

But to bring my tale back to matters of the present day, and to Efrel:

It was into this same hidden chamber on a night some thirty years ago that Pellin Othrin, then Monarch of Pellin, carried a screaming and naked girl — and though she was his teenaged cousin, Wehrle, no man dared interfere. What they did there no man ever learned, for at dawn Wehrle crawled forth half-lifeless and with madness in her staring eyes. Pellin Othrin was silent as to what had transpired, nor did any man dare inquire. Not long after, Lyrde, Othrin's wife, who had borne him no children, fell strangely ill and died. While the ashes of her pyre were yet warm, Othrin announced that he would make Wehrle his new queen. Some wondered that he would wed the unfortunate girl, for they knew Othrin had no germ of pity in his heart. Nor could they understand why Othrin slew the physician and nurse who attended the birth of their daughter a few months later, for the child was perfect in every way.

This daughter was Efrel. Wehrle's madness grew deeper after Efrel's birth, so that at times she had to be restrained from attacking the child. Pellin Othrin placed his wife in private chambers with attendants constantly on guard against her rages. When Efrel was old enough to leave her mother's breast, she was given over to a nurse, and afterward no more was said of Wehrle, nor did any man ask. As Efrel grew from infancy, Othrin kept her by his side and gave personal attention to every detail of her education — in statecraft and in the secret delvings of the Pellin lords.

One night Pellin Othrin was found strangled in his chambers, though no outcry had been heard. His guards could not explain how the assassin had slipped past them, nor guess what strangler's cord had circled their lord's body with livid red stigmata, nor yet account for the seaweed that hung in his beard.

His sudden death left Pellin without male heir, but there was precedent in Pellin's long history when the island had been ruled by a woman. And Pellin Othrin taught his daughter well. Thus Efrel ascended the ancient throne of Pellin as Queen. It was not to be long before she would be Empress as well.

Of Efrel it is said that she pursued the study of demonology and the black arts with a passion beyond that of any of her unhallowed ancestors. Perhaps she was spurred on by the desire to rekindle the ancient glory of the House of Pellin, which was inexorably drifting toward obscurity within the growing Empire. Possibly she sought ways to revitalize the anemic blood of her line, whose heirs were fewer and sicklier with each generation, and the madness that haunted the House of Pellin grew stronger apace.

Then, again, there is a persistent rumor that Efrel is only half human — that her real father was not Pellin Othrin, but a demon of his conjuration, who had lain with Wehrle on that night when sanity was driven from her. Certainly there is some little to be offered in defense of this whispered theory. It might explain Efrel's obsessive interest in sorcery and other arcane researches, for one thing. And further, it might account for her inhuman beauty — or for her vitality that is like a weed to the anemic blooms that others of her line resemble. Perhaps her unnatural parentage gave her power to inflame Netisten Maril, who in his late thirties was as cold and unapproachable a man as ever.

Netisten Maril saw Efrel for the first time when she was presented to him at court one day. She moved gracefully in a clinging swirl of a gown pieced from the opalescent scales of blind sea-snakes dredged from the Sorn-Ellyn. When introductions were effected by their servants as court etiquette prescribed, the seductress explained to Maril that she had come from Pellin to pay her respects to him and to remain for a while in the Imperial Court, such being the privilege of one of royal lineage. From that moment Maril thought of little else but Efrel, for her exotic beauty and her aura of mystery (and perhaps her glamour) had thoroughly conquered his long slumbering passions. Rekindled after so long, they blazed anew with pent-up fire — and it was evident to all that Thovnos would very soon have a new queen.

To be sure, the turn of events dismayed Leyan, as well as many others, who foretold that there could be nothing but misfortune from a union with ill-famed Pellin. But Maril was totally in love with this pale-skinned beauty of midnight tresses and eyes so dark they shone like onyx. Even those who hated the court's newest star granted that her beauty transcended in every particular that of any other woman of their experience — including M'Cori, who under Leyan's shelter was advancing in the Imperial Court as an ingenue of uncommon loveliness. And objections to the Emperor's imminent marriage were effectively hushed when Maril ordered a trusted advisor beheaded after becoming enraged at his well-meant advice.

So they were married, and the Empire settled back to make the best of the new situation. However, to her chagrin, Efrel soon discovered that although she had won into Maril's bed, she could not insinuate herself onto his throne. For Maril was a man of strong will who kept the affairs of his personal life unmixed with affairs of the Empire. Thus Efrel found her ambitions of ruling behind the throne stillborn for all her wiles and secret glamour, and the many nobility she had brought as entourage remained without influence or important position.

And as time went by, Efrel felt even her hold on Maril's affections loosening — for strong passions too often exhaust the spirit and burn out quickly. But more important, despite Maril's enthusiastic efforts, he was unable to get Efrel pregnant. Again a male heir eluded him, and this renewed frustration blighted his passion for her. Of his own virility there could be no question; it must then be Efrel who was barren. In his dark moods perhaps Maril remembered the old rumors concerning Efrel's inhuman parentage — for it is common that hybrids are sterile. Angrily he severed all but the most formal relations with his wife.

Despairing of realizing her ambitions with Maril, Efrel then turned to intrigue. Seeking out Leyan, she easily seduced him with her ready beauty — and with the promise to aid Leyan in his bid for the Imperial tone. For if Netisten Maril died without male heir, Leyan would be his successor. The idea had, of course, often occurred to Leyan, but he was well aware of his half-brother's careful measures to prevent assassination, and that he would be the obvious culprit in the event of success. But many a man has lost all caution in a woman's embrace, and so it was with Leyan.

The two conspired to murder Netisten Maril with a slow-acting poison of Efrel's devising, whose certain toxins would mimic a natural illness. Any resistance at court to Leyan's succession they would quell with an army secretly loyal to them. The plot was well underway, and several of the nobility had sworn allegiance to Leyan in return for promised rewards under his reign. Then disaster struck the conspirators.

Maril had always been on the alert for conspiracy, especially from his half-brother. He had taken extensive precautions, and his spy system was more effective than either Efrel or Leyan had realized. Thus Maril learned of the plan before it could mature. One night he surprised the two together in Efrel's bedchamber and announced to them that all who had entered into conspiracy with them were being arrested even at that moment.

Leyan came out from the sheets with time to draw his sword, if not draw on his pants, before Maril's guards could intervene. But Maril with characteristic rashness ordered his men not to interfere and welcomed his brother's attack. Then followed a desperate bit of swordplay — for Leyan might still win an empire should he win this duel, and the only alternative was certain death. For what those who watched swore was fully half an hour, though exaggeration is understandable, these two seasoned veterans fought — each skilled from constant training and hardened from many campaigns. Leyan was judged to be the better swordsman, but Maril, I think by design, had confronted his brother while he was groggy from wine and recent loveplay. Further, Leyan was naked, and Maril wore mail.

Gradually Maril forced him back, slowly wearing down his frantic defenses, parrying his superior swordplay with growing confidence. A small cut here, a barely parried thrust there — slashes that mail would turn and bare flesh could not. Finally Leyan moved a heartbeat too slow to counter the deceptive slash of Maril's' powerful sword arm. His brother's blade clove through his side, and down toppled Leyan — his final curses strangled by the blood that filled sundered lungs. His fate was the easiest of the conspirators.

Efrel then tried suicide, it is said — but the guards were too swift and stopped her dagger short of her breast. Maril left her beside the corpse under close guard — there to ponder the fate that would await her with the new day.

At dawn Maril sent out criers to tell Thovnosten's populace of the aborted conspiracy — and to summon them to the execution at noon. The people flocked to the central square, eager for the spectacle and the promised food and drink given in celebration of their loyalty to Netisten Maril. Peddlers, hawkers, and vendors descended like vultures from the cloudless sky.

Efrel arrived clad in her most splendid gown and jewelry. Those with memories for such things recognized it as the gown she wore when first she bewitched Maril. She was enthroned at the side of Netisten Maril as usual, but instead of ladies-in-waiting, there were guards to see to her comfort. Then while Efrel watched, the six lords who had sworn allegiance to Leyan were led out and bound to frames erected during the night. After attention had been given to their tongues with red-hot pincers and to their limbs with iron rods, their families and servants were brought out. Slowly, without breaking the neck — so to prolong the agony — every man, woman, and child of them was hanged before the lords' eyes. And once they had witnessed the deaths of all their households, the conspirators were cunningly impaled and hung like spitted steers over slow fires. A ghastly penalty, but such is the punishment just laws demand for conspiracy against our lawful government.

Throughout the long afternoon — for it was near dusk when the last lord had died — Efrel had been forced to watch the gruesome spectacle — her torture made worse because she was still treated with every show of respect. What must have passed through her mind only the gods know. She knew Maril to be without pity — a man overruled by his volcanic emotions. She knew that mercy was not to be hoped for. But perhaps mingled with dread anticipation there was a scrap of hope that Maril might deal mercifully with one whom he once had loved. Foolish hope, if hope there was.

When the last gruesome carcass had ceased to writhe, and the crowd shuffled with boredom, awaiting a finale worthy of their long attention, Maril turned to Efrel.

"For you, Efrel — deceptive whore with serpent's kisses — I have devised a less common death. One that suits your animal lusts and noble blood. I've found a consort equal to your gentle character and pristine morals." As she shrank in fear from the rage that twisted his face and choked his voice, Maril signed to his guard.

Then several strong slaves came into the square. They led a fiercely heaving wild bull. To restrain the animal called for all their sweaty effort, for it was driven mad with pain and drugs. More so were those who held Efrel compelled to exert all their strength — for the girl had become frenzied at the sight of her fate.

They carried the struggling girl, beautiful despite her terror in all her exquisite finery, into the square. There they cuffed her wrists to two long silver chains that were fastened to a collar about the bull's neck. A section of the crowd was moved aside, and the bull and the Empress were led into a narrow street leading through the city and beyond the gates.

As she saw the hopelessness of her plight, Efrel's terror gave way to venomous fury. She cursed Netisten Maril and vowed vengeance in a manner that chilled the souls of those already sated with torture. She swore by strange gods that she would return to bring red flames and utter ruin to all Thovnos, to wrest from Maril his throne and all that was his. Maril only laughed at her and signaled the slaves to release the bull.

With a last shriek of inhuman hatred, Efrel was jerked from her feet and dragged across the paving as the maddened bull plunged away. The enraged beast plummeted down the winding, cobbled streets as it sought to find the freedom of its native meadows — pounding headlong past walls and buildings and taunting creatures, past tenements and hovels and paving that gave way to dirt. It never gave a thought to the slight burden that bounced and smacked behind its hooves — a mewing, broken thing that left a trail of blood and scraped flesh upon the rough pavement over which it passed.

"The whore leaves us with her new consort!" roared Maril. "There'll be little of the bride left for the groom by the time he carries her past our walls — but I wish him better luck with it! Let her serpent's carcass lie unburied wherever it chances to fall — and let no man again speak her name to me!" With that Netisten Maril contrived to dismiss the matter from his thoughts.

Better would it have been for Maril had he first made certain of her death. A number of Efrel's loyal retainers had eluded Maril's wrath. They caught the bull as it reached the twilight-hung outskirts of the city, and there they killed it and stopped its flight. Although they did this seeking only to recover their queen's body for proper burial, they discovered to their utter astonishment that the mutilated body still lived!

Again the half-human, half-demon parentage seems to apply — for surely only an inhuman vitality could survive such an ordeal. Yet, live she did — for the Pellinites immediately bore her to the ship they had hidden in a secret cove and set sail for their homeland. Fearing relentless pursuit should Maril learn that Efrel still lived, all were sworn to secrecy — agreeing to say no more than that they had reclaimed their queen's corpse. And all human logic would suspect nothing further.

This was nearly two years ago. In this time Efrel has recovered — thanks to her unnatural vitality and to the skill of the court physicians. But she is no longer a woman of unearthly beauty — only a hideously mutilated wreck of humanity that hides from the sight of men. Life is held in her ruined body only by an all-consuming lust for vengeance upon Netisten Maril and all that is his. In her hidden chambers within Dan-Legeh, Efrel spins her web of vengeance, and only a trusted elite are privy to her commands.

Unceasingly since her return to strength has she intrigued to gather an army about her. She has delved ever deeper into the occult mysteries, seeking to marshall forces of the other planes for her vengeance. The others of her family are powerless or unwilling to halt the destructive designs of her fiendish energy. Her hidden conspiracy against Thovnos and its Monarch progresses daily, and she seeks everywhere for those who will aid her in this. Soon the magnitude of the venture must alert Maril to its existence — assuming he does not already suspect.

In some unknown manner Efrel became aware of your presence here, milord — and she is convinced that your generalship is essential for her victory in the rebellion. Accordingly, she has sent me to you as an emissary to secure your aid.

In conclusion, Efrel offers this proposition: Assume leadership of her naval forces, and when victory is ours, your reward shall be the island kingdom of your choice — saving Thovnos and Pellin.

There was quiet as Imel finished his narrative. Kane sipped his wine and brooded over the tale. The tomb beetle had finally given up its obsession with the lamplight and escaped on some other errand.

At length Kane turned to Imel and said, "Well, your story does interest me. I'll have to look over your Queen's set-up before I decide definitely, but what you say sounds attractive. Dramatic, but in content your account is in keeping with various things I've heard from time to time.

"The main problem, though, is how to get out of here. I assume you have made some sort of arrangements?"

Imel felt his insides slowly unknot as the tension left him. The first part of his mission was going to be a success. The rest would be on more familiar ground for him. "Yes. We have a small craft, fast and well-manned, hidden in a cove along the coast maybe thirty miles from here. If we reach it, I think we can run or fight through any blockade the Combine may have sent out — these Lartroxians never were worth much on the seas."

"Our light cavalry is good enough," growled Arbas, feeling something approaching patriotism.

"That's true," conceded Imel. "And herein is our greatest danger. They have mounted patrols covering the roads and passes through the mountains, so we'll have to sneak through them or plan a running fight. Fortunately, the authorities have grown lax in their search for you, Kane, and we won't have as much trouble as we would have had, say, two months ago."

"Yeah. I know about those damned patrols. I was waiting for them to grow laxer still," said Kane. "There are definite advantages to biding your time..."

"Advantages we can't wait for, I'm afraid. We've already pressed our luck by waiting this long. If the ship is discovered, everything is ruined. We don't dare hold off any later than tomorrow night."

"How many men do you have with you?"

"Seven — no, six," Imel corrected.

"Well, that should be enough men to carry us through a running fight, though that many will be ticklish to slip past any large patrols unseen." Kane rubbed his beard in thought. "Coming along, Arbas?"

"No, thanks," the assassin replied. "My trade affords me both wealth and excitement enough for my tastes. Conspiracy on so large a scale is not to my liking."

They passed another hour settling details and swapping anecdotes over a jar of wine, and Imel began to think that Kane could be almost likable if you just avoided his eyes. The man was an enigma: gigantic, of savage strength, a hardened warrior; withal he was no barbarian outlaw, but a man of cold intelligence whose knowledge was extensive in whatever area their conversation touched.

At last when the storm had somewhat abated, Arbas and Imel slipped out and began to pick their course carefully back along the rain-slick ledge. They were almost beyond the tombs when the light of Arbas's lantern caught something white moving toward them.

"Watch it!" hissed Arbas and whipped out his sword. Biting back the taste of fear that the weird apparition had churned in his gut, Imel did likewise — hoping it was only soldiers that they had to deal with.

Arbas threw open the lantern shield. The white object suddenly fell with a slopping thud. Half-seen in the flickering light, emaciated figures with leprous flesh crouched and snarled then scurried off into the shadows. The shapes disappeared into the night, although an occasional pair of luminous eyes could be glimpsed beyond the lantern light.

Stealthily the two men approached the motionless object, and Imel suddenly felt recognition and with it, sickness. It was the corpse of the unfortunate bodyguard who had followed him and been cut down by Kane. The mystery of his presence here was clear at first glance. His body had been partially eaten, the fleshy parts of his face, arms, and legs gnawed away. Entrails hung across the ledge.

"Ghouls!" cursed Arbas. "Those were ghouls carrying him back to their dens to ripen!" He studied the shadows with grim intensity. "Well, let's just hope those carrion-eaters haven't the courage to attack two armed men with a light!"

"Ghouls!" Imel echoed. "What kind of man would choose as his lair these ghoul-infested tombs?"

II
Of Weavers and Webs

The storm began with renewed fury after Arbas had left with Efrel's emissary. Lightning flung forked tongues against the eroded escarpment; thunder blasted the pitted stone, shook the mouldering sleepers in their beds of plundered decay. Within Kane's lair, the reverberating echoes sounded distant and unreal. Flickers of bluish light stole past the curtained doorway in fitful effulgence.

Kane hunched in his chair, drinking cup after cup of wine. Ordinarily he would have drunk no more than constant vigilance permitted. Tonight his mood was blacker than the storm outside, and enemies human or inhuman might steal upon him at their peril. His cruel face was set in dark rage, and the death-fires in his cold blue eyes matched the flickering hell of the storm.

Kane drained his cup with a grunt and reached carefully for the wine jar. It was empty. Kane swore and flung it into a corner of the crypt, already littered with broken glass of earlier jars. The thick glass struck something soft and bounded away without shattering. Kane muttered a curse and went to retrieve it. He intended to smash it properly.

The wine bottle had bounded onto a mound of rotted debris in a disused section of the crypt. It hung in the air a few inches clear of the wreckage. Its thick, black-green glass was smeared with blood and ichor.

Kane took a pull from the new bottle he had broken open as he crossed the chamber. His uncanny eyes focused in the near-darkness.

A cave spider had spun her web across the niches with their mouldering coffins and sardonic skeletons. As large as Kane's hand, the white-furred arachnid had snared a bat. The heavy bottle, flung aimlessly in Kane's blind wrath, had struck weaver and prey together — pulping them against the debris. Clotted with fur and chitin and venom and gore, the chance missile spun slowly in the thick web. It was a thing of beauty, the web, and meticulously woven...

Kane laughed mirthlessly. His blade slashed the web to make a shroud.

III
Escape to the Ship

The rain had stopped, but the quiet of the night was broken intermittently by rumbles of distant thunder. High among the splintered rocks that guarded the unfrequented roadway leading up to the escarpment, Kane crouched behind a boulder. Beside him lay a small pack of personal belongings along with an assortment of weapons. Crossbow at hand, Kane scanned the darkened roadway for sign of Imel and his men. From the trail below he was impossible to be seen — even by eyes that might search intently. Kane had told Imel to meet him at a point farther along the cliffs — but always wary of treachery, he chose to await the renegade from this point of vantage.

Regretfully he considered the priceless volumes of black knowledge which he had been forced to leave behind. Well, he had committed most of them to memory, and the Black Priest would recover them presently and return the accursed tomes to their niches within his shadowy vaults. There had been a very early transcription of Alorri-Zrokros's monumental *Book of the Elders* that had particularly captured his admiration. The later transcriptions could be deadly from errors and omissions, Kane well knew. Presumably he might have found room to include just this one bulky volume in his pack, but he knew the crumbling parchment would never survive the frantic dash to escape the Combine's vengeance that lay ahead. Perhaps he would return to Lartroxia when those who now hunted him were dead and their curses forgotten...

His keen ears caught the sound of hooves on stone. Riders were coming up the road — but who were they? Kane cocked his weapon past its safety stop, then searched along the path with eyes that saw more in darkness than man should.

Eight riders and nine horses — presumably an extra mount saddled for him. Their approach was furtive; soldiers would be watchful, but more confident. Kane strained his eyes and recognized Imel on the lead horse. Certain that this was his party, Kane fired the crossbow bolt across their path, drumming it into the trunk of a dead tree. It brought them to an effective, albeit abrupt, halt.

"Don't piss in your pants! It's me!" Kane called to the startled riders. Gathering his kit, he scrambled down over the boulders. Muttered profanity greeted him as he paused to cut the quarrel from the hardened trunk where the iron head was bored with force that would pierce the best mail as if it were silk.

"Have you been followed?" asked Kane, wrenching the bolt free.

"We don't think so — though it's a damn fool who says for sure. Did you have to shake the crap out of us like that? I was damn well sure we'd run into an ambush!"

Kane recognized the angry growl. "Arbas! So you're still with us! Surely sentiment hasn't driven you to see me off."

"Bindoff decided I'd better go along as guide in case we have to start dodging patrols," Arbas explained, watching Kane stow his gear on the horse they provided him. "I told him you could get lost in these hills as well as I could, but he was persuasive."

"An assassin for a guide. I like that," chuckled Kane. He swung his heavy frame into the saddle and made certain his battle-axe was in easy reach. "Let's ride, then."

The nine riders retraced their way up the neglected road. When they finally reached the main roadway, they headed southwest for the coast. One man rode ahead to scout for patrols. It was Imel's plan to force their way to the hidden ship by following as rapid a course as possible — speed rather than stealth, and trust to luck that they might not run into anything a quick fight could not carry them through. Drumming hoofbeats muffled their flight along the sodden road beneath storm-heavy midnight skies.

Twice along the way they had to leave the road to make a wide detour of army outposts that kept a check on all travellers. Then the ride was suddenly halted as Essen, the scout, rushed back upon them.

Savagely reining in his plunging horse, he gasped out, "Five of them! They heard me turn back, and they're hot after me!"

Five. They had blundered upon a small patrol.

"Keep on running, and we'll ambush them," ordered Kane, taking charge without thinking twice. "Quick — the rest of you over here and take cover in the trees. They'll ride past hot on the trail and never look up. You with bows — get ready and we'll cut them down!"

He gave a quick critical glance at the terrain, then snapped, "You there without a bow — down the road and head off anyone who gets past us. Hurry, damn you!"

With a loud thrashing but not undue confusion, Kane's commands were carried out. Imel kept silent as he slid behind cover. He had had no illusions about who was commanding the band, anyway. Barely had they withdrawn into the shadow of the trees and readied their weapons when four Combine cavalrymen tore into view.

Hoping that Imel had carefully selected his party, Kane fired his crossbow and sent the iron quarrel drilling through the eye of the lead rider. A deadly chorus of *twangs* followed on his shot, and two other riders catapulted from their saddles — each with a pair of shafts quivering in his chest. The fourth rider raced through unscathed — saved not by bad marksmanship, but because there had been no time for the archers to call their targets.

"Stop him, Labe! Damn it man, stop him!" shouted Imel, alerting the survivor to his new danger. He jerked free his sword just in time to meet the attack of the Pellinite who lay waiting for him. Desperately the soldier traded blows with his adversary — knowing the others would be on him in an instant. Then, using a trick that caught the inferior horseman unaware, the cavalryman crashed his mount into the other. Startled, Labe swayed off-balance, and the cavalryman slashed his blade downward through unguarded shoulder and into the other's spine.

Ripping his sword free from the blood gushing corpse, the soldier bolted across the road for the shelter of the woods. He had just left the roadway when a searing pain pierced his throat and lifted him head over heels from his saddle. He fell in a broken jumble on the forest floor, blood pouring hotly over the quarrel that skewered his neck.

Kane lowered his crossbow, thankful that the brief struggle had given him time to get off a second shot. The crossbow's greater range and power balanced against the additional time it required to load and fire; someday Kane hoped to find a bow with equal power that was practical to use from horseback — not that a crossbow was much fun to manage on a running mount.

Essen rode back warily, having assumed from the disappearance of his pursuers that the skirmish was over. Kane questioned him, "Did I hear you right that there were five horsemen?"

"Yes, Five — I'm certain."

Kane made a remark about cavalrymen's mothers. "It seems then they weren't the eager fools I had hoped. They must have kept a man behind in case they ran into more than they could handle. Lato devour their cautious souls! If only they had been overconfident!"

"Now what?" Imel wanted to know.

"How far is it to your cove?"

"From Imel's description I'd guess we're maybe halfway," Arbas answered without enthusiasm.

Kane caught the assassin's eye and shrugged. "Well, the dice are cast now. The other soldier will have the whole Combine on the alert by now. It's suicide to bypass the roadway and try to slip through the forest now. Heavy patrols will be combing the area in an hour — they'll cordon us and close in. Our best chance now is to ride like the Pack of Volutio — and gamble we can beat them to the ship. So let's move out!"

Off they galloped, leaving the dead to watch silently the lightning-flecked heavens.

They had ridden perhaps an hour with no sign of pursuit. Twice more they had to break their course to bypass army posts, and Kane cursed the delay this entailed. Imel watched landmarks carefully, and concluded that they had only about another mile to travel before they could leave the main road and cut through an expanse of forest to reach the cove.

He was about to ride forward to tell Kane, who had moved slightly ahead, when the red-bearded man signaled a halt. Essen was returning from point at a gallop, and Kane wondered what the scout had learned.

A burst of lightning lit the landscape in a brief, sharp glare. In that split second of light, Kane caught sight of the large, dark-red blotch that soaked Essen's tunic — and the wind carried to his sensitive nostrils the odor of blood.

"No man wounded like that rides that well!" muttered Kane. His hand streaked for his dagger.

As his fingers closed on its hilt, the rider plunged into him. "Die — you treacherous hellspawn!" shrieked the man in Essen's tunic. His dagger flashed toward Kane's chest.

Clamping his knees against his mount's flank, Kane kept his balance as their horses collided. With a motion too quick to follow, he caught the descending arm with his left hand, halting the thrusting blade. The assailant screamed as Kane's inhuman grip snapped the bones in his wrist like brittle twigs — but the scream had hardly begun before it choked into a gurgle. Kane's other fist drove his own dagger deep into the man's belly and ripped upward in a disembowelling stroke.

The corpse fell heavily to the road, and the cloak was pulled back from his face. "That isn't Essen," observed one of the men sagaciously.

The horse on which the unknown attacker had ridden whinnied in wild pain. It rolled to its knees, then collapsed drunkenly upon the body of its rider. It kicked spasmodically for a moment and lay still. Its eyes were glazed in the lightning glare.

"His dagger cut the horse in falling," said Arbas, who had been closest to Kane.

Kane nodded. "Yes, a poisoned dagger — very pretty. They must have done for Essen, then sent this son of a bitch back for me on a suicide mission. By Tloluvin, the bastards really want me!"

He laughed bitterly. "One consolation, though. The Combine wouldn't have tried a stunt like this unless they're desperate. My guess is their soldiers at this end haven't had time to prepare for us yet."

"If they need time, we're giving them enough with stalling on our asses here," Imel snapped. "We've like a mile to cover before we can leave the road. So let's get out of here!"

"Right — only this is going to be tense," Kane warned. "Maybe we'll be in the clear once we leave the road — but this dumb fool's friends are almost certainly waiting for us before then. So we'll have to take things slow and careful until then, or they'll get us all like they did Essen. Just pray to your gods that we can get past them before reinforcements arrive.

"So don't panic and run into something — spread out a little and watch close! Fortunately the trees are thinning out some, so there's not as much cover for them — but look sharp for anything that doesn't fit!"

They moved on slowly, feeling the gnawing terror of hunted creatures.

Each moment they expected to hear the deadly hiss of an arrow. Never could a man be certain if he would draw a second breath before a hidden archer sealed his death. Muscles twitched under the painful strain. Flesh crawled in anticipation of an iron-fanged bite. Each shadow held a dozen crouching soldiers.

It was a very well-hidden ambush. Kane rode into it with almost no warning. However, the Combine soldiers were a little too widely dispersed, and too eager to strike. In the darkness and confusion, they were uncertain as to the number of Kane's men, perhaps. As it was, they failed to use their cover to maximum advantage and struck prematurely before their trap could close.

The tense silence of the night was abruptly slashed as the ambushers' arrows stabbed through the Pellinite ranks.

One arrow skidded across the top of Kane's shoulder, deflected by the chain mail he wore. "Split off into the woods!" he roared, thankful that someone had overrated his archery skill in attempting a difficult head shot. "Surround them and force the bastards into the road!" Kane thought it unlikely that his handful of men could surround anyone, but the attackers didn't know that.

One of his band was hit in the thigh, but otherwise the volley had somehow left them unscathed. Arrows shivered past them in the darkness as they instinctively sought cover. Desperately Kane spurred his mount from the road, bellowing for the others to follow.

Weaving rapidly through the trees, they crashed into the Combine cavalry patrol. Kane felt a surge of relief as he judged the soldiers numbered less than ten, with only a few armed with bows. No wonder their old-maid's caution — this was only a vanguard of the larger force Kane was certain must be moving toward them. The surprise of Kane's break for the sea after months of inaction, while it was generally assumed he must have fled or been killed — and not knowing the size of Kane's band — worked against the Combine patrol. Now, battle cries ringing, the cavalrymen galloped headlong from their ambush to meet their enemy hand-to-hand.

"Keep them apart! Don't let them form a charge!" yelled Kane, still not daring to believe that the main body of cavalry was yet to enter the combat. He lunged to parry the slash of the first soldier to meet him. Furiously they traded blows — the long curved blade of the cavalryman dancing nimbly back from Kane's massive broadsword. Then Kane hewed one mighty stroke against the other's saber that drove down the narrow blade, smashed its guard aside, and chopped through the arm that held it. The horseman had scarce time to realize his wound, before Kane's return slashed through his ribs.

Whirling about, Kane just met the charge of another horseman on his opposite flank. The swordsman was good — Arbas's opinion of the Combine's cavalry was well justified — and it took all Kane's effort to cope with the lighter blade. And now another cavalryman galloped up on Kane's other side — facing him with death from two sides at once.

Seeing his new danger, Kane swiftly reached for the battle-axe at hand on his saddle. Instead of attacking Kane's unprotected flank, the newcomer discovered too late — as had so many before him — that Kane could use his right arm with almost the proficiency of his left. Risking all on one effort, Kane slung the heavy axe around in one awful blow that no sword or shield could turn. The assailant was hurled from his horse, his chest a torn ruin.

The momentary diversion proved nearly fatal to Kane. Wrenched off balance by the heavy axe, it was all he could do to deflect a quick thrust from his other opponent. Knocked aside at the final instant, the blade still slipped under Kane's guard to smash agonizingly into his side. The mail held true and stopped the edge, but its force drove the chain links cutting and bruising into his flesh. Kane snarled in pain and relentlessly forced the other back. The soldier's guard faltered under the strain, and Kane disabled him with a cut to the shoulder. As the Lartroxian frantically sought to raise his crippled sword arm, Kane thrust his blade through his unprotected abdomen.

Sending his steed hurtling over the dead, Kane recovered his axe and turned to the battle behind him. Three of the Pellinites were down, including the man who had been hit during the ambush. Three of the cavalrymen survived. One was engaged in a ringing interchange with Imel, who was bleeding from two minor cuts on his arm and other shoulder. As Kane watched, Imel dispatched the man with a sudden thrust to his heart. Arbas was occupied with another of the horsemen in a cat-like duel, but was slowly getting the upper hand. The other Pellinite fought gamely with the remaining cavalryman in an uncertain match that Imel decided by charging the unsuspecting soldier from behind and running him through.

With a sudden burst of desperate energy, the surviving soldier of the Combine forced Arbas back in his saddle, then plunged his blade into the neck of the assassin's horse. Trumpeting in pain, the horse crumpled, throwing Arbas heavily to the ground. Landing clear of the horse's flailing body, Arbas lay dazed by the impact. He groped dully for his fallen sword. The soldier hurtled madly upon him, leaning from his saddle to deliver the decapitating blow.

Kane's arm snapped forward. His flashing axe clove through the soldier's helmet and skull to bury its razor edge in his chest.

Recovering quickly, Arbas lurched to his feet and seized the bridle of the riderless horse. Sword in hand, he swung into the gore-spattered saddle. "Thanks! Are we even yet?"

"I'm one up on you at least," grunted Kane dourly. "Four of us left? Better than we deserve. We may still make it — if we don't run into any more trouble. Let's get out of here — Arbas, leave the bastard's ears on his head!"

The assassin reluctantly abandoned his trophy. With a pounding of hooves the victors vanished into the darkness as rain began to fall. Pushing their tired mounts to the fullest, they raced for the trail that led to the cove. Trees flashed monotonously by in the drizzle, and mist grew deeper with the approach of dawn. It seemed impossible that they would not miss the turn-off.

Then Imel shouted, "There it is! That's it just ahead!" Triumphantly he pointed to where an almost indistinct trail left the roadway. "We're in the clean" He laughed. Spirits rising with escape in sight at last, the fugitives dashed for the trail.

No sooner had they reached it than shouts and the clamour of many riders reached their ears. Bursting into view and bearing rapidly down upon them was a force of fifty or more cavalry. The trap had closed — reinforcements had gathered. The Combine's indefatigable hunters had finally caught up with their prey. Clearly only speed could snatch them from death's touch now.

Kane snarled in rage. "May their wives and daughters rot with pox — the bastards have sighted us! Lead on to your craft, Imel. And ride for your life!"

The headlong flight was a panic-ridden nightmare to Imel. Hoping desperately that he would not blunder off the trail in the darkness, he plummeted through the dripping forest. Branches heavy with wet foliage overhung the path, forcing him to bend low against his weary mount's froth-spattered neck. Night-prowling forest beasts started from the path ahead and fled crashing through the underbrush. It seemed inevitable that a clutching root, a sudden trunk or branch would end the ride in plunging disaster.

The trees had thinned out barely enough to permit their rushing passage, and in the darkness this sparse cover prevented their pursuers from getting any exact idea as to their course. This alone saved them at first — and made it possible to stretch a scant head start into a respectable lead as the minutes flew by.

The horses were ready to give out, when the trees suddenly vanished altogether, and they streaked out of the forest onto a wide gravel beach. The rain-wet stones glistened in the lightning blasts. With relief Imel discerned his ship waiting a few hundred yards offshore.

"A boat! A boat! Where's the rowboat?" he yelled, gazing frenziedly through the rain and grey mist. "I ordered them to have the rowboat at ready!"

"There!" called Kane. He pointed to where several sailors were running toward them from a beached rowboat.

"Thank Onthe! They did as I ordered!" gasped Imel jubilantly. He raced toward them, shouting, "Cast off! Cast off! Double wages to each of you for this — but damn you, cast off!"

Doggedly clinging to his kit, Kane leaped to the beach and sent his mount pelting off into the mist. Imel had picked his horses well, or they could never have made it. In mad haste they piled into the rowboat and put out from shore.

Scarcely had the boat cleared the surf when the Combine cavalry streamed out of the woods and onto the beach. The released mounts had momentarily confused them in the night. Straining mightily, the rowers pulled over the cove toward the ship, taking them out of range of the hail of arrows and curses that followed from the shore. The pouring rain served as cover, and none of the missiles reached its target.

"Goodbye, dear friends — and thanks for your most courteous hospitality!" shouted Kane and laughed derisively. "Someday I'll return to repay you in kind!"

Curses of baffled rage answered him from the mist cloaked beach — along with floundering splashes as a few reckless ones attempted to swim after them. But the Pellinite craft was set to sail, and the Lartroxians were helpless to stop them.

Kane wiped the froth and spray from his beard and flowing red hair. He grinned at Arbas. "Well, then, so you have decided to come along after all. It seems that expediency remains your god."

"An assassin's services are in demand in any realm," shrugged Arbas philosophically.

IV
Passage to Pellin

$\mathcal{A}$rbas carefully adjusted the telescope for the tenth time and squinted through the brass tube with determined concentration. Kane watched him with amusement. "Damn it, Kane!" he muttered in annoyance. "I still can't even find their frigging sails in this charlatan's toy!"

He lowered the telescope and regarded it with a frown, the powerful muscles of his lean arms twitching in eagerness to crumple the frail instrument.

"Don't!" interceded Kane in anticipation of the other's whim. "That little toy required weeks of painstaking craftsmanship to turn out, and I think friend Imel values it more highly than the jewellery he loads himself down with."

Arbas snorted and closed the telescope with callous irreverence, "Right. Our well-dressed friend likes his pretty toys. Sure don't want to piss him off. No, wouldn't want that!"

"I don't think you like Imel," Kane remarked.

Arbas grinned at some pleasant thought. "No. No, I just don't appreciate the finer things, I guess."

"I don't think Imel likes you very much, either."

The assassin raised the telescope once again. He worked its sectioned tube smartly. "No. Don't think Imel appreciates the finer things, either."

"You propose a quandary."

"It's a natural talent." Arbas pressed his lips together and sighted through the lens resolutely. "Ah — think maybe I just caught a glimpse there. Yeah, the Combine of Southern Lartroxia lost its greatest philosopher when Arbas left the dusty path of scholarship for the alleys of Nostoblet."

Kane spat into the sea. "Yeah, that's what you've told me on occasion. Though when you ever graced the halls of academe is still a puzzle — unless it was to stalk some sage whose ideas offended someone with wealth."

"I was one of the most promising students of the city — a rising young star, no less. I'd already begun to gather students about *me* — when one day I wondered whether they must be as bored with it all as I was…" Arbas sighed.

"In the tale's last retelling wasn't there a girl…"

"All that and more. My memoirs will someday fill a shelf. Stirring adventure, ribald wit, biting social commentary, ageless wisdom. If you'll cut the sarcasm, I might feel moved to devote a volume to our lurid association."

He fumbled with the instrument, nearly dropping it into the sea. "And if this damned ship would stop pitching, I might be able to hold this diabolical device on target long enough to focus it. Why don't they carve these lenses large enough to see something through them, anyway?

"Yeah, and I'll spend several pages telling how I carved my name in Imel's heart, for no payment other that the gratitude of my fellow man — and to the dismay of jewellers and tailors all over the Island Empire. Hey, I'm getting the hang of it now, I think. You get the object in view, then adjust the sections."

"I think you'll find the Imperial aristocracy attach considerable importance to the refinements of dress," Kane pointed out. "Prestige is extremely important to them, and a man's appearance should reflect his wealth and rank — just as their elaborate court etiquette and code of conduct is a mark of breeding. They have made a fine art of snobbery, it seems. Imel probably feels the strain of his efforts to improve his station in their society, and we have been a trifle rough with him. Anyway, he fights well enough in a scramble — so watch him. Besides, we're allies for the moment, don't forget."

"Didn't know you were an authority on the customs and mores of the Thovnosian Empire," Arbas scoffed.

"Heads up! Here comes our man now," interjected Kane, changing the subject.

The Thovnosian's spirits had improved considerably once he had escaped the pressures of his mission to the mainland. Decent food and drink, a bath, and a long sleep had driven the harassed look from his features. To be treated with due respect by his men after a week of skulking undercover in the slums of Nostoblet had bolstered his self-image, and a change to finer garments had restored a swagger to his step. With highest gratification he had watched his body-slave commit his ragged costume to the sea. Now — bathed, massaged with scented oils, his face shaved clean, his long hair meticulously combed down to his shoulders — clothed in dark green silk hose and shirt, brown woolen jacket with silver tracery, soft leather knee boots — resplendent with four costly rings, gem-set cloak pin at his throat, jewel-pommeled dagger with silver-studded scabbard and belt — now he once again considered himself a whole man, and no relation to the sixth son of an impoverished and wine-besotted petty-gentry father, who had been driven from home years back.

He sauntered across the main deck and sprang up the stairs onto the high stern deck, where Kane and Arbas stood gazing across the sea. There was hard muscle beneath the silk, Arbas conceded. Although the slender Thovnosian renegade was maybe fifty pounds lighter than the broad shouldered assassin, he was of equal height — and Arbas had seen that he could wield a blade with dangerous speed and skill. There was a deceptive frankness about his thin face — a boyishness contributed to by clean-shaven features and a hint of freckles under the tan.

Imel nodded greeting to Kane and raised a quizzical eyebrow to the seemingly preoccupied assassin. "Teaching our landlubber to use a telescope?" he queried. He had heard with profound regret that Arbas had shown no seasickness despite a reckless appetite.

Arbas bristled. He had been to sea for several short excursions and considered himself a bit of an old salt — if somewhat unfamiliar with a telescope.

"Arbas actually is an old hand with a glass," Kane offered smoothly. "He's fascinated with the precise powers of resolution your instrument demonstrates."

"Hmmm." Imel brushed back a windblown lock of brown hair. "I thought I saw him looking through it backward a moment ago."

"I was admiring the flawless workmanship," growled Arbas, fending for himself. Though expensive, telescopes were not a rarity. But when a man seldom needs to see farther than across an alley, such devices were uncommon — and Arbas had far more use for eyes that saw all about him, rather than at great distance.

Imel discreetly dropped the matter. He gestured toward the two sails that rose in the distance over their wake. "Still following us, are they?" he observed. "If I may borrow this."

He accepted the telescope and expertly trained it on first one, then the other of the pursuing vessels. Silently he watched them, lips pursed in concentration.

He handed the glass to Kane. "Well, as you have by now observed for yourself," he glanced blandly at Arbas, "both ships are indeed Combine vessels. That lets out our other vague conjecture that they might be curious pirates."

The sails had first been sighted late in the morning. Imel had arisen at the lookout's cry, but had not deemed the matter of more pressing importance than his own grooming. The sails had persisted into the afternoon, and from idle speculation it had become quite certain that they were being pursued.

"The Lartroxians were always an obstinate people," mused Kane. "The claws of their vengeance reach farther than I had anticipated.

"They saw us escape by ship, and so knew that we must sail through the mouth of the Bay of Lartroxia. In the darkness we slipped past any patrol vessels that waited there, but they have other ships stationed along the coastal islands. At first light of day, they must have alerted all craft within range of their signal mirrors. Knowing our point of departure, they had only to plot an intercept course for all possible routes leading out of the Bay of Lartroxia. Simple enough," Kane concluded. "All things considered, it's a bit surprising that only two ships were able to pick up our wake."

"Not so surprising considering the general ineptitude of the Combine's navy," Imel remarked — displaying a deep-water sailor's scorn for those who seldom sailed out of sight of land.

"Still, two ships discovered us," Arbas pointed out. "And to my untutored eye it would seem that they're gaining"

Kane studied the ships in question carefully through the glass. "Gaining slowly, but closing on us nonetheless," he acknowledged. "The Combine has a few large vessels in their navy, after all, and we appear to have drawn two of their finest. They're biremes — with that long, slender hull some shipbuilders are experimenting with of late, trying to design an oared vessel that's as fast as a good craft under full sail. The trick is balancing keel enough for the sail without too much drag under oars. They're carrying more sail than a bireme should — see how high their masts stand. Works great until a strong wind turns them bottom up, which usually happens if the ballast and keel aren't altered just so."

He uneasily contemplated their own small ship. Imel had picked a blockade runner, with an eye toward combining secrecy, speed, and fighting power — in order of descending importance. His choice was a lean racing hull that was built low to the waves and displayed all the sail her design could handle. She was also fitted with a single row of oars, which could be unshipped in a calm. The crew were picked fighting men, but of necessity few in number. The pursuing biremes had easily twice their size and strength.

"I think it will be unfortunate for us if it comes to an open battle," Kane went on. "And that seems rather likely. With the wind they're slowly gaining on us. Should the wind die, they have over three times our rowing speed, at a guess. Our only chance is to lose them both in the darkness — if we can hold our lead until after nightfall."

Imel's confidence seemed undimmed. "They can't overtake us before morning," he estimated coolly. "And whether we lose them in the night or not, before dawn we'll have reached the northernmost limits of the Sorn-Ellyn — assuming the wind holds. They won't follow us very far into the Sorn-Ellyn."

"A questionable prediction, considering the Combine's well-demonstrated tenacity," Arbas commented sarcastically. "Besides which, from your lurid account I recall that the Sorn-Ellyn isn't a very lucky stretch of water to sail across. Perhaps your men would prefer to take their chances with the Combine's navy."

Imel smiled without rancour. "Efrel herself commanded me to sail across the Sorn-Ellyn. We did so unscathed on our voyage to Nostoblet; we shall do so again on our return. I have complete confidence in Efrel's wisdom in such matters. And I don't believe the Lartroxians will follow us across the Sorn-Ellyn."

Kane shrugged, having nothing more feasible to put forward as an alternative. Arbas still looked dubious.

"Perhaps, Arbas, you might care to make some sort of bet on this matter," Imel suggested suavely. "Say that prized dirk of yours against my jewelled dagger. A token bet, and I give you ridiculous odds — a blade of dubious origin against one set with gems of obvious value."

Arbas ran his finger along his long mustaches in thought, not wanting to permit the other to outface him. At length he shook his head. "No. No, I don't like that bet. To my way of thinking, a knife's worth lies in its blade and not in a garish hilt. I've seen pimps in Nostoblet who'd be embarrassed to wear that thing. But aside from that, it occurs to me that if I should win the bet, it is most unlikely that I'd live long enough to enjoy my prize."

"I hadn't thought you so cautious," chided Imel. "We shall see in the morning, though."

The remainder of the day passed uneventfully, with the Combine ships gaining enough on them by nightfall to discern with unaided eye their double-tiered oars. Still the wind held for them. The Pellinite blockade runner sailed unerringly toward the ill famed Sorn-Ellyn.

After darkness hid their pursuers from view, Kane sat up for several hours drinking wine and throwing dice with Arbas. Neither man gave full attention to the game, though, as their ears were strained to catch the first sounds of the biremes closing in on them in the night. Their craft ran without lights, a black arrow in the starless darkness. In the distance the lights of the biremes bobbed up through the mist now and again. They were on a converging course with the blockade-runner — and gaining.

The game at last broke up when Kane forgot what his previous point had been, and Arbas was at a loss to remember as well. Arbas stoically collected his small pile of winnings and left for his hammock. Kane was in a dark mood and remained on deck with the wine. At length he lay back on a mound of rigging and spare sail, and lapsed into a fitful sleep.

His dreams were troubled, but he slept on without ever quite returning to full consciousness. Then toward dawn he started suddenly from his dreams — uncertain what had been going through his mind, not knowing why he had awakened. *There.* His hand closed comfortably about his swordhilt. Again the sound. From far off in the night it came.

The creaking of timber? The shouting of men? He concentrated on the sound. No. It sounded more like the splintering of timber. Voices howled in terror. Sounds too dim to distinguish. And silence.

Silence.

In alarm Kane reeled to his feet. The wind had died with the approach of dawn. Above him the sails hung limp, listlessly rippling with a vagrant night breeze. Kane considered arousing the ship to man the oars, but discarded the idea. The Combine vessels would be in a similar position, and in the darkness the sound of oars would give away the position of the first ship to utilize them. Presumably the watch had already informed Imel, and he had reached a similar decision. Perhaps they might drift awhile until dawn. Then they could at least appraise their position.

He lay awake, watching for the first light in the east. After maybe an hour the sky began to turn grey, and he went to the rail grimly. Hearing shuffling and scraping on the deck behind him, he turned to see Imel emerge from his cabin, stretching luxuriously.

The Thovnosian yawned his way over to him. Kane wondered how much of his air of unconcern was assumed. "Morning," greeted Imel. "I had the watch wake me soon as it grew light. See, you beat me to the sunrise anyway. Can you see anything yet?"

Kane shook his head. Mists still obscured the waves, with a blanket deeper than the night's darkness. Then the rising sun seared through, and the sea around them was empty as far as he could see in the fading mists of dawn.

"Damned wind hasn't started up yet, either," Imel observed with a curse. "That's going to mean another night on the Sorn-Ellyn, unless it picks up before noon. I'll get the men to their oars."

His orders were carried out. The sleepy crew filed onto deck — grumbling that fighting men should have to do the work of galley slaves — another luxury that space had precluded. The sky grew brighter and the mist cleared. Still the sea remained empty.

The craft slowly got underway as the rowers worked her up to speed. The sun appeared and climbed out of the sea. There was no sign of either Combine bireme to be seen, even after Kane slowly scanned the horizon through the telescope.

"They didn't follow us into the Sorn-Ellyn after all," Imel reminded them, after it was certain that they were alone on the ocean. "Even a Lartroxian's persistence must have a limit, it seems. Efrel once again has called the game down to the last exigency." For all his complacency, there was a note of relief in Imel's smooth tone.

"So it seems," agreed Kane softly. His full attention was directed through the telescope at that moment.

In the distance he could make out scattered fragments of wreckage. Bits of broken timbers, cargo of a ship's store, unidentifiable flotsam. It was from a large vessel — and a recent wreck, as the debris would have drifted far apart before long. There were no bodies floating in the tangle.

But there was nothing to run aground against here in the Sorn-Ellyn. Could the biremes have collided? A simple collision could not have splintered the hull into insignificant fragments. What then?

Kane handed the telescope to Arbas. He doubted that they would again catch sight of pursuing sails.

V
Gods in Darkness

It was late at night, and all aboard ship slept soundly, when the seaman on watch saw standing at the rail a dark figure in a hooded cloak. Glad for the companionship on this lonely night, he joined him there in silence. The other's face was hidden in the shadow of his hood, so the watch was uncertain as to the tall stranger's identity. He pondered little over the mystery as he leaned on the rail, looking out over the nighted ocean.

A strong breeze was sending the ship knifing over the foam-flecked black waves, rippling water that coldly reflected the pale light of the gibbous moon above. Looking up, the sailor saw only a few stars, and those gleamed evilly — like cats' eyes in the firelight. For the heavens were obscured by heavy clouds. Strange clouds — racing across the skies in the night wind, and forming fantastic patterns as they passed over the dead-white moon. Weird, titanic figures that writhed grotesquely, as if possessed with life — contorting ominously about the few leering stars and watched over by an insane moon.

"Look at the skies!" exclaimed the seaman in wonder. "Why do the clouds roll about so wildly?"

"They are gods in darkness," came the rasping reply. "And they weave the lattice of man's fate from the infinite shades of cosmic darkness. You see their shadows now — for the forces of evil are gathering in celebration of the coming days."

The words seemed cracked and distorted, echoing across eons of time and space. The seaman started at these eldritch tones, and looked around at the speaker.

There was no one beside him at the rail.

Part Two

VI
Within the Black Citadel

Approached from its northern coast, Pellin was a dark, forbidding island. Its cliffs were sheer columns of black basalt, broken and eroded by the winds and pounding surf. Beyond the headland, the soil was thin and infertile. Trees grew sparse and stunted along the cliff, and farther inland black and gnarled trunks struggled above a forest of vines and underbrush.

At intervals could be seen barren spots where even this vegetation refused to take root. From these wastelands strange piles of basalt gleamed darkly in the sun — weird masses of stone too regular to be called the work of nature, too unthinkably ancient to be the work of man. Cyclopean ruins that had brooded over the sea for lonely centuries.

To the southern side of the island lay the wide harbor of Prisarte, main city of the island and seat of Efrel's power. The harbor was well protected, with fortifications guarding the narrow straits that opened into its large bay, now filled with many ships as Efrel prepared for war. The bay itself was surrounded by dry docks and shipbuilding yards, warehouses and barracks, unlovely structures of timber and basalt, with a few lavishly constructed palaces of the nobility easily discernible.

But dominating the entire view was Dan-Legeh, black fortress of Prisarte — the looming ancestral castle of the Pellin blood since time immemorial. Dan-Legeh was a bizarre megalithic structure, whose towering walls were strangely reminiscent of the ancient ruins that haunted the desolate regions of the island. Various sections of the fortress had obviously been annexed to the original over the years. One glance might notice a tower that seemed somehow out of place; another look might reveal a wall of one construction awkwardly joined to another wall of different masonry. The additions were ancient themselves, relics of attempts to make Dan-Legeh more acceptable for human usage. They looked discordant, ajar with the original. Legend told that the fortress had stood here before man first came to the island, but Pellin was a land that abounded with such myths.

Dan-Legeh was an ominous hulking mass, silhouetted against the sunset as Kane sailed into the harbor of Prisarte. A thin wind was blowing, and the city lay under the long shadow of its fortress. Dusk had fallen by the time Kane and his associates touched shore to meet the armed escort there awaiting them. The twilight grew deeper as they approached Dan-Legeh, riding along the narrow gloomy streets to the clanking of accouterments and the deceptive flicker of torchlight. Night closed over them when they finally stood before the mighty drawbridge and barbicans that guarded the main entrance to the citadel.

An officer stepped forward to meet them as they entered Dan-Legeh — a powerful nobleman from his extravagant attire and splendid accouterments. He was tall and slender of build — with the pale, handsome features and glowing black hair of the Pellinite aristocracy. His slenderness was that of a cat — silk-smooth muscles and perfect coordination. A man beautiful and deadly as the black panther. His eyes were as expressionless as a cat's as he came toward them.

"Congratulations, Imel," he said by way of greeting, "on fulfillment of a most difficult mission. I knew our confidence was well placed. Well done."

He went on crisply, "You, then, must be Kane." He hesitated over the name, as one does in repeating an obscenity in polite company.

The two men regarded one another in cool appraisal for a moment. Kane instantly sensed a deep feeling of hatred and rivalry on the part of the Pellinite. His rigid stance and haughty mien made it clear that he had been opposed to Kane's presence in Pellin since Imel's mission had been planned. Only his mistress's command and a sense of *noblesse oblige* barred him from overt hostility. Kane found ironic amusement in that the first to welcome him to Pellin should be a deadly enemy whom he had never before met.

The Pellinite lord looked at him with barely restrained contempt. Their eyes met, and he hastily glanced away. His manner became more cautious — calculating.

"I am Oxfors Alremas," he announced. "My will is here subservient to none but that of Efrel." He paused to let this sink in, then recollecting himself, he went on unconvincingly: "I welcome you to Pellin and to Dan-Legeh. There will be dinner served for you presently. First, though, let me guide you to your quarters. I suspect you will need to wash away the salt of your voyage. More suitable garments await you there, should you care to dress in accordance with your new position."

Biting his lip pensively, Imel watched Kane and Arbas leave with Alremas. Then, shaking his head as if to clear it, he turned to the remaining soldiers and ordered them back to their barracks. As for himself, a change to better clothes was in order as well, certainly. And then to the banquet Alremas had mentioned.

Moving away, Imel thought of wine, laughter, and the roguish company of the court ladies. He felt curiously relieved that Kane was no longer his responsibility.

VII
Queen of Night

Kane found his quarters to be of truly imperial splendour. His taste for luxury was entranced by the costly furs, silks, and tapestries that covered the spacious rooms. Gracing the chambers throughout were many expensive and beautiful statues, ornamental pieces and *objets d'art* that complemented the exquisitely done furnishings. And there was a fine sunken pool for bathing, in which Kane found pleasure with the lovely slave girl sent to him as a personal servant.

Dinner was similarly magnificent. The banquet was served in a gigantic firelit great hall, with countless dishes of roasted meat and cups of foaming ale or wine carried all about by scampering serving wenches. The great hall was filled with almost two hundred guests for the most part, nobility and officers. Loud talk and laughter rose from the long wooden tables to the high vaulted ceiling.

But it seemed to Kane that the laughter was a little thin and strained; their voices held a nervous quality not wholly hidden. Moreover, the shadows in the great hall were somehow too deep. More than once his eyes caught quick traces of movement from the shadowy curtains. And throughout the meal his keen senses were aware of some hidden surveillance — one of almost inhuman intensity.

Although its place was set, the master seat of the head table stood vacant. Kane sat at the head table with Oxfors Alremas on one side and Imel on the other. Arbas was several places down — the Pellinites were uncertain of his status, but assumed he was of some importance since he had come with Kane. Conversation with the others at the table was guarded and kept to matters of commonplace. So Kane bided his time, waiting for things to develop. Of Efrel there was still no sign.

As the meal drew to a close Alremas turned to Kane, who was just emptying his tankard. "Now that you have had a chance to recover somewhat from your journey, I'm to take you to Efrel."

Kane nodded impassively and rose to follow him. Alremas led him through a bewildering progression of stone stairways and long, winding passageways. The interior of the fortress was far more extensive than outward appearances indicated. Again Kane sensed that much of the walls and stairways were alien to the original external construction — perhaps additions made after the original portions had collapsed with age. Always the outside wall could be distinguished by its cyclopean architecture — megalithic blocks of basalt cunningly fitted. To raise such a wall would have demanded an engineering genius of a degree unknown in this age.

At length they stopped before a heavy door of iron-studded oak. Alremas knocked loudly with his dagger hilt, and the door was opened by a huge slave.

The obese servant Kane recognized as the typical eunuch bodyguard of a lady's private chambers. What was not typical was that this man stood close to seven feet in stature, and his massive form hinted of considerable strength under the rubbery blanket of fat. A parang of formidable length hung in a sheath at his belt. His face was without expression.

"Leave your weapons with the eunuch," growled Alremas. He gave Kane a glowering look and strode away down the shadowy passageway.

Crossing the threshold, Kane entered a spacious anteroom — boudoir seemed an inappropriate term for such a chamber. The room was brightly lit and decorated in a bizarre fashion. It bore an obvious feminine touch in its furnishings, but there were other objects of a sinister, diabolical nature — weird paintings and bits of statuary, strangely bound volumes, unusual pieces of apparatus and alchemical impedimenta, exotic incenses and unfamiliar scents. From somewhere Kane sensed an indefinable aura of evil. It was a macabre hybrid of a sorcerer's study and a lady's boudoir.

At one end of the room was a curtained doorway. The curtain was only a thin veil, and no light shone behind it. A person watching from the room beyond would be able to observe occurrences on the other side, while he himself remained invisible.

Not particularly relishing the situation, Kane sat down and watched the curtain. He had not long to wait.

"So, then. You are Kane." The low voice from beyond the veil was an eerie one. Its accents were beautiful and feminine, but somehow distorted and maimed. It was as if the speaker had difficulty forming the words in her throat — as if the speaker were struggling to articulate a rage beyond sane expression.

"And you are Efrel?" Kane inquired.

Her answer was a hateful titter. "Yes — and *no*! I *was* Efrel. I suppose convenience dictates that I still be called by this name. But I am not Efrel. Efrel is dead. Two years dead. But I am dead — and I am Efrel! Or was Efrel, since Efrel is dead. So where does that leave us, Kane? It doesn't matter. Yes, do call me Efrel. It will do for now.

"But the dead do not always die! Beware, Netisten Maril, of the dead that yet live!" The last was a maddened shriek. Silence followed as Efrel fought to control her passion.

She began again. "Yes, I am Efrel. And by now Imel should have told you of my past — and something about your place in my plans."

Kane nodded. "Imel told me that you intend to avenge yourself upon Netisten Maril, and to reestablish Pellin as the center of power in the Empire. According to him, I was summoned to command your naval forces in the coming war. At this point, however, it isn't at all clear to me why you don't rely on one of your own generals for this. Oxfors Alremas seems definitely to feel the position of command should be his."

Again laughter. "Poor Alremas. Dear Alremas. He was always faithful to me — in bed and in battle. I think he has assumed all the while that he should hold the reins of power in my new Empire — and leave my pretty hands for more delicate pursuits. It was cruel of me to indulge his conceit, don't you think? I believe he hates you for usurping the position he had taken for granted. Poor faithful Alremas.

"He comes of proud blood, though, and I'm afraid his jealousy may now detract from his usefulness. And, of course, I couldn't forgive him that transgress. But Alremas couldn't manage this task, anyway. He's better at roles that suit his feline cunning — intrigue rather than outright war. No, he couldn't be my general. Enough of Alremas. You will be given command over him, as well as command of the rest of my forces."

Alremas might have further thoughts on that, mused Kane. He continued, "But neither can I understand why you should choose me to command your rebellion — for that matter, how did you know of me? Granted, I have enjoyed some fame as a general in several campaigns within the continent east of your islands. But I have only recently come this far into the western reaches of Lartroxia. I wasn't aware that any tales were told of me in these distant regions."

"Are you so sure of this, Kane?" Efrel's voice was edged with mordant mockery. "No. You know why I have summoned you. I have summoned you, Kane — evoked you as I might a demon. The people do not lie when they say I am a sorceress. It is true that I have delved deeply into the mysteries of the black arts, of the ancient gods who have not yet entirely forgotten their home of old…

"But of this you will know more later. For now it pleases me to entertain you with a story. A tale which you already know well — or the demon who whispered at to me is a liar."

Efrel's Tale

My tale goes back over two centuries, to days when Thovnos and Pellin were but two of the many disunited islands in this region. Tresli, Josten, Fisitia, Parwi, Raconos, Quarnora, and all the other lesser islands — unstable independent realms and holdings. Petty kingdoms weakened and impoverished from recurrent internecine wars between the islands.

In addition to its larger land masses, this region is dotted with a vast number of tiny islands. Islands which provided countless harbors and bases for fishermen — or for pirates. Yes, there were a great many pirates here in those troubled years. For the advantages of inexhaustible places of refuge, ineffectual retaliation by the authorities, and heavy interisland commerce made this region a true paradise for their kind.

But such pirates were never much more than a dangerous nuisance — for like the islands, they were weak and unorganized. They were but jackals, stealthy killers who preyed upon the helpless and the unwary. A single well armed escort would send the jackals scurrying to their lairs.

Then there came into the islands a stranger from the Southern Lands. He was a ruthless and deadly fighter in combat, as well as a genius at naval strategy and tactics. In a few years he built up an unassailable pirate stronghold on the rocky island of Montes. His rivals he either absorbed or destroyed. Under his formidable command was a gigantic pirate fleet established — a bloody, deadly sword that first swept the seas of commerce and soon threatened the very ports themselves.

Arrogant squadrons of the pirate fleet prowled the seas at will, attacking any ships that they encountered. Spies in every port kept them informed of the merchants' shipments and of their desperate countermeasures. No secrets escaped the pirates. No convoy was too well guarded for them to dare. Even the largest warships of the islands' rulers fell prey to them, and it invited certain disaster for any vessel to venture away from its harbor.

Eventually the pirates had the sea to themselves, for not even a fishing boat risked leaving its port. The sea wolves had driven away their prey. It seemed that the pirates must now disband and seek more prosperous sea lanes elsewhere, but their leader had more ambitious designs than this. With the seas barren of commerce, he drew his fleet together and turned his might against the cities of the coast. Now he struck at the very sources of the riches he had plundered upon the sea.

Out of the night, his ravening fleet would sail into some sleeping port. A short battle would wipe out all organized resistance, and the city would be his to plunder. Then with ruthless efficiency was the stricken seaport utterly despoiled of its wealth. His pirate hordes would overflow the streets with bloodshed and rapine — taking whatever they wanted in booty and women. When the city was sacked, they made a pyre of their carnage and sailed into a dawn reddened from its blazing ruin.

And the man who commanded the pirates — the man whose evil genius had forged this awesome weapon of destruction — he was named *Kane*.

But the success of the pirates was ultimately to prove their undoing. The warring island lords at last realized that they were in extreme danger from Kane's pirate empire. Forgetting their private quarrels, they followed their enemy's example and united themselves under one overlord — the house of Pellin, chosen because of its prestige and power. The new Empire gathered together its scattered forces and pieced together a fleet powerful enough to challenge the pirates. After long and inconclusive months of skirmishes and chase, the Imperial fleet under the command of Netisten Ehbuhr of Thovnos attacked Kane on the sea before his pirate stronghold on Montes. The fighting was vicious and the issue long in doubt — for both admirals were brilliant commanders, and it was evident that the fate of the islands would be decided by this desperate battle. Throughout the day the struggle raged across the sea, but as the evening approached, the vastly greater numbers of ships and fighting men that the Empire could draw upon swung the balance of battle.

Realizing he was too badly outnumbered to continue the fight on the sea, Kane withdrew the shattered remains of his fleet into the harbor of his cliff-top fortress. The siege that followed wore on for hard and bloody days, but the catapults and trebuchets of the Empire gradually smashed down the stronghold's defenses. At a fearsome cost in lives, Netisten Ehbuhr forced his way into the devastated citadel, and in one deadly battle the grim survivors of the pirate horde were slain.

The battle was a costly one for the new Empire as well, and many noble lives met red doom at Montes — including the principal lords of the house of Pellin. Thus was Netisten Ehbuhr able to usurp control of the new Empire for himself and his line — for there were none to oppose the hero of Montes among the surviving aristocracy. And so the usurper line of Netisten has sat upon the Imperial throne for all but the infancy of the Empire's existence — stealing the throne that rightly belongs to Pellin!

And a most curious thing was discovered after the last of the pirates had fallen. Although many soldiers had seen Kane fighting alongside his men up until the very end of the final battle, his body was never discovered. No trace of Kane was ever found, even though the victors searched meticulously through the blackened ruins and crimson heaps of the slain for his body. Some maintained that Kane's men had hidden his corpse to save it from dishonor. Others laughed at this conceit and argued that the pirate lord must have escaped through some secret tunnel, slipped past their lines and sailed away from another part of the island.

It was strange, to be sure. For years thereafter, those who dwelt beside the sea still felt the gnawing fear that one night Kane and his black fleet would return to wreak bloody vengeance for his defeat at Montes. Even today his name is a curse — an anathema of evil, terror, and rapine.

And so the dread name of Kane the pirate lord has merged into the dark legends of our people. A demonic figure was this Kane of old. His past was shrouded in rumors and myth even in his lifetime, and his death could never be proven. He flashed through our troubled history like some all-destroying comet, appearing suddenly from the blackness of night and as abruptly vanishing to regions unimagined. Men told that Kane was a giant in stature, more powerful than ten strong men. In battle no man could stand before him, for he fought with a sword in either hand — wielding easily weapons that another warrior could scarcely lift. His hair was red as blood, and he feasted on the still beating hearts of his enemies. His eyes were the eyes of Death himself, and they cast a blue flame that could shrivel the souls of his victims. His only delight was in rapine and slaughter, and after each victory his banquet halls echoed with the tortured screams of captive maidens.

Of course, these legends grew wilder and more luridly exaggerated with each retelling. But histories and accounts written at that time speak of the dread pirate lord with superstitious awe, and their authors credit him with almost superhuman attributes. And though they curse and vilify Kane as the most evil man of the age, they nonetheless record with grudging admiration his indomitable prowess in battle.

This much is commonplace — old tales that all of us have heard as children. But I have powers at my command beyond the frightened dreams of the common folk. You have heard their whispers. Know then that I hold power over the demons of darkness, whose wisdom is not blinded by the cringing frailties of the mortal mind. On countless nights have I summoned forth these creatures of an alien plane — commanded them to obey my will, listened as they whispered to me knowledge that has been eons-hidden from the minds of man. And they have told me many strange secrets.

It was of a certain demon from beyond our stars that I demanded to be told the name of the general who would surely lead my forces to victory in the coming war. My lovely demon that night told me that the triumph or failure of my vengeance hung balanced upon forces so powerful, as to defy control or even prediction by a creature of its plane. But as I pressed the demon to obey my commands to the full limit of its powers, it was forced to name to me the man who could best aid me in my revenge.

The name that the demon snarled was *Kane*.

I cursed the creature then for its mockery. And cringing from my fury, it fawned and cackled to me of certain secrets that no other man in all our Empire has ever known. The demon told me of the fate of the pirate lord, Kane, after he fled the defeat at Montes.

Those who knew the pirate's cunning had guessed well. For this Kane of old did not die at Montes, but had escaped the massacre to sail away into the West with the last of his reavers. Across the limitless Western Sea Kane wandered, to spread his curse through many a strange land upon its far shores. And as the years passed and his enemies grew old, this Kane mysteriously remained young. For by means of a curse to which my demon gave only vague hints, Kane the pirate lord had escaped age as well as death.

Thus while new generations trod the inescapable path from womb to grave, Kane lived on to wander the earth. In the Empire his dark fame became legend, and from legend melted into myth. But more incredible than any myth — none of us has ever dreamt that our ancient enemy yet stalked the land. More than two centuries have crept past, and none ever guessed Kane's secret. And now — so my demon swore to me — from out of the East, Kane has returned to our shores.

It was of *you* the demon whispered, Kane! You are the man my demon named as the general I must have to achieve my vengeance! And by oaths it dared not perjure, the demon swore to me that in Nostoblet I would find the same man who brought terror and death to this region two centuries ago.

And thus, Kane, I know beyond doubt that it is the Kane of dread legend who stands before me now!

If Kane was surprised, he gave no sign of unease. His only acknowledgment was a slight nod and a trace of a cold smile.

"You carry your years well, Kane. You seem unchanged from the descriptions these old volumes give of you."

"Rather colorful descriptions, from your words," Kane commented sardonically.

"Then you are that same Kane of whom so many fearsome legends tell!"

"You have already told me this yourself."

Efrel laughed at her cleverness. But there was no mirth in her sudden command: "Gravter! Kill him!"

Startled by the unexpected death sentence from beyond the veiled doorway, Kane whirled from his seat to meet the sudden danger. All the while his mistress had spoken to her guest, the huge eunuch had stood motionless in the shadow at his post by the door. At her command Gravter tore the heavy-bladed parang from its sheath — leaping for Kane's back as Efrel's words yet hung on the air. His thick-lipped mouth gaped wide in a silent shout of murder-lust.

Cursing his own weaponless state, Kane had just enough time to recognize the danger — then Gravter was upon him. The colossus of rubbery flesh was a blur as he charged, his parang swinging down in a drawing arc. With quickness that belied a man of his bulk, Kane slipped past the slashing blade and kicked the eunuch's legs from under him. It took Gravter a fraction of a second to regain his balance — time enough for Kane to snatch up a heavy silver candlestick.

Eyeing the candlestick, Gravter moved confidently. Warily the two combatants circled in a fighting crouch, poised to strike or retreat at any instant. The eunuch feinted, and Kane swung the candlestick clumsily to meet his threat. Eyes derisively crinkled, Gravter opened his mouth and uttered a bizarre coughing hiss. Within his slobbering jaws remained only the gnarled and blackened stump of his tongue. Again he made a feint, which Kane, distracted by the mutilated mouth, again parried awkwardly.

Certain of his adversary now, Gravter swung his curved blade for Kane's belly. But Kane was no longer there. With bewildering speed he sidestepped the duped eunuch's stroke and lashed out cobra-quick with the candlestick. The silver club clashed against the hilt of the heavy knife, ripping it from Gravter's benumbed fist.

With the hideous croak of a tongueless man seeking to voice his rage, the eunuch grappled with Kane — who foolhardily flung the badly bent candlestick after Gravter's parang. Although a castrado, Gravter was powerfully muscled, and he had been trained to perfection for his duties as bodyguard. Many times the towering giant had broken men with his bare hands for the amusement of his mistress. Massively built, a skillful wrestler — any ordinary man was doomed once caught in Gravter's blubbery grasp. But as the eunuch wrestled now with Kane, he encountered a man far more powerful than any he had been pitted against. Sweat trickled on Gravter's near-naked body. Desperately he sought to crush his adversary beneath his 350 pounds of muscle and bone and rubbery bulk.

A statue would have been easier to wrestle down than the iron-muscled fighter Gravter now contended against. Displaying a master's knowledge of wrestling holds, Kane broke each grapple Gravter attempted — and only the eunuch's oily flesh enabled him to wriggle free from Kane's clawing grasp. Strips of skin tore away, as the two surged together. A sudden twist, and Kane wrenched Gravter's arm behind his back in an irresistible vise. Gravter struggled helplessly, one arm rendered useless, as Kane bore him to the floor. A muffled snap. Gravter convulsed. Grimly Kane broke the eunuch's other arm, and his hopeless groan of animal pain was the loudest sound uttered throughout the tense struggle. Ignoring the grotesque flailing of the castrado's twisted arms, Kane seized Gravter's fat throat in his mighty left hand and slowly strangled him.

Contemptuously tossing the corpse aside, Kane came to his feet and moved toward the curtain — his blood-lust thoroughly aroused, his eyes blazing pools of blue hell.

Efrel's insane laughter greeted him. "Easy! Softly now! You have just proven your identity to me, Kane! It is said in the legends that your hands are your deadliest weapon — they called you Kane the Strangler, along with many other lurid names. Peace now! I only wished to test the old tales for their validity. I have no use for a legend whose prowess has been exaggerated out of all proportion — no matter if he is seemingly deathless."

Kane smiled humorlessly, his mood as dangerous as an enraged tiger's. "Well, your curiosity is satisfied. You know who I am. So now let's have a look at you!"

He ripped aside the veil…

…and looked into horror.

Efrel lay tittering on a couch of costly silks and precious furs — their luxurious beauty utterly defiled by the hideousness that lounged upon them. The mistress of Dan-Legeh was a maimed, broken caricature of a woman — evil malignancy taken material form. A black aura of vengeful malice exuded from this twisted monstrosity, made all the more loathsome by her jewels and gown of green silk.

Hanging from the wall above her couch was a nearly life-sized full-length painting of another woman. The lady of the painting was one of the most beautiful that Kane had ever seen. She reclined upon a fur-strewn couch, seductively attired in the filmiest of silk veils. Her skin was a luminous white, her figure a compelling synthesis of feminine loveliness and licentiousness. The artist must have spent weeks seeking to portray the exquisite delicacy of her face, the dark glowing eyes, the silken black hair.

The girl in the painting, and the girl on the couch before him. Perfect beauty and mutilated depravity. It was a mind-destroying contrast of absolute extremes. And in one awful moment, Kane understood that both of these women were Efrel.

She had been tied by her wrists, so that her arms were relatively unscarred — at least no bone was laid bare. The remainder of her entire body was hideously scarred. Her flesh was but shapeless masses of twisted tissue; in places pallid bone shone beneath the expanses of scar. Jagged stumps of rib poked through her side, where flesh had been stripped bare by her ride. One leg was amputated just below the knee, torn away or too maimed to be salvaged. On her other leg, her foot was no more than a flattened stump below her ankle.

Worst of all was her face. It must have dragged the earth after Efrel had lost consciousness. Long strands of black silky hair grew from the few patches on her scalp that were more than just splotches of scar tissue. Most of the flesh of her face had been scraped away; her ears were scraggly stumps of gristle, her nose but a gaping pit. Efrel's difficulty of speech was easily accounted for. Her cheeks had been fearfully lacerated, and her mouth was drawn into a shapeless slit that was unable to cover the broken bits of her teeth. One eye was horror, the other worse because it had been unmarred. This one dark eye was still beautiful in this hideous travesty of a human face — an onyx in a maggot pile.

The creature called Efrel should not be alive; clearly no human form could survive such mutilation. Yet she lived. And the malevolent force of vengeance that somehow kept her living blazed forth insanely from her one eye — an eye which looked straight into Kane's eyes without flinching.

Kane stared dispassionately at the horror on the couch, his manner portraying no emotion other than urbane curiosity. He laughed mirthlessly. "Yes, I am Kane. And I see that you are Efrel. Now that we have introduced ourselves, why have you summoned me to Dan-Legeh?"

"What? Business? So soon?" tittered Efrel, all shackles of sanity cast far aside. "Why do you speak to me now of business? See! You are in the intimate bedchamber of the Empire's most beautiful lady! See me there on the wall! See me here before you! Have I changed so? Do you not find me beautiful still? Am I not the most lovely and desirable woman your eyes have ever beheld? Once I was!"

"Compared with what lies within your flayed carcass, you are still a beautiful woman," Kane thought aloud, revulsion rising within him.

Another burst of insane laughter. "So gallant, Kane? But I know the evil that lurks behind your eyes! And we are two of a kind, you and I! Mated in evil!"

She opened her arms to him. "Come, Kane the Pirate! Come, Kane the Deathless! If you are truly to take Alremas's place, remember that he was once more than general to me! Come, Kane, my lover!"

Kane went to her side. The tattered lips writhed against his.

On the floor, the dead eyes of the strangled eunuch watched in horror.

VIII
Conspiracy in Prisart

Sipping sweet wine from a splendid crystal chalice, Kane thoughtfully looked over a number of closely written sheets of parchment. The body of Gravter had been carried off, and another attendant stood watch beyond the door. Kane's sword hung at his belt once again, as Dan-Legeh's macabre mistress had altogether accepted him into her confidence. Efrel, Kane sourly mused, was fully satisfied with him.

Now she emerged from her bedchamber to bring another stack of papers to the lamplit table where Kane sat. For all her broken limbs and maimed flesh, Efrel was not bedridden. To the stump below her right knee was strapped a bizarrely carved wooden leg. Set with costly gems and embellished with strange carvings, it resembled a demon's forepaw from some drugged nightmare. Thus Efrel was able to walk about, although her task was difficult, and she required the aid of a cane to hobble for any distance.

She extended the papers to Kane triumphantly. "Here are a few other documents that will interest you: lists of the ships of war under Maril's command, the numbers of fighting men he can muster, secret pledges of fealty to me from various lords, the current status of my own forces — all these things are tabulated here. Wouldn't Maril give a fortune to read it!"

Kane glanced up from one of the statements. "You've done an extraordinarily thorough job here of gathering and assimilating information — excellent work in accounting for your own preparations, as well as in finding out your enemy's strengths and weaknesses. I'm impressed."

Efrel made what might have been a smile. "Yes, my spies are very efficient. Most efficient. There is little I do not know of my enemies. Where my human servants fail me, I have other means of gathering information."

Kane's eyebrows rose slightly, but he moved on. "Yeah, so I see. Well, these show you have made thorough preparations. I'll need to study these more carefully, of course — but for the moment, just where do things stand? I mean, can you give me a quick summary, say, of the present stage of your overall plans?"

Painfully dropping into a chair, Efrel waited a moment before beginning. "It is growing late, and dawn cannot be far off. I'm tired, and so I shall make this brief. Later we can work out details together — I'm certain your own knowledge will prove invaluable in this venture."

She began speaking with deliberate slowness, her voice rising with tension at each phrase. "I have spent these past several years plotting to overthrow the usurper rule of Netisten Maril. Of the failure of my first effort, you already know. I paid an inconceivable penalty for that failure, but the gods of darkness were moved to spare their daughter for a second attempt.

"*This* time I have spun my web more cunningly. *This* time I have summoned to my command forces powerful beyond human imagination. *This* time I will not — I cannot fail. I *must* restore the rule of the house of Pellin to this region. I *must* claim the Imperial throne that was predestined to be mine. I *must* avenge myself upon Netisten Maril and all his thrice-damned line. I *must* have my vengeance!"

This last utterance was almost a shriek. Her next words were whispered. "And no man, no god, no devil shall obstruct my vengeance."

It was a moment before Efrel went on. "As you see, I have prepared well for this. Yes, prepared well — and Maril still has learned nothing of my plans. I have been secretly building up Pellin's navy. Many a ship that floats at anchor in some southern harbor waits not for cargo, but for my commands. My emissaries have sought out the clandestine allegiance of many of the island lords — great lords as well as those from the lesser islands. Imel, whom you have met, is typical of my new servants — a renegade noble from Thovnos itself. Like the scions of other noble houses which have dwindled under the Netisten rule, he recognized the chance to seize the rich holdings that would restore the prestige of his blood. In some instances promises of expanded power, or of unbridled pillage and looting have brought a noble over to me. Or it may happen that some lord who hated me has suddenly died, and a secret friend to my cause has taken his place. Armies of mercenaries have given their allegiance through my proxy lords. I've even enlisted whole regiments from bands of pirates, recruited hunted criminals for my service — so you, Kane, should be among congenial souls.

"Thus, piece by piece, I have added to my forces — amassed an army of vengeance without Maril's suspicion. The exact strength that I can muster at this moment is recorded here. I estimate that perhaps as many as one hundred ships will sail behind my battle pennant and there are many more who will join me once they have seen our initial success. Fighting men and galley slaves I can produce in the thousands, and my workers labor day and night over new arms and armor and engines of war."

"What you say is impressive, certainly," interrupted Kane. "But withal we'll be heavily outnumbered by the Imperial navy. As near as I can tell from your documents here, Maril still has the firm allegiance of the monarchs of the other six major islands in the Empire, not to mention that the majority of the smaller islands are largely under his direct control. He can easily muster a fleet three times our strength, and every vessel a first-class fighting ship. He has only to call upon his lords to render to him the support that they are pledged to give their Emperor. And in manpower we're even worse out-stripped."

Kane scowled at the sheaf of documents. "Hell, if Maril scrapes the bottom of the barrel the way you have, he can command better than four times our number of ships, and man them better, too. As I found out once before in these islands, no amount of daring and ingenuity can conquer an enemy whose resources are vastly superior to your own. It ultimately has to come down to human terms — man against man — and in the final balance the stronger force will be victor and the weaker will be dead"

"Of course!" Efrel dismissed Kane's forebodings. "But as I have told you, I have more than human powers at my command. These scribbled sheets of parchment do not hint of the hidden forces that I shall unleash in good time — but only at the proper moment may I do so."

She paused to relish Kane's obvious curiosity. "Listen, Kane! See to the organization of my mundane powers. I know you have the genius to forge these disparate fragments into a fighting unit — an army that shall conquer despite our inferior numbers and my thrown-together fleet. Your reward for this victory will be a kingdom — power in the Empire second only to my own.

"Only see to your army, and don't speak to me of balances and of odds. For I tell you, Kane — when the time comes to strike, I can turn the tides of war for us! No man dare guess from what secret realms Efrel shall summon forth an irresistible power. They who shall answer my call will smash aside any petty advantage Maril may have over us in numbers and strength."

Kane pounced to draw her out. "You interest me. What manner are these supernatural powers that you claim to command? If they are so potent, why do you need me?"

Sensing his challenge, Efrel again became evasive. Her nightmarish face assumed a vague interpretation of a cunning smile. "Later, Kane, when it is time to take you into my fullest confidence. Later I shall tell you all. But now the dawn breaks."

IX
The Prisoner in Thovnosten

There exists an unmistakable aura about a prison cell. A man blind and deaf can sense this quality, even though he cannot see the walls and bars, or hear the curses, the pleas, the rattle of chains. The prison may be a filthy hole buried in some forgotten dungeon; it may be a royal suite offering every convenience and luxury. Regardless of its station or the range of accommodation, every prison denies its inmates two priceless rights — freedom and human dignity.

For every prison there stands some form of barrier — a rusty chain, a mouldering wall, a surly guard, or perhaps only an obsequious but adamant attendant at the door. Some definite barrier imposes its will upon the imprisoned and says to him *This far you may go, but no farther; this much you may do, but nothing more.* As surely as a prison robs a man of his freedom to choose for himself his movements and actions, the some does it strip from him his dignity as an independent individual. And from this denial arises that characteristic rancid atmosphere which every prison exudes — an invisible miasma of tension, compounded of hatred and fear, apathy and pain, frustrated hope and inexpressible despair.

M'Cori sensed this. Her heartbeat raced in subconscious panic as she followed the guards, and she breathed rapidly as if the air were growing stale. It *was* stale, she thought uneasily. No fresh air, no sunlight, no companionship — a lingering death by suffocation. Shivering, she repressed this painful line of thought. As she descended the stairway, she gathered close the vagrant folds of her silken gown, dreading that a touch might absorb some intangible taint from the stones. She wore a light cloak about her white shoulders, although the bodies of the guards showed beads of sweat outside their dirty harness.

A half-dozen guards waited vigilantly outside the heavy door that opened into an underground room from which there was no other exit. They stood with weapons ready, suspiciously awaiting the approach of the others. A challenge was sounded and answered. The newcomers advanced, and the guards relaxed somewhat as they recognized the daughter of their Emperor.

"He's been asking for you, milady," explained the captain courteously. He peered through the tiny barred spyhole in the thick door. Inside were posted four more guards. "It's all right. Open her up," he ordered them. "The Lady M'Cori has come to pay a visit."

The captain of the guard thrust his keys into the two massive locks on his side of the door, while from within heavy bolts were pulled back. The door swung open ponderously, and the guards within stepped back to allow their captain to enter the antechamber. Another key turned the lock on the door of thick bars that stood inside. The guards watched tensely as this final barrier creaked open, but of the inmate of Thovnosten's most secure cell there was no sign.

The captain held the door. "If you please, milady, no more than half an hour. Your father's orders, you know."

Nodding halfheartedly, she crossed the threshold. Again she experienced that same tremor of trapped hopelessness, and she wondered if ever again they two should meet beyond its chill shadow. She called softly, "Lages?"

The room was silent in subterranean darkness but for a single lamp and the torches outside. It was spacious enough so that much of the chamber was lost in shadow beyond the flickering light. As her wide eyes grew accustomed to the gloom, M'Cori could make out the spartan accommodations of the cell.

For this cell was no dank pit where prisoners were left to rot in chains, although no man had escaped from here in all the dungeon's long history. This was a very special cell. Here the monarchs and emperors of Thovnos chose to incarcerate political prisoners whose threat to their established order demanded that they be imprisoned beyond hope of escape — yet whose rank required certain considerations and privileges. Death was a more certain warden, but it was often expedient to confine a popular figure herein — until public sympathy waned, and his demise could be handled discreetly, conveniently.

M'Cori thought she could discern a still figure stretched upon the chamber's narrow bed. She moved closer, a note of alarm rising in her voice. "Lages?"

The figure on the bed started as she stepped close. He gasped hoarsely and blindly struck out at her. M'Cori cried out, as a powerful blow of his arm slammed back her hesitant touch.

The youth shook himself awake. "M'Cori!" he breathed. "It's you! By Horment, I'm sorry I startled you, M'Cori. I was in the midst of a nightmare and I…"

His voice trailed off as he haphazardly brushed his fingers through his disordered brown hair and wiped the cold sweat from his stubbled face. He fumbled for his water jug.

"Hate to strike a light, darling — I'm such a mess," he apologized. "Didn't really expect you until tomorrow, or I would have straightened the place up. Hey, what are you doing here in the middle of the night?"

His voice became edged. "M'Cori! Don't hide anything back! Have they…?"

She hurried to his side, cutting short his sudden panic. "No, Lages! Stop it, please! Father has decided nothing yet. Nothing has changed."

Her eyes clouded. "Lages, it isn't night. It's the middle of the day."

Lages cursed and swung to his feet. "Wait — I'll strike some more light. Middle of the day, do you say? Damn it, I've slept too long again. Wait — I'll make it day down here, too. High noon, if you like. I'm getting to be a vegetable down here, damn it all — a mushroom. Day, night, what difference! I eat when I'm hungry, I sleep when I'm tired. Lately I'm not too hungry, so I sleep most of the time. Someday I'll just not bother waking up, and I'll snore away here until the world outside has long forgotten Lages. There! Two lamps for morning, three for noon, and I'll blow one out for evening. Midday, you said — that means all three."

He turned to her then and saw the horror reflected in her face. Uneasily Lages realized that his words were bordering on a lunatic's raving. He straightened his rumpled clothing and muttered reassuringly, "Forgive me, sweetheart. That nightmare still has my nerves all shot to hell. Get used to talking to myself down here, and I forget how to converse intelligently."

He smiled crookedly, and she brightened hopefully. "Sorry if I frightened you," he went on, trying to push away the nightmare.

The nightmare that haunted him with every sleep. The nightmare of the young man who lay trapped and helpless in his cell — who cowered like a whipped slave in a dark corner, as he heard the footsteps of his executioners marching closer. Closer, ever closer. Never quite reaching the door — before the slave began to scream in spineless terror. And then Lages would wake up, screaming.

Someday the footsteps would reach the door and enter. Someday he would not wake up. He shuddered. It was degrading enough to have to wait here, wait to be led out and slaughtered like some condemned felon. But to be tormented by the fear that his enemies would find him groveling on the floor...

He knew he did not fear death. Even so ignominious a death as doubtless lay in store for him. Distasteful. Something to be fought, to be avoided as long as possible. But he did not fear death. Then why the nightmare — why the dreams of cowardice? Could any man say for certain how he would ultimately face death? His captivity was eating away at his mind. Perhaps his manhood was rotting away as well. Maybe in another month — or another... For the thousandth time he cursed the fate that had let him be taken alive by his enemies.

The cell was no longer silent. Someone was speaking. Speaking to him. It was M'Cori. Gods, he had all but dismissed her from his thoughts. Hoping she had not noticed his withdrawn silence, Lages started to smile — and realized he had been smiling blankly for several minutes now. Had she noticed? She appeared not to have. Was she then behaving discreetly toward one whose mind was starting to wander? He forced himself to concentrate on her nervous account of the past week's court gossip, of a newly arrived troubadour, and similar inanities.

She sensed that he had returned to her, and cut short her chatter — looking toward him anxiously. Outside the barred doorway, the guards stood impassively. Lages wondered if Maril enjoyed hearing their reports of his increasingly disordered conduct.

"Has your father made any further mention of me?" he asked, already knowing the answer.

She shook her head solemnly, rippling the waves of blond hair. He noticed her perfume for the first time and remembered that he should have complimented her on her appearance. Clearly she had spent hours planning and preparing for this half-hour. She was gowned and groomed as if to attend a banquet. He wondered if it were too late to express his appreciation — without giving her the impression he hadn't noticed earlier. He decided it was not.

"No, Father pretends that he has forgotten all about you. Never does he mention your name. It's his favorite trick when anything happens that disturbs him deeply. Darling, I'm sure he means to spare you. Why else would he have kept you alive these last—?"

"These last two months," Lages finished for her. "There's any number of reasons, but don't worry yourself over it. After all, I've lasted two years under Maril's thumb, and I'm still not down."

But damn close to it now, he told himself. Third time is the last.

Lages had been at sea while Efrel was weaving her conspiracy with Leyan, and consequently he had not been implicated in the plot. Certain of his son's loyalty to him, Leyan had postponed involving Lages until the final moment. Thus the first knowledge Lages received of his father's tragic fate came when he returned to port, and his fellow officers reluctantly declared him under Imperial arrest. Showing unwonted mercy, Maril did not execute Lages with the others of the conspirators' households, but chose instead to keep him under careful surveillance.

Enraged over his father's death, Lages had recklessly plotted to kill Netisten Maril. His abortive conspiracy had never a chance to take form, and Maril this time placed Lages under genteel confinement. He imprisoned his nephew within a suite of rooms inside the Imperial palace, extracting from Lages his solemn promise to engage in no further conspiracy against his uncle. Again the Emperor departed from character to show mercy.

With the help of some friends, Lages made a daring escape from his gilded prison. Gathering together a number of his uncle's enemies, Lages this time organized an almost successful attempt to assassinate the Emperor and seize the throne. In his hatred of his uncle, Lages gave little thought to the fact that he was being used by powers whose only ambition was to gain control of the Empire for themselves. Using Lages for a figurehead, his fellow conspirators had developed a considerable popular following for the fiery youth. Again Netisten Maril had crushed the conspiracy, and Lages once more became his prisoner.

But this time there was to be no escape for Lages, no one that he could turn to for help. He was buried alive. Only M'Cori was privileged to visit him, and she would never betray her father — or so Maril believed. The weeks had dragged by, while Maril ferreted out the last of Lages's co-conspirators. And Lages knew that this time Netisten Maril would grant no reprieve to the nephew who hated him.

"I brought you a few things," M'Cori was saying. She held up her basket with the delighted air of a child bestowing treasured gifts upon a favorite playmate. It was this ingenuousness — this ability utterly to divorce herself from her surroundings, from reality, to draw others into her enchantment that made him love M'Cori, so Lages told himself.

"A sword and a set of keys, I hope," he said with unconvincing levity.

M'Cori flashed a smile. "I'm afraid your guards confiscated that along with the battle-axe I had tucked away in my coiffure."

She blushed nicely as he took this chance to pay some painfully awaited compliments. "They missed the magic ring of invisibility I slipped into my decolletage, though," she added wickedly.

"Where is it, then?" he asked.

"I can't find it myself now," she laughed. "Its charm must work too well."

"Might I help you search for it?" Lages suggested.

M'Cori kicked at him playfully and reached into her basket. Lages caught the secret promise in her averted eyes, though this was hardly the time and place.

"Here," she said, extending a heavy flask. "I stole a bottle of Father's imported brandy from his most secret cellar bin."

Lages sighed his appreciation. "What other surprises, little magician?"

"Well, here's a book. I thought you might want to read."

"What sort of book?"

M'Cori kept her eyes lowered as she proffered the opulently bound volume. "Well, it's poetry. Written by Pacin of Tresli. I know you'll think it's awfully tender stuff. But it's mine. My favorite book. I read it a lot. I mean, I thought you might like to look through his poems — if you knew that I liked them and that they mean a lot to me. Then you'd have something that was dear to me. Something to keep with you while you're down here."

"Thank you, M'Cori," Lages said gallantly. "I'll read these poems over carefully at night. If it would please you, I'll even learn them all by heart. Recite them to you like your personal minstrel."

She laughed at his proposal, but there was a faint catch before she continued. "Here's one more present I brought." Carefully she reached into her basket and lifted out a small bouquet of wild flowers. Timidly she displayed the handful of colored fragrance to Lages — hoping desperately that he would accept them, terribly afraid that he would laugh, or be insulted.

"Flowers, M'Cori?" he asked her in wonder.

"I picked them with my own hands in the meadow this morning. My maids think I'm mad," she said hesitantly. "Oh, darling, I know it's silly for a girl to bring flowers to a man! Only I keep thinking of you locked away from the sunlight down here. I thought something full of life like these flowers — I thought maybe then it would be like... like..."

"Like capturing a fragment of the sunlight and bringing it here to me,"

Lages finished for her.

M'Cori nodded and smiled her appreciation of his understanding. Since she had nothing more to say, she let Lages hold her close for a while. Kissing, they were oblivious to the impassive scrutiny of the guards.

She nestled her head under his chin and clung to him in silence. Lages felt each beat of her heart against his chest. He felt her relax slowly in his arms — content for the moment, like a child at rest. He wondered if she had gone to sleep, so still she lay, when abruptly she pushed away from him.

She ran her soft hands over his face in elaborate disdain. "Your face is like a scrub brush! You've scratched me to ribbons! Why don't you either scrape that mess off, or let it grow out?" She looked at him in appraisal. "You'd look sort of dashing with a full beard, you know. If you kept it trimmed neatly."

Lages started to protest, but realized she was just trying to goad him out of his apathy. Instead he told her slowly, "You're my last hope, M'Cori. I would have given up — gone mad with despair long ago, if it weren't for you."

The captain of the guard discreetly cleared his throat from the doorway. "Milady, you'll have to go now. I've let you stay almost an hour already, and your father will have my hide if he finds out."

Reluctantly she got up to leave. "I'll be back, beloved," she whispered. "And you'll get out of here — I know you will. I'll keep begging Father to parole you — at least to move you to a cell in the tower. I know he means to spare your life, Lages!"

He found himself almost sharing her optimism. "Sure, darling. Keep trying, in any way you know how. I know you're doing everything you can for me. And I'll be waiting for your next visit"

"Goodby, Lages," she called from the door. "Don't forget the priestess's prophecy."

He listened to her departing footsteps. Yes, the prophecy. Don't forget the prophecy.

Long ago — how long ago? They were three half-wild kids on a spree at a holiday carnival. M'Cori, Roget, and Lages — they had slipped away from Leyan and run amuck through the throngs and stalls. In one dark booth they had discovered an ancient crone, who swore to them that she was the last priestess of Lato, a devil-worship suppressed decades before by the priests of Horment. She said that if they would let her taste a drop of their blood, she would tell their fortunes.

An exchange of dares had made it impossible to back out. Solemnly each had pricked a finger with Roget's dagger and thrust the ruby-spotted tip into the hag's toothless mouth. She had sucked so rapaciously that it seemed their fingers would be stripped of flesh.

For Roget she forecast fame and glory as a warrior; for Lages, a kingdom to rule; for M'Cori, marriage to her dearest love, who would be a prince and would father her seven strong sons. They had left quarreling over whose fortune was the brightest, and when Leyan at last found them, he had been tremendously alarmed at their adventure. They never saw the old priestess again.

He shrugged, feeling the bitterness return. Prophecies and childhood dreams. True, Roget had found fame and renown as a warrior, but he had encountered death as well — shot from ambush by some unknown assassin after his glorious triumph over the rebels on Fisitia.

And the man whose throne Roget had died to preserve had butchered their father. Now Lages was the rebel. And his fortune was almost played out.

Grimly Lages contemplated M'Cori's gifts. Insipid poems. Arid flowers. Just the thing he needed to escape this cell, this fate. At worst they only reminded him of his imprisonment here below ground.

He snatched up the bouquet in his fist and glared at it angrily. Whether he wanted to trample the blossoms into the floor, or press them to his lips — Lages could not decide.

X

The Emperor's Spy

Cassi was a hunted man. Most of his life he had been a hunted man. Childhood in the alleys of Thovnosten leads either to rapid maturity or to early death — for survival there is a merciless game whose winners are the strong and the clever. Cassi had been a scrawny child, but his mind was sharp and cunning as a rat's. This natural talent eventually established him as one of the Empire's most resourceful thieves. And when the youth had finally been captured, he cheated the waiting gallows with an unprecedented escape from the Imperial dungeons. Never again could the Imperial guard ensnare him, and his colleagues marveled at his incredible fortune.

Withal, there were a few — a very few — who knew him instead to be one of the Empire's most capable spies. For Netisten Maril had recognized in Cassi a craftiness that could render great service to the Emperor. Maril had himself arranged for Cassi's escape, once he had procured his loyalty, and the fabulous thefts that made Cassi almost legendary among the Empire's underworld were clandestine payments for some valued item of information.

Vague suspicions impelled Maril to send his spy to Pellin. He had maintained a careful watch upon this island ever since the collapse of its Queen's conspiracy. The reports he received had been purely routine, and his nephew's treason had later necessitated his full attention. Otherwise he might have felt alarm, when one by one of his spies on Pellin ceased to make their reports. Those few who did return from that island assured him that all was peaceful there, that the Pellinites were unconcerned over the death of their Queen. But Maril was no fool, and he knew that a spy was a weapon not difficult to turn upon its wielder. A great many separately insignificant circumstances throughout the Empire hinted to him that some plot might be festering unseen. So the Emperor ordered Cassi to go to Pellin.

And Cassi found his master's suspicions vindicated.

A rumor had persisted for some months throughout the slums and waterfront dives where Cassi skulked. There was a haven, so men whispered, that promised wealth and safety for any rogue, regardless of his crimes, in return for his cooperation and obedience in some secret venture. Just where this haven was, or what was expected of them once there, no one would say. Talk was that some mastermind contemplated an Empire-wide smuggling ring, or that a newly formed pirate band was recruiting hands, or that one of the island lords sought to raise a private army in secret, or a host of other wild guesses.

Cassi's own information had tied the rumor to Pellin, so he acted on intuition and made known his interest in this refuge. On cue, the Imperial guard began making things very hot for the thief, and very shortly Cassi made contact with those who promised sanctuary and riches. He was then taken to Pellin, along with a shipload of companions who would have provided a full day of hangings in Justice Square.

On arrival they were taken to newly erected barracks that housed hundreds of other green recruits, chosen from the dregs and the gutters of the Empire's underworld. Here they were given food, weapons and equipment, and the promise of gold. To earn their keep, they were ordered to drill for battle each day. Although the pretense of secrecy was maintained, it was obvious to the dullest of them that open rebellion was planned. Talk flowed endlessly — gloating prospects of plundering an Empire, excited speculation on all aspects of the bold venture, wild conjectures regarding the sinister stranger who directed all preparations.

As soon as he found it discreet, Cassi slipped away to make contact with Netisten Maril's spy network on Pellin. After failing to turn up several of those he sought, he finally contacted one Tolsyt, who was also the chief wine merchant to Dan-Legeh.

The wineshop stank of stale vinegar and sour sweat. It had the look of an empty tavern after the bar has closed — seedy and abandoned in the stark absence of customers. Tolsyt himself looked only half the role of a fat, jolly wine dealer. He was quite plump, certainly — although a noticeable looseness to his skin hinted that he had lost a number of pounds recently. But he was not jolly at all. He was scared. And he looked as though he hadn't seen a sober day in months.

"All right, what's happened here?" Cassi demanded, as soon as he caught the frightened wine merchant alone and satisfied him of his identity. "By Lato's black heart! You people must have known something was going on in Pellin for months! Why were there no reports? Why did the few agents who returned to Thovnos never tell us a damn thing about this blatant conspiracy? And Maril has more than doubled his intelligence force here — where are all the others?"

"Dead. All dead." Tolsyt's soft voice answered simply. "By the gods, how they died!"

His words quavered. Cassi noted in alarm that his eyes were damp with tears, though his face was drained of emotion.

Cassi exploded. "Dead! Everyone dead but you! Do you expect me to swallow that line of bullshit?" His eyes were narrow; now they drew narrower. Cassi was a small man, of drab and undistinguished appearance. An asp is small and unimpressive as well, until it strikes.

The other man smiled stupidly through his tears. "Dead, yes. All but me. Just Tolsyt alone. There were a few others whom she must have bought over to her service. These few she spared so they could bear false reports to Netisten Maril — poisoned lies about quiet, peaceful Pellin. They earned their pay well, it seems. Maybe they told her where to find their former comrades. Maybe she tore betrayal from some of the others with her hellish instruments of torture.

"If you only had seen what she did to them. She was proud — hung their carcasses up before the walls of Dan-Legeh, so everyone could admire her art. Must have spent days at her sport. Flayed, burnt, broken bodies—"

"And why not you?" cut in Cassi suspiciously.

"Maril always took into consideration the chance of betrayal, you know that," Tolsyt answered. "He even employed two separate spy networks on Pellin, neither one supposedly aware of the other. And he used a few completely independent spies. And, of course, there were other agents just like me — assigned to watch over one segment of the network without anyone else knowing our identity. Guess that's why I'm still alive — no one here knew I was Maril's agent.

"She found all the others, though. All the men I knew, and Horment knows how many others that Efrel claimed were spies. Maybe her demons told her their names. I only know they didn't tell her mine. I didn't dare try to warn Maril, to try to help the others — I was afraid even to try to escape. I did nothing to give any hint of my true business here."

He winced under the other's sneer. "If you had been here, it would have been the same with you, Cassi. Watching the witch hunt us down like a weasel in a rabbit warren. Living in endless dread of the day she'd hang your shredded corpse up on the walls of Dan-Legeh."

"So you believe their propaganda that Efrel still lives?" Cassi asked contemptuously. What jest of fate had preserved this coward's worthless life, he mused, while better men had died horribly.

Tolsyt snorted in a flash of anger — the first indication he had given that some backbone remained to him. "Efrel alive? You can bet your sweet ass she's alive! That's not just a rumor they've cooked up to fire the public's imagination. Everyone here knows Efrel is still alive — no matter if no one has seen her. But it's Efrel's hand in this rebellion. Who did you think was behind this entire affair? Alremas? Kane?

"Oh, you're a real bright one, aren't you just? Sneaking in here after all of us lie butchered. Knowing right exactly what's been done wrong. Doubting the words of the only man who was smart enough to escape the damned witch."

Cassi scowled at the wine merchant in dubious appraisal. He needed the man, but wasn't certain whether he could rely on his help — or even trust Tolsyt. Perhaps more than luck had spared the agent's life.

"Why did no one escape the island?" Cassi demanded suspiciously.

"Few had the chance, she struck so fast. And no ship leaves Pellin except under closest surveillance — not even a fishing boat. Something always happens to ships that try to slip away in secret."

"They're all caught?" Cassi frowned skeptically. "No blockade can stop every boat."

"Out there there's worse things waiting than Efrel's navy," Tolsyt shuddered. "Candon and Mosna escaped. Stole a small boat, and sailed off into the fogbound night. I watched them leave. I saw them the next day, too. Hung up outside Dan-Legeh, all pale and bloated — and their bodies covered with puckered gouges and welts, like they'd been whipped and branded all over. That was all anyone knew about it. They sailed out to sea one night, and the next morning they were dragged out of Dan-Legeh and hung up to feed the crows. And I don't know how many other attempts failed just the same way."

Cassi changed the subject. "What do you know about this man Kane?"

"No more than what you will have heard. Nobody knows anything much about Kane. Efrel brought him in to take charge of her rebellion. Oxfors Alremas had to step down for him, so the two are deadly enemies. Alremas is too popular and too powerful a lord to dispose of easily, and Kane is doing his work too well for Alremas to recover his leadership. Something has to break there in time."

"What about these... stories they tell about Kane?"

Tolsyt shrugged. "You mean, that people say he is the Kane of old? Red Kane the Pirate, come from the past to wreak vengeance on the Empire that destroyed him two centuries ago? For all I know, it may be true. Why not? Efrel was destroyed by the Empire, too. She still lives — why not Kane? Everything else about this conspiracy defies the laws of nature. Why did Maril ever take a sorceress to his bed?"

"Ask him when he gets here," advised Cassi caustically. "And you may be certain that Maril *will* be here with his fleet to destroy this cancer — as soon as I make my report to him. And that I'll do just as soon I can find a way to get back to Thovnosten — without joining your not-so-lucky colleagues," he added pointedly.

Tolsyt seemed ready to dismiss the matter. "Sure, you go on and make your report. Just swim back to Maril and tell him his late wife and a centuries-old pirate are sort of planning on pulling his throne out from under him. You do that. I'll just wait right here for the Imperial fleet to land."

Reluctantly Cassi decided he would have to trust Tolsyt. "I'll work something out. For the moment, I'm going to scout around and see what other information I can pick up. Then tomorrow, say, you are going to get us into Dan-Legeh. If Efrel really is alive, Maril will want to know."

Tolsyt's plump face blanched. "Me? Like hell I will! That's suicide! Maril paid me to spy for him, not to get myself killed. I'm through with this."

"I don't think you are," Cassi told him pleasantly. There was casual cruelty written in his eyes. "I need to get into Dan-Legeh, and since you furnish wine to the fortress, you've got an excuse to pay a visit with your new assistant. And don't even think about crossing me, Tolsyt. I know ways to make a man die horribly, too."

"But I'm not due to make my delivery there for a week," the other protested.

"Tomorrow, Tolsyt. You've just gotten in some stuff, and you know the
chief steward there will be interested."

He turned his back on the vintner's pleading and hurried from the shop.
After wasting time to check on the other agents whose names he had been
given, Cassi was forced to admit that Tolsyt had not exaggerated. It seemed
incredible that Maril's entire intelligence network had been utterly wiped out,
but that was the case. He would have to rely on Tolsyt, then.

The preparations for the rebellion were extensive, Cassi noted, as he walked
through the city. Armed men were everywhere, and dozens of forges spewed
forth weapons and armor. Ranks of soldiers drilled on several of the open
fields beyond the walls, and Cassi had already learned that a number of military camps existed farther inland. The rebels must plan to strike soon, he
realized, since the scope of operations had now reached a point where it was
obvious that some major plot was underway. Enforced isolation and clever
lies could cover up only so much. He would have to get word to Maril soon.

The harbor was filled with ships, and hundreds of workmen toiled at building new vessels and refitting old ones. He spotted some unusual construction
in one corner of the harbor and decided to risk a closer look. Munching on
some rather green apples he had acquired from an unwary peddler, Cassi
strolled over toward the docks.

He gazed at the work in puzzlement. Workers were constructing a number
of gigantic catapults, weapons of a size sometimes used to besiege cities. They
were fitting these catapults into huge barges — clumsy vessels equipped with
long rows of oars for propulsion. Cassi frowned. When completed, these lumbering vessels would scarcely be seaworthy. They certainly could not be rowed
as far as Thovnos; and if Kane planned on using them to besiege Thovnosten,
the practical course of action would be to transport the bulky catapults dis-
assembled in the holds of his warships and set them up once landed.

It was growing late. Cassi decided he had best get back to his barracks
before someone took notice of his overlong sightseeing excursion. With all
the confusion here in Prisarte, it was unlikely that anyone cared — but then
the Pellinites had demonstrated their efficiency at ferreting out spies.

Riders were approaching. Cassi stepped back to let them pass, and was
startled to recognize Imel on one of the horses. He had already learned of the
Thovnosian's treason, for Imel had been given a high rank in the rebel army.
Moving cautiously, Cassi kept to the shadow of a shop awning. He had seen
Imel on numerous occasions around Thovnosten, but fortunately the ren-
egade did not know him.

On another of the horses rode a dark-haired man of rather tough appearance. He wore leather trousers and a vest with silver conchos. Broad bands of
muscle bunched on his arms and chest as the wind whipped his vest. Cassi
did not recognize him.

Although the spy had never before seen him, the third rider could only be
Kane. There was no mistaking his massive build — even his mount stood

seventeen hands at a guess. Kane wore boots and trousers similar to those of his companion, along with a fine rust-colored jupon that matched his beard. The red hair and primitive features followed the descriptions of Kane — and one look at his demonic blue eyes removed any doubt. With a shiver Cassi looked away. He found himself wondering whether the tales whispered of Kane might not be true after all. Certainly there were many bizarre mysteries on this earth, and who could say what manner of creature a demented sorceress might summon to her aid?

The riders paused within a few yards of him, and Cassi listened carefully to hear their conversation while he idly looked over the shop's assortment of fruits.

"Seems to be coming along as fast as feasible, anyway," Imel was saying. "I still don't quite see how it's going to be very practical, though. I mean, how much accuracy can you get on any target over maybe a quarter of a mile?"

"They'll do the job they're made for," Kane asserted. "I've seen it done a few times. True, their use is rather limited — but they're devastating when you *can* utilize them. Anyway, catapults are essential to any siege, so we'd have had to construct them eventually. And if we can just get the time to drill them properly, their crews can get pretty damned accurate with the things. With a fireball you don't need to be too accurate, so long as you get it to any target where it can splatter."

He shrugged. "I think we've got time to check on Alremas before dark yet. He ought to have some thoughts on how his group did during battle maneuvers at sea today. Getting hungry myself. Arbas, are those apples any good yet?"

The dark-haired man grunted. "Not much. All I've seen so far have been on the green side. But then if you like green apples, it doesn't matter. Had some orange wedges that were pretty good."

"Well, it was a thought," Kane muttered as they rode away.

As they left, Cassi selected a bunch of grapes and paid for them. The proprietor had been watching too closely this time. He wandered off in the direction of his barracks, spitting seeds as he walked.

XI
Ebb Tide and Undercurrent

The water was cold and as black as the basalt of Dan-Legeh's walls. Kane stuck his foot in it and cursed.

"Sure you know what you're doing?" Arbas inquired. Kane declined comment. The night was starless beneath a heavy blanket of sea mist, and a cold wind made a scattering of whitecaps across the inky water. The tide was out, and the surf made a sobbing moan against the rocks where they stood. The mist was sour with the scents of kelp and stale sea. Blacker in the blackness, the towers of Dan-Legeh stabbed through the fog into the night above them.

"Just don't let some bastard swipe my stuff — and save some of that brandy for me," Kane growled, gingerly wading out into the ebbing surf. His boots and clothing lay piled upon his cloak, along the kelp-wreathed rocks of the headland. Kane's sword and scabbard waited there as well, but the hulking man kept his heavy-bladed dagger strapped to his naked waist.

Arbas watched him with a dubious expression. Shaking his head, the assassin took a long pull from the brandy flask. He was used to Kane's mad schemes, and used to seeing Kane pull them off. If this time were different, well then, he'd wait until the tide turned or the brandy gave out.

Swimming out across the mist-shrouded surf, Kane made his way toward the cliffs below Dan-Legeh. He was confident no human eye could pick him out on a night like this, though Kane found his own course through the darkness without apparent difficulty.

When Kane reached the base of the cliffs, he dived. Salt water stung his eyes, and the cold numbed his flesh. Strands of kelp clutched at him, entangled his thrashing limbs — and it took all of his strength to swim against the sucking undercurrents. Kane was a powerful swimmer, but he knew better than to dare for long the treacherous undertow here. If he faltered, the current would drag him down to the bottomless depths of the Sorn-Ellyn — and Kane had an idea of what would welcome him there.

He dived as deeply beneath the moaning surf as he dared — swimming down until the pressure lanced his skull with intolerable agony, until the undertow sucked at his aching limbs with a current almost beyond his power to resist, until his chest shuddered with pent-up breath. There was nothing to indicate he had neared the bottom of the sea beneath the cliffs there.

Kane sensed movement far below his deepest dive.

He returned to the surface, gulping air in great gasps. His hand gripped his knife. A chill touch enwrapped his leg. It was only a trailing strand of kelp.

Again Kane sensed movement from below. Quickly he swam for the kelp-strewn rocks — scrambling onto a slimy knob to catch his breath. Behind him, the sea convulsed for an instant. Kane drew back into the cover of the seaweed and broken rocks, watching.

A head broke through the surface and stared about. Kane pressed closer to the clammy rock. Against the choppy whitecaps and the boiling surf, the face was a pale blotch. The waves about the other swimmer swirled from the passage of other shapes. The swimmer dived again, and did not return, although Kane watched a long time.

He swam back closer to the shoreline. Because he did so, Kane found the body that was wedged in the rocks.

It was a man's body, naked, looking dead and drowned in that pale, bloated manner that dead and drowned things have. The crabs had not been at their work so well yet that Kane could not examine the wounds that scored the man's bloodless flesh. Kane had once seen a man enwrapped with chains that had been heated white-hot. These wounds called that vision to mind, although closer examination showed they were not burns, but puckered gouges.

Kane left the crabs to their meal. He was chilled from more than the icy surf when he clambered back to where Arbas waited.

The assassin tossed Kane the flask, grinning as Kane turned it up. Kane's teeth chattered as he towelled himself with his cloak and struggled to drag clothes over his still-damp flesh.

"If you've had enough skinny-dipping for one night, let's go find a warm fire and a keg of that same brandy," Arbas prescribed. "I've been fighting off hungry crabs for a good hour, waiting for you to get back. What did you do — run into a pretty little mermaid?"

Kane looked at him strangely for a moment; then he wrestled some more with his boots. "I did see another swimmer out there," he commented in a low voice. "I don't think she saw me."

Arbas suspected a jest. "Was she a sea sprite?"

"It was Efrel."

XII
Two Went In...

The next day Cassi bribed a sergeant to put him on sick call. Once on his own, the Emperor's spy hurried to Tolsyt's wineshop, where he exchanged his soldier's harness for a duty smock and wine-stained apron. Tolsyt received him glumly and told him that he had picked up a wagonload of choice Lartroxian wine to take to the fortress. His breath indicated that he had sampled the vintage thoroughly. The two climbed onto the wagon seat and drove slowly through the crowded streets to Dan-Legeh, Tolsyt wearing the mien of a man driving his own funeral coach.

Still, he played his part well enough when they reached the fortress. The guards passed them through the gates with little argument and called for the chief steward, who presently came to inspect their wares. It was a good vintage. Tolsyt was a better vintner than spy, although he was too worried to haggle well, and the steward purchased the wine at a bargain price.

They took their time unloading the barrels, then loaded the wagon with empty kegs — dawdling until mealtime, whereupon they received permission to eat with the kitchen servants.

Having more or less established their presence within Dan-Legeh, Cassi and Tolsyt casually took an after-dinner stroll through the fortress, talking with the servants and listening to the conversations of the soldiers. The very multitudes of people who thronged the sprawling citadel formed a cover for them. To anyone who gave them notice, they appeared to be merely a pair of loafers gawking at the sights.

Cassi beckoned his companion aside. "We'll split off now," he told him. "I want to do some snooping around the north wing and see what we can hear from the servants in the living quarters of the Pellin lords. It might get ticklish if we're spotted hanging around there, but any names or scraps of information we can dig up will be worth plenty. So keep your eyes and ears open. I'd still like to know something definite about Efrel. All we've heard so far doesn't prove a thing."

"Damn it, Cassi! Let's get out of here now!" Tolsyt begged. "We've found out enough for Maril, already. All the servants swear that Efrel is alive and keeps to the northern wing of the fortress. Come on, we know enough. They'll kill us if they find us wandering around any farther."

But Cassi silenced his protests with threatening curses and ordered the panic-stricken vintner to do as he was told. Tolsyt left him with dragging steps at an intersection of the labyrinthian corridors. The man was close to breaking, Cassi realized. But he would have to risk him — and Cassi was quite willing to sacrifice Tolsyt if necessity demanded.

Cautiously he strode along the hallways, casting a curious eye into whatever open doorways he passed. His steps were bold, and he assumed the appearance of a man who was going about his accustomed business. Now and again he stepped behind tapestries or into open doorways, choosing to avoid confrontation with those whom he heard approaching.

He began to sense an oppressive tension as he approached the northern wing of Dan-Legeh. There were fewer people in evidence now, which only made it all the more difficult to account for his own presence. Still he pressed on, determined to earn Maril's richest bounty by bringing him the first-hand information the Emperor would demand with regard to the conspiracy's leaders.

He rounded a corner and found himself facing two lounging guardsmen. Cassi felt the chill of their suspicious stares.

"Where the hell do you think you're headed, buddy?" one of them growled.

The small of his back was cold with sweat, but Cassi smiled ingratiatingly. "Gosh, am I glad to see you guys!" he blurted in his best yokel accent. "How does a guy get out of this place? I been walking pretty near for an hour, and I just keep getting lost. Wow, this place sure gives me the creeps! How do you guys stand it being in here all day?"

"What were you doing in the first place, buddy?" the guard continued suspiciously.

Cassi hitched his belt awkwardly. "Well, you see I was delivering a load of wine with the boss. Ten hogsheads of that real quality Lartroxian stuff — man, it's the best you can get, too. Well, after that we ate us a bite, and the boss he sort of dozed off for a bit like he does. So I decided to take me a look at this huge palace jerks is always talking about back home — so I could tell them all about it, you know. Thought maybe I'd even see some of that elegant indoor plumbing these bluebloods put in even for the servants to use, so they say."

He paused, smiling amiably — wondering whether he were laying it on too thick. He hadn't been able to bring a weapon with him in his role of a vintner's flunky — but even if he could lay hands on a sword, he knew he could never cut his way out of the fortress.

The other guardsman looked him over contemptuously, noting the wine stains that blotched his clothing. "Hell, let him go, Joren," he yawned. "Kane would skin our asses if we bothered him about this hayseed."

He glowered at the spy. "Turn around and go back, boy. This is off limits, get it? Keep left when you get to the main corridor, go straight past three cross passages, right on the fourth, then straight toward the kitchen smells.

Hell, find somebody else down at that end and ask them. Now beat it, boy — and you better plan on crapping in your britches before you come looking for plumbing around the north wing again!"

Cassi thanked them profusely and slunk off. The secret pleasure of making fools of the guards compensated for their bullying treatment, he told himself. But he had been marked and warned off. Now he would have to try another avenue of approach to learn anything here. Wondering how Tolsyt fared, Cassi cut across the route the guard had directed and turned into a hallway that felt dank and disused. He hoped he might catch up with Tolsyt before the other man encountered the same pair of guards.

He was uncertain as to the exact course his companion might have taken — or even how far Tolsyt might have gone before his courage failed. When Cassi had last seen him, Tolsyt was headed down a flight of stairs, evidently intending to work his way to the north wing through the lower levels of the fortress. With this in mind, Cassi descended the precipitous stairways into the colossal citadel's foundations — marveling yet again at the immensity of this legendary structure.

Skillfully he picked his way through the maze of murky chambers and dusty corridors. Stealth was imperative in these seldom frequented nether reaches, so that Cassi stepped into concealment to avoid meeting chance intruders. Thus, when he caught the faint scuff of furtive footsteps, Cassi was quick to slip behind an ancient tapestry.

Cassi cautiously looked down the gloomy corridor, wondering whether he was being cut off by suspicious guards. After a moment he caught sight of the intruder. It was only Tolsyt, creeping down the torch-lit passage toward him. The vintner was maybe a hundred feet from his own hiding place — but Cassi easily recognized his portly silhouette, even though the light was too poor to reveal his features. Cassi started to call out to the wine merchant — he would learn how Tolsyt had done, then decide if they dared risk further snooping. But instead of hailing Tolsyt, Cassi could only gape in terror.

As Cassi stared, Tolsyt's movements suddenly were becoming stiff and slow-paced. The vintner moved his plump limbs as if they were weighted with stone — he struggled like a man seized in quicksand, dragging himself to an uncanny standstill. Tolsyt's face was frozen in a grimace of stark terror. A hoarse bleat of fear started from his lips, became a groaning rattle as even his tongue failed him. All voluntary motion ceased. He stood paralyzed in a stance of terrified flight trapped into helpless immobility. It was as if Cassi watched a scene from a common nightmare.

For an instant Cassi fought back headlong panic. Then there came to his ears the shivery squeal of stone and oiled metal sliding together. The torches flared brightly as a faint breeze caught their flame. A section of the musty tapestries billowed outward, disclosing a concealed door that swung open from the stones of the corridor wall.

Two figures stepped out from the darkness beyond the doorway. One, Cassi recognized as Kane, for the man carried a torch that threw light on his features and cast a hulking shadow about him. Beside him hobbled a creature who looked only remotely human. She limped along on a grotesquely carved wooden leg, most of her body swathed in clinging folds of silk. The silhouette of her body against the torchlight was vaguely feminine, but strangely deformed. When she turned her face toward where he crouched, Cassi had to stifle a cry. Cassi knew beyond all doubt that Efrel the sorceress yet lived. There was one eye to remind him of the beautiful Efrel he had seen at the court of Thovnosten, but the hideously disfigured face was beyond the most depraved imagination. He only felt relief that the torchlight shone no more brightly.

She regarded the helpless vintner in amusement. "So you see, Kane, my alarm system does not fail when meddlers trespass upon my sanctuary. There's little here to tempt a thief, and after we saw the fool creeping about so inquisitively, there can be no doubt."

Efrel uttered a joyful cry, like a child with a new toy. "A spy! A fat little spy! Prowling about, little fat mousie? Were you going to bear tales to your master?" She laughed delightfully. "And after I'd thought I had purged my realm of such vermin. Poor little spy. Are you frightened?"

"What spell holds him like a statue?" Kane wanted to know.

"What spell holds you, little mouse?" she mocked. "The spell of my beauty, perhaps? No, Kane. He's too shy. It's something else, I think.

"Did you not see Efrel cast her spell then?" She tittered. "But I remember now. I told you to watch my fat little spy through the peephole, while I turned his limbs to clay. No matter. Perhaps I'll show you on another day. No one else of the Pellin line has ever mastered it — but Efrel is mistress of Dan-Legeh and all who venture within my halls. It is a simple spell, but a potent one. It is quickly cast, and steals from my victim all powers of voluntary movement.

"See, my fat spy can only stand and breathe. Wait, I hear his soft little heart pounding away in its plump nest, and I think my mousie is standing in a puddle that wasn't there before. But he can move his limbs and head only as I will him to do — he is my automaton now. Were he one man or a hundred, my spell would make him dance to my command. Will you see my little puppet walk?"

"I'd rather hear him talk," Kane rumbled. "Make him tell us his mission here. Ask him who else spies on us. Where can—"

"I can make him speak only such words as I command his lips to form," interrupted Efrel impatiently. "But come, my little spy, join us within my secret chambers, where you so dearly wanted to pry. We will show Kane a game or two with my pretty toys, and soon I think you'll beg to tell us all the secrets your fat little mind holds."

"He may have accomplices here in the fortress," Kane suggested. "We should order all gates barred immediately. If you summon some of your servants, we might learn immediately on what pretext he came to Dan-Legeh — and who else came with him. It won't take more than a few minutes to determine this, regardless of the obstinacy of his tongue — which I judge to be ready to spill over with words right now."

"Kane, at times you display a depressing boorishness." There was an insane tone of menace in the sorceress's words that silenced Kane. "Spies are rare visitors to Dan-Legeh these days. Since my last pets languished here, I've thought of several new tricks to play on them. This one will speak to us presently. But first I intend to have my sport, and I mean for you to watch."

She whispered soothingly. "Come, fat little mousie!"

His face still set in a mask of abject horror, Tolsyt followed her beckoning finger. With awkward steps he plodded through the doorway and into the concealed passageway beyond. Kane frowned in chagrin, but entered behind him.

Efrel's words drifted back as the door slid shut. "Dear little spy. What games shall we two play? I wonder if you were one of those who whispered of my plans to Netisten Maril a lifetime ago? Do you know how it feels to have your flesh torn from your bones? Shall we play that game, too? Poor little plump spy — I think you're frightened of me."

The closing door cut short her mocking laughter. Warily Cassi stepped out of his concealment. Tolsyt had maybe had more nerve than Cassi had credited him with. At any rate, Tolsyt had managed to reach a sector of the fortress important enough for Efrel to guard it with some manner of alarm. Clearly Tolsyt had blundered upon something — and in doing so had drawn Efrel and her henchman to investigate.

Cassi licked his thin lips. At least the wine merchant had succeeded in flushing the sorceress from her lair — but whatever knowledge he had gained was lost forever now. Cassi regretted that loss, though he felt no regret at his companion's fate — only relief that it had not been his own.

With a sudden rush of fear, Cassi realized that Efrel and Kane would soon be party to Tolsyt's every secret regarding the two spies' operations in Prisarte. Only Efrel's sadistic lusts had kept Tolsyt from spilling everything on the spot. Cassi hurried through the passageways as fast as discretion permitted. It would only be a short time before Kane had the pieces together, he knew. Had it not been for Efrel's interference, Kane's men would be combing the fortress for him this very moment.

The minutes dragged by as Cassi rushed through the endless passages. Valuable time was lost in ducking out of sight to wait for soldiers to pass by, or in ambling casually along once the spy reached the safety of the kitchen area. But his luck still held.

Returning a few nods and greetings from acquaintances made earlier in the day, he eased himself onto the wagon seat. He clucked to the horses, and the wagon-load of empty wine barrels rattled toward the servants' gate. The guards waved him through without interest, and there remained only the main entrance gates to pass.

The sergeant of the guard looked at him quizzically. "What happened to your master?" he drawled.

Cassi swore. "The fat bastard sent me back to haul back a second load by himself. I'll be busting a gut, while he loafs around pinching the kitchen maids."

The guards laughed. "Well, go on, then," grunted the sergeant. "I guess you'll have to hustle to get through by dark, anyway."

Cassi let out a deep breath as he rode from under Dan-Legeh's shadow. The horses were impatient from their long wait, so he let them jog along. As soon as he reached the empty wineshop, he jumped off and raced to pull on his soldier's gear. No one noticed as he strode from the building and hurried for the docks, but he knew his time was fast running out.

He knew he must get off the island at all costs before the alarm went out for his capture. Holing up somewhere in the hills was out of the question — even if he escaped, he would have no means of getting his information to Netisten Maril. Not that Cassi felt any extraordinary loyalty to the man who had saved his neck from the gallows, but the Emperor paid generously for his services, and this mission could make Cassi rich as any lord.

He had considered and discarded a number of hazy plans on his way to the docks, based on his knowledge of the Pellinites' blockade. Once at the waterfront, Cassi sighted a ponderous trireme in the process of casting off. It was as good a chance as any, he decided. Raking his memory for bits of information he might work from, Cassi ran toward the vessel and jumped on board even as it slid away from its mooring.

He smiled cheerfully at the milling sailors and marines, who gazed at him curiously. Sitting against the rail to catch his breath, Cassi pulled off his newly issued helmet and wiped his face with his forearm. Below him, the slaves rattled their oars into place. The ship began to get under way.

An officer approached him with a frown. "You! What's your story?" he barked.

Cassi clumsily clapped on his helmet and snapped a salute. "Better late than never, sir! I... uh... was sick this morning and I didn't wake up till they threw me... I mean, I got here as quick as I could, but I got turned around..." He sputtered on sheepishly, keeping an eye on the receding shoreline.

The officer spat. "Shit! You damned marines can't even spend a night in a whorehouse and bear up the next day. I ought to have you flogged as an example, soldier! Shitload of good that would do, with your sort of gutter-scrapings. Where Kane digs up scum like you, and how he expects trained officers to make fighting men out of you, is more than I can figure!"

The angry officer continued to chew him out for the benefit of all those on deck, while above them the sails filled with wind and the trireme plowed out to sea. Out of breath, he thumbed through his rollbook. "What did you say your name was, soldier?" he growled.

Cassi told him, and watched him run his finger along several dirty pages of names. "This is the *Sorpath*, I guess?" he queried as the officer came to end of his roll and started over.

The officer looked stricken. "The *Sorpath* sailed for battle maneuvers this morning," he said heavily. "You stupid ass! You're on the wrong ship! This is the *Hast-Endab*, and we're bound for two weeks of patrol south around Fisitia!"

Cassi burst into astonished protests of innocence. He'd thought it was before noon yet, and how could he recognize a new ship, and he didn't have time to ask, and he couldn't read what it said on the bow, and...

By the time the officer finished cussing him out, the ship had put not a few miles behind them. "Damn well got a notion to feed you to the fish!" he concluded. "But I'm stuck with you, so you'll get to fill in for the ones who didn't make it out of the whorehouses for this crew. Lato knows how Kane expects disciplined troops out of the crap he keeps handing us for recruits! Stay out of my way, soldier! That's all!"

Orders Cassi gladly planned to obey. He joined the laughing marines, weakened and sick as the tension slipped from him. All that remained for him was to find a way to jump ship when the propitious moment came.

He lapsed into a dream of the rewards Netisten would heap upon him in a few days. It amused Cassi that he, a gutter-born thief, had boldly entered and then escaped the diabolical web Efrel was spinning.

XIII
Two Enemies Meet

Netisten Maril sat on the obsidian-and-gold Imperial throne in his high-vaulted audience hall. About him rose the towering walls of his palace at Thovnosten, capital city of Thovnos and of the Empire. His black-bearded face was dark with barely restrained anger, and he nervously tapped the golden throne arm with his dagger hilt, adding a new pattern of tiny dents across the soft metal. The Emperor glared at the assembled counselors, evidently chafing for an excuse to cut a few throats. He usually needed little excuse.

Maril was a well-built man, still in his early forties. If his prime of life had passed the Emperor, there lay no hint in his hard-muscled frame. His aristocratic face was lined with traces of frequently vented rage — creases and suffused veins that matched the thin white scars on his weathered skin, hallmarks of past battles. Here was a man who held on to what he claimed for his own — a man who had never yielded ground to an opponent, and considered any man a weakling who would yield for him. It made for a volcanic temper and a domineering, uncompromising spirit. The Emperor was a dangerous man to cross, and he was dangerous now. Netisten Maril had just learned that his power in the Empire was seriously threatened by an enemy whom he believed he had utterly destroyed.

A guardsman entered the doorway from the hallway beyond the throne room. "They're bringing him up now, milord," he announced, resuming his post.

Maril grunted, and watched the doorway with hostile eyes.

An unarmed youth of about twenty-five entered, followed by two other guards, who stopped at the door to let him enter alone. Lages carried his powerful body well erect as he stalked toward the black-and-gold throne. Exercise had passed the time and kept him in shape, but the paleness of his complexion evidenced the more than two months he had spent in his cell. His appearance was somewhat shabby withal — his long brown hair unkempt, and his clothing carelessly chosen and hastily arranged. Lages had been given only a short time to prepare for this audience — and he fully expected it to end in an audience with the headsman. His expression was sullen, his well-muscled body tense. His brown eyes quickly surveyed the room — searching for M'Cori. But the girl was not present. Only Maril's most trusted counselors — and the ever vigilant guards. Arrogantly, he drew himself up and glared back at Maril.

Maril fought down his resentment and forced himself to speak calmly. "Well, Lages — I hope this last stay in my dungeons has taught you a little something."

No answer came but an insolent glare.

Maril shrugged. "I could have killed you. I *should* have killed you. Only your high rank and your innocence in your father's treasonous plot spared you when I punished the original nest of conspirators. Then the first time when you so rashly attempted my life, I spared you out of acknowledgment that your father's death had robbed you of sanity. A questionable premise — a stupidity compounded by my accepting your promise of honorable conduct as the valid word of a gentleman. But when you broke your vow and escaped to let that pack of jackals make a puppet and a fool of you — when you again tried to plot against me! By all rights and reason, I should have executed you on the spot. If it hadn't been for the old friendship I bore your family, and my daughter's unreasonable fondness for your worthless carcass—"

"Leave M'Cori out of this, you damned butcher!" Lages exploded. "And your lies of friendship as well. You hate me nearly as much as I hate you, and you've never cared a damn for M'Cori's feelings. There's only one single reason why you haven't eliminated me, and it's the same reason today as you had two years ago. We two are the last direct heirs of the Netisten blood, and you're too proud to let that blood die out. If you could possibly get a male heir, I'd be dead in an instant. So spare me these accusations of my having violated your mercy — I've seen what mercy you showed my father and his friends."

"You insolent bastard's son! Your father was a traitor to the Empire, and I killed him in a fair fight!"

"You murdered him in bed when you found he'd seduced your wife! Couldn't you even get it up for Efrel?"

Maril snarled in rage and leaped from his throne, dagger poised to strike. Lages jumped back into a fighter's crouch — eyes wild, watching the object of his hatred warily. Bare-handed and in the presence of his guards, he would kill the man at first opening.

"Milords! Stop it!" shouted a counselor. "For the sake of us all, don't fight among yourselves now! It will only mean ruin for the Empire and death for all of us!" Several of them started to move toward the two — hesitantly, as they knew what it was to interfere with Maril when he was enraged.

With difficulty, Maril regained control of himself. Lowering his dagger, he ordered, "Get out! All of you get out! I'll call for you when I want you!"

With backward glances, the court nervously filed out of the audience chamber. The guards followed, with the reluctance of sailors leaving a burning ship.

"Now then," intoned Maril, once they were alone. "Despite your perversity, your obstinance. Despite your hostility and past treason. Despite all reason and judgment. I'm going out on a limb to show you mercy one final time. I may be a complete fool, but I'm going to give you a last chance to redeem yourself.

"If you can prove to me once more that you can be trusted, I'll let pass what has happened between us. I'll release you from confinement and restore to you all the privileges of your station. I'll give you leadership over the Imperial fleet. I'll even place you as my second-in-command, as though you were my son and true heir. Remember that you can still ascend my throne someday, Lages. But cross me just once again, and I swear to you I'll kill you even if you were my only son!"

Lages was startled — dumbfounded — for he knew the Emperor to be implacable. He had come to this audience fully expecting death; instead, his enemy offered to return his freedom and high position. Amazement at this incredible turn of fortune broke through his armor of hatred.

"What makes you think you dare trust me?" he wanted to know, wondering suddenly what devious trick Maril intended with this offer of full pardon.

Maril settled back on his throne, watching Lages carefully. "I think I know your heart, Lages. Even if you won't admit it, you know I did the only thing I could with your father. It wasn't some petty court intrigue — it was high treason he entered into. Custom and law alike demand only one end for conspiracy against the Empire. If Leyan was your father, don't forget he was also my brother. That was why I dealt with him as I did — giving him his chance either to kill me or to die honorably in equal combat"

Lages clenched his fists, but held back the anger in his reply. "Perhaps that's true — I won't say. A man's motives are his secret alone. But I know one thing for certain: custom also demands that I avenge the death of my father."

Maril nodded acknowledgment. "Yes, I realize this. Another reason why I haven't executed you."

"That doesn't mean I've tried to kill you only to satisfy custom. This quarrel is a blood feud between the two of us — man to man. I swear to you, there's no pleasure I'd crave more than to savour your death by these hands!" He raised both fists before him to punctuate his words.

Maril's eyes burned with reflected fury — but he answered with a harsh laugh. "Nevertheless, you're going to have to put aside our feud for now, nephew. Instead — if I understand your heart as I think I do — you're actually going to help me..."

"I'll help strangle you with your own guts!"

Maril ignored the outburst. "Yes, help me. We both seek to avenge your father."

Lages was taken off guard. "What do you mean?" he asked quietly, wondering wherein lay the cruel jest. Such deviousness was as alien to Maril's temperament as the show of mercy he had thus far extended to his deadly enemy.

Maril smiled coldly, pressing his advantage. "I didn't kill your father; you should know that. Sure, it was my hand that put a sword through his flesh — but I didn't kill him. Leyan was my brother; I had never desired his death, until fate demanded it. I'm no more responsible for Leyan's death than is the sword that cut him down. My hand and my sword were merely instruments of the dark fate that has caught us all up in its web — an evil fate woven by a cunning fiend who has plotted to destroy all of our blood.

"No, Lages. It was not I who murdered Leyan. It was the scheming witch who poisoned my brother's mind against me — who lured him into a black conspiracy to fulfill her own twisted motives. It was Efrel who murdered your father. I say to you that Efrel murdered Leyan, just as surely as if her hand had plunged the blade into his heart!"

Lages stood silently scowling. The circumstances of Efrel's guilt had occurred to him before, to be sure — but the furious rush of his emotions would not let reason channel his rage to the dead sorceress. Often on sleepless nights he had tossed about in frustrated agony of spirit — cursing the beautiful enchantress who had destroyed so many with her treacherous schemes. But it was Maril whose victory meant his father's ruin and the collapse of his own hopes. Maril lived while the others died, and this Lages could not endure.

"Yes, Efrel." The Emperor saw uncertainty in Lages's face and drove relentlessly with his argument. "You knew in your heart that the witch was to blame for Leyan's downfall, but you wouldn't acknowledge it — even to yourself. Efrel was beyond your revenge, and I was someone tangible to focus your hatred on — an obvious villain when grief and shame fired your senses with blood-madness. So you raged at Netisten Maril, forgetting the venomous creature who seduced your father to his own destruction."

Struggling beneath an intolerable emotional strain, Lages bent his head and said in almost a whisper, "*Efrel!* Yes, what you say is true. I realize that now. Perhaps I've known it secretly all this time. But Efrel is dead, and I — "

"*No!*" interrupted Maril. A note of awe — almost of terror — entered his voice. "No, Efrel is *not* dead! In her lair on Pellin the sorceress still lives. I tell you, Efrel still lives — and by all the gods, I can't understand how or why!"

"What! How do you know this?" Lages's troubled thoughts reeled from yet another incredible reversal of what he had considered solid actuality. "It can't be true! What jest do you — "

"I've sensed something has been afoot for months now," Maril cut him off. "Agents have brought me reports of unusual movements of ships and men throughout the Empire. A number of my lords have been restive; others have discreetly withdrawn from my surveillance. And there's been an alarmingly high mortality among my spies. Especially have I found it difficult to obtain information pertaining to Pellin. The few humdrum reports of peaceful activity there made a suspicious contrast to the associated information — and to the sinister fact that most of my agents on Pellin had ceased to report at all. It was obvious that a plot was taking shape against me, but I have been unable to secure any specific information — nothing that I could pin down and move to destroy."

Maril scowled. "Of course, your own ill-advised efforts not only called for all my attention, but until recently obscured this deeper threat to the Empire. I had assumed, not unnaturally, that you somehow had a hand in the plot I sensed was taking shape." He did not add that one reason he had spared Lages was to seek to draw out his imagined co-conspirators.

"Then this morning, Cassi, one of my most capable spies, returned to me from Pellin, where he had ventured along with a band of cutthroats who had been told there would be work for them there. Even Cassi was barely able to escape from that accursed isle to make his report. He was half-dead when he finally was picked up by a fishing boat off Fisitia — after he'd jumped off a rebel warship at night and paddled toward the mainland with just a cork-stuffed pair of pants to keep afloat.

"But Cassi brought away with him the information I've been seeking. He tells me that Efrel is still alive — although badly disfigured after her ride through our city. Cassi saw her in the cellars of Dan-Legeh with his own eyes, so he swears. He can't explain how she managed to live through it, but her punishment did nothing to cripple the hellish cunning of her mind — and now the fires of hatred eat at her evil soul. Over the months Efrel has made far-reaching preparations to conquer Thovnos and to seize the throne of Empire. Cassi says the witch has amassed a dangerously large following for her rebellion. He also tells me that Efrel has appointed as her general some enigmatic outlander whom she brought in from the Lartroxian mainland. He calls himself Kane."

"Kane? I know of only one man to bear that name."

"Yes." Maril's voice lost its domineering assuredness. "This is another strange thing that plagues my mind. Cassi got close to the man on two occasions, and he says Kane even looks like the monster of legend. Further, he says that the rebels boast among themselves that their new leader and Red Kane, whose pirate hordes pillaged our coasts two centuries ago, are one and the same man!"

He paused for a moment, lost in speculation. "Wait, I'll summon Cassi. He should be somewhat rested from his ordeal. We'll listen to his complete report now."

Maril bellowed for the guards. Bodies crowded the doorway in an instant. "Guardsman! Bring Cassi to me!"

"The Kane of old, uncle?" Lages shook his head in bewilderment. "No, that doesn't seem possible. More likely this is more of the witch's cunning. Efrel has found someone of chance resemblance to Kane and is using his legend to give her rebels confidence."

"That's what I thought, Lages," replied Maril, noting with pleasure that his nephew had once again acknowledged their relationship. It was beginning to look as if he would be able to count on his loyalty after all. "But then again, it isn't possible that Efrel should have lived. Who can say what powers that sorceress commands? Events are taking a weird turn, and I don't like it. Not at all. I fear nothing of flesh or of steel — but sorcery..."

Maril spoke with compelling earnestness. "Then, I can count on your loyalty in this matter, can't I? Will you give me your word of honor to end this pointless feud? Will you fight at my side to destroy this witch whose black crimes and foul lusts have affronted the gods and brought doom to the house of Netisten?"

According to his code, there was only one answer Lages could give. He nodded thoughtfully. "Yes. You can count on my loyalty. I give my oath to help you destroy the witch. If it is true that Efrel has escaped her deserved fate, you can be certain that I'll never rest until she and her hellish conspiracy are wiped out. Efrel has my father's death to answer for, and neither a resurrected pirate lord nor all her sorcerous powers shall save the scheming whore from my vengeance!"

"I knew I could trust you to see reason," exulted Maril. He grasped his nephew's hand with convincing enthusiasm. "There's still hope that the rebellion can be nipped in the bud. We'll get a full report from Cassi — precise details on Efrel's plans and defenses, the names of the traitors in our midst. Then I'll send the Imperial fleet to Prisarte under your command. As much of the Imperial navy as we can mobilize in a short week should be enough to crush the rebels and burn the city and its fortress to clean ashes."

A guardsman entered the throne room. His face was pallid, and he was alone.

"Where's Cassi?" Maril demanded.

The guardsman licked his lips. "Milord, I think you had best see to this for yourself."

Maril glared at the unhappy guard. With an oath, the Emperor heaved himself from his throne and stalked from the hall.

Lages stood in the empty audience hall, arms folded across his broad chest, eyes pensive. His brow furrowed in speculation. Too many revelations in one hour left his mind in turmoil. This morning he was a prisoner, disgraced and awaiting execution. It was not yet noon and he was free, restored to his rank, given command of the Imperial fleet, promised succession to the throne. Glory and power were his to strive for. The gods had given him the chance to win vengeance on Efrel, his place on the Imperial throne, and M'Cori for his wife. Ambitious plans — but with daring and ability, a strong man could conquer anything.

So the gods had chosen to alter the woven pattern of his fate. He smiled, remembering the prophecy. The priestess had known Lages was favored by the gods.

Lages's smile twisted into a snarl. "This changes nothing, dear uncle," he whispered to the shadows. "I gave you my word to be loyal until Efrel is slain. After that…"

Only the shadows heard his mirthless laugh.

XIV
...And One Came Out

Cassi opened one eye, saw the silken sheets and lush fur coverings of his bed, opened the other eye, saw the luxurious appointments of his quarters. He yawned, stretched overtaxed muscles and stiffened limbs. He was in the Imperial palace of Thovnosten. He was longer a hunted man.

He was a wealthy man. Cassi scratched the stubble of his pointed jaw and mused upon the extent of the Emperor's generosity. From now on, he would live the life of an aristocrat — no more prowling about the alleys of Thovnosten. He would live in a splendid manor, stay drunk and well fed and well laid, worry how to keep his former colleagues from stealing his jewels and costly furnishings.

Something had awakened him. He glowered at the doorway to his chambers. Netisten Maril had posted enough guards there to keep out an army. The security was comforting, but right now Cassi wanted to sleep. If the fools would make a little less noise…

"Sir? Are you awake?" A guardsman stood at attention on the threshold.

Cassi savoured the sight of a member of the Imperial guard addressing him in such manner. He curled his lips to reply. "I am now. What is it?" He let his tone insinuate that the interruption had better not be over some trifle.

"Someone to see you, sir."

"Tell him to go bugger himself," Cassi yawned. A man of his station could not entertain casual callers, and if Maril wanted him, the guards would not be so circumspect.

"But I'd prefer that you do that for me, milord," purred a new voice.

Cassi sat up. Sleep was the last thing on his mind.

"Netisten Maril sent me to you," she smiled. "Do you like me?"

She was lithe as a dancer, with a tight figure that pressed against the clinging folds of the sheer silk gown that she wore. Her hair was short and tightly curled, extravagantly dyed in the colors of autumn leaves. Her face was as somber and coquettish as a child's and her nails were long and lacquered in black. Cassi guessed she could barely have reached her middle teens.

"Come here," he grinned.

"Milord, our orders are to admit no one but the Emperor himself," the guard protested. "There is danger that — "

She chuckled in a surprisingly throaty tone. "Do I look so dangerous, milord?"

Black-nailed fingers plucked at the fastenings of her gold-and-yellow gown. The folds of silk floated down upon her ankles. She was willowy and white, and she had followed the pattern of autumn-hued dyes throughout. She made a leisurely pirouette.

"Do you fear me, milord?" she smiled. "Do I hide weapons upon my person?"

"Come here," Cassi invited thickly.

The guardsman interjected, "Milord, our orders are to — "

"To hell with your orders, fool!" Cassi sneered. "My friend, Netisten Maril, sends me evidence of his favor. Now, go!"

She laughed as they closed the door. "What is your pleasure, milord?" She stepped away from her pile of silks, and danced toward him like some fantastic butterfly.

"We'll think of something, you and I," Cassi grinned, making way for her on the bed.

She was accomplished, Cassi had to admit. After awhile, he lifted her up and rolled astride her. "Maril shows his gratitude in a fine style," he gasped between kisses. "Ahhh... Watch your nails, bitch! My back is sunburned, and salted as a sailor's... Ahh..."

Her breath came in sudden gasps as her nails dug into the flesh of his back. "Do they not call this ecstasy *the little death*?" she panted, biting at his ear.

Cassi felt his orgasm shudder through him. He was still dizzy and shaken, wondering at her words, when the venom encrusted beneath her raking nails fired his veins with final agony.

She licked the froth from his dead lips, and winked as she sauntered past the guards.

XV
A Tower at Dawn

The night skies were pale with the approach of dawn. Two figures stood side by side on a tower before the harbor gate of Thovnosten, watching the stars go out. Lages stood straight and proud as if the months of imprisonment had been but a bad dream, forgotten now. The youth was resplendent in his silvered mail, crested helmet, and scarlet cloak of an Imperial general. M'Cori stood beneath the shelter of his arm, silent as the first light of dawn high lighted the cascade of fine blond hair that spilled over her shoulders. Caught at her delicate throat by an emerald pin, a splendid cloak of white ermine held back the cold sea breeze. The wind fluttered her gown against her slender form, whipped strands of hair across her patrician features. She was fragile and beautiful as some exquisite porcelain goddess — pale and golden with eyes green as the sea below them.

"It's dawn," said Lages simply.

"Dawn. And now you must sail." M'Cori stared down at the fleet tossing at anchor below them. She counted slowly, the syllables falling softly under each breath. "Only twenty-four ships. So few to meet the witch's traitor fleet."

"These are all the warships we can have at battle-ready on such short notice. In a month we could have another hundred, but in a month Efrel will have mobilized her forces, too. It's best we attack now, while her preparations are incomplete. And don't forget — our vessels are every one of them first-class warships, well armed and manned by trained soldiers. We'll only be facing a mob of undisciplined renegades. It's a pity that Cassi didn't get the chance to tell us all he knew. From what he indicated, their fleet probably consists of a handful of real warships and a motley scattering of jury-rigged merchants and barges converted to haul troops and supplies. We'll sweep them from the seas."

She seemed to disregard his confidence. "I'm losing you again, dearest — again, after all those weeks in prison. Lages, I lied — at times I was sure Father meant to kill you. He would have eventually, if he hadn't needed you to fight Efrel.

"Now you're free. Free — only to leave me again, after but a few days of happiness together. I almost wish you had remained in that cell. You were safe there, and I could visit you whenever I wished."

Lages turned on her. "Like a pet bird in a cage! Something to bring sweets and flowers to! A man prefers death to an existence such as that!"

He caught himself. He hadn't meant to snap at her like that. Horment! She was only concerned with his safety. Her baffling system of illogic at times was infuriating. He started to apologize — but, feeling awkward, said nothing. Instead he looked at the skies and knew he had to leave.

"I love you, M'Cori," he whispered.

She threw her white arms around his mailed shoulders and clung to him desperately. After a moment he gently loosened their embrace. Feeling a keen desire to possess her — and at the same instant a longing to be free of her — Lages marched down the steps from the tower and to the harbor.

Through her tears, M'Cori watched the fleet sail out.

XVI
Visions of Black Prometheus

Cut deep into the basalt beneath Dan-Legeh lay the secret chamber of Efrel. Few were those who came here willingly, and fewer those who left again. In this darkened vault — a great hollow of cunningly hewn stone, where the flickering cressets cast the brightest light that ever would shine here — Efrel engaged in her sorceries and experiments in the black arts. For ages past, the chamber had been put to this accursed usage by the Pellin lords, and the expansive room was filled with debris of evil enterprises centuries forgotten.

The chamber was a vast, shadowy cavern, and great oil lamps — most of them unlit for centuries — were positioned at frequent intervals to give illumination. The lamps stood on tripods half the height of a man, and many gallons of oil filled their tanks to feed the lambent flames. The center of the chamber was taken up with a wide pool of inky water — a black mirror-like surface encircled by a low wall with curious carvings in bas-relief. About the pool stood a number of man-sized statues of some obscenely tentacled sea demon. A visitor might wonder if this were not the fane of some forgotten devil cult, whose acolytes were now dust with their gods. The pool gave back the torchlight like polished jet, and no conception of its depth could be realized from peering within. It must be very deep, for its level rose and fell with the tides — indicating communication with the sea.

Around this circular pool were arranged the apparatus and paraphernalia of Efrel's supernatural delvings — strangely bound tomes of forbidden knowledge, weirdly shaped alembics and retorts and other alchemical devices, caskets and vials filled with powders and elixirs and preserved objects of dubious origins, eldritch carvings on the floor and walls. The stained and freshly oiled instruments of torture were the least abhorrent objects within the chamber.

Efrel was not alone in this place. Before her, imprisoned within the borders of a meticulously ordered pentagram, reared the serpentine coils of her familiar demon — a creature of hideous malevolence summoned by Efrel from another plane of existence. The demon was no stranger to Efrel or to this chamber. The sorceress was wont to evoke her monstrous pet in order to gain certain knowledge that no human resource could supply. For this purpose she had summoned her creature once again.

The pentagram defied its wrathful efforts to break free. Disappointed, the demon abandoned the attempt. Glaring at the triumphant sorceress, it spoke in its harsh, whispering tones: "I see that you have succeeded in bringing Kane to your side. To be sure, he seems to be most energetic in his services to you. How does your new lover suit you?"

Efrel smiled at the demon's leering snicker. "I am completely satisfied with your recommendation. Kane is exactly the man I needed for this venture. He has given me invaluable lessons in treachery, introduced new strategy and tactics for my navy, organized all aspects of my rebellion with an incomparable ability."

She paused, then went on to the reason for this evocation. "Kane seems to me more than human, somehow. Kane is a unique combination — a man of incredible strength, ruthless daring, intellectual genius, and evil to the core. There's something utterly inhuman about his eyes — they are the mark of a killer, or my every instinct lies! Yes, I can make good use of Kane. A deadly weapon, to be sure — and as treacherous as he is dangerous. I will use Kane, but I won't trust him an inch!"

The demon laughed mockingly. "I see like recognizes like. Can you be certain, though, that you can control him? I wonder."

Efrel snarled in anger. "I can handle Kane! He's but a man — for all his black heart and long life. The fool has an inkling of but a fraction of my powers, while I know Kane for what he is. Kane can withhold no mysteries from Efrel!

"But this is why I have summoned you. Thus far you have told me very little of Kane. Only that Red Kane the pirate lord still lived, that he was the one man who could gain victory for me, that he could be found on the Lartroxian coast. Tonight I intend to devote this entire evocation to learning everything about Kane. Tell me now, who — or what — is Kane? What has he done during these decades since he terrorized the Empire? Who was he before he appeared in our realm to lead his pirate horde on their reign of carnage? And how has he escaped death for these two centuries?"

Again the demon laughed. "There are many things you may not know of Kane. Even in my world there are mysteries concerned with Kane that have escaped our wisdom. Even to tell you what we know of him would require far more time than your evocation can hold me here. But while your spell lasts, I shall tell you a little of the man you have called forth from the past.

"I obey your command. Behold now, as I show to you but a few tableaux of past moments in Kane's fantastic history."

The outlines of the underground chamber suddenly began to fade. The massive lamps, the grotesque statues, the circular pool, the instruments of torture, the sorcerous paraphernalia all grew indistinct before her eyes, dissolved into blackness. Efrel seemed to stand vertiginously in the midst of infinite oblivion, with only the sardonic demon visible in the cosmic darkness.

Then light began to form out of the chaos. Wavering images began to take shape before her, tumbling kaleidoscopic patterns of time. Flashing in front of her eyes now were frozen instants of the past — brief glimpses of Kane's past life, wrested from eternity by the demon's supernatural 'powers and projected onto her consciousness.

Efrel saw Kane running through a ruined city, a slim girl dashing at his side. Behind them thundered a dozen vicious looking bandits — triumph on their cruel faces as they urged their mounts after the fugitives. The city's towers were broken and toppled, its buildings gutted and fire-scarred. Horizons were strangely foreshortened, as if the city were built upon a pinnacle above a plain. The rubble-choked streets gave Kane a short lead over the riders — and as he momentarily escaped their sight, he leaped through a darkened doorway, pulling the girl after him.

Kane lay naked across a mouldering bed, in a room where moonlight spilled through a window curtained with dusty cobwebs. Beyond the window stretched the crumbling parapets of a fortress that had slumbered in ruin for decades. A deserted village could dimly be seen in the valley below. Kane seemed to give no notice to the decay rampant about him as he lay there, weakly, in a dream. Stepping close to him in the musty chamber was a pale-skinned woman, her porcelain figure veiled with rotting silk. The moonlight shone white upon her long fangs as she smiled at the man who awaited her.

A gore-spattered Kane reeled, locked in combat with a towering demon of twice his bulk. Doll-sized imps scampered about the thrashing legs of the combatants — stabbing at Kane with tiny razor-edged spears. Several of the imps lay crushed and sundered upon the red earth. Behind them, a naked girl stood bound to a rock, watching the battle in terror. Desolate mountains and black stones ringed the figures, and from the cliff beside them yawned a black cave that seemed to drop off straight into the bowels of earth. Kane's sword was broken, and he slashed desperately with the jagged forte — holding away the demon's jaws with his free arm.

Kane slipped stealthily along empty streets in a city where no window showed a light against the darkness. There were no signs of destruction, but the buildings stood as if deserted for several years. Here there the moonlight disclosed a scattering of dry bones. Torches followed behind Kane as half a dozen grim-faced men stalked him through the dead city.

The night exploded into a chaos of bloodshed and flame. Kane strode through the pillaged streets of a city, sword red in his fist — laughing mightily as his pirate horde rioted all about him. Barbaric figures smashed down doors of houses, slaying all who confronted them. Howling warriors raced through streets, loaded down with riches and plunder. Women and children were being cut down alongside their men, as the younger girls were carried off, bare-limbed and screaming, into the darkness. Kane seized a wine bottle from a passing looter and poured its contents over his blood-flecked smile.

Kane ran up a long flight of stairs, pursued by a slavering white-furred creature, half man and half wolf. Below them lay a castle hall — its tables overturned and its floors crimson with blood. Strewn about were the torn and broken bodies of scores of men and grey wolves. At the top of the stairway, Kane suddenly turned to hurl himself upon the hulking werewolf. Locked in a bone-crushing embrace, man and were-beast hurtled back down the stairs, bounding through the railing near the bottom and crashing to the hall floor. The stunning impact threw them apart. Kane shook the pain from his head groggily as the werewolf champed its reddened fangs and lunged for him.

Stars shone down upon a tower jutting far into the nighted sky. Wearing robes of a fantastic pattern, Kane hunched in concentration over a table strewn with strange volumes and scrolls of rust red writing. He was muttering to himself while he worked over pages of diagrams and calculations. Often he referred to the dark tomes of necromantic lore that lay before him. An intricate system of pentagrams and occult glyphics covered much of the tower walls, while a terrified girl wept in chains in one corner.

Kane sat upon an immense throne of obsidian; on his head was a crown of unfaceted jewels. A snarling lion lay at his feet, causing the courtiers who stood beside his throne to keep their distance. Their manner of dress was unfamiliar, nor was the race immediately recognizable. Kane's face was twisted with anger, and his lips formed strange syllables as he made some decree to those assembled before his throne. Consternation shuddered through their ranks at his words — but they slunk away when he leaped up in fury and brandished his scepter as if it were a mace.

Shambling man-sized creatures, who looked like monstrous hybrids of man and frog, stood watching Kane in the shattered chamber of some colossal prehuman structure. Great bronze swords were clutched in webbed fists as they waited in the shadows of the cracked and leaning walls. Slimy water covered much of the floor, and fleshy vines stole through jagged apertures to enshroud looming machines of unguessable nature. A gigantic crystal filled the center of the chamber — a sullen dome nearly a hundred yards across, composed of a substance that resembled bloodstone. The scarlet veins of the crystal suddenly seemed to glow with life. Blinding flashes of coruscant energy burst from long-slumbering pillars of machinery, driving the amphibian creatures back in fear. An eerie light of green, veined with red, shot forth from the depths of the awakened crystal and bathed Kane in its fire.

Kane stood in what appeared to be a cavern, stretching endlessly far beneath the earth. Jagged stalactites hung like black clouds from the cavern roof a mile above; about him the horizon vanished over a smoking plain of shattered rock and angry lava pits. In this nightmare vision of Hell, Kane was not alone. Dark creatures of blighted beauty stood around him — bizarre demons with leathery wings, and beautiful faces that glowed with evil wisdom. They wheeled about Kane in attitudes half of menace, part curiosity. Kane spoke earnestly to one who seemed to be their leader — a tall demonic figure of perfect beauty and consummate evil, whose eyes shone like yellow suns.

Kane rolled on the floor of a fantastic temple, struggling with another man before its smoking altar. Kane's eyes were wild with murder-lust, as he wrestled there on the stones. His powerful hands were locked about his opponent's throat who now flailed only weakly at Kane's grinning face. The livid face of the man he strangled bore a striking resemblance to Kane's own primitive features.

The pictures flashed through Efrel's mind at a bewildering speed — taking shape, then dissolving, almost faster than she could recognize each scene. It was a whirlpool of images that spun past on and on — some only an instant's glimpse of Kane's face, others complete tableaux that lasted for perhaps a minute. The demon's grating voice reached her ears through the phantasmagoria — while Efrel sought to comprehend the frozen moments of Kane's incredible saga as they burst from the vault of eternity.

"Two centuries — they are nothing to Kane. Years are only flickering moments to a man who has seen ages roll past him, empires rise and crumble, mankind emerge from infancy, and the elder races pass into darkness. You have badly underestimated Kane — as you can see now, Efrel. He is not, as you had supposed, a mere pirate lord who has been kept living past his time by a freak of fate. No, Efrel! Pirate, thief, beggar, king, sorcerer, warrior, scholar, general, poet, assassin — his roles have been myriad. This man who measures centuries like years has been many things in his endless wandering.

"Kane was one of the first true men — born into a hostile world of strange ancient beings. In this dawn world of humanity, Kane defied the insane god who created his race — an experiment that had turned out far from the creator's expectations. This demented elder god dabbled at creating a race of mindless creatures whose only existence would be to amuse and delight him. He almost succeeded, until Kane rebelled against this stifling paradise and spurred the young race to independent will. He killed his own brother, who sought to oppose his heresy, thus bringing violent death as well as rebellion to the infant mankind. Disgusted at the failure of his depraved design, the god abandoned his creation. And for his act of defiance, Kane was cursed with immortality — doomed to roam this world under the shadow of violence and death. His blighted wandering will cease only when Kane himself can be destroyed by the violence to which he first gave expression. And to distinguish Kane from the rest of mankind whom he has renounced are his hellish eyes — killer's eyes — the Mark of Kane!

"For centuries he has wandered from place to place, and wherever he lingers, he brings death and destruction with him. He is a harbinger of death — a lord of chaos. To tear down, to kill and destroy is his very nature. For was it not Kane who first introduced murder to a newborn race? This Kane, Efrel, is the man you have chosen to league yourself with.

"To be sure, Kane is still a man — and a steel blade through Kane's heart will kill him as dead as any other man. But yet, Kane is not quite human. Natural death is closed to him, and his body has not aged an hour from the inception of the curse. Injuries quickly heal, to leave his body as it was at the moment of that curse. Only through violence can death claim him, and Kane has so far proved too strong for those who have sought to destroy him. For violence and death are the proper element of this lord of chaos, and herein he is master.

"But no man can live for centuries and remain altogether human. His mind is filled with the wisdom and experiences of centuries. He has seen things of which others can only dream; he has tasted knowledge that would drive sanity from the mind of another man. And he is not sane as your world reckons sanity. Kane's thoughts are not like those of another man, for he sees all things in the perspective of centuries. Lives of others are flashing motes of light. Time stands still for him, and everything you hold to be permanent Kane considers no more than ever-changing phenomena. All that remains permanent for Kane is his own existence, and to make this interminable existence endurable is all that drives him on. His motives are unguessable, his actions unthinkable to human minds — for he lives in a world of flux in which he himself is the only stationary force.

"This then is he whom you have presumed to use to gain your revenge. And certainly Kane can accomplish all that you wish — I did not lie to you when I advised you to seek him out. Kane is your weapon; manipulate him if you can. Only remember that no pentagram holds safely this demon you have evoked. Beware, Efrel — not even the queen of night dares kindle her fire with the comet!"

With a final mocking laugh, the demon vanished. The darkness of infinity burst into a final vortex of images, then collapsed like a cosmic bubble. The chamber lay as before, altered only by the empty pentagram.

Shaken by the creature's revelations, Efrel sat alone in the darkened chamber, thinking over what she had learned and cursing the unreliability of demonic aid. Uneasily, she recalled an ancestor who had asked to be showered with wealth — and was buried under an avalanche of gold.

At length she smiled confidently. After all, Kane had never encountered Efrel in his wandering. She whispered to the darkness, "So, then! This knowledge I shall not fear, for it shall be my strength. As I know Kane's secret, thus shall it be easier to deal with him, when I know that I must. Let Kane first conquer an empire for me — then there will be time to test Kane's immortality!"

XVII
Call to Battle

Kane drew on his battle gear, with movements sure and rapid from long practice. Although only just awakened, he moved about in the cold dawn-lit chamber as if he had been up for hours. Adjusting his mail hauberk, Kane wondered to himself — how many times had he done this before? How many battles had the dawn watched him prepare to fight? Not so many that the familiar chill in his guts ever failed to appear. Musing whether this last-minute uncertainty would ever leave him, he buckled on his greaves.

Over his shoulder, Kane called to Efrel, "When is it estimated that the Imperial fleet will reach us? And do we know its exact strength?"

It seemed to him that Efrel watched him with a strange intensity from her seat in a darkened corner of the bedchamber. "My information tells me their fleet left at dawn five days ago," the sorceress replied, "sailing under good winds until yesterday's calm. So, assuming they will push on at their best speed to take us by surprise, the Imperial forces should enter our waters sometime between late morning and early tomorrow. As to their fleet, my informant counted twenty-four first-line warships — eleven of them triremes."

"Is Netisten Maril commanding them?" Kane inquired, fitting a greave over his other boot. Above the greaves, trousers of heavy leather ran from high boot tops to protect knee and thigh in the interval below the mail skirts of his hauberk.

"No. My spies tell me the Emperor has finally made peace with his nephew, Lages, and is sending him instead. Knowing Maril, he's being cautious in his old age — or likely he hopes that Lages will destroy both himself and my fleet. At any rate, he only now has received word of my conspiracy — so he's trying to hit us quickly before my plans can reach fruition. Hence the relatively small fleet."

Kane grunted and buckled his two-handed broadsword across his back. For a moment, he considered leaving it in favor of a shorter blade for the close fighting — when a short, chopping blade had an advantage in the press of bodies. Still, the broadsword had a nice balance, and he felt confident his arm could swing it without tiring. Its greater reach might prove useful, he decided.

Kane continued, "Are you certain that this is the full extent of their attack? This could be just the vanguard of a larger fleet. Try to draw us out and…"

"No. This one fleet is all Maril has sent. It would take him weeks to mobilize the entire Imperial navy, of course. Anyway, my source assured me that there are no other warships moving against Pellin at the moment."

"Where the hell's Alremas?" muttered Kane, selecting a long dagger, flat-bladed and weighted for throwing. "Your source seems amazingly sure of himself. Will his head roll if he's made an error, I wonder? Who is this mysterious informant, anyway — another one of your demons?"

"Not a demon." Efrel smirked at his ignorance. "But creatures of this plane — creatures who dwell in hidden places of this world, whose secrets few humans have fathomed. They watch our foolish wars, unsuspected by forgetful mankind. Dare you guess? I assure you, Kane, my information comes from creatures as alien to mankind as any demon from the outer dimensions!"

She paused enticingly. "But I will tell you more of this at another time. Efrel does not share her secrets needlessly."

Imel burst in, out of breath. Busily the renegade fretted with the fastenings of his magnificent cuirass. He winced at the thought of how the crimson lacquer the gold tracery would look by the end of the day, but at least he knew he would cut an imposing figure — victor or corpse.

"Have all the officers been alerted?" snapped Kane, taking his anger at Efrel out on Imel.

"Yes. I've seen to that personally."

"And the men?"

"The trumpeters have sounded the call to arms in every barracks, and the fleet has acknowledged. The marines will be ready to board in an hour. Meanwhile, we've managed to arouse the entire city. Things are moving in good order, all things considered."

Kane scowled as Imel fidgeted with his cuirass. "I hope you can swim with that thing on — you'll never get it off in the water. All right — see that everything moves with all possible dispatch. Lages and the Imperial fleet may be here in a matter of hours, and I want to have every available ship manned and ready to meet them. So get to it and stop preening yourself! And tell Alremas to get his ass up here, if you see him!"

"Yes, milord!" saluted Imel. He wheeled smartly from the chamber, almost colliding with Arbas. The assassin sprang agilely aside and entered the room cursing to himself.

"Battle alert already, Kane?" Arbas queried. "Thought we were supposed to have more time. Did that damned spy screw things up?"

"It seems he did. But things couldn't have gone on like this much longer. Fortunately, Maril hasn't sent the entire Imperial fleet, but it's still going to be touch and go. I'll want you with me on the *Ara-Teving* — I'd like someone at my back I can trust. In the meantime check around on how preparations are going. Your pal, Imel, will be glad for any help you can give him, but mostly let me know where there's any problem."

As Arbas left, Kane turned to Efrel. "Now we'll see how well I was able to get your navy kicked into shape in the past weeks. And don't worry about a court martial if my leadership turns out to have been ineffective. But to return to my earlier questions. You tell me that your information on Maril's fleet has come from these inhuman allies you keep hinting about. That you should keep them a mystery from your general seems pointless to me. That's your affair, though. In any case, I hope you've called for their aid against Lages — we can use whatever supernatural powers you command."

Efrel ignored his prodding. "You'll have to fight this battle completely on your own, Kane. As you know, the Imperial fleet will be protected against all commonplace sorceries. And the time is not right for me to call upon those forces to which I've often alluded. Otherwise I'd never have needed you, would I?"

Kane started to argue further, but at that moment Oxfors Alremas leisurely entered the chamber.

"Well, you managed to take your sweet time getting here!" Kane growled.

Alremas gave him an angry glare. "I'm not accustomed to being ordered around like a common soldier. And don't send that renegade parvenu calling for me next time, either! I may be forced to act as second-in-command to you for the moment, but don't forget that you only usurp the position that I—"

He caught sight of Efrel and checked himself. "Good morning, my Queen," he greeted her calmly.

Efrel raised herself. "And good morning to you, Oxfors Alremas." She hobbled to the door. "I have things to do myself now, so I'll take leave of you, Kane. I'm sure Alremas will give you his full cooperation. Won't you, Alremas?" She smiled at him with serpentine menace, then limped for the stair.

All the rebellious spirits seemed drained from Alremas as he dazedly turned to Kane.

"Now then," began Kane, "if I may have your gracious attention, there's a battle to be fought. Lages is commanding a fleet of some twenty-four warships that will reach here in a matter of hours. Almost half of these are triremes, and all of them are first-class fighting ships. As you know, we haven't dared to mass our own forces for the danger of discovery, so all we can mobilize at this moment are five triremes and seven other real warships. Add to this about twenty-six converted merchants, barges, and smaller craft — and we're left with a damn small fleet to take on the Imperials. Also Efrel tells me she can't help out at this time with whatever secret powers she makes boast to control.

"So we're going to have a close fight of it, and we'll need every available man and ship. And I want them ready as soon as possible! I don't intend for Lages to catch us in the harbor. We'll put out and wait for him on the open sea, where we can count on enough room to maneuver. If this patchwork navy has just followed through with the program I've drilled into it, we should be able to give Lages a more dangerous game than he had thought to play.

"We've planned this out before to the last detail, so you understand what you're to do. Now by Lord Tloluvin's red eyes, get busy and see that my plans are carried out! Our personal quarrel can wait until Thovnosten is taken. I'll see you on board the *Kelkin* in an hour for final orders. That's all."

Alremas snarled something that was hardly a salute, and stalked out.

Kane buckled on a crested helmet and snatched up his axe. "If you survive today's battle, then I'm going to have to deal with you myself, Oxfors Alremas!" he muttered, scowling after the Pellinite lord. It occurred to him as he left to check on the battle preparations that his enemy was doubtlessly thinking along similar patterns.

XVIII
Fire on the Sea

They met the Imperial fleet about an hour before noon. From his flagship, the *Ara-Teving*, Kane observed the approaching fleet. Lages had wasted no time, and without Efrel's mysterious intelligence, he almost certainly would have ripped through the rebel blockade and descended upon Prisarte before any effective resistance could be mounted. Lages had made use of yesterday's calm to beach his warships and unstep his mainmasts for battle. Under oars, his fleet was advancing at ramming speed.

Through his telescope, Kane admired the beauty of the long warships — their double or triple rows of oars knifing the water strongly and evenly, their jibsails taut in the wind, driving their ram-mounted hulls through the choppy sea. Then Kane grimly surveyed his own navy — a motley fleet of refitted antiques and converted merchants, with a few first-line warships like the *Ara-Teving* and the *Kelkin*. But they would have to do the job, he realized, thankful that there had been time for all the ships to move into formation here at a point some fifteen miles from the harbor of Prisarte. Whatever its worth as a fighting force, Efrel's newborn fleet now awaited the Imperial onslaught.

"Well, what do you think?" asked Arbas from beside Kane.

"No different. If all their warships hit us in a wedge, we're going to be in a really bad position — if not to say, a hopeless position. So we'll have to make certain that all of them don't reach our formation — and that's why I designed these special barges. Now we're going to know the truth about this floating artillery that I've been getting so much lip about."

He pointed to the ten ponderous barges that were slowly being rowed out into a position slightly in advance of the rest of the fleet. The barges had been carefully converted according to Kane's dictate. Each hull was dominated by a gigantic catapult — not the small petrary that some warships carried, but a massive siege engine of the type that normally was constructed to breach a walled town or fortress.

Baskets of broken rocks along with stones of a hundred pounds or more filled the hold of each barge. But there was a stranger type of missile provided for the catapults as well — on which Kane was gambling for victory against a superior force. Special bundles of cloth, matting, kindling, and thatch had been bound together into a ball some two feet thick. Each bundle of tinder had then been soaked through with a mixture of saltpeter and sulfur, stirred into pitch, tar, and other combustible oils. The fireballs, a weapon Kane had used in past sieges, burned with an intense flame as they soared through the air — and on hitting they burst into dozens of fiery fragments. One such missile could burn a ship, or divert the greater part of the crew to fighting its spreading flames.

The only other cargo the unwieldy barges carried was a crew of slave rowers and a team of soldiers trained to man the catapults. These crafts were far too slow and awkward for any use except as seagoing artillery — and because of the danger of heavy seas, they could not be safely rowed very far from port.

Judging the Imperial fleet to be within range, Kane gave the signal to commence firing. Ten catapults lashed forth their long throwing arms — the recoil forcing the barges dangerously low into the sea. A rain of rocks and fireballs arched high through the air toward the oncoming fleet. At least half were far off the mark, but a few rocks fell among the fleet. Hurriedly the catapult crews rewound their instruments, adjusted the slings, and fired again.

The second volley was more deadly.

From his flagship, the *Mon-Ossa*, Lages watched in amazement as the trireme next to his took two of the fireballs at once. The blazing missiles splattered the decks and the men with a wave of clinging, inextinguishable flame.

"Forward, full speed!" Lages shouted. Battle pennants relayed his command, increasing the pace from ramming speed. The Thovnosian general seethed in frustration, for his fleet was still a good distance out of bowshot. "Full speed, forward — and close with them! We've got to get in where their catapults can't reach us! Archers! Fire as soon as we get in range! Silence those damned catapults!"

A massive stone smashed into a bank of oarsmen behind him, leaving a bloody, confused tangle of splintered timber and crushed flesh. Unsteadily, his ship veered into another's path as the slaves on the untouched side continued to row without break. The other warship slid past at spitting distance, its captain only narrowly avoiding collision. To Lages's left, a smaller warship took a fireball in its hold and began to belch great clouds of black smoke. Other vessels were flaming now across the wedge formation. And still the missiles fell relentlessly among them.

Lages bawled out orders and cursed the rowers for their laziness. The catapults had found their range at a good half-mile away. They were pounding his fleet into blazing wreckage, well beyond effective archery range. Oars frothing the waves, the Imperial fleet bored through the deadly hail.

Kane observed with satisfaction the effects of the catapult barrage. By now the catapults were no longer firing in volley, but at will — as fast as their crews could reload. Already several of the Imperial warships were noticeably crippled — and four ships, two triremes included, burned out of control. A sudden rushing, ripping tear alerted Kane that Lages had ordered his archers to open fire — too soon, for their first volley fell short into the sea before the slowly backwatering barges.

"Move forward!" shouted Kane. "Ramming speed!"

Battle pennants relayed his orders to the other warships. As the rebel navy surged forward to meet the Imperial fleet, Kane called for his own archers to prepare to fire. In a moment Lages's fleet would be at too close quarters for the retreating catapult barges to continue their attack. And then the rebel navy would speedily come into bowshot.

Kane laughed recklessly, senses inflamed with the thrill of battle. The decks were dashed with sand to blot the blood that would shortly make footing slippery. The mainmasts were unstepped — the impact of ramming would have sent them crashing onto the decks. Plowing through the sea under the rhythmic stroke of long oars, his fleet of warships bore down on the Imperials at a speed of some four knots. The dice had been cast, and the battle was upon them.

As the formations began to close now, a hail of arrows from the Imperial fleet fell upon the retreating line of barges. An iron-barbed shaft struck a crewman on one barge in the chest. Reeling in pain, he fell back against the brazier used to ignite the fireballs — knocking it into the barge's hold. The scattering coals instantly caught the remaining store of fireballs. With a sudden roar, the barge exploded into a spewing column of oily flame and shrieking men.

Undaunted by the hissing arrows, the rest of the catapult crews continued to fire — until their own warships advanced past them and into their line of fire. Useless in the close-quarters fighting, they withdrew to Prisarte before the Imperial fleet could take revenge for their murderous barrage.

The two fleets rushed together amidst a black rain of iron-barbed arrows and jagged rocks fired from small deck-mounted petraries. And through the hail of death they met.

A mighty Imperial trireme rammed a converted merchant that had rashly advanced before her sister warships — almost knocking its broken hull out of the water. Two biremes collided nearly head-on, leaving the rebel vessel crippled in the water and the other ship sinking. Cries of "Ramming speed!" were drowned out in a dreadful fury of splintering timber, screams of pain, and bestial roars.

Shouting orders savagely, Kane directed his flagship against the nearest enemy trireme. Reaching ramming speed, the rowers desperately hauled in their oars at the final instant — just as Kane skillfully heaved the ship's wheel to the right. The *Ara-Teving* veered aside from her opponent and glanced along her hull — splintering the oars and maiming the rowers on one side of the enemy warship. Still under momentum, the *Ara-Teving* shot past, then returned her own oars to the water and pulled away, leaving the Imperial warship dead in the water for the smaller vessels to swarm over.

Across the seething battleline, the rebel warships were attempting the same maneuver — not always with equal success. Unable to avoid her opponent's grappling irons, the *Hast-Endab* was trapped between two triremes before oars could be returned. As the grapples caught, a double wave of Imperial marines leaped onto her decks. Two converted merchants raced to the stricken warship's aid, and the ensuing conglomeration took on the appearance of a floating island. The air was torn with the cries of dying and injured combatants, the clash of arms, sounds of crashing and splintering timber. Arrows fell everywhere.

The *Mon-Ossa* advanced into the melee somewhat after the initial contact, as Lages had lost way until the crippled oarbank could be cleared. Sighting the Imperial flagship, Kane gave the order to ram, determined to take the warship and demoralize the Imperials with her defeat. Lages saw the rebel trireme bearing down on his ship, but the damaged oarbanks cost him some maneuverability. He sought to veer, but could not entirely evade the bronze-capped ram.

The two flagships smashed together, and with the thundering impact came the roaring battle cries of the soldiers. The two sides rushed upon each other as fierce hand-to-hand combat prevailed over both decks.

Kane leaped into the fray, his great sword cutting a path to the other ship. Confident that he could wield the long blade effectively with his left arm, he tossed aside his shield and ripped a cutlass from the side of a corpse, hefted it in his right hand. Although left-handed, Kane had trained himself to use his right arm with equal prowess. Having full use of both hands made Kane doubly deadly in a close fight — as those who tore at him quickly learned.

Driving back the enemy marines, Kane reached the high prow of the *Ara-Teving* and leaped onto the *Mon-Ossa*'s decks. A host of Imperial soldiers rushed to meet him. Kane smashed down the first with his broadsword, briefly parried the blade of the second before finishing him with a sudden gutting slash of the cutlass, then whirled to spit a third marine on his broadsword. Shouting for his crew to follow him, Kane tore into the ranks of the Imperials, his two blades leaving a gory trail. Snarling faces and glittering blades whirled about him in a crimson vortex. It was close work for the first minutes. Kane's mail held true, though his bare flesh bled from minor gashes — cheap payment for the lives he took. Then his crew was spilling over the rails to give him support.

In the first wave, Arbas was fighting like a blood-mad panther. Recklessly the dark-haired assassin ripped into the Imperial marines. Kane wished he could find a lull to watch an artist at work — for the assassin's deadliness lay not only in his stealth, but in his raw fighting ability as well.

Calmly and deliberately, Kane slashed through the Imperial forces, his senses inflamed with the rush of battle and the ecstasy of killing. Much as he longed to lose himself in an orgy of death and carnage, Kane kept his bloodlust in check, and it was intellect, not emotion, that governed his actions.

An officer in the red cloak of an Imperial general broke through the reeling marines to hurl himself against Kane. "You must be Kane!" he shouted, swinging a vicious upward slash that Kane barely knocked aside. "Well then, know that I am Lages! Today I command this fleet, pirate! Tomorrow your death shall make me Emperor!"

"You will never be Emperor, then!" snarled Kane, and pressed his attack with increased fury. "But I'll give you a crown of good steel!"

Lages was an excellent swordsman, but Kane's lightning-swift, two-bladed attack baffled him. He had seen men fight with sword and dagger before, but never with two swords. And Kane wielded with complete ease a sword that most men would use with both hands. Taunts that sneered on his lips now passed unspoken as Lages struggled for breath. In spite of his skill, Lages found himself being forced back steadily to the ship's railing. For the first time his confidence began to waver. Had the weeks in prison so weakened him? Was this Kane truly the monster of old, against whom legend claimed no man could prevail?

But Lages was a strong man. His notched buckler continued to turn back the rain of blows Kane hammered against him, while his reddened blade stabbed to pierce his enemy's guard. In growing panic, Lages realized that less and less was he on the offensive — that now he was hard pressed even to weave a defense against Kane's relentless attack. Grimly he sought to keep Kane's blades away from his aching flesh. His shield was being cut to pieces; his sword was dulled from parrying Kane's steel. Finally came one blinding-fast stroke that could not be parried. Kane's cutlass moved like reflected light and slashed across Lages's sword arm. In agony, Lages felt his sword arm go nerveless, his blade clatter to the slippery deck.

"Goodbye, Lages!" Kane laughed, and raised his broadsword for the killing blow. "Go join your fleet in hell!"

Frantically, Lages jumped back to avoid the blade, tripped over the ship's broken railing, and fell into the sea below. The waves slammed against him with stunning force, and the icy water closed above him, His armor weighted him down, dragging him under. Lages sank, struggling desperately to force his gashed arm to unbuckle his heavy cuirass.

"Lages is down! Lages is down!" The hopeless cry ran from ship to ship among the Imperials.

Kane started for the rail to make certain of his kill, but was swept back as a pack of vengeance-mad Imperial marines flung themselves against him. Fighting desperately, Kane needed all his strength to beat back their crazed onslaught, and for a timeless interval, steel clangoured against steel faster than mind or eye could follow. But their attack finally wavered before the figure of death they had centered upon, and from behind rebel soldiers quickly cut through to Kane's aid.

Then suddenly, there were no more to fight. The Imperial flagship was taken.

Kane wiped the sweat and gore from his face and gasped for breath. He stood covered with blood, some of it his own. But around him he could see that the tide of battle was with him. The catapult attack had broken the Imperial formation, and the glancing-ramming tactics had disabled enough of the warships for the smaller rebel craft to swarm over them. Dismayed by the fall of their flagship, the survivors of Lages's fleet would fight for retreat, not victory.

Kane grinned. It began to look as if his efforts on Efrel's behalf had not been in vain.

Arbas came up, limping badly, a crude bandage soaked with blood decorating his thigh. "Come on, Kane! This ship is sinking! Oh, shit! Some son of a bitch damn near cut my leg off! Damn, was that a fight!"

"Damn!" Kane frowned at the assassin's crimson trouser leg. "Looks like someone cut you straight to the artery! Get a tighter bandage on that mess before you bleed to death! And we're not through this fight yet, Arbas."

Kane bellowed to his men. "Back to the *Ara-Teving*, men! Bring whatever of our wounded you see! Get the lead out, damn it! Hurry!"

Giving Arbas a hand, Kane left the sinking *Mon-Ossa*. The assassin was cursing with each step, but still game. Kane decided his femoral artery was spared — otherwise Arbas would have bled out by now.

The *Ara-Teving* backed away from the wreck and moved to another quarter of the battle. A rebel bireme and an Imperial trireme were locked in combat nearby, and Kane gave the order to ram the enemy warship. As the *Ara-Teving* rowed away, no one gave a thought to a bleeding figure who floated on a piece of wreckage in their wake. The water was filled with such.

Lages clutched the broken timber and tried to paddle with his good arm. The salt water was like acid on his slashed arm, and he cursed with breath better saved for swimming. He could not die here now! Not with so much to live for! His fleet lay stricken about him — already assuming that their leader was dead, as the *Mon-Ossa* lifted her stern and sank. Had Lages not won free of his armor, he would be lying on the bottom a thousand fathoms below. Withal, at the moment there seemed small odds of escaping either drowning or capture. He desperately looked about him for aid.

At this point Lages caught sight of an Imperial trireme — by some miracle unscathed in the melee — rowing straight toward him. The trireme had dispatched the two rebel vessels that had tried to take it and was now steering for another quarter of the battle.

Lages waved with his good arm and shouted hoarsely. *Rescue?* In horror, he realized that he lay directly in the vessel's path. "By Horment, no!" he prayed. "Don't let me die, run down by my own men!"

But someone aboard the Imperial warship recognized the thrashing figure in the water — thanks to the scarlet cloak that Lages had flung across the broken timber as he struggled to cling to it. The trireme slowed under momentum and swerved before it could hit him. Lages caught the rope they threw to him and clambered aboard.

"Thank Horment!" he gasped. "And thanks to all of you here! You won't go unrewarded for this! Who's captain here?"

An officer ran up — Lages recognized him as one of his old comrades. "Oh, it's you, Gable!" Lages laughed shakily. "Your ship has saved me from becoming fish food, and I won't forget that!"

"I thought we were hauling a ghost on board, milord," Gable told him. "The *Mon-Ossa* lies on the bottom, and men say Kane sent you there to captain her."

Lages swore. "I'll settle with Kane another time. But what do you think of the battle? What's happened since I was given up for dead?"

"It goes against us, milord," Gable answered glumly. "Other than our ship, I can see only two biremes that are still moving freely. The fireballs hurt us bad. Now these damned rebels have us hemmed in — they're grappling and are overwhelming the rest of our fleet that is still afloat."

"I feared as much!" groaned Lages. "So it's hopeless, then. Kane *is* the devil that legend declares him to be! All right, signal the retreat. We'll try to get back to Thovnosten with what we can save."

The lone Imperial trireme moved away from the battle, and fled for Thovnosten. The two biremes and several other crippled warships tried to follow suit — but the rebel fleet closed in, and only one bireme was able to escape. No chase was given — as the rebels were too busy massacring the survivors of the Imperial fleet.

And so out of twenty-four proud ships, two limped back to Thovnosten, leaving the rest to the victors and to the sea.

Meanwhile the rebel forces were inexorably overwhelming ship after ship of those trapped by their grappling irons. And as each craft was taken, the victorious rebels moved on to reinforce their comrades on board another stricken warship. The Imperial marines fought gallantly, but their position was hopeless, and the wise ones surrendered their ships for whatever mercy they might find in Prisarte.

Having finished with her second opponent, the *Ara-Teving* drove on against another. In yet one area of the battle, the issue was going against the rebels. The *Ara-Teving*'s sister ship, the *Kelkin*, was caught between two Imperial triremes, and the Imperial soldiers were slowly beating down the outmanned rebels. Despite his feelings about Alremas, Kane could not risk losing the best warship next to his own in Efrel's entire navy.

Kane ordered the attack, thinking by fighting to save Alremas he might at best achieve some stature among the aloof Pellinites. At his command, the *Ara-Teving* pulled alongside one Imperial trireme and quickly grappled. Leading his crew, Kane rushed over the rails to attack the Imperial marines from behind. Giving them little time to realize this new threat, Kane burst into the enemy ranks, hewing about him with his twin blades. The Imperial marines gave back and faltered under the renewed rebel strength. Their apparent victory now cruelly loomed as defeat. With the rage of a cornered beast, they fought to the death without regard for wounds or danger.

To his disgust, Kane saw that Oxfors Alremas was still fighting — Kane had hoped the Imperials would kill the Pellin lord for him and save him from a thorny problem. Grudgingly, he admired the Pellinite's intricate swordplay. The man fenced with brilliance, and there was speed and endurance within that foppish frame. Kane had not thought Alremas tough enough for a melee such as this. If only the bastard weren't too popular a figure to murder, Kane mused with regret. Arbas would handle that matter most willingly.

On Kane fought, striking death all about him. Alremas would wait until another day. For now there was the dirty, bloody work of mopping up the last of the stubborn resistance. At length the fighting ceased. The last Imperial soldier had fallen or surrendered.

A weary cheer went through the rebel ranks. Half their number lay dead or badly wounded, and half their warships were broken wreckage. But the captured Imperial warships would more than replace the loss of their fighting ships, and more soldiers could always be found. It had been a decisive victory over a more powerful, better-equipped enemy, and the men had a right to be jubilant.

Sensing the popular feeling, Kane presented himself upon the prow of his flagship. Kane was now an even more awe-inspiring figure — his mail hauberk torn, his bare arms and face gashed, his body splattered with blood from helm to toe. He raised his gory broadsword in salute to the men he had led to victory.

Amidst wild cheers of "Hail, Kane! Hail, Kane! Hail, Red Kane!" he led his fleet in a triumphant return to Prisarte. It was with secret satisfaction that Kane noted it was his name and not Efrel's that the men roared out in adulation.

Part Three

XIX
Return to Thovnosten

Netisten Maril was in a volcanic temper — his most common mood when confronted by any obstacle. "Only two ships return! By Horment! By the thrice-damned Tloluvin! This is intolerable — impossible! How could Kane deal such a smashing defeat to the Imperial navy! By Lato, I knew I should have commanded the expedition myself. You let a mob of rebels and pirates rout the finest warships on the Western Sea!"

Trying to keep his own temper in check, Lages stonily listened to his uncle's raging. His wounds were giving him pain, and each time he tried without success to break into Maril's stream of invective, his own temper flared. At length, Maril ran out of breath and lapsed into fitful silence, his livid face twisted in uncomprehending dismay.

Bitterly Lages began, "All right, so we took a beating. Well, a tantrum won't reverse things, and if you want to scream curses at anyone, then take your anger out on Kane. The men fought valiantly throughout the battle, and I doubt that you could have commanded them better yourself. We tried to take Efrel by surprise, and we made a mistake. Kane was waiting for us with a far stronger fleet than we had ever anticipated. He used a few ingenious tricks to offset our superior fleet, and we got hit bad. Now we've shown our hand, lost a significant portion of our total naval strength, and let Kane win a tremendous strategic victory as well. Okay, it was your idea to attempt a sudden attack — I'm not saying I wouldn't have ordered the same. The strategy failed, and let's leave it at that!"

Unappeased, Maril muttered an incoherent snarl as an attempt to reply, then subsided. He smoothed his black beard while he continued to glower at his nephew.

Hurriedly Lages continued. "So let's take stock of things. We know we have a major rebellion on our hands — a plot that has been taking shape for many months. Now we know where its center is, and who its leaders are. The battle will have drawn everything into the open. Now that open warfare has broken out, we can assume that Efrel will summon to Pellin all the aid that has been promised to her through secret alliances. Kane's victory is going to pull in a wave of support from those more cautious traitors who were undecided before — so the witch will probably have a considerable following once the news of our defeat tempts shaky loyalties. And with Kane as her general, Efrel's rebellion constitutes as deadly a threat to us and to our Empire as the Netisten blood has ever faced.

"Now then, we lost twenty-two ships and maybe five thousand men and slaves. But this only represents about half of Thovnos's navy, when you consider the warships that were out on patrol or otherwise unavailable at the time we sailed. Then, if we make a real effort, we can convert a good number of merchant vessels to warships and man them with freshly recruited troops. That was Kane's own game, so we know that it works. So much for Thovnos itself. Now, we can call upon the lords of all the islands in the Empire to render their support, since Efrel does pose a threat to the entire Empire. I doubt if her conspiracy can have netted too much support from among the great houses, so we can probably assume that Tresli, Fisitia, Josten, Quarnora, Raconos, and Parwi will remain loyal — along with many of the lesser islands. Counting their support, I'd estimate we can mobilize a fleet of maybe three hundred warships, plus around another hundred serviceable conversions and the like.

"The rebels took heavy losses, too. I'd be surprised if Kane can muster a hundred ships of all descriptions — and he'll be hard pressed to man them in any fashion. So we can probably count on outnumbering the rebels a good four to one, maybe better. That means this first defeat hasn't cost us the war by any means. We'll gather our forces, go back to Pellin with a real invasion fleet, and level that damned witch's fortress to the ground!

"But let's worry about that tomorrow. I've hardly slept for days. I'm exhausted and I ache all over. So if you'll forgive me, dear uncle, I'm going to my chambers."

Without waiting any further, Lages wheeled and stalked from the audience hall. Maril muttered a few dark thoughts about insolent youths and fell into gloomy thought.

Lages was painfully removing his battle-stained clothing when M'Cori burst into his chambers. "M'Cori!" he smiled. "Hold it a second" He shrugged a clean, loose-fitting shirt across his grimy shoulders and started to shove the tails back under his belt.

Ignoring his efforts to look presentable, M'Cori hurried his bodyservant out of the room. "I had to come and see you right away. Oh, Lages — I thank all the gods that you've come back! Everyone is talking about the disaster — about Efrel's vow of revenge! I heard that Kane almost killed you — that they almost didn't see you in the water!" She fell into his arms, trembling violently.

Lages held her close, disregarding the pain in his arm. For a while they stood in a tight embrace, Lages murmuring soothingly in her ear. Eventually they kissed.

"And Kane," began M'Cori, in control of herself again, "they say that he truly is that Kane whose legendary pirate hordes almost conquered the Empire in the first years of our history. They say Efrel has brought him back from the dead to create an invincible army for her conspiracy."

"That I can believe, now that I've seen him!" Lages exclaimed. "The man isn't human! He looked like some sort of demon of death out there — all covered with blood, and with that insane light in his killer's eyes! He was slaughtering our men like sheep. In battle Kane was as much within his element as a shark in the sea we fought upon — and just as deadly."

M'Cori gasped, and Lages went on reassuringly, "But that's all nonsense about him. I know he's human enough. He was definitely wounded in several places. An incredible warrior he may be, with an uncanny resemblance to Red Kane the pirate, but this Kane is no supernatural demon from out of the past. I know his measure now, and when we meet again, I'll kill him — no matter who he really is. I'll make you a matched set of drinking mugs from his skull and from Efrel's."

M'Cori seemed entranced at the thought. "Ugh! That's a gruesome present! You've been paying too much attention to those gory old sagas the minstrels wail. How could anyone drink out of a skull — even those wild heroes in the tales! It wouldn't hold water even. That's an awful idea, Lages. Give them to Father instead."

Her mind wasn't half on her words, Lages knew. He was very much aware of her thinly gowned figure pressing against his bare chest. Dreamily it seemed as though her heart beat in cadence with his own — possibly that was why his own pulse was throbbing. He thought about all the years he had known M'Cori, wondered when there had been a time that he had not loved her. He had been an utter fool to have let the tumultuous events of the past few years interfere with their relationship. Those years were lost forever now, he realized, and the future was uncertain. How many times had death come within a breath of costing him the years to come?

Lages whispered to her then, not daring to raise his voice for fear it would shake. "Listen to me, M'Cori! When this is all over, Maril should be reconciled with me. And I'm through with this blood feud now. I'll no longer be a fugitive; I won't be a landless traitor's son, trying to prove himself worthy of the Emperor's grace. I'm going to ask Maril for your hand, M'Cori — and I know he'll consent."

He looked at her with painful intensity, as if he would hear her thoughts before she could form the words. "And will you have me? Will you be my wife, M'Cori?"

M'Cori clasped him with fierce passion. The words had been formed years before. "Oh, Lages — beloved! You know the answer to that!"

She kissed him deeply. For the next minutes Lages forgot all about his exhaustion and pain. Forgot about the web of darkness whose patterns were not yet completely woven.

XX

From the Ancient Seas

Late one night several days after the battle, Kane sat reading over reports in the tower room he had chosen for his headquarters. Assuming that repairs on the captured warships and others could be completed in time, his fleet had about broken even — maybe better, since the acquisition of a few fast-class warships more than made up for the loss of many of the less serviceable craft. Casualties had been high, though, which was more serious. A lot of replacements had to be found. Common soldiers were not too hard to scare up, but trained officers were another story.

Assuming Arbas recovered in time, he could probably be trusted with a command. The assassin was a loner, Kane knew, but he was a formidable swordsman, and as such could command the respect and obedience of his men — making him a good battle leader, even though he cared for none of the responsibilities of long-term leadership. Arbas just might be talked into it, Kane reflected, if he could appeal to the assassin's ego. And perhaps Imel could persuade some more of his acquaintants to come over to his side. The aristocracy had all the experience and mystique needed to command — the common folk were used to taking orders from their superiors. The same tradition of subservience to the nobility caused problems with promotions from the ranks.

Kane laid the papers aside. Some sixth sense detected the presence of Efrel even before his keen hearing caught the clump of her wooden leg on the stairs. What cause drove her up such a difficult climb, he wondered? He had chosen this tower room for his study partly because it made such excursions inconvenient for Efrel.

Kane considered his relationship with the sorceress a difficult one. At present she was altogether pleased with him, but catering to the whims of a madwoman taxed even Kane's nerves. Her attitude of elaborate secrecy and incessant insinuation annoyed him far more than he cared to show, and her unpredictable seizures of raving insanity were trying, to say the least. Kane's jaded senses found slight fascination in seeking to satisfy Efrel's almost bestial lusts, but there always persisted a deeper feeling of disgust that could not be dispelled. Unconsciously Kane found himself counting each step of the passageway by the echoing thump of Efrel's demon's-paw limb. There was an almost hypnotic rhythm to her progress, he decided.

Soon Efrel's maimed figure limped through the doorway. He looked at her expectantly. "Good evening, Kane," she began in her strange voice — beautiful tones as mutilated as her nightmarish body. "So I find you here working late hours like a clerk."

"A good general should know his strengths and weakness to the smallest detail," Kane stated, somewhat annoyed. Actually it had been insomnia, not diligence, that kept him here so late. "Success in battle isn't won by accepting the standards and incompetence of others. So many hot-headed amateurs think wars are fought by throwing two armies together and letting justice and the gods grant victory to their cause. My sword has dulled its edge on such fools, settled causes past counting."

"Don't take offense — I was only jesting. Certainly, after last week's victory I have no criticisms either of your ability or your philosophy."

Efrel sank into a chair beside Kane. "But I came to tell you that Imel has once more proved his worth to me. Another of his highborn friends has yielded to his persuasion. Imel has just informed me that Lord Gall of Tresli has thrown his lot in with us. He's the most powerful lord on that island, as you should know, and he'll come to us presently with a fleet of eighteen warships. I must find some new way to show Imel my appreciation."

Kane smiled. "There's a coincidence — I was just wondering if Imel might come through for us. Buy him a new wardrobe, and he'll win over all of Tresli. But this is good news. I've needed a fresh fleet to guard Pellin's waters — in case Maril sends another expedition sooner than expected. If I were in his place, I'd attempt a raid of some sort — a quick strike to disrupt operations in Prisarte. But after the beating we gave Lages, I imagine Maril will wait to bring the entire might of the Imperial navy against us before he mounts another attack."

"Offers of aid are pouring in from every quarter," Efrel exulted. "Every adventurous rogue, every greedy nobleman, all those who have cause to hate the house of Netisten — they are rallying to me as news of our victory spreads throughout the Empire."

The sorceress paused to gloat, and her eye caught sight of the puckered seams of the minor gashes Kane had suffered in the battle. Strange, she mused, only slight scabs or pinkish scars marked them now. So the immortal had strong recuperative powers, as well. She recalled the demon's words that Kane could receive no permanent scar, since his body never altered from its original state. Considering his past career, she wondered whether his body might not otherwise be as scarred as her own. It was pleasant to think that another creature might live through such mutilation.

Kane was speaking. "Yes, I can see that response to our cause is mounting. But, as Hedusi complained:

Speak no more to me of numbers,

Though truth, your words are lies —
Fill my goblet drop by drop,
While you pour from the amphora."

"I've never heard the proverb in that form before," returned Efrel.

Kane had forgotten the passage's antiquity. Vexed at having been trapped into pedantry, he told her bitterly, "It isn't a proverb originally. It's a familiar quotation from one of Gorovin's plays. Don't tell me that Gorovin's work has been lost here in the East."

"So Kane is a scholar as well as a warrior. How unusual! We must talk together at length over the knowledge you've acquired over the centuries." Efrel had caught Kane's unconscious reference to the Thovnosian Empire as the East. This was clearly the West with respect to the Lartroxian supercontinent, and if Kane had not merely made a slip of the tongue... She wondered how long Kane had lived in the semi-mythical lands beyond the Western Sea.

"You wouldn't like Gorovin," Kane said caustically. "No one ever gets flayed alive in his plays. But my meaning should be clear — certainly I've repeated myself often enough. We can't take on Netisten Maril and the entire Empire with just bits and pieces from here and there — not when he has the resources of his Empire to draw upon. Why, most of these recruits we've gathered since the battle are useless against seasoned troops. Just sword-meat to waste the strength of the Imperial forces. If I'm to be of any real use to you, I'm going to have to be told exactly what manner of supernatural powers you've made an allegiance with. Tell me what this mysterious force is that you've so devilishly hinted of all along. Then maybe I can make plans accordingly."

Efrel laughed wildly, and for a moment Kane feared that she was entering into another of her spells of incoherent madness. But the sorceress was merely enjoying her moment of triumph, and presently she grew calmer. Efrel must have been anticipating the unveiling of this final mystery for some time, judging from her secret amusement. She assumed a grimace that her torn features interpreted as a mysterious smile — Kane had grown to recognize the expression — and asked: "What do you know of the Scylredi?"

Though the direction Efrel's revelation was taking was not an unsuspected one, Kane remained impassive. His thoughts at that moment might have shaken the sorceress, but he only said, "I have heard a few bizarre tales of the Scylredi from the seamen of this region. Some sort of malevolent sea gods, they say."

Efrel tittered scornfully. "Yes, so they say. Garbled legends and old wives' tales. They are but frightened guesses — pale shadows of the hidden truth. Listen, Kane!

"In the eons before man walked the earth — when the sea was a vast, teeming wilderness of primitive life, its oceans far more immense than those of today — the race of creatures known to mankind as the Scylredi arose and flourished. Most of the continents we know today had not yet risen from the primeval sea, and only a few jungle-choked land masses stood out from the boundless seas of Elder Earth. The Scylredi lived beneath this ancient sea and created for themselves a civilization beyond man's wildest conception. Here in this very region they built their cities, for at that time all these islands lay upon the ocean floor.

"They were a strange race, these creatures of awesome antiquity. Nothing on earth truly resembled them, even then. Were they some freak of evolution, a race from another world — or perhaps, like man, the result of some insane god's whimsy? Who can say at this distant age? The most ancient writings that I have studied are uncertain on so many points. But then, this earth has held many strange races about which mankind can only speculate, and all but a fragment of the secrets of prehuman history has been lost forever.

"Whatever their origin, the Scylredi were as gods themselves. They had control of powers both natural and supernatural. They used the great beasts of the primordial sea for their own purposes, controlling fantastic monsters known to mankind only through legend. With their knowledge of the physical sciences, they built great submarine seacraft — unearthly engines in which they traveled the oceans and waged war with the other inhuman races of Elder Earth. That age was a far more violent world than the earth of our day, and there were many powerful forces the prehuman races must constantly contend against in the battle to survive. They were versed in the elder sorceries, as well — the secrets of the gulfs beyond our stars — and legend only hints at some of the hideous deeds that were committed by the Scylredi in their wars.

"Magnificent fortresses they raised — huge basalt structures that surpassed human imagination. The ruins of these great castles can be seen today — on hillsides where they have crumbled for millennia, ever since the waters receded from these islands. This very fortress, Dan-Legeh, is their creation. For the Scylredi, it is only a minor citadel, and built after their race had declined. It was an age of giants, and the Scylredi commanded both sorcery and science in their constant battle for supremacy in that prehistoric age of chaos.

"But as the centuries passed, their power slipped from them. Perhaps it was the shrinking of the great seas, or the cooling of the earth that caused their decline. It is recorded that there was a long period of horrific warfare between the Scylredi and some other race of elder beings. The conflict was waged with weapons of unimaginable power. Many of their colossal basalt castles were blasted into fused rubble, their gigantic seacraft destroyed, their fearsome servants annihilated, and the greater part of the Scylredi were killed. Both races lay near to extinction upon the termination of that war, and the scattered survivors were left to mourn amidst the ruins of their vanished civilizations.

"Then mighty quakes and tremors shook the earth. Mountains rose from the muck, and great cracks split apart the ocean floor. The waters receded, as the ocean floor buckled and heaved forth to form new lands. The ruins of the Scylredi's titanic fortresses were left to moulder in the sun. And Dan-Legeh itself finally emerged, to dry beneath lonely grey skies until the day some centuries-removed ancestor of mine conquered his superstitious fears and adapted the fortress for his own use. Surely you have noticed the alienness of this citadel. The innumerable additions and modifications man has made — new walls and chambers, stairways and ceilings — they can't disguise this inhuman heritage.

"As for the Scylredi themselves, their numbers were dwindling. Creatures of preternaturally long lives, they were slow to reproduce — but this was only a fragment of their dilemma. Most of the great beasts that had served them were dead; their fortresses were virtually destroyed, as were the strange machines they had created. Their power broken, the Scylredi were too weakened to confront that hostile age. As time passed, they were not prepared to cope with the changing world — and after the oceans receded, their remnants withdrew into the depths of the Sorn-Ellyn, to the north of what is today Pellin.

"Here in this deep trench whose abyss has never been plumbed, the last survivors of this once mighty race yet dwell. Few men have guessed that they still survive, or that there is truth to the many legends concerning these vanished sea demons. Seldom do they venture forth, and the seas over this abyss are shunned by the wise. Still, it is not uncommon to hear tales whispered among the seamen of poor fools who have strayed into the Sorn-Ellyn and paid horribly for their trespass. The Scylredi care little for the puny race of man — the weaklings who fell heir to their ancient home.

"But I have not been bound by human ignorance or weakness. Through my sorceries I have established contact with the Scylredi. I have learned to communicate with them, and have drawn them to me from their lair in the depths of the Sorn-Ellyn. Far below this fortress is cut from the bedrock a gigantic chamber. You have seen my pretty toys there on the day we played with that fat little spy. Here also is where I perform my incantations and rituals of the black arts. But the chamber has other uses than you may have guessed. Located there is a circular pool. I saw you peering into it; it is very deep, this pool — bottomless, to be truthful. For the pool is nothing less than one end of a tremendous tunnel that runs beneath this island and terminates within the Sorn-Ellyn. The Scylredi cut this and other such tunnels through the rock beneath our feet in the age when Dan-Legeh was still their citadel. Through this tunnel I am able to communicate with the Scylredi at will.

"It is through the Scylredi that I have been able to keep in close touch with the maneuvers of my enemies. Here, too, lies the secrets of the fortuitous disasters which have destroyed a few of those who sought to invade my waters, or to escape the island. It is to the Scylredi that I look for aid against Netisten Maril. With their assistance I shall be avenged in full. Not even the entire might of the Empire can stand before the power of the Scylredi, when they arise to my command!

"For although they have kept from the sight of man for centuries in that great abyss, they are not stripped of all the power that once was theirs. Not all of their undersea craft have been destroyed. They have fantastic machines, built by an alien science of a scope far beyond human comprehension. Colossal metal ships that move at tremendous speed beneath the sea, propelled by a power that is not pure magic but of a science which even they no longer fully understand. They have weapons that can burn right through the stoutest warship. Their submarine craft can lash out with fearful streams of elemental flame — controlled bolts of energy that can blast to cinders all that they strike. True, they have only a few of these seacraft, and the power that drives them is almost exhausted, but a small number of such weapons can destroy countless warships.

"And they still have a number of their great sea creatures under their command. Alongside us will fight creatures known only in the most dread legends — the Oraycha. Many tales are spread of the Oraycha, the primeval monsters of whom the octopus and squid are only puny descendants. Only a few of these gigantic beasts survive today, but whatever regions these creatures haunt are seas over which no sane man dare sail. It is no lurid myth that an Oraycha can drag down an entire ship in its tentacles. With their alien science, the Scylredi have been laboring to produce devices that will enable the Oraycha to distinguish my ships from the enemy fleet. The Oraycha will be able to range beneath our embattled navies — to ensnare and annihilate any warship that lacks a protective talisman.

"This then is the power to which I have sworn allegiance. The Scylredi are the source of my secret strength — the power I shall wield to complete my vengeance. What do you think now, Kane? With such allies as these, can Netisten Maril stand before me? Efrel shall be Empress of a new Empire, and the Scylredi shall lend an invincible might to my rule!"

Kane had been listening intently throughout, but if he felt astonishment at anything Efrel told him, he kept his emotions hidden. His voice held no hint of amazement or uncertainty, although his thoughts were in considerable turmoil. "If the Scylredi truly come up to your expectations, then perhaps you will be Empress of the island Empire," he acceded. "But I would like to see personally what the Scylredi have to offer us, though. Obviously their powers are limited, or you would never have relied on my own efforts for your cause."

Efrel giggled. "Jealous, Kane? But I still require human warriors, as well. And you shall see the Scylredi, if you wish — if you are prepared to confront a nightmare from earth's dreaming infancy."

Kane ignored her taunt and pressed on. "But what really interests me about your secret alliance comes down to this: Why should the Scylredi aid you? These are no demons that you can command with spells and conjurations. What have you offered these creatures in return for their intercession?"

She eyed him slyly before explaining. "I told you that the Scylredi are god-like. Alorri-Zrokros even postulates that they are gods, fallen from the sky to dwell on earth. And it is natural that gods require worship. Fallen gods or fallen devils — they still dream of ancient glory. The Scylredi have speculated that through their elder sorcery and the rituals of mass worship, they will be restored to their original power. Worshipped as gods, they will become gods once more. It is evident that a god draws strength from the supernatural bonds that link the faithful to him. The Scylredi mean to absorb the psychic energies of untold thousands of neophytes.

"And so the answer to your question should be obvious. The Scylredi shall

help me to fulfill my revenge, to achieve my ambition to rule as Empress —
and in return I shall establish the worship of the Scylredi as the one religion
of the new Empire. Efrel shall be Empress; the Scylredi shall be gods. Ah, they
have told me of the rituals they will require — and they're magnificent! I
shall be priestess as well as Empress. They will demand numerous human
sacrifices, of course. You should see what the Scylredi can do with a living
human, Kane! A few spies have already learned."

She doubled with a fit of insane laughter. "Think of it! Was ever an Empire
bought more cheaply? Only for a yearly payment of a few hundred lives. It's
absurdly cheap — more than that starve to death every week in the Empire.
Well, how about it, Kane? You sit there so quietly. Does the bargain seem too
repulsive?"

Kane smiled thinly. "I think you know enough about my past to realize
that human life means nothing to me. And what manner of demons you
choose to make your pact with is your own affair. My only apprehension
concerns whether you can trust the Scylredi to carry through with their part
of the bargain. Supernatural weapons have often proved unwieldy, I have
learned."

Still tittering, Efrel rose and hobbled to the doorway. "Yes, I knew you
would be the last to get cold feet over this alliance. You only complain of
distrust, where sane men should feel overwhelming dread."

Pausing at the stairs, she shot back, "Imagine — Kane scrupling over taking human life!" She limped on down the stairway, her maddened laughter
rising back after her.

Kane sat on the window ledge for a longtime after, looking out over the
darkened sea. *The Scylredi.* There had been certain hints of such an alliance —
ones he should have pursued further than he had. Those statues he had barely
glimpsed by the pool beneath Dan-Legeh were one thing that had made him
suspect Efrel's secret. There had been other such hints, but such an alliance
had seemed too alien to be credible. Kane had feared that something unforeseen might complicate matters for him — a force entering the picture that he
could not control, a factor defying manipulation.

He had seen a Scylred once long ago — a long-dead one floating in the
sea. Kane had recognized it primarily from the description given by Alorri-
Zrokros in his ancient treatise on the prehuman races, *Book of the Elders.*

Death could not have made the bloated form much uglier. It had been
more than half again as large as a man, and vaguely analogous to man in
form. Only where legs should have been, its lower trunk sprouted six thick
tentacles, and likewise from its upper trunk grew two longer tentacles in place
of arms. Alorri-Zrokros claimed that these tentacles were armed with suckers
that could draw the lifeblood from its victim. He had dwelled upon the
creature's feeding habits with customary morbid detail. At the other end of
the central trunk, where the head should be, was a short projection that was
encircled near its extremity with half a dozen or more eyes. At the base of this
grotesque head was a large, gaping toothless cavity that served the function
vaguely of a mouth. Water was drawn in here, passed over gill bars, and jetted

out from the base of the trunk. Like the octopus the creature resembled, the Scylred was capable of jetting through the water at considerable velocity. An altogether hideous creature from the earth's infancy, and if Alorri-Zrokros could be believed, its soul was even more monstrous.

Withal, it was not this that bothered Kane — although he bore universal hatred and distrust toward all forms of gods. What now disturbed him was the realization that here was a means by which Efrel might dispose of him should the occasion arise — or more likely, a factor that would complicate his disposing of Efrel. For to remain in a secondary position was utterly alien to Kane's nature. And Kane knew that the defeat of Netisten Maril would only be the first phase of the crimson pattern fate was weaving for the days to come.

XXI
Of Games and Goals

There was a thin wind blowing from the sea, carrying away some of the stench of the waterfront, but not much. The stars were high and lost beneath cloud. Enough of the moon was left to show the cobbled streets.

Imel led the way through the moonlit streets. His stride was quick and nervous. "I thought I'd see if you could do something with him," he said. "You're his friend. You know his moods."

"Some of them, I guess," Arbas grunted, limping to keep pace with the renegade.

"I thought I ought to do something," Imel muttered. "Does he get like this very often?"

Arbas shrugged. "I don't really know him that well. But I've seen him like this a few times. He gets this way when the mood is on him. Doesn't sleep, starts smoking too much opium, washes it down with too much brandy. Any other man would be out cold for a week, but Kane..."

"Here," said Imel, indicating the waterfront dive.

There was no sign over the door, but the smell of sour wine and stale vomit and urine was familiar to the assassin. He cautiously pushed past the filthy leather curtain and peered into the darkened interior. A man's body lay across the threshold, smashed and crumpled. Arbas stepped over it.

"Kane?" he called softly.

The figure who reclined across the tavern bar lifted his head. "Come on in, Arbas," Kane muttered.

The assassin entered the poorly lit common room. Imel followed uneasily. There was another broken body lying amidst the wreckage of a table.

"Looks like you've got the place all to yourself," Arbas observed.

"Almost," Kane agreed. He lifted the bottle to his lips, drank, and tossed it to Arbas. A thin-faced whore handed him another from behind the bar. Her eyes darted anxiously from the newcomers' faces to Kane's.

"The tavern keeper left," Kane said. "My friend here has been telling me her life story. It's very interesting."

"What are you doing?" Arbas asked casually, passing the bottle to Imel.

"I was looking for a quiet place to get drunk."

The girl's face was abnormally pallid beneath its rouge. Arbas glanced down and saw a third body sprawled behind the bar at her feet.

"Some quiet place," the assassin commented.

"It got a lot quieter after a while," Kane told him.

Imel sighed and slumped onto a bench. His men had reported the brawl to him. By then Kane had been recognized, and by that time there was no longer reason to interfere. While it might be permissible for a general to have a drink with the rank and file, the renegade was uncertain as to the propriety of brawling with them.

Kane frowned at Imel's troubled face. "Drink up." he invited. "You look upset. Want to borrow my girl friend?"

The idea brought a harsh laugh from Kane. He rolled off the bar, gathered a fresh bottle in each huge fist, and made his way across the littered room. He was still laughing as he slid into a chair at a corner table.

Arbas nodded to Imel, and the two drew up chairs beside Kane. The whore watched uncertainly from behind the dirty bar, eyeing the doorway.

"Kane, you're getting too old for this," Arbas said sarcastically.

Kane's laughter rumbled in his chest, around the mouth of the upturned bottle.

"Arbas," said Kane, "you ever make it with a one-legged lady?"

The assassin shook his head and tilted back his own bottle.

"Imel." Kane turned to the Thovnosian. "You ever made it with a one-legged lady?"

Imel took a long pull from his bottle, hoping grimly that there were no other ears within hearing. The brandy made the sordid room seem to glow, and suddenly he began to laugh with Kane.

"Time was," Kane began, pushing his other bottle toward his companions. "Time was, when an Empress took you to her bed, it was something worth fighting for. Go out the next day, spill your guts all over the field of battle — what the hell, let's die for the kisses of her imperial highness. Why not? Men die for stupider causes. But this…"

Arbas was laughing now as well. The whore slipped from behind the bar and fled into the night. No one paid her heed

"Imel," Kane muttered, "your girl friend got away."

"She was too thin," the Thovnosian allowed, working on his second bottle.

"All those poor old heroes of legend," Kane mourned. "Gone out and died for their lady's love. All we three got between us is a one-legged madwoman, and I can't even give her away."

"Got to be a better reason than that for getting killed," Imel agreed.

"Well, what's your reason?" Kane asked.

"Best reason of all," the renegade answered with drunken candour. "I'm fighting for myself. Things work out right by the time this is all over, I'll be one of the greatest lords in the new Empire. Lands and riches, power and prestige. No more putting up with sneers from the likes of Oxfors Alremas.

My blood is as good as the proudest of them — all I need is the wealth and the power."

"If you live to enjoy it," Arbas said cheerfully. He returned from the bar with a fresh round of heavy green bottles.

"I threw my lot in with the winning side," Imel rejoined. "I know the risks. Every goal worth striving for has its price."

"And the trick is to avoid paying the price," the assassin grinned.

Imel toasted him. "I'll risk it. So what was there worth living for otherwise? But what about you, Arbas? You with your boasts of having studied at the great university at Nostoblet. Why does a would-be philosopher leave the dusty libraries and lecture halls to sell his blade for bloodstained gold?"

"Same reason you offer, Imel," Arbas drawled. "I'm just a bit more selective about whom I kill than your average soldier of fortune. Lucrative work, though it doesn't carry the glory of battlefield slaughter."

"Then what are you doing here with Kane?"

"Well, why not? I'm getting paid"

"That's no answer."

"It's as good as any. Hell, does any man really control his fate? Does he ever really know why he does what he does? We act out the dramas that the gods place us in, follow the web of our fates — and what matter the reasons we rationalize to explain our lives and our actions?"

Imel belched. "Horment! You should have stayed at the university. But what about you, Kane? Can you explain why you're here? Or are you gong to spout philosophical nonsense like Arbas here?"

Kane laughed bitterly. "It's a game I play. An old game with an old enemy. And tonight I find I grow weary of it."

He was on his feet and through the door before they quite realized he was moving. They scrambled after him, following his mordant laughter through the darkness.

XXII
Up from the Abyss

Under sail, the *Ara-Teving* stabbed her bronze ram through the black waves of the Sorn-Ellyn. Half a mile to her starboard, the bleak cliffs of Pellin's northern coast thrust into the star-flecked night. A scatter of fish-scale clouds drifted high across the lonely moon. The trireme had sailed from Prisarte that dawn. Nightfall found the *Ara-Teving* cutting across the unfathomed waters of the Sorn-Ellyn.

"This is the place," Efrel told Kane.

The *Ara-Teving* lost headway as Kane gave the order to take in sail. The trireme drifted slowly in the thin wind. Efrel, bundled in a hooded cloak of ermine, made her way to the prow and stood there silently at the rail, staring out across the jet-black sea.

Arbas followed her gaze. "So this is where we're to meet our new allies," he remarked dubiously. "When you told me what Efrel had in mind, I was startled that you would accept at face value the ravings of a madwoman. Now that I'm out here, I'm not so skeptical. Were it not for the black line of cliffs off there, I'd swear we were adrift on the seas of hell. No wonder even the Pellinites shun these waters!"

"The bottom of the sea here is as close to the floor of hell as you'll ever see in this life," Kane murmured. "As for the Scylredi and their giant pets, they still haunt these waters — make no doubt. We've already seen evidences of their presence — during our flight from the Lartroxian coast, and later in Prisarte. What I find astonishing is that Efrel claims the Scylredi still have functional seacraft after untold millennia. The prehuman races created strange machines and weapons through their knowledge of alien technology, but I haven't seen a functional relic of Elder Earth in... Well, in a long time."

Arbas, who in his university days had come across only a few vague allusions to the races of Elder Earth — an age now lost in the veils of myth — declined to press Kane for details. "I see crumbling piles of basalt that Efrel claims were once Scylredi fortresses," he commented. "How can anything mechanical outlast columns of basalt?"

"My thought as well," Kane mused. "If the seacraft were built at the close of the age, as was Dan-Legeh, and maintained carefully over the eons — who can say what is possible or impossible when we speak of the science of Elder Earth? We know far more of our own black sorceries than of prehuman science."

Kane frowned and went on. "There is another possibility. I had wondered why Efrel sought me out to lead her rebellion, and why she waited so long to tell me of her secret alliance."

Imel, who had been listening in gloomy silence, broke in. "Presumably for a number of good reasons. First, Efrel needs a human navy and invasion force. Second, she needed an immediate defense against Maril's retaliation once the Emperor learned of the plot — as she knew he must. Third, she needed a smashing initial victory to swing support to her cause. Finally, the Scylredi demanded some convincing show of strength on Efrel's part, before they chose to interfere in human wars."

"Good," Kane grinned. "Exactly as Efrel has told me — along with the fact that time was needed for the Scylredi to devise a means by which they and their creatures could distinguish our vessels from the Imperial fleet. It all fits."

"Then what's bothering you?" Imel wanted to know.

"Suppose these aren't relics from prehuman earth that the Scylredi intend to use," Kane said. "Suppose these are new seacraft that the Scylredi have been constructing to aid Efrel — and that they weren't ready until just now."

Arbas glanced quickly at Kane's brooding face. "Go on.

"If that guess is correct," Kane suggested, "then we know that the Scylredi still have some measure of their ancient knowledge and power. And after untold millennia, Efrel has somehow persuaded them to use this power to intervene in human affairs."

He paused, staring across the jet-black sea. "I wonder whether, having called the Scylredi forth, Efrel will find them less willing to return to their lost realm."

Efrel's glad shout cut short his speculation.

"They come!"

The trireme's hull seemed to reverberate with a high-pitched humming from far below. Crewmen looked at one another uneasily. Men shouted and pointed out to sea.

The black waters of the Sorn-Ellyn boiled and heaved. And the *Ara-Teving* no longer floated alone on the sea.

There were four of them, and they rose up out of the water like a school of gigantic black whales, circling about the *Ara-Teving*. Only no whales had ever existed to match the size of these metallic leviathans, nor could any creature of the sea swim with their blurring speed.

A cry of astonishment and of fear went up from the crew. Kane felt a soaring thrill — how long had it been since he had seen a marvel to compare with this?

The Scylredi seacraft were perhaps three times the length of Kane's flagship, although not much broader than the trireme's hull at its widest. Their shape was basically that of an elongated teardrop — ovoid toward the bow and tapering to a point at the stern. Arranged like a crown at the pointed stern, a ring of ovoid protrusions emanated a pale-green glow. Steam rose in a trailing vapor from the lambent cluster — each unit perhaps ten feet in length, and constructed either of near-opaque crystal or semi-translucent metal. At regular intervals along the sloping metal hulls were positioned other conical or ovoid protuberances — these black and apparently lifeless. Otherwise, the Scylredi submarines were featureless.

For a moment the four metallic leviathans hovered upon the surface. Although the crew had been warned what to expect, the appearance of these alien seacraft left every man of them shaken and afraid. Then — as effortlessly as a shark turns for its prey — the submarines accelerated and sped out across the waves, leaving the *Ara-Teving* shuddering in their backwash. Streaking at a level just below the waves, the submarines tore through the sea — silent, save for the roar of cleft water and the uncanny drone of their engines. Kane could follow their lightning-fast course by the glow of their propulsive units. He roughly estimated their speed to be in excess of sixty knots. From the jet of steam that spewed from their wakes, he guessed that considerable heat was being generated by their engines.

Out across the Sorn-Ellyn, until their pallid green wakes dwindled and vanished. Kane waited. As suddenly as before — the whining hum from the depths, the upheaval of black water — the Scylredi seacraft once again breached the waves about the awe-stricken humans and their puny wooden ship.

"Look now, Kane!" came Efrel's shrill cackle.

Kane felt his hair tingle — as in the instant before a lightning storm closes.

Near the bow of one of the alien seacraft, a conical protrusion suddenly glowed into violet incandescence. From this cone of lurid brilliance, a bolt of crackling energy lashed forth to play across the basalt cliffs of the half-mile-distant shoreline. The beam of energy struck the headland — and instantly trees and vegetation flared into roaring flame, rocks splintered and shattered.

In another second all four submarines had opened fire — coruscant bolts of energy lancing forth from the turrets spaced along their black hulls. The flames of hell burst forth from the night, where the fury of their ravening bolts struck the cliff. The sea rose in gouts of shrieking steam, as red-hot masses of basalt crumbled away in a semi-molten avalanche and crashed into the hissing surf below. The stunted forest was ablaze in one instant, white-hot ash in the next. Across a hundred-foot section of shoreline, it was as if a purple-flamed volcano had suddenly erupted.

As abruptly as it began, the barrage of violent energy ceased. Kane let his breath out and realized he had been holding it throughout. His vision was dazzled from the storm of destroying lightning. Against the coastline, a sullen red wound glowed through the haze of steam and smoke.

The crew were too stunned to feel panic. This was just as well.

"Look now, Kane!" Efrel howled. "Look again!"

Kane followed the sorceress's triumphant gesture. The four Scylredi craft had moved out from the *Ara-Teving* and now formed a square. Kane stared at the square of black water in their midst.

A gasp went up from the crew.

Rising from the waves now, looping black tentacles lashed through the air and slapped spitefully at the submarine hulls. The sea convulsed—and then a titanic writhing mass of tentacles thrashed forth from the sea. For an instant, an immense bloated bulk lurched above the surface. Kane had a fleeting impression of a central body as enormous as the largest whale, of impossible lengths of coiling tentacles whose girth was more than a man might reach around, of a huge gnashing beak that might crush a warship's hull as effortlessly as a parrot cracks an almond, of pallid eyes as wide as an open doorway that stared back at him with malevolent intelligence.

The monstrosity from earth's dawn breached, then plunged beneath the inky waves. Kane knew then that the Oraycha was fully as terrible as legend had portrayed the monster to be. And Kane knew he was glad it was gone. It gave him a chill to think of such a creature lurking in the depths beneath the *Ara-Teving*. He wondered whether the Scylredi could keep such a beast under control...

In another moment the Scylredi submarines had vanished as well. The *Ara-Teving* drifted alone on the sea once more — with a panicstricken crew and only a dying red glow from the smouldering shoreline to prove all had not been an insane nightmare.

Efrel threw back her heart in laughter. The ermine hood fell back, and Kane looked upon the face of nightmare, howling at a pallid moon.

"Get the men moving!" Kane snapped to Imel. "Let's get out of these waters before the shock wears off."

"What do you think now, Kane?" Efrel exalted. "Did I lie? You asked to be shown, and did I not show you? Do you still fear Netisten Maril and his fleet? Do you still doubt that Efrel commands powers beyond the frightened dreams of mankind?"

"But do you command this power?" Kane wondered aloud.

XXIII
Night in M'Cori's Chamber

Light was dim in M'Cori's bedchamber. The faint candle glow fell softly on the two figures who lay together on her bed, where M'Cori lovingly caressed Lages's hard-muscled back. He lay there quietly, resting for the moment and enjoying the soothing movements of her hands. Lages gave a contented sigh.

"Indolent brute!" M'Cori exclaimed, and teasingly slapped him across his buttocks. He grabbed her roughly and pulled the soft, giggling girl against him. The fastenings of her gown had been loosened earlier in their embraces, and as they kissed, Lages drew it down from her shoulders. She made a low sound in her throat and snuggled against his bare chest. After a moment, she giggled and playfully pushed him away.

"What liberties do you presume, cad!" she cried, mimicking a role from a romantic drama. "It seems you take a lady's favors too lightly. Would you ruin me?"

Jumping into the act, Lages struck an affected pose — somewhat unsteadily after the wine they had enjoyed — and declaimed: "Ah, fair lady! Spurn not my advance! It reflects but the undying ardor of a poor soldier about to face death in battle!"

M'Cori gasped and fell back upon the pillows. Her face was pale as she dug her fist against her mouth and bit down on the knuckles to hold back the tears.

Lages cursed himself for his oafishness. Damn it! Always saying the wrong thing! She was trying so hard to forget — to find lighthearted refuge from the tension of the gathering conflict — and he had to remind her. The past months had been hard for her, he knew. For all her infectious gaiety, she was at heart fragile as a child. At times Lages, feared he would break her with his coarse hands and rough manner.

He touched one naked shoulder and turned her to him. Her sea-green eyes were filled with tears again, but she looked at him and uttered no cry. "You'll never come back," she said softly. "I know it."

Lages laughed and shook her gently. "M'Cori, M'Cori! This is so silly! You said the same thing the last time, remember? And this time there will be much less risk. We know what Kane's tactics are, and we know how to face them. Why, we've even fitted some of our warships with catapults like his. And we'll have the rebels overwhelmingly outnumbered.

"I won't even be in command," he added, not without considerable chagrin. "Your father is commanding this fleet himself." He noted with satisfaction that M'Cori felt no such concern for her father. Maril had never warmed toward his daughter, for all his fond words.

Her hair was in disorder, and coils of blond tresses had fallen across her breasts. Lages lifted back each strand with a cautious finger. The pain was going from her eyes now. There was hidden strength beneath her delicate appearance.

"Remember your prophecy, M'Cori," he prompted, feeling the pulse of her heart upon his fingertips. "You aren't going to give up on that, after you've kept faith this long, are you?"

M'Cori's face was dreamy. "So long ago," she mused. "I wonder if that woman really was a priestess of Lato." Color had returned to her face now. Her lips were half-parted.

He looked down at her pale beauty reflected in the candlelight. "When we are man and wife, you'll have to grow accustomed to my absences whenever the Empire is threatened."

She looked up at him in resignation. "Let's live for now," she whispered, and reached for him.

XXIV
Night in Efrel's Chamber

The giant oil lamps blazed brightly in an effort to dispel the inky darkness of the subterranean chamber. Their harsh, glaring light illuminated a scene as ghastly as any the chamber had witnessed in many centuries.

Kane stood beside Efrel in the shadows and watched as a nervous guard of trusted soldiers escorted a party of prisoners into the hidden chamber. The prisoners, some sixty men who had been captured during the battle of three months previous, were unbound, but made no move to escape. Instead, they marched with stiff, wooden legs, their faces frozen in masks of absolute hopelessness. Caught in Efrel's paralytic spell, they were powerless to control their movements as they marched inexorably to their doom. Like mindless robots, the Imperials were drawn by the witch's mental commands into the chamber. The fear in their eyes grew deeper as they helplessly stepped ever closer to their fate. The cause of their anguish could be found in the black pool of water toward which they were being lured by invisible tethers.

The wide pool was not calm and mirror-like tonight, as it usually was. The water boiled and stirred with swift movement beneath its dark surface, and undulating shadows could be glimpsed from time to time. Sometimes a black shape would lift itself above the water, then resubmerge faster than the eye could form a distinct image. Nightmare lurked within the pool tonight. The very air reeked with deadly horror, and the prisoners sensed their doom.

Efrel was speaking. "Netisten Maril is going to make his move very soon, from all indications. He has gathered together just about all the support he's going to get, and the feverish preparations he's been making are about to draw to completion. I assume you are prepared to mobilize on a moment's notice."

"Of course," asserted Kane. "You've already seen that my men are at battle-ready, the fleet gathered together and ready to sail. Just make certain your pretty friends over there are ready when I need them."

He reflected upon the all but insurmountable difficulties he had been plagued with in order to fit the Scylredi and their terrifying weapons into a unified attack formation. Aside from the obvious problems of coordination, there had been tremendous problems arising from the necessity for absolute secrecy. These difficulties proved trivial compared to that of handling the reaction among the men, once they learned the nature of their secret allies. Kane had shown and told them as little as possible, and had maintained discipline with an iron hand. No one left the island except on specific orders.

In the weeks since that night when he had visited the Sorn-Ellyn with Efrel, there had been countless meetings with the Scylredi in Efrel's hidden chamber. Here, surrounded by the relics of centuries of sorcerous delvings, Kane had watched Efrel communicate with the hideous creatures.

Communication was through mental telepathy — although how Efrel was able to exchange thoughts with such inhuman monsters remained a mystery to Kane. Kane had cultivated his own psychic abilities far beyond the limits of most men, but he was able to understand nothing that passed between Efrel and the Scylredi. If the Scylredi could form a mental contact with a human mind, they chose to do so only with Efrel — or else the witch could draw upon incredible psychic powers in her own right. However the sorceress accomplished the feat, Kane had been able to work out the details for the coming battle through her interpretation.

It mattered little to Kane. The prospect of linking minds with a Scylred did not greatly appeal to him. He was far more interested in the secret of Efrel's spell of paralysis. She guarded that secret well — as she guarded all her secrets. Kane thought he recognized the basic enchantment and toyed with the thought of attempting a counterspell with one of the prisoners.

Efrel broke in on his revery. "This should be the talismans coming up to us now."

Kane followed her gesture toward the surface of the pool where a stubby, miniature version of the Scylredi seacraft was just breaking the water. The tiny submarine moved closer to the low wall at the edge of the pool. A hatch slip open across its spheroid bow.

Kane spoke sharply, and a line of uneasy soldiers stepped alongside the wall next to the vessel. With shaky hands, they withdrew the heavy containers that waited within the water-filled hold. One man gasped and almost fell in — as a black loop of tentacle lifted a container to him.

"Be careful, you clumsy ass!" barked Kane. "We'll need every one of those talismans."

The bulky containers held dozens of heavy, egg-shaped globes of metal — featureless objects about the size of a man's head. These talismans were the solution to the major problem of coordination, and their production had been essential before the Scylredi could serve effectively as allies. With these devices, it was possible for the Scylredi to distinguish the rebel warships from the Imperial craft. Products of Scylredi science, the metal eggs emitted a constant drone inaudible to human ears, but which the Scylredi — and their giant servants, the Oraycha — could hear and understand. Each ship in the rebel fleet must carry one of these talismans against its keel — or risk destruction by Efrel's inhuman allies when the fighting became close.

Unloaded, the submarine departed. An aura of awful expectancy settled over the chamber. Imel, in charge of the work crew, gladly led the line of porters from the chamber. Arbas stood with his arms folded across his thick chest, waiting to see if Kane would leave.

"One final thing, Kane," reminded Efrel, watching the pool's surface intently. "Remember that neither Netisten Maril nor M'Cori is to be killed or injured in the least. I'd like to have Lages alive, too, but with him it isn't essential. Regardless of the cost, Maril and M'Cori *must* be delivered to me unharmed. Kill a thousand men if it is necessary, but bring them to me so that they may suffer the full vengeance that I promised to wreak upon the house of Netisten! I have elaborate plans regarding those two, and I will not be thwarted in this. See that it is understood by all your men."

"Certainly!" Kane assured her — as if hearing this for the first time. In her insane obsession with vengeance, Efrel had impressed this command upon him a hundred times. "Just you see that your ugly friends leave Maril's flagship to me."

Efrel nodded. "They understand. One conspicuous ship they can single out and avoid."

Turning from him, she raised her hand in a beckoning gesture. In agonized terror, the Imperial prisoners jerked forward — puppets dancing on invisible strings. Their muscles twitched with desperate effort, but they could not break free of the spell. Cringing strides carried them closer to the pool, then to the very edge. And over.

Instantly the water came alive — as hordes of the waiting Scylredi rose to seize the struggling captives. Released at the final moment from the spell, their doomed screams echoed throughout the cavernous chamber.

Kane watched in fascination as the tormented victims were dragged beneath the surface in a snare of slimy black tentacles — to be sported with, torn apart, sucked bloodless by these creatures from the lost past.

Scarlet froth lapped along the pool's edge as the last tortured face sank into the bottomless well. Alorri-Zrokros had not lied in regard to the Scylredi's feeding habits.

XXV
Battle for Empire

The sea wind blowing through his red hair, Kane stood at the bow of the *Ara-Teving* and watched through his telescope as the Imperial fleet crawled across the blue horizon. The sea was dark with ships — warships of all descriptions, flying the red banner of Thovnos, the blue banner of Raconos, the green-and-black flag of Fisitia ... Kane gave up trying to count. Warships were here from every quarter of the Empire, rallying to their Emperor to meet the threat of Efrel's insurrection.

The Imperial armada must outnumber his own navy about four to one, Kane decided. Maril was confident in his numbers, and for this reason the Emperor had elected to move first and crush the rebel navy in one decisive encounter. Kane had predicted such a move — and as he regarded his own fleet, he considered Maril's strategy justified.

A disparate formation of outmoded, overhauled and refitted vessels, with only a scattering of first-class warships. Response to Efrel's rebellion had been good — but almost entirely from those minor powers who stood to gain the most from this venture. Withal, Efrel had won a number of the more powerful lords over to her cause, and their warcraft along with those of Pellin formed the backbone of Kane's fleet. Altogether Kane had nearly a hundred vessels under his command — a powerful navy, but pitifully outnumbered and outclassed by the Imperial armada. They would be slaughtered, if the Scylredi failed to come through.

On the deck of his own flagship, Netisten Moral felt no misgivings as the rebel fleet came into view. "By Horment!" he laughed to his captain. "That pox-eaten witch put together a bigger navy than I'd thought she could. I didn't know there were that many derelicts afloat on the entire Western Sea! A damn lot of good it will do her. We're going to roll over these damned rebels like a tidal wave on a mud flat!"

He grinned as an aide handed him his crested helmet. "By nightfall we should be in Prisarte, watching the city burn. I'm going to teach them a lesson here that will quell any thoughts of rebellion for the next century. Pellin has been poisoning the body of the Empire like a rotting cancer for too long. Today I'm going to excise and then cauterize this stinking abscess once and for all. And as for Efrel and her so-called deathless general…"

A shout of alarm roared across the vanguard of the Imperial formation. Maril cut short his gloating to see the cause. Stunned, the Emperor pointed and demanded incredulously, "What in all the seven hells of Lord Tloluvin is that?"

From out of the sea between the two opposing armadas, the four submarine warcraft of the Scylredi breached like a pack of colossal killer whales. Soundless, save for the uncanny ultrasonic whine of their engines, the alien submarines bore down on the Imperial fleet.

Whatever the strange craft might be, their hostile intent was obvious. Maril shouted for his petraries to open fire.

From across the gigantic armada, deck-mounted catapults — smaller than those Kane had used, and more conventionally armed — lashed forth their deadly missiles. A storm of rocks and pitch-soaked fireballs arched across the sea and fell among the Scylredi sea craft. Flame splashed harmlessly across the metallic hulls; rocks struck the impervious leviathans with resounding crashes and glanced aside.

The petraries had scarcely fired a first volley when the Scylredi craft attacked. Crackling bolts of violet energy lanced from their conical turrets. Across the Imperial front, warships suddenly exploded in a hissing roar of flame.

It was as if the Imperial fleet had been caught up in some unthinkable lightning storm on the blazing seas of hell. Ravening bolts of energy devastated the vanguard of the armada, wreaking havoc throughout the proud fleet. Doomed soldiers screamed in horror as they saw their comrades and sister ships blasted into a charred mass — waited for the next destroying bolt to send them to hell. Here was terror that no human weapon could counter, no defense confront. In desperation the catapult crews kept up their ineffectual fire — only to be answered with a continuous barrage of coruscant death from the Scylredi warcraft.

"Keep firing!" yelled Maril, trying to maintain order in the burning chaos wrought by the Scylredi. "Ram them! Whip the oarsmen to full speed!"

Somehow his orders were relayed. Across the deadly waters, his captains desperately sought to close with the Scylredi submarines.

Again and again the violet beams lashed out to destroy. Ships by the score exploded into flaming oblivion. Like a burning, broken thing, the Imperial armada advanced resolutely against the Scylredi craft. Charred debris clotted the steaming waves. The ocean seemed to boil from the heat. Reeking billows of smoke filled the air, almost obscuring the stench of ozone.

Then Maril felt the deck lift under his feet, as a lance of destroying energy struck the Imperial flagship. Where the bolt fell, the stern of the warship exploded into a pillar of flame — as the intense heat seared timber and flesh in a wash of incandescent flame. A gaping hole was blasted through the hull. Steam shrieked through ruptured planks as the sea gushed into the blazing wound. The warship tilted sharply on its keel.

"Abandon ship." Maril shouted needlessly.

Panic swept the flagship. Men jumped from the flaming hell of the deck into a wreckage-strewn sea. Most were pulled down instantly by the weight of their weapons and mail.

Maril quickly flung off helmet, cuirass, and greaves. He gained the rail, even as the flagship began its final roll, and dived into the water. Cutting the littered surface with clean, powerful strokes, he swam in the direction of the nearest ship. A drowning marine clutched at his leg, dragging him down. The Emperor broke free with a curse and a kick to the wretch's face.

"Here, Uncle!" The cry was that of Lages, whose warship had been alongside Maril's flagship.

Swimming through the chaos of charred wreckage and drowning men, Maril reached the other ship. A rope was hurled down to him, which Maril quickly seized. Dodging the oars, he pulled himself aboard.

"Lages!" he cried, and grasped his nephew's hand. "No longer do I regret sparing your life! Someone bring me a sword! I won't let another good blade go to the bottom before it's well oiled with stinking rebel blood!"

Lages smiled grimly and cursed. "What hellish weapon is this that Kane has brought against us? The men are being slaughtered, our ships blown out of the water — and we have yet to strike a blow."

"I don't know what it is," shouted Maril. "But I see Efrel's hand in this. And if we can't destroy the sorceress's demon ships, all we can do is get close to Kane's fleet — where they can't fire on us for fear of hitting the rebel ships. Full speed, forward! If stones and fireballs bounce off their armor flanks, we'll see how they take to being rammed!"

The Imperial armada surged through the water, through sheer force of numbers bearing down on the Scylredi craft. Slowly, taking awful casualties, they closed with the submarines. The Scylredi warcraft hovered motionlessly upon the surface — firing into the onrushing fleet as fast as their weapons could be charged.

The first line of warships came abreast of the alien seacraft. One trireme attempted to ram and smashed full into midships of one of the submarines. The trireme's bow crumpled under the impact, doing no damage to the metallic hull other than to knock the submarine backward in the water. In another instant, the warship and the poor fools aboard were consumed in a ripping blast of flame.

But during the uproar, a second trireme rammed at full speed into the stern of another Scylredi submarine, tearing into one of the ovoid projections there. The force of the suicidal collision drove the bronze-capped ram through the glowing ovoid — buried its sharp beak deep within the submarine's droning engines.

Almost on impact, the Scylredi craft exploded into an incandescent ball of searing white flame. A blinding light brighter than the sun engulfed both vessels. With a fantastic concussion, trireme and alien warcraft were annihilated in one awesome blast. Roaring steam spewed in great, scalding clouds into the sky. Bits of cinder and fused metal ripped the sea apart. Ships closest to the blast burst into flame from the heat.

And with the explosion, the remaining three submarine craft dived beneath the surface and disappeared. Either they feared to join their sister ship in death now that a point of weakness had been found — or they chose to let others continue the battle.

With this deadly obstruction gone, the Imperial fleet surged forward to meet Kane's forces. The soldiers cheered at the destruction of one alien warship and now were in a frenzy to do battle with a tangible, human foe. But Maril was painfully conscious that well over half his fleet had gone to a fiery death beneath the deadly weapons of Efrel's demonic allies.

Only a few hundred yards separated the two fleets. Already the air was filled with missiles and arrows, and the battle cries made a roar like angry surf. Then new terror struck — a weapon fully as dreadful and as unexpected as the attack of the Scylredi warcraft — and war cries shuddered into a tocsin of horror.

A slimy black tentacle — thicker than a man's body — suddenly lashed through the waves and wrapped itself around one of the lead warships. Even as the Imperials froze in disbelief, a flurry of tentacles snaked out of the water to seize the doomed ship. Soldiers screamed in horror as a nightmare from the ocean's pits climbed to the surface behind its tentacles — a bloated mountain of rubbery flesh, two dead-white eyes glaring at the hated sunlight. One of the sea's most fearsome legends had come to life.

The Oraycha tightened its grip on the warship. Timbers cracked and splintered in its crushing embrace. Its monstrous, yellowed beak gaped wide as a castle doorway, then snapped together, smashing through the ship's stout hull. Shrieking, flinging themselves into the churning sea, the helpless soldiers were pulled down to hell with their crumpled ship.

More tentacles were breaking water now. More of these monstrosities of primordial evolution arose from the ocean depths to attack the Imperial fleet. With appalling ease, the gigantic Oraycha crushed ship after ship. An uncanny intelligence seemed to direct the monsters' methodical attack.

Shaking off the numbing grip of terror that the sight of such abominations had aroused, the Imperial forces pressed forward to meet this new threat. Arrows were less than pinpricks to the monsters, and sword blows had no more effect than against a tree trunk. Attempts to ram proved futile, as the Oraycha moved too quickly. Those foolhardy enough to attempt to ram one discovered that the creatures would dive beneath them and seize their warship from below in a fatal grasp.

The soldiers fought valiantly against the sea monsters. One reckless captain hurled a spear deep into the eye of an Oraycha, as it rose to attack his ship. Those near the scene felt, rather than heard, a soul-searing hiss of agony as black blood geysered from the wound. A gigantic tentacle spasmed upward, then fell to smash the captain into his deck. With a convulsive movement, the enraged creature crushed the warship into kindling.

Emitting great gouts of black ink, the wounded Oraycha attacked one ship after another, tearing at them in a murderous frenzy. Then, as it wrapped itself around one vessel, a trireme seized the chance to bore in from behind and bury its bronze ram into the creature's head. Mortally wounded, the Oraycha lashed about in one last orgy of destruction — before sinking to the bottom in a coiling, writhing mass.

On another stricken ship, the soldiers cast flaming pitch upon the monster that ensnared them. As the flames burned into its slimy flesh, the Oraycha released the warship and plunged beneath the sea. Leaking badly from sprung timbers, the ship was quickly engulfed in flame. Her men scrambled off into a sea whipped to froth by the monster's agony. They might as well have stayed on the burning decks.

Somehow, through all this turmoil and chaos, the two fleets came together. Shouting their war cries, the Imperial soldiers leaped upon the rebels — carrying them back in the first rush of their charge. Ship smashed against ship, and waves of vicious hand to hand combat washed over the decks as the opposing forces clashed. The battle exploded into maddened carnage — with each warship, each man, fighting for life.

Kane saw with satisfaction that the Oraycha had further depleted the Imperial armada. Now their numbers were nearly even — and if his disreputable-looking navy could just fight together, he could wrest a victory out of this battle yet.

An Imperial trireme bore down on him. With experience of countless battles, Kane swung the *Ara-Teving* aside and struck the other ship a glancing blow with the bronze ram. With a moan of protesting timbers, the two ships grappled.

Throwing down the shield he had held against arrows, Kane drew his two swords and rushed to meet the Imperial marines. Cutlass and broadsword flashed like lethal silver through the air. Leaden impact flowed from steel to muscle, and Kane howled at the first shock of combat. The twin blades swung back again, spraying a line of scarlet behind them. Kane laughed wildly as an avalanche of shining steel and snarling faces swept to overwhelm him. With powerful left-handed blows, he cut down all who rose to meet his challenge.

The sand-strewn deck lurched beneath his feet, and only Kane's lightning-quick reflexes saved him from falling onto his opponent's thrusting swordpoint. A second Imperial trireme had struck the *Ara-Teving*, and now her soldiers poured over in an all-out effort to take the rebel flagship.

Shouting orders deliberately, Kane directed his men to meet the new menace. His role of commander was a dangerous encumbrance in this close fighting, he realized — even as a group of marines used the distraction to try to slay the rebel leader. Surrounded by vengeful warriors, Kane found himself hard pressed. Laying about him with deadly precision, Kane chopped off a hand of one assailant, laid open an exposed belly of another. He unerringly struck wherever a target presented itself — taking a dreadful toll of his attackers. Only a man of Kane's fantastic prowess could have parried the vortex of steel that sought for him — and many a rash fool died under his flashing blades.

Not all blows could be wholly parried, and deflected blades struck painfully against his mailed body. His hauberk was snagged and bloody, thin slashes bled down face and forearms, and an unseen archer almost skewered his throat with an arrow. It seemed inescapable that some assailant must soon slip beneath Kane's guard and deal him a major wound. Once crippled, Kane knew he would instantly be dragged down, cut to pieces by the jackals. Heedless of his danger, Kane taunted and jeered at his frantic assailants. Covered with blood that matched his red hair, Kane fought on viciously — exulting each time his sword struck home.

Then the Imperial marines began to fall back, leaving a mound of bodies about Kane. Cutting his way across the blood-soaked sand of the decks was Arbas. For the first time Kane realized that Arbas had grappled his warship into the melee, had thrown his men against the overwhelming Imperial force. His entrance had been well timed, and numbers now swung to more favorable odds for the rebels.

"Hey, assassin!" greeted Kane. "How's business today?" Arbas's appearance gave him respite to waste breath on bravado. Kane rested his aching muscles and grinned at his friend.

"There's death enough that the market's flooded!" complained Arbas. He paused to hurl a fallen dagger through the throat of a soldier on the other side of the deck.

"There's a damn fine throw," the burly assassin applauded. "But finesse is wasted in this melee. Kane, I'm afraid my office as captain will be short-lived. My ship took a ram earlier, and she's leaking badly. In fact, docking her to this mess was the only course left to me, short of swimming."

"Then we'll combine what's left of our crews on the *Ara-Teving*," Kane declared.

Arbas nodded, then yelled, "Hey, watch that son of a bitch at the bow — up there by the jibsail!"

Kane leaped back as an arrow struck at his feet. Savagely, Kane tore a fallen spear out of the decking and hurled it at the hidden archer. Bow and quiver fell to the deck as the spear ripped through the jibsail. The sniper hung writhing across the bowsprit, like an impaled figurehead.

Kane grunted in satisfaction. "Let's hit them hard, Arbas! Clear our decks, and cut loose."

Arbas glanced at the sea, then cursed. "Damn! This is going to be crowded in a minute! Here comes more company, and the marines are going to be swarming over us like stink on shit!"

Two more Imperial warships, a trireme and a bireme, were converging on the embattled *Ara-Teving*. Kane looked at the fighting around him, estimated his strength, and realized that his situation would be serious, if not hopeless, when these new warships locked into the melee.

But then the trireme suddenly stopped in her rush. A maze of black tentacles lashed from the depths to ensnare the warship. While her sister ship watched helplessly, the trireme was crushed in the grip of the colossal sea creature. Men spilled into the sea and wallowed about, striving piteously to reach their comrades on board the bireme. Hundred-foot tentacles stirred the sea about the struggling wretches, killing with a zeal that only intelligence could have lusted for.

The Oraycha were hunting beneath the battle-locked fleets now. In response to the ultrasonic impulses of the talismans, they were continuing to single out and destroy the Imperial warships.

Kane had no time to watch further. There was hot, deadly fighting before the reinforcements from the bireme together with the marines from the initial fray could be cleared from the decks. Despite Arbas's men, it was a smaller crew that finally disentangled the *Ara-Teving* from the floating battlefield and moved on to another foe. Arbas shook his head philosophically as he watched his own abandoned vessel tilt awash with the waves.

Aboard the new Imperial flagship, as all across the battle formation, fighting was similarly hard and without quarter. Twice Lages and Maril had rammed and destroyed rebel warships, and twice they had beaten off attacks against their own ship. Their luck could not continue. They were caught between two rebel warships at once as a glancing blow of one ram tore a great wound below their flagship's waterline.

Lages fought silently beside his uncle on the pitching deck, marveling at Maril's endurance and skill. The choleric Emperor had not held his throne through the strength and ability of other men — and he was still the formidable warrior the court poets exalted him to be. But it was evident that their soldiers were slowly falling back before the rebel advance, and Lages realized that soon their ship would be taken. They well knew what capture meant for them, so the two fought recklessly — planning to die with their swords dripping in enemy blood rather than surrender to Efrel's mercy.

Then help came from a most unexpected quarter. One of the rebel warships was suddenly seized in the death-dealing grip of an Oraycha. The creature's inhuman senses had been confused by the proximity of the grappled warships and had attacked the wrong vessel. As the one ship disappeared into broken wreckage, the Imperial marines took new spirit.

"On to the other warship! We're not through with these rebels yet!" Maril shouted, and swung his blade with new zeal. "Kill the gutter-scum! They can't stand against us on even terms!"

With desperate fury, the Imperials jumped from their rapidly settling decks onto the rebel warship. The struggle dragged bloodily on across the other ship, until slowly the rebels were beaten down. There was neither quarter nor mercy — on the decks or in the sea. At last only an exhausted, tattered band of the Imperials stood on the decks of the rebel bireme.

Taking over the ship for his own, Maril ordered his crew to pick up survivors from the sea in an effort to rebuild their strength before moving on to another fight. Grimly he reflected that this was his third flagship of the day.

So the battle raged everywhere, and victory hung in the balance as the hours wore on. At first the advantage had been with the Imperial armada. But as the battle formation closed into a chaotic melee, their superior warships could not be used to best advantage. It was not an ordered battle they fought now, but a maelstrom of brawling violence. Strategy had long been lost in the chaos. Through it all, the relentless attacks of the Oraycha were slowly cutting down the advantage the Imperials had enjoyed in numbers.

It was a grisly, merciless struggle to the death. On both sides, fighting was vicious and desperate — for both sides knew the price of defeat. But the Scylredi's devastating attack and the crushing embraces of the Oraycha had taken a hideous toll, and now Kane's generalship began to assert itself. The scales of battle shifted, and gradually Kane's forces gained the upper hand.

Nonetheless, the battle was far from won — as the violence increased inversely with the falling numbers of the combatants. It was a dirty, personal struggle of man against man, ship against ship — with only one fate for the vanquished.

Imel arrived too late to save his close friend, Lord Gall of Tresli, who fell at last on the decks of his warship, surrounded by a moraine of Imperial dead. Thirsting for vengeance, Imel saw to it that no Imperial soldier left the ship alive. The renegade seemed obsessed with the lust to destroy all those who called him traitor. As the day dragged to a gory close, his gleaming battle gear was sodden with the blood of his countrymen — and the foppish youth was a grim and haggard stranger to his men.

Elsewhere, Lord Bremnor of the backwater island of Olan — an indifferent swordsman himself — killed the famed warrior, Gostel of Parwi, by an amazingly lucky thrust. Lord Bremnor had scarce time to enjoy his new renown, for he was slain by a hidden archer while leading his soldiers onto an Imperial warship.

In another quarter of the battle, a victorious rebel crew had but a moment to celebrate their triumph over the Imperial trireme they had just taken when an Oraycha seized the vessel and smashed it into a broken coffin for victor and vanquished alike.

And so the battle went on...

The *Ara-Teving* pulled near her sister ship, the *Kelkin*, where Kane saw a reduced force of the Pellinites striving to meet the onslaught of a fresh wave of Imperial marines. Oxfors Alremas was battling desperately, trying to rally his weary men.

Seizing this chance to rid himself of his enemy, Kane unobtrusively picked up a fallen spear. All eyes were fixed on the *Kelkin* as the *Ara-Teving* closed to succor the beleaguered trireme. Waiting for a moment when none of his crew watched him, Kane hurled the spear across the water at Alremas's back. Hard pressed, Alremas chose that moment to stumble to his knees beneath an axe blow to his notched shield. Kane's spear shot past the vacated space and buried its iron blade in the axe-wielder's chest.

"Nice throw, milord!" came the shout from one marine. A murmur of approval passed through the men of both ships as word sped that Kane had saved Alremas through a miraculous spear cast.

Kane swore. His throw had been witnessed, after all, although his intent was favorably misconstrued. Aware that this was too open a place for murder, Kane raised his fist in acknowledgment of the praise, seething inwardly at the thought that the axeman might have killed Alremas. Then they were upon the Imperial warship, and Kane was too busy rescuing his enemy to hatch further schemes.

Looking across the faltering battle, Netisten Maril came to the shocking realization that his forces were being defeated. Of his giant armada of some four hundred warships, only about twenty-five remained afloat — mostly in crippled condition.

The Emperor had almost lost this third flagship, when one of his own warships had seen the Pellinite banners and nearly rammed him. The remaining Imperial warships were being slowly and relentlessly overwhelmed by the rebel navy — still with maybe forty ships afloat, and the constant threat of the Oraycha giving them confidence. Their exact strengths were a little uncertain, because of the frequent exchange of control of an embattled warship. Maril had been told of one trireme that had changed hands three times.

This morning the thought had been inconceivable; as the shadows lengthened it was inescapable. The entire might of the Thovnosian Empire had been brutally annihilated by the forces of an insane sorceress. Efrel had conquered. Total defeat was inevitable if he remained on the field.

"I'm going to order a retreat," he bleakly informed Lages. "We'll at least try to save something to use to defend Thovnos."

His nephew grimly worked to stanch the flow of blood from his side, where a dagger point had forced the joint of his cuirass. Lages said nothing. There were no words to say.

Giving the signal to retreat, Maril headed for Thovnosten with his captured warship. The surviving Imperial warships followed suit — those that were able to escape the melee. What looked at first to be pursuit, turned out instead to be a number of other captured rebel warships, whose new masters little realized that they may have owed their lives to the droning impulses of the Scylredi talismans fixed to their prizes' keels. Altogether, fourteen ships left the wreckage of the battle and made for Thovnosten.

"They're in flight!" shouted Arbas. "We've beaten them at last! Kane, you've defeated the largest armada ever assembled in this part of the world — maybe even the damn biggest fleet in history!"

"It soothes some old wounds," said Kane, thinking of a similar battle with an opposite ending, two centuries before. His eyes grew clouded in revery.

"Shall we chase them?" Arbas wanted to know. "Hell, if Efrel's sea demons hadn't turned tail, we could've sent them out to blast every mother's son of them. But we might still overtake them before dark."

"No. We'll let them run," Kane decided. He was limping somewhat, and his right arm was hard to use from a deep gash that continued to seep through the crude bandage. Even Kane's fantastic strength had been pushed past limit in the grueling, day-long battle.

"We'll hold our position and consolidate our victory," he concluded. "There's plenty of salvageable material in the water that we're going to need — and the men need a chance to lick their wounds and celebrate. We'll mop up here and head for Prisarte.

"Efrel won't like it that we've let her enemy escape, but we'll finish Maril later. Right now I could see a bath, a drink, and some soft kisses to draw out the pain of battle. We just may burn down Prisarte tonight by ourselves."

He scowled wearily at the dwindling warships. Evidently the Oraycha had tired of their sport and were feeding by now. The sea was an overflowing storm sewer of death. The water was filled with the wreckage of hundreds of ships, the bodies of thousands of men. And Kane could see other dark shapes feasting among the debris that were not Oraycha.

XXVI
A Victory Toast

The riot and jubilation that claimed Prisarte did not penetrate into the northern wing of Dan-Legeh. In the night beyond the black citadel, the city resounded with the rebels' victory celebration. Taverns and bordellos overflowed into the streets and alleys, where mobs of revellers feasted and drank and caroused without care or thought for the next battle.

Oxfors Alremas stood stiffly in Efrel's private chambers, sipping pale wine from a crystal chalice. The Pellinite lord was impeccably groomed, resplendent in brocaded houppelande and silken hose. He might have just emerged from a court ball, rather than from a grueling and bloody day of battle.

"The joy of my victory is made tasteless by the escape of Netisten Maril," Efrel murmured.

Alremas wiped his lips with a perfumed handkerchief. "I should consider it ill grace to criticize a man who has saved my life," he said urbanely. "However, I do feel that Kane should have given pursuit. There was sufficient time to overtake the fugitive survivors before darkness. I imagine that Kane had had enough fighting for the day. Certainly, he lost no time upon landing to go out drinking and brawling with the common soldiers."

"The gods of darkness have granted me victory," Efrel mused. "In a matter of days Thovnosten will have fallen to me. Then let Netisten Maril be dragged from the smoking ruins of his lost majesty, be brought to me in chains and disgrace. My vengeance shall have the more savor for the anticipation of a few more days."

"I suggest that you remind Kane that the Emperor is to be taken alive," Alremas told her. "It is churlish to disparage one's superior officer, but I must say that Kane showed little concern for capturing Maril. Looking back upon the conduct of his men. during the battle, it's a wonder that Maril wasn't killed in the melee."

Efrel's one eye glared at him balefully. "That must not happen," she hissed. "Netisten Maril must be brought to me alive — at any cost!"

"I shall do all in my power to see that your wishes are obeyed," promised

Alremas.

"And M'Cori," Efrel breathed. "M'Cori must also be brought to me — untouched and unharmed! Do you understand?"

"I understand, my Queen," Alremas assured her. "And I shall continue to remind Kane of your commands."

He set aside his chalice and knelt beside her couch. "Efrel, let me command the invasion fleet. Kane has served his purpose. The man is dangerous. You think you use him — but I fear that Kane uses you instead."

"Enough!" snarled Efrel. "I use men as I please — and discard them when it pleases me! See that my wishes are obeyed, Oxfors Alremas — and beware that your jealousy of Kane does not detract from your usefulness to me! You may go now."

Alremas stood up, saluted stiffly, and withdrew from Efrel's presence. Hatred smouldered in his eyes.

Efrel finished her wine and felt the rush of anger subside. Reclining upon her couch, she stared at the painting on the wall.

Efrel of another life stared down at her.

Efrel loosened her fur pelisse and let its folds fall away from her naked flesh. Her unblemished hands trailed across the hideous expanses of twisted scar and torn flesh. She gazed entranced upon the girl of naked beauty in the painting, caressed her mutilated body. Were these maimed legs once those ivory thighs of the painting? Were these tattered breasts those same rouge-crowned hillocks? Was this mass of scar and broken rib once that slim white belly? Was this face…

There were tears in that eye that could yet distill tears.

"Soon," Efrel crooned to herself. "Soon…"

XXVII
Attack on Thovnosten

A week after the defeat of the Imperial armada, Kane watched the coastline of Thovnos climb out of the sea. This day he commanded a fleet of some seventy-five ships of all descriptions, crowded to the rails with fighting men for the invasion of Thovnosten. This was to be the final assault, for Kane estimated Maril's strength to be too decimated to withstand a full-scale attack. The only difficulty would be in penetrating the city's defenses, and Kane trusted to the Scylredi to accomplish this task.

Whatever their reaction over the loss of one of their irreplaceable submarine craft, Efrel had succeeded in maintaining their support in the rebellion. But, so the sorceress warned Kane, the energy that powered their engines and terrible weapons was almost exhausted. Unable to replenish this energy source, the Scylredi had made only sparing use of their warcraft for centuries. Efrel had persuaded them to consume some final reservoirs of this precious energy, but the Scylredi insisted that their annihilating rays be utilized only where it was absolutely essential.

As he had expected, Kane encountered no resistance on the passage to Thovnos. Maril had realized it would only be a foolish waste of strength to oppose Kane's fleet with the remnants of his own force. The Emperor had gathered together everything at his command to mount a desperate defense of Thovnosten — knowing that he must preserve his capital from Efrel's power at all costs. The sea was barren of Imperial warships now. Without incident, the rebel fleet took up position outside the harbor of Thovnosten.

Thovnosten's harbor was too wide to be blocked, but through the glass Kane could see that at strategic places wrecks had been sunk and sharp poles driven into the bottom, in an effort to stop the invaders. They would have to proceed carefully if the Scylredi did not remove all obstructions, and that would expose the ships to the defenders' fire. And this was only the outer perimeter of the harbor defenses. The surviving warships of the great battle were armed and ready to repel the invaders within the harbor. Kane noted dozens of fishing boats and other nondescript hulls drawn up before the Imperial fleet. Fireboats and other pleasantries, Kane decided.

The walls of the city were lined with defenders. Every able-bodied man in the city must have turned out to hold the walls. Also visible were great numbers of catapults — along with mounds of boulders and vats of flaming oil to be hurled down on the attackers. The city gates were strong and well fortified — work for a massive battering ram, assuming men could endure the constant fire from the walls. Altogether, Thovnosten was well prepared to withstand the rebel assault, and the city's defenders were determined not to yield. Ordinarily Kane would never have considered taking the stronghold, except by long siege.

But Efrel's inhuman allies fought with weapons no human defenses could withstand. Beyond the harbor, the Scylredi warcraft now surfaced to signal the start of the final assault.

Deadly bolts of violet heat crackled forth from the submarines and sliced into the walls of Thovnosten. Hundreds of screaming defenders died in searing blast after blast as the very stones shattered to cinder under the incandescent heat. Catapults and siege machinery flashed into charred heaps, while kettles of oil exploded into gigantic fireballs. Howling mobs fled in terror. The frightened tales of the battle's survivors had only been halfway believed. Now the horrors of prehuman science rose up from the ocean depths to confront the race that dared to declare itself masters of the earth.

From the city came an answering hail of arrows and missiles of all kinds. The rain of death glanced harmlessly off the metal hulls, or fell among the recklessly advancing warships with more serious effect. But as the lashes of destroying energy raked the walls of the city, the return fire became ragged — and failed. Columns of black, reeking smoke boiled up from the battlements. Screaming figures stumbled from the wall, trailing flame as they plummeted to the smouldering ground below.

Then the Scylredi turned their fire against the city gates. With a thundering concussion, the iron gates were blasted into a flaming gout of molten fragments and fused cinder — leaving gaping holes in the cracked walls. Thovnosten's heart was guarded now only by tumbled heaps of flaming timber and splintered rubble.

Turning from the smouldering walls, the submarines unleashed a salvo of quick bursts of coruscant hellfire into the waiting ships. Fireships exploded amidst the lines of warships. The last of the Imperial navy withered beneath the destroying barrage. Then, as suddenly as it had began, the firing ceased and the warcraft submerged. But in less than ten minutes, their awesome attack had annihilated the defenses of Thovnosten.

"Now! Let's get in there before they pick themselves up!" shouted Kane — and the rebel fleet drove into the harbor.

Several captains were careless, smashing their ships into hidden obstructions — but the great part of the rebel fleet entered the harbor unscathed and rushed to meet what remained of the Imperial navy. Ship crashed into ship as the Imperial forces recklessly attacked the rebels. They knew theirs to be a suicide mission, and they fought like maddened devils to take as many souls as possible with them into the eternal night.

Fishing boats filled with combustible materials were set afire and driven into the ranks of the invaders. In the close quarters, precise maneuvering was impossible — and the blazing fireboats smashed against several warships, showering them with flame. And as the battle dragged on, a scattered but steadily increasing rain of arrows and missiles descended upon the struggling warships. The survivors were quickly returning to the smoking walls.

But the resistance was ineffectual. Defenses geared to the repulsion of a natural enemy had been shattered by an inhuman force. The rebel invasion fleet pressed relentlessly forward, and although a number of ships were lost, the desperate defenders were driven back. Decks swarming with rebel soldiers, the last of the Imperial fleet was overrun — helpless against the irresistible strength of Kane's hordes. The rebel fleet landed, and thousands of soldiers rushed ashore to carry the battle into the city. Following Kane's commands, the rebel forces now split into three sections, each entering the city through a different breach in the walls. This would cut the regrouping defenders off from each other — and make it impossible for the Thovnosians to throw their remaining strength against any single front.

Taking several arrows on his shield, Kane jumped ashore and pushed to the glowing ruin of the main gate. His men were milling about the smouldering wreckage — momentarily checked as the Thovnosians concentrated their shattered forces to defend the major portal. The soldiers shouted a welcome as he joined them, and confidently they followed him into the hard fighting around the breach in the wall. Like a demon of death, Kane cut through the defenders — smashing them aside with powerful razor-edged strokes. For this heavy fighting Kane chose to carry his short-hafted battle-axe. Swinging the double-bitted weapon with his strong left arm, Kane ripped men apart in crimson eruptions of dismembered limbs, entrails, and gore. Behind the bludgeon of his axe, the cutlass Kane wielded in his right hand flashed like a serpent's fang. Heedless of arrows in the dense melee, Kane discarded his buckler and trusted to his mail to turn the steel that stabbed past his guard.

On through the ranks of the Thovnosians, Kane led his men in an irresistible wedge. The streets and the rabble of the walls were choked with fallen bodies as the Thovnosians fought valiantly to repel the invaders. But they were relentlessly crushed against the smoking ruins and the corpses of their comrades. Sensing victory, the rebels stormed over the windrows of dead and began a three-headed invasion of the city itself.

For hours fierce fighting raged, but Thovnosten now was doomed. Her defenses were annihilated, and thousands of the enemy were pouring into her streets. No organized resistance could be thrown against the raiders, and the small pockets of defenders were cut down to a man. Soon the fighting ebbed, to be replaced by waves of looting and rapine.

The rebels ran from house to house — killing all who could not flee, seizing what they wanted, and setting fire to the rest. The smoke-filled streets of the Imperial capital echoed with the shrieks of tortured women, the wails of children, the screams of the injured and dying. It was a dream become reality for the pirates and cutthroats recruited by Kane — as all men returned to their true state of bestiality and reveled in the mad glory of rape and pillage.

Racing through the orgy of rape and unbridled destruction, Kane led a strong force of raiders to the Imperial palace. Here the resistance was still organized, and the fighting was fierce and unyielding. Another band of rebels led by Imel quickly joined them at the beleaguered walls. If the Thovnosian renegade felt any remorse over the sack of his native capital, he failed to show it.

"Where's Alremas?" Kane shouted.

"Working his way around from behind," came Imel's answer. "He should get here in ten or twenty minutes."

Kane felt bitterness that his enemy seemed invulnerable in these affairs. "Look, you know your way around here. When we break through, take some men and capture M'Cori. Remember — bring her to me unharmed. I'll handle the resistance until Alremas can bring up his reserve."

Imel nodded and returned to his men. Sending a party under Arbas to mock up mantlets and battering rams from the wreckage, Kane began the assault on the stronghold. The defense from the palace walls was rugged and determined — but rebel archers kept the defenders pinned down effectively, until the improvised battering ram could drive its way through the main gate. With Kane in the lead, the rebels poured through the palace gardens and courts, into the halls themselves. The palace guard fought valiantly, but they were steadily driven back by Kane's superior force.

"Kane!" A haggard figure in armor suddenly loomed before Kane. Netisten Maril had watched his Empire crumble about him — and now after hours of furious fighting in a vain effort to blunt the rebel drive, he had returned to defend his palace. "By Horment, at least I'll have the satisfaction of sending your black soul down to the Seventh Hell!"

"There have been many who have tried!" sneered Kane. "And Lord Tloluvin now watches over them all!"

With a bull-like bellow of rage, Maril rushed upon Kane. The Emperor was a powerful man, and he fought driven by an insane fury. Here at last was the man who had brought about the ruin of his vast Empire. If victory had eluded the Emperor, at least vengeance was within his grasp. Kane gave ground slowly under Maril's violent attack, stopping blow after blow with his sword — smashing at the Emperor's shield with his axe. Recklessly Maril avoided the flashing battle-axe in Kane's left-hand and pressed his attack in a storm of steel lightning and thunderous clangour. Berserk strength guided his furious swordplay.

A sudden twist of Maril's longer blade caught Kane in his right arm — gashing painfully through the partially healed wound he carried there. The cutlass clattered from Kane's grasp, and he now faced Maril with one arm useless. A red lust to kill overwhelmed Kane's senses. Ignoring the pain, Kane carefully circled Maril, watching for an opening. His axe wove a glittering pattern as he snarled defiance.

But Maril was too reckless in his eagerness to finish his hated enemy. One slip was all Kane needed. Kane feinted with the heavy axe and recoiled as Maril's blade swept wildly past his head. For an instant the Emperor was over-extended with the impetus of his decapitating stroke. With blinding speed, Kane's axe swung out and clove through Maril's cuirass and ribcage. His eye still brimming with hatred, Netisten Maril crumpled to the floor and died in a rush of blood at Kane's feet.

"Well, you've killed him," observed Arbas, who had been watching the duel with great interest. "Efrel, I think, will not be amused. And to make things perfect, I see our friend, Alremas, has broken through just in time to witness the Emperor's last stand. I'm sure he won't waste time telling Efrel who killed him. Kane, maybe we should take our time about getting back to Pellin."

Kane cursed and examined his badly wounded arm. "Screw her! I'll talk to Efrel! I wasn't about to let Maril kill me just to satisfy her whim! I've handed Efrel the Imperial throne — and if Imel comes through with M'Cori, she should be happy enough."

Imel, in the meantime, had fought his way to M'Cori's chambers. There the renegade and his men finally cut down the last of those who had been stationed on guard and forced an entrance into her rooms. The rebels fell upon the screaming servant girls, then swaggered into M'Cori's presence.

M'Cori fought down her gnawing terror, and rose defiantly to meet the grinning intruders. Thoughts of suicide had raced through her mind, but the idea was too repulsive. While there was life, there was hope — and until she knew that Lages was slain, she refused to relinquish all hope.

Savouring her beauty, Imel cursed Efrel for reserving M'Cori for her own uses. The girl would make a nice prize for the sorceress's most valued servant. "Come along quietly, and I promise you won't be harmed," he told his blond captive. He smiled reassuringly. "You're an honored prisoner, after all. We're to escort you to the Empress at Prisarte."

"Nothing is lower than a renegade!" spat M'Cori.

"Better a victorious renegade than a defeated patriot," Imel shrugged. He ordered her bound, then led her back to Kane. There would be less principled girls elsewhere in the plundered city.

Meanwhile in the red chaos of the streets, Lages still carried on a desperate resistance. Separating from his uncle early in the battle to meet the multiple rebel attack, Lages had been bypassed by the main thrust of the invaders. As a result of this chance, he and a ragged band of Imperial soldiers still roamed the riot-filled streets, cutting down scattered looters. Knowing that the Imperial capital was lost, Lages fought on without thought of escape, intending to die amidst the ashes of his city.

Then a messenger reached him with word of the palace's fall, of the Emperor's death and M'Cori's capture. At this news Lages broke into a sui-cidal frenzy, howling for his men to follow him in an impossible attempt to rescue M'Cori. But his weary soldiers held him back, convinced him that it would be senseless to throw all their lives away in a hopeless attack against Kane and his army of marauders.

At last Lages realized the hopelessness of the situation. He gave orders to spread the word for all loyalists to join him, then grudgingly retreated with his battle-worn band. Picking up stragglers as they passed, he moved out of the burning city and into the hills of Thovnos, where he could organize guerrilla resistance to the Empire's conquerors.

And thus fell the Thovnosian Empire, in ashes and blood — at the hand of the man who had indirectly been responsible for its creation.

XXVIII
The Hand of Kane

Throughout the city of Prisarte, there was wild celebration among the victorious rebels. The tension of battle broke loose into jubilant hysteria. Captured gold and wine flowed freely, as drunken revelry and raucous gaiety prevailed.

Within the black fortress of Dan-Legeh, the atmosphere was otherwise. Efrel was in a towering rage. For an hour she had shrieked and cursed insanely at Kane. His crushing defeat of the Thovnosian Empire meant nothing to her in this state of madness. All the sorceress knew was that Kane had slain her enemy himself. His colossal stupidity had forever destroyed her long-cherished dream of vengeance. For months she had been kept alive through her hatred for the man who had shamed and mutilated her — and now Netisten Maril was beyond even her revenge.

Oxfors Alremas watched smugly as Kane stoically withstood Efrel's endless tirade. At times she could only utter a shrill, incoherent shriek of impassioned rage. Never had Alremas seen her in such wrath. He judged with satisfaction that he no longer would have to worry about Kane. With his rival's fall from favor, he should be able to convince Efrel that Kane was too dangerous to have around. Then, it was just a matter of legal murder.

Kane gave up all efforts to reason with the sorceress. Realizing that she was beyond rationality, he braced himself and waited for her anger to slacken. It took some time, but finally her tirade ceased.

Before she could began again, Kane rushed to speak: "In every particular but this, I have fulfilled your every command. When before this have you had any reason to criticize me or my methods? And despite what some lying tongues say, I only meant to disarm Maril. The fool refused to surrender — he all but threw himself against my axe. So how am I to blame for his death? Forget this one whim of vengeance. Haven't I delivered the Empire into your hands? I have accomplished everything else I agreed to perform in your service. And remember, you still have M'Cori to work your revenge upon."

A strange light came into Efrel's eye. Her attention seemed no longer fixed an Kane, but on some secret thought. "Yes, but another was responsible for her capture," she hissed.

"May I point out a slight dissimilarity between capturing a teenage girl and subduing a seasoned warrior? Anyway, it was all carried out according to my orders."

Kane added shrewdly: "Lages is still on the loose — and with an army of sorts under his command. Until he and his guerrillas are destroyed, you will always have that threat hanging over you. Perhaps you feel that another should deal with Lages."

Efrel snarled in frustration, "No, damn you! I still want you to root out the last shreds of Imperial resistance. When you have accomplished this, you may then claim your reward. Now get out of my sight — before I treat you to the fate I had reserved for Maril!"

"Thank you for your benevolence," said Kane drily — trying to mask his feelings. "I assure you that Lages will straightway be delivered to you for this pleasure."

He hastily left the council room, his face taut with cold anger. Arbas was waiting around outside. "I wasn't sure you'd come out of that with your hide intact!" he began. "You know, you could hear her howls all over this fortress. Damn! I've never heard anyone in such a rage!"

Kane grunted and walked on in silence. "Let's go where we can talk," he finally muttered.

"Any alehouse should do for that. There's too much noise and drunkenness for spying tonight. Anyway," the assassin added reflectively, "it's a good occasion to get drunk, if nothing else."

So they eventually found their way to a bustling tavern, where crowds of battle-weary soldiers mixed drink and women in loud celebration. Picking their way to a relatively deserted corner of the room, they took up mugs of ale and sat down. Arbas eyed the dancing girls calculatingly, but there was real concern beneath his festive air.

"I think you know what I have to say," Kane began in a low voice. "I never intended to leave that madwoman in control of the new Empire. I had hoped to bide my time until the choice moment. Now it looks as though I'm going to have to move faster than I'd planned."

He frowned, remembering Alremas's supercilious smile during his ordeal with Efrel. "Anyway, there's no other course left to me. Alremas looked at me like I was an old friend with a fatal disease. This war has depleted Efrel's strength as much as the Empire's. I can count on enough men to do the job. The mercenaries from outside the Empire will follow me — as will most of those who were in on this for motives of pure gain. Imel will side with me, I know. Efrel can only count on the Pellinites to support her claim to rule."

The assassin sipped his beer thoughtfully. "You figure you can swing enough support, then? I mean, you'll be up against all of Pellin — and Efrel's sorcery."

"I think so. I intend a *coup d'état*, not a conquest. We'll strike fast and secretly. By the time anyone knows what's going on, it will be too late to do anything. Besides, we've got M'Cori — and unless I'm mistaken, she's going to bring us some more help."

"What do you mean?" Arbas asked, belching and refilling their mugs.

"Lages is holed up somewhere on Thovnos with quite a few men. We can make use of their swords. When I offer him a chance to save M'Cori from Efrel, I'm certain the fool will join us. Afterward, something can happen to him."

Kane's eyes looked beyond the room. "I almost had this place in my grasp once before. I don't mean to let it slip away again."

XXIX
The Vengeance of Efrel

Far beneath the revelry of the night outside, smoky yellow flames from the great oil lamps gave light to a shadowy scene of bizarre antithesis. In her subterranean chamber, Efrel stood gloating over the chained form of M'Cori.

The tableau presented absolute extremes of the feminine soul. M'Cori crouched in chains before her captor. Ingenuous, blond and fair-skinned, face and figure of fragile loveliness — M'Cori was truly a child of light. Before her strutted a cold-hearted girl of spider-like cunning. Efrel — black-haired and pale-skinned, uncanny beauty corrupted into hideous mutilation. Efrel, a queen of night. A soul that loved the world of daylight was ensnared by a soul of malevolent hatred.

M'Cori moved as far back as the chains anchored to the floor would permit — recoiling in horror from the evil mockery of femininity that leered at her. Efrel watched her terrified captive with unutterable delight.

"M'Cori, dear — don't you recognize me?" she taunted. "Have you forgotten Efrel? It's true that I was much lovelier at your father's court — but your father saw to that, didn't he? It's a pity Maril died without once more enjoying the beauty that his malice had moulded. Did you weep for Efrel when she died, M'Cori?"

She tittered at the expression of absolute horror frozen on her captive's face. "But as I remember, you never did care much for Efrel, did you? Efrel was too dark a spirit to meet favor in your dear little thoughts. Well, that's forgiven — all is forgiven — because you're going to make it up to me now."

She stared intently at the fragile beauty of M'Cori. "M'Cori will be spared the fate I had planned for her father. Pretty M'Cori, you shouldn't be frightened of Efrel. No flaying knife shall caress lovely M'Cori's soft skin. Ah, you always were so beautiful a child, weren't you? Some even claimed more beautiful than I was. Beautiful child, let me see more of you!" Savagely, Efrel's hands clawed out at her captive and tore away the silken shoulders of M'Cori's gown.

M'Cori jerked back from her clutching fingers. "Efrel! Why are you doing this to me?" she stammered. "I have never wished you harm! I was promised I would be treated as an honored prisoner. Instead you chain me in your dungeons — threaten me with torture!"

Efrel cackled wildly. "Torture you? No, no — rest assured that I won't harm one hair of your golden body. Oh, no! But as you will learn, pretty one, I have every right to examine all your beauty."

She swayed before her captive, like a serpent before a hypnotized bird. "Do you know what I have planned for you, dear M'Cori? Not torture, I promise you.

"Have you ever studied the arts of the occult sphere? Sweet M'Cori, you're trembling. How careless of me to forget — your bright little world revolves around happier pastimes. M'Cori has always lived in a flower garden world — her life is a game of adventures and childish laughter. So it is not strange that you should show such revulsion toward sorcery.

"For Efrel it was otherwise. I was far younger than you, beautiful child, when first I ripped a virgin's heart from her breast and offered it to a howling demon from the world beyond night. But M'Cori read foolish love poetry, instead of blood-stained grimoires. Withal, we might be sisters for the nearness of our ages — but you frolicked in the sunlight, while Efrel danced in sulfur-lit darkness. Yet I wonder if you could stand here in my place — dreaming the dreams of hatred and vengeance that I know — had it been M'Cori, and not Efrel, that Netisten Maril gave to the bull. My gods spared me to fulfill my curse. Would yours have done the same?

"Still I see only horror in your eyes. Sweet M'Cori only feels compassion for pretty things. When you saved a struggling butterfly from his webbed prison, M'Cori darling, did you ever shed a tear for the spider you thus left to starve? Have you ever thought, dear child, what you might have become had our lives been reversed? Would you feel sympathy for the spider, had you been born a child of night? Had there been dark Pellin blood in your heart, instead of tepid Netisten blood — perhaps lovely M'Cori would have learned to chant spells, rather than to recite sugary poems. Perhaps M'Cori would have abandoned her flower gardens to the conqueror weeds and spent her nights poring over cryptic lines paged on human skin.

"But I was speaking of sorcery. If your childhood had passed like mine, perhaps then M'Cori would know of an ancient spell of transmigration. She might know that through certain magics, the soul can be excised from its earthly body and projected through the cosmos, that through potent sorceries a captive soul may be stolen from its natural breast and imprisoned within another body. She might even know how to perform the difficult spell through which the human soul may be exchanged from one body to another — wrested from its corporeal form, and imprisoned within the body of the adept.

"Efrel knows such a spell, pretty one."

Efrel swayed closer to her cringing captive. One hand lifted her chin, the other slipped the torn gown away from M'Cori's shoulders. The girl's face was blank with frightened wonder.

"Now do you understand why your body interests me so? Dear M'Cori, you stare at me so innocently — without comprehension. Must I tell you what your naive mind refuses to accept?

"Your body will soon be my own."

She laughed with insane pleasure at M'Cori's scream of horror. "Yes! Yes, my lovely one! That is why I've spared you from these instruments of crude torture. No harm shall come to pretty, pretty M'Cori. Because before very long your body will be mine, and your spirit will be trapped in this shattered hull that once was Efrel! Think of the irony of it! Maril's own daughter — imprisoned within the mutilated flesh he had lusted for and then destroyed. And the woman he had doomed to a hideous death — alive and beautiful once again in his own daughter's body."

Numb with fear and shock, M'Cori watched the sorceress fall to the floor in maddened laughter. In a half-faint, she huddled in her chains and watched as in a dream while the cavorting, taunting madwoman hopped about her, tearing away her clothing and greedily pawing over her body. Efrel's scarred face giggled inches from her own. Sharp nails clutched at her bare flesh. Torn lips whispered intolerable demands and promises into her ears.

M'Cori tried to crawl away, but chains fettered her wrists and ankles. She tried to struggle free, but the sorceress's mad strength was too much for her. Her screams were lost in the shadows of the hidden chamber. Her garments were in shreds now. Efrel's hands crawled over her naked flesh. She was pinned beneath the sorceress's writhing body, naked now as well. Tattered lips caressed her face, sucked at her lips, bit her breasts. M'Cori moaned in revulsion as Efrel forced her legs apart and bent her helpless body to serve her lusts.

Sick with loathing, M'Cori writhed helplessly beneath the bestial assault of the raving sorceress. Her soul shriveled with the horror of it as a wave of evil crushed her to the stones, smothered her sobbing breath. Pain and nausea and shame shook her violated flesh in great paroxysms. She felt herself falling into a deep black well, and somewhere in the nightmare came oblivion.

Sometime later, when M'Cori awoke, she was unable for a moment to orient herself. In her hollow weakness, it seemed for a space that she still lay tossing in the delirium of a fever-dream. Then she saw the dark stones, the chains, the torn clothing, her scratched and bruised flesh — and knew that the nightmare was reality.

Groggily she sat up, praying that the scene of horror might yet dissolve into fragments of dream. The walls did not waver, and the sickness remained. Weird odors filled the air; bluish lights flickered in the darkness. Looking about, M'Cori saw that she now was chained in the center of a great circle.

An evil laugh drew a gasp from her. "Back with me so soon, my darling?" Efrel jeered. "Was it passion that made you faint beneath my tender caresses, pretty child? Touching modesty from one who is not even a virgin."

She laughed cruelly and bent to examine a large parchment-paged volume. Around her were stacks of other strangely bound works of varying stages of antiquity — along with jars and vials of paints, chalks, incenses, and the dubious powders and elixirs of her black art. From the vast quantities of occult paraphernalia the sorceress had drawn together, it was evident that Efrel was at work on some great necromantic project.

"You look interested," sneered the sorceress. "Well, you should be. After all, this spell will be of no little personal interest to you, won't it? Besides, this is a very intriguing spell — and a most difficult one, as well. I shall need a few days just to get everything in readiness to begin the actual conjuration. But I have prepared well for this triumph, so you won't be inconvenienced too long. A few days are nothing to one who has already suffered a lifetime of agony and shame as this crippled monster your father made me.

"Poor pretty M'Cori, I hope the delay won't tire you. But we shall find ways to amuse one another from time to time, you and I. And if you find yourself bored, just take a last long look at your lovely body. You may find your new one a considerable change"

M'Cori stretched out on the cold stones and sobbed wretchedly.

XXX
An Unexpected Alliance

"**I** don't know why I don't cut out your black heart!" snarled Lages, by way of greeting.

Kane shrugged. "For the same reason that you agreed to this meeting. Because you want to see M'Cori again — and you know that if you don't act quickly, you won't like what you'll see."

He waited for that barb to sink in. Announcing that he intended to mop up Lages's guerilla force without delay, Kane had sailed for Thovnos almost immediately following his last meeting with Efrel. With him Kane had brought a good-sized force loyal to him — former pirates and brigands, mercenaries, and a few ambitious adventurers like Imel. The Thovnosten renegade Kane left in Prisarte, to gather more men and to stand ready at the Pellin stronghold when he returned. Efrel, Kane learned, had withdrawn into her hidden chamber, with the command that on no account was she to be interrupted. Her action boded ill for M'Cori, but was perfect for Kane's designs.

Finding where Lages and his band were holed up was not too difficult for a man of Kane's resources — although arranging a meeting had been more of a problem. Desperation and the tempting possibilities of Kane's proposal had caused Lages to take the risk. They had arranged to meet in an isolated region of the great forest that covered much of Thovnos. Here they each brought fifty men along with them — well armed and suspicious of traps. Kane guessed that Lages probably had many more within calling distance — but then, so did he.

"I assume you understand what I'm proposing," Kane prompted.

"Your emissary was clear enough," replied Lages sullenly. "Only tell me why I should trust you? Regardless of the legends they tell of Red Kane, you've done enough to our Empire in the past year to make the name of Kane a curse for centuries to come. I know you have no scruples against luring me out of hiding — then springing a trap and slaughtering us to a man."

"That's true enough," Kane conceded graciously. "You have no reason to trust me. Only consider: I found out where you and your band were hidden easily enough. If I really wanted to destroy you, I would simply have brought up the large army at my command, encircled you, and wiped out every last one of you. And by doing so, I wouldn't have had to risk my own neck trying to hold a conference with you.

"And now consider this: Efrel has your friend, M'Cori — and you can be sure the witch has something most unpleasant in store for her. Efrel would probably suspect my treachery, in fact — if she weren't so preoccupied with her captive.

"Oh, I don't think she's done too much to her yet!" Kane interjected, to halt an outburst from Lages. "She's going to make whatever she does to her last a long time. Probably only mental anguish to start with — nothing that will leave physical scars. I've seen that Efrel likes to savour her games. But you can be certain that you'll have to act pretty damn fast to save M'Cori — and skulking around here in the hills isn't going to accomplish anything. Besides, if I can't make an ally of you, I'll have no choice but to wipe you out myself."

Kane leaned forward earnestly, pressing his advantage. "Actually my men and I would be hunting you down even now, if I had not discovered that Efrel intends to dispose of me as soon as I have destroyed all resistance to her rule. The witch's treachery went too far when she plotted against me.

"Moreover, I've grown disgusted with her methods — with these hideous sea demons she has formed a pact with. Despite the lies you've heard of me, I only entered Efrel's service to command her military forces, same as any mercenary general would do. Black sorcery and wholesale massacre sicken me — to say nothing of the unhallowed bargain the witch made with the Scylredi. I sold her my sword as her general, not wizard — and I fight with weapons of steel, not inhuman magic. I'm through fighting for that madwoman — even if I weren't certain of her plot to kill me once I've done her work.

"So here's my proposal: I want Efrel dead. You want Efrel dead. You help me, and together we'll accomplish this. In return, you'll get M'Cori back again — and, if you pledge loyalty, I'll let you have Thovnos back as well. Of course, I'll retain the throne of Emperor for myself, and establish my seat of power on another island."

"All very logical — but I still can't trust you!" Lages growled, thinking how long he would allow Kane to usurp the Imperial throne.

"So? Take a chance. All you've ever backed were losing causes. Staying here in the hills is only going to get you killed. Throw in with me, and you'll end up with your girl and a kingdom to rule. You know that it's a better deal than Netisten Maril ever really planned to give you."

Lages bristled, but turned it over at length. Really there was little choice — and he knew it. It was a madman's gamble, but Kane was his only hope. "All right," he concluded. "I'm in with you. But if this is a trap, Kane — I warn you…"

"I knew you could listen to reason," congratulated Kane, grasping his hand. Lages knew a flash of *déjà vu*. "Now we've got to make plans fast."

XXXI
Gather the Gods

On a dark night some five days after his departure from Thovnos, Kane sailed into the harbor of Prisarte, his fleet crowded to the gunwales with almost a thousand Imperial soldiers. Together with another seven hundred of his own men left with Imel in Prisarte, Kane calculated he had strength enough to take Dan-Legeh by stealthy attack and hold it until the city grew accustomed to his being in command. No one noticed anything amiss, as the soldiers disembarked from the warships in the darkness. It appeared at first glance as though Kane had returned from a normal campaign.

Quickly Kane met with Imel and informed him of Lages's alliance. The renegade filled Kane in on developments since his departure. Imel was enthusiastic.

"I've brought over as much support as I dared. I could have gotten a lot more, but it would have risked discovery. They'll back you once you make your move. Only the Pellinites will stay loyal to Efrel, I think. After all, to most of the men Kane is their leader — not some mad sorceress in Dan-Legeh.

"So far there's been no trouble. Efrel hasn't been seen for days. Word has it, the witch is still locked up in her secret chamber with M'Cori — only Lord Tloluvin knows what sort of torments the girl has endured in this time. And most of the Pellinites are still too busy celebrating to pay attention to what's going on. We should take the place with ease."

"Don't count Efrel out just because you don't see her," warned Kane. "That witch is sure to have a few deadly tricks left to her yet. Don't forget we're attacking her in her own lair."

"Well, the Scylredi can't help her on land," said Imel with considerable relief.

"That's true." Kane scratched his beard in thought. This night would settle the fate of too many opposing ambitions. Perhaps his own, as well. He grinned ruthlessly and drew his sword.

"Let's get started," Kane ordered.

"Your time grows short!" hissed Efrel, drawing a final detail to the pair of complicated pentagrams on the stone floor. Weak from terror and the foul drugs she had been forced to swallow, M'Cori lay moaning within one of the complex figures. In the other Efrel had positioned herself, along with several articles she would need for her final incantations.

Efrel was haggard from lack of sleep, but her deranged mind drove her on to the completion of her grand design — pausing only to take meals and snatches of rest. The spell of transmigration was complicated and difficult in the extreme. Many of the components had to be prepared explicitly for the spell, and often many pages of incantations had to be read over a single phase. Two full days had gone to the preparation of an ordinary-looking paste that had to be used to form a tiny, but essential, figure within the twin pentagrams.

Now the last preparation was complete. Sealing her pentagram, Efrel moved to the center and fastened a chain to her ankle. "When you awake to find yourself in my body, I wouldn't want you to wander about and hurt yourself," she told M'Cori solicitously. "After all, it will take you quite a while to get used to walking on only one leg."

Efrel paused a moment to savour the despairing sobs of her captive; then she took up her grimoire and began the final incantations.

To M'Cori's drug-clouded mind, the abominable incantation went on forever. An eerie chill stole over her body — a numbness that invaded every fiber of her being. Waves of nausea racked her, broken by searing blasts of intolerable pain. An all-pervasive lethargy made even breathing an unendurable effort. Slowly she felt her soul being sucked down into a whirlpool of darkness, her physical self drifting farther and farther away from consciousness...

The guards at the city gate still thought nothing amiss when a gang of fellow soldiers staggered up to them and demanded in drunken tones to be let out. Then suddenly knives flashed, and the Pellinite guards died without an outcry. Quickly the gates were opened, and Kane slipped through — followed by silent files of his soldiers.

"All right, here we split off and head for Dan-Legeh from different routes," he ordered. "Each group captain remember: Keep together, move fast, and try to raise as little hell as possible. Tell people anything, and try to avoid fighting until you reach the fortress. This has to be finished before the Pellinites can suspect anything. Good luck!"

Kane tersely whispered final instructions to Imel and Lages, then strode away with Arbas at the head of his own band.

The march through the streets was largely uneventful, and only a few occasions, necessitated swordplay. But as Kane's men converged on Dan-Legeh, the populace knew something was astir — and the wise ones bolted their doors and prepared to mind their own business.

At Dan-Legeh, the guards had been alerted by the sight of a small army advancing through the streets toward the citadel. The fortress's basalt walls were bristling with men and weapons — hastily summoned in the middle of the night. Even so, discipline had been lax following the great victory, and a good percentage of the men were still out celebrating. The reduced garrison looked nervously down upon the encircling soldiers. An attack on Dan-Legeh at this moment was absurd to contemplate — thus only a skeleton force had grudgingly remained to man the stronghold.

"What's going on out there?" demanded the captain of the guard from time to time. Only silence answered him. Lies could do nothing but verify their suspicions.

Finally Kane judged his men were in position — and shouted a challenge. "This is General Kane! I've uncovered a full-scale plot by Oxfors Alremas to seize control of the army! I've come to arrest the conspirators! As your general, I'm ordering you to surrender Dan-Legeh to my men! If you don't, I'll pull it down on your heads!"

The captain was not buying any. "Treason, is it! We owe allegiance to Pellin, not to a devil of a pirate mercenary!"

"Open fire!" yelled Kane, and a volley of arrows shot from his soldiers' ranks, raking the parapets. Their fire was answered, and the battle for Dan-Legeh began. The Pellinites were short of men and unprepared, but they had the security of a formidable fortress. Kane knew it was going to be a bloody struggle, and that it must be quickly concluded.

Using anything for shelter, Kane's soldiers kept up a deadly fire at the defenders. Arrows and spears fell in an invisible hail of death, and the night air was filled with shouts and cries of pain. Curious citizens came to investigate — and quickly fled, or were cut down by those in the rear. Alarm of the combat immediately spread to the soldiers encamped beyond the city walls — but those who were loyal to Pellin found the gates of the city held by Kane's men. Then, as word of Kane's *coup d'état* circulated, they were instantly set upon by factions loyal to Kane. Fighting erupted throughout the city.

A moat surrounded the fortress, crossed at the main gate by a drawbridge. Improvised bridges of wagons and other loose material allowed men to cross to the walls, advancing beneath interlocked shields and crude mantlets. Covered by punishing fire from Kane's archers, they finally succeeded in climbing to the top of the wall, although initial casualties were spectacular. But the Pellinite guard had no reserve to replace its fallen, while Kane's force outnumbered them heavily. A death blow was struck when some of Kane's men atop the wall succeeded in overturning a vat of boiling pitch onto the soldiers who rushed to repel them. By the time the Pellinites struggled over the flaming pile of dead, Kane's soldiers occupied a section of the battlement.

A foothold was established. Then more and more men were swarming up the ropes and ladders, forcing back the desperate defenders of the gate. It was a vicious fight, but finally Kane's men reached the controls of the drawbridge and dropped it. The main gate swung open. At the head of his soldiers, Kane led the howling band into the fortress itself.

The pain passed, then the sickness. Even the cosmic blackness at last began to fade into grey.

Light.

One eye opened. Images took shape. Images subtly distorted from their familiar patterns.

Two eyes opened. Emotion shook their unaccustomed focus. Tears blurred the shapes that leaped from the gloom.

Hesitant fingers softly caressed the smooth lines of her face.

A laugh of ghoulish triumph echoed from lips that had never formed such tones before.

Efrel was admiring her new body in incredulous delight when Oxfors Alremas came dashing into the chamber. He gaped at the uncanny scene before him in astonishment.

"Hello, Alremas," smiled Efrel, and posed provocatively. "How do you like me now?"

Alremas gasped in stunned disbelief and stared at the blond beauty who spoke to him with Efrel's inflections. He was unutterably shocked, even though Efrel had hinted to him of her intended revenge. His mouth opened foolishly for a moment, before he found speech.

"Efrel! By Lato — have you really done it! Have you indeed transferred your spirit into M'Cori's body?"

Efrel laughed prettily. "Shall I prove it, then? On the night of my sixteenth birthday, I met you in the gardens as you had begged me to do, and you suggested that we move back from the path to talk..."

Alremas stood stunned as she finished the anecdote. None other had ever known of his attempted seduction that had proven the reverse once they entered the shadows.

"Now take that silver dagger from the stand, and open this pentagram," she ordered. The tone and inflection were Efrel, although the voice was M'Cori. "There's keys there too for these chains. Hurry up! I want to feel what it is to walk about again."

Collecting himself, Alremas rushed to comply, explaining in agitated tones: "You've got to come immediately! The fortress is under attack! Kane has risen against you! He's at the gate this moment with hundreds of men behind him. I understand the devil has even brought Lages with him. Things look bad for us!"

Efrel's beautiful face was demonic in rage. "Hurry with these chains, you fool! I should never have let him live after he killed Maril! Another general could have finished with Lages and his pathetic remnant of the Imperial army. Curse his thrice-damned soul! Kane shall pay for this treachery as no man has ever suffered! I'll prepare a reception for Kane that he wasn't expecting!"

The last chain fell loose. Howling imprecations, Efrel ran up the stairs from the chamber — not even pausing to cover her nakedness.

Behind her in the silent chamber, M'Cori slowly regained consciousness. She opened her single eye, gazed at her body — and screamed.

With the entrance to Dan-Legeh secured, Kane's forces quickly overran the guards along the wall and passed into the sprawling citadel. Inside, soldiers were boiling up like bees from an invaded hive. The Pellinites fought hard, but Kane had the strength of numbers. Foot by bloody foot, he and his men gained ground.

His right arm was nearly healed — thanks to his preternatural recuperative powers — and Kane was able to use it sparingly. A long dagger in his right fist, sword in his left, Kane fought like a madman. Faces rose and fell about him as he steadily hewed his way through the stubborn Pellinite resistance. Behind him, his men kept up the relentless pressure.

With M'Cori primarily in his thoughts, Lages soon separated from Kane in the spreading melee. With a band of his own men, he pushed his way through the maze-like corridors of Dan-Legeh, searching for his beloved. Doubt tortured him, as Lages had no certainty that M'Cori still lived — or whether she would want to live if he did rescue her. Perhaps she had been murdered at the inception of the attack.

Lages and his men encountered fewer and fewer soldiers as they followed through the winding hallways, getting ever farther from the central battle as they descended to the lower levels. Leaving the fight to Kane, Lages pressed on, intending to search the fortress dungeons for M'Cori. If he was too late…

Then he saw her. In the darkened passageway beyond, naked and terror-stricken, running toward him, her blond hair flowing past her white body.

"M'Cori!" he cried, crushing her trembling body against him. "Thank all the gods that I've found you safe! What have they done to you! Kane said that Efrel was going to…"

Efrel buried her face in his shoulder and sobbed. "*Kane!* Don't speak that accursed name to me! I've only now escaped from his private chambers. Oh, Lages — it was terrible! That first night he came in and forced me to do his will! I fought but he was always too strong. He'd beat me until I couldn't take any more pain — I had to surrender to his depraved lusts. I begged him not to…"

The hallway swam before Lages in a crimson haze. "Kane told me you were imprisoned by Efrel," he began in a strange voice. "I joined forces with him to rescue you and to kill the witch."

"Oh, I know! Kane boasted to me of his plans before he left for Thovnos. Lages, Efrel was never behind this conspiracy! She died months ago on Thovnos. This has all been a plot by Kane. He found some mutilated beggar-woman to pretend to be Efrel, and used that deception to form the nucleus for the rebellion he has secretly led all along. Now the Pellinites have began to suspect his ruse, and they've started a move to get rid of Kane. Kane had to destroy them before that could happen. So Kane tricked you into helping him solidify his phantom rule."

Her face twisted in terror. Hysterical tears choked her words. "Oh, darling, now he'll kill you, and take me again to… *No!* Kill me now! Please! I couldn't endure his lusts for another night!"

Lages felt a roaring in his brain. He fought to speak coherently. "Hide in the lower chambers. I'll come for you when this is over. There's no need to fear Kane any more. I'll bring you that treacherous devil's heart!"

Lages turned and ran down the hall babbling of treachery, ordering his men to spread the word to attack Kane's followers.

Efrel doubled up with laughter.

The first group Lages came upon was led by Imel, who with a few score men was searching the lower levels for Pellinite survivors.

"Treachery! Kill the lying bastards!" shouted Lages. "We've been betrayed!"

After only a moment's hesitation, Lages's men turned on the rebels. The passageway flamed into a seething, deadly brawl.

"What the hell!" Imel yelled, and pulled his blade up just in time to miss being spitted by Lages's rush.

"I've found out the truth of your schemes!" snarled Lages, slashing wildly. "Did Kane take me for a fool?"

"You've gone mad!" rejoined Imel, retreating in confusion.

The halls erupted into a chaos of struggling soldiers. The Imperial soldiers were in the majority, and the rebels were falling fast. Only the cry of "Treachery!" was understood in the confusion — but it was enough to detonate the barely restrained antipathy between the Imperials and the rebels.

Imel realized his plight and fought with renewed vigor. But Lages fenced with blood-mad rage behind his blade, and his powerful strokes were numbing Imel's arm, slashing apart his buckler. The renegade felt panic gibber through his brain. Frantically he sought to defend himself — but against a better and stronger swordsman. He was the only rebel left standing now. Bitterly Imel remembered Arbas's long-ago warning and cursed the day he had become involved with Kane.

His defense was faltering, and he knew it. A sudden blow glanced off Imel's sword and struck him across the ribs. Imel gasped in pain and dropped his guard. With a powerful stroke, Lages clove in Imel's skull.

"There's one traitor down!" he roared. "Now where's the blackest of them all?"

The Imperial soldiers raced through the labyrinthine hallways, picking up support as they went. Throughout the citadel, soldiers who had just fought side by side suddenly turned on one another. Constant suspicion and smouldering enmity exploded in a violent reaction.

At length, Lages burst into the great hall, where he found the bulk of Kane's forces still engaged in a tense struggle with the last of the Pellinite guard. Shouting for vengeance, the Imperials attacked their allies of a moment gone.

Utter chaos enveloped the citadel as three forces locked in a battle to the death. In the confusion it became difficult to follow any one faction. For the combatants, it was sufficient to accept that any man not personally known to them was probably an enemy.

Lages caught sight of Kane — battling at the head of the stairway to the balcony above the great hall. "Now I'll kill you, you prince of traitors!" Lages roared, and charged Kane. "You've hidden from death for the last time!"

One glance told Kane not to argue. "You crazy son of a bitch!" he growled, and met the youth's attack.

"This is for what you did to M'Cori! And to Maril! And to the entire Empire!" Lages shouted, as he smashed blow after wild blow against Kane. But in Kane he had an opponent stronger than himself — and a better swordsman, as well. He was not able to wear down Kane's guard as he had done to Imel, nor could he force Kane to remain on the defensive.

Fighting silently, Kane knocked aside every slash, parried every thrust, backing Lages to the stairs. Kane was bleeding from several fresh cuts, and his injured right arm was beginning to throb agonisingly. Setting his teeth in a death's-head grin, Kane hurried to finish his assailant. Methodically he pressed his attack upon Lages, but the youth again and again eluded him. Anger and hysteria gave seemingly boundless strength to Lages, and he desperately fought toe to toe with Kane, taking Kane's steel on his shield, striking grimly with his own blade

The end struck blindingly. Kane countered a vicious thrust — then feinted with the long dagger in his right hand. Lages swerved his shield to meet the dagger blade — for an instant he left an opening — and Kane hewed his broadsword into his adversary's right side. The blade slashed deep — cleaving through cuirass and bone. With a cry of mortal agony, Lages fell backward from the force of the blow, plummeted down the stairs and into blackness.

Kane watched Lages's body roll down the staircase, then turned to meet a new threat. The battle was too hot to waste time sorting out the puzzle. Killing the vengeful Imperial soldier nearest him, Kane wondered what could have happened to make Lages attack him. The matter defied logic.

A Pellinite leaped back to avoid Kane's sword thrust and was neatly skewered by Arbas. The assassin was also puzzled over the sudden reversal of Kane's well-laid plans, but his fighting skill had lost none of its professional polish. Grimly Arbas fought beside Kane, knowing that whatever strange twist fate had taken, Kane would be in at the finish.

"Kane!" The cry was a demand.

"What now?" wondered Kane — and whirled to face Oxfors Alremas.

"I've waited for this moment!" hissed the Pellinite lord. "I've known you for a treacherous pirate from the first. Well, Efrel knows that, too, now — and it's a pity I've got to kill you instead of saving you for her vengeance. Still, this is one pleasure I'll share with no one — not even Efrel."

It was a fine speech, but Kane saved his own breath to reply with a flicker of killing steel.

The Pellinite fenced with amazing speed, fighting with catlike grace. Kane had to move fast to parry each thrust, and his right arm was rapidly becoming useless. Yet Alremas had seldom faced a left-handed swordsman, and Kane's speed astounded him. He had thought such a big man would be slow and awkward. Relentlessly he found himself forced to give ground before Kane's attack. With unfaltering skill his opponent parried Alremas's every stroke.

Then, with a rush of exaltation, Alremas saw his sword tip stab into Kane's thigh below the skirt of his hauberk. *That should slow the devil down,* he thought with a smile, lunging to press home his momentary advantage. It was the last enjoyment Alremas ever would know. Even as his smile broadened, Kane's sword deflected the thrusting blade, spun in a tight arc, and chopped through Alremas's neck. The Pellinite lord dropped dead at his rival's feet, but his head fled away down the stairway.

Pressing his right hand to the wound in his thigh, Kane cursed and looked about. him. In the interval while he and Alremas dueled atop the staircase, the remaining Pellinites all seemed to have fallen or fled, and the Imperials were steadily being wiped out by the survivors of Kane's force. Within the citadel, it would only be a matter of hunting down the fugitives. And things must be going well for his men outside, or Pellinite reinforcements would have swamped them by now. If nothing else, Lages's sudden change of heart had ultimately resulted in the destruction of the last imperial forces.

Tying a bandage to his thigh, Kane smiled wearily. "Well, Arbas," he began, "it looks as if the Empire is mine at last."

The assassin rolled Alremas's head cautiously with his boot and nodded. The head nodded back at the prodding of his toe.

At that moment Kane felt an uncanny stiffness stealing over him. His muscles seemed to constrict, refuse to obey him. *Was Alremas's sword a poisoned blade,* Kane wondered in anguish.

Then he saw Arbas's consternation — saw that all about the blood-covered hall, fighters were halting in their combat. Everywhere in the embattled citadel, soldiers felt an unnatural rigor seize their flesh, all power slip from their limbs, as their minds became prisoners within their own bodies.

With one tremendous effort, Kane forced his head to turn about. His astonished eyes beheld a naked girl, completing a series of cryptic passes — *M'Cori?*

Consciousness returned to Lages through a haze of pain. Slowly he forced himself erect, wincing at the agony in his side. Kane's blade had driven deep, and Lages coughed blood. Several ribs were smashed, and his left arm seemed broken by the fall. He gazed around him in wonder. Except for a mountain of corpses, the great hall was empty.

How long had he been unconscious? Surely there must be someone around yet — someone must be victorious. The fighting must have moved elsewhere, Lages decided. He wondered bleakly if Kane yet lived. The dead on the floor told him that his own men had suffered serious losses.

Bending painfully, Lages picked up his fallen sword. "Got to find M'Cori!" his pain-fogged brain told him, and he repeated to the dead. He forced himself to walk. His steps were dream-like; his legs seemed numb and apart from the rest of him. Remembering that he had told M'Cori to hide in the lower levels, Lages started walking in that direction.

The corridors seemed to be endless. Door after door Lages passed, calling M'Cori's name weakly. Only the dead returned his searching gaze. He passed by the corpse of Imel, the ruined face glared at him accusingly. On and on he staggered through the black stone maze. Were none but the dead left to challenge him?

Then it seemed to Lages that he could hear M'Cori's voice. He listened bewilderedly. It was so hard to listen, to concentrate — even to breathe. But there again came the sound. He felt sure it wasn't delirium. From far below, he seemed to hear the sound of M'Cori's voice.

A black doorway yawned from the wall before him. Yes. It was from here that her voice arose. Gripping his sword tightly, Lages entered the doorway and started down the long dark stairs.

The stairs went on forever, and Lages began to believe he would never see the end. But the voice grew stronger, so he forced himself onward. Then, quite illogically, the infinite stairway came to an end. Lages found himself standing on a low balcony, with wide steps leading down to the floor of a fantastic cavern.

There was a huge black pool, and standing all around were a few hundred soldiers. It was strange the way they just stood there — like so many statues, Lages decided. Then he recognized with astonishment that the soldiers were both his men and Kane's. Yes! There was Kane himself — and with him was Efrel.

But the greatest shock of all came to Lages when he beheld M'Cori — pacing back and forth before the eerily motionless figures. What could it mean? Had M'Cori somehow captured all these warriors? The scene was altogether incredible. In dreamy bewilderment, Lages started to call out to M'Cori.

Then the words she spoke penetrated into his consciousness.

"Ah, Kane! If you could only have seen how surprised you looked, when you felt my little spell stealing away your strength! Now here you stand — with all those traitors who followed you. Completely helpless, unable to walk or even nod your head, except at my command. Remember those others you have seen under my spell? Remember their fate? Won't it be delightful to stand there utterly helpless like this, when the Scylredi come for you? Just like in the nightmare, when you want to run, to scream — but can't. Didn't you once describe the spell in such words? And now you will have the added sophistication of knowing how this nightmare will end."

She laughed in cruel triumph: "And haven't you any words to praise my new body? Beautiful, isn't it? I haven't had the heart to cover it yet. It was so kind of you, dear M'Cori, to give me your body. I'm sure your father would be amazed at your generosity. A pity Maril never lived to see my vengeance completed. But I haven't asked you how well you like your new body. Speak to me — pretty, pretty M'Cori!"

"Can't you just kill me and be done?" came the hopeless response from the mutilated form.

Efrel sneered. "What? You want death so soon? Stupid little bitch! I begged your father for a quick, clean death — and look what mercy he showed me! What a disappointment I can't arrange for you to savour the thrill of being dragged by a bull through a jeering city! But there's not much left on those bones to maim further — is there, M'Cori?

"Well, I have the body of the beautiful M'Cori now!" she exulted. "And you'll have to be content with the maimed one your father gave to me? At any event, if it's death you wish, you won't have long to wait. The Scylredi will soon be here to feed. I give you freedom. I'll let you decide whether to dine with the Scylredi — or live yet a while in your new body."

Slowly understanding dawned on Lages. To his tortured mind came the realization that somehow Efrel had stolen his beloved's body. A crime monstrous beyond imagination had been perpetrated by the sorceress. Cobwebs of delirium melted, and he saw things clearly. Strength suddenly flowed back into his frame. The pain was gone.

With a hoarse shout of "*Efrel!*" Lages jumped from the low balcony and raced for the malevolent creature who masqueraded as M'Cori.

Efrel whirled in amazement as the blood-smeared swordsman charged toward her. She raised her hand to cast the spell that had trapped her other enemies — the spell that gave her power over all who entered her fortress. There was no time to halt the vengeful specter.

Lages plunged his sword into the breast of the body he had loved — impaled the desecrated beauty on cold steel.

Efrel screamed as bright blood spurted from the wound. Her fingers tore futilely at the blade. Her eyes blazed with intense concentration, then momentarily went blank.

And Lages looked into the eyes of the girl he loved. Escaping the dying shell, Efrel had reversed the psychic bonds, returned to her own body — and returned M'Cori's soul to her violated flesh.

"Lages... thank you... I..."

The weak voice trailed off, and Lages looked into dead eyes once more.

He started to cry out her name. But the words were choked, as a great rush of blood filled his throat and the last flame of strength failed. Lages fell lifeless over M'Cori's body.

The interval had lasted only a matter of seconds. But it had been sufficient to break the full concentration of Efrel's spell. With a mind trained in studies of the supernatural, Kane fought to escape the weakened enchantment. Summoning up every ultimate reserve of his psychic energy, Kane forced his lips to obey his will. Slowly he croaked the words of the counterspell that he had learned in centuries of delving into the black arts. If only he had correctly identified Efrel's secret spell...

The spell snapped, and Kane was free. Around him the others began to shake off their trance.

But on the floor the twisted body of the sorceress was stirring. In its old flesh, Efrel's spirit was quickly resuming control. Her eyes flashed open in a blaze of insane hatred. Rising to her feet before the stuporous soldiers, she opened her mouth to cast her spell again.

With lightning speed, Kane snatched a spear from the grip of a soldier whose hand had never received the command to release it. Before Efrel could utter a syllable of the spell, he cast the spear straight through her heart.

The force of impact threw the sorceress backward onto the floor. She writhed upon the black stones like an impaled serpent, clawing at the spear that pierced her maimed flesh. Her strength failed.

Efrel uttered a last hideous shriek: "*Father!*" Then crimson laughter sprayed from her lips, and came no more.

Then came a final horror to surpass all that had transpired. As Efrel's mutilated body fell back in death, its outlines began to blur. The arms lost their joints, the fingers foreshortened. The head retreated into the trunk, as mouth and nose parted into a gaping hole, while ruined eyes grew round and white. Skin color darkened, and glistening slime oozed across the bloated hide. The mutilated legs grew boneless and attenuated. Before their eyes, the corpse of Efrel began to assume the maimed form of a Scylred.

Shaking the numbness from his brain, Kane seized one of the great oil lamps. He lifted the huge copper vessel on high — then brought it smashing down upon the transforming corpse. A flood of flaming oil engulfed the half-human, half-Scylred abomination. Clouds of putrid smoke steamed up from the crackling pyre.

At that same instant — Efrel's last cry still an echoing ghost — the black pool erupted with Scylredis. Scores of them had been summoned to the sacrifice. Now the feast began. The sea demons reached out and seized those nearest to the pool's edge, pulling them down into the black water. Yet in the grip of the horror they had endured, the soldiers were too slow in recognizing the doom that had come to claim them.

"Get back!" shouted Kane. Dragging the dazed Arbas with him, he hurtled toward the stairway.

For now looping from the pool were the immense black tentacles of an Oraycha. Somehow the boneless monster had passed through the vast tunnel along with its masters. Like a giant scythe, the tentacles swept across the chamber — smashing dozens of men to the stones in each blow, catching them up in its suckered grasp. The lamps were hurled to the floor, spilling oil in spreading pools that blazed briefly across the bare stones.

Kane gained the stairway, followed by Arbas and several of the others. Behind them the subterranean chamber dissolved into a nightmare of screaming men and feasting black shapes.

Darkness swallowed up the entire chamber and all those who were in it.

XXXII
Farewell

From the deck of the *Ara-Teving*, Kane watched the ruin-haunted coasts of Pellin drop from sight.

He had escaped from the carnage within Dan-Legeh only to find his forces on the short end of the battle. The heavy losses that resulted from the fight with Lages's men — and the horror in the subterranean chamber — had dealt a mortal blow to his plans. With all of Prisarte raised against Kane, the battle with the Pellinites was going against him. Fighting his way clear, Kane had gathered together as many of his followers as escaped on the *Ara-Teving*. With ship and crew, Kane set sail, leaving behind him the chaos of his own creation.

"What was it that happened to Efrel there in her chamber?" asked Arbas from beside him, finding pause at last to reflect. Even the assassin's irreverent tones were tinged with a note of awe.

"The tales of Efrel's demon parentage were true," Kane answered pensively. "Somehow, by some dark sorcery — who knows what Pellin Othrin intended to achieve that night — Efrel was the offspring of an unhallowed coupling of human and Scylred. No wonder her mother went insane that night in the sorcerer's chamber.

"Efrel was beautiful, certainly — appeared completely human. But that's not uncommon among were-beasts — which is roughly what Efrel was, although she couldn't change form at will. I often wondered how she could communicate so well with such alien creatures — her bond with them was a deeper one than any had guessed. Her half-demon heritage explains a lot of other things, now that I think back on it. As to what took place in the end — like a werebeast, Efrel assumed her true form in death."

Kane spat into the water in the direction of the vanishing coastline. "So it seems as though no one could achieve his ambition in this game. And this region is too hot for me to linger in now. After all that has happened, it would be impossible for me to raise another army large enough to consolidate any strong position within these islands.

"No, I think I'll head on south and see what's happening around the more civilized parts of the world. It has been quite a while since I tried my luck in the Southern Lands. With a trireme and a good crew, there's no telling what I might find to do."

He grinned at his companion. "Care to come along, Arbas? I'll show you lands where a man can carve out a kingdom."

"No, thanks," decided Arbas. "Just drop me off somewhere where I can get a ship back to the Combine and the alleys of Nostoblet. I have a feeling that my calling is to be an assassin, not a soldier of fortune. And anyway, I've noticed that people who come in contact with you don't live long lives."

Kane laughed. "Perhaps another time."

Two weeks later, in the southern port of Castakes, Arbas watched Kane sail away on another voyage of his eternal wandering. The sun was just beginning to rise, and perhaps it was only his imagination that colored the dawn skies so deep a red.